The Complete Works of
WASHINGTON
IRVING

Henry A. Pochmann (1965–1973)
Herbert L. Kleinfield (1973–1976)
Richard Dilworth Rust
General Editors

BRACEBRIDGE HALL

Bracebridge Hall

WASHINGTON IRVING

BRACEBRIDGE HALL
OR
THE HUMOURISTS

A Medley
by Geoffrey Crayon, Gent.

Under this cloud I walk gentlemen; pardon my rude
assault. I am a traveller, who, having surveyed most
of the terrestrial angles of this globe, am hither
arrived to peruse this little spot.

CHRISTMAS ORDINARY

Edited by
Herbert F. Smith

Twayne Publishers
Boston
1977

Published by Twayne Publishers

A Division of G. K. Hall & Co.

Copyright © 1977 by

G. K. Hall & Co.

All Rights Reserved

The Complete Works of Washington Irving

Volume IX

CENTER FOR EDITIONS OF
AMERICAN AUTHORS

AN APPROVED TEXT

MODERN LANGUAGE
ASSOCIATION OF AMERICA

®

Library of Congress Cataloging in Publication Data

Irving, Washington, 1783–1859.
Bracebridge Hall.

(The complete works of Washington Irving; v. 9)
Includes bibliographical references and index.
I. Title.
PS2057.A1   1977   818'.2'07   77–22164
ISBN 0–8057–8506–X

Manufactured in the United States of America

ACKNOWLEDGMENTS

Much as I would like to express my gratitude individually to the many people who have helped me with this edition, the mere listing of several dozen names would be self-defeating. They know who they are, and they must be aware of my gratitude. Let two men who together gave aid and comfort to whole generations of American scholars stand for all the rest: this edition would never have been begun without the aid and friendship of Harry Hayden Clark; it would never have been finished without the counsel and advice of Henry A. Pochmann.

For permission to consult and make use of Irving manuscripts, special thanks are due to the New York Public Library, Astor, Lenox, and Tilden Foundations, the Columbia University Library, and the Clifton Waller Barrett Collection of the University of Virginia Library. Financial support from the University of Wisconsin, the University of Victoria, and the National Endowment for the Humanities allowed me time and travel to complete my research and do what seemed endless collations.

And for aid in those endless collations and forgiveness when she was not aiding me, I will be forever grateful to my wife, Virginia.

H. F. S.

University of Victoria
June 1977

CONTENTS

VOLUME II

EDITORIAL APPENDIX

ILLUSTRATIONS

FRONTISPIECE

Bracebridge Hall
Randolph Caldecott illustration of the Bracebridge family mansion

INTERIOR ILLUSTRATIONS

The Lovers
(following page 24)

Ready-Money Jack
(following page 38)

Stable Yard on a Rainy Day
(following page 50)

Gypsy Encampment
(following page 92)

Traveler and Goblin
(following page 230)

Dolph Heyliger and The Doctor
(following page 256)

INTRODUCTION

Geoffrey Crayon noted in the sketch "The Voyage" in *The Sketch Book,* that when his ship lost sight of America en route to the Old World, "It seemed as if I had closed one volume of the world and its concerns."[1] The next volume he would open was *The Sketch Book,* and after it, *Bracebridge Hall. The Sketch Book* is a truly transatlantic work, facing both East and West: twenty-six of its essays describe English life; only four deal with America—but two of those four, "Rip Van Winkle" and the "Legend of Sleepy Hollow," are probably the best known of his writings. Yet the bulk of *The Sketch Book* remains English, and its sequel was to be even more an English work.

Irving has given several accounts of his first impressions of England. In *The Sketch Book* he remarks, "I had no friend to meet, no cheering to receive. I stepped upon the land of my forefathers—but felt that I was a stranger in the land."[2] In the first essay of *Bracebridge Hall* he takes another tone:

> Indeed it is difficult to describe the whimsical medley of ideas that throng upon [the American traveler's] mind on landing among English scenes. He, for the first time, sees a world about which he has been reading and thinking in every stage of his existence. The recollected ideas of infancy, youth, and manhood; of the nursery, the school, and the study, come swarming at once upon him; and his attention is distracted between great and little objects; each of which, perhaps, awakens an equally delightful train of remembrances.
>
> But what more especially attracts his notice are those peculiarities which distinguish an old country and an old state of society from a new one. I have never yet grown familiar enough with the crumbling monuments of past ages, to blunt the intense interest with which I at first beheld them.[3]

The very different tone of the two statements is appropriate to the two works in which they appear. *The Sketch Book,* for all its comparative brilliance when examined side by side with its less-successful sequel, is

1. *The Sketch Book,* Author's Revised Edition (New York, 1849), I, 20; the Author's Revised Edition is hereafter cited as ARE.
2. *Ibid.,* p. 27.
3. See above, p. 4.

a relatively tentative work. Geoffrey Crayon, that unique persona, is prominent throughout. The experience of England is distilled in his alembic, and he communicates his own flavor to the liquor. In essays like "The Mutability of Literature" and "Boar's Head Tavern, Eastcheap," how prominent he is! And the relative success of these sketches compared with those smelling more of the lamp (like the Christmas essays) rests heavily on the sensibility of the narrator. In the best of *The Sketch Book*, it is not England we are seeing, but Geoffrey Crayon in the act of seeing England.

Impressionism in *The Sketch Book* gives way to the more intensified and more bookish study of old English customs in *Bracebridge Hall*. *The Sketch Book* describes one brief holiday in a representative English country house named Bracebridge Hall, chosen apparently because it typified one aspect of English life in the context of a work devoted to sampling the variety of experiences available to Crayon in England. *Bracebridge Hall*, on the other hand, focuses almost entirely on the one circumstance of the old customs and manners of English country life in an age when they were at the crossroads of reform and experiencing the rise of the middle class and the beginnings of the industrial revolution. The first work offers us God's plenty; the second is a sociological study, suitably limited for a doctoral dissertation, well footnoted, and, according to most modern critics, about as interesting. Nevertheless, if one is to examine the origins of *Bracebridge Hall*, he must concern himself first with Irving's sources and attitudes leading to *The Sketch Book*. Only when he understands what led Irving to a sampling of English customs can he turn his attention to the more specific sequel.

The attractions Irving found in England were the ancient traditions and manners of an England "rich in the accumulated treasures of age," where he could "tread ... in the footsteps of antiquity ... loiter about the ruined castle ... meditate on the falling tower."[4] These qualities are, of course, prominently displayed in both *The Sketch Book* and *Bracebridge Hall*, though in a far greater variety in the former. Irving's enthusiasm for all things smacking of English antiquity filled his notebooks for *The Sketch Book* and inclined him toward the deeper researches of *Bracebridge Hall*. It propelled him from the London of the Boar's Head Tavern through Stratford-on-Avon to the country settings of "Rural Funerals" and "May-Day," from Westminster Abbey, where he meditated on "The Mutability of Literature," to Aston Hall, near the Van Warts in Birmingham, one reputed original of Bracebridge Hall.

That manorial England was a subject of consuming interest not only

4. *The Sketch Book*, ARE p. 17.

for Irving but for the English as well is attested by the lengthy debate among literary antiquarians as to what English manor house was the original of Bracebridge Hall. Three manor houses have been championed by a variety of persons in a debate which waxed furious in the 1890's and is still going on, albeit with a good deal less seriousness.[5] These are Brereton Hall in Cheshire, Barlborough Hall in Derbyshire, and Aston Hall in Birmingham. Evidence could be supplied for the general appropriateness and for Irving's involvement, at one time or another, with each. No doubt Irving found it convenient to "tread . . . in the footsteps of antiquity" in the relative comfort of such surroundings whenever he could. But the debate is a purely academic one. Bracebridge Hall is a noumenal English manor, while even Aston Hall, for which Stanley T. Williams argues forcefully, is phenomenal.[6] Irving doubtless blended details from a number of English manor houses and parks into his descriptions. If Aston Hall has any right to be named as the original of Bracebridge Hall, it must be because Irving knew it slightly better than any other, since Birmingham and the Van Warts' "Castle Van Tromp" was the closest thing to an English home that he knew in those years.

If the terms of the question are shifted slightly to include not what specific place presented Irving with physical details of architecture and furnishings and the like for Bracebridge Hall, but instead what experience in England provided him with more details of English country life and the general ambiance of a country squire, a different model for Bracebridge Hall emerges. Curiously, it is not even English, but Scottish. There is no doubt that the one encounter Irving had during

5. See, for example, Notes and Queries, 8th ser., 1 (May 28, 1892), 427; 2 (October 8, 1892), 288, among many others. For the latest addition to the genre, see Ben Harris McClary, "A Bracebridge Hall Christmas for Van Buren: an Unpublished Irving Letter," English Language Notes 8 (September, 1970), 18–22.

6. Stanley T. Williams, The Life of Washington Irving (New York, 1935), I, 204, 438–439; II, 284; hereafter cited as STW. Williams seems to accept the Van Wart tradition that Irving had spent a Christmas at Aston Hall, although there is no evidence in his journals or letters supporting such a remarkable event. The Aston Hall identification was also promoted by Randolph Caldecott's use of scenes from the mansion for illustrations in his popular volume of the Christmas chapters from The Sketch Book. The tradition has continued into such varied modern publications as Volume III of Irving's Journals and Notebooks (ed. Walter A. Reichart [Madison: University of Wisconsin Press, 1970], 355 n. 795, and a series of articles in Country Life beginning with the issue of September 3, 1953 (p. 697). One regrets that the identification with Aston Hall has not more reality behind it upon discovering the real-life irony that James Watt, son of the well-known Scottish inventor at the time of the industrial revolution, and himself an inventor, was the last resident of Aston Hall before it was turned over to the city of Birmingham (Country Life, August 27, 1953, p. 622).

the years preceding *The Sketch Book* which struck him most forcefully was the visit he made to Sir Walter Scott's home, Abbotsford, at the end of August and beginning of September, 1817. As he wrote shortly afterward in a letter to Peter Irving dated September 6, 1817, "The few days that I passed there were among the most delightful of my life, and worth as many years of ordinary existence."[7] There seems no reason to doubt him. The visit forms the material for a lengthy essay published in *Abbotsford and Newstead Abbey* (1835), in which Irving gives full expression to his admiration for the man Scott and life at Abbotsford. Even without that evidence, the letters Irving sent immediately after the visit vouch for its effect upon him. The letter cited above goes on for pages about the delights of Abbotsford, and was followed by another of September 20, also to Peter Irving, announcing Irving's intention to visit Scott again: "I want to set out another evening there; Scott reading, occasionally, from Prince Arthur; telling border stories or characteristic anecdotes; Sophy Scott singing with charming naiveté a little border song; the rest of the family disposed in listening groups, while grey hounds, spaniels, and cats bask in unbounded indulgence before the fire. Every thing around Scott is perfect character and picture."[8]

That Irving studied that "perfect character and picture" and reproduced at least part of it in *Bracebridge Hall* is also evident. Much of the color of "Story-Telling" and "The Manuscript" might derive directly from these evenings at Abbotsford. Several specific anecdotes in *Bracebridge Hall* have a direct source in Irving's visit to Abbotsford. Irving noted that Scott had been teaching his son Walter "to ride, to shoot, and to tell the truth."[9] Exactly the same phrase appears in *Bracebridge Hall* as an old Persian maxim repeated by the squire to his sons.[10] The anecdote in "English Country Gentlemen" in which the steward voices his independence of the squire over some alteration of the grounds, then observes that "he had been turning the matter over in his mind, and, upon the whole, he believed he would take his honour's advice,"[11] is again a direct quotation from an encounter between Scott and his steward, Purdie. It went unfootnoted in all editions of *Bracebridge Hall* until the Author's Revised Edition of 1849, where Irving admitted its source.[12] In the same footnote, Irving remarked that "the author is

7. Pierre M. Irving, *The Life and Letters of Washington Irving* (New York, 1862–1864), I, 383; hereafter cited as PMI.
8. PMI, I, 385.
9. *Ibid.*, p. 383.
10. See above, p. 70.
11. See above, p. 157.
12. *Bracebridge Hall*, ARE, p. 250.

indebted for several of his traits of the squire to observations made on Sir Walter Scott during that visit; though he had to be cautious and sparing in drawing from that source." The problem of identification of any real place with Bracebridge Hall is implicit in that last statement, the more so if one wishes to read *Bracebridge Hall* as any sort of fictionalized biography with Scott as the squire, Tommy Purdie as the steward, and the like. Irving, as a friend and admirer of Scott, could idealize the life of a country squire as Scott practiced it at Abbotsford; Irving as Geoffrey Crayon must criticize to some extent the self-contradictory materials of English landed society pursuing a pastoral existence into the age of steam.

The creation of the Hall, the squire, and several other characters for the Christmas visit chapters was a new departure for the text of *The Sketch Book*. Three sketches are devoted to the Christmas festivities at Bracebridge Hall, "Christmas Eve," "Christmas Day," and "Christmas Dinner." The group is introduced twice: first by a general essay, "Christmas," in which Bracebridge Hall and its denizens are not mentioned, then by a chapter entitled "The Stage-Coach," at the conclusion of which Geoffrey Crayon is invited by Frank Bracebridge, "a sprightly, good-humoured young fellow, with whom I had once travelled on the continent," to spend the approaching holidays at his family hall. A similar division between specific creative imagination and general folklore and customs is apparent in the three Christmas chapters. A large part of them derives, as Stanley T. Williams has pointed out, from Irving's youthful admiration of the *Spectator* papers, especially of Sir Roger de Coverley.[13] But an even more significant influence was Irving's fearsome love of "black-letter volumes." Undeniably, some of the Christmas pastimes described in these chapters survived in England to Irving's day; but it is equally certain that the direct source for many, perhaps most, of them was not in life but in literature, in the sixteenth- and seventeenth-century writings which pack Irving's notebooks of this period (and which account for an enormous number of the chapter epigraphs in both *The Sketch Book* and *Bracebridge Hall*).

Thus these Christmas chapters of *The Sketch Book* smell doubly of the lamp. Irving himself was pleased with them, but he seems to have sensed the risk inherent in them for an American audience. In his letter to Ebenezer transmitting them, on October 28, 1819, to New York for publication, he voiced his uncertainty: "Whether No. V will please or not, I cannot say, but it has cost me more trouble and more odd research than any of the others."[14]

13. STW, II, 282.
14. PMI, I, 447.

Apparently it did not please Ebenezer, because in his next letter to his brother Irving felt the need to defend it:

The article you object to, about Christmas, is written for peculiar tastes—those who are fond of what is quaint in literature and customs. The scenes there depicted are formed upon humors and customs peculiar to the English, and illustrative of their greatest holyday. The old rhymes which are interspersed are but selections from many which I found among old works in the British Museum, little read even by Englishmen, and which will have a value with some literary men who relish these morsels of antiquated humor. When an article is studied out in this manner, it cannot have that free flowing spirit and humor that one written off-hand has; but then it compensates to some peculiar minds by the points of character and manners which it illustrates. Had I not thought so, I certainly would not have taken the trouble which the article cost me. If it possesses the kind of merit I mention, and pleases the peculiar, though perhaps few tastes to which I have alluded, my purpose in writing the article is satisfied, and it will go to keep up the variety which is essential to a work of the kind.[15]

The problem, along with the letter it provoked, is symbolic. Here, at the very germ and conception of *Bracebridge Hall*, Irving shows his unease at the "studied . . . manner" necessary to write the kind of work to please "the peculiar, though perhaps few tastes" of antiquarians. In the larger context of *The Sketch Book* the difficulty is minimal; Irving is right in his final comment about the variety necessary for a work like *The Sketch Book*. But viewing this letter from the critical shadows into which *Bracebridge Hall* has moved, how ironically prophetic it sounds!

But his diffidence and defensiveness about the Christmas visit to Bracebridge Hall were only a local and temporary disturbance in his general euphoria as a result of the enormous popular success of *The Sketch Book* in America. "I . . . shall be quite satisfied if I deserve half the praise they give me in the American journals," Irving wrote on September 13, 1819; "they always overdo these matters in America."[16] His eye was fixed rather more interestedly upon the English literary public, and there he was not at first successful. On October 27, the day before Irving sent off the Christmas visit essays to America, he received a rejection from John Murray of the already published Numbers

15. *Ibid.*, pp. 447–48.
16. *Ibid.*, pp. 434–35.

I and II of *The Sketch Book*. He asked Scott to intercede with Constable, and when that was not successful, had the volume published at his own expense by John Miller, whose business promptly failed. With the success of the early sketches, however, he finally succeeded in having Murray accept the remainder of *The Sketch Book*. It is perhaps not a coincidence that Murray's first publication of *The Sketch Book* began with the Christmas visit sketches. The "peculiar tastes" for which that selection was written were more congenial to the English temper than the American. Nor could Irving have missed the lesson implicit in this history. Numbers I through IV of *The Sketch Book*, which included "Rip Van Winkle," had to be published at the author's expense, while the Christmas visit essays, for all the objections raised by its first American reader, Ebenezer, attracted the Prince of Publishers, John Murray. If Irving was to aim for the English audience, he might well look to the future possibilities of combinations of *Spectator* scenes with even more antiquated black-letter traditions.

The result of the English publication of *The Sketch Book* is well known: like Byron, Irving awoke one morning to find himself famous. He began to be lionized by English literary society, and he began to be importuned to cash in on his new popularity with another work, two rather opposed impulses. What was to be the nature of the new work? One obvious answer was another *Sketch Book*, and in a letter of September 28, 1821, to his brother Ebenezer, Irving records that Ebenezer had asked for "an additional number" of the earlier work.[17] The obvious alternative—structured fiction, a novel—was rather too daring for Irving. He had begun thinking about a novel, tentatively entitled "Rosalie," in 1818, and perhaps he thought of returning to it. "Buckthorne and His Friends" was written during this period, and it is possible that he visualized it even this early as part of a novel. He definitely did so later when he was in Dresden after the publication of *Bracebridge Hall*. The pressure upon him to write a novel must have been considerable from both friends and critics. A friendly busybody in the *Port Folio*, for example, was willing even to pick the style of novel he should write, though he did allow Irving some choice. It should be a prototype of "a series of novels, on the plan of those of Miss Edgeworth, or, if he likes that better, of the author of Waverly."[18] Apparently Thomas Moore rescued him from this dilemma. He suggested that Irving take the characters and locale of the Christmas visit at Bracebridge Hall and work them into a book-length production. It was not to be a novel, but the setting and the group of characters already gathered for *The*

17. *Ibid.*, II, 58.
18. *Port Folio*, March 21, 1821, pp. 134–35; quoted in STW, II, 290.

Sketch Book would provide a foundation, as Moore wrote, "for the purpose of making a slight thread of a story on which to string his remarks and sketches of human manner and feeling."[19] Neither as structured as a novel nor as diffuse as the series of essays and stories in *The Sketch Book*, the proposed work must have seemed a logical step forward for Irving.

But the other result of *The Sketch Book*, his new literary and social prominence, was to hamper Irving's work on *Bracebridge Hall* through the entire period of its composition. One might imagine from some of his comments that he was impervious to the blandishments of society: "I have advances made me by society, that were I a mere seeker of society, would be invaluable," he wrote to Brevoort sometime in June, 1821, "but I dread so much being put out in my pursuits and distracted by the mere hurry of fashionable engagements that I keep aloof and neglect opportunities which I may perhaps at some future day look back to with regret."[20] These are admirable sentiments for the working writer, but it is hard to believe that Irving lived up to the letter of them. The fact remains that Irving apparently accomplished little on *Bracebridge Hall* for a year or more, while he found much solace in the society of London and Paris. It was not until March 19, 1821, that Thomas Moore recorded that Irving had written, within the past ten days, "about one hundred and thirty pages of the size of those in the 'Sketch Book.' "[21] That was an extraordinary rate of composition, even for a writer like Irving who drew heavily upon notebooks for material. He was not to keep it up, though the pressure for the new work was to continue. By July of the same year, in response to a subtle spurring from Murray, who wrote to ask him to "tell me how you are and what you are about," Irving had to reply:

> I have been leading a "miscellaneous" kind of life at Paris, if I may use a literary phrase. I have been rather distracted by engagements, in spite of all my efforts to keep out of society. Anacreon Moore is living here, and has made me a gayer fellow than I could have wished; but I found it impossible to resist the charm of his society. Paris is like an English watering-place, with the advantage of the best kind of amusements, and excellent society.
>
> I have scribbled at intervals, and have a mass of writings by

19. Entry for March 19, 1821, in *Memoirs, Journals, and Correspondence of Thomas Moore*, ed. Lord John Russell (London, 1853–1856), III, 211; quoted in PMI, II, 39.

20. Irving to Brevoort, June or July (?), 1821; quoted in PMI, II, 48.

21. Entry for March 19, 1821, in *Memoirs, Journals, and Correspondence of Thomas Moore*, III, 211.

me; rather desultory, as must be the case when one is so much interrupted; but I hope, in the fulness of time, to get them into some order.[22]

Many years later, in 1850, he recalled in a letter to John Murray III that he had actually completed a "rough manuscript" of *Bracebridge Hall* by July, 1821.[23] Rough it must have been indeed, since he required six more months to produce a manuscript good enough to be sent to America, but, as we shall see, still very imperfect. As he wrote to Ebenezer on September 28, for part of the time he was "so much out of health" that he could not write at all. But his "bilious attacks" of this period fed his anxiety "to get something into print," the more so as Murray was eager to have something, and Irving judged that the success of *The Sketch Book* "would ensure a run to anything I should now bring forward."[24] All in all, this period of composition seems to have been an unhappy, unhealthy, anxious time. It was not entirely without its successes, however. Parts of the new book that he showed his friends seemed to be well received. Leslie recalled with pleasure years afterward the composition of "The Stout Gentleman," as did George Bancroft on the occasion of Irving's reading to him of "St. Mark's Eve." And one essay originally intended for *Bracebridge Hall*, "Buckthorne and His Critics," was so successful that Irving accepted Leslie's recommendation that he hold it out from the work in progress and use it as "the groundwork of a novel."[25]

Sometime around the beginning of 1822, Irving began to draft what he considered a fair copy of the still rather "desultory" manuscript of *Bracebridge Hall*. This copy he sent off to Ebenezer in New York in two installments, Volume I on January 29, and Volume II on February 25, 1822. His instructions to Ebenezer about American publication of the book were given in a letter accompanying the first volume of manuscript. This letter is so interesting in itself and so significant to the history surrounding *Bracebridge Hall* that it is reproduced.

London, Jan. 29, 1822.

My Dear Brother:

By the packet from Liverpool which brings this letter I forward you a parcel, containing the first volume of BRACEBRIDGE HALL, or

22. Irving to Murray, July 6, 1821; quoted in *ibid.*, II, 49.

23. Irving to John Murray III, Sunnyside, September 22, 1850; quoted in Ben H. McClary, *Washington Irving and the House of Murray* (Knoxville: University of Tennessee Press, 1969), p. 198.

24. PMI, II, 57–58; see also Irving to Peter Irving, September 6, 1821, *ibid.*, II, 54.

25. *Ibid.*, II, 51, 54–57. "Buckthorne" was printed in *Tales of a Traveller*.

THE HUMOURISTS, a MEDLEY in two volumes. I had hoped to have
sent both volumes, but I have not been able to get the second
volume ready in time for this opportunity, though I have tried until
the last moment. You will receive it, however, by the next opportunity, and very probably before you can have made the necessary
arrangements for printing. At any rate, put the first volume to press
immediately and publish it *as soon as possible*, with or without
the second volume. As it is not like a novel, but rather a connected
series of tales and essays, it is of no great importance that they
should be published together; but it is of the greatest importance
that some part of the work should appear as early as possible, to
give me some chance of securing copyright. I shall have to put
it to press here in a very short time, as the season is advancing,
and my publisher is very impatient; besides, the public has been
expecting something from me for some time past, and it will not
do to let expectation get too high. If the work is not got out very
soon therefore in America, there will be a chance of an English
copy getting out beforehand, and thus throwing me at the mercy
of American publishers. Should the number of copies make any
material difference in the time of getting out the work, you had
better let the first edition be rather small; and put another to press
the moment I furnish you with proof sheets of the English edition,
in which there will doubtless be many alterations, as I have not
had time to revise some parts of the work sufficiently, and am apt
to make alterations to the last moment.

The work had better be printed in duodecimo; and to save time
in binding, let the volumes be put up in lettered covers like the
Sketch Book. The second edition can be got up in better style.
The first volume runs, as near as I can guess, between 340 and
350 pages of the American edition of the Sketch Book. The second
volume will be about the same size. You can make your estimates
accordingly. Put what price you think proper. I do not care about
its being a very high one. *I wish, expressly, Moses Thomas to have
the preference over every other publisher.* I impress this upon you,
and beg you to attend to it as earnestly as if I had written three
sheets full on the subject. Whatever may have been his embarrass-
ments and consequent want of punctuality, he is one who shewed
a disposition to serve me, and who did serve me in the time of
my necessity, and I should despise myself could I for a moment
forget it. Let him have the work on better terms than other publishers, and do not be deterred by the risk of loss.

I have not had time to page the work, but must beg you to
do it. I have given a table of contents in the order in which the

papers are to be put, and have numbered each with a pencil for *your* direction. These numbers are *not* to be printed over the papers. Perhaps it will be best to advertise the work as in the press, to secure orders in time.

I have no time left to say any thing further. I have fagged until the last moment, and am now fit to go to bed. My health is still unrestored. This work has kept me from getting well, and my indisposition on the other hand has retarded the work. I have now been about five weeks in London, and have only once been out of doors, about a month since, and that made me worse.[26]

The urgent tone of this letter is a result of the extraordinary pressures Irving was feeling. To begin with, there was Murray in the background, pressing him to complete a work in time to benefit from his recent success with *The Sketch Book*. Even without Murray's importuning on this point, Irving was enough of a businessman to sense the advantages to be gained by speed in these circumstances. Yet his health would not allow him to progress at his normal pace. The more he drove himself, the more his health suffered; if he should try to relax and improve his health, the pressure of time and need must have made him more anxious. Still, he might have put off the considerable effort of drafting a manuscript for an American edition had it not been for the circumstances surrounding international copyright. To protect himself from transatlantic pirates, he had to have the work published nearly simultaneously in England and America. If he should choose the normal method to achieve this protection—sending proofs of one publisher to be reset by another, either the Murray proofs to America or the American proofs to Murray—he would have to delay publication at least several months to assure simultaneous publication. His solution to the problem was, essentially, to throw away the first American edition of *Bracebridge Hall*—to use it merely as a tool to block violation of his copyright. The manuscript he sent to Ebenezer was imperfect; he was to make more than a thousand substantive revisions for the English edition, yet none of them could possibly be incorporated in the first American edition. Some of the stories and essays in the first American edition were so corrupt they were almost unreadable, notably "The Student of Salamanca." Four whole new essays appear in the English text which are not present in the American. Yet, faced with his pressures and problems, Irving must have felt he had little choice. As it was, sending the imperfect manuscript to Ebenezer committed him to completion of the English text—which, as the letter states clearly, was to be heavily

26. Irving to Ebenezer Irving; quoted in PMI, II, 71–73.

corrected—in a matter of months, else the American text would appear before the English and could be pirated by unscrupulous English publishers.

To all of these unusual circumstances a final fillip may be added. Irving made these arrangements without the benefit of any firm commitment by Murray. It was not until after he had sent off both volumes of *Bracebridge Hall* to America that he was approached by Colburn; Irving, however, went to Murray with his manuscript. Irving received one thousand guineas for the work during an often-described interview. Murray asked what Irving wanted for the manuscript, and Irving replied that his price was fifteen hundred guineas. Murray countered with an offer for one thousand guineas, which Irving accepted at once, perhaps surprising Murray, who expected him to haggle.[27] The anecdote has been told, correctly and incorrectly, by several biographers with sundry points to make about the relationship between Irving and Murray, but none seems to have taken into consideration the fact that Irving was in no position to bargain, since a pirateable American edition was already in the mail. Had he not made some arrangement before the American text came out, any English publisher could reprint the work without so much as a token royalty!

The two parts of the American manuscript arrived in New York within eight days of each other near the beginning of April, 1822, though the second volume was mailed almost a month after the first. Apparently Moses Thomas was the publisher, though all copies bear the name of C. S. Van Winkle on the title page.[28] The first American

---

27. Pierre M. Irving, II, 76–78, tells the story this way. Stanley T. Williams (STW, I, 207) gives a different account and a different final sum, 1200 guineas. Page 170 of John Murray's Ledger B under Bracebridge Hall reads, "To Irving for [*illegible*] copyright . . . £1050", that is, one thousand guineas (John Murray archives).

28. This anomaly is perhaps the most enigmatic circumstance of all the bibliographical problems about *Bracebridge Hall*. Jacob Blanck notes (*Bibliography of American Literature*, V, 19; hereafter cited as BAL) that the two copies he had seen in original bindings bore the inscription "PUBLISHED BY / M. & S. Thomas. / Philadelphia" on the spine. Research for this volume discovered no exceptions to this finding. In view of this evidence, coupled with the emphasis Irving placed in his letter to Ebenezer quoted above that Moses Thomas publish the book, one must conclude that was perhaps technically the case, and that Van Winkle's name on the title page was a result of the curious arrangement among American publishers described in William Charvat, *Literary Publishing in America, 1790–1850* (Philadelphia: University of Pennsylvania Press, 1969), especially pp. 44–51. This arrangement divided the risk of new publications among publisher, printer, jobber, and retailer in the various publishing centers of America with "a system of distribution so complicated that the publishers were almost as confused as the historian who tries to read their surviving records and correspondence"

edition was published on May 21, 1822, just two days before the date usually given for the first English edition.[29] Perhaps it is not surprising that even though the text of this edition was very bad and was to be repudiated by Irving specifically in an apologetic "Advertisement to the Second Edition," few reviewers in America condemned it as they should have. One, after admitting that he picked up the book "predisposed to admire, and almost predetermined to applaud," confessed that it fell short of his expectations, but quickly added that it was, nevertheless, "a very considerable book." This reviewer seemed most preoccupied with Irving's failure to condemn things English. He was particularly annoyed with "the overflowing delight, with which he contemplates every object of the old world, whether it be Fentern [sic] Abbey, Conway Castle, or Mr. Newberry's print shop!" It is interesting that the reviewer knew no better than to repeat the typographical error, unique in the first American edition, of "Fentern Abbey" for "Tintern Abbey."[30]

Edward Everett, reviewing the work for the *North American Review*, took the opportunity to extol Irving's work as a whole and *Bracebridge Hall* in particular, "not because we have anything to say of value, after the unequivocal tribute the great English and American public have paid to his success, but because we would fain call him in as an auxiliary in the battle we have occasionally waged in behalf of our country's reputation."[31] He finds he has "no hesitation in pronouncing Bracebridge quite equal to any thing, which the present age of British literature has produced in this department [the familiar essay]." Thus it is no surprise when Everett discovers the one major flaw of *Bracebridge Hall* to be that the author does not remain American enough:

> Mr. Irving traverses Bracebridge Hall, explores the grounds, goes in and out of the housekeeper's room, and the hunter's lodge, visits the village school and the rustic fair, not like the stranger from another world, struck at the sort of life, which he had never before witnessed, but as one of the inmates. In doing so, we maintain

---

(*ibid.*, p. 45). Irving probably insisted upon Thomas because his American profits on *The Sketch Book* were so considerable—some nine thousand dollars in two years, a princely profit for those times and circumstances. But Thomas was near bankruptcy by 1822, and it is likely that he jobbed all of the printing and distribution of *Bracebridge Hall*, supplying little more to the work than his name on the too-tender spine.

29. McClary, *Irving and the House of Murray* (p. 42), gives May 17 as the date when the book was registered in Stationers' Hall. Publication date was May 23.

30. *North American Review* 4 (July, 1822), p. 205.

31. *Ibid.*, p. 209.

that he has mistaken his powers . . . he should at least have acted
on the principle, announced in his preface as that on which his
interest in England rested. A well educated American, kindly received in good company in England . . . might surely be called upon
to produce a work of a strongly marked original character.[32]

All in all, it was to be expected that the American reading public,
including its reviewers, should be willing to take to its heart even this
most imperfect version of *Bracebridge Hall*; Irving had guessed well
at the uncritical reception anything he wrote might receive across the
Atlantic. He had other fish to fry—in this case an English sole over
an American cod.

Once the American manuscript was safely out of the way, Irving
began working strenuously on the perfection of *Bracebridge Hall*.
Judging from a comparison of the extant manuscripts, the correction
that took place for the fair copy that became the American manuscript
was something less than half the correction given the English manuscript. Many sections of the British manuscript were rewritten entirely,
four new sections were added, the order of essays in Volume I was
changed, and hardly a page of manuscript escaped some substantive
revision.[33] No evidence exists concerning the precise method Irving used
to correct manuscript, present copy to Murray, and then to correct
proof, but the press of time must have been such that the process was
continuous and interlocking. That is, he must have sent off several
corrected chapters at a time, worked on the next installments until
proof was returned to him, then corrected proof for an earlier segment
while correcting manuscript for a later one. The result was a very
carelessly produced work, and one that continued to undergo correction
even after publication. In this matter the evidence, though circumstantial, is convincing.

Irving began a continuous pagination of his English manuscript which
carries through "Family Reliques." He then shifted the position of "The
Widow" and "The Lovers" and gave up his pagination. He seems to
have done little or no correction of punctuation, which is extremely
eccentric in the manuscripts, probably accepting all revisions of his
punctuation by Murray's compositors without protest. His carelessness
in this matter, as well as some retrospective concern, is expressed in a
letter to Brevoort about the American text of *The Sketch Book*. He
suggested that that work appeared to him "to be a little too *highly
pointed*. I don't know whether my manuscript was so, or whether it
is the scrupulous precision of the printer. High pointing is apt to injure

32. *Ibid.*, p. 213.
33. These matters are discussed at length in the Textual Commentary.

the fluency of the style if the reader attends to all the stops."[34] The English manuscript of *Bracebridge* is punctuated by no known system beyond the author's whim, and Irving apparently cared so little for such matters that even when one compositor overloaded the work with colons and semicolons, he paid no attention.

He did pay a good deal of attention to the substance of his text. The amount of correction done to the English manuscript after the American copy was sent off varies widely from essay to essay. Most of the essays show only an occasional verbal change, but two at least, "Hawking" and "Falconry," were so heavily corrected that Irving produced several pages of new manuscript. Nevertheless, the heaviest revisions came when the book was in proof. Several pages of manuscript bear mute testimony to Irving's revisions in proof by the compositors' marks for the beginnings of gatherings that do not correspond to the equivalent places in the Murray text. Probably Irving was revising for several specific purposes. One, of course, was simple fluency in the narrative—the revisions for "Hawking" and "Falconry" are of this sort. Another was for consistency. *Bracebridge Hall* is a long text, its composition was hurried, and corrections were made at several stages of production at virtually the same time. It is to be expected that Homer should nod. Irving apparently got confused about some purely physical events—Master Simon's and General Harbottle's encounters with the radical, discussed in the Textual Commentary, pages 000–00, is an example. He attempted to correct these in proof, but, as we shall see, was not always successful or consistent.

A third purpose in correction was to achieve a coherent and modern English style. Irving, the American upstart directing his prose toward Murray, the English Prince of Booksellers, was not fully conversant with what he probably considered the best modern English style. His expression was naturally somewhat antiquarian, somewhat American, and he tried to revise it to consistent modern practice in England. One journal entry of this period is representative. A "shewn" is to be replaced by a "showed," which was corrected in proof.[35] On the other hand, both the English and the American manuscripts are fairly consistent in a preference for English spellings over American, *-our* over *-or*, "relique" in preference to "relic."

Evidence is plentiful that the first English edition underwent considerable correction after May 11, 1822, when Irving sent off the last proof, to sometime before May 30, when Murray recorded payment to the printer Davison for four thousand copies of *Bracebridge Hall.*

34. Irving to Brevoort, July 28, 1819; quoted in PMI, I, 245.

35. In *Journals and Notebooks* (III, 183), Irving noted, "B B hall vol. 2 361 / line 3, showed, for shewn." See Twayne edition, 295.11.

What is not known is to what extent Irving participated in these revisions. We do know that he added a paragraph to the last essay, doubtless when he received an early set of printed sheets to ship to Ebenezer, as he had promised to do when he mailed the manuscript for the first American edition. This paragraph was incorporated into the second American edition, also published by Van Winkle in 1822, and into about three-quarters of the total number of copies of the first English edition. Clearly, Irving transmitted the paragraph to both publishers, and it was added to the run of the 1822 John Murray edition, creating a second state of that first edition. There are a number of other variants in the first English edition, but no evidence whether Irving was involved in them, directly or indirectly. A cancel occurs in some copies of the first state in Volume I, pages 93–94; a number of corrections were made, at first piecemeal, and then massively, including finally the resetting of every gathering in both volumes. These variants suggest at least three states of this first English edition and a concealed second edition in the fourth state; and, except for the added paragraph marking the second state, there is no sure evidence of Irving's hand. External indications are particularly ambiguous. No evidence seems to have survived about Irving's movements between May 7, when he saw Thomas Moore off to Paris from Dover,[36] to June 11, when he wrote Brevoort a note mentioning that "about three weeks since" he had "launched a new work which you have doubtless long since seen in America. The English edition has many alterations and additions, as I got into better health and spirits after I sent my manuscript to America, and was enabled to improve the work while printing."[37] It is tempting to read that last phrase, "to improve the work while printing," as a definite indication that Irving corrected the work while it was in press, but he could as easily mean that he corrected it when it was already in print, that is, in proof. And his comment that the work was "launched" three weeks before his letter tends to indicate that he personally was through with it at or before publication, which was on May 23, 1822.[38] Although the whole pressrun was probably complete by that date, he might still have had a hand in the corrections

36. *Memoirs, Journals, and Correspondence of Thomas Moore*, III, 351.
37. Quoted in PMI, II, 80.
38. Murray's account book gives May 30 as the date of payment to Davison for four thousand copies; no date is given for the payment to Ross (?) for the binding, but the page entry for the daybook seems to read 156, very close to the page reference to the payment to Davison, 157. Therefore it seems likely that the whole pressrun was printed and bound before May 30, indeed, possibly by publication date, May 23 (John Murray, Ledger B, p. 170. Murray archives). Blanck (BAL, V, 20) quotes a letter, dated December, 1964, from the heirs of Murray on this subject: "4,000 copies printed made up of 3,000 plus a run-on of 1,000.

of the later states, but evidence of his involvement or lack of it is entirely internal, and for that reason the problem is considered at greater length in the Textual Commentary.

That Murray had been correct in urging Irving to get the book out is suggested by the eager critical attention it received upon publication.[39] The first review appeared only two days after publication, in the May 25 issue of the *Literary Chronicle and Weekly Review*. Within the next few months every important literary journal in England reviewed it, and extracts from it were printed in periodicals all over England. In general the reviews were favorable, though the work sometimes suffered by comparison with *The Sketch Book*. Such was the case with the review in the *London Magazine*, which intimated that Irving was in danger of being spoiled by his success.[40] The *Gentleman's Magazine* concluded also that *Bracebridge Hall* was not as successful as *The Sketch Book*, and gave a perceptive explanation: "Although the author's delineations are full of humour, and gentlemanly pleasantry, as sketches of society in England, the volumes are comparatively worthless, as no one ever heard of a family residing in any part of these united kingdoms at this present time, whose peculiarities and traits of character bear any sort of resemblance to the sketches which Mr. Irving has professed to give of them. He can only have read of such persons in old books of a hundred years' standing; no such beings exist now a days."[41] The review in *The Literary Gazette* for June 1, 1822, also compared it unfavorably with *The Sketch Book*, and the *Blackwood's* review not only announced its inferiority to its predecessor but qualified its own enthusiastic reception of *The Sketch Book*. The reviewer was particularly aroused to irony at what he sensed to be the egotism of Irving's self-proclaimed position as literary liberalizer of English taste:

> Mr. Irving is evidently an amiable and a well-meaning man; and we like him the better for the good-natured vanity which he

---

No means of knowing the time interval between these printings but evidently very short and, in many cases, "run-on' may mean that the whole lot were printed without a gap of time." There seems no reason to dispute this conclusion.

39. A thorough survey of the reviews of *Bracebridge Hall* and other works by Irving may be found in W. B. Cairns, *British Criticisms of American Writings, 1815–1833*, University of Wisconsin Studies in Language and Literature, No. 14 (1922), especially pp. 71–85; STW covers the same ground, though not as thoroughly, I, 206–12.

40. *London Magazine* 6 (1822) 436; quoted in Cairns, *British Criticisms*, p. 77.

41. *Gentleman's Magazine* 92 (1822) 54; quoted in Cairns, *British Criticisms*, p. 73.

betrays, in asserting that his philanthropic labours have been crowned with success. That England has of late evinced friendly sentiments towards America, there can be no doubt; but as those sentiments were chiefly marked by the reception of the Sketch Book, it is evident that they preceded that talented work, and that the success of Mr. Irving's book was more owing to our liberal feelings, than our liberal feelings to Mr. Irving's book.[42]

The consensus of these comparisons may be observed in the summary given by the *Literary Gazette* for August 28, 1824, in a review of Irving's next work, *Tales of a Traveller*: "The Sketch Book and Brace-bridge Hall are the foundations of [Irving's] celebrity, and the former especially continues to be read with undiminished pleasure."[43]

Of the individual sketches in the book, "The Stout Gentleman" is the one most frequently singled out for praise, while almost as many reviewers indicated their own taste for sentimentality by giving "Annette Delarbre" special mention. Almost all praise the style, and many comment, not at all invariably unfavorably, on the relationship between this work and Addison's essays. Irving is given much credit for his sympathetic insight into English character, although one review finds him too unsympathetic to the English military type in his presentation of General Harbottle. All, of course, comment on the fact that he is an American, but the range of values associated with this quality is enormous. Some echo Irving's observation in the first chapter, "It has been a matter of marvel to my European readers, that a man from the wilds of America should express himself in tolerable English"; others take a more sympathetic attitude. Perhaps the extreme is in the review in *The British Critic*:

> We need only say, that the style and taste, as well as the matter of the present, as of all our author's compositions, is of the best kind. To say that they are extraordinary, when considered as the production of a person born and educated on the other side of the Atlantic, would be neither gracious nor just; for they are strikingly so in themselves. Without this qualification, viewing his productions as compositions only, we much doubt whether we could name any contemporary writer whose attempts, in that light species of writing, of which the first model in our language was furnished by Addison, would easily stand a comparison with those of this American essay-ist. It may seem strange to bring Addison and a citizen of New

42. *Blackwood's Magazine* 11 (June, 1822), 691.
43. *Literary Gazette* 8 (August 28, 1824), 545.

York together in the same sentence . . . in spite, however, of the apparent improbability of the fact, so it is.[44]

On the whole, the verdict, though not quite unanimous, was overwhelming; *Bracebridge Hall* might disappoint in comparison to *The Sketch Book*, but it was at a high level of literary creation nevertheless. The wisdom of following Tom Moore's suggestion was made clear to Irving in the *succès d'estime* of the book.

With the book fairly launched in England on May 23, 1822, Irving turned his attention to righting the wrong he had done the American reading public with the publication of the first American edition—published only two days before the English, as was noted before, but several months and thousands of emendations earlier than the equivalent English text in terms of his attention. He seems to have taken some of the earliest sheets of the first English edition, added a paragraph to the last essay and perhaps a line to the first page, along with an apologetic "Advertisement," and shipped the bundle forthwith to Ebenezer. He must have hurried, since the second American edition, like the first, is dated 1822 and is published by Van Winkle, this time with no mention of Moses Thomas on the spine or elsewhere. This second American edition, for all its immensely superior text, presented itself in a much more modest format, a squat duodecimo in small print. Doubtless the price reduction implied in the format was necessary to compete with the well-printed quarto first American edition.

The first American edition represents a complete textual dead end. It was never reprinted in any form, and, with only a few exceptions, its readings are universally inferior to the later forms of the text. The second American edition has a more interesting history. It was reprinted in 1826 by Van Winkle with a few corrections, almost certainly not authorial. Then, in 1828, Irving signed a seven-year contract with the Carey publishing firm of Philadelphia, leasing the American copyright of *Bracebridge Hall* and three other works for a yearly payment of approximately six hundred dollars. A third American edition was then printed by Carey and Lea, Philadelphia, in 1830. The text was almost certainly taken from the 1826 printing of the second American edition; many of the errors of the 1822 text disappear in this edition, while most of the 1826 readings are duplicated. Although there is some indication that Irving himself made corrections for the 1829 edition of *Knickerbocker's History* published by Carey,[45] no evidence, internal or external, suggests that he had any hand in the 1830 edition of *Brace-*

44. *British Critic*, n. s. 18 (September, 1822), p. 299; quoted in Cairns, *British Criticisms*, pp. 77–78.

45. Letter to the editor of this volume from Mr. Michael Black, March 28, 1967.

bridge Hall. The text includes no new readings of any significance and transmits many of the corruptions of the 1826 printing of the second American edition. Nor is there evidence that Irving modified the text in later reprintings by Carey and Lea and their successors. The work was reprinted in 1831 and 1833, twice in 1835, the later text bearing an 1836 copyright and the deceptive rubric, "A New Edition," in 1838, 1839, and finally 1841. Irving's seven-year contract was renewed in 1835 for another seven years, perhaps explaining the two editions in that year. It was not renewed in 1842, and the work went out of print in America with the 1841 printing until the appearance of the Author's Revised Edition by Putnam at the end of 1849.

Meanwhile, in the Old World, the book enjoyed a further international success. To begin with, John Murray managed to realize a fairly satisfactory profit on his original one-thousand-guinea speculation. Total costs for producing the first edition were £2200, while income from the 3976 copies sold at sixteen shillings each came to £3180 16s., leaving him a profit of £980.[46] In 1823 he reprinted the work in a smaller octavo, producing three thousand copies.[47] This edition was reissued in 1824, 1825, and 1829. Also in 1823, Baudry and Didot produced an edition of the work, which was reprinted in 1827 by Galignani and again in 1834 by Baudry. This edition was derived from the 1823 Murray edition. The first translation was by M. Jean Cohen, entitled *Le Château de Bracebridge* (Paris, 1822), and Irving himself noticed a copy for sale while walking on the Quai in Paris. He made the terse notation in his journal "—4 vols—5 francs."[48]

Then, in 1845, Murray added *Bracebridge Hall* to his Home and Colonial Library, deriving the text of this fourth English edition from the 1825 reprinting of the third English edition, in which form it stayed in print until 1866. Again, on the Continent, Bohn printed an edition of *Bracebridge Hall* in a series of cheap English reprints, which moved Murray to institute a copyright suit in 1850.[49]

When Irving returned to America in 1846 it was to be welcomed as a literary immortal, a classic. "Very well, then—," as Stanley T. Williams reconstructed his thought, "something should be devised to . . . swell the income of Mr. Irving."[50] On July 26, 1848, Irving contracted with George P. Putnam for the Author's Revised Edition, a reissue of all his writings, to be revised for posterity, a truly formidable task. The real purpose of the series, as Williams hints, was to salvage works

46. Murray Ledger B, p. 170, Murray archives.
47. *Ibid.,* p. 290.
48. Irving, *Journals and Letters,* III, 215; entry for August 16, 1823.
49. See McClary, *Irving and the House of Murray,* pp. 191, 200.
50. STW, II, 213.

like *Mahomet* that Irving had cluttering his trunk, but it necessarily included the gruelling drudgery of revising his works published earlier. Perhaps the most succinct attestation of the speed and effort involved is the fact that *Bracebridge Hall*, the sixth numbered volume in the series, was completed and published less than eighteen months after the contract was signed. As Irving wrote in 1849, "I have had more toil of head and fagging of the pen for the last eighteen months than in any other period of my life."[51]

The amount of revision for the Author's Revised Edition of *Bracebridge Hall* and the authority of these revisions are the subject of considerable discussion in the Textual Commentary to this volume, and need not be mentioned here. It should only be noted that the text of *Bracebridge Hall* that appears in the Author's Revised Edition, reprinted many times thereafter, is the one on which almost all critical and historical commentary has been based. Probably nothing can circumvent the critical neglect which *Bracebridge Hall* has suffered, but the restoration of its text to something at least approaching the form Irving originally intended for it may serve to wipe away a cobweb or two.

51. Irving to his niece, Mrs. Sarah Storrow; quoted in STW, II, 202.

BRACEBRIDGE HALL

Volume I

THE AUTHOR

WORTHY READER!

On again taking pen in hand, I would fain make a few observations at the outset, by way of bespeaking a right understanding. The volumes which I have already published have met with a reception far beyond my most sanguine expectations. I would willingly attribute this' to their intrinsic merits; but, in spite of the vanity of authorship, I cannot but be sensible that their success has, in a great measure, been owing to a less flattering cause. It has been a matter of marvel, that a man from the wilds of America should express himself in tolerable English. I was looked upon as something new and strange in literature; a kind of demi-savage, with a feather in his hand, instead of on his head; and there was a curiosity to hear what such a being had to say about civilized society.

This novelty is now at an end, and of course the feeling of indulgence which it produced. I must now expect to bear the scrutiny of sterner criticism, and to be measured by the same standard with contemporary writers; and the very favour which has been shown to my previous writings, will cause these to be treated with the greater rigour; as there is nothing for which the world is apt to punish a man more severely, than for having been over-praised. On this head, therefore, I wish to forestall the censoriousness of the reader; and I entreat he will not think the worse of me for the many injudicious things that may have been said in my commendation.

I am aware that I often travel over beaten ground, and treat of subjects that have already been discussed by abler pens. Indeed, various authors have been mentioned as my models, to whom I should feel flattered if I thought I bore the slightest resemblance; but in truth I write after no model that I am conscious of, and I write with no idea of imitation or competition. In venturing occasionally on topics that have already been almost exhausted by English authors, I do it, not with the presumption of challenging a comparison, but with the hope that some new interest may be given to such topics, when discussed by the pen of a stranger.

If, therefore, I should sometimes be found dwelling with fondness on subjects that are trite and common-placed with the reader, I beg the circumstances under which I write may be kept in recollection. Having been born and brought up in a new country, yet educated from infancy in the literature of an old one, my mind was early filled with historical and poetical associations, connected with places, and manners, and customs of Europe; but which could rarely be applied to those of my own country. To a mind thus peculiarly prepared, the most ordinary objects and scenes, on arriving in Europe, are full of strange matter and interesting novelty. England is as classic ground to an American as Italy is to an Englishman; and old London teems with as much historical association as mighty Rome.

Indeed, it is difficult to describe the whimsical medley of ideas that throng upon his mind on landing among English scenes. He for the first time sees a world about which he has been reading and thinking in every stage of his existence. The recollected ideas of infancy, youth, and manhood; of the nursery, the school, and the study, come swarming at once upon him; and his attention is distracted between great and little objects; each of which, perhaps, awakens an equally delightful train of remembrances.

But what more especially attracts his notice are those peculiarities which distinguish an old country and an old state of society from a new one. I have never yet grown familiar enough with the crumbling monuments of past ages, to blunt the intense interest with which I at first beheld them. Accustomed always to scenes where history was, in a manner, in anticipation; where every thing in art was new and progressive, and pointed to the future rather than to the past; where, in short, the works of man gave no ideas but those of young existence, and prospective improvement; there was something inexpressibly touching in the sight of enormous piles of architecture, gray with antiquity, and sinking to decay. I cannot describe the mute but deep-felt enthusiasm with which I have contemplated a vast monastic ruin, like Tintern Abbey, buried in the bosom of a quiet valley, and shut up from the world, as though it had existed merely for itself; or a warrior pile, like Conway Castle, standing in stern loneliness on its rocky height, a mere hollow yet threatening phantom of departed power. They spread a grand, and melancholy, and, to me, an unusual charm over the landscape; I for the first time beheld signs of national old age, and empire's decay, and proofs of the transient and perishing glories of art, amidst the ever-springing and reviving fertility of nature.

But, in fact, to me every thing was full of matter; the footsteps of history were every where to be traced; and poetry had breathed over and sanctified the land. I experienced the delightful freshness of feeling of a child, to whom every thing is new. I pictured to myself a set of inhabitants and a mode of life for every habitation that I saw, from the aristocratical mansion, amidst the lordly repose of stately groves and solitary parks, to the straw-thatched cottage, with its scanty

garden and its cherished woodbine. I thought I never could be sated
with the sweetness and freshness of a country so completely carpeted
with verdure; where every air breathed of the balmy pasture, and the
honeysuckled hedge. I was continually coming upon some little document of poetry in the blossomed hawthorn, the daisy, the cowslip,
the primrose, or some other simple object that has received a supernatural value from the muse. The first time that I heard the song of
the nightingale, I was intoxicated more by the delicious crowd of
remembered associations than by the melody of its notes; and I shall
never forget the thrill of ecstasy with which I first saw the lark rise,
almost from beneath my feet, and wing its musical flight up into the
morning sky.

In this way I traversed England, a grown-up child, delighted by
every object great and small; and betraying a wondering ignorance,
and simple enjoyment, that provoked many a stare and a smile from
my wiser and more experienced fellow-travellers. Such too was the
odd confusion of associations that kept breaking upon me as I first
approached London. One of my earliest wishes had been to see this
great metropolis. I had read so much about it in the earliest books
that had been put into my infant hands; and I had heard so much
about it from those around me who had come from the "old countries,"
that I was familiar with the names of its streets and squares, and
public places, before I knew those of my native city. It was, to me,
the great centre of the world, round which every thing seemed to
revolve. I recollect contemplating so wistfully when a boy, a paltry
little print of the Thames, and London Bridge, and St. Paul's, that
was in front of an old magazine; and a picture of Kensington Gardens,
with gentlemen in three-cornered hats and broad skirts, and ladies in
hoops and lappets, that hung up in my bedroom; even the venerable
cut of St. John's Gate, that has stood, time out of mind, in front of
the Gentleman's Magazine, was not without its charms to me; and I
envied the odd looking little men that appeared to be loitering about
its arches.

How then did my heart warm when the towers of Westminster
Abbey were pointed out to me, rising above the rich groves of St.
James's Park, with a thin blue haze about their gray pinnacles! I could
not behold this great mausoleum of what is most illustrious in our
paternal history, without feeling my enthusiasm in a glow. With what
eagerness did I explore every part of the metropolis! I was not content
with those matters which occupy the dignified research of the learned
traveller; I delighted to call up all the feelings of childhood, and
to seek after those objects which had been the wonders of my infancy.

London Bridge, so famous in nursery song; the far-famed Monument; Gog and Magog, and the Lions in the Tower, all brought back many a recollection of infantine delight, and of good old beings, now no more, who had gossiped about them to my wondering ear. Nor was it without a recurrence of childish interest that I first peeped into Mr. Newberry's shop, in St. Paul's Church-yard, that fountain-head of literature. Mr. Newberry was the first that ever filled my infant mind with the idea of a great and good man. He published all the picture books of the day; and, out of his abundant love for children, he charged "nothing for either paper or print, and only a penny-halfpenny for the binding!"

I have mentioned these circumstances, worthy reader, to show you the whimsical crowd of associations that are apt to beset my mind on mingling among English scenes. I hope they may, in some measure, plead my apology, should I be found harping upon stale and trivial themes, or indulging an over-fondness for any thing antique and obsolete. I know it is the humour, not to say cant of the day, to run riot about old times, old books, old customs, and old buildings; with myself, however, as far as I have caught the contagion, the feeling is genuine. To a man from a young country all old things are in a manner new; and he may surely be excused in being a little curious about antiquities, whose native land, unfortunately, cannot boast of a single ruin.

Having been brought up, also, in the comparative simplicity of a republic, I am apt to be struck with even the ordinary circumstances incident to an aristocratical state of society. If, however, I should at any time amuse myself by pointing out some of the eccentricities, and some of the poetical characteristics of the latter, I would not be understood as pretending to decide upon its political merits. My only aim is to paint characters and manners. I am no politician. The more I have considered the study of politics, the more I have found it full of perplexity; and I have contented myself, as I have in my religion, with the faith in which I was brought up, regulating my own conduct by its precepts; but leaving to abler heads the task of making converts.

I shall continue on, therefore, in the course I have hitherto pursued; looking at things poetically, rather than politically; describing them as they are, rather than pretending to point out how they should be; and endeavouring to see the world in as pleasant a light as circumstances will permit.

I have always had an opinion that much good might be done by keeping mankind in good humour with one another. I may be wrong in my philosophy, but I shall continue to practise it until convinced of its fallacy. When I discover the world to be all that it has been represented by sneering cynics and whining poets, I will turn to and abuse it also; in the mean while, worthy reader, I hope you will not think lightly of me, because I cannot believe this to be so very bad a world as it is represented.

Thine truly,

GEOFFREY CRAYON

THE HALL

The ancientest house, and the best for housekeeping in this
county or the next; and though the master of it write but
squire, I know no lord like him.

MERRY BEGGARS

The reader, if he has perused the volumes of the Sketch Book, will
probably recollect something of the Bracebridge family, with which
I once passed a Christmas. I am now on another visit at the Hall,
having been invited to a wedding which is shortly to take place.
The squire's second son, Guy, a fine, spirited young captain in the
army, is about to be married to his father's ward, the fair Julia Templeton. A gathering of relations and friends has already commenced, to
celebrate the joyful occasion; for the old gentleman is an enemy to
quiet, private weddings. "There is nothing," he says, "like launching a
young couple gaily, and cheering them from the shore; a good outset
is half the voyage."

Before proceeding any further, I would beg that the squire might
not be confounded with that class of hard-riding, fox-hunting gentlemen
so often described, and, in fact, so nearly extinct in England. I use
this rural title partly because it is his universal appellation throughout
the neighbourhood, and partly because it saves me the frequent repetition of his name, which is one of those rough old English names at
which Frenchmen exclaim in despair.

The squire is, in fact, a lingering specimen of the old English
country gentleman; rusticated a little by living almost entirely on his
estate, and something of a humourist, as Englishmen are apt to become
when they have an opportunity of living in their own way. I like
his hobby passing well, however, which is, a bigoted devotion to old
English manners and customs; it jumps a little with my own humour,
having as yet a lively and unsated curiosity about the ancient and
genuine characteristics of my "father land."

There are some traits about the squire's family also, which appear
to me to be national. It is one of those old aristocratical families, which,
I believe, are peculiar to England, and scarcely understood in other
countries; that is to say, families of the ancient gentry, who, though
destitute of titled rank, maintain a high ancestral pride: who look
down upon all nobility of recent creation, and would consider it a
sacrifice of dignity to merge the venerable name of their house in a
modern title.

This feeling is very much fostered by the importance which they enjoy on their hereditary domains. The family mansion is an old manor-house, standing in a retired and beautiful part of Yorkshire. Its inhabitants have been always regarded through the surrounding country, as "the great ones of the earth;" and the little village near the Hall looks up to the squire with almost feudal homage. An old manor-house, and an old family of this kind, are rarely to be met with at the present day; and it is probably the peculiar humour of the squire that has retained this secluded specimen of English housekeeping in something like the genuine old style.

I am again quartered in the pannelled chamber, in the antique wing of the house. The prospect from my window, however, has quite a different aspect from that which it wore on my winter visit. Though early in the month of April, yet a few warm, sunshiny days have drawn forth the beauties of the spring, which, I think, are always most captivating on their first opening. The parterres of the old fashioned garden are gay with flowers; and the gardener has brought out his exotics, and placed them along the stone balustrades. The trees are clothed with green buds and tender leaves; when I throw open my jingling casement, I smell the odour of mignionette, and hear the hum of the bees from the flowers against the sunny wall, with the varied song of the throstle, and the cheerful notes of the tuneful little wren.

While sojourning in this strong hold of old fashions, it is my intention to make occasional sketches of the scenes and characters before me. I would have it understood, however, that I am not writing a novel, and have nothing of intricate plot, or marvellous adventure, to promise the reader. The Hall of which I treat, has, for aught I know, neither trap-door, nor sliding-pannel, nor donjon-keep; and indeed appears to have no mystery about it. The family is a worthy well-meaning family, that, in all probability, will eat and drink, and go to bed, and get up regularly, from one end of my work to the other; and the squire is so kind-hearted an old gentleman that I see no likelihood of his throwing any kind of distress in the way of the approaching nuptials. In a word, I cannot foresee a single extraordinary event that is likely to occur in the whole term of my sojourn at the Hall

I tell this honestly to the reader, lest, when he finds me dallying along, through every-day English scenes, he may hurry ahead, in hopes of meeting with some marvellous adventure further on. I invite him, on the contrary, to ramble gently on with me, as he would saunter out into the fields, stopping occasionally to gather a flower, or listen to a bird, or admire a prospect, without any anxiety to arrive at the end of his career. Should I, however, in the course of my loiterings about this old mansion, see or hear any thing curious, that might serve to vary the monotony of this every-day life, I shall not fail to report it for the reader's entertainment:

> For freshest wits I know will soon be wearie,
> Of any book, how grave so e'er it be,
> Except it have odd matter, strange and merrie,
> Well sauc'd with lies and glared all with glee.*

* Mirror for Magistrates.

THE BUSY MAN

A decayed gentleman, who lives most upon his own mirth and
my master's means, and much good do him with it. He does
hold my master up with his stories, and songs, and catches,
and such tricks and jigs, you would admire – he is with him
now.

JOVIAL CREW

By no one has my return to the Hall been more heartily greeted than
by Mr. Simon Bracebridge, or Master Simon, as the squire most commonly calls him. I encountered him just as I entered the park, where
he was breaking a pointer, and he received me with all the hospitable
cordiality with which a man welcomes a friend to another one's house.
I have already introduced him to the reader as a brisk old bachelor-
looking little man; the wit and superannuated beau of a large family connexion, and the squire's factotum. I found him, as usual, full of bustle;
with a thousand petty things to do, and persons to attend to, and in
chirping good-humour; for there are few happier beings than a busy
idler; that is to say, a man who is eternally busy about nothing.

I visited him, the morning after my arrival, in his chamber, which is
in a remote corner of the mansion, as he says he likes to be to himself,
and out of the way. He has fitted it up in his own taste, so that it is
a perfect epitome of an old bachelor's notions of convenience and
arrangement. The furniture is made up of odd pieces from all parts of
the house, chosen on account of their suiting his notions, or fitting some
corner of his apartment; and he is very eloquent in praise of an ancient
elbow chair, from which he takes occasion to digress into a censure on
modern chairs, as having degenerated from the dignity and comfort of
high-backed antiquity.

Adjoining to his room is a small cabinet, which he calls his study.
Here are some hanging shelves, of his own construction, on which are
several old works on hawking, hunting, and farriery, and a collection or
two of poems and songs of the reign of Elizabeth, which he studies out
of compliment to the squire; together with the Novelist's Magazine, the
Sporting Magazine, the Racing Calendar, a volume or two of the Newgate Calendar, a book of peerage, and another of heraldry.

His sporting dresses hang on pegs in a small closet; and about the
walls of his apartment are hooks to hold his fishing-tackle, whips, spurs,
and a favourite fowling-piece, curiously wrought and inlaid, which he
inherits from his grandfather. He has also a couple of old single-keyed
flutes, and a fiddle, which he has repeatedly patched and mended him-

11

self, affirming it to be a veritable Cremona; though I have never heard him extract a single note from it that was not enough to make one's blood run cold.

From this little nest his fiddle will often be heard, in the stillness of midday, drowsily sawing some long-forgotten tune; for he prides himself on having a choice collection of good old English music, and will scarcely have any thing to do with modern composers. The time, however, at which his musical powers are of most use, is now and then of an evening, when he plays for the children to dance in the Hall, and he passes among them and the servants for a perfect Orpheus.

His chamber also bears evidence of his various avocations: there are half-copied sheets of music; designs for needlework; sketches of landscapes, very indifferently executed; a camera lucida; a magic lantern, for which he is endeavouring to paint glasses; in a word, it is the cabinet of a man of many accomplishments, who knows a little of every thing, and does nothing well.

After I had spent some time in his apartment, admiring the ingenuity of his small inventions, he took me about the establishment, to visit the stables, dog-kennel, and other dependencies, in which he appeared like a general visiting the different quarters of his camp; as the squire leaves the control of all these matters to him, when he is at the Hall. He inquired into the state of the horses; examined their feet; prescribed a drench for one, and bleeding for another; and then took me to look at his own horse, on the merits of which he dwelt with great prolixity, and which, I noticed, had the best stall in the stable.

After this I was taken to a new toy of his and the squire's, which he termed the falconry, where there were several unhappy birds in durance, completing their education. Among the number was a fine falcon, which Master Simon had in especial training, and he told me that he would show me, in a few days, some rare sport of the good old-fashioned kind. In the course of our round, I noticed that the grooms, game-keeper, whippers-in, and other retainers, seemed all to be on somewhat of a familiar footing with Master Simon, and fond of having a joke with him, though it was evident they had great deference for his opinion in matters relating to their functions.

There was one exception, however, in a testy old huntsman, as hot as a pepper-corn; a meagre, wiry old fellow, in a thread-bare velvet jockey-cap, and a pair of leather breeches, that, from much wear, shone as though they had been japanned. He was very contradictory and pragmatical, and apt, as I thought, to differ from Master Simon now and then, out of mere captiousness. This was particularly the case with respect to the treatment of the hawk, which the old man seemed to have under his peculiar care, and, according to Master Simon, was in a fair way to ruin: the latter had a vast deal to say about *casting*, and *imping*, and *gleaming*, and *enseaming*, and giving the hawk the *rangle*, which I saw was all heathen Greek to old Christy; but he maintained his point notwithstanding, and seemed to hold all this technical lore in utter disrespect.

I was surprised at the good humour with which Master Simon bore his contradictions till he explained the matter to me afterwards. Old Christy is the most ancient servant in the place, having lived among dogs and horses the greater part of a century, and been in the service of Mr. Bracebridge's father. He knows the pedigree of every horse on the place, and has bestrode the great-great grandsires of most of them. He can give a circumstantial detail of every fox-hunt for the last sixty or seventy years, and has a history for every stag's head about the house, and every hunting trophy nailed to the door of the dog-kennel.

All the present race have grown up under his eye, and humour him in his old age. He once attended the squire to Oxford when he was a student there, and enlightened the whole university with his hunting lore. All this is enough to make the old man opinionated, since he finds on all these matters of first-rate importance, he knows more than the rest of the world. Indeed, Master Simon had been his pupil, and acknowledges that he derived his first knowledge in hunting from the instructions of Christy; and I much question whether the old man does not still look upon him as rather a greenhorn.

On our return homewards, as we were crossing the lawn in front of the house, we heard the porter's bell ring at the lodge, and shortly afterwards, a kind of cavalcade advanced slowly up the avenue. At sight of it my companion paused, considered it for a moment, and then, making a sudden exclamation, hurried away to meet it. As it approached I discovered a fair fresh-looking elderly lady, dressed in an old-fashioned riding-habit, with a broad-brimmed white beaver hat, such as may be seen in Sir Joshua Reynolds' paintings. She rode a sleek white pony, and was followed by a footman in rich livery, mounted on an over-fed hunter. At a little distance in the rear came an ancient cumbrous chariot, drawn by two very corpulent horses, driven by as corpulent a coachman, beside whom sat a page dressed in a fanciful green livery. Inside of the chariot was a starched prim personage, with a look somewhat between a lady's companion and a lady's maid, and two pampered curs, that showed their ugly faces and barked out of each window.

There was a general turning out of the garrison to receive this new comer. The squire assisted her to alight, and saluted her affectionately; the fair Julia flew into her arms, and they embraced with the romantic fervour of boarding-school friends: she was escorted into the house by Julia's lover, towards whom she showed distinguished favour; and a line of the old servants, who had collected in the Hall, bowed most profoundly as she passed.

I observed that Master Simon was most assiduous and devout in his attentions upon this old lady. He walked by the side of her pony up the avenue; and, while she was receiving the salutations of the rest of the family, he took occasion to notice the fat coachman; to pat the sleek carriage horses, and, above all, to say a civil word to my lady's gentlewoman, the prim, sour-looking vestal in the chariot.

I had no more of his company for the rest of the morning. He was swept off in the vortex that followed in the wake of this lady. Once indeed he paused for a moment, as he was hurrying on some errand of the good lady's, to let me know that this was Lady Lillycraft, a sister of the squire's, of large fortune, which the captain would inherit, and that her estate lay in one of the best sporting countries in all England.

FAMILY SERVANTS

Verily old servants are the vouchers of worthy housekeeping.
They are like rats in a mansion, or mites in a cheese, bespeaking the antiquity and fatness of their abode.

In my casual anecdotes of the Hall, I may often be tempted to dwell
on circumstances of a trite and ordinary nature, from their appearing
to me illustrative of genuine national character. It seems to be the
study of the squire to adhere, as much as possible, to what he considers
the old landmarks of English manners. His servants all understand his
ways, and for the most part have been accustomed to them from infancy;
so that, upon the whole, his household presents one of the few tolerable
specimens that can now be met with, of the establishment of an English
country gentleman of the old school.

By the bye, the servants are not the least characteristic part of the
household: the housekeeper, for instance, has been born and brought up
at the Hall, and has never been twenty miles from it; yet she has a stately
air that would not disgrace a lady that had figured at the court of
Queen Elizabeth.

I am half inclined to think that she has caught it from living so much
among the old family pictures. It may, however, be owing to a consciousness of her importance in the sphere in which she has always moved; for
she is greatly respected in the neighbouring village, and among the
farmers' wives, and has high authority in the household, ruling over
the servants with quiet, but undisputed sway.

She is a thin old lady, with blue eyes and pointed nose and chin. Her
dress is always the same as to fashion. She wears a small, well-starched
ruff, a laced stomacher, full petticoats, and a gown festooned and open
in front, which, on particular occasions, is of ancient silk, the legacy of
some former dame of the family, or an inheritance from her mother, who
was housekeeper before her. I have a reverence for these old garments,
as I make no doubt they have figured about these apartments in days
long past, when they have set off the charms of some peerless family
beauty; and I have sometimes looked from the old housekeeper to the
neighbouring portraits, to see whether I could not recognize her
antiquated brocade in the dress of some one of those long-waisted dames
that smile on me from the walls.

Her hair, which is quite white, is frizzed out in front, and she wears
over it a small cap, nicely plaited, and brought down under the chin.

Her manners are simple and primitive, heightened a little by a proper dignity of station.

The Hall is her world, and the history of the family the only history she knows, excepting that which she has read in the Bible. She can give a biography of every portrait in the picture gallery, and is a complete family chronicle.

She is treated with great consideration by the squire. Indeed, Master Simon tells me that there is a traditional anecdote current among the servants, of the squire's having been seen kissing her in the picture gallery, when they were both young. As, however, nothing further was ever noticed between them, the circumstance caused no great scandal; only she was observed to take to reading Pamela shortly afterwards, and refused the hand of the village innkeeper, whom she had previously smiled on.

The old butler, who was formerly footman, and a rejected admirer of hers, used to tell the anecdote now and then, at those little cabals that will occasionally take place among the most orderly servants, arising from the common propensity of the governed to talk against administration; but he has left it off, of late years, since he has risen into place, and shakes his head rebukingly when it is mentioned.

It is certain that the old lady will, to this day, dwell on the looks of the squire when he was a young man at college; and she maintains that none of his sons can compare with their father when he was of their age, and was dressed out in his full suit of scarlet, with his hair craped and powdered, and his three-cornered hat.

She has an orphan niece, a pretty, soft-hearted baggage, named Phœbe Wilkins, who has been transplanted to the Hall within a year or two, and been nearly spoiled for any condition of life. She is a kind of attendant and companion of the fair Julia's; and from loitering about the young lady's apartments, reading scraps of novels, and inheriting second-hand finery, has become something between a waiting-maid and a slip-shod fine lady.

She is considered a kind of heiress among the servants, as she will inherit all her aunt's property; which, if report be true, must be a round sum of good golden guineas, the accumulated wealth of two housekeepers' savings; not to mention the hereditary wardrobe, and the many little valuables and knick-knacks treasured up in the housekeeper's room. Indeed the old housekeeper has the reputation among the servants and the villagers of being passing rich; and there is a japanned chest of drawers and a large iron-bound coffer in her room, which are supposed, by the housemaids, to hold treasures of wealth.

The old lady is a great friend of Master Simon, who, indeed, pays a little court to her, as to a person high in authority; and they have many discussions on points of family history, in which, notwithstanding his extensive information, and pride of knowledge, he commonly admits her superior accuracy. He seldom returns to the Hall, after one of his visits to the other branches of the family, without bringing Mrs. Wilkins some remembrance from the ladies of the house where he has been staying.

Indeed all the children of the house look up to the old lady with habitual respect and attachment, and she seems almost to consider them as her own, from their having grown up under her eye. The Oxonian, however, is her favourite, probably from being the youngest, though he is the most mischievous, and has been apt to play tricks upon her from boyhood.

I cannot help mentioning one little ceremony, which, I believe, is peculiar to the Hall. After the cloth is removed at dinner, the old housekeeper sails into the room and stands behind the squire's chair, when he fills her a glass of wine with his own hands, in which she drinks the health of the company in a truly respectful yet dignified manner, and then retires. The squire received the custom from his father, and has always continued it.

There is a peculiar character about the servants of old English families that reside principally in the country. They have a quiet, orderly, respectful mode of doing their duties. They are always neat in their persons, and appropriately, and, if I may use the phrase, technically dressed; they move about the house without hurry or noise; there is nothing of the bustle of employment, or the voice of command; nothing of that obtrusive housewifery that amounts to a torment. You are not persecuted by the process of making you comfortable; yet every thing is done, and is done well. The work of the house is performed as if by magic, but it is the magic of system. Nothing is done by fits and starts, nor at awkward seasons; the whole goes on like well-oiled clock-work, where there is no noise nor jarring in its operations.

English servants, in general, are not treated with great indulgence, nor rewarded by many commendations; for the English are laconic and reserved towards their domestics; but an approving nod and a kind word from master or mistress goes as far here, as an excess of praise or indulgence elsewhere. Neither do servants often exhibit any animated marks of affection to their employers; yet, though quiet, they are strong in their attachments; and the reciprocal regard of masters and servants, though not ardently expressed, is powerful and lasting in old English families.

The title of "an old family servant" carries with it a thousand kind associations in all parts of the world; and there is no claim upon the home-bred charities of the heart more irresistible than that of having been "born in the house." It is common to see gray-headed domestics of this kind attached to an English family of the "old school," who continue in it to the day of their death, in the enjoyment of steady unaffected kindness, and the performance of faithful, unofficious duty. I think such instances of attachment speak well for both master and servant, and the frequency of them speaks well for national character.

These observations, however, hold good only with families of the description I have mentioned; and with such as are somewhat retired, and pass the greater part of their time in the country. As to the powdered menials that throng the halls of fashionable town residences, they equally reflect the character of the establishments to which they belong; and I know no more complete epitomes of dissolute heartlessness, and pampered inutility.

But the good "old family servant!"–The one who has always been linked, in idea, with the home of our heart; who has led us to school in the days of prattling childhood; who has been the confidant of our boyish cares, and schemes, and enterprises; who has hailed us as we came home at vacations, and been the promotor of all our holiday sports; who, when we, in wandering manhood, have left the paternal roof, and only return thither at intervals, will welcome us with a joy inferior only to that of our parents; who, now grown gray and infirm with age, still totters about the house of our fathers in fond and faithful servitude; who claims us, in a manner, as his own; and hastens with querulous eagerness to anticipate his fellow-domestics in waiting upon us at table; and who, when we retire at night to the chamber that still goes by our name, will linger about the room to have one more kind look, and one more pleasant word about times that are past – who does not experience towards such a being a feeling of almost filial affection?

I have met with several instances of epitaphs on the gravestones of such valuable domestics, recorded with the simple truth of natural feeling. I have two before me at this moment; one copied from a tomb-stone of a churchyard in Warwickshire:

"Here lieth the body of Joseph Batte, confidential servant to George Birch, Esq. of Hamstead Hall. His grateful friend and master caused this inscription to be written in memory of his discretion, fidelity, diligence, and continence. He died (a bachelor) aged 84, having lived 44 years in the same family."

The other was taken from a tombstone in Eltham churchyard:

"Here lie the remains of Mr. James Tappy, who departed this life on the 8th of September, 1818, aged 84, after a faithful service of 60 years in one family; by each individual of which he lived respected, and died lamented by the sole survivor."

Few monuments, even of the illustrious, have given me the glow about the heart that I felt while copying this honest epitaph in the churchyard of Eltham. I sympathised with this "sole survivor" of a family mourning over the grave of the faithful follower of his race, who had been, no doubt, a living memento of times and friends that had passed away; and in considering this record of long and devoted service, I called to mind the touching speech of Old Adam in "As You Like It," when tottering after the youthful son of his ancient master:

> "Master, go on, and I will follow thee
> To the last gasp, with truth and loyalty!"

NOTE – I cannot but mention a tablet which I have seen somewhere in the chapel of Windsor Castle, put up by the late king to the memory of a family servant, who had been a faithful attendant of his lamented daughter, the Princess Amelia. George III possessed much of the strong, domestic feeling of the old English country gentleman; and it is an incident curious in monumental history, and creditable to the human heart, a monarch erecting a monument in honour of the humble virtues of a menial.

THE WIDOW

She was so charitable and pitious
She would weep if that she saw a mous
Caught in a trap, if it were dead or bled;
Of small hounds had she, that she fed
With rost flesh, milke, and wastel bread,
But sore wept she if any of them were dead,
Or if man smote them with a yard smart.

CHAUCER

Notwithstanding the whimsical parade made by Lady Lillycraft on her arrival, she has none of the petty stateliness that I had imagined; but, on the contrary, she has a degree of naïveté, and simple-heartedness, if I may use the phrase, that mingles well with her old fashioned manners and harmless ostentation. She dresses in rich silks, with long waist; she rouges considerably, and her hair, which is nearly white, is frizzed out, and put up with pins. Her face is pitted with the small-pox, but the delicacy of her features shows that she may once have been beautiful; and she has a very fair and well-shaped hand and arm, of which, if I mistake not, the good lady is still a little vain.

I have had the curiosity to gather a few particulars concerning her. She was a great belle in town between thirty and forty years since, and reigned for two seasons with all the insolence of beauty, refusing several excellent offers; when, unfortunately, she was robbed of her charms and her lovers by an attack of the small-pox. She retired immediately into the country, where she sometime after inherited an estate, and married a baronet, a former admirer, whose passion had suddenly revived; "having," as he said, "always loved her mind rather than her person."

The baronet did not enjoy her mind and fortune above six months, and had scarcely grown very tired of her, when he broke his neck in a fox-chase, and left her free, rich, and disconsolate. She has remained on her estate in the country ever since, and has never shown any desire to return to town, and revisit the scene of her early triumphs and fatal malady. All her favourite recollections, however, revert to that short period of her youthful beauty. She has no idea of town but as it was at that time; and continually forgets that the place and people must have changed materially in the course of nearly half a century. She will often speak of the toasts of those days as if still reigning; and, until very recently, used to talk with delight of the royal family, and the beauty of the young princes and princesses. She cannot be brought to think of the present king otherwise than as an elegant young man, rather wild, but who danced a minuet divinely; and before he came to the crown, would often mention him as the "sweet young prince."

She talks also of the walks in Kensington Garden, where the gentlemen appeared in gold-laced coats and cocked hats, and the ladies in hoops, and swept so proudly along the grassy avenues; and she thinks the ladies let themselves sadly down in their dignity, when they gave up cushioned head-dresses, and high-heeled shoes. She has much to say too of the officers who were in the train of her admirers; and speaks familiarly of many wild young blades, that are now, perhaps, hobbling about watering-places with crutches and gouty shoes.

Whether the taste the good lady had of matrimony discouraged her or not, I cannot say; but, though her merits and her riches have attracted many suitors, she has never been tempted to venture again into the happy state. This is singular too, for she seems of a most soft and susceptible heart; is always talking of love and connubial felicity; and is a great stickler for old-fashioned gallantry, devoted attentions, and eternal constancy, on the part of the gentlemen. She lives, however, after her own taste. Her house, I am told, must have been built and furnished about the time of Sir Charles Grandison. Everything about it is somewhat formal and stately; but has been softened down into a degree of voluptuousness, characteristic of an old lady very tender-hearted and romantic, and that loves her ease. The cushions of the great arm-chairs and wide sofas almost bury you when you sit down on them. Flowers of the most rare and delicate kind are placed about the rooms and on little japanned stands; and sweet bags lie about the tables and mantel-pieces. The house is full of pet dogs, Angola cats, and singing birds, who are as carefully waited upon as she is herself.

She is dainty in her living, and a little of an epicure, living on white meats, and little ladylike dishes, though her servants have substantial old English fare, as their looks bear witness. Indeed, they are so indulged, that they are all spoiled; and when they lose their present place, they will be fit for no other. Her ladyship is one of those easy-tempered beings that are always doomed to be much liked, but ill served by their domestics, and cheated by all the world.

Much of her time is past in reading novels, of which she has a most extensive library, and has a constant supply from the publishers in town. Her erudition in this line of literature is immense; she has kept pace with the press for half a century. Her mind is stuffed with love-tales of all kinds, from the stately amours of the old books of chivalry, down to the last blue-covered romance, reeking from the press; though she evidently gives the preference to those that came out in the days of her youth, and when she was first in love. She maintains that there are no novels written now-a-days equal to Pamela and Sir Charles Grandison; and she places the Castle of Otranto at the head of all romances.

She does a vast deal of good in her neighbourhood, and is imposed upon by every beggar in the county. She is the benefactress of a village adjoining to her estate, and takes an especial interest in all its love-affairs. She knows of every courtship that is going on; every love-lorn damsel is sure to find a patient listener and a sage adviser in her ladyship. She takes great pains to reconcile all love-quarrels, and should any faithless swain persist in his inconstancy, he is sure to draw on himself the good lady's violent indignation.

I have learned these particulars partly from Frank Bracebridge, and partly from Master Simon. I am now able to account for the assiduous attention of the latter to her ladyship. Her house is one of his favourite resorts, where he is a very important personage. He makes her a visit of business once a year, when he looks into all her affairs; which, as she is no manager, are apt to get into confusion. He examines the books of the overseer, and shoots about the estate, which, he says, is well stocked with game, notwithstanding that it is poached by all the vagabonds in the neighbourhood.

It is thought, as I before hinted, that the captain will inherit the greater part of her property, having always been her chief favourite; for, in fact, she is partial to a red coat. She has now come to the Hall to be present at his nuptials, having a great disposition to interest herself in all matters of love and matrimony.

THE LOVERS

Rise up, my love, my fair one, and come away: for lo the
winter is past, the rain is over and gone; the flowers appear
on the earth, the time of the singing of birds is come, and
the voice of the turtle is heard in the land.

SONG OF SOLOMON

To a man who is a little of a philosopher, and a bachelor to boot; and
who, by dint of some experience in the follies of life, begins to look
with a learned eye upon the ways of man, and eke of woman; to
such a man, I say, there is something very entertaining in noticing
the conduct of a pair of young lovers. It may not be as grave and
scientific a study as the loves of the plants, but it is certainly as
interesting.

I have therefore derived much pleasure, since my arrival at the Hall,
from observing the fair Julia and her lover. She has all the delightful,
blushing consciousness of an artless girl, inexperienced in coquetry,
who has made her first conquest; while the captain regards her with that
mixture of fondness and exultation, with which a youthful lover is apt
to contemplate so beauteous a prize.

I observed them yesterday in the garden, advancing along one of the
retired walks. The sun was shining with delicious warmth, making great
masses of bright verdure, and deep blue shade. The cuckoo, that "har-
binger of spring," was faintly heard from a distance; the thrush
piped from the hawthorn, and the yellow butterflies sported, and toyed,
and coquetted in the air.

The fair Julia was leaning on her lover's arm, listening to his conversation, with her eyes cast down, a soft blush on her cheek, and a quiet
smile on her lips, while in the hand that hung negligently by her side
was a bunch of flowers. In this way they were sauntering slowly along,
and when I considered them, and the scene in which they were moving,
I could not but think it a thousand pities that the season should ever
change, or that young people should ever grow older, or that blossoms
should give way to fruit, or that lovers should ever get married.

From what I have gathered of family anecdote, I understand that
the fair Julia is the daughter of a favourite college friend of the squire;
who after leaving Oxford, had entered the army, and served for many
years in India, where he was mortally wounded in a skirmish with the
natives. In his last moments he had, with a faltering pen, recommended
his wife and daughter to the kindness of his early friend.

The widow and her child returned to England helpless, and almost hopeless. When Mr. Bracebridge received accounts of their situation, he hastened to their relief. He reached them just in time to soothe the last moments of the mother, who was dying of a consumption, and to make her happy in the assurance that her child should never want a protector.

The good squire returned with his prattling charge to his strong hold, where he has brought her up with a tenderness truly paternal. As he has taken some pains to superintend her education, and form her taste, she has grown up with many of his notions, and considers him the wisest, as well as the best of men. Much of her time, too, has been passed with Lady Lillycraft, who has instructed her in the manners of the old school, and enriched her mind with all kinds of novels and romances. Indeed, her ladyship has had a great hand in promoting the match between Julia and the captain, having had them together at her country seat, the moment she found there was an attachment growing up between them; the good lady being never so happy as when she has a pair of turtles cooing about her.

I have been pleased to see the fondness with which the fair Julia is regarded by the old servants at the Hall. She has been a pet with them from childhood, and every one seems to lay some claim to her education; so that it is no wonder that she should be extremely accomplished. The gardener taught her to rear flowers, of which she is extremely fond. Old Christy, the pragmatical huntsman, softens when she approaches; and as she sits lightly and gracefully in her saddle, claims the merit of having taught her to ride; while the housekeeper, who almost looks upon her as a daughter, intimates that she first gave her an insight into the mysteries of the toilet, having been dressing-maid in her young days to the late Mrs. Bracebridge. I am inclined to credit this last claim, as I have noticed that the dress of the young lady had an air of the old school, though managed with native taste, and that her hair was put up very much in the style of Sir Peter Lely's portraits in the picture-gallery.

Her very musical attainments partake of this old-fashioned character; and most of her songs are such as are not at the present day to be found on the piano of a modern performer. I have, however, seen so much of modern fashions, modern accomplishments, and modern fine ladies, that I relish this tinge of antiquated style in so young and lovely a girl; and I have had as much pleasure in hearing her warble one of the old songs of Herrick, or Carew, or Suckling, adapted to some simple old melody, as I have had from listening to a lady amateur sky-lark it up and down through the finest bravura of Rossini or Mozart.

We have very pretty music in the evenings, occasionally, between her

The Lovers

An engraving reproduced in the Geoffrey Crayon edition of *Bracebridge Hall*
(New York: G. P. Putnam's Sons, 1868).

and the captain, assisted sometimes by Master Simon, who scrapes, dubiously, on his violin; being very apt to get out, and to halt a note or two in the rear. Sometimes he even thrums a little on the piano, and takes a part in a trio, in which his voice can generally be distinguished by a certain quavering tone, and an occasional false note.

I was praising the fair Julia's performance to him after one of her songs, when I found he took to himself the whole credit of having formed her musical taste, assuring me that she was very apt; and, indeed, summing up her whole character in his knowing way, by adding, that "she was a very nice girl, and had no nonsense about her."

FAMILY RELIQUES

My Infelice's face, her brow, her eye,
The dimple on her cheek: and such sweet skill
Hath from the cunning workman's pencil flown,
These lips look fresh and lively as her own.
False colours last after the true be dead.
Of all the roses grafted on her cheeks,
Of all the graces dancing in her eyes,
Of all the music set upon her tongue,
Of all that was past woman's excellence
In her white bosom; look, a painted board
Circumscribes all!

DEKKER

An old English family mansion is a fertile subject for study. It abounds with illustrations of former times, and traces of the tastes, and humours, and manners, of successive generations. The alterations and additions, in different styles of architecture; the furniture, plate, pictures, hangings; the warlike and sporting implements of different ages and fancies; all furnish food for curious and amusing speculation. As the squire is very careful in collecting and preserving all family reliques, the Hall is full of remembrances of the kind. In looking about the establishment, I can picture to myself the character and habits that have prevailed at different eras of the family history. I have mentioned on a former occasion the armour of the crusader which hangs up in the Hall. There are also several jack-boots, with enormously thick soles and high heels, that belonged to a set of cavaliers, who filled the Hall with the din and stir of arms during the time of the Covenanters. A number of enormous drinking vessels of antique fashion, with huge Venice glasses, and green hock-glasses, with the apostles in relief on them, remain as monuments of a generation or two of hard-livers, that led a life of roaring revelry, and first introduced the gout into the family.

I shall pass over several more such indications of temporary tastes of the squire's predecessors; but I cannot forbear to notice a pair of antlers in the great hall, which is one of the trophies of a hard-riding squire of former times, who was the Nimrod of these parts. There are many traditions of his wonderful feats in hunting still existing, which are related by old Christy, the huntsman, who gets exceedingly nettled if they are in the least doubted. Indeed, there is a frightful chasm, a few miles from the Hall, which goes by the name of the Squire's Leap, from his having cleared it in the ardour of the chase; there can be no doubt of the fact, for old Christy shows the very dints of the horse's hoofs on the rocks on each side of the chasm.

Master Simon holds the memory of this squire in great veneration, and has a number of extraordinary stories to tell concerning him, which he repeats at all hunting dinners; and I am told that they wax more and more marvellous the older they grow. He has also a pair of Rippon spurs which belonged to this mighty hunter of yore, and which he only wears on particular occasions.

The place, however, which abounds most with mementos of past times, is the picture gallery; and there is something strangely pleasing, though melancholy, in considering the long rows of portraits which compose the greater part of the collection. They furnish a kind of narrative of the lives of the family worthies, which I am enabled to read with the assistance of the venerable housekeeper, who is the family chronicler, prompted occasionally by Master Simon. There is the progress of a fine lady, for instance, through a variety of portraits. One represents her as a little girl, with a long waist and hoop, holding a kitten in her arms, and ogling the spectator out of the corners of her eyes, as if she could not turn her head. In another we find her in the freshness of youthful beauty, when she was a celebrated belle, and so hard-hearted as to cause several unfortunate gentlemen to run desperate and write bad poetry. In another she is depicted as a stately dame, in the maturity of her charms; next to the portrait of her husband, a gallant colonel in full-bottomed wig and gold-laced hat, who was killed abroad; and, finally, her monument is in the church, the spire of which may be seen from the window, where her effigy is carved in marble, and represents her as a venerable dame of seventy-six.

In like manner I have followed some of the family great men through a series of pictures, from early boyhood to the robe of dignity, or truncheon of command, and so on by degrees, until they were garnered up in the common repository, the neighbouring church.

There is one group that particularly interested me. It consisted of four sisters of nearly the same age, who flourished about a century since, and, if I may judge from their portraits, were extremely beautiful. I can imagine what a scene of gaiety and romance this old mansion must have been, when they were in the hey-day of their charms; when they passed like beautiful visions through its halls, or stepped daintily to music in the revels and dances of the cedar gallery; or printed, with delicate feet, the velvet verdure of these lawns. How must they have been looked up to with mingled love, and pride, and reverence, by the old family servants; and followed with almost painful admiration by the aching eyes of rival admirers! How must melody, and song, and tender serenade, have breathed about these courts, and their echoes whispered to the loitering tread of lovers! How must these very turrets have made the hearts of the young galliards thrill, as they first discerned them from afar, rising from among the trees, and pictured to themselves the beauties casketed like gems within these walls! Indeed I have discovered about the place several faint records of this reign of love and romance, when the Hall was a kind of Court of Beauty. Several of the old romances in the library have marginal notes expressing sympathy and approbation, where there are long speeches extolling ladies' charms, or protesting eternal fidelity, or bewailing the cruelty of some tyrannical fair one. The interviews, and declarations, and parting scenes of tender lovers, also bear evidence of having been frequently read, and are scored, and marked with notes of admiration, and have initials written on the margins; most of which annotations have the day of the month and year annexed to them. Several of the windows, too, have scraps of poetry engraved on them with diamonds, taken from the writings of the fair Mrs. Philips, the once celebrated Orinda. Some of these seem to have been inscribed by lovers; and others, in a delicate and unsteady hand, and a little inaccurate in the spelling, have evidently been written by the young ladies themselves, or by female friends, who have been on visits to the Hall. Mrs. Philips seems to have been their favourite author, and they have distributed the names of her heroes and heroines among their circle of intimacy. Sometimes, in a male hand, the verse bewails the cruelty of beauty, and the sufferings of constant love; while in a female hand it prudishly confines itself to lamenting the parting of female friends. The bow-window of my bed-room, which has, doubtless, been inhabited by one of these beauties, has several of these inscriptions. I have one at this moment before my eyes, called "Camilla parting with Leonora:"

> "How perished is the joy that's past,
>   The present how unsteady!
> What comfort can be great and last,
>   When this is gone already?"

And close by it is another, written, perhaps, by some adventurous lover, who had stolen into the lady's chamber during her absence:

> "THEODOSIUS TO CAMILLA.
> I'd rather in your favour live,
>   Than in a lasting name;
> And much a greater rate would give
>   For happiness than fame.
>   THEODOSIUS. 1700."

When I look at these faint records of gallantry and tenderness; when I contemplate the fading portraits of these beautiful girls, and think too that they have long since bloomed, reigned, grown old, died, and passed away, and with them all their graces, their triumphs, their rivalries, their admirers; the whole empire of love and pleasure in which they ruled – "all dead, all buried, all forgotten," I find a cloud of melancholy stealing over the present gaieties around me. I was gazing, in a musing mood, this very morning, at the portrait of the lady, whose husband was killed abroad, when the fair Julia entered the gallery, leaning on the arm of the captain. The sun shone through the row of windows on her as she passed along, and she seemed to beam out each time into brightness, and relapse into shade, until the door at the bottom of the gallery closed after her. I felt a sadness of heart at the idea, that this was an emblem of her lot: a few more years of sunshine and shade, and all this life, and loveliness, and enjoyment, will have ceased, and nothing be left to commemorate this beautiful being but one more perishable portrait; to awaken, perhaps, the trite speculations of some future loiterer, like myself, when I and my scribblings shall have lived through our brief existence and been forgotten.

AN OLD SOLDIER

I've worn some leather out abroad; let out a heathen soul or
two; fed this good sword with the black blood of pagan
Christians; converted a few infidels with it. – But let that
pass.

THE ORDINARY

The Hall was thrown into some little agitation, a few days since, by
the arrival of General Harbottle. He had been expected for several days,
and had been looked for, rather impatiently, by several of the family.
Master Simon assured me that I would like the general hugely, for he
was a blade of the old school, and an excellent table companion. Lady
Lillycraft, also, appeared to be somewhat fluttered, on the morning
of the general's arrival, for he had been one of her early admirers;
and she recollected him only as a dashing young ensign, just come upon
the town. She actually spent an hour longer at her toilette, and made
her appearance with her hair uncommonly frizzed and powdered, and
an additional quantity of rouge. She was evidently a little surprised and
shocked, therefore, at finding the lithe dashing ensign transformed into
a corpulent old general, with a double chin; though it was a perfect
picture to witness their salutations; the graciousness of her profound
curtsy, and the air of the old school with which the general took off
his hat, swayed it gently in his hand, and bowed his powdered
head.

All this bustle and anticipation has caused me to study the general
with a little more attention than, perhaps, I should otherwise have done;
and the few days that he has already passed at the Hall have enabled
me, I think, to furnish a tolerable likeness of him to the reader.

He is, as Master Simon observed, a soldier of the old school, with
powdered head, side locks, and pigtail. His face is shaped like the stern
of a Dutch man of war, narrow at top, and wide at bottom, with full
rosy cheeks and a double chin; so that, to use the cant of the day, his
organs of eating may be said to be powerfully developed.

The general, though a veteran, has seen very little active service,
except the taking of Seringapatam, which forms an era in his history.
He wears a large emerald in his bosom, and a diamond on his finger,
which he got on that occasion, and whoever is unlucky enough to notice
either, is sure to involve himself in the whole history of the siege. To
judge from the general's conversation, the taking of Seringapatam is the
most important affair that has occurred for the last century.

On the approach of warlike times on the continent, he was rapidly promoted, to get him out of the way of younger officers of merit; until having been hoisted to the rank of general, he was quietly laid on the shelf. Since that time his campaigns have been principally confined to watering places; where he drinks the waters for a slight touch of the liver which he got in India; and plays whist with old dowagers, with whom he has flirted in his younger days. Indeed he talks of all the fine women of the last half century, and, according to hints which he now and then drops, has enjoyed the particular smiles of many of them.

He has seen considerable garrison duty, and can speak of almost every place famous for good quarters, and where the inhabitants give good dinners. He is a diner out of first-rate currency, when in town; being invited to one place, because he has been seen at another. In the same way he is invited about to country-seats, and can describe half the seats in the kingdom, from actual observation; nor is any one better versed in court gossip, and the pedigrees and intermarriages of the nobility.

As the general is an old bachelor, and an old beau, and there are several ladies at the Hall, especially his quondam flame Lady Lillycraft, he is put rather upon his gallantry. He commonly passes some time, therefore, at his toilette, and takes the field at a late hour every morning, with his hair dressed out and powdered, and a rose in his button-hole. After he has breakfasted, he walks up and down the terrace in the sunshine, humming an air, and hemming between every stave, carrying one hand behind his back, and with the other touching his cane to the ground, and then raising it up to his shoulder. Should he, in these morning promenades, meet any of the elder ladies of the family, as he frequently does Lady Lillycraft, his hat is immediately in his hand, and it is enough to remind one of those courtly groups of ladies and gentlemen, in old prints of Windsor Terrace, or Kensington Garden.

He talks frequently about "the service," and is fond of humming the old song,

> Why, soldiers, why,
> Should we be melancholy, boys?
> Why, soldiers, why,
> Whose business 'tis to die!

I cannot discover, however, that the general has ever run any great risk of dying, excepting from an apoplexy, or an indigestion. He criticises all the battles on the continent, and discusses the merits of the commanders, but never fails to bring the conversation, ultimately, to Tippoo Saib and Seringapatam. I am told that the general was a perfect champion at drawing-rooms, parades, and watering-places, during the late war, and was looked to with hope and confidence by many an old lady, when labouring under the terror of Bonaparte's invasion.

He is thoroughly loyal, and attends punctually on levees when in town. He has treasured up many remarkable sayings of the late king, particularly one which the king made to him on a field-day, complimenting him on the excellence of his horse. He extols the whole royal family, but especially the present king, whom he pronounces the most perfect gentleman and best whist-player in Europe. The general swears rather more than is the fashion of the present day; but it was the mode in the old school. He is, however, very strict in religious matters, and a stanch churchman. He repeats the responses very loudly in church, and is emphatical in praying for the king and royal family.

At table his loyalty waxes very fervent with his second bottle, and the song of "God save the King" puts him into a perfect ecstacy. He is amazingly well contented with the present state of things, and apt to get a little impatient at any talk about national ruin and agricultural distress. He says he has travelled about the country as much as any man, and has met with nothing but prosperity; and to confess the truth, a great part of his time is spent in visiting from one country seat to another, and riding about the parks of his friends. "They talk of public distress," said the general this day to me, at dinner, as he smacked a glass of rich burgundy, and cast his eyes about the ample board; "they talk of public distress, but where do we find it, sir? I see none. I see no reason any one has to complain. Take my word for it, sir, this talk about public distress is all humbug!"

THE WIDOW'S RETINUE

Little dogs and all!

LEAR

In giving an account of the arrival of Lady Lillycraft at the Hall, I ought to have mentioned the entertainment which I derived from witnessing the unpacking of her carriage, and the disposing of her retinue. There is something extremely amusing to me in the number of factitious wants, the loads of imaginary conveniences, but real incumbrances, with which the luxurious are apt to burthen themselves. I like to watch the whimsical stir and display about one of these petty progresses. The number of robustious footmen and retainers of all kinds bustling about, with looks of infinite gravity and importance, to do almost nothing. The number of heavy trunks, and parcels, and bandboxes belonging to my lady; and the solicitude exhibited about some humble, odd-looking box, by my lady's maid; the cushions piled in the carriage to make a soft seat still softer, and to prevent the dreaded possibility of a jolt; the smelling-bottles, the cordials, the baskets of biscuit and fruit; the new publications; all provided to guard against hunger, fatigue, or ennui; the led horses to vary the mode of travelling; and all this preparation and parade to move, perhaps, some very good-for-nothing personage about a little space of earth!

I do not mean to apply the latter part of these observations to Lady Lillycraft, for whose simple kindheartedness I have a very great respect, and who is really a most amiable and worthy being. I cannot refrain, however, from mentioning some of the motley retinue she has brought with her; and which, indeed, bespeak the overflowing kindness of her nature, which requires her to be surrounded with objects on which to lavish it.

In the first place, her ladyship has a pampered coachman, with a red face, and cheeks that hang down like dew-laps. He evidently domineers over her a little with respect to the fat horses; and only drives out when he thinks proper, and when he thinks it will be "good for the cattle."

She has a favourite page to attend upon her person: a handsome boy of about twelve years of age, but a mischievous varlet, very much spoiled, and in a fair way to be good for nothing. He is dressed in green, with a profusion of gold cord and gilt buttons about his clothes. She always has one or two attendants of the kind, who are replaced by others as soon as they grow to fourteen years of age. She has brought two dogs

with her also, out of a number of pets which she maintains at home.
One is a fat spaniel, called Zephyr – though heaven defend me from such
a zephyr! He is fed out of all shape and comfort; his eyes are nearly
strained out of his head; he wheezes with corpulency, and cannot walk
without great difficulty. The other is a little, old, gray-muzzled curmudgeon, with an unhappy eye, that kindles like a coal if you only
look at him; his nose turns up; his mouth is drawn into wrinkles, so
as to show his teeth; in short, he has altogether the look of a dog far
gone in misanthropy, and totally sick of the world. When he walks, he
has his tail curled up so tight that it seems to lift his feet from the
ground; and he seldom makes use of more than three legs at a time,
keeping the other drawn up as a reserve. This last wretch is called
Beauty.

These dogs are full of elegant ailments unknown to vulgar dogs; and
are petted and nursed by Lady Lillycraft with the tenderest kindness.
They are pampered and fed with delicacies by their fellow-minion, the
page; but their stomachs are often weak and out of order, so that they
cannot eat; though I have now and then seen the page give them a
mischievous pinch, or thwack over the head, when his mistress was not
by. They have cushions for their express use, on which they lie before
the fire, and yet are apt to shiver and moan if there is the least draught
of air. When any one enters the room, they make a most tyrannical
barking that is absolutely deafening. They are insolent to all the other
dogs of the establishment. There is a noble stag-hound, a great favourite
of the squire's, who is a privileged visitor to the parlour; but the moment
he makes his appearance, these intruders fly at him with furious rage;
and I have admired the sovereign indifference and contempt with
which he seems to look down upon his puny assailants. When her ladyship drives out, these dogs are generally carried with her to take the
air; when they look out of each window of the carriage, and bark at
all vulgar pedestrian dogs. These dogs are a continual source of misery
to the household; as they are always in the way, they every now and
then get their toes trod on, and then there is a yelping on their part, and
a loud lamentation on the part of their mistress, that fill the room with
clamour and confusion.

Lastly, there is her ladyship's waiting-gentlewoman, Mrs. Hannah,
a prim, pragmatical old maid; one of the most intolerable and intolerant
virgins that ever lived. She has kept her virtue by her until it has turned
sour, and now every word and look smacks of verjuice. She is the very
opposite to her mistress, for one hates, and the other loves, all mankind.
How they first came together I cannot imagine; but they have lived
together for many years; and the abigail's temper being tart and en-

croaching, and her ladyship's easy and yielding, the former has got the complete upper hand, and tyrannises over the good lady in secret.

Lady Lillycraft now and then complains of it, in great confidence, to her friends, but hushes up the subject immediately, if Mrs. Hannah makes her appearance. Indeed, she has been so accustomed to be attended by her, that she thinks she could not do without her; though one great study of her life is to keep Mrs. Hannah in good humour, by little presents and kindnesses.

Master Simon has a most devout abhorrence, mingled with awe, for this ancient spinster. He told me the other day, in a whisper, that she was a cursed brimstone – in fact, he added another epithet, which I would not repeat for the world. I have remarked, however, that he is always extremely civil to her when they meet.

READY MONEY JACK

My purse, it is my privy wyfe,
This song I dare both syng and say,
It keepeth men from grievous stryfe
When every man for hymself shall pay.
As I ryde in ryche array
For gold and sylver men wyll me floryshe;
By thys matter I dare well saye,
Ever gramercy myne owne purse.
BOOK OF HUNTING

On the skirts of the neighbouring village there lives a kind of small potentate, who, for aught I know, is a representative of one of the most ancient legitimate lines of the present day; for the empire over which he reigns has belonged to his family time out of mind. His territories comprise a considerable number of good fat acres; and his seat of power is in an old farm-house, where he enjoys, unmolested, the stout oaken chair of his ancestors. The personage to whom I allude is a sturdy old yeoman of the name of John Tibbets, or rather Ready Money Jack Tibbets, as he is called throughout the neighbourhood.

The first place where he attracted my attention was in the church-yard on Sunday; where he sat on a tombstone after the service, with his hat a little on one side, holding forth to a small circle of auditors; and, as I presumed, expounding the law and the prophets; until, on drawing a little nearer, I found he was only expatiating on the merits of a brown horse. He presented so faithful a picture of a substantial English yeoman, such as he is often described in books, heightened, indeed, by some little finery, peculiar to himself, that I could not but take note of his whole appearance.

He was between fifty and sixty, of a strong, muscular frame, and at least six feet high, with a physiognomy as grave as a lion's, and set off with short, curling, iron-gray locks. His shirt-collar was turned down, and displayed a neck covered with the same short, curling, gray hair; and he wore a coloured silk neckcloth, tied very loosely, and tucked in at the bosom, with a green paste brooch on the knot. His coat was of dark green cloth, with silver buttons, on each of which was engraved a stag, with his own name, John Tibbets, underneath. He had an inner waistcoat of figured chintz, between which and his coat was another of scarlet cloth, unbuttoned. His breeches were also left unbuttoned at the knees, not from any slovenliness, but to show a broad pair of scarlet garters. His stockings were blue, with white

clocks; he wore large silver shoe-buckles; a broad paste buckle in his
hatband; his sleeve-buttons were gold seven shilling pieces; and he
had two or three guineas hanging as ornaments to his watch-chain.

On making some inquiries about him, I gathered, that he was
descended from a line of farmers that had always lived on the same
spot, and owned the same property; and that half of the churchyard
was taken up with the tombstones of his race. He has all his life
been an important character in the place. When a youngster, he was
one of the most roaring blades of the neighbourhood. No one could
match him at wrestling, pitching the bar, cudgel play, and other
athletic exercises. Like the renowned Pinner of Wakefield, he was
the village champion, carried off the prize at all the fairs, and threw
his gauntlet at the country round. Even to this day the old people
talk of his prowess, and undervalue, in comparison, all heroes of the
green that have succeeded him; nay, they say, that if Ready Money
Jack were to take the field even now, there is no one could stand
before him.

When Jack's father died, the neighbours shook their heads, and
predicted that young hopeful would soon make way with the old
homestead; but Jack falsified all their predictions. The moment he
succeeded to the paternal farm he assumed a new character; took a
wife; attended resolutely to his affairs, and became an industrious,
thrifty farmer. With the family property he inherited a set of old
family maxims, to which he steadily adhered. He saw to every thing
himself; put his own hand to the plough; worked hard; ate heartily;
slept soundly; paid for every thing in cash down; and never danced
except he could do it to the music of his own money in both pockets.
He has never been without a hundred or two pounds in gold by him,
and never allows a debt to stand unpaid. This has gained him his
current name, of which, by the bye, he is a little proud; and has caused
him to be looked upon as a very wealthy man by all the village.

Notwithstanding his thrift, however, he has never denied himself
the amusements of life, but has taken a share in every passing
pleasure. It is his maxim, that "he that works hard can afford to play."
He is, therefore, an attendant at all the country fairs and wakes, and
has signalized himself by feats of strength and prowess on every
village green in the shire. He often makes his appearance at horse
races, and sports his half guinea, and even his guinea at a time;
keeps a good horse for his own riding, and to this day is fond of
following the hounds, and is generally in at the death. He keeps up
the rustic revels, and hospitalities too, for which his paternal farm-
house has always been noted; has plenty of good cheer and dancing

at harvest-home, and, above all, keeps the "merry night,"* as it is termed, at Christmas.

With all his love of amusement, however, Jack is by no means a boisterous jovial companion. He is seldom known to laugh even in the midst of his gaiety; but maintains the same grave, lion-like demeanour. He is very slow at comprehending a joke; and is apt to sit puzzling at it, with a perplexed look, while the rest of the company is in a roar. This gravity has, perhaps, grown on him with the growing weight of his character; for he is gradually rising into patriarchal dignity in his native place. Though he no longer takes an active part in athletic sports, yet he always presides at them, and is appealed to on all occasions as umpire. He maintains the peace on the village-green at holiday games, and quells all brawls and quarrels by collaring the parties and shaking them heartily, if refractory. No one ever pretends to raise a hand against him, or to contend against his decisions; the young men having grown up in habitual awe of his prowess, and in implicit deference to him as the champion and lord of the green.

He is a regular frequenter of the village inn, the landlady having been a sweetheart of his in early life, and he having always continued on kind terms with her. He seldom, however, drinks any thing but a draught of ale; smokes his pipe, and pays his reckoning before leaving the tap-room. Here he "gives his little senate laws;" decides bets, which are very generally referred to him; determines upon the characters and qualities of horses; and indeed plays now and then the part of a judge, in settling petty disputes between neighbours, which otherwise might have been nursed by country attorneys into tolerable law-suits. Jack is very candid and impartial in his decisions, but he has not a head to carry a long argument, and is very apt to get perplexed and out of patience if there is much pleading. He generally breaks through the argument with a strong voice, and brings matters to a summary conclusion, by pronouncing what he calls the "upshot of the business," or, in other words, "the long and the short of the matter."

Jack once made a journey to London a great many years since, which has furnished him with topics of conversation ever since. He saw the old king on the terrace at Windsor, who stopped, and pointed him out to one of the princesses, being probably struck with Jack's truly yeoman-like appearance. This is a favourite anecdote with him, and has no doubt had a great effect in making him a most loyal subject

---

* MERRY NIGHT. A rustic merry-making in a farm-house about Christmas, common in some parts of Yorkshire. There is abundance of homely fare, tea, cakes, fruit, and ale; various feats of agility, amusing games, romping, dancing, and kissing withal. They commonly break up at midnight.

Ready-Money Jack

An engraving reproduced in the Geoffrey Crayon edition of *Bracebridge Hall* (New York: G. P. Putnam's Sons, 1868).

ever since, in spite of taxes and poors' rates. He was also at Bartholomew-fair, where he had half the buttons cut off his coat; and a gang of pickpockets, attracted by his external show of gold and silver, made a regular attempt to hustle him as he was gazing at a show; but for once they found that they had caught a tartar; for Jack enacted as great wonders among the gang as Samson did among the Philistines. One of his neighbours, who had accompanied him to town, and was with him at the fair, brought back an account of his exploits, which raised the pride of the whole village; who considered their champion as having subdued all London, and eclipsed the achievements of Friar Tuck, or even the renowned Robin Hood himself.

Of late years the old fellow has begun to take the world easily; he works less, and indulges in greater leisure, his son having grown up, and succeeded to him both in the labours of the farm, and the exploits of the green. Like all sons of distinguished men, however, his father's renown is a disadvantage to him, for he can never come up to public expectation. Though a fine active fellow of three and twenty, and quite the "cock of the walk," yet the old people declare he is nothing like what Ready Money Jack was at his time of life. The youngster himself acknowledges his inferiority, and has a wonderful opinion of the old man, who indeed taught him all his athletic accomplishments, and holds such a sway over him, that I am told, even to this day, he would have no hesitation to take him in hands, if he rebelled against paternal government.

The squire holds Jack in very high esteem, and shows him to all his visitors as a specimen of old English "heart of oak." He frequently calls at his house, and tastes some of his home-brewed, which is excellent. He made Jack a present of old Tusser's "Hundred Points of good Husbandrie," which has furnished him with reading ever since, and is his text book and manual in all agricultural and domestic concerns. He has made dog's ears at the most favourite passages, and knows many of the poetical maxims by heart.

Tibbets, though not a man to be daunted or fluttered by high acquaintances, and though he cherishes a sturdy independence of mind and manner, yet is evidently gratified by the attentions of the squire, whom he has known from boyhood, and pronounces "a true gentleman every inch of him." He is also on excellent terms with Master Simon, who is a kind of privy counsellor to the family; but his great favourite is the Oxonian, whom he taught to wrestle and play at quarter-staff when a boy, and considers the most promising young gentleman in the whole county.

BACHELORS

The Bachelor most joyfully
  In pleasant plight doth pass his daies,
Goodfellowship and companie
  He doth maintain and kepe alwaies.

EVAN'S OLD BALLADS

There is no character in the comedy of human life that is more difficult to play well, than that of an old Bachelor. When a single gentleman, therefore, arrives at that critical period, when he begins to consider it an impertinent question to be asked his age, I would advise him to look well to his ways. This period, it is true, is much later with some men than with others; I have witnessed more than once the meeting of two wrinkled old lads of this kind, who had not seen each other for several years, and have been amused by the amicable exchange of compliments on each other's appearance that takes place on such occasions. There is always one invariable observation; "Why, bless my soul! you look younger than when last I saw you!" Whenever a man's friends begin to compliment him about looking young, he may be sure that they think he is growing old.

I am led to make these remarks by the conduct of Master Simon and the general, who have become great cronies. As the former is the youngest by many years, he is regarded as quite a youthful blade by the general, who moreover looks upon him as a man of great wit and prodigious acquirements. I have already hinted that Master Simon is a family beau, and considered rather a young fellow by all the elderly ladies of the connexion; for an old bachelor, in an old family connexion, is something like an actor in a regular dramatic corps, who seems "to flourish in immortal youth," and will continue to play the Romeos and Rangers for half a century together.

Master Simon, too, is a little of the camelion, and takes a different hue with every different companion. He is very attentive and officious, and somewhat sentimental, with Lady Lillycraft; copies out little namby-pamby ditties and love-songs for her, and draws quivers, and doves, and darts, and Cupids to be worked on the corners of her pocket handkerchiefs. He indulges, however, in very considerable latitude with the other married ladies of the family; and has many sly pleasantries to whisper to them, that provoke an equivocal laugh and a tap of the fan. But when he gets among young company, such as Frank Bracebridge, the Oxonian, and the general, he is apt to put on the mad wag, and to talk in a very bachelor-like strain about the sex.

40

In this he has been encouraged by the example of the general, whom he looks up to as a man that has seen the world. The general, in fact, tells shocking stories after dinner, when the ladies have retired, which he gives as some of the choice things that are served up at the Mulligatawney club: a knot of boon companions in London. He also repeats the fat jokes of old Major Pendergast, the wit of the club, and which, though the general can hardly repeat them for laughing, always make Mr. Bracebridge look grave, he having a great antipathy to an indecent jest. In a word, the general is a complete instance of the declension in gay life, by which a young man of pleasure is apt to cool down into an obscene old gentleman.

I saw him and Master Simon, an evening or two since, conversing with a buxom milkmaid in a meadow; and from their elbowing each other now and then, and the general's shaking his shoulders, blowing up his cheeks, and breaking out into a short fit of irrepressible laughter, I had no doubt they were playing the mischief with the girl.

As I looked at them through a hedge, I could not but think they would have made a tolerable group for a modern picture of Susannah and the two elders. It is true, the girl seemed in no wise alarmed at the force of the enemy; and I question, had either of them been alone, whether she would not have been more than they would have ventured to encounter. Such veteran roysters are daring wags when together, and will put any female to the blush with their jokes; but they are as quiet as lambs when they fall singly into the clutches of a fine woman.

In spite of the general's years, he evidently is a little vain of his person, and ambitious of conquests. I have observed him on Sunday in church, eying the country girls most suspiciously; and have seen him leer upon them with a downright amorous look, even when he has been gallanting Lady Lillycraft, with great ceremony, through the church-yard. The general, in fact, is a veteran in the service of Cupid rather than of Mars, having signalized himself in all the garrison towns and country quarters, and seen service in every ball-room of England. Not a celebrated beauty but he has laid siege to; and, if his word may be taken in a matter wherein no man is apt to be over veracious, it is incredible the success he has had with the fair. At present he is like a worn-out warrior, retired from service; but who still cocks his beaver with a military air, and talks stoutly of fighting whenever he comes within the smell of gunpowder.

I have heard him speak his mind very freely over his bottle, about the folly of the captain in taking a wife; as he thinks a young soldier should care for nothing but his "bottle and kind landlady." But, in fact, he says, the service on the continent has had a sad effect upon the young men; they have been ruined by light wines and French quadrilles. "They've nothing," he says, "of the spirit of the old service. There are none of your six-bottle men left, that were the souls of a mess-dinner, and used to play the very deuce among the women."

As to a bachelor, the general affirms that he is a free and easy man, with no baggage to take care of but his portmanteau; but a married man, with his wife hanging on his arm, always puts him in mind of a chamber candlestick, with its extinguisher hitched to it. I should not mind all this if it were merely confined to the general; but I fear he will be the ruin of my friend, Master Simon, who already begins to echo his heresies, and to talk in the style of a gentleman that has seen life, and lived upon the town. Indeed, the general seems to have taken Master Simon in hand, and talks of showing him the lions when he comes to town, and of introducing him to a knot of choice spirits at the Mulligatawney club; which, I understand, is composed of old nabobs, officers in the company's employ, and other "men of Ind," that have seen service in the East, and returned home burnt out with curry, and touched with the liver complaint. They have their regular club, where they eat Mulligatawney soup, smoke the hookah, talk about Tippoo Saib, Seringapatam, and tiger-hunting; and are tediously agreeable in each other's company.

WIVES

Believe me, man, there is no greater blisse
Than is the quiet joy of loving wife;
Which whoso wants, half of himselfe doth misse;
Friend without change, play-fellow without strife,
Food without fulnesse, counsaile without pride,
Is this sweet doubling of our single life.

SIR P. SIDNEY

There is so much talk about matrimony going on round me, in consequence of the approaching event for which we are assembled at the Hall, that I confess I find my thoughts singularly exercised on the subject. Indeed, all the bachelors of the establishment seem to be passing through a kind of fiery ordeal; for Lady Lillycraft is one of those tender, romance-read dames of the old school, whose mind is filled with flames and darts, and who breathe nothing but constancy and wedlock. She is for ever immersed in the concerns of the heart; and, to use a poetical phrase, is perfectly surrounded by "the purple light of love." The very general seems to feel the influence of this sentimental atmosphere; to melt as he approaches her ladyship, and, for the time, to forget all his heresies about matrimony and the sex.

The good lady is generally surrounded by little documents of her prevalent taste; novels of a tender nature; richly bound little books of poetry, that are filled with sonnets and love tales, and perfumed with rose-leaves; and she has always an album at hand, for which she claims the contributions of all her friends. On looking over this last repository the other day, I found a series of poetical extracts, in the squire's handwriting, which might have been intended as matrimonial hints to his ward. I was so much struck with several of them, that I took the liberty of copying them out. They are from the old play of Thomas Davenport, published in 1661, intitled "The City Night-cap;" in which is drawn out and exemplified, in the part of Abstemia, the character of a patient and faithful wife, which, I think, might vie with that of the renowned Griselda.

I have often thought it a pity that plays and novels should always end at the wedding, and should not give us another act, and another volume, to let us know how the hero and heroine conducted themselves when married. Their main object seems to be merely to instruct young ladies how to get husbands, but not how to keep them: now this last, I speak it with all due diffidence, appears to me to be a desideratum in modern married life. It is appalling to those who have not yet adventured into the holy state, to see how soon the flame of romantic love burns out, or rather is quenched in matrimony; and how deplorably the passionate, poetic lover declines into the phlegmatic, prosaic husband. I am inclined to attribute this very much to the defect just mentioned in the plays and novels, which form so important a branch of study of our young ladies; and which teach them how to be heroines, but leave them totally at a loss when they come to be wives. The play from which the quotations before me were made, however, is an exception to this remark; and I cannot refuse myself the pleasure of adducing some of them for the benefit of the reader, and for the honour of an old writer, who has bravely attempted to awaken dramatic interest in favour of a woman, even after she was married!

The following is a commendation of Abstemia to her husband Lorenzo:

> She's modest, but not sullen, and loves silence;
> Not that she wants apt words (for when she speaks,
> She inflames love with wonder), but because
> She calls wise silence the soul's harmony.
> She's truly chaste; yet such a foe to coyness,
> The poorest call her courteous; and, which is excellent,
> (Though fair and young) she shuns to expose herself
> To the opinion of strange eyes. She either seldom
> Or never walks abroad but in your company;
> And then with such sweet bashfulness, as if
> She were venturing on crack'd ice, and takes delight
> To step into the print your foot hath made,
> And will follow you whole fields; so she will drive
> Tediousness out of time with her sweet character.

Notwithstanding all this excellence, Abstemia has the misfortune to incur the unmerited jealousy of her husband. Instead, however, of resenting his harsh treatment with clamorous upbraidings, and with the stormy violence of high, windy virtue, by which the sparks of anger are so often blown into a flame; she endures it with the meekness of conscious, but patient, virtue; and makes the following beautiful appeal to a friend who has witnessed her long suffering:

> ——Hast thou not seen me
> Bear all his injuries, as the ocean suffers
> The angry bark to plough thorough her bosom,
> And yet is presently so smooth, the eye
> Cannot perceive where the wide wound was made?

Lorenzo, being wrought on by false representations, at length repudiates her. To the last, however, she maintains her patient sweetness, and her love for him, in spite of his cruelty. She deplores his error, even more than his unkindness; and laments the delusion which has turned his very affection into a source of bitterness. There is a moving pathos in her parting address to Lorenzo after their divorce:

        —— Farewell, Lorenzo,
Whom my soul doth love: if you e'er marry,
May you meet a good wife; so good, that you
May not suspect her, nor may she be worthy
Of your suspicion: and if you hear hereafter
That I am dead, inquire but my last words,
And you shall know that to the last I lov'd you.
And when you walk forth with your second choice,
Into the pleasant fields, and by chance talk of me,
Imagine that you see me, lean and pale,
Strewing your path with flowers. –
But may she never live to pay my debts: (weeps)
If but in thought she wrong you, may she die
In the conception of the injury.
Pray make me wealthy with one kiss: farewell, sir:
Let it not grieve you when you shall remember
That I was innocent: nor this forget,
Though innocence here suffer, sigh, and groan,
She walks but thorow thorns to find a throne.

In a short time Lorenzo discovers his error, and the innocence of his injured wife. In the transports of his repentance, he calls to mind all her feminine excellence; her gentle, uncomplaining, womanly fortitude under wrongs and sorrows:

      ——Oh, Abstemia!
How lovely thou lookest now! now thou appearest
Chaster than is the morning's modesty,
That rises with a blush, over whose bosom
The western wind creeps softly; now I remember
How, when she sat at table, her obedient eye
Would dwell on mine, as if it were not well,
Unless it look'd where I look'd: oh how proud
She was, when she could cross herself to please me!
But where now is this fair soul? Like a silver cloud

She hath wept herself, I fear, into the dread sea,
And will be found no more.

It is but doing right by the reader, if interested in the fate of
Abstemia by the preceding extracts, to say, that she was restored to
the arms and affections of her husband, rendered fonder than ever, by
that disposition in every good heart, to atone for past injustice, by an
overflowing measure of returning kindness:

Thou wealth worth more than kingdoms; I am now
Confirmed past all suspicion; thou art far
Sweeter in thy sincere truth than a sacrifice
Deck'd up for death with garlands. The Indian winds
That blow from off the coast, and cheer the sailor
With the sweet savour of their spices, want
The delight flows in thee.

I have been more affected and interested by this little dramatic picture than by many a popular love tale; though, as I said before, I do
not think it likely either Abstemia or patient Grizzle stand much chance
of being taken for a model. Still I like to see poetry now and then
extending its views beyond the wedding-day, and teaching a lady how
to make herself attractive even after marriage. There is no great need
of enforcing on an unmarried lady the necessity of being agreeable; nor
is there any great art requisite in a youthful beauty to enable her to
please. Nature has multiplied attractions round her. Youth is in itself
attractive. The freshness of budding beauty needs no foreign aid to set
it off; it pleases merely because it is fresh, and budding, and beautiful.
But it is for the married state that a woman needs the most instruction,
and in which she should be most on her guard to maintain her powers
of pleasing. No woman can expect to be to her husband all that he
fancied her when he was a lover. Men are always doomed to be duped,
not so much by the arts of the sex, as by their own imaginations. They
are always wooing goddesses, and marrying mere mortals. A woman
should therefore ascertain what was the charm that rendered her so
fascinating when a girl, and endeavour to keep it up when she has
become a wife. One great thing undoubtedly was, the chariness of
herself and her conduct, which an unmarried female always observes.
She should maintain the same niceness and reserve in her person and
habits, and endeavour still to preserve a freshness and virgin delicacy
in the eye of her husband. She should remember that the province of
woman is to be wooed, not to woo; to be caressed, not to caress. Man

is an ungrateful being in love; bounty loses instead of winning him. The secret of a woman's power does not consist so much in giving, as in withholding. A woman may give up too much even to her husband. It is to a thousand little delicacies of conduct that she must trust to keep alive passion, and to protect herself from that dangerous familiarity, that thorough acquaintance with every weakness and imperfection incident to matrimony. By these means she may still maintain her power, though she has surrendered her person, and may continue the romance of love even beyond the honey-moon.

"She that hath a wise husband," says Jeremy Taylor, "must entice him to an eternal dearnesse by the veil of modesty, and the grave robes of chastity, the ornament of meeknesse, and the jewels of faith and charity. She must have no painting but blushings; her brightness must be purity, and she must shine round about with sweetnesses and friendship; and she shall be pleasant while she lives, and desired when she dies."

I have wandered into a rambling series of remarks on a trite subject, and a dangerous one for a bachelor to meddle with. That I may not, however, appear to confine my observations entirely to the wife, I will conclude with another quotation from Jeremy Taylor, in which the duties of both parties are mentioned; while I would recommend his sermon on the marriage ring to all those who, wiser than myself, are about entering the happy state of wedlock.

"There is scarce any matter of duty but it concerns them both alike, and is only distinguished by names, and hath its variety by circumstances and little accidents; and what in one is called love, in the other is called reverence; and what in the wife is obedience, the same in the man is duty. He provides, and she dispenses; he gives commandments, and she rules by them; he rules her by authority, and she rules him by love; she ought by all means to please him, and he must by no means displease her."

STORY TELLING

A favourite evening pastime at the Hall, and one which the worthy squire is fond of promoting, is story telling, "a good old-fashioned fire-side amusement," as he terms it. Indeed, I believe he promotes it chiefly because it was one of the choice recreations in those days of yore, when ladies and gentlemen were not much in the habit of reading. Be this as it may, he will often, at supper table, when conversation flags, call on some one or other of the company for a story, as it was formerly the custom to call for a song; and it is edifying to see the exemplary patience, and even satisfaction, with which the good old gentleman will sit and listen to some hackneyed tale that he has heard for at least a hundred times.

In this way one evening the current of anecdotes and stories ran upon mysterious personages that have figured at different times, and filled the world with doubt and conjecture; such as the Wandering Jew, the Man with the Iron Mask, who tormented the curiosity of all Europe; the Invisible Girl, and last, though not least, the Pigfaced Lady.

At length one of the company was called upon that had the most unpromising physiognomy for a story teller that ever I had seen. He was a thin, pale, weazen-faced man, extremely nervous, that had sat at one corner of the table, shrunk up, as it were, into himself, and almost swallowed up in the cape of his coat, as a turtle in its shell.

The very demand seemed to throw him into a nervous agitation, yet he did not refuse. He emerged his head out of his shell, made a few odd grimaces and gesticulations, before he could get his muscles into order, or his voice under command, and then offered to give some account of a mysterious personage that he had recently encountered in the course of his travels, and one whom he thought fully entitled of being classed with the Man with the Iron Mask.

I was so much struck with his extraordinary narrative, that I have written it out to the best of my recollection, for the amusement of the reader. I think it has in it all the elements of that mysterious and romantic narrative, so greedily sought after at the present day.

THE STOUT GENTLEMAN

A STAGE COACH ROMANCE

"I'll cross it, though it blast me!"
HAMLET

It was a rainy Sunday, in the gloomy month of November. I had been
detained, in the course of a journey, by a slight indisposition, from
which I was recovering; but I was still feverish, and was obliged to
keep within doors all day, in an inn of the small town of Derby. A wet
Sunday in a country inn! whoever has had the luck to experience one
can alone judge of my situation. The rain pattered against the casements; the bells tolled for church with a melancholy sound. I went
to the windows in quest of something to amuse the eye; but it seemed
as if I had been placed completely out of the reach of all amusement.
The windows of my bed-room looked out among tiled roofs and stacks
of chimneys, while those of my sitting-room commanded a full view
of the stable-yard. I know of nothing more calculated to make a man
sick of this world than a stable-yard on a rainy day. The place was
littered with wet straw that had been kicked about by travellers and
stable-boys. In one corner was a stagnant pool of water, surrounding
an island of muck; there were several half-drowned fowls crowded
together under a cart, among which was a miserable, crest-fallen cock,
drenched out of all life and spirit; his drooping tail matted, as it were,
into a single feather, along which the water trickled from his back; near
the cart was a half-dozing cow, chewing the cud, and standing patiently
to be rained on, with wreaths of vapour rising from her reeking hide;
a wall-eyed horse, tired of the loneliness of the stable, was poking his
spectral head out of a window, with the rain dripping on it from the
eaves; an unhappy cur, chained to a doghouse hard by, uttered something every now and then, between a bark and a yelp; a drab of a
kitchen wench tramped backwards and forwards through the yard in
pattens, looking as sulky as the weather itself; every thing, in short,
was comfortless and forlorn, excepting a crew of hard-drinking ducks,
assembled like boon companions round a puddle, and making a riotous
noise over their liquor.

I was lonely and listless, and wanted amusement. My room soon
became insupportable. I abandoned it, and sought what is technically

49

called the travellers'-room. This is a public room set apart at most inns for the accommodation of a class of wayfarers, called travellers, or riders; a kind of commercial knights errant, who are incessantly scouring the kingdom in gigs, on horseback, or by coach. They are the only successors that I know of at the present day, to the knights errant of yore. They lead the same kind of roving adventurous life, only changing the lance for a driving-whip, the buckler for a pattern-card, and the coat of mail for an upper Benjamin. Instead of vindicating the charms of peerless beauty, they rove about, spreading the fame and standing of some substantial tradesman, or manufacturer, and are ready at any time to bargain in his name; it being the fashion now-a-days to trade, instead of fight, with one another. As the room of the hostel, in the good old fighting times, would be hung round at night with the armour of way-worn warriors, such as coats of mail, falchions, and yawning helmets; so the travellers'-room is garnished with the harnessing of their successors, with box coats, whips of all kinds, spurs, gaiters, and oil-cloth covered hats.

I was in hopes of finding some of these worthies to talk with, but was disappointed. There were, indeed, two or three in the room; but I could make nothing of them. One was just finishing his breakfast, quarrelling with his bread and butter, and huffing the waiter; another buttoned on a pair of gaiters, with many execrations at Boots for not having cleaned his shoes well; a third sat drumming on the table with his fingers and looking at the rain as it streamed down the window-glass; they all appeared infected by the weather, and disappeared, one after the other, without exchanging a word.

I sauntered to the window and stood gazing at the people, picking their way to church, with petticoats hoisted midleg high, and dripping umbrellas. The bell ceased to toll, and the streets became silent. I then amused myself with watching the daughters of a tradesman opposite; who, being confined to the house for fear of wetting their Sunday finery, played off their charms at the front windows, to fascinate the chance tenants of the inn. They at length were summoned away by a vigilant vinegar-faced mother, and I had nothing further from without to amuse me.

What was I to do to pass away the long-lived day? I was sadly nervous and lonely; and every thing about an inn seems calculated to make a dull day ten times duller. Old newspapers, smelling of beer and tobacco smoke, and which I had already read half a dozen times. Good for nothing books, that were worse than rainy weather. I bored myself to death with an old volume of the Lady's Magazine. I read all the common-placed names of ambitious travellers scrawled

Stable Yard on a Rainy Day

An engraving reproduced in the Geoffrey Crayon edition of *Bracebridge Hall*
(New York: G. P. Putnam's Sons, 1868).

on the panes of glass; the eternal families of the Smiths and the Browns, and the Jacksons, and the Johnsons, and all the other sons; and I decyphered several scraps of fatiguing inn-window poetry which I have met with in all parts of the world.

The day continued lowering and gloomy; the slovenly, ragged, spongy clouds drifted heavily along; there was no variety even in the rain; it was one dull, continued, monotonous patter – patter – patter, excepting that now and then I was enlivened by the idea of a brisk shower, from the rattling of the drops upon a passing umbrella.

It was quite *refreshing* (if I may be allowed a hackneyed phrase of the day) when, in the course of the morning, a horn blew, and a stage coach whirled through the street, with outside passengers stuck all over it, cowering under cotton umbrellas, and seethed together, and reeking with the steams of wet box-coats and upper Benjamins.

The sound brought out from their lurking-places a crew of vagabond boys, and vagabond dogs, and the carroty-headed hostler, and that non-descript animal ycleped Boots, and all the other vagabond race that infest the purlieus of an inn; but the bustle was transient; the coach again whirled on its way; and boy and dog, and hostler and Boots, all slunk back again to their holes; the street again became silent, and the rain continued to rain on. In fact, there was no hope of its clearing up; the barometer pointed to rainy weather; mine hostess's tortoise-shell cat sat by the fire washing her face, and rubbing her paws over her ears; and, on referring to the Almanack, I found a direful prediction stretching from the top of the page to the bottom through the whole month, "expect – much – rain – about – this – time!"

I was dreadfully hipped. The hours seemed as if they would never creep by. The very ticking of the clock became irksome. At length the stillness of the house was interrupted by the ringing of a bell. Shortly after I heard the voice of a waiter at the bar: "The stout gentleman in No. 13, wants his breakfast. Tea and bread and butter, with ham and eggs; the eggs not to be too much done."

In such a situation as mine every incident is of importance. Here was a subject of speculation presented to my mind, and ample exercise for my imagination. I am prone to paint pictures to myself, and on this occasion I had some materials to work upon. Had the guest up stairs been mentioned as Mr. Smith, or Mr. Brown, or Mr. Jackson, or Mr. Johnson, or merely as "the gentleman in No. 13," it would have been a perfect blank to me. I should have thought nothing of it; but "The Stout Gentleman!" – the very name had something in it of the picturesque. It at once gave the size; it embodied the personage to my mind's eye; and my fancy did the rest.

He was stout, or, as some term it, lusty; in all probability, therefore, he was advanced in life, some people expanding as they grow old. By his breakfasting rather late, and in his own room, he must be a man accustomed to live at his ease, and above the necessity of early rising; no doubt a round, rosy, lusty old gentleman.

There was another violent ringing. The stout gentleman was impatient for his breakfast. He was evidently a man of importance; "well to do in the world;" accustomed to be promptly waited upon; of a keen appetite, and a little cross when hungry; "perhaps," thought I, "he may be some London Alderman; or who knows but he may be a Member of Parliament?"

The breakfast was sent up, and there was a short interval of silence; he was, doubtless, making the tea. Presently there was a violent ringing; and before it could be answered, another ringing still more violent. "Bless me! what a choleric old gentleman!" The waiter came down in a huff. The butter was rancid, the eggs were over-done, the ham was too salt: – the stout gentleman was evidently nice in his eating; one of those who eat and growl, and keep the waiter on the trot, and live in a state militant with the household.

The hostess got into a fume. I should observe that she was a brisk, coquettish woman; a little of a shrew, and something of a slammer-kin, but very pretty withal; with a nincompoop for a husband, as shrews are apt to have. She rated the servants roundly for their negligence in sending up so bad a breakfast, but said not a word against the stout gentleman; by which I clearly perceived that he must be a man of consequence, intitled to make a noise and to give trouble at a country inn. Other eggs, and ham, and bread and butter were sent up. They appeared to be more graciously received; at least there was no further complaint.

I had not made many turns about the travellers'-room, when there was another ringing. Shortly afterwards there was a stir and an inquest about the house. The stout gentleman wanted the Times or the Chronicle newspaper. I set him down, therefore, for a whig; or rather, from his being so absolute and lordly where he had a chance, I suspected him of being a radical. Hunt, I had heard, was a large man; "who knows," thought I, "but it is Hunt himself?"

My curiosity began to be awakened. I inquired of the waiter who was this stout gentleman that was making all this stir; but I could get no information. Nobody seemed to know his name. The landlords of bustling inns seldom trouble their heads about the names or occupations of their transient guests. The colour of a coat, the shape or size of the person, is enough to suggest a travelling name. It is either the tall gentleman, or the short gentleman, or the gentleman in black, or the gentleman in snuff-colour; or, as in the present instance, the stout gentleman. A designation of the kind once hit on answers every purpose, and saves all further inquiry.

Rain – rain – rain! pitiless, ceaseless rain! No such thing as putting a foot out of doors, and no occupation nor amusement within. By and by I heard some one walking over head. It was in the stout gentleman's room. He evidently was a large man by the heaviness of his tread; and an old man from his wearing such creaking soles. "He is doubtless," thought I, "some rich old square-toes of regular habits, and is now taking exercise after breakfast."

I now read all the advertisements of coaches and hotels that were stuck about the mantel-piece. The Lady's Magazine had become an abomination to me; it was as tedious as the day itself. I wandered out, not knowing what to do, and ascended again to my room. I had not been there long, when there was a squall from a neighbouring bed-room. A door opened and slammed violently; a chambermaid, that I had remarked for having a ruddy, good-humoured face, went down stairs in a violent flurry. The stout gentleman had been rude to her!

This sent a whole host of my deductions to the deuce in a moment. This unknown personage could not be an old gentleman; for old gentlemen are not apt to be so obstreperous to chambermaids. He could not be a young gentleman; for young gentlemen are not apt to inspire such indignation. He must be a middle-aged man, and confounded ugly into the bargain, or the girl would not have taken the matter in such terrible dudgeon. I confess I was sorely puzzled.

In a few minutes I heard the voice of my landlady. I caught a glance of her as she came tramping up stairs; her face glowing, her cap flaring, her tongue wagging the whole way. "She'd have no such doings in her house, she'd warrant! If gentlemen did spend money freely, it was no rule. She'd have no servant maids of hers treated in that way, when they were about their work, that's what she wouldn't!"

As I hate squabbles, particularly with women, and above all with pretty women, I slunk back into my room, and partly closed the door; but my curiosity was too much excited not to listen. The landlady marched intrepidly to the enemy's citadel, and entered it with a storm. The door closed after her. I heard her voice in high, windy clamour for a moment or two. Then it gradually subsided, like a gust of wind in a garret; then there was a laugh; then I heard nothing more.

After a little while my landlady came out with an odd smile on her face, adjusting her cap, which was a little on one side. As she went down stairs I heard the landlord ask her what was the matter; she said, "Nothing at all, only the girl's a fool." – I was more than ever perplexed what to make of this unaccountable personage, who could put a good-natured chambermaid in a passion, and send away a termagant landlady in smiles. He could not be so old, nor cross, nor ugly either.

I had to go to work at his picture again, and to paint him entirely different. I now set him down for one of those stout gentlemen that are frequently met with swaggering about the doors of country inns. Moist, merry fellows, in Belcher handkerchiefs, whose bulk is a little assisted by malt-liquors. Men who have seen the world, and been sworn at Highgate; who are used to tavern life; up to all the tricks of tapsters, and knowing in the ways of sinful publicans. Free-livers on a small scale; who are prodigal within the compass of a guinea; who call all the waiters by name, touzle the maids, gossip with the landlady at the bar, and prose over a pint of port, or a glass of negus, after dinner.

The morning wore away in forming of these and similar surmises. As fast as I wove one system of belief, some movement of the unknown would completely overturn it, and throw all my thoughts again into confusion. Such are the solitary operations of a feverish mind. I was, as I have said, extremely nervous; and the continual meditation on the concerns of this invisible personage began to have its effect: – I was getting a fit of the fidgets.

Dinner-time came. I hoped the stout gentleman might dine in the travellers'-room, and that I might at length get a view of his person; but no – he had dinner served in his own room. What could be the meaning of this solitude and mystery? He could not be a radical; there was something too aristocratical in thus keeping himself apart from the rest of the world, and condemning himself to his own dull company throughout a rainy day. And then, too, he lived too well for a discontented politician. He seemed to expatiate on a variety of dishes, and to sit over his wine like a jolly friend of good-living. Indeed, my doubts on this head were soon at an end; for he could not have finished his first bottle before I could faintly hear him humming a tune; and on listening, I found it to be "God save the King." 'Twas plain, then, he was no radical, but a faithful subject; one that grew loyal over his bottle, and was ready to stand by king and constitution, when he could stand by nothing else. But who could he be! My conjectures began to run wild. Was he not some personage of distinction travelling incog.? "God knows!" said I, at my wit's end; "it may be one of the royal family, for aught I know, for they are all stout gentlemen!"

The weather continued rainy. The mysterious unknown kept his room, and, as far as I could judge, his chair, for I did not hear him move.

In the mean time, as the day advanced, the travellers'-room began to be frequented. Some, who had just arrived, came in buttoned up in box-coats; others came home who had been dispersed about the town. Some took their dinners, and some their tea. Had I been in a different mood, I should have found entertainment in studying this peculiar class of men. There were two especially, who were regular wags of the road, and up to all the standing jokes of travellers. They had a thousand sly things to say to the waiting-maid, whom they called Louisa, and Ethelinda, and a dozen other fine names, changing the name every time, and chuckling amazingly at their own waggery. My mind, however, had become completely engrossed by the stout gentleman. He had kept my fancy in chase during a long day, and it was not now to be diverted from the scent.

The evening gradually wore away. The travellers read the papers two or three times over. Some drew round the fire and told long stories about their horses, about their adventures, their overturns, and breakings-down. They discussed the credits of different merchants and different inns; and the two wags told several choice anecdotes of pretty chambermaids, and kind landladies. All this passed as they were quietly taking what they called their night-caps, that is to say, strong glasses of brandy and water and sugar, or some other mixture of the kind; after which they one after another rang for "Boots" and the chambermaid, and walked off to bed in old shoes cut down into marvellously uncomfortable slippers.

There was only one man left; a short-legged, long-bodied, plethoric fellow, with a very large, sandy head. He sat by himself, with a glass of port wine negus, and a spoon; sipping and stirring, and meditating and sipping, until nothing was left but the spoon. He gradually fell asleep bolt upright in his chair, with the empty glass standing before him; and the candle seemed to fall asleep too, for the wick grew long, and black, and cabbaged at the end, and dimmed the little light that remained in the chamber. The gloom that now prevailed was contagious. Around hung the shapeless, and almost spectral, box-coats of departed travellers, long since buried in deep sleep. I only heard the ticking of the clock, with the deep-drawn breathings of the sleeping toper, and the drippings of the rain, drop – drop – drop, from the eaves of the house. The church bells chimed midnight. All at once the stout gentleman began to walk over head, pacing slowly backwards and forwards. There was something extremely awful in all this, especially to one in my state of nerves. These ghastly great coats, these guttural breathings, and the creaking footsteps of this mysterious being. His steps grew fainter and fainter, and at length died away. I could bear it no longer. I was wound up to the desperation of a hero of romance. "Be he who or what he may," said I to myself, "I'll have a sight of him!" I seized a chamber candle, and hurried up to number 13. The door stood ajar. I hesitated – I entered: the room was deserted. There stood a large, broad-bottomed elbow-chair at a table, on which was an empty tumbler, and a "Times" newspaper, and the room smelt powerfully of Stilton cheese.

The mysterious stranger had evidently but just retired. I turned off, sorely disappointed, to my room, which had been changed to the front of the house. As I went along the corridor, I saw a large pair of boots, with dirty, waxed tops, standing at the door of a bed-chamber. They doubtless belonged to the unknown; but it would not do to disturb so redoubtable a personage in his den; he might discharge a pistol, or something worse, at my head. I went to bed, therefore, and lay awake half the night in a terribly nervous state; and even when I fell asleep, I was still haunted in my dreams by the idea of the stout gentleman and his wax-topped boots.

I slept rather late the next morning, and was awakened by some stir and bustle in the house, which I could not at first comprehend; until getting more awake, I found there was a mail-coach starting from the door. Suddenly there was a cry from below, "The gentleman has forgot his umbrella! look for the gentleman's umbrella in No. 13!" I heard an immediate scampering of a chambermaid along the passage, and a shrill reply as she ran, "here it is! here's the gentleman's umbrella!"

The mysterious stranger then was on the point of setting off. This was the only chance I should ever have of knowing him. I sprang out of bed, scrambled to the window, snatched aside the curtains, and just caught a glimpse of the rear of a person getting in at the coach-door. The skirts of a brown coat parted behind, and gave me a full view of the broad disk of a pair of drab breeches. The door closed – "all right!" was the word – the coach whirled off: – and that was all I ever saw of the stout gentleman!

FOREST TREES

"A living gallery of aged trees."

One of the favourite themes of boasting with the squire is the noble trees on his estate, which, in truth, has some of the finest that I have seen in England. There is something august and solemn in the great avenues of stately oaks that gather their branches together high in air, and seem to reduce the pedestrians beneath them to mere pigmies. "An avenue of oaks or elms," the squire observes, "is the true colonnade that should lead to a gentleman's house. As to stone and marble, any one can rear them at once, they are the work of the day; but commend me to the colonnades that have grown old and great with the family, and tell by their grandeur how long the family has endured."

The squire has great reverence for certain venerable trees, gray with moss, which he considers as the ancient nobility of his domain. There is the ruin of an enormous oak, which has been so much battered by time and tempest, that scarce any thing is left; though he says Christy recollects when, in his boyhood, it was healthy and flourishing, until it was struck by lightning. It is now a mere trunk, with one twisted bough stretching up into the air, bearing a green branch at the end of it. This sturdy wreck is much valued by the squire; he calls it his standard-bearer, and compares it to a veteran warrior beaten down in battle, but bearing up his banner to the last. He has actually had a fence built round it, to protect it as much as possible from further injury.

It is with great difficulty that the squire can ever be brought to have any tree cut down on his estate. To some he looks with reverence, as having been planted by his ancestors; to others with a kind of paternal affection, as having been planted by himself; and he feels a degree of awe in bringing down with a few strokes of the axe, what it has cost centuries to build up. I confess I cannot but sympathize, in some degree, with the good squire on the subject. Though brought up in a country overrun with forests, where trees are apt to be considered mere incumbrances, and to be laid low without hesitation or remorse, yet I could never see a fine tree hewn down without concern. The poets, who are naturally lovers of trees, as they are of every thing that is beautiful, have artfully awakened great interest in their favour, by representing them as the habitations of sylvan deities; insomuch that every great tree had its tutelar genius, or a nymph, whose existence was limited to its duration. Evelyn, in his Sylva, makes several pleasing and fanciful allusions to this superstition. "As the fall," says he, "of a very aged oak, giving a crack like thunder, has often been heard at many miles distance; constrained though I often am to fell them with reluctancy, I do not at any time remember to have heard the groans of those nymphs (grieving to be dispossessed of their ancient habitations) without some emotion and pity." And again, in alluding to a violent storm that had devastated the woodlands, he says; "Methinks I still hear, sure I am that I still feel, the dismal groans of our forests; the late dreadful hurricane having subverted so many thousands of goodly oaks, prostrating the trees, laying them in ghastly postures, like whole regiments fallen in battle by the sword of the conqueror, and crushing all that grew beneath them. The public accounts," he adds, "reckon no less than three thousand *brave oaks* in one part only of the forest of Dean blown down."

I have paused more than once in the wilderness of America, to contemplate the traces of some blast of wind, which seemed to have rushed down from the clouds, and ripped its way through the bosom of the woodlands; rooting up, shivering and splintering the stoutest trees, and leaving a long track of desolation. There was something awful in the vast havoc made among these gigantic plants; and in considering their magnificent remains, so rudely torn and mangled, and hurled down to perish prematurely on their native soil, I was conscious of a strong movement of the sympathy so feelingly expressed by Evelyn. I recollect, also, hearing a traveller, of poetical temperament, expressing the kind of horror which he felt on beholding, on the banks of the Missouri, an oak of prodigious size, which had been, in a manner, overpowered by an enormous wild grape-vine. The vine had clasped its huge folds round the trunk, and from thence had wound about every branch and twig, until the mighty tree had withered in its embrace. It seemed like Laocoon struggling ineffectually in the hideous coils of the monster Python. It was the lion of trees perishing in the embraces of a vegetable boa.

I am fond of listening to the conversation of English gentlemen on rural concerns, and of noticing with what taste and discrimination, and what strong, unaffected interest they will discuss topics, which in other countries are abandoned to mere woodmen, or rustic cultivators. I have heard a noble earl descant on park and forest scenery with the science and feeling of a painter. He dwelt on the shape and beauty of particular trees on his estate, with as much pride and technical precision as though he had been discussing the merits of statues in his collection. I found that he had even gone considerable distances to examine trees which were celebrated among rural amateurs; for it seems that trees, like horses, have their established points of excellence; and that there are some in England which enjoy very extensive celebrity among tree-fanciers from being perfect in their kind.

There is something nobly simple and pure in such a taste; it argues, I think, a sweet and generous nature, to have this strong relish for the beauties of vegetation, and this friendship for the hardy and glorious sons of the forest. There is a grandeur of thought connected with this part of rural economy. It is, if I may be allowed the figure, the heroic line of husbandry. It is worthy of liberal, and freeborn, and aspiring men. He who plants an oak looks forward to future ages, and plants for posterity. Nothing can be less selfish than this. He cannot expect to sit in its shade, nor enjoy its shelter; but he exults in the idea, that the acorn which he has buried in the earth shall grow up into a lofty pile, and shall keep on flourishing, and increasing, and benefiting mankind, long after he shall have ceased to tread his paternal fields. Indeed it is the nature of such occupations to lift the thoughts above mere worldliness. As the leaves of trees are said to absorb all noxious qualities of the air, and to breathe forth a purer atmosphere, so it seems to me as if they drew from us all sordid and angry passions, and breathed forth peace and philanthropy. There is a serene and settled majesty in woodland scenery, that enters into the soul, and dilates and elevates it, and fills it with noble inclinations. The ancient and hereditary groves, too, that embower this island, are most of them full of story. They are haunted by the recollections of great spirits of past ages, who have sought for relaxation among them from the tumult of arms, or the toils of state, or have wooed the muse beneath their shade. Who can walk, with soul unmoved, among the stately groves of Penshurst, where the gallant, the amiable, the elegant Sir Philip Sidney passed his boyhood; or can look without fondness upon the tree that is said to have been planted on his birthday; or can ramble among the classic bowers of Hagley; or can pause among the solitudes of Windsor Forest, and look at the oaks around, huge, gray, and time-worn, like the old castle towers, and not feel as if he were surrounded by so many monuments of long-enduring glory? It is, when viewed in this light, that planted groves, and stately avenues, and cultivated parks, have an advantage over the more luxuriant beauties of unassisted nature. It is that they teem with moral associations, and keep up the ever-interesting story of human existence.

It is incumbent then, on the high and generous spirits of an ancient nation, to cherish these sacred groves that surround their ancestral mansions, and to perpetuate them to their descendants. Republican as I am by birth, and brought up as I have been in republican principles and habits, I can feel nothing of the servile reverence for titled rank, merely because it is titled; but I trust that I am neither churl nor bigot in my creed. I can both see and feel how hereditary distinction, when it falls to the lot of a generous mind, may elevate that mind into true nobility. It is one of the effects of hereditary rank, when it falls thus happily, that it multiplies the duties, and, as it were, extends the existence of the possessor. He does not feel himself a mere individual link in creation, responsible only for his own brief term of being. He carries back his existence in proud recollection, and he extends it forward in honourable anticipation. He lives with his ancestry, and he lives with his posterity. To both does he consider himself involved in deep responsibilities. As he has received much from those that have gone before, so he feels bound to transmit much to those who are to come after him. His domestic undertakings seem to imply a longer existence than those of ordinary men; none are so apt to build and plant for future centuries, as noble-spirited men, who have received their heritages from foregone ages.

I cannot but applaud, therefore, the fondness and pride with which I have noticed English gentlemen, of generous temperaments, and high aristocratic feelings, contemplating those magnificent trees, which rise like towers and pyramids, from the midst of their paternal lands. There is an affinity between all nature, animate and inanimate; the oak, in the pride and lustihood of its growth, seems to me to take its range with the lion and the eagle, and to assimilate, in the grandeur of its attributes, to heroic and intellectual man. With its mighty pillar rising straight and direct towards heaven, bearing up its leafy honours from the impurities of earth, and supporting them aloft in free air and glorious sunshine, it is an emblem of what a true nobleman *should be;* a refuge for the weak, a shelter for the oppressed, a defence for the defenceless; warding off from them the peltings of the storm, or the scorching rays of arbitrary power. He who is *this,* is an ornament and a blessing to his native land. He who is *otherwise,* abuses his eminent advantages; abuses the grandeur and prosperity which he has drawn from the bosom of his country. Should tempests arise, and he be laid prostrate by the storm, who would mourn over his fall? Should he be borne down by the oppressive hand of power, who would murmur at his fate? – "why cumbereth he the ground?"

A LITERARY ANTIQUARY

Printed bookes he contemnes, as a novelty of this latter age;
but a manuscript he pores on everlastingly; especially if the
cover be all moth-eaten, and the dust make a parenthesis
betweene every syllable.

MICRO-COSMOGRAPHIE, 1628

The squire receives great sympathy and support, in his antiquated
humours, from the parson, of whom I made some mention on my former
visit to the Hall, and who acts as a kind of family chaplain. He has been
cherished by the squire almost constantly since the time that they were
fellow students at Oxford; for it is one of the peculiar advantages of
these great universities, that they often link the poor scholar to the rich
patron, by early and heart-felt ties, that last through life, without the
usual humiliations of dependence and patronage. Under the fostering
protection of the squire, therefore, the little parson has pursued his
studies in peace. Having lived almost entirely among books, and those,
too, old books, he is quite ignorant of the world, and his mind is as
antiquated as the garden at the Hall, where the flowers are all arranged
in formal beds, and the yew-trees clipped into urns and peacocks.

His taste for literary antiquities was first imbibed in the Bodleian
Library at Oxford; where, when a student, he past many an hour
foraging among the old manuscripts. He has since, at different times,
visited most of the curious libraries in England, and has ransacked many
of the cathedrals. With all his quaint and curious learning, he has
nothing of arrogance or pedantry; but that unaffected earnestness and
guileless simplicity which seem to belong to the literary antiquary.

He is a dark, mouldy little man, and rather dry in his manner; yet,
on his favourite theme, he kindles up, and at times is even eloquent.
No fox-hunter, recounting his last day's sport, could be more animated
than I have seen the worthy parson, when relating his search after
a curious document, which he had traced from library to library, until
he fairly unearthed it in the dusty chapter-house of a cathedral. When,
too, he describes some venerable manuscript, with its rich illumina-
tions, its thick creamy vellum, its glossy ink, and the odour of the
cloisters that seems to exhale from it, he rivals the enthusiasm of a
Parisian epicure, expatiating on the merits of a Perigord pie, or a
Paté de Strasbourg.

His brain seems absolutely haunted with love-sick dreams about
gorgeous old works in "silk linings, triple gold bands, and tinted leather,

locked up in wire cases, and secured from the vulgar hands of the mere reader;" and, to continue the happy expressions of an ingenious writer, "dazzling one's eyes like eastern beauties, peering through their jealousies."*

He has a great desire, however, to read such works in the old libraries and chapter-houses to which they belong; for he thinks a black-letter volume reads best in one of those venerable chambers where the light struggles through dusty lancet windows and painted glass; and that it loses half its zest if taken away from the neighbourhood of the quaintly-carved oaken book-case and Gothic reading-desk. At his suggestion the squire has had the library furnished in this antique taste, and several of the windows glazed with painted glass, that they may throw a properly tempered light upon the pages of their favourite old authors.

The parson, I am told, has been for some time meditating a commentary on Strutt, Brand, and Douce, in which he means to detect them in sundry dangerous errors in respect to popular games and superstitions; a work to which the squire looks forward with great interest. He is, also, a casual contributor to that long-established repository of national customs and antiquities, the Gentleman's Magazine, and is one of those that every now and then make an inquiry concerning some obsolete custom or rare legend; nay, it is said that several of his communications have been at least six inches in length. He frequently receives parcels by coach from different parts of the kingdom, containing mouldy volumes and almost illegible manuscripts; for it is singular what an active correspondence is kept up among literary antiquaries, and how soon the fame of any rare volume, or unique copy, just discovered among the rubbish of a library, is circulated among them. The parson is more busy than common just now, being a little flurried by an advertisement of a work, said to be preparing for the press, on the mythology of the middle ages. The little man has long been gathering together all the hobgoblin tales he could collect, illustrative of the superstitions of former times; and he is in a complete fever, lest this formidable rival should take the field before him.

Shortly after my arrival at the Hall, I called at the parsonage, in company with Mr. Bracebridge and the general. The parson had not been seen for several days, which was a matter of some surprise, as he was an almost daily visitor at the Hall. We found him in his study; a small dusky chamber, lighted by a lattice window that looked into the church-yard, and was overshadowed by a yew-tree. His chair was surrounded by folios and quartos, piled upon the floor, and his table

* D'Israeli. Curiosities of Literature.

was covered with books and manuscripts. The cause of his seclusion was a work which he had recently received, and with which he had retired in rapture from the world, and shut himself up to enjoy a literary honeymoon undisturbed. Never did boarding-school girl devour the pages of a sentimental novel, or Don Quixote a chivalrous romance, with more intense delight than did the little man banquet on the pages of this delicious work. It was Dibdin's Bibliographical Tour; a work calculated to have as intoxicating an effect on the imaginations of literary antiquaries, as the adventures of the heroes of the round table, on all true knights; or the tales of the early American voyagers on the ardent spirits of the age, filling them with dreams of Mexican and Peruvian mines, and of the golden realm of El Dorado.

The good parson had looked forward to this Bibliographical expedition as of far greater importance than those to Africa, or the North Pole. With what eagerness he had seized upon the history of the enterprise! with what interest had he followed the redoubtable bibliographer and his graphical squire in their adventurous roamings among Norman castles and cathedrals, and French libraries, and German convents and universities; penetrating into the prison houses of vellum manuscripts, and exquisitely illuminated missals, and revealing their beauties to the world!

When the parson had finished a rapturous eulogy on this most curious and entertaining work, he drew forth from a little drawer a manuscript, lately received from a correspondent, which had perplexed him sadly. It was written in Norman French, in very ancient characters, and so faded and mouldered away as to be almost illegible. It was apparently an old Norman drinking song, that might have been brought over by one of William the Conqueror's carousing followers. The writing was just legible enough to keep a keen antiquity hunter on a doubtful chase; here and there he would be completely thrown out, and then there would be a few words so plainly written as to put him on the scent again. In this way he had been led on for a whole day, until he had found himself completely at fault.

The squire endeavoured to assist him, but was equally baffled. The old general listened for some time to the discussion, and then asked the parson, if he had read Captain Morris's, or George Stevens', or Anacreon Moore's bacchanalian songs; on the other replying in the negative, "Oh, then," said the general, with a sagacious nod, "if you want a drinking song, I can furnish you with the latest collection – I did not know you had a turn for those kind of things; and I can lend you the Encyclopedia of Wit into the bargain. I never travel without them; they're excellent reading at an inn."

It would not be easy to describe the odd look of surprise and perplexity of the parson, at this proposal; or the difficulty the squire had
in making the general comprehend, that though a jovial song of the
present day was but a foolish sound in the ears of wisdom, and beneath
the notice of a learned man, yet a trowl, written by a tosspot several
hundred years since, was a matter worthy of the gravest research, and
enough to set whole colleges by the ears.

I have since pondered much on this matter, and have figured to
myself what may be the fate of our current literature, when retrieved,
piecemeal, by future antiquaries, from among the rubbish of ages.
What a Magnus Apollo, for instance, will Moore become, among sober
divines and dusty schoolmen! Even his festive and amatory songs, which
are now the mere quickeners of our social moments, or the delights of
our drawing-rooms, will then become matters of laborious research and
painful collation. How many a grave professor will then waste his
midnight oil, or worry his brain through a long morning, endeavouring
to restore the pure text, or illustrate the biographical hints of "Come,
tell me, says Rosa, as kissing and kissed;" and how many an arid old
book-worm, like the worthy little parson, will give up in despair, after
vainly striving to fill up some fatal hiatus in "Fanny of Timmol!"

Nor is it merely such exquisiite authors as Moore that are doomed
to consume the oil of future antiquaries. Many a poor scribbler, who is
now, apparently, sent to oblivion by pastry-cooks and cheesemongers,
will then rise again in fragments, and flourish in learned immortality.

After all, thought I, time is not such an invariable destroyer as he is
represented. If he pulls down, he likewise builds up; if he impoverishes
one, he enriches another; his very dilapidations furnish matter for new
works of controversy, and his rust is more precious than the most
costly gilding. Under his plastic hand trifles rise into importance; the
nonsense of one age becomes the wisdom of another; the levity of
the wit gravitates into the learning of the pedant, and an ancient
farthing moulders into infinitely more value than a modern guinea.

THE FARM-HOUSE

―――"Love and hay
Are thick sown, but come up full of thistles."
BEAUMONT AND FLETCHER

I was so much pleased with the anecdotes which were told me of Ready
Money Jack Tibbets, that I got Master Simon, a day or two since, to
take me to his house. It was an old-fashioned farm-house, built of
brick, with curiously twisted chimneys. It stood at a little distance from
the road, with a southern exposure, looking upon a soft, green slope
of meadow. There was a small garden in front, with a row of beehives
humming among beds of sweet herbs and flowers. Well-scoured milking-
tubs, with bright copper hoops, hung on the garden paling. Fruit-trees
were trained up against the cottage, and pots of flowers stood in the
windows. A fat, superannuated mastiff lay in the sunshine at the door;
with a sleek cat sleeping peacefully across him.

Mr. Tibbetts was from home at the time of our calling, but we were
received with hearty and homely welcome by his wife; a notable,
motherly woman, and a complete pattern for wives; since, according
to Master Simon's account, she never contradicts honest Jack, and
yet manages to have her own way, and to control him in every thing.

She received us in the main room of the house, a kind of parlour and
hall, with great brown beams of timber across it, which Mr. Tibbets is
apt to point out with some exultation, observing, that they don't put
such timber in houses now-a-days. The furniture was old-fashioned,
strong, and highly polished; the walls were hung with coloured prints
of the story of the Prodigal Son, who was represented in a red coat
and leather breeches. Over the fire-place was a blunderbuss, and a
hard-favoured likeness of Ready Money Jack, taken, when he was a
young man, by the same artist that painted the tavern sign; his mother
having taken a notion that the Tibbetses had as much right to have a
gallery of family portraits as the folks at the Hall.

The good dame pressed us very much to take some refreshment, and
tempted us with a variety of household dainties, so that we were
glad to compound by tasting some of her home-made wines. While we
were there, the son and heir-apparent came home; a good-looking young
fellow, and something of a rustic beau. He took us over the premises,
and showed us the whole establishment. An air of homely but substantial plenty prevailed throughout; every thing was of the best materials,
and in the best condition. Nothing was out of place, or ill-made; and

you saw every where the signs of a man that took care to have the
worth of his money, and that paid as he went.

The farm-yard was well stocked; under a shed was a taxed cart, in
trim order, in which Ready Money Jack took his wife about the country.
His well-fed horse neighed from the stable, and when led out into the
yard, to use the words of young Jack, "he shone like a bottle;" for he
said the old man made it a rule that every thing about him should fare
as well as he did himself.

I was pleased to see the pride which the young fellow seemed to
have of his father. He gave us several particulars concerning his habits,
which were pretty much to the effect of those I have already mentioned.
He had never suffered an account to stand in his life, always providing
the money before he purchased any thing; and, if possible, paying in
gold and silver. He had a great dislike to paper-money, and seldom went
without a considerable sum in gold about him. On my observing that
it was a wonder he had never been waylaid and robbed, the young fellow
smiled at the idea of any one venturing upon such an exploit, for I
believe he thinks the old man would be a match for Robin Hood and all
his gang.

I have noticed that Master Simon seldom goes into any house without
having a world of private talk with some one or other of the family,
being a kind of universal counsellor and confidant. We had not been
long at the farm, before the old dame got him into a corner of her
parlour, where they had a long, whispering conference together; in which
I saw by his shrugs that there were some dubious matters discussed,
and by his nods that he agreed with every thing she said.

After we had come out, the young man accompanied us a little
distance, and then, drawing Master Simon aside into a green lane, they
walked and talked together for nearly half an hour. Master Simon, who
has the usual propensity of confidants to blab every thing to the next
friend they meet with, let me know that there was a love affair in
question; the young fellow having been smitten with the charms of
Phœbe Wilkins, the pretty niece of the housekeeper at the Hall. Like
most other love concerns, it had brought its troubles and perplexities.
Dame Tibbets had long been on intimate, gossiping terms with the
housekeeper, who often visited the farm-house; but when the neighbours spoke to her of the likelihood of a match between her son and
Phœbe Wilkins, "Marry come up!" she scouted the very idea. The girl
had acted as lady's maid, and it was beneath the blood of the Tibbetses,
who had lived on their own lands time out of mind, and owed reverence
and thanks to nobody, to have the heir-apparent marry a servant!

These vapourings had faithfully been carried to the housekeeper's ear, by one of their mutual, go-between friends. The old housekeeper's blood, if not as ancient, was as quick as that of Dame Tibbets. She had been accustomed to carry a high head at the Hall, and among the villagers; and her faded brocade rustled with indignation at the slight cast upon her alliance by the wife of a petty farmer. She maintained that her niece had been a companion rather than a waiting-maid to the young ladies. "Thank heavens, she was not obliged to work for her living, and was as idle as any young lady in the land; and when somebody died, would receive something that would be worth the notice of some folks, with all their ready money."

A bitter feud had thus taken place between the two worthy dames, and the young people were forbidden to think of one another. As to young Jack, he was too much in love to reason upon the matter; and being a little heady, and not standing in much awe of his mother, was ready to sacrifice the whole dignity of the Tibbetses to his passion. He had lately, however, had a violent quarrel with his mistress, in consequence of some coquetry on her part, and at present stood aloof. The politic mother was exerting all her ingenuity to widen this accidental breach; but, as is most commonly the case, the more she meddled with this perverse inclination of her son, the stronger it grew. In the mean time Old Ready Money was kept completely in the dark; both parties were in awe and uncertainty as to what might be his way of taking the matter, and dreaded to awaken the sleeping lion. Between father and son, therefore, the worthy Mrs. Tibbets was full of business, and at her wits' end. It is true there was no great danger of honest Ready Money's finding the thing out, if left to himself; for he was of a most unsuspicious temper, and by no means quick of apprehension; but there was daily risk of his attention being aroused by those cobwebs which his indefatigable wife was continually spinning about his nose.

Such is the distracted state of politics in the domestic empire of Ready Money Jack; which only shows the intrigues and internal dangers to which the best regulated governments are liable. In this perplexed situation of their affairs, both mother and son have applied to Master Simon for counsel; and, with all his experience in meddling with other people's concerns, he finds it an exceedingly difficult part to play, to agree with both parties, seeing that their opinions and wishes are so diametrically opposite.

HORSEMANSHIP

A coach was a strange monster in those days, and the sight of
one put both horse and man into amazement. Some said it
was a great crabshell brought out of China, and some imagined
it to be one of the pagan temples, in which the canibals
adored the divell.

TAYLOR, THE WATER POET

I have made casual mention, more than once, of one of the squire's
antiquated retainers, old Christy the huntsman. I find that his crabbed
humour is a source of much entertainment among the young men
of the family; the Oxonian, particularly, takes a mischievous pleasure
now and then in slyly rubbing the old man against the grain, and
then smoothing him down again; for the old fellow is as ready to
bristle up his back as a porcupine. He rides a venerable hunter called
Pepper, which is a counterpart of himself, a heady, cross-grained
animal, that frets the flesh off its bones; bites, kicks, and plays all
manner of villanous tricks. He is as tough, and nearly as old as his
rider, who has ridden him time out of mind, and is, indeed, the only
one that can do any thing with him. Sometimes, however, they have
a complete quarrel, and a dispute for mastery, and then, I am told,
it is as good as a farce to see the heat they both get into, and the
wrongheaded contest that ensues; for they are quite knowing in each
other's ways, and in the art of teasing and fretting each other. Notwithstanding these doughty brawls, however, there is nothing that
nettles old Christy sooner than to question the merits of his horse;
which he upholds as tenaciously as a faithful husband will vindicate
the virtues of the termagant spouse, that gives him a curtain lecture
every night of his life.

The young men call old Christy their "professor of equitation," and
in accounting for the appellation, they let me into some particulars
of the squire's mode of bringing up his children. There is an odd
mixture of eccentricity and good sense in all the opinions of my
worthy host. His mind is like modern Gothic, where plain brick-work
is set off with pointed arches and quaint tracery. Though the main
groundwork of his opinions is correct, yet he has a thousand little
notions, picked up from old books, which stand out whimsically on
the surface of his mind.

Thus, in educating his boys, he chose Peachem, Markam, and such
like old English writers, for his manuals. At an early age he took

68

the lads out of their mother's hands, who was disposed, as mothers
are apt to be, to make fine, orderly children of them, that should keep
out of sun and rain, and never soil their hands, nor tear their clothes.

In place of this, the squire turned them loose to run free and wild
about the park, without heeding wind or weather. He was also particularly attentive in making them bold and expert horsemen; and
these were the days when old Christy, the huntsman, enjoyed great
importance, as the lads were put under his care to practise them at
the leaping-bars, and to keep an eye upon them in the chase.

The squire always objected to their riding in carriages of any kind,
and is still a little tenacious on this point. He often rails against the
universal use of carriages, and quotes the words of honest Nashe to
that effect. "It was thought," says Nashe, in his Quaternio, "a kind
of solecism, and to savour of effeminacy, for a young gentleman in
the flourishing time of his age to creep into a coach, and to shrowd
himself from wind and weather: our great delight was to out-brave
the blustering Boreas upon a great horse; to arm and prepare ourselves
to go with Mars and Bellona into the field was our sport and pastime;
coaches and caroches we left unto them for whom they were first
invented, for ladies and gentlemen, and decrepit age and impotent
people."

The squire insists that the English gentlemen have lost much of
their hardiness and manhood since the introduction of carriages. "Compare," he will say, "the fine gentleman of former times, ever on horseback,
booted and spurred, and travel-stained, but open, frank, manly, and
chivalrous, with the fine gentleman of the present day, full of affectation
and effeminacy, rolling along a turnpike in his voluptuous vehicle. The
young men of those days were rendered brave, and lofty, and generous
in their notions, by almost living in their saddles, and having their
foaming steeds 'like proud seas under them.' There is something," he
adds, "in bestriding a fine horse that makes a man feel more than
mortal. He seems to have doubled his nature, and to have added to
his own courage and sagacity the power, the speed, and stateliness of
the superb animal on which he is mounted."

"It is a great delight," says old Nashe, "to see a young gentleman
with his skill and cunning, by his voice, rod and spur, better to
manage and to command the great Bucephalus, than the strongest
Milo, with all his strength; one while to see him make him tread, trot
and gallop the ring; and one after to see him make him gather up
roundly; to bear his head steadily; to run a full career swiftly; to
stop a sudden lightly; anon after to see him make him advance, to
yorke, to go back and side long, to turn on either hand; to gallop

the gallop galliard; to do the capriole, the chambetta, and dance the curvetty."

In conformity to these ideas, the squire had them all on horseback at an early age, and made them ride, slap dash, about the country, without flinching at hedge, or ditch, or stone wall, to the imminent danger of their necks.

Even the fair Julia was partially included in this system; and, under the instructions of old Christy, has become one of the best horse-women in the county. The squire says it is better than all the cosmetics and sweeteners of the breath that ever were invented. He extols the horsemanship of the ladies in former times, when Queen Elizabeth would scarcely suffer the rain to stop her accustomed ride. "And then think," he will say, "what nobler and sweeter beings it made them. What a difference must there be, both in mind and body, between a joyous high-spirited dame of those days, glowing with health and exercise, freshened by every breeze that blows, seated loftily and gracefully on her saddle, with plume on head, and hawk on hand, and her descendant of the present day, the pale victim of routs and ball-rooms, sunk languidly in one corner of an enervating carriage."

The squire's equestrian system has been attended with great success, for his sons, having passed through the whole course of instruction without breaking neck or limb, are now healthful, spirited, and active, and have the true Englishman's love for a horse. If their manliness and frankness are praised in their father's hearing, he quotes the old Persian maxim, and says, they have been taught "to ride, to shoot, and to speak the truth."

It is true the Oxonian has now and then practised the old gentleman's doctrines a little in the extreme. He is a gay youngster, rather fonder of his horse than his book, with a little dash of the dandy; though the ladies all declare that he is "the flower of the flock." The first year that he was sent to Oxford, he had a tutor appointed to overlook him, a dry chip of the university. When he returned home in the vacation, the squire made many inquiries about how he liked his college, his studies, and his tutor.

"Oh, as to my tutor, sir, I've parted with him some time since."

"You have; and, pray, why so?"

"Oh, sir, hunting was all the go at our college, and I was a little short of funds; so I discharged my tutor, and took a horse, you know."

"Ah, I was not aware of that, Tom," said the squire, mildly.

When Tom returned to college his allowance was doubled, that he might be enabled to keep both horse and tutor.

LOVE-SYMPTOMS

I will now begin to sigh, read poets, look pale, go neatly,
and be most apparently in love.

MARSTON

I should not be surprised if we should have another pair of turtles
at the Hall, for Master Simon has informed me, in great confidence,
that he suspects the general of some design upon the susceptible heart
of Lady Lillycraft. I have, indeed, noticed a growing attention and
courtesy in the veteran towards her ladyship; he softens very much
in her company, sits by her at table, and entertains her with long
stories about Seringapatam, and pleasant anecdotes of the Mulligatawney club. I have even seen him present her with a full blown
rose from the hot-house, in a style of the most captivating gallantry,
and it was accepted with great suavity and graciousness; for her ladyship delights in receiving the homage and attention of the sex.

Indeed, the general was one of the earliest admirers that dangled
in her train during her short reign of beauty; and they flirted together
for half a season in London, some thirty or forty years since. She
reminded him lately, in the course of a conversation about former
days, of the time when he used to ride a white horse, and to canter
so gallantly by the side of her carriage in Hyde Park; whereupon I
have remarked that the veteran has regularly escorted her since, when
she rides out on horseback; and, I suspect, he almost persuades himself
that he makes as captivating an appearance as in his youthful days.

It would be an interesting and memorable circumstance in the
chronicles of Cupid, if this spark of the tender passion, after lying
dormant for such a length of time, should again be fanned into a
flame, from amidst the ashes of two burnt out hearts. It would be
an instance of perdurable fidelity, worthy of being placed beside those
recorded in one of the squire's favourite tomes, commemorating the
constancy of the olden times; in which times, we are told, "Men and
wymmen coulde love togyders seven yeres, and no licours lustes were
betwene them, and thenne was love, trouthe and feythfulnes; and lo in
lyke wyse was used love in Kyng Arthurs dayes."*

Still, however, this may be nothing but a little venerable flirtation,
the general being a veteran dangler, and the good lady habituated
to these kind of attentions. Master Simon, on the other hand, thinks

---

* Morte d'Arthur.

71

the general is looking about him with the wary eye of an old campaigner; and now that he is on the wane, is desirous of getting into
warm winter quarters. Much allowance, however, must be made
for Master Simon's uneasiness on the subject, for he looks on Lady
Lillycraft's house as one of his strong holds, where he is lord of the
ascendant; and, with all his admiration of the general, I much doubt
whether he would like to see him lord of the lady and the establishment.

There are certain other symptoms, notwithstanding, that give an
air of probability to Master Simon's intimations. Thus for instance, I
have observed that the general has been very assiduous in his attentions
to her ladyship's dogs, and has several times exposed his fingers to
imminent jeopardy, in attempting to pat Beauty on the head. It is
to be hoped his advances to the mistress will be more favourably
received, as all his overtures towards a caress are greeted by the
pestilent little cur with a wary kindling of the eye, and a most
venomous growl.

He has, moreover, been very complaisant towards my lady's gentlewoman, the immaculate Mrs. Hannah, whom he used to speak of
in a way that I do not choose to mention. Whether she has the same
suspicions with Master Simon or not, I cannot say; but she receives
his civilities with no better grace than the implacable Beauty; un-
screwing her mouth into a most acid smile, and looking as though
she could bite a piece out of him. In short, the poor general seems
to have as formidable foes to contend with as a hero of ancient fairy
tale; who had to fight his way to his enchanted princess through
ferocious monsters of every kind, and to encounter the brimstone terrors
of some fiery dragon.

There is still another circumstance which inclines me to give very
considerable credit to Master Simon's suspicions. Lady Lillycraft is
very fond of quoting poetry, and the conversation often turns upon
it, on which occasions the general is thrown completely out. It happened the other day that Spenser's Fairy Queen was the theme for
the great part of the morning, and the poor general sat perfectly silent.
I found him not long after in the library, with spectacles on nose, a
book in his hand, and fast asleep. On my approach he awoke, slipt
the spectacles into his pocket, and began to read very attentively.
After a little while he put a paper in the place, and laid the volume
aside, which I perceived was the Fairy Queen. I have had the curiosity
to watch how he got on in his poetical studies; but, though I have
repeatedly seen him with the book in his hand, yet I find the paper
has not advanced above three or four pages; the general being extremely apt to fall asleep when he reads.

FALCONRY

Ne is there hawk which mantleth on her perch,
Whether high tow'ring or accousting low,
But I the measure of her flight doe search,
And all her prey and all her diet know.

SPENSER

There are several grand sources of lamentation furnished to the worthy squire, by the improvement of society, and the grievous advancement of knowledge; among which there is none, I believe, that causes him more frequent regret than the unfortunate invention of gunpowder. To this he continually traces the decay of some favourite custom, and, indeed, the general downfall of all chivalrous and romantic usages. "English soldiers," he says, "have never been the men they were in the days of the cross-bow and the long-bow; when they depended upon the strength of the arm, and the English archer could draw a clothyard shaft to the head. These were the times when at the battles of Cressy, Poictiers, and Agincourt, the French chivalry was completely destroyed by the bowmen of England. The yeomanry, too, have never been what they were, when, in times of peace, they were constantly exercised with the bow, and archery was a favourite holiday pastime."

Among the other evils which have followed in the train of this fatal invention of gunpowder, the squire classes the total decline of the noble art of falconry. "Shooting," he says, "is a skulking, treacherous, solitary sport in comparison; but hawking was a gallant, open, sun-shiny recreation; it was the generous sport of hunting carried into the skies."

"It was, moreover," he says, "according to Braithwate, the stately amusement of 'high and mounting spirits;' for, as the old Welsh proverb affirms, in those times 'You might know a gentleman by his hawk, horse, and grayhound.' Indeed, a cavalier was seldom seen abroad without his hawk on his fist; and even a lady of rank did not think herself completely equipped, in riding forth, unless she had her tassel-gentel held by jesses on her delicate hand. It was thought in those excellent days, according to an old writer, 'quite sufficient for noblemen to winde their horn, and to carry their hawke fair; and leave study and learning to the children of mean people.' "

Knowing the good squire's hobby, therefore, I have not been surprised at finding that, among the various recreations of former times which he has endeavoured to revive in the little world in which he rules, he has bestowed great attention on the noble art of falconry. In this he, of course, has been seconded by his indefatigable coadjutor, Master Simon; and even the parson has thrown considerable light on their labours, by various hints on the subject, which he has met with in old English works. As to the precious work of that famous dame Juliana Barnes; the Gentleman's Academie, by Markham; and the other well-known treatises that were the manuals of ancient sportsmen, they have them at their fingers' ends; but they have more especially studied some old tapestry in the house, whereon is represented a party of cavaliers and stately dames, with doublets, caps, and flaunting feathers, mounted on horse, with attendants on foot, all in animated pursuit of the game.

The squire has discountenanced the killing of any hawks in his neighbourhood, but gives a liberal bounty for all that are brought him alive; so that the Hall is well stocked with all kinds of birds of prey. On these he and Master Simon have exhausted their patience and ingenuity, endeavouring to "reclaim" them, as it is termed, and to train them up for the sport; but they have met with continual checks and disappointments. Their feathered school has turned out the most untractable and graceless scholars; nor is it the least of their trouble to drill the retainers who were to act as ushers under them, and to take immediate charge of these refractory birds. Old Christy and the gamekeeper both, for a time, set their faces against the whole plan of education; Christy having been nettled at hearing what he terms a wild-goose chase put on a par with a fox-hunt; and the gamekeeper having always been accustomed to look upon hawks as arrant poachers, which it was his duty to shoot down, and nail, in terrorem, against the out-houses.

Christy has at length taken the matter in hand, but has done still more mischief by his intermeddling. He is as positive and wrongheaded about this, as he is about hunting. Master Simon has continual disputes with him as to feeding and training the hawks. He reads to him long passages from the old authors I have mentioned; but Christy, who cannot read, has a sovereign contempt for all book-knowledge, and persists in treating the hawks according to his own notions, which are drawn from his experience, in younger days, in the rearing of game-cocks.

The consequence is, that, between these jarring systems, the poor birds have had a most trying and unhappy time of it. Many have fallen victims to Christy's feeding and Master Simon's physicking; for the latter has gone to work *secundem artem*, and has given them all the vomitings and scourings laid down in the books; never were poor hawks so fed and physicked before. Others have been lost by being but half "reclaimed," or tamed: for on being taken into the field, they have "raked" after the game quite out of hearing of the call, and never returned to school.

All these disappointments had been petty, yet sore grievances to the squire, and had made him to despond about success. He has lately, however, been made happy by the receipt of a fine Welsh falcon, which Master Simon terms a stately highflyer. It is a present from the squire's friend, Sir Watkyn Williams Wynne; and is, no doubt, a descendant of some ancient line of Welsh princes of the air, that have long lorded it over their kingdom of clouds, from Wynnstay to the very summit of Snowden, or the brow of Penmanmawr.

Ever since the squire received this invaluable present, he has been as impatient to sally forth and make proof of it, as was Don Quixote to assay his suit of armour. There have been some demurs as to whether the bird was in proper health and training; but these have been overruled by the vehement desire to play with a new toy; and it has been determined, right or wrong, in season or out of season, to have a day's sport in hawking to-morrow.

The Hall, as usual, whenever the squire is about to make some new sally on his hobby, is all agog with the thing. Miss Templeton, who is brought up in reverence for all her guardian's humours, has proposed to be of the party, and Lady Lillycraft has talked also of riding out to the scene of action and looking on. This has gratified the old gentleman extremely; he hails it as an auspicious omen of the revival of falconry, and does not despair but the time will come when it will be again the pride of a fine lady to carry about a noble falcon in preference to a parrot or a lap-dog.

I have amused myself with the bustling preparations of that busy spirit, Master Simon, and the continual thwartings he receives from that genuine son of a pepper-box, old Christy. They have had half a dozen consultations about how the hawk is to be prepared for the morning's sport. Old Nimrod, as usual, has always got in a pet, upon which Master Simon has invariably given up the point, observing, in a good-humoured tone, "Well, well, have it your own way, Christy; only don't put yourself in a passion;" a reply which always nettles the old man ten times more than ever.

HAWKING

The soaring hawk, from fist that flies,
Her falconer doth constrain
Sometimes to range the ground about
To find her out again;
And if by sight, or sound of bell,
His falcon he may see,
Wo ho! he cries, with cheerful voice –
The gladdest man is he.

HANDEFULL OF PLEASANT DELITES

At an early hour this morning the Hall was in a bustle, preparing for the sport of the day. I heard Master Simon whistling and singing under my window at sunrise, as he was preparing the jesses for the hawk's legs, and could distinguish now and then a stanza of one of his favourite old ditties:

"In peascod time, when hound to horn
Gives note that buck be kill'd;
And little boy with pipe of corn
Is tending sheep a-field," &c.

A hearty breakfast, well flanked by cold meats, was served up in the great hall. The whole garrison of retainers and hangers-on were in motion, reinforced by volunteer idlers from the village. The horses were led up and down before the door; every body had something to say, and something to do, and hurried hither and thither; there was a direful yelping of dogs; some that were to accompany us being eager to set off, and others that were to stay at home being whipped back to their kennels. In short, for once, the good squire's mansion might have been taken as a good specimen of one of the rantipole establishments of the good old feudal times.

Breakfast being finished, the chivalry of the Hall prepared to take the field. The fair Julia was of the party, in a hunting dress, with a light plume of feathers in her riding-hat. As she mounted her favourite galloway, I remarked, with pleasure, that old Christy forgot his usual crustiness, and hastened to adjust her saddle and bridle. He touched his cap as she smiled on him and thanked him; and then, looking round at the other attendants, gave a knowing nod of his head, in which I read pride and exultation at the charming appearance of his pupil.

Lady Lillycraft had likewise determined to witness the sport. She was dressed in her broad white beaver, tied under the chin, and a riding-habit of the last century. She rode her sleek, ambling pony, whose motion was as easy as a rocking-chair; and was gallantly escorted by the general, who looked not unlike one of the doughty heroes in the old prints of the battle of Blenheim. The parson, likewise, accompanied her on the other side; for this was a learned amusement in which he took great interest; and, indeed, had given much council, from his knowledge of old customs.

At length every thing was arranged, and off we set from the Hall. The exercise on horseback puts one in fine spirits; and the scene was gay and animating. The young men of the family accompanied Miss Templeton. She sat lightly and gracefully in her saddle, her plumes dancing and waving in the air; and the group had a charming effect as they appeared and disappeared among the trees, cantering along with the bounding animation of youth. The squire and Master Simon rode together, accompanied by old Christy, mounted on Pepper. The latter bore the hawk on his fist, as he insisted the bird was most accustomed to him. There was a rabble rout on foot, composed of retainers from the Hall, and some idlers from the village, with two or three spaniels, for the purpose of starting the game.

A kind of corps de reserve came on quietly in the rear, composed of Lady Lillycraft, General Harbottle, the parson, and a fat footman. Her ladyship ambled gently along on her pony, while the general, mounted on a tall hunter, looked down upon her with an air of the most protecting gallantry.

For my part, being no sportsman, I kept with this last party, or rather lagged behind, that I might take in the whole picture; and the parson occasionally slackened his pace and jogged on in company with me.

The sport led us at some distance from the Hall, in a soft meadow, reeking with the moist verdure of spring. A little river ran through it, bordered by willows, which had put forth their tender early foliage. The sportsmen were in quest of herons which were said to keep about this stream.

There was some disputing, already, among the leaders of the sport. The squire, Master Simon, and old Christy, came every now and then to a pause, to consult together, like the field officers in an army; and I saw, by certain motions of the head, that Christy was as positive as any old wrong-headed German commander.

As we were prancing up this quiet meadow every sound we made was answered by a distinct echo, from the sunny wall of an old building that lay on the opposite margin of the stream; and I paused to listen to this "Spirit of a sound," which seems to love such quiet and beautiful places. The parson informed me that this was the ruin of an ancient grange, and was supposed, by the country people, to be haunted by a dobbie, a kind of rural sprite, something like Robin-good-fellow. They often fancied the echo to be the voice of the dobbie answering them, and were rather shy of disturbing it after dark. He added, that the squire was very careful of this ruin, on account of the superstition connected with it. As I considered this local habitation of an "airy nothing," I called to mind the fine description of an echo in Webster's Duchess of Malfy:

> _____ "'Yond side o' th' river lies a wall,
> Piece of a cloister, which in my opinion
> Gives the best echo that you ever heard;
> So plain in the distinction of our words,
> That many have supposed it a spirit
> That answers."

The parson went on to comment on a pleasing and fanciful appellation which the Jews of old gave to the echo, which they called Bath-kool, that is to say, "the daughter of the voice;" they considered it an oracle, supplying in the second temple the want of the urim and thummim, with which the first was honoured.* The little man was just entering very largely and learnedly upon the subject, when we were startled by a prodigious bawling, shouting, and yelping. A flight of crows, alarmed by the approach of our forces, had suddenly rose from a meadow; a cry was put up by the rabble rout on foot. "Now, Christy! now is your time, Christy!" The squire and Master Simon, who were beating up the river banks in quest of a heron, called out eagerly to Christy to keep quiet; the old man, vexed and bewildered by the confusion of voices, completely lost his head; in his flurry he slipped off the hood, cast off the falcon, and away flew the crows, and away soared the hawk.

I had paused on a rising ground, close to Lady Lillycraft and her escort, from whence I had a good view of the sport. I was pleased with the appearance of the party in the meadow, riding along in the direction that the bird flew; their bright beaming faces turned up to the bright skies as they watched the game; the attendants on foot scampering along, looking up, and calling out, and the dogs bounding and yelping with clamorous sympathy.

The hawk had singled out a quarry from among the carrion crew.

---

* Bekker's Monde enchanté.

It was curious to see the efforts of the two birds to get above each other; one to make the fatal swoop, the other to avoid it. Now they crossed athwart a bright feathery cloud, and now they were against the clear blue sky. I confess, being no sportsman, I was more interested for the poor bird that was striving for its life, than for the hawk that was playing the part of a mercenary soldier. At length the hawk got the upper hand, and made a rushing stoop at her quarry, but the latter made as sudden a surge downwards, and slanting up again evaded the blow, screaming and making the best of his way for a dry tree on the brow of a neighbouring hill; while the hawk, disappointed of her blow, soared up again into the air, and appeared to be "raking" off. It was in vain old Christy called, and whistled, and endeavoured to lure her down; she paid no regard to him: and, indeed, his calls were drowned in the shouts and yelps of the army of militia that had followed him into the field.

Just then an exclamation from Lady Lillycraft made me turn my head. I beheld a complete confusion among the sportsmen in the little vale below us. They were galloping and running towards the edge of a bank; and I was shocked to see Miss Templeton's horse galloping at large without his rider. I rode to the place to which the others were hurrying, and when I reached the bank, which almost overhung the stream, I saw at the foot of it, the fair Julia, pale, bleeding, and apparently lifeless, supported in the arms of her frantic lover.

In galloping heedlessly along, with her eyes turned upward, she had unwarily approached too near the bank; it had given way with her, and she and her horse had been precipitated to the pebbled margin of the river.

I never saw greater consternation. The captain was distracted; Lady Lillycraft fainting; the squire in dismay, and Master Simon at his wits' ends. The beautiful creature at length showed signs of returning life; she opened her eyes; looked around her upon the anxious group, and comprehending in a moment the nature of the scene, gave a sweet smile, and putting her hand in her lover's, exclaimed, feebly, "I am not much hurt, Guy!" I could have taken her to my heart for that single exclamation.

It was found, indeed, that she had escaped almost miraculously, with a contusion of the head, a sprained ankle, and some slight bruises. After her wound was stanched, she was taken to a neighbouring cottage, until a carriage could be summoned to convey her home; and when this had arrived, the cavalcade, which had issued forth so gaily on this enterprise, returned slowly and pensively to the Hall.

I had been charmed by the generous spirit shown by this young creature, who, amidst pain and danger, had been anxious only to relieve the distress of those around her. I was gratified, therefore, by the universal concern displayed by the domestics on our return. They came crowding down the avenue, each eager to render assistance. The butler stood ready with some curiously delicate cordial; the old housekeeper was provided with half a dozen nostrums, prepared by her own hands, according to the family receipt book; while her niece, the melting Phœbe, having no other way of assisting, stood wringing her hands, and weeping aloud.

The most material effect that is likely to follow this accident is a postponement of the nuptials, which were close at hand. Though I commiserate the impatience of the captain on that account, yet I shall not otherwise be sorry at the delay, as it will give me a better opportunity of studying the characters here assembled, with which I grow more and more entertained.

I cannot but perceive that the worthy squire is quite disconcerted at the unlucky result of his hawking experiment, and this unfortunate illustration of his eulogy on female equitation. Old Christy too is very waspish, having been sorely twitted by Master Simon for having let his hawk fly at carrion. As to the falcon, in the confusion occasioned by the fair Julia's disaster, the bird was totally forgotten. I make no doubt she has made the best of her way back to the hospitable Hall of Sir Watkyn Williams Wynne; and may very possibly, at this present writing, be pluming her wings among the breezy bowers of Wynnstay.

ST. MARK'S EVE

O 'tis a fearful thing to be no more.
Or if to be, to wander after death!
To walk as spirits do, in brakes all day,
And, when the darkness comes, to glide in paths
That lead to graves; and in the silent vault,
Where lies your own pale shroud, to hover o'er it,
Striving to enter your forbidden corpse.

DRYDEN

The conversation this evening at supper-table took a curious turn on the subject of a superstition, formerly very prevalent in this part of the country, relative to the present night of the year, which is the Eve of St. Mark's. It was believed, the parson informed us, that if any one would watch in the church porch on this eve, for three successive years, from eleven to one o'clock at night, he would see, on the third year, the shades of those of the parish who were to die in the course of the year, pass by him into church, clad in their usual apparel.

Dismal as such a sight would be, he assured us that it was formerly a frequent thing for persons to make the necessary vigils. He had known more than one instance in his time. One old woman, who pretended to have seen this phantom procession, was an object of great awe for the whole year afterwards, and caused much uneasiness and mischief. If she shook her head mysteriously at a person, it was like a death warrant; and she had nearly caused the death of a sick person by looking ruefully in at the window.

There was also an old man, not many years since, of a sullen, melancholy temperament, who had kept two vigils, and began to excite some talk in the village, when, fortunately for the public comfort, he died shortly after his third watching; very probably from a cold that he had taken, as the night was tempestuous. It was reported about the village, however, that he had seen his own phantom pass by him into the church.

This led to the mention of another superstition of an equally strange and melancholy kind, which, however, is chiefly confined to Wales. It is respecting what are called corpse candles, little wandering fires, of a pale bluish light, that move about like tapers in the open air, and are supposed to designate the way some corpse is to go. One was seen at Lanylar, late at night, hovering up and down, along the bank of the Istwith, and was watched by the neighbours until they were tired, and went to bed. Not long afterwards there came a comely country lass, from Montgomeryshire, to see her friends, who dwelt on the opposite side of the river. She thought to ford the stream at the very place where the light had been first seen, but was dissuaded on account of the height of the flood. She walked to and fro along the bank, just where the candle had moved, waiting for the subsiding of the water. She at length endeavoured to cross, but the poor girl was drowned in the attempt.*

There was something mournful in this little anecdote of rural superstition, that seemed to affect all the listeners. Indeed, it is curious to remark how completely a conversation of the kind will absorb the attention of a circle, and sober down its gaiety, however boisterous. By degrees I noticed that every one was leaning forward over the table, with eyes earnestly fixed upon the parson, and at the mention of corpse candles which had been seen about the chamber of a young lady who died on the eve of her wedding-day, Lady Lillycraft turned pale.

I have witnessed the introduction of stories of the kind into various evening circles; they were often commenced in jest, and listened to with smiles; but I never knew the most gay or the most enlightened of audiences, that were not, if the conversation continued for any length of time, completely and solemnly interested in it. There is, I believe, a degree of superstition lurking in every mind; and I doubt if any one can thoroughly examine all his secret notions and impulses without detecting it, hidden, perhaps, even from himself. It seems, in fact, to be a part of our nature, like instinct in animals, acting independently of our reason. It is often found existing in lofty natures, especially those that are poetical and aspiring. A great and extraordinary poet of our day, whose life and writings evince a mind subject to powerful exaltation, is said to believe in omens and secret intimations. Cæsar, it is well known, was greatly under the influence of such belief; and Napoleon had his good and evil days, and his presiding star.

As to the worthy parson, I have no doubt that he is strongly inclined to superstition. He is naturally credulous, and passes so much of his time searching out popular traditions and supernatural tales, that his mind has probably become infected by them. He has lately been immersed in the Demonolatria of Nicholas Remigius, concerning supernatural occurrences in Lorraine, and the writings of Joachimus Camerarius, called by Vossius the Phœnix of Germany; and he entertains the ladies with stories from them, that make them almost afraid to

* Aubrey's Miscel.

go to bed at night. I have been charmed myself with some of the wild, little superstitions which he has adduced from Blefkénius, Scheffer, and others; such as those of the Laplanders about the domestic spirits which wake them at night, and summon them to go and fish; of Thor, the deity of thunder, who has power of life and death, health and sickness, and who, armed with the rainbow, shoots his arrows at those evil demons that live on the tops of rocks and mountains, and infest the lakes; of the Juhles or Juhlafolket, vagrant troops of spirits, which roam the air, and wander up and down by forests and mountains, and the moonlight sides of hills.

The parson never openly professes his belief in ghosts, but I have remarked that he has a suspicious way of pressing great names into the defence of supernatural doctrines, and making philosophers and saints fight for him. He expatiates at large on the opinions of the ancient philosophers about larves, or nocturnal phantoms, the spirits of the wicked, which wandered like exiles about the earth; and about those spiritual beings which abode in the air, but descended occasionally to earth, and mingled among mortals, acting as agents between them and the gods. He quotes also from Philo the rabbi, the contemporary of the apostles, and, according to some, the friend of St. Paul, who says that the air is full of spirits of different ranks; some destined to exist for a time in mortal bodies, from which, being emancipated, they pass and repass between heaven and earth, as agents or messengers in the service of the deity.

But the worthy little man assumes a bolder tone when he quotes from the fathers of the church; such as St. Jerome, who gives it as the opinion of all the doctors, that the air is filled with powers opposed to each other; and Lactantius, who says that corrupt and dangerous spirits wander over the earth, and seek to console themselves for their own fall by effecting the ruin of the human race; and Clemens Alexandrinus, who is of opinion that the souls of the blessed have knowledge of what passes among men, the same as angels have.

I am now alone in my chamber, but these themes have taken such hold of my imagination, that I cannot sleep. The room in which I sit is just fitted to foster such a state of mind. The walls are hung with tapestry, the figures of which are faded, and look like unsubstantial shapes melting away from sight. Over the fireplace is the portrait of a lady, who, according to the housekeeper's tradition, pined to death for the loss of her lover in the battle of Blenheim. She has a most pale and plaintive countenance, and seems to fix her eyes mournfully upon me. The family have long since retired. I have heard their steps die away, and the distant doors clap to after them. The murmur of voices, and the peal of remote laughter, no longer reach the ear. The clock from the church, in which so many of the former inhabitants of this house lie buried, has chimed the awful hour of midnight.

I have sat by the window and mused upon the dusky landscape, watching the lights disappearing, one by one, from the distant village; and the moon rising in her silent majesty, and leading up all the silver pomp of heaven. As I have gazed upon these quiet groves and shadowy lawns, silvered over, and imperfectly lighted by streaks of dewy moon-shine, my mind has been crowded by "thick coming fancies" concerning those spiritual beings which

> "_____ walk the earth
> Unseen, both when we wake and when we sleep."

Are there, indeed, such beings? Is this space between us and the deity filled up by innumerable orders of spiritual beings, forming the same gradations between the human soul and divine perfection, that we see prevailing from humanity downwards to the meanest insect? It is a sublime and beautiful doctrine, inculcated by the early fathers, that there are guardian angels appointed to watch over cities and nations; to take care of the welfare of good men, and to guard and guide the steps of helpless infancy. "Nothing," says St. Jerome, "gives us a greater idea of the dignity of our soul, than that God has given each of us, at the moment of our birth, an angel to have care of it."

Even the doctrine of departed spirits returning to visit the scenes and beings which were dear to them during the body's existence, though it has been debased by the absurd superstitions of the vulgar, in itself is awfully solemn and sublime. However lightly it may be ridiculed, yet the attention involuntarily yielded to it whenever it is made the subject of serious discussion; its prevalence in all ages and countries, and even among newly discovered nations, that have had no previous interchange of thought with other parts of the world, prove it to be one of those mysterious, and almost instinctive beliefs, to which, if left to ourselves, we should naturally incline.

In spite of all the pride of reason and philosophy, a vague doubt will still lurk in the mind, and perhaps will never be perfectly eradi-cated; as it is concerning a matter that does not admit of positive demonstration. Every thing connected with our spiritual nature is full of doubt and difficulty. "We are fearfully and wonderfully made;" we are surrounded by mysteries, and we are mysteries even to ourselves. Who yet has been able to comprehend and describe the nature of the soul, its connexion with the body, or in what part of the frame it is situated? We know merely that it does exist; but whence it came, and when it entered into us, and how it is retained, and where it is seated, and how it operates, are all matters of mere speculation, and contradictory theories. If, then, we are thus ignorant of this spiritual essence, even while it forms a part of ourselves, and is continually present to our consciousness, how can we pretend to ascertain or to deny its powers and operations when released from its fleshly prison-house? It is more the manner, therefore, in which this superstition has been degraded, than its intrinsic absurdity, that has brought it into contempt. Raise it above the frivolous purposes to which it has been applied, strip it of the gloom and horror with which it has been surrounded, and there is none of the whole circle of visionary creeds that could more delightfully elevate the imagination, or more tenderly affect the heart. It would become a sovereign comfort at the bed of death, soothing the bitter tear wrung from us by the agony of our mortal separation. What could be more consoling than the idea, that the souls of those whom we once loved were permitted to return and watch over our welfare? That affectionate and guardian spirits sat by our pillows when we slept, keeping a vigil over our most helpless hours? That beauty and innocence, which had languished into the tomb, yet smiled unseen around us, revealing themselves in those blest dreams wherein we live over again the hours of past endearment? A belief of this kind would, I should think, be a new incentive to virtue; rendering us circumspect even in our most secret moments, from the idea that those we once loved and honoured were invisible witnesses of all our actions.

It would take away, too, from that loneliness and destitution which we are apt to feel more and more as we get on in our pilgrimage through the wilderness of this world, and find that those who set forward with us, lovingly and cheerily, on the journey, have one by one dropped away from our side. Place the superstition in this light, and I confess I should like to be a believer in it. I see nothing in it that is incompatible with the tender and merciful nature of our religion, nor revolting to the wishes and affections of the heart.

There are departed beings that I have loved as I never again shall love in this world; – that have loved me as I never again shall be loved! If such beings do ever retain in their blessed spheres the attachments which they felt on earth; if they take an interest in the poor concerns of transient mortality, and are permitted to hold communion with those whom they have loved on earth, I feel as if now, at this deep hour of night, in this silence and solitude, I could receive their visitation with the most solemn, but unalloyed, delight.

In truth, such visitations would be too happy for this world; they would be incompatible with the nature of this imperfect state of being. We are here placed in a mere scene of spiritual thraldom and restraint. Our souls are shut in and limited by bounds and barriers; shackled by mortal infirmities, and subject to all the gross impediments of matter. In vain would they seek to act independently of the body, and to mingle together in spiritual intercourse. They can only act here through their fleshly organs. Their earthly loves are made up of transient embraces and long separations. The most intimate friendship, of what brief and scattered portions of time does it consist! We take each other by the hand, and we exchange a few words and looks of kindness, and we rejoice together for a few short moments, and then days, months, years intervene, and we see and know nothing of each other. Or granting that we dwell together for the full season of this our mortal life, the grave soon closes its gates between us, and then our spirits are doomed to remain in separation and widowhood; until they meet again in that more perfect state of being, where soul will dwell with soul in blissful communion, and there will be neither death, nor absence, nor any thing else to interrupt our felicity.

---

* * * In the foregoing paper I have alluded to the writings of some of the old Jewish rabbins. They abound with wild theories; but among them are many truly poetical flights; and their ideas are often very beautifully expressed. Their speculations on the nature of angels are curious and fanciful, though much resembling the doctrines of the ancient philosophers. In the writings of the Rabbi Eleazer is an account of the temptation of our first parents and the fall of the angels, which the parson pointed out to me as having probably furnished some of the ground-work for "Paradise Lost."

According to Eleazer, the ministering angels said to the Deity, "What is there in man that thou makest him of such importance? Is he any thing else than vanity? for he can scarcely reason a little on terrestrial things." To which God replied, "Do you imagine that I will be exalted and glorified only by you here above? I am the same below that I am here. Who is there among you that can call all the creatures by their names?" There was none found among them that could do so. At that moment Adam arose, and called all the creatures by their name. Seeing which, the ministering angels said among themselves, "Let us consult together how we may cause Adam to sin against the Creator, otherwise he will not fail to become our master."

Sammaël, who was a great prince in the heavens, was present at this council, with the saints of the first order, and the seraphim of six bands. Sammaël chose several out of the twelve orders to accompany him, and descended below, for the purpose of visiting all the creatures which God had created. He found none more cunning and more fit to do evil than the serpent.

The rabbi then treats of the seduction and the fall of man; of the consequent fall of the demon, and the punishment which God inflicted on Adam, Eve, and the serpent. "He made them all come before him; pronounced nine maledictions on Adam and Eve, and condemned them to suffer death; and he precipitated Sammaël and all his band from heaven. He cut off the feet of the serpent, which had before the figure of a camel (Sammaël having been mounted on him), and he cursed him among all beasts and animals."

GENTILITY

—— True Gentrie standeth in the trade
Of virtuous life, not in the fleshly line;
For bloud is knit, but Gentrie is divine.
MIRROR FOR MAGISTRATES

I have mentioned some peculiarities of the squire in the education of his sons; but I would not have it thought that his instructions were directed chiefly to their personal accomplishments. He took great pains also to form their minds, and to inculcate what he calls good old English principles, such as are laid down in the writings of Peachem and his contemporaries. There is one author of whom he cannot speak without indignation, which is Chesterfield. He avers that he did much, for a time, to injure the true national character, and to introduce, instead of open manly sincerity, a hollow perfidious courtliness. "His maxims," he affirms, "were calculated to chill the delightful enthusiasm of youth, to make them ashamed of that romance which is the dawn of generous manhood, and to impart to them a cold polish and a premature worldliness.

"Many of Lord Chesterfield's maxims would make a young man a mere man of pleasure; but an English gentleman should not be a mere man of pleasure. He has no right to such selfish indulgence. His ease, his leisure, his opulence, are debts due to his country, which he must ever stand ready to discharge. He should be a man at all points; simple, frank, courteous, intelligent, accomplished, and informed; upright, intrepid, and disinterested; one that can mingle among freemen; that can cope with statesmen; that can champion his country and its rights either at home or abroad. In a country like England, where there is such free and unbounded scope for the exertion of intellect, and where opinion and example have such weight with the people, every gentleman of fortune and leisure should feel himself bound to employ himself in some way towards promoting the prosperity or glory of the nation. In a country where intellect and action are trammelled and restrained, men of rank and fortune may become idlers and triflers with impunity; but an English coxcomb is inexcusable; and this, perhaps, is the reason why he is the most offensive and insupportable coxcomb in the world."

The squire, as Frank Bracebridge informs me, would often hold forth in this manner to his sons when they were about leaving the paternal roof; one to travel abroad, one to go to the army, and one to the university. He used to have them with him in the library, which is hung with the portraits of Sydney, Surrey, Raleigh, Wyat, and others. "Look at those models of true English gentlemen, my sons," he would say with enthusiasm; "those were men that wreathed the graces of the most delicate and refined taste around the stern virtues of the soldier; that mingled what was gentle and gracious, with what was hardy and manly; that possessed the true chivalry of spirit, which is the exalted essence of manhood. They are the lights by which the youth of the country should array themselves. They were the patterns and the idols of their country at home; they were the illustrators of its dignity abroad. 'Surrey,' says Camden, 'was the first nobleman that illustrated his high birth with the beauty of learning. He was acknowledged to be the gallantest man, the politest lover, and the completest gentleman of his time.' And as to Wyat, his friend Surrey most amiably testifies of him, that his person was majestic and beautiful, his visage 'stern and mild;' that he sung, and played the lute with remarkable sweetness; spoke foreign languages with grace and fluency, and possessed an inexhaustible fund of wit. And see what a high commendation is passed upon these illustrious friends: 'They were the two chieftains, who, having travelled into Italy, and there tasted the sweet and stately measures and style of the Italian poetry, greatly polished our rude and homely manner of vulgar poetry from what it had been before, and therefore may be justly called the reformers of our English poetry and style.' And Sir Philip Sydney, who has left us such monuments of elegant thought, and generous sentiment, and who illustrated his chivalrous spirit so gloriously in the field. And Sir Walter Raleigh, the elegant courtier, the intrepid soldier, the enterprising discoverer, the enlightened philosopher, the magnanimous martyr. These are the men for English gentlemen to study. Chesterfield, with his cold and courtly maxims, would have chilled and impoverished such spirits. He would have blighted all the budding romance of their temperaments. Sydney would never have written his Arcadia, nor Surrey have challenged the world in vindication of the beauties of his Geraldine. These are the men, my sons," the squire will continue, "that show to what our national character may be exalted, when its strong and powerful qualities are duly wrought up and refined. The solidest bodies are capable of the highest polish; and there is no character that may be wrought to a more exquisite and unsullied brightness, than that of the true English gentleman."

When Guy was about to depart for the army, the squire again took him aside, and gave him a long exhortation. He warned him against that affectation of cool-blooded indifference, which he was told was cultivated by the young British officers, among whom it was a study to "sink the soldier" in the mere man of fashion. "A soldier," said he, "without pride and enthusiasm in his profession, is a mere sanguinary hireling. Nothing distinguishes him from the mercenary bravo but a spirit of patriotism, or a thirst for glory. It is the fashion, now-a-days, my son," said he, "to laugh at the spirit of chivalry; when that spirit is really extinct, the profession of the soldier becomes a mere trade of blood." He then set before him the conduct of Edward the Black Prince, who is his mirror of chivalry; valiant, generous, affable, humane; gallant in the field; but when he came to dwell on his courtesy towards his prisoner, the king of France; how he received him into his tent, rather as a conqueror than as a captive; attended on him at table like one of his retinue; rode uncovered beside him on his entry into London, mounted on a common palfrey, while his prisoner was mounted in state on a white steed of stately beauty; the tears of enthusiasm stood in the old gentleman's eyes.

Finally, on taking leave, the good squire put in his son's hands, as a manual, one of his favourite old volumes, the Life of the Chevalier Bayard, by Godefroy; on a blank page of which he had written an extract from the Morte d'Arthur, containing the eulogy of Sir Ector over the body of Sir Launcelot of the Lake, which the squire considers as comprising the excellencies of a true soldier. "Ah, Sir Lancelot! thou wert head of all Christian knights; now there thou liest: thou were never matched of none earthly knights-hands. And thou wert the curtiest knight that ever bare shield. And thou were the truest friend to thy lover that ever bestrood horse; and thou were the truest lover of a sinfull man that ever loved woman. And thou were the kindest man that ever strook with sword; and thou were the goodliest person that ever came among the presse of knights. And thou were the meekest man and the gentlest that ever eate in hall among ladies. And thou were the sternest knight to thy mortal foe that ever put speare in the rest."

FORTUNE TELLING

Each city, each town, and every village,
Affords us either an alms or pillage.
And if the weather be cold and raw,
Then in a barn we tumble on straw.
If warm and fair, by yea-cock and nay-cock,
The fields will afford us a hedge or a hay-cock.

MERRY BEGGARS

As I was walking one evening with the Oxonian, Master Simon, and the general, in a meadow not far from the village, we heard the sound of a fiddle, rudely played, and looking in the direction from whence it came, we saw a thread of smoke curling up from among the trees. The sound of music is always attractive; for, wherever there is music, there is good humour, or good-will. We passed along a footpath, and had a peep, through a break in the hedge, at the musician and his party, when the Oxonian gave us a wink, and told us that if we would follow him we should have some sport.

It proved to be a gipsy encampment, consisting of three or four little cabins, or tents, made of blankets and sail cloth, spread over hoops that were stuck in the ground. It was on one side of a green lane, close under a hawthorn hedge, with a broad beech-tree spreading above it. A small rill tinkled along close by, through the fresh sward, that looked like a carpet.

A tea-kettle was hanging by a crooked piece of iron, over a fire made from dry sticks and leaves, and two old gipsies, in red cloaks, sat crouched on the grass, gossiping over their evening cup of tea; for these creatures, though they live in the open air, have their ideas of fireside comforts. There were two or three children sleeping on the straw with which the tents were littered; a couple of donkeys were grazing in the lane, and a thievish-looking dog was lying before the fire. Some of the younger gipsies were dancing to the music of a fiddle, played by a tall slender stripling, in an old frock coat, with a peacock's feather stuck in his hatband.

As we approached, a gipsy girl, with a pair of fine roguish eyes, came up, and, as usual, offered to tell our fortunes. I could not but admire a certain degree of slattern elegance about the baggage. Her long black silken hair was curiously plaited in numerous small braids, and negligently put up in a picturesque style that a painter might have been proud to have devised. Her dress was of figured chintz, rather ragged, and not over clean, but of a variety of most harmonious and agreeable colours; for these beings have a singularly fine eye for colours. Her straw hat was in her hand, and a red cloak thrown over one arm.

The Oxonian offered at once to have his fortune told, and the girl began with the usual volubility of her race; but he drew her on one side, near the hedge, as he said he had no idea of having his secrets overheard. I saw he was talking to her instead of she to him, and by his glancing towards us now and then, that he was giving the baggage some private hints. When they returned to us, he assumed a very serious air. "Zounds!" said he, "it's very astonishing how these creatures come by their knowledge; this girl has told me some things that I thought no one knew but myself!"

The girl now assailed the general: "Come, your honour," said she, "I see by your face you're a lucky man; but you're not happy in your mind; you're not, indeed, sir: but have a good heart, and give me a good piece of silver, and I'll tell you a nice fortune."

The general had received all her approaches with a banter, and had suffered her to get hold of his hand; but at the mention of the piece of silver, he hemmed, looked grave, and turning to us, asked if we had not better continue our walk. "Come, my master," said the girl, archly, "you'd not be in such a hurry, if you knew all that I could tell you about a fair lady that has a notion for you. Come, sir, old love burns strong; there's many a one comes to see weddings that go away brides themselves!" – Here the girl whispered something in a low voice, at which the general coloured up, was a little fluttered, and suffered himself to be drawn aside under the hedge, where he appeared to listen to her with great earnestness, and at the end paid her half-a-crown with the air of a man that has got the worth of his money.

The girl next made her attack upon Master Simon, who, however, was too old a bird to be caught, knowing that it would end in an attack upon his purse, about which he is a little sensitive. As he has a great notion, however, of being considered a royster, he chucked her under the chin, played her off with rather broad jokes, and put on something of the rake-helly air, that we see now and then assumed on the stage, by the sad-boy gentlemen of the old school. "Ah, your honour," said the girl, with a malicious leer, "you were not in such a tantrum last year, when I told you about the widow you know who; but if you had taken a friend's advice, you'd never have come away from Doncaster races with a flea in your ear!"

There was a secret sting in this speech that seemed quite to disconcert Master Simon. He jerked away his hand in a pet, smacked his whip, whistled to his dogs, and intimated that it was high time to go home. The girl, however, was determined not to lose her harvest. She

Gypsy Encampment

An engraving reproduced in the Geoffrey Crayon edition of *Bracebridge Hall* (New York: G. P. Putnam's Sons, 1868).

now turned upon me, and, as I have a weakness of spirit where there is a pretty face concerned, she soon wheedled me out of my money, and, in return, read me a fortune; which, if it prove true, and I am determined to believe it, will make me one of the luckiest men in the chronicles of Cupid.

I saw that the Oxonian was at the bottom of all this oracular mystery, and was disposed to amuse himself with the general, whose tender approaches to the widow have attracted the notice of the wag. I was a little curious, however, to know the meaning of the dark hints which had so suddenly disconcerted Master Simon; and took occasion to fall in the rear with the Oxonian on our way home, when he laughed heartily at my questions, and gave me ample information on the subject.

The truth of the matter is, that Master Simon has met with a sad rebuff since my Christmas visit to the Hall. He used at that time to be joked about a widow, a fine dashing woman, as he privately informed me. I had supposed the pleasure he betrayed on these occasions resulted from the usual fondness of old bachelors for being teased about getting married, and about flirting, and being fickle and false-hearted. I am assured, however, that Master Simon had really persuaded himself the widow had a kindness for him; in consequence of which he had been at some extraordinary expense in new clothes, and had actually got Frank Bracebridge to order him a coat from Stultz. He began to throw out hints about the importance of a man's settling himself in life before he grew old; he would look grave whenever the widow and matrimony were mentioned in the same sentence; and privately asked the opinion of the squire and parson about the prudence of marrying a widow with a rich jointure, but who had several children.

An important member of a great family connexion cannot harp much upon the theme of matrimony without its taking wind; and it soon got buzzed about that Mr. Simon Bracebridge was actually gone to Doncaster races, with a new horse; but that he meant to return in a curricle with a lady by his side. Master Simon did, indeed, go to the races, and that with a new horse; and the dashing widow did make her appearance in her curricle; but it was unfortunately driven by a strapping young Irish dragoon, with whom even Master Simon's self-complacency would not allow him to venture into competition, and to whom she was married shortly after.

It was a matter of sore chagrin to Master Simon for several months, having never before been fully committed. The dullest head in the family had a joke upon him; and there is no one that likes less to be bantered than an absolute joker. He took refuge for a time at Lady Lillycraft's, until the matter should blow over; and occupied himself by looking over her accounts, regulating the village choir, and inculcating loyalty into a pet bullfinch, by teaching him to whistle "God save the King."

He has now pretty nearly recovered from the mortification; holds up his head, and laughs as much as any one; again affects to pity married men, and is particularly facetious about widows, when Lady Lillycraft is not by. His only time of trial is when the general gets hold of him, who is infinitely heavy and persevering in his waggery, and will interweave a dull joke through the various topics of a whole dinner-time. Master Simon often parries these attacks by a stanza from his old work of "Cupid's Solicitor for Love:"

> " 'Tis in vain to wooe a widow over long,
>   In once or twice her mind you may perceive;
>   Widows are subtle, be they old or young,
>   And by their wiles young men they will deceive."

LOVE-CHARMS

——Come, do not weep, my girl,
Forget him, pretty pensiveness; there will
Come others, every day, as good as he.
SIR J. SUCKLING

The approach of a wedding in a family is always an event of great importance, but particularly so in a household like this, in a retired part of the country. Master Simon, who is a pervading spirit, and, through means of the butler and housekeeper, knows every thing that goes forward, tells me that the maid-servants are continually trying their fortunes, and that the servants'-hall has of late been quite a scene of incantation.

It is amusing to notice how the oddities of the head of a family flow down through all the branches. The squire, in the indulgence of his love of every thing that smacks of old times, has held so many grave conversations with the parson at table, about popular superstitions and traditional rites, that they have been carried from the parlour to the kitchen by the listening domestics, and, being apparently sanctioned by such high authority, the whole house has become infected by them.

The servants are all versed in the common modes of trying luck, and the charms to ensure constancy. They read their fortunes by drawing strokes in the ashes, or by repeating a form of words, and looking in a pail of water. St. Mark's eve, I am told, was a busy time with them; being an appointed night for certain mystic ceremonies. Several of them sowed hemp-seed to be reaped by their true lovers; and they even ventured upon the solemn and fearful preparation of the dumb-cake. This must be done fasting, and in silence. The ingredients are handed down in traditional form. "An eggshell full of salt, an eggshell full of malt, and an eggshell full of barley-meal." When the cake is ready, it is put upon a pan over the fire, and the future husband will appear; turn the cake, and retire; but if a word is spoken, or a fast is broken, during this awful ceremony, there is no knowing what horrible consequences would ensue!

The experiments, in the present instance, came to no result; they that sowed the hemp-seed forgot the magic rhyme that they were to pronounce, so the true lover never appeared; and as to the dumb-cake, what between the awful stillness they had to keep, and the awfulness of the midnight hour, their hearts failed them when they had put the cake in the pan; so that, on the striking of the great house-clock in the servants'-hall, they were seized with a sudden panic, and ran out of the room, to which they did not return until morning, when they found the mystic cake burnt to a cinder.

The most persevering at these spells, however, is Phœbe Wilkins, the housekeeper's niece. As she is a kind of privileged personage, and rather idle, she has more time to occupy herself with these matters. She has always had her head full of love and matrimony. She knows the dream-book by heart, and is quite an oracle among the little girls of the family, who always come to her to interpret their dreams in the mornings.

During the present gaiety of the house, however, the poor girl has worn a face full of trouble; and, to use the housekeeper's words, "has fallen into a sad hystericky way lately." It seems that she was born and brought up in the village, where her father was parish clerk, and she was an early playmate and sweetheart of young Jack Tibbets. Since she has come to live at the Hall, however, her head has been a little turned. Being very pretty, and naturally genteel, she has been much noticed and indulged; and being the housekeeper's niece, she has held an equivocal station between a servant and a companion. She has learnt something of fashions and notions among the young ladies, which have effected quite a metamorphosis; insomuch that her finery at church on Sundays has given mortal offence to her former intimates in the village. This has occasioned the misrepresentations which have awakened the implacable family pride of Dame Tibbets. But what is worse, Phœbe, having a spice of coquetry in her disposition, showed it on one or two occasions to her lover, which produced a downright quarrel; and Jack, being very proud and fiery, has absolutely turned his back upon her for several successive Sundays.

The poor girl is full of sorrow and repentance, and would fain make up with her lover; but he feels his security, and stands aloof. In this he is doubtless encouraged by his mother, who is continually reminding him what he owes to his family; for this same family pride seems doomed to be the eternal bane of lovers.

As I hate to see a pretty face in trouble, I have felt quite concerned for the luckless Phœbe, ever since I heard her story. It is a sad thing to be thwarted in love at any time, but particularly so at this tender season of the year, when every living thing, even to the very butterfly, is sporting with its mate; and the green fields, and the budding groves, and the singing of the birds, and the sweet smell of the flowers, are enough to turn the head of a love-sick girl. I am told that the coolness of young Ready Money lies very heavy at poor Phœbe's heart. Instead of singing about the house as formerly, she goes about pale and sighing, and is apt to break into tears when her companions are full of merriment.

Mrs. Hannah, the vestal gentlewoman of my Lady Lillycraft, has had long talks and walks with Phœbe, up and down the avenue, of an evening; and has endeavoured to squeeze some of her own verjuice into the other's milky nature. She speaks with contempt and abhorrence of the whole sex, and advises Phœbe to despise all the men as heartily as she does. But Phœbe's loving temper is not to be curdled; she has no such thing as hatred or contempt for mankind in her whole composition. She has all the simple fondness of heart of poor, weak, loving woman; and her only thoughts at present are how to conciliate and reclaim her wayward swain.

The spells and love-charms, which are matters of sport to the other domestics, are serious concerns with this love-stricken damsel. She is continually trying her fortune in a variety of ways. I am told that she has absolutely fasted for six Wednesdays and three Fridays successively, having understood that it was a sovereign charm to ensure being married to one's liking within the year. She carries about, also, a lock of her sweetheart's hair, and a riband he once gave her, being a mode of producing constancy in a lover. She even went so far as to try her fortune by the moon, which has always had much to do with lovers' dreams and fancies. For this purpose she went out in the night of the full moon, knelt on a stone in the meadow, and repeated the old traditional rhyme:

"All hail to thee, moon, all hail to thee;
I pray thee, good moon, now show to me
The youth who my future husband shall be."

When she came back to the house, she was faint and pale, and went immediately to bed. The next morning she told the porter's wife that she had seen some one close by the hedge in the meadow, which she was sure was young Tibbets; at any rate, she had dreamt of him all night; both of which, the old dame assured her, were most happy signs. It has since turned out that the person in the meadow was old Christy, the huntsman, who was walking his nightly rounds with the great stag-hound; so that Phœbe's faith in the charm is completely shaken.

THE LIBRARY

Yesterday the fair Julia made her first appearance down stairs since her accident; and the sight of her spread an universal cheerfulness through the household. She was extremely pale, however, and could not walk without pain and difficulty. She was assisted, therefore, to a sofa in the library, which is pleasant and retired, looking out among trees; and so quiet that the little birds come hopping upon the windows, and peering curiously into the apartment. Here several of the family gathered round, and devised means to amuse her, and make the day pass pleasantly. Lady Lillycraft lamented the want of some new novel to while away the time; and was almost in a pet, because the "Author of Waverley" had not produced a work for the last three months.

There was a motion made to call on the parson for some of his old legends or ghost stories; but to this Lady Lillycraft objected, as they were apt to give her the vapours. General Harbottle gave a minute account, for the sixth time, of the disaster of a friend in India, who had his leg bitten off by a tyger whilst he was hunting; and was proceeding to menace the company with a chapter or two about Tippoo Saib.

At length the captain bethought himself, and said, he believed he had a manuscript tale lying in one corner of his campaigning trunk, which, if he could find, and the company were desirous, he would read to them. The offer was eagerly accepted. He retired, and soon returned with a roll of blotted manuscript, in a very gentlemanlike, but nearly illegible, hand, and a great part written on cartridge paper.

"It is one of the scribblings," said he, "of my poor friend, Charles Lightly, of the dragoons. He was a curious, romantic, studious, fanciful fellow; the favourite, and often the unconscious butt of his fellow officers, who entertained themselves with his eccentricities. He was in some of the hardest service in the peninsula, and distinguished himself by his gallantry. When the intervals of duty permitted, he was fond of roving about the country, visiting noted places, and was extremely fond of Moorish ruins. When at his quarters, he was a great scribbler, and passed much of his leisure with his pen in his hand.

"As I was a much younger officer, and a very young man, he took me, in a manner, under his care, and we became close friends. He used often to read his writings to me, having a great confidence in my taste, for I always praised them. Poor fellow! he was shot down close by me at Waterloo. We lay wounded together for some time, during a hard contest that took place near at hand. As I was least hurt, I tried to relieve him, and to stanch the blood which flowed from a wound in his breast. He lay with his head in my lap, and looked up thankfully in my face, but shook his head faintly, and made a sign that it was all over with him; and, indeed, he died a few minutes afterwards, just as our men had repulsed the enemy, and came to our relief. I have his favourite dog and his pistols to this day, and several of his manuscripts, which he gave to me at different times. The one I am now going to read, is a tale which he said he wrote in Spain, during the time that he lay ill of a wound received at Salamanca."

We now arranged ourselves to hear the story. The captain seated himself on the sofa, beside the fair Julia, who I had noticed to be somewhat affected by the picture he had carelessly drawn of wounds and dangers in a field of battle. She now leaned her arm fondly on his shoulder, and her eye glistened as it rested on the manuscript of the poor, literary dragoon. Lady Lillycraft buried herself in a deep, well-cushioned elbow-chair. Her dogs were nestled on soft mats at her feet; and the gallant general took his station, in an arm-chair, at her side, and toyed with her elegantly ornamented work-bag. The rest of the circle being all equally well accommodated, the captain began his story; a copy of which I have procured for the benefit of the reader.

THE STUDENT OF SALAMANCA

What a life doe I lead with my master; nothing but blowing
of bellowes, beating of spirits, and scraping of croslets! It is
a very secret science, for none almost can understand the
language of it. Sublimation, almigation, calcination, rubifica-
tion, albification, and fermentation; with as many termes un-
possible to be uttered as the arte to be compassed.

LILLY'S GALLATHEA

Once upon a time, in the ancient city of Grenada, there sojourned a
young man of the name of Antonio de Castros. He wore the garb
of a student of Salamanca, and was pursuing a course of reading in
the library of the university; and, at intervals of leisure, indulging his
curiosity by examining those remains of Moorish magnificence for which
Grenada is renowned.

Whilst occupied in his studies, he frequently noticed an old man of
a singular appearance, who was likewise a visitor to the library. He
was lean and withered, though apparently more from study than from
age. His eyes, though bright and visionary, were sunk in his head, and
thrown into shade by overhanging eyebrows. His dress was always the
same: a black doublet, a short black cloak, very rusty and threadbare,
a small ruff, and a large overshadowing hat.

His appetite for knowledge seemed insatiable. He would pass whole
days in the library absorbed in study, consulting a multiplicity of
authors, as though he were pursuing some interesting subject through
all its ramifications; so that, in general, when evening came, he was
almost buried among books and manuscripts.

The curiosity of Antonio was excited, and he inquired of the attendants concerning the stranger. No one could give him any information,
excepting that he had been for some time past a casual frequenter of
the library; that his reading lay chiefly among the works treating of
the occult sciences, and that he was particularly curious in his inquiries
after Arabian manuscripts. They added, that he never held communication with any one, excepting to ask for particular works; that, after
a fit of studious application, he would disappear for several days, and
even weeks, and when he revisited the library, he would look more
withered and haggard than ever. The student felt interested by this
account; he was leading rather a desultory life, and had all that capricious curiosity which springs up in idleness. He determined to make
himself acquainted with this book-worm, and find out who and what
he was.

The next time that he saw the old man at the library he commenced his approaches, by requesting permission to look into one of the volumes with which the unknown appeared to have done. The latter merely bowed his head in token of assent. After pretending to look through the volume with great attention, he returned it with many acknowledgements. The stranger made no reply.

"May I ask, senor," said Antonio, with some hesitation, "may I ask what you are searching after in all these books?"

The old man raised his head, with an expression of surprise, at having his studies interrupted for the first time, and by so intrusive a question. He surveyed the student with a side glance from head to foot: "Wisdom, my son," said he, calmly; "and the search requires every moment of my attention." He then cast his eyes upon his book and resumed his studies.

"But, father," said Antonio, "cannot you spare a moment to point out the road to others? It is to experienced travellers, like you, that we strangers in the paths of knowledge must look for directions in our journey."

The stranger looked disturbed: "I have not time enough, my son, to learn," said he, "much less to teach. I am ignorant myself of the path of true knowledge; how then can I show it to others?"

"Well, but father——."

"Senor," said the old man, mildly, but earnestly, "you must see that I have but few steps more to the grave. In that short space have I to accomplish the whole business of my existence. I have no time for words; every word is as one grain of sand of my glass wasted. Suffer me to be alone."

There was no replying to so complete a closing of the door of intimacy. The student found himself calmly, but totally repulsed. Though curious and inquisitive, yet he was naturally modest, and on afterthoughts he blushed at his own intrusion. His mind soon became occupied by other objects. He passed several days wandering among the mouldering piles of Moorish architecture, those melancholy monuments of an elegant and voluptuous people. He paced the deserted halls of the Alhambra, the paradise of the Moorish kings. He visited the great court of the lions, famous for the perfidious massacre of the gallant Abencerrages. He gazed with admiration at its mosaic cupolas, gorgeously painted in gold and azure; its basins of marble, its alabaster vase, supported by lions, and storied with inscriptions.

His imagination kindled as he wandered among these scenes. They were calculated to awaken all the enthusiasm of a youthful mind. Most of the halls have anciently been beautified by fountains. The fine taste of the Arabs delighted in the sparkling purity and reviving freshness of water, and they erected, as it were, altars on every side, to that delicate element. Poetry mingles with architecture in the Alhambra. It breathes along the very walls. Wherever Antonio turned his eye, he beheld inscriptions in Arabic, wherein the perpetuity of Moorish power and splendour within these walls was confidently predicted. Alas! how has the prophecy been falsified! Many of the basins, where the fountains had once thrown up their sparkling showers, were dry and dusty. Some of the palaces were turned into gloomy convents, and the bare-foot monk paced through those courts, which had once glittered with the array, and echoed to the music of Moorish chivalry.

In the course of his rambles, the student more than once encountered the old man of the library. He was always alone, and so full of thought as not to notice any one about him. He appeared to be intent upon studying those half-buried inscriptions, which are found, here and there, among the Moorish ruins, and seem to murmur from the earth the tale of former greatness. The greater part of these have since been translated; but they were supposed by many, at the time, to contain symbolical revelations, and golden maxims of the Arabian sages and astrologers. As Antonio saw the stranger apparently deciphering these inscriptions, he felt an eager longing to make his acquaintance, and to participate in his curious researches; but the repulse he had met with at the library deterred him from making any further advances.

He had directed his steps one evening to the sacred mount, which overlooks the beautiful valley watered by the Darro, the fertile plain of the Vega, and all that rich diversity of vale and mountain, that surrounds Grenada with an earthly paradise. It was twilight when he found himself at the place, where, at the present day, are situated the chapels known by the name of the Sacred Furnaces. They are so called from grottoes, in which some of the primitive saints are said to have been burnt. At the time of Antonio's visit, the place was an object of much curiosity. In an excavation of these grottoes, several manuscripts had recently been discovered, engraved on plates of lead. They were written in the Arabian language, excepting one, which was in unknown characters. The pope had issued a bull, forbidding any one, under pain of excommunication, to speak of these manuscripts. The prohibition had only excited the greater curiosity; and many reports were whispered about, that these manuscripts contained treasures of dark and forbidden knowledge.

As Antonio was examining the place from whence these mysterious manuscripts had been drawn, he again observed the old man of the library, wandering among the ruins. His curiosity was now fully awakened; the time and place served to stimulate it. He resolved to

watch this groper after secret and forgotten lore, and to trace him
to his habitation. There was something like adventure in the thing,
that charmed his romantic disposition. He followed the stranger, therefore, at a little distance; at first cautiously, but he soon observed him
to be so wrapped in his own thoughts, as to take little heed of external
objects.

They passed along the skirts of the mountain, and then by the shady
banks of the Darro. They pursued their way, for some distance from
Grenada, along a lonely road that led among the hills. The gloom of
evening was gathering, and it was quite dark when the stranger stopped
at the portal of a solitary mansion.

It appeared to be a mere wing, or ruined fragment, of what had once
been a pile of some consequence. The walls were of great thickness;
the windows narrow, and generally secured by iron bars. The door was
of planks, studded with iron spikes, and had been of great strength,
though at present it was much decayed. At one end of the mansion was
a ruinous tower, in the Moorish style of architecture. The edifice had
probably been a country retreat, or castle of pleasure, during the
occupation of Grenada by the Moors, and rendered sufficiently strong
to withstand any casual assault in those warlike times.

The old man knocked at the portal. A light appeared at a small
window just above it, and a female head looked out. It might have
served as a model for one of Raphael's saints. The hair was beautifully
braided, and gathered in a silken net; and the complexion, as well as
could be judged from the light, was that soft, rich brunette, so becoming in southern beauty.

"It is I, my child," said the old man. The face instantly disappeared,
and soon after a wicket-door in the large portal opened. Antonio, who
had ventured near to the building, caught a transient sight of a delicate female form. A pair of fine black eyes darted a look of surprise at
seeing a stranger hovering near, and the door was precipitately closed.

There was something in this sudden gleam of beauty that wonderfully
struck the imagination of the student. It was like a brilliant flashing from
its dark casket. He sauntered about, regarding the gloomy pile with
increasing interest. A few simple, wild notes, from among some rocks
and trees at a little distance, attracted his attention. He found there a
group of Gitanas, a vagabond gipsy race, which at that time abounded
in Spain, and lived in hovels and caves of the hills about the neighbourhood of Grenada. Some were busy about a fire, and others were listening to the uncouth music which one of their companions, seated on
a ledge of the rock, was making with a split reed.

Antonio endeavoured to obtain some information of them concerning the old building and its inhabitants. The one who appeared to be their spokesman was a gaunt fellow, with a subtle gait, a whispering voice, and a sinister roll of the eye. He shrugged his shoulders on the student's inquiries, and said that all was not right in that building. An old man inhabited it, whom nobody knew, and whose family appeared to be only a daughter and a female servant. He and his companions, he added, lived up among the neighbouring hills; and as they had been about at night, they had often seen strange lights, and heard strange sounds from the tower. Some of the country people, who worked in the vineyards among the hills, believed the old man to be one that dealt in the black art, and were not over fond of passing near the tower at night; "but for our parts," said the Gitano, "we are not a people that trouble ourselves much with fears of that kind."

The student endeavoured to gain more precise information, but they had none to furnish him. They began to be solicitous for a compensation for what they had already imparted; and recollecting the loneliness of the place, and the vagabond character of his companions, he was glad to give them a gratuity, and to hasten homewards.

He sat down to his studies, but his brain was too full of what he had seen and heard; his eye was upon the page, but his fancy still returned to the tower, and he was continually picturing the little window, with the beautiful head peeping out; or the door half open, and the nymph-like form within. He retired to bed, but the same objects haunted his dreams. He was young and susceptible; and the excited state of his feelings, from wandering among the abodes of departed grace and gallantry, had predisposed him for a sudden impression from female beauty.

The next morning he strolled again in the direction of the tower. It was still more forlorn by the broad glare of day than in the gloom of evening. The walls were crumbling, and weeds and moss were growing in every crevice. It had the look of a prison rather than a dwelling-house. In one angle, however, he remarked a window which seemed an exception to the surrounding squalidness. There was a curtain drawn within it, and flowers standing on the window-stone. Whilst he was looking at it the curtain was partially withdrawn, and a delicate white arm, of the most beautiful roundness, was put forth to water the flowers.

The student made a noise to attract the attention of the fair florist. He succeeded. The curtain was further drawn, and he had a glance of the same lovely face he had seen the evening before; it was but a mere glance; the curtain again fell, and the casement closed. All this was calculated to excite the feelings of a romantic youth. Had he seen the unknown under other circumstances, it is probable that he would not have been struck with her beauty; but this appearance of being shut up and kept apart gave her the value of a treasured gem. He passed and repassed before the house several times in the course of the day, but saw nothing more. He was there again in the evening. The whole aspect of the house was dreary. The narrow windows emitted no rays of cheerful light, to indicate that there was social life within. Antonio listened at the portal, but no sound of voices reached his ear. Just then he heard the clapping to of a distant door, and fearing to be detected in the unworthy act of eaves-dropping, he precipitately drew off to the opposite side of the road, and stood in the shadow of a ruined archway.

He now remarked a light from a window in the tower. It was fitful and changeable; commonly feeble and yellowish, as if from a lamp; with an occasional glare of some vivid metallic colour, followed by a dusky glow. A column of dense smoke would now and then rise in the air, and hang like a canopy over the tower. There was altogether such a loneliness and seeming mystery about the building and its inhabitants, that Antonio was half inclined to indulge the country people's notions, and to fancy it the den of some powerful sorcerer, and the fair damsel he had seen to be some spell-bound beauty.

After some time had elapsed, a light appeared in the window where he had seen the beautiful arm. The curtain was down, but it was so thin that he could perceive the shadow of some one passing and repassing between it and the light. He fancied that he could distinguish that the form was delicate; and from the alacrity of its movements, it was evidently youthful. He had not a doubt but this was the bed-chamber of his beautiful unknown.

Presently he heard the sound of a guitar, and a female voice singing. He drew near cautiously, and listened. It was a plaintive Moorish ballad, and he recognised in it the lamentations of one of the Abencerrages on leaving the walls of lovely Grenada. It was full of passion and tenderness. It spoke of the delights of early life; the hours of love it had enjoyed on the banks of the Darro, and among the blissful abodes of the Alhambra. It bewailed the fallen honours of the Abencerrages, and imprecated vengeance on their oppressors. Antonio was affected by the music. It singularly coincided with the place. It was like the voice of past times echoed in the present, and breathing among the monuments of its departed glories.

The voice ceased; after a time the light disappeared, and all was still. "She sleeps!" said Antonio, fondly. He lingered about the building with the devotion with which a lover lingers about the bower of sleeping beauty. The rising moon threw its silver beams on the gray walls, and glittered on the casement. The late gloomy landscape gradually became flooded with its radiance. Finding, therefore, that he could no longer move about in obscurity, and fearful that his loiterings might be observed, he reluctantly retired.

The curiosity which had at first drawn the young man to the tower was now seconded by feelings of a more romantic kind. His studies were almost entirely abandoned. He maintained a kind of blockade of the old mansion; he would take a book with him, and pass a great part of the day under the trees in its vicinity; keeping a vigilant eye upon it, and endeavouring to ascertain what were the walks of his mysterious charmer. He found, however, that she never went out except to mass, when she was accompanied by her father. He waited at the door of the church, and offered her the holy water, in the hopes of touching her hand; a little office of gallantry common in catholic countries. She, however, modestly declined, without raising her eyes to see who made the offer, and always took it herself from the font. She was attentive in her devotion; her eyes were never taken from the altar or the priest; and, on returning home, her countenance was almost entirely concealed by her mantilla.

Antonio had now carried on the pursuit for several days, and was hourly getting more and more interested in the chase, but never a step nearer to the game. His lurkings about the house had probably been noticed, for he no longer saw the fair face at the window, nor the white arm put forth to water the flowers. His only consolation was to repair nightly to his post of observation and listen to her warbling, and if by chance he could catch a sight of her shadow, passing and repassing before the window, he thought himself most fortunate.

As he was indulging in one of these evening vigils, which were complete revels of the imagination, the sound of approaching footsteps made him withdraw into the deep shadow of the ruined archway, opposite to the tower. A cavalier approached, wrapped in a large Spanish cloak. He paused under the window of the tower, and after a little while began a serenade, accompanied by his guitar, in the usual style of Spanish gallantry. His voice was rich and manly; he touched the instrument with skill, and sang with amorous and impassioned eloquence. The plume of his hat was buckled by jewels that sparkled in the moon-beams; and, as he played on the guitar, his cloak falling off from one shoulder, showed him to be richly dressed. It was evident that he was a person of rank.

The idea now flashed across Antonio's mind, that the affections of his unknown beauty might be engaged. She was young, and doubtless susceptible; and it was not in the nature of Spanish females to be deaf and insensible to music and admiration. The surmise brought with it a feeling of dreariness. There was a pleasant dream of several days suddenly dispelled. He had never before experienced any thing of the tender passion; and, as its morning dreams are always delightful, he would fain have continued in the delusion.

"But what have I to do with her attachments?" thought he, "I have no claim on her heart, nor even on her acquaintance. How do I know that she is worthy of affection? Or if she is, must not so gallant a lover as this, with his jewels, his rank, and his detestable music, have completely captivated her? What idle humour is this that I have fallen into? I must again to my books. Study, study will soon chase away all these idle fancies!"

The more he thought, however, the more he became entangled in the spell which his lively imagination had woven round him; and now that a rival had appeared, in addition to the other obstacles that environed this enchanted beauty, she appeared ten times more lovely and desirable. It was some slight consolation to him to perceive that the gallantry of the unknown met with no apparent return from the tower. The light at the window was extinguished. The curtain remained undrawn, and none of the customary signals were given to intimate that the serenade was accepted.

The cavalier lingered for some time about the place, and sang several other tender airs with a taste and feeling that made Antonio's heart ache; at length he slowly retired. The student remained with folded arms, leaning against the ruined arch, endeavouring to summon up resolution enough to depart; but there was a romantic fascination that still enchained him to the place. "It is the last time," said he, willing to compromise between his feelings and his judgment, "it is the last time; then let me enjoy the dream a few moments longer."

As his eye ranged about the old building to take a farewell look, he observed the strange light in the tower, which he had noticed on a former occasion. It kept beaming up and declining as before. A pillar of smoke rose in the air, and hung in sable volumes. It was evident the old man was busied in some of those operations that had gained him the reputation of a sorcerer throughout the neighbourhood.

Suddenly an intense and brilliant glare shone through the casement, followed by a loud report, and then a fierce and ruddy glow. A figure appeared at the window, uttering cries of agony or alarm; but immediately disappeared, and a body of smoke and flame whirled out of the narrow aperture. Antonio rushed to the portal, and knocked at it with vehemence. He was only answered by loud shrieks, and found that the females were already in helpless consternation. With an exertion of desperate strength he forced the wicket from its hinges, and rushed into the house.

He found himself in a small vaulted hall, and by the light of the moon which entered at the door, he saw a staircase to the left. He hurried up it to a narrow corridor, through which was rolling a volume of smoke. He found here the two females in a frantic state of alarm; one of them clasped her hands, and implored him to save her father.

The corridor terminated in a spiral flight of steps, leading up to the tower. He sprang up it to a small door, through the chinks of which came a glow of light, and smoke was spuming out. He burst it open, and found himself in an antique vaulted chamber, furnished with furnace, and various chemical apparatus. A shattered retort lay on the stone floor; a quantity of combustibles, nearly consumed, with various half-burnt books and papers, were sending up an expiring flame, and filling the chamber with stifling smoke. Just within the threshold lay the reputed conjuror. He was bleeding, his clothes were scorched, and he appeared lifeless. Antonio caught him up, and bore him down the stairs to a chamber in which there was a light, and laid him on a bed. The female domestic was despatched for such appliances as the house afforded; but the daughter threw herself frantically beside her parent, and could not be reasoned out of her alarm. Her dress was all in disorder; her dishevelled hair hung in rich confusion about her neck and bosom, and never was there beheld a lovelier picture of terror and affliction.

The skilful assiduities of the scholar soon produced signs of returning animation in his patient. The old man's wounds, though severe, were not dangerous. They had evidently been produced by the bursting of the retort; in his bewilderment he had been enveloped in the stifling metallic vapours, which had overpowered his feeble frame, and had not Antonio arrived to his assistance, it is possible he might never have recovered.

By slow degrees he came to his senses. He looked about with a bewildered air at the chamber, the agitated group around, and the student who was leaning over him.

"Where am I?" said he, wildly.

At the sound of his voice his daughter uttered a faint exclamation of delight. "My poor Inez!" said he, embracing her; then putting his hand to his head, and taking it away stained with blood, he seemed suddenly to recollect himself and to be overcome with emotion.

"Ay!" cried he, "all is over with me! all gone! all vanished! gone in a moment! the labour of a lifetime lost!"

His daughter attempted to soothe him, but he became slightly delirious, and raved incoherently about malignant demons, and about the habitation of the green lion being destroyed. His wounds being dressed, and such other remedies administered as his situation required, he sunk into a state of quiet. Antonio now turned his attention to the daughter, whose sufferings had been little inferior to those of her father. Having with great difficulty succeeded in tranquillizing her fears, he endeavoured to prevail upon her to retire, and seek the repose so necessary to her frame, proffering to remain by her father until morning. "I am a stranger," said he, "it is true, and my offer may appear intrusive; but I see you are lonely and helpless, and I cannot help venturing over the limits of mere ceremony. Should you feel any scruple or doubt, however, say but a word, and I will instantly retire."

There was a frankness, a kindness, and a modesty mingled in Antonio's deportment that inspired instant confidence; and his simple scholar's garb was a recommendation in the house of poverty. The females consented to resign the sufferer to his care, as they would be the better able to attend to him on the morrow. On retiring, the old domestic was profuse in her benedictions; the daughter only looked her thanks; but as they shone through the tears that filled her fine black eyes, the student thought them a thousand times the most eloquent.

Here, then, he was, by a singular turn of chance, completely housed within this mysterious mansion. When left to himself, and the bustle of the scene was over, his heart throbbed as he looked round the chamber in which he was sitting. It was the daughter's room, the promised land towards which he had cast so many a longing gaze. The furniture was old, and had probably belonged to the building in its prosperous days; but every thing was arranged with propriety. The flowers that he had seen her attend stood in the window; a guitar leaned against a table, on which stood a crucifix, and before it lay a missal and a rosary. There reigned an air of purity and serenity about this little nestling place of innocence; it was the emblem of a chaste and quiet mind. Some few articles of female dress lay on the chairs; and there was the very bed on which she had slept; the pillow on which her soft cheek had reclined! The poor scholar was treading enchanted ground; for what fairy land has more of magic in it than the bed-chamber of innocence and beauty?

From various expressions of the old man in his ravings, and from what he had noticed on a subsequent visit to the tower, to see that the fire was extinguished, Antonio had gathered that his patient was an alchymist. The philosopher's stone was an object eagerly sought after by visionaries in those days; but in consequence of the superstitious prejudices of the times, and the frequent persecutions of its votaries, they were apt to pursue their experiments in secret; in lonely houses, in caverns and ruins, or in the privacy of cloistered cells.

In the course of the night the old man had several fits of restlessness and delirium; he would call out upon Theophrastus, and Geber, and Albertus Magnus, and other sages of his art; and anon would murmur about fermentation and projection, until, towards daylight, he once more sunk into a salutary sleep. When the morning sun darted his rays into the casement, the fair Inez, attended by the female domestic, came blushing into the chamber. The student now took his leave, having himself need of repose, but obtained ready permission to return and inquire after the sufferer.

When he called again, he found the alchymist languid and in pain, but apparently suffering more in mind than in body. His delirium had left him, and he had been informed of the particulars of his deliverance, and of the subsequent attentions of the scholar. He could do little more than look his thanks, but Antonio did not require them; his own heart repaid him for all that he had done, and he almost rejoiced in the disaster that had gained him an entrance into this mysterious habitation. The alchymist was so helpless as to need much assistance; Antonio remained with him therefore the greater part of the day. He repeated his visit the next day, and the next. Every day his company seemed more pleasing to the invalid; and every day he felt his interest in the latter increasing. Perhaps the presence of the daughter might have been at the bottom of this solicitude.

He had frequent and long conversations with the alchymist. He found him, as men of his pursuits were apt to be, a mixture of enthusiasm and simplicity; of curious and extensive reading on points of little utility, with great inattention to the every-day occurrences of life, and profound ignorance of the world. He was deeply versed in singular and obscure branches of knowledge, and much given to visionary speculations. Antonio, whose mind was of a romantic cast, had himself given some attention to the occult sciences, and he entered upon those themes with an ardour that delighted the philosopher. Their conversations frequently turned upon astrology, divination, and the great secret. The old man would forget his aches and wounds, rise up like a spectre in his bed, and kindle into eloquence on his favourite topics. When gently admonished of his situation, it would but prompt him to another sally of thought.

"Alas, my son!" he would say, "is not this very decrepitude and suffering another proof of the importance of those secrets with which we are surrounded? Why are we trammelled by disease, withered by old age, and our spirits quenched, as it were, within us, but because we have lost those secrets of life and youth which were known to our parents before their fall? To regain these have philosophers been ever since aspiring; but just as they are on the point of securing the precious secrets for ever, the brief period of life is at an end; they die, and with them all their wisdom and experience. 'Nothing,' as De Nuysment observes, 'nothing is wanting for man's perfection but a longer life, less crossed with sorrows and maladies, to the attaining of the full and perfect knowledge of things.'"

At length Antonio so far gained on the heart of his patient, as to draw from him the outlines of his story.

Felix de Vasquez, the alchymist, was a native of Castile, and of an ancient and honourable line. Early in life he had married a beautiful female, a descendant from one of the Moorish families. The marriage displeased his father, who considered the pure Spanish blood contaminated by this foreign mixture. It is true, the lady traced her descent from one of the Abencerrages, the most gallant of Moorish cavaliers, who had embraced the christian faith on being exiled from the walls of Grenada. The injured pride of the father, however, was not to be appeased. He never saw his son afterwards; and on dying left him but a scanty portion of his estate; bequeathing the residue, in the piety and bitterness of his heart, to the erection of convents, and the performance of masses for souls in purgatory. Don Felix resided for a long time in the neighbourhood of Valladolid in a state of embarrassment and obscurity. He devoted himself to intense study, having, while at the university of Salamanca, imbibed a taste for the secret sciences. He was enthusiastic and speculative; he went on from one branch of knowledge to another, until he became zealous in the search after the grand Arcanum.

He had at first engaged in the pursuit with the hopes of raising himself from his present obscurity, and resuming the rank and dignity to which his birth entitled him; but, as usual, it ended in absorbing every thought, and becoming the business of his existence. He was at length aroused from this mental abstraction by the calamities of his household. A malignant fever swept off his wife and all his children, excepting an infant daughter. These losses for a time overwhelmed and stupefied him. His home had in a manner died away from around him, and he felt lonely and forlorn. When his spirit revived within him, he determined to abandon the scene of his humiliation and disaster; to bear away the child that was still left him, beyond the scene of contagion, and never to return to Castile until he should be enabled to reclaim the honours of his line.

He had ever since been wandering and unsettled in his abode. Sometimes the resident of populous cities, at other times of absolute solitudes. He had searched libraries, meditated on inscriptions, visited adepts of different countries, and sought to gather and concentrate the rays which had been thrown by various minds upon the secrets of alchymy. He had at one time travelled quite to Padua to search for the manuscripts of Pietro d'Abano, and to inspect an urn which had been dug up near Este, supposed to have been buried by Maximus Olybius, and to have contained the grand elixir.*

While at Padua he had met with an adept versed in Arabian lore, who talked of the invaluable manuscripts that must remain in the Spanish libraries, preserved from the spoils of the Moorish academies and universities; of the probability of meeting with precious unpublished writings of Geber, and Alfarabius, and Avicenna, the great physicians of the Arabian schools, who, it was well known, had treated much of alchymy; but above all, he spoke of the Arabian tablets of lead, which had recently been dug up in the neighbourhood of Grenada, and which, it was confidently believed among adepts, contained the lost secrets of the art.

The indefatigable alchymist once more bent his steps for Spain, full of renovated hope. He had made his way to Grenada: he had wearied himself in the study of Arabic, in decyphering inscriptions, in rummaging libraries, and exploring every possible trace left by the Arabian sages.

In all his wanderings he had been accompanied by Inez; through the rough and the smooth, the pleasant and the adverse; never complaining, but rather seeking to soothe his cares by her innocent and playful caresses. Her instruction had been the employment and the delight of his hours of relaxation. She had grown up while they were wandering, and had scarcely ever known any home but by his side.

---

* This urn was found in 1533. It contained a lesser one, in which was a burning lamp betwixt two small vials, the one of gold, the other of silver, both of them full of a very clear liquor. On the largest was an inscription, stating that Maximus Olybius shut up in this small vessel elements which he had prepared with great toil. There were many disquisitions among the learned on the subject. It was the most received opinion, that this Maximus Olybius was an inhabitant of Padua, that he had discovered the great secret, and that these vessels contained liquor, one to transmute metals to gold, the other to silver. The peasants who found the urns, imagining this precious liquor to be common water, spilt every drop, so that the art of transmuting metals remains as much a secret as ever.

He was family, friends, home, every thing to her. He had carried her in his arms when they first began their wayfaring; had nestled her, as an eagle does its young, among the rocky heights of the Sierra Morena; she had sported about him in childhood in the solitudes of the Bateucas; had followed him, as a lamb does the shepherd, over the rugged Pyrenees, and into the fair plains of Languedoc; and now she was grown up to support his feeble steps among the ruined abodes of her maternal ancestors.

His property had gradually wasted away in the course of his travels and his experiments. Still hope, the constant attendant of the alchymist, had led him on; ever on the point of reaping the reward of his labours, and ever disappointed. With the credulity that often attended his art, he attributed many of his disappointments to the machinations of the malignant spirits that beset the path of the alchymist, and torment him in his solitary labours. "It is their constant endeavour," he observed, "to close up every avenue to those sublime truths, which would enable man to rise above the abject state into which he has fallen, and to return to his original perfection." To the evil offices of these demons he attributed his late disaster. He had been on the very verge of the glorious discovery; never were the indications more completely auspicious; all was going on prosperously, when, at the critical moment which should have crowned his labours with success, and have placed him at the very summit of human power and felicity, the bursting of a retort had reduced his laboratory and himself to ruins.

"I must now," said he, "give up at the very threshold of success. My books and papers are burnt; my apparatus is broken. I am too old to bear up against these evils. The ardour that once inspired me is gone; my poor frame is exhausted by study and watchfulness, and this last misfortune has hurried me towards the grave." He concluded in a tone of deep dejection. Antonio endeavoured to comfort and re-assure him; but the poor alchymist had for once awakened to a consciousness of the worldly ills that were gathering around him, and had sunk into despondency. After a pause, and some thoughtfulness and perplexity of brow, Antonio ventured to make a proposal.

"I have long," said he, "been filled with a love for the secret sciences, but have felt too ignorant and diffident to give myself up to them. You have acquired experience; you have amassed the knowledge of a lifetime; it were a pity it should be thrown away. You say you are too old to renew the toils of the laboratory; suffer me to undertake them. Add your knowledge to my youth and activity, and what shall we not accomplish? As a probationary fee, and a fund on which to proceed, I will bring into the common stock a sum of gold, the residue of a legacy, which has enabled me to complete my education. A poor scholar cannot boast much; but I trust we shall soon put ourselves beyond the reach of want; and if we should fail, why, I must depend, like other scholars, upon my brains to carry me through the world."

The philosopher's spirits, however, were more depressed than the student had imagined. This last shock, following in the rear of so many disappointments, had almost destroyed the reaction of his mind. The fire of an enthusiast, however, is never so low, but that it may be blown again into a flame. By degrees the old man was cheered and reanimated by the buoyancy and ardour of his sanguine companion. He at length agreed to accept of the services of the student, and once more to renew his experiments. He objected, however, to using the student's gold, notwithstanding that his own was nearly exhausted; but this objection was soon overcome; the student insisted on making it a common stock and common cause; – and then how absurd was any delicacy about such a trifle, with men who looked forward to discovering the philosopher's stone!

While, therefore, the alchymist was slowly recovering, the student busied himself in getting the laboratory once more in order. It was strewed with the wrecks of retorts and alembics, with old crucibles, boxes and phials of powders and tinctures, and half-burnt books and manuscripts.

As soon as the old man was sufficiently recovered, the studies and experiments were renewed. The student became a privileged and frequent visitor, and was indefatigable in his toils in the laboratory. The philosopher daily derived new zeal and spirits from the animation of his disciple. He was now enabled to prosecute the enterprise with continued exertion, having so active a coadjutor to divide the toil. While he was poring over the writings of Sandivogius, and Philalethes, and Dominus de Nuysment, and endeavouring to comprehend the symbolical language in which they have locked up their mysteries, Antonio would occupy himself among the retorts and crucibles, and keep the furnace in a perpetual glow.

With all his zeal, however, for the discovery of the golden art, the feelings of the student had not cooled as to the object that first drew him to this ruinous mansion. During the old man's illness, he had frequent opportunities of being near the daughter; and every day made him more sensible to her charms. There was a pure simplicity, and an almost passive gentleness in her manners; yet with all this was mingled something, whether mere maiden shyness, or a consciousness of high descent, or a dash of Castilian pride, or perhaps all united, that prevented undue familiarity, and made her difficult of approach.

The danger of her father, and the measures to be taken for his relief, had at first overcome this coyness and reserve; but as he recovered and her alarm subsided, she seemed to shrink from the familiarity she had indulged with the youthful stranger, and to become every day more shy and silent.

Antonio had read many books, but this was the first volume of womankind that he had ever studied. He had been captivated with the very title-page; but the further he read the more he was delighted. She seemed formed to love; her soft black eye rolled languidly under its long silken lashes, and wherever it turned, it would linger and repose; there was tenderness in every beam. To him alone she was reserved and distant. Now that the common cares of the sick room were at an end, he saw little more of her than before his admission to the house. Sometimes he met her on his way to and from the laboratory, and at such times there was ever a smile and a blush; but, after a simple salutation, she glided on and disappeared.

"'Tis plain," thought Antonio, "my presence is indifferent, if not irksome to her. She has noticed my admiration, and is determined to discourage it; nothing but a feeling of gratitude prevents her treating me with marked distaste – and then has she not another lover, rich, gallant, splendid, musical? how can I suppose she would turn her eyes from so brilliant a cavalier, to a poor obscure student, raking among the cinders of her father's laboratory?"

Indeed, the idea of the amorous serenader continually haunted his mind. He felt convinced that he was a favoured lover; yet, if so, why did he not frequent the tower? Why did he not make his approaches by noon-day? There was mystery in this eaves-dropping and musical courtship. Surely Inez could not be encouraging a secret intrigue! Oh, no! she was too artless, too pure, too ingenuous! But then the Spanish females were so prone to love and intrigue; and music and moonlight were so seductive, and Inez had such a tender soul languishing in every look. – "Oh!" would the poor scholar exclaim, clasping his hands, "Oh that I could but once behold those loving eyes beaming on me with affection!"

It is incredible to those who have not experienced it, on what scanty aliment human life and human love may be supported. A dry crust, thrown now and then to a starving man, will give him a new lease of existence; and a faint smile, or a kind look, bestowed at casual intervals, will keep a lover loving on, when a man in his sober senses would despair.

When Antonio found himself alone in the laboratory his mind would be haunted by one of these looks, or smiles, which he had received in passing. He would set it in every possible light, and argue on it with all the self-pleasing, self-teasing logic of a lover.

The country around him was enough to awaken that voluptuousness of feeling so favourable to the growth of passion. The window of the tower rose above the trees of the romantic valley of the Darro, and looked down upon some of the loveliest scenery of the Vega, where groves of citron and orange were refreshed by cool springs and brooks of the purest water. The Xenel and the Darro wound their shining streams along the plain, and gleamed from among its bowers. The surrounding hills were covered with vineyards, and the mountains crowned with snow seemed to melt into the blue sky. The delicate airs that played about the tower were perfumed by the fragrance of myrtle and orange blossoms, and the ear was charmed with the fond warbling of the nightingale, which, in these happy regions, sings the whole day long. Sometimes, too, there was the idle song of the muleteer, sauntering along the solitary road; or the notes of the guitar from some group of peasants dancing in the shade. All these were enough to fill the head of a young lover with poetic fancies; and Antonio would picture to himself how he could loiter among those happy groves, and wander by those gentle rivers, and love away his life with Inez.

He felt at times impatient at his own weakness, and would endeavour to brush away these cobwebs of the mind. He would turn his thought, with sudden effort, to his occult studies, or occupy himself in some perplexing process; but often, when he had partially succeeded in fixing his attention, the sound of Inez' lute, or the soft notes of her voice, would come stealing upon the stillness of the chamber, and, as it were, floating round the tower. There was no great art in her performance; but Antonio thought he had never heard music comparable to this. It was perfect witchcraft to hear her warble forth some of her national melodies; those little Spanish romances and Moorish ballads that transport the hearer, in idea, to the banks of the Guadalquiver, or the walls of the Alhambra, and make him dream of beauties, and balconies, and moonlight serenades.

Never was poor student more sadly beset than Antonio. Love is a troublesome companion in a study at the best of times; but in the laboratory of an alchymist his intrusion is terribly disastrous. Instead of attending to the retorts and crucibles, and watching the process of some experiment intrusted to his charge, the student would get entranced in one of these love-dreams, from which he would often be aroused by some fatal catastrophe. The philosopher, on returning from his researches in the libraries, would find every thing gone wrong, and Antonio in despair over the ruins of the whole day's work. The old man, however, took all quietly, for his had been a life of experiment and failure.

"We must have patience, my son," would he say, "as all the great masters that have gone before us have had. Errors, and accidents, and delays, are what we have to contend with. Did not Pontanus err two hundred times before he could obtain even the matter on which to found his experiments? The great Flamel, too, did he not labour four and twenty years, before he ascertained the first agent? What difficulties and hardships did not Cartilaceus encounter, at the very threshold of his discoveries? And Bernard de Treves, even after he had attained a knowledge of all the requisites, was he not delayed full three years? What you consider accidents, my son, are the machinations of our invisible enemies. The treasures and golden secrets of nature are surrounded by spirits hostile to man. The air about us teems with them. They lurk in the fire of the furnace, in the bottom of the crucible and the alembic, and are ever on the alert to take advantage of those moments when our minds are wandering from intense meditation on the great truth that we are seeking. We must only strive the more to purify ourselves from those gross and earthly feelings which becloud the soul, and prevent her from piercing into nature's arcana."

"Alas!" thought Antonio, "if to be purified from all earthly feeling requires that I should cease to love Inez, I fear I shall never discover the philosopher's stone!"

In this way matters went on for some time at the alchymist's. Day after day was sending the student's gold in vapour up the chimney; every blast of the furnace made him a ducat the poorer, without apparently helping him a jot nearer to the golden secret. Still the young man stood by, and saw piece after piece disappearing without a murmur; he had daily an opportunity of seeing Inez, and felt as if her favour would be better than silver or gold, and that every smile was worth a ducat.

Sometimes, in the cool of the evening, when the toils of the laboratory happened to be suspended, he would walk with the alchymist in what had once been a garden belonging to the mansion. There were still the remains of terraces and balustrades, and here and there a marble urn, or mutilated statue overturned, and buried among weeds and flowers run wild. It was the favourite resort of the alchymist in his hours of relaxation, where he would give full scope to his visionary flights. His mind was tinctured with the Rosycrucian doctrines. He believed in elementary beings; some favourable, others adverse to his pursuits; and in the exaltation of his fancy, had often imagined that he held communion with them in his solitary walks about the whispering groves and echoing walls of this old garden.

When accompanied by Antonio, he would prolong these evening recreations. Indeed, he sometimes did it out of consideration for his disciple, for he feared lest his too close application, and his incessant seclusion in the tower, should be injurious to his health. He was delighted and surprised by this extraordinary zeal and perseverance in so young a tyro, and looked upon him as destined to be one of the great luminaries of the art. Lest the student should repine at the time lost in these relaxations, the good alchymist would fill them up with wholesome knowledge, in matters connected with their pursuits; and would walk up and down the alleys with his disciple, imparting oral instruction, like an ancient philosopher. In all his visionary schemes there breathed a spirit of lofty, though chimerical, philanthropy, that won the admiration of the scholar. Nothing sordid, nor sensual; nothing petty nor selfish seemed to enter into his views, in respect to the grand discoveries he was anticipating. On the contrary his imagination kindled with conceptions of widely dispensated happiness. He looked forward to the time when he should be able to go about the earth relieving the indigent, comforting the distressed; and, by his unlimited means, devising and executing plans for the complete extirpation of poverty, and all its attendant sufferings and crimes. Never were grander schemes for general good, for the distribution of boundless wealth and universal competence, devised, than by this poor, indigent alchymist in his ruined tower.

Antonio would attend these peripatetic lectures with all the ardour of a devotee; but there was another circumstance which may have given a secret charm to them. The garden was the resort also of Inez, where she took her walks of recreation; the only exercise that her secluded life permitted. As Antonio was duteously pacing by the side of his instructor, he would often catch a glimpse of the daughter, walking pensively about the alleys in the soft twilight. Sometimes they would meet her unexpectedly, and the heart of the student would throb with agitation. A blush too would crimson the cheek of Inez, but still she passed on, and never joined them.

He had remained one evening, until rather a late hour, with the alchymist in this favourite resort. It was a delightful night after a sultry day, and the balmy air of the garden was peculiarly reviving. The old man was seated on a fragment of a pedestal, looking like a part of the ruin on which he sat. He was edifying his pupil by long lessons of wisdom from the stars, as they shone out with brilliant lustre in the dark blue vault of a southern sky; for he was deeply versed in

Behmen, and other of the Rosicrucians, and talked much of the signature of earthly things, and passing events, which may be discerned in the heavens; of the power of the stars over corporeal beings, and their influence on the fortunes of the sons of men.

By degrees the moon rose, and shed her gleaming light among the groves. Antonio apparently listened with fixed attention to the sage, but his ear was drinking in the melody of Inez' voice, who was singing to her lute in one of the moonlight glades of the garden. The old man having exhausted his theme, sat gazing in silent reverie at the heavens. Antonio could not resist an inclination to steal a look at this coy beauty, who was thus playing the part of the nightingale, so sequestered and musical. Leaving the alchymist in his celestial reverie, he stole gently along one of the alleys. The music had ceased, and he thought he heard the sound of voices. He came to an angle of a copse that had screened a kind of green recess, ornamented by a marble fountain. The moon shone full upon the place, and by its light, he beheld his unknown serenading rival at the feet of Inez. He was detaining her by the hand, which he covered with kisses; but at sight of Antonio he started up and half drew his sword, while Inez, disengaged, fled back to the house.

All the jealous doubts and fears of Antonio were now confirmed. He did not remain to encounter the resentment of his happy rival at being thus interrupted, but turned from the place in sudden wretchedness of heart. That Inez should love another would have been misery enough; but that she should be capable of a dishonourable amour, shocked him to the soul. The idea of deception in so young and apparently artless a being, brought with it that sudden distrust in human nature, so sickening to a youthful and ingenuous mind; but when he thought of the kind, simple parent she was deceiving, whose affections all centered in her, he felt for a moment a sentiment of indignation, and almost of aversion.

He found the alchymist still seated in his visionary contemplation of the moon. "Come hither, my son," said he, with his usual enthusiasm; "come, read with me in this vast volume of wisdom, thus nightly unfolded for our perusal. Wisely did the Chaldean sages affirm, that the heaven is as a mystic page, uttering speech to those who can rightly understand; warning them of good and evil, and instructing them in the secret decrees of fate."

The student's heart ached for his venerable master; and, for a moment he felt the futility of all his occult wisdom. "Alas! poor old man!" thought he, "of what avails all thy study? Little dost thou dream, while busied in airy speculations among the stars, what a treason against thy happiness is going on under thine eyes; as it were, in thy very bosom! – Oh Inez! Inez! where shall we look for truth and innocence; where shall we repose confidence in woman, if even you can deceive?"

It was a trite apostrophe, such as every lover makes when he finds his mistress not quite such a goddess as he had painted her. With the student, however, it sprung from honest anguish of heart. He returned to his lodgings in pitiable confusion of mind. He now deplored the infatuation that had led him on until his feelings were so thoroughly engaged. He resolved to abandon his pursuits at the tower, and trust to absence to dispel the fascination by which he had been spellbound. He no longer thirsted after the discovery of the grand elixir: the dream of alchymy was over; for without Inez, what was the value of the philosopher's stone?

He rose, after a sleepless night, with the determination of taking his leave of the alchymist, and tearing himself from Grenada. For several days did he rise with the same resolution, and every night saw him come back to his pillow to repine at his want of resolution, and to make fresh determinations for the morrow. In the meanwhile he saw less of Inez than ever. She no longer walked in the garden, but remained almost entirely in her apartment. When she met him, she blushed more than usual; and once hesitated, as if she would have spoken; but after a temporary embarrassment, and still deeper blushes, she made some casual observation, and retired. Antonio read in this confusion, a consciousness of fault, and of that fault's being discovered. "What could she have wished to communicate? Perhaps to account for the scene in the garden; – but how can she account for it, or why should she account for it to me? What am I to her? – or rather, what is she to me?" exclaimed he, impatiently; with a new resolution to break through these entanglements of the heart, and fly from this enchanted spot for ever.

He was returning that very night to his lodgings, full of this excellent determination, when, in a shadowy part of the road, he passed a person, whom he recognized, by his height and form, for his rival. He was going in the direction of the tower. If any lingering doubts remained, here was an opportunity of settling them completely. He determined to follow this unknown cavalier, and, under favour of the darkness, observe his movements. If he obtained access to the tower, or in any way a favourable reception, Antonio felt as if it would be a relief to his mind, and would enable him to fix his wavering resolution.

The unknown, as he came near the tower, was more cautious and stealthy in his approaches. He was joined under a clump of trees by another person, and they had much whispering together. A light was burning in the chamber of Inez, the curtain was down, but the casement was left open, as the night was warm. After some time, the light was extinguished. A considerable interval elapsed. The cavalier and his companion remained under covert of the trees, as if keeping watch. At length they approached the tower with silent and cautious steps. The cavalier received a dark lantern from his companion, and threw off his cloak. The other then softly brought something from the clump of trees, which Antonio perceived to be a light ladder. He placed it against the wall, and the serenader gently ascended. A sickening sensation came over Antonio. Here was indeed a confirmation of every fear. He was about to leave the place, never to return, when he heard a stifled shriek from Inez' chamber.

In an instant the fellow that stood at the foot of the ladder lay prostrate on the ground. Antonio wrested a stiletto from his nerveless hand, and hurried up the ladder. He sprang in at the window, and found Inez struggling in the grasp of his fancied rival: the latter, disturbed from his prey, caught up his lantern, turned its light full upon Antonio, and drawing his sword, made a furious assault; luckily the student saw the light gleam along the blade, and parried the thrust with the stiletto. A fierce but unequal combat ensued. Antonio fought exposed to the full glare of the light, while his antagonist was in shadow. His stiletto, too, was but a poor defence against a rapier. He saw that nothing would save him but closing with his adversary and getting within his weapon; he rushed furiously upon him, and gave him a severe blow with the stiletto; but received a wound in return from the shortened sword. At the same moment a blow was inflicted from behind, by the confederate, who had ascended the ladder; it felled him to the floor, and his antagonists made their escape.

By this time the cries of Inez had brought her father and the domestic to the room. Antonio was found weltering in his blood, and senseless. He was conveyed to the chamber of the alchymist, who now repaid in kind the attentions which the student had once bestowed upon him. Among his varied knowledge he possessed some skill in surgery, which at this moment was of more value than even his chymical lore. He stanched and dressed the wounds of his disciple, which on examination proved less desperate than he had at first apprehended. For a few days, however, his case was anxious, and attended with danger. The old man watched over him with the affection of a parent. He felt a double debt of gratitude towards him on account of his daughter and himself; he loved him too as a faithful and zealous disciple; and he dreaded lest the world should be deprived of the promising talents of so aspiring an alchymist.

An excellent constitution soon medicined his wounds; and there was a balsam in the looks and words of Inez, that had a healing effect on still severer wounds which he carried in his heart. She displayed the strongest interest in his safety; she called him her deliverer, her preserver. It seemed as if her grateful disposition sought, in the warmth of its acknowledgments, to repay him for past coldness. But what most contributed to Antonio's recovery, was her explanation concerning his supposed rival. It was some time since he had first beheld her at church, and he had ever since persecuted her with his attentions. He had beset her in her walks, until she had been obliged to confine herself to the house, except when accompanied by her father. He had besieged her with letters, serenades, and every art by which he could urge a vehement, but clandestine and dishonourable suit. The scene in the garden was as much of a surprise to her as to Antonio. Her persecutor had been attracted by her voice, and had found his way over a ruined part of the wall. He had come upon her unawares; was detaining her by force, and pleading his insulting passion, when the appearance of the student interrupted him, and enabled her to make her escape. She had forborne to mention to her father the persecution which she suffered; she wished to spare him unavailing anxiety and distress, and had determined to confine herself more rigorously to the house; though it appeared that even here she had not been safe from his daring enterprise.

Antonio inquired whether she knew the name of this impetuous admirer? She replied, that he had made his advances under a fictitious name; but that she had heard him once called by the name of Don Ambrosio de Loxa.

Antonio knew him, by report, for one of the most determined and dangerous libertines in all Grenada. Artful, accomplished, and, if he chose to be so, insinuating; but daring and headlong in the pursuit of his pleasures; violent and implacable in his resentments. He rejoiced to find that Inez had been proof against his seductions, and had been inspired with aversion by his splendid profligacy; but he trembled to think of the dangers she had run, and he felt solicitude about the dangers that must yet environ her.

At present, however, it was probable the enemy had a temporary quietus. The traces of blood had been found for some distance from the ladder, until they were lost among thickets; and as nothing had been heard or seen of him since, it was concluded that he had been seriously wounded.

As the student recovered from his wounds, he was enabled to join Inez and her father in their domestic intercourse. The chamber in which they usually met had probably been a saloon of state in former times. The floor was of marble; the walls partially covered with remains of tapestry; the chairs, richly carved and gilt, were crazed with age, and covered with tarnished and tattered brocade. Against the wall hung a long, rusty rapier, the only relique that the old man retained of the chivalry of his ancestors. There might have been something to provoke a smile in the contrast between the mansion and its inhabitants; between present poverty and the traces of departed grandeur; but the fancy of the student had thrown so much romance about the edifice and its inmates, that every thing was clothed with charms. The philosopher, with his broken-down pride, and his strange pursuits, seemed to comport with the melancholy ruin he inhabited; and there was a native elegance of spirit about the daughter, that showed she would have graced the mansion in its happier days.

What delicious moments were these to the student! Inez was no longer coy and reserved. She was naturally artless and confiding; though the kind of persecution she had experienced from one admirer had rendered her, for a time, suspicious and circumspect towards the other. She now felt an entire confidence in the sincerity and worth of Antonio, mingled with an overflowing gratitude. When her eyes met his, they beamed with sympathy and kindness; and Antonio, no longer haunted by the idea of a favoured rival, once more aspired to success.

At these domestic meetings, however, he had little opportunity of paying his court, except by looks. The alchymist supposing him, like himself, absorbed in the study of alchymy, endeavoured to cheer the tediousness of his recovery by long conversations on the art. He even brought several of his half-burnt volumes, which the student had once rescued from the flames, and rewarded him for their preservation, by reading copious passages. He would entertain him with the great and good acts of Flamel, which he effected through means of the philosopher's stone, relieving widows and orphans, founding hospitals, building churches, and what not; or with the interrogatories of King Kalid, and the answers of Morienus, the Roman hermit of Hierusalem; or the profound questions which Elardus, a necromancer of the province of Catalonia, put to the Devil, touching the secrets of alchymy, and the Devil's replies.

All these were couched in occult language, almost unintelligible to the unpractised ear of the disciple. Indeed, the old man delighted in the mystic phrases and symbolical jargon in which the writers that have treated of alchymy have wrapped their communications; rendering them incomprehensible except to the initiated. With what rapture would he elevate his voice at a triumphant passage, announcing the grand discovery! "Thou shalt see," would he exclaim in the words of Henry Kuhnrade,* "the stone of the philosophers (our king) go forth of the bedchamber of his glassy sepulchre into the theatre of this world; that is to say, regenerated and made perfect, a shining carbuncle, a most temperate splendour, whose most subtle and depurated parts are inseparable, united into one with a concordial mixture, exceeding equal, transparent as chrystal, shining red like a ruby, permanently colouring or ringing, fixt in all temptations or tryals; yea, in the examination of the burning sulphur itself, and the devouring waters, and in the most vehement persecution of the fire, always incombustible and permanent as a salamander!"

The student had a high veneration for the fathers of alchymy, and a profound respect for his instructor; but what was Henry Kuhnrade, Geber, Lully, or even Albertus Magnus himself, compared to the countenance of Inez, which presented such a page of beauty to his perusal? While, therefore, the good alchymist was doling out knowledge by the hour, his disciple would forget books, alchymy, every thing but the lovely object before him. Inez, too, unpractised in the science of the heart, was gradually becoming fascinated by the silent attentions of her lover. Day by day she seemed more and more perplexed by the kindling and strangely pleasing emotions of her bosom. Her eye was often cast down in thought. Blushes stole to her cheek without any apparent cause, and light, half-suppressed sighs, would follow these short fits of musing. Her little ballads, though the same that she had always sung, yet breathed a more tender spirit. Either the tones of her voice were more soft and touching, or some passages were delivered with a feeling which she had never before given them. Antonio, besides his love for the abstruse sciences, had a pretty turn for music; and never did philosopher touch the guitar more tastefully. As, by degrees, he conquered the mutual embarrassment that kept them asunder, he ventured to accompany Inez in some of her songs. He had a voice full of fire and tenderness; as he sang, one would have thought, from the kindling blushes of his companion, that he had been pleading his own passion in her ear. Let those who would keep two youthful hearts asunder beware of music. Oh! this leaning over chairs, and conning the same music book, and entwining of voices, and melting away in harmonies! – the German waltz is nothing to it.

The worthy alchymist saw nothing of all this. His mind could admit

---

* Amphitheatre of the Eternal Wisdom.

of no idea that was not connected with the discovery of the grand arcanum, and he supposed his youthful coadjutor equally devoted. He was a mere child as to human nature; and, as to the passion of love, whatever he might once have felt of it, he had long since forgotten that there was such an idle passion in existence. But, while he dreamed, the silent amour went on. The very quiet and seclusion of the place were favourable to the growth of romantic passion. The opening bud of love was able to put forth leaf by leaf, without an adverse wind to check its growth. There was neither officious friendship to chill by its advice, nor insidious envy to wither by its sneers, nor an observing world to look on and stare it out of countenance. There was neither declaration, nor vow, nor any other form of Cupid's canting school. Their hearts mingled together, and understood each other without the aid of language. They lapsed into the full current of affection, unconscious of its depth, and thoughtless of the rocks that might lurk beneath its surface. Happy lovers! who wanted nothing to make their feliciy complete, but the discovery of the philosopher's stone!

At length Antonio's health was sufficiently restored to enable him to return to his lodgings in Grenada. He felt uneasy, however, at leaving the tower, while lurking danger might surround its almost defenceless inmates. He dreaded lest Don Ambrosio, recovered from his wounds, might plot some new attempt, by secret art, or open violence. From all that he had heard, he knew him to be too implacable to suffer his defeat to pass unavenged, and too rash and fearless, when his arts were unavailing, to stop at any daring deed in the accomplishment of his purposes. He urged his apprehensions to the alchymist and his daughter, and proposed that they should abandon the dangerous vicinity of Grenada.

"I have relations," said he, "in Valentia, poor indeed, but worthy and affectionate. Among them you will find friendship and quiet, and we may there pursue our labours unmolested." He went on to paint the beauties and delights of Valentia with all the fondness of a native, and all the eloquence with which a lover paints the fields and groves which he is picturing as the future scenes of his happiness. His eloquence, backed by the apprehensions of Inez, was successful with the alchymist, who, indeed, had led too unsettled a life to be particular about the place of his residence; and it was determined, that, as soon as Antonio's health was perfectly restored, they should abandon the tower, and seek the delicious neighbourhood of Valentia*

* Here are the strongest silks, the sweetest wines, the excellent'st almonds, the best oyls and beautifull'st females of all Spain. The very bruit animals make themselves beds of rosemary, and other fragrant flowers hereabouts; and when one is

To recruit his strength, the student suspended his toils in the laboratory, and spent the few remaining days, before departure, in taking a farewell look at the enchanting environs of Grenada. He felt returning health and vigour as he inhaled the pure temperate breezes that play about its hills; and the happy state of his mind contributed to his rapid recovery. Inez was often the companion of his walks. Her descent, by the mother's side, from one of the ancient Moorish families, gave her an interest in this once favourite seat of Arabian power. She gazed with enthusiasm upon its magnificent monuments, and her memory was filled with the traditional tales and ballads of Moorish chivalry. Indeed the solitary life she had led, and the visionary turn of her father's mind, had produced an effect upon her character, and given it a tinge of what, in modern days, would be termed romance. All this was called into full force by this new passion; for, when a woman first begins to love, life is all romance to her.

In one of their evening strolls, they had ascended to the mountain of the Sun, where is situated the Generaliffe, the palace of pleasure, in the days of Moorish dominion, but now a gloomy convent of capuchins. They had wandered about its garden, among groves of orange, citron, and cypress, where the waters, leaping in torrents, or gushing in fountains, or tossed aloft in sparkling jets, fill the air with music and freshness. There is a melancholy mingled with all the beauties of this garden, that gradually stole over the feelings of the lovers. The place is full of the sad story of past times. It was the favourite abode of the lovely queen of Grenada, where she was surrounded by the delights of a gay and voluptuous court. It was here, too, amidst her own bowers of roses, that her slanderers laid the base story of her dishonour, and struck a fatal blow to the line of the gallant Abencerrages.

The whole garden has a look of ruin and neglect. Many of the fountains are dry and broken; the streams have wandered from their marble channels, and are choked by weeds and yellow leaves. The reed whistles to the wind where it had once sported among roses, and shaken perfume from the orange blossom. The convent bell flings its sullen sound, or the drowsy vesper hymn floats along these solitudes, which once resounded with the song, and the dance, and the lover's serenade. Well may the Moors lament over the loss of this earthly paradise; well may they

---

at sea, if the winde blow from the shore, he may smell this soyl before he come in sight of it many leagues off, by the strong oderiferous scent it casts. As it is the most pleasant, so it is also the temperat'st clime of all Spain, and they commonly call it the second Italy, which made the Moors, whereof many thousands were disterr'd, and banish'd hence to Barbary, to think that Paradise was in that part of the heavens which hung over this citie.   HOWELL'S LETTERS.

remember it in their prayers, and beseech heaven to restore it to the faithful; well may their ambassadors smite their breasts when they behold these monuments of their race, and sit down and weep among the fading glories of Grenada!

It is impossible to wander about these scenes of departed love and gaiety, and not feel the tenderness of the heart awakened. It was then that Antonio first ventured to breathe his passion, and to express by words what his eyes had long since so eloquently revealed. He made his avowal with fervour, but with frankness. He had no gay prospects to hold out: he was a poor scholar, dependent on his "good spirits to feed and clothe him." But a woman in love is no interested calculator. Inez listened to him with downcast eyes, but in them was a humid gleam that showed her heart was with him. She had no prudery in her nature; and she had not been sufficiently in society to acquire it. She loved him with all the absence of worldliness of a genuine woman; and, amidst timid smiles and blushes, he drew from her a modest acknowledgment of her affection.

They wandered about the garden with that sweet intoxication of the soul which none but happy lovers know. The world about them was all fairy land; and, indeed, it spread forth one of its fairest scenes before their eyes, as if to fulfil their dream of earthly happiness. They looked out from between groves of orange upon the towers of Grenada below them; the magnificent plain of the Vega beyond, streaked with evening sunshine, and the distant hills tinted with rosy and purple hues; it seemed an emblem of the happy future that love and hope were decking out for them.

As if to make the scene complete, a group of Andalusians struck up a dance, in one of the vistas of the garden, to the guitars of two wandering musicians. The Spanish music is wild and plaintive, yet the people dance to it with spirit and enthusiasm. The picturesque figures of the dancers; the girls with their hair in silken nets that hung in knots and tassels down their backs, their mantillas floating round their graceful forms, their slender feet peeping from under their basquinas, their arms tossed up in the air to play the castanets, had a beautiful effect on this airy height, with the rich evening landscape spreading out below them.

When the dance was ended, two of the parties approached Antonio and Inez; one of them began a soft and tender Moorish ballad, accompanied by the other on the lute. It alluded to the story of the garden, the wrongs of the fair queen of Grenada, and the misfortunes of the Abencerrages. It was one of those old ballads that abound in this part of Spain, and live, like echoes, about the ruins of Moorish greatness. The heart of Inez was at that moment open to every tender impression; the tears rose into her eyes as she listened to the tale. The singer approached nearer to her; she was striking in her appearance; young, beautiful, with a mixture of wildness and melancholy in her fine black eyes. She fixed them mournfully and expressively on Inez, and suddenly varying her manner, sang another ballad, which treated of impending danger and treachery. All this might have passed for a mere accidental caprice of the singer, had there not been something in her look, manner, and gesticulation, that made it pointed and startling.

Inez was about to ask the meaning of this evidently personal application of the song, when she was interrupted by Antonio, who gently drew her from the place. Whilst she had been lost in attention to the music, he had remarked a group of men, in the shadows of the trees, whispering together. They were enveloped in the broad hats and great cloaks, so much worn by the Spanish, and while they were regarding himself and Inez attentively, seemed anxious to avoid observation. Not knowing what might be their character or intention, he hastened to quit a place where the gathering shadows of evening might expose them to intrusion and insult. On their way down the hill, as they passed through the woods of elms, mingled with poplars and oleanders, that skirts the road leading from the Alhambra, he again saw these men, apparently following at a distance; and he afterwards caught sight of them among the trees on the banks of the Darro. He said nothing on the subject to Inez, nor her father, for he would not awaken unnecessary alarm; but he felt at a loss how to ascertain or to avert any machinations that might be devising against the helpless inhabitants of the tower.

He took his leave of them late at night, full of this perplexity. As he left the dreary old pile, he saw some one lurking in the shadow of the wall, apparently watching his movements. He hastened after the figure, but it glided away, and disappeared among some ruins. Shortly after he heard a low whistle, which was answered from a little distance. He had no longer a doubt but that some mischief was on foot, and turned to hasten back to the tower, and put its inmates on their guard. He had scarcely turned, however, before he found himself suddenly seized from behind by some one of Herculean strength. His struggles were in vain; he was surrounded by armed men. One threw a mantle over him that stifled his cries, and enveloped him in its folds; and he was hurried off with irresistible rapidity.

The next day passed without the appearance of Antonio at the alchymist's. Another, and another day succeeded, and yet he did not come; nor had any thing been heard of him at his lodgings. His absence caused, at first, surprise and conjecture, and at length alarm. Inez recollected the singular intimations of the ballad-singer upon the mountain, which seemed to warn her of impending danger, and her mind was full of vague forebodings. She sat listening to every sound at the gate, or footstep on the stairs. She would take up her guitar and strike a few notes, but it would not do; her heart was sickening with suspense and anxiety. She had never before felt what it was to be really lonely. She now was conscious of the force of that attachment which had taken possession of her breast; for never do we know how much we love, never do we know how necessary the object of our love is to our happiness, until we experience the weary void of separation.

The philosopher, too, felt the absence of his disciple almost as sensibly as did his daughter. The animating buoyancy of the youth had inspired him with new ardour, and had given to his labours the charm of full companionship. However, he had resources and consolations of which his daughter was destitute. His pursuits were of a nature to occupy every thought, and keep the spirits in a state of continual excitement. Certain indications, too, had lately manifested themselves, of the most favourable nature. Forty days and forty nights had the process gone on successfully; the old man's hopes were constantly rising, and he now considered the glorious moment once more at hand, when he should obtain not merely the major lunaria, but likewise the tinctura solaris, the means of multiplying gold, and of prolonging existence. He remained, therefore, continually shut up in his laboratory, watching his furnace; for a moment's inadvertency might once more defeat all his expectations.

He was sitting one evening at one of his solitary vigils, wrapped up in meditation; the hour was late, and his neighbour, the owl, was hooting from the battlement of the tower, when he heard the door open behind him. Supposing it to be his daughter coming to take her leave of him for the night, as was her frequent practice, he called her by name, but a harsh voice met his ear in reply. He was grasped by the arms, and looking up, perceived three strange men in the chamber. He attempted to shake them off, but in vain. He called for help, but they scoffed at his cries.

"Peace, dotard!" cried one, "think'st thou the servants of the most holy inquistion are to be daunted by thy clamours? Comrades, away with him!"

Without heeding his remonstrances and entreaties, they seized upon his books and papers, took some note of the apartment and the utensils, and then bore him off a prisoner.

Inez, left to herself, had passed a sad and lonely evening; seated by a casement which looked into the garden, she had pensively watched star after star sparkle out of the blue depths of the sky, and was indulging a crowd of anxious thoughts about her lover, until the rising tears began to flow. She was suddenly alarmed by the sound of voices that seemed to come from a distant part of the mansion. There was not long after a noise of several persons descending the stairs. Surprised at these unusual sounds in their lonely habitation, she remained for a few moments in a state of trembling, yet indistinct apprehension, when the servant rushed into the room, with terror in her countenance, and informed her that her father was carried off by armed men.

Inez did not stop to hear further, but flew down stairs to overtake them. She had scarcely passed the threshold, when she found herself in the grasp of strangers. – "Away! – away!" cried she, wildly; "do not stop me – let me follow my father."

"We come to conduct you to him, senora," said one of the men, respectfully.

"Where is he, then?"

"He is gone to Grenada," replied the man: "an unexpected circumstance requires his presence there immediately; but he is among friends."

"We have no friends in Grenada," said Inez, drawing back; but then the idea of Antonio rushed into her mind; something relating to him might have called her father thither. "Is senor Antonio de Castros with him?" demanded she with agitation.

"I know not, senora," replied the man. "It is very possible. I only know that your father is among friends, and is anxious for you to follow him."

"Let us go, then," cried she, eagerly. The men led her a little distance to where a mule was waiting, and, assisting her to mount, they conducted her slowly towards the city.

Grenada was on that evening a scene of fanciful revel. It was one of the festivals of the Maestranza, an association of the nobility to keep up some of the gallant customs of ancient chivalry. There had been a representation of a tournament in one of the squares; the streets would still occasionally resound with the beat of a solitary drum, or the bray of a trumpet, from some straggling party of revellers. Sometimes they were met by cavaliers, richly dressed in ancient costumes, attended by their squires, and at one time they passed in sight of a palace brilliantly illuminated, from whence came the mingled sounds of music and the dance. Shortly after they came to the square, where the mock tournament had been held. It was thronged by the populace, recreating themselves among booths and stalls where refreshments were sold, and the glare of torches showed the temporary galleries, and gay-coloured awnings, and armorial trophies, and other paraphernalia of the show. The conductors of Inez endeavoured to keep out of observation, and to traverse a gloomy part of the square; but they were detained at one place by the pressure of a crowd surrounding a party of wandering musicians, singing one of those ballads of which the Spanish populace are so passionately fond. The torches which were held by some of the crowd, threw a strong mass of light upon Inez, and the sight of so beautiful a being, without mantilla or veil, looking so bewildered, and conducted by men, who seemed to take no gratification in the surrounding gaiety, occasioned expressions of curiosity. One of the ballad-singers approached, and striking her guitar with peculiar earnestness, began to sing a doleful air, full of sinister forebodings. Inez started with surprise. It was the same ballad-singer that had addressed her in the garden of Generaliffe. It was the same air that she had then sung. It spoke of impending dangers; they seemed, indeed, to be thickening around her. She was anxious to speak with the girl, and to ascertain whether she really had a knowledge of any definite evil that was threatening her; but as she attempted to address her, the mule, on which she rode, was suddenly seized, and led forcibly through the throng by one of her conductors, while she saw another addressing menacing words to the ballad-singer. The latter raised her hand with a warning gesture as Inez lost sight of her.

While she was yet lost in perplexity, caused by this singular occurrence, they stopped at the gate of a large mansion. One of her attendants knocked, the door was opened, and they entered a paved court. "Where are we?" demanded Inez, with anxiety. "At the house of a friend, senora," replied the man. "Ascend this staircase with me, and in a moment you will meet your father."

They ascended a staircase that led to a suite of splendid apartments. They passed through several until they came to an inner chamber. The door opened, some one approached; but what was her terror at perceiving, not her father, but Don Ambrosio!

The men who had seized upon the alchymist had, at least, been more honest in their professions. They were, indeed, familiars of the inquisition. He was conducted in silence to the gloomy prison of that horrible tribunal. It was a mansion whose very aspect withered joy, and almost shut out hope. It was one of those hideous abodes which the bad passions of men conjure up in this fair world, to rival the fancied dens of demons and the accursed.

Day after day went heavily by without any thing to mark the lapse of time, but the decline and re-appearance of the light that feebly glimmered through the narrow window of the dungeon, in which the unfortunate alchymist was buried, rather than confined. His mind was harassed with uncertainties and fears about his daughter, so helpless and inexperienced. He endeavoured to gather tidings of her from the man who brought his daily portion of food. The fellow stared, as if astonished, at being asked a question in that mansion of silence and mystery, but departed without saying a word. Every succeeding attempt was equally fruitless.

The poor alchymist was oppressed by many griefs; and it was not the least that he had been again interrupted in his labours on the very point of success. Never was alchymist so near attaining the golden secret – a little longer, and all his hopes would have been realized. The thoughts of these disappointments afflicted him more even than the fear of all that he might suffer from the merciless inquisition. His waking thoughts would follow him into his dreams. He would be transported in fancy to his laboratory, busied again among retorts and alembics, and surrounded by Lully, by D'Abano, by Olybius, and the other masters of the sublime art. The moment of projection would arrive; a seraphic form would rise out of the furnace, holding forth a vessel, containing the precious elixir; but, before he could grasp the prize, he would awake, and find himself in a dungeon.

All the devices of inquisitorial ingenuity were employed to ensnare the old man, and to draw from him evidence that might be brought against himself, and might corroborate certain secret information that had been given against him. He had been accused of practising necromancy and judicial astrology, and a cloud of evidence had been secretly brought forward to substantiate the charge. It would be tedious to enumerate all the circumstances, apparently corroborative, which had been industriously cited by the secret accuser. The silence which prevailed about the tower, its desolateness, the very quiet of its inhabitants, had been adduced as proofs that something sinister was perpetrated within. The alchymist's conversations and soliloquies in the garden had been overheard and misrepresented. The lights and strange appearances at night, in the tower, were given with violent exaggerations. Shrieks and yells were said to have been heard from thence at midnight, when, it was confidently asserted, the old man raised familiar spirits by his incantations, and even compelled the dead to rise from their graves, and answer to his questionings.

The alchymist, according to the custom of the inquisition, was kept in complete ignorance of his accuser; of the witnesses produced against him; even of the crimes of which he was accused. He was examined generally, whether he knew why he was arrested, and was conscious of any guilt that might deserve the notice of the holy office? He was examined as to his country, his life, his habits, his pursuits, his actions, and opinions. The old man was frank and simple in his replies; he was conscious of no guilt, capable of no art, practised in no dissimulation. After receiving a general admonition to bethink himself whether he had not committted any act deserving of punishment, and to prepare, by confession, to secure the well-known mercy of the tribunal, he was remanded to his cell.

He was now visited in his dungeon by crafty familiars of the inquisition; who, under pretence of sympathy and kindness, came to beguile the tediousness of his imprisonment with friendly conversation. They casually introduced the subject of alchymy, on which they touched with great caution and pretended indifference. There was no need of such craftiness. The honest enthusiast had no suspicion in his nature: the moment they touched upon his favourite theme, he forgot his misfortunes and imprisonment, and broke forth into rhapsodies about the divine science.

The conversation was artfully turned to the discussion of elementary beings. The alchymist readily avowed his belief in them; and that there had been instances of their attending upon philosophers, and administering to their wishes. He related many miracles said to have been performed by Apollonius Thyaneus through the aid of spirits or demons; insomuch that he was set up by the heathens in opposition to the Messiah; and was even regarded with reverence by many Christians. The familiars eagerly demanded whether he believed Apollonius to be a true and worthy philosopher. The unaffected piety of the alchymist protected him even in the midst of his simplicity, for he condemned Apollonius as a sorcerer and an impostor. No art could draw from him an admission that he had ever employed or invoked spiritual agencies in the prosecution of his pursuits, though he believed himself to have been frequently impeded by their invisible interference.

The inquisitors were sorely vexed at not being able to enveigle him into a confession of a criminal nature; they attributed their failure to craft, to obstinacy, to every cause but the right one, namely, that the harmless visionary had nothing guilty to confess. They had abundant proof of a secret nature against him; but it was the practice of the inquisition to endeavour to procure confession from the prisoners. An auto da fé was at hand; the worthy fathers were eager for his conviction, for they were always anxious to have a good number of culprits condemned to the stake, to grace these solemn triumphs. He was at length brought to a final examination.

The chamber of trial was spacious and gloomy. At one end was a huge crucifix, the standard of the inquisition. A long table extended through the centre of the room, at which sat the inquisitors and their secretary; at the other end a stool was placed for the prisoner.

He was brought in, according to custom, bare-headed and bare-legged. He was enfeebled by confinement and affliction; by constantly brooding over the unknown fate of his child, and the disastrous interruption of his experiments. He sat bowed down and listless; his head sunk upon his breast; his whole appearance that of one "past hope, abandoned, and by himself given over."

The accusation alleged against him was now brought forward in a specific form; he was called upon by name, Felix de Vasquez, formerly of Castile, to answer to the charges of necromancy and demonology. He was told that the charges were amply substantiated; and was asked whether he was ready, by full confession, to throw himself upon the well-known mercy of the holy inquisition.

The philosopher testified some slight surprise at the nature of the accusation, but simply replied, "I am innocent."

"What proof have you to give of your innocence?"

"It rather remains for you to prove your charges," said the old man. "I am a stranger and a sojourner in the land, and know no one out of the doors of my dwelling. I can give nothing in my vindication but the word of a nobleman and a Castilian."

The inquisitor shook his head, and went on to repeat the various inquiries that had before been made as to his mode of life and pursuit. The poor alchymist was too feeble and too weary at heart to make any but brief replies. He requested that some man of science might examine his laboratory, and all his books and papers, by which it would be made abundantly evident that he was merely engaged in the study of alchymy.

To this the inquisitor observed, that alchymy had become a mere covert for secret and deadly sins. That the practisers of it were apt to scruple at no means to satisfy their inordinate greediness of gold. Some had been known to use spells and impious ceremonies; to conjure the aid of evil spirits; nay, even to sell their souls to the enemy of mankind, so that they might riot in boundless wealth while living.

The poor alchymist had heard all patiently, or, at least, passively. He had disdained to vindicate his name otherwise than by his word; he had smiled at the accusations of sorcery, when applied merely to himself; but when the sublime art, which had been the study and passion of his life, was assailed, he could no longer listen in silence. His head gradually rose from his bosom; a hectic colour came in faint streaks to his cheek; played about there, disappeared, returned, and at length kindled into a burning glow. The clammy dampness dried from his forehead; his eyes, which had been nearly extinguished, lighted up again, and burned with their wonted and visionary fires. He entered into a vindication of his

favourite art. His voice at first was feeble and broken; but it gathered
strength as he proceeded, until it rolled in a deep and sonorous volume.
He gradually rose from his seat as he rose with his subject; he threw
back the scanty black mantle which had hitherto wrapped his limbs;
the very uncouthness of his form and looks gave an impressive effect to
what he uttered; it was as though a corpse had become suddenly
animated.

He repelled with scorn the aspersions cast upon alchymy by the
ignorant and vulgar. He affirmed it to be the mother of all art and
science, citing the opinions of Paracelsus, Sandivogius, Raymond
Lully, and others, in support of his assertions. He maintained that it
was pure and innocent, and honourable both in its purposes and
means. What were its objects? The perpetuation of life and youth, and
the production of gold. "The elixir vitæ," said he, "is no charmed potion,
but merely a concentration of those elements of vitality which nature
has scattered through her works. The philosopher's stone, or tincture, or
powder, as it is variously called, is no necromantic talisman, but consists
simply of those particles which gold contains within itself for its
reproduction; for gold, like other things, has its seed within itself, though
bound up with inconceivable firmness, from the vigour of innate fixed
salts and sulphurs. In seeking to discover the elixir of life, then," continued he, "we seek only to apply some of nature's own specifics against
the disease and decay to which our bodies are subjected; and what
else does the physician, when he tasks his art, and uses subtle compounds and cunning distillations to revive our languishing powers, and
avert the stroke of death for a season?

"In seeking to multiply the precious metals, also, we seek but to
germinate and multiply, by natural means, a particular species of nature's
productions; and what else does the husbandman, who consults times
and seasons, and, by what might be deemed a natural magic, from the
mere scattering of his hand, covers a whole plain with golden vegetation? The mysteries of our art, it is true, are deeply and darkly hidden;
but it requires so much the more innocence and purity of thought to
penetrate unto them. No, father! the true alchymist must be pure in
mind and body; he must be temperate, patient, chaste, watchful, meek,
humble, devout. 'My son,' says Hermes Trismegestes, the great master
of our art, 'My son, I recommend you above all things to fear God'.
And indeed it is only by devout castigation of the senses and purification
of the soul, that the alchymist is enabled to enter into the sacred chambers of truth. 'Labour, pray, and read,' is the motto of our science. As
De Nuysement well observes, 'these high and singular favours are
granted unto none, save only unto the sons of God (that is to say,

the virtuous and devout), who, under his paternal benediction, have obtained the opening of the same, by the helping hand of the queen of arts, divine Philosophy.' Indeed, so sacred has the nature of this knowledge been considered, that we are told it has four times been expressly communicated by God to man, having made a part of that cabalistical wisdom which was revealed to Adam to console him for the loss of Paradise; and to Moses in the bush, and to Solomon in a dream, and to Esdras by the angel.

"So far from demons and malign spirits being the friends and abettors of the alchymist, they are the continual foes with which he has to contend. It is their constant endeavour to shut up the avenues to those truths which would enable him to rise above the abject state into which he has fallen, and return to that excellence which was his original birthright. For what would be the effect of this length of days, and this abundant wealth, but to enable the possessor to go on from art to art, from science to science, with energies unimpaired by sickness, uninterrupted by death? For this have sages and philosophers shut themselves up in cells and solitudes; buried themselves in caves and dens of the earth; turning from the joys of life, and the pleasance of the world; enduring scorn, poverty, persecution. For this was Raymond Lully stoned to death in Mauritania. For this did the immortal Pietro D'Abano suffer persecution at Padua, and when he escaped from his oppressors by death, was despitefully burnt in effigy. For this have illustrious men of all nations intrepidly suffered martyrdom. For this, if unmolested, have they assiduously employed the latest hour of life, the expiring throb of existence; hoping to the last that they might yet seize upon the prize for which they had struggled, and pluck themselves back even from the very jaws of the grave!

"For, when once the alchymist shall have attained the object of his toils; when the sublime secret shall be revealed to his gaze, how glorious will be the change in his condition! How will he emerge from his solitary retreat, like the sun breaking forth from the darksome chamber of the night, and darting his beams throughout the earth! Gifted with perpetual youth and boundless riches, to what heights of wisdom may he attain! How may he carry on, uninterrupted, the thread of knowledge, which has hitherto been snapped at the death of each philosopher! And, as the increase of wisdom is the increase of virtue, how may he become the benefactor of his fellow-men; dispensing with liberal, but cautious and discriminating hand, that inexhaustible wealth which is at his disposal; banishing poverty, which is the cause of so much sorrow and wickedness; encouraging the arts; promoting discoveries, and enlarging all the means of virtuous enjoyment! His life will be the connecting band of generations. History will live in his recollection; distant ages will speak with his tongue. The nations of the earth will look to him as their preceptor, and kings will sit at his feet and learn wisdom. Oh glorious! Oh celestial alchymy!" –

Here he was interrupted by the inquisitor, who had suffered him to go on thus far, in hopes of gathering something from his unguarded enthusiasm. "Senor," said he, "this is all rambling, visionary talk. You are charged with sorcery, and in defence you give us a rhapsody about alchymy. Have you nothing better than this to offer in your defence?"

The old man slowly resumed his seat, but did not deign a reply. The fire that had beamed in his eye gradually expired. His cheek resumed its wonted paleness; but he did not relapse into inanity. He sat with a steady, serene, patient look, like one prepared not to contend but to suffer.

His trial continued for a long time, with cruel mockery of justice, for no witnesses were ever, in this court, confronted with the accused, and the latter had continually to defend himself in the dark. Some unknown and powerful enemy had alleged charges against the unfortunate alchymist, but who he could not imagine. Stranger and sojourner as he was in the land; solitary and harmless in his pursuits, how could he have provoked such hostility? The tide of secret testimony, however, was too strong against him; he was convicted of the crime of magic, and condemned to expiate his sins at the stake, at the approaching auto da fé.

While the unhappy alchymist was undergoing his trial at the inquisition, his daughter was exposed to trials no less severe. Don Ambrosio, into whose hands she had fallen, was, as has before been intimated, one of the most daring and lawless profligates in all Grenada. He was a man of hot blood and fiery passions, who stopped at nothing in the gratification of his desires; yet with all this he possessed manners, address, and accomplishments, that had made him eminently successful among the sex. From the palace to the cottage he had extended his amorous enterprises; his serenades harassed the slumbers of half the husbands of Grenada; no balcony was too high for his adventurous attempts; nor any cottage too lowly for his perfidious seductions. Yet he was as fickle as he was ardent; success had made him vain and capricious; he had no sentiment to attach him to the victim of his arts, and many a pale cheek and fading eye, languishing amidst the sparkling of jewels; and many a breaking heart, throbbing under the rustic boddice, bore testimony to his triumphs and his faithlessness.

He was sated, however, by easy conquests, and wearied of a life of continual and prompt gratification. There had been a degree of difficulty and enterprise in the pursuit of Inez, that he had never before experienced. It had aroused him from the monotony of mere sensual life, and stimulated him with the charm of adventure. He had become an epicure in pleasure; and now that he had this coy beauty in his power, he was determined to protract his enjoyment, by the gradual conquest of her scruples, and downfall of her virtue. He was vain of his person and address, which he thought no woman could long withstand; and it was a kind of trial of skill, to endeavour to gain by art and fascination, what he was secure of obtaining at any time by violence.

When Inez, therefore, was brought into his presence by his emissaries, he affected not to notice her terror and surprise; but received her with formal and stately courtesy. He was too wary a fowler to flutter the bird when just entangled in the net. To her eager and wild inquiries about her father, he begged her not to be alarmed; that he was safe, and had been there, but was engaged elsewhere in an affair of moment, from which he would soon return; in the mean time he had left word, that she should await his return in patience. After some stately expressions of general civility, Don Ambrosio made a ceremonious bow and retired.

The mind of Inez was full of trouble and perplexity. The stately formality of Don Ambrosio was so unexpected as to check the accusations and reproaches that were springing to her lips. Had he had evil designs, would he have treated her with such frigid ceremony when he had her in his power? But why, then, was she brought to his house? Was not the mysterious disappearance of Antonio connected with this? A thought suddenly darted into her mind. Antonio had again met with Don Ambrosio – they had fought – Antonio was wounded – perhaps dying! – It was him to whom her father had gone. – It was at his request that Don Ambrosio had sent for them to soothe his dying moments! These, and a thousand such horrible suggestions harassed her mind; but she tried in vain to get information from the domestics; they knew nothing but that her father had been there, had gone, and would soon return.

Thus passed a night of tumultuous thought and vague yet cruel apprehensions. She knew not what to do, or what to believe: whether she ought to fly, or to remain; but if to fly, how was she to extricate herself? and where was she to seek her father? As the day dawned without any intelligence of him, her alarm increased; at length a message was brought from him, saying that circumstances prevented his return to her, but begging her to hasten to him without delay.

With an eager and throbbing heart did she set forth with the men that were to conduct her. She little thought, however, that she was merely changing her prison-house. Don Ambrosio had feared lest she should be traced to his residence in Grenada; or that he might be interrupted there before he could accomplish his plan of seduction. He had her now conveyed, therefore, to a mansion which he possessed in one of the mountain solitudes in the neighbourhood of Grenada; a lonely, but beautiful retreat. In vain, on her arrival, did she look around for her father, or Antonio; none but strange faces met her eye; menials profoundly respectful, but who knew nor saw any thing but what their master pleased.

She had scarcely arrived before Don Ambrosio made his appearance, less stately in his manner, but still treating her with the utmost delicacy and deference. Inez was too much agitated and alarmed to be baffled by his courtesy, and became vehement in her demand to be conducted to her father.

Don Ambrosio now put on an appearance of the greatest embarrassment and emotion. After some delay, and much pretended confusion, he at length confessed that the seizure of her father was all a stratagem; a mere false alarm to procure him the present opportunity of having access to her, and endeavouring to mitigate that obduracy, and conquer that repugnance, which he declared had almost driven him to distraction.

He assured her that her father was again at home in safety, and occupied in his usual pursuits; having been fully satisfied that his daughter was in honourable hands, and would soon be restored to him. It was in vain that she threw herself at his feet, and implored to be set at liberty; he only replied, by gentle entreaties, that she would pardon the seeming violence he had to use; and that she would trust a little while to his honour. "You are here," said he, "absolute mistress of every thing; nothing shall be said or done to offend you; I will not even intrude upon your ear the unhappy passion that is devouring my heart. Should you require it, I will even absent myself from your presence; but to part with you entirely at present, with your mind full of doubts and resentments, would be worse than death to me. No, beautiful Inez, you must first know me a little better, and know by my conduct, that my passion for you is as delicate and respectful as it is vehement."

The assurance of her father's safety had relieved Inez from one cause of torturing anxiety, only to render her fears the more violent on her own account. Don Ambrosio, however, continued to treat her with artful deference, that insensibly lulled her apprehensions. It is true she found herself a captive, but no advantage appeared to be taken of her helplessness. She soothed herself with the idea that a little while would suffice to convince Don Ambrosio of the fallacy of his hopes, and that he would be induced to restore her to her home. Her transports of terror and affliction, therefore, subsided, in a few days, into a passive, yet anxious melancholy, with which she awaited the hoped-for event.

In the mean while all those artifices were employed that are calculated to charm the senses, ensnare the feelings, and dissolve the heart into tenderness. Don Ambrosio was a master of the subtil arts of seduction. His very mansion breathed an enervating atmosphere of languor and delight. It was here, amidst twilight saloons and dreamy chambers, buried among groves of orange and myrtle, that he shut himself up at times from the prying world, and gave free scope to the gratification of his pleasures.

The apartments were furnished in the most sumptuous and voluptuous manner; the silken couches swelled to the touch, and sunk in downy softness beneath the slightest pressure. The paintings and statues all told some classic tale of love, managed, however, with an insidious delicacy; which, while it banished the grossness that might disgust, was the more calculated to excite the imagination. There the blooming Adonis was seen, not breaking away to pursue the boisterous chase, but crowned with flowers, and languishing in the embraces of celestial beauty. There Acis wooed his Galatea in the shade, with the Sicilian sea spreading in halcyon serenity before them. There were depicted groups of fauns and dryads, fondly reclining in summer bowers, and listening to the liquid piping of the reed; or the wanton satyrs surprising some wood-nymph during her noontide slumber. There, too, on the storied tapestry, might be seen the chaste Diana, stealing, in the mystery of moonlight, to kiss the sleeping Endymion; while Cupid and Psyche, entwined in immortal marble, breathed on each other's lips the early kiss of love.

The ardent rays of the sun were excluded from these balmy halls; soft and tender music from unseen musicians floated around, seeming to mingle with the perfumes that were exhaled from a thousand flowers. At night, when the moon shed a fairy light over the scene, the tender serenade would rise from among the bowers of the garden, in which the fine voice of Don Ambrosio might often be distinguished; or the amorous flute would be heard along the mountain, breathing in its pensive cadences the very soul of a lover's melancholy.

Various entertainments were also devised to dispel her loneliness, and to charm away the idea of confinement. Groups of Andalusian dancers performed, in the splendid saloons, the various picturesque dances of their country; or represented little amorous ballets, which turned upon some pleasing scene of pastoral coquetry and courtship.

Sometimes there were bands of singers, who, to the romantic guitar, warbled forth ditties full of passion and tenderness.

Thus all about her enticed to pleasure and voluptuousness; but the heart of Inez turned with distaste from this idle mockery. The tears would rush into her eyes as her thoughts reverted from this scene of profligate splendour, to the humble but virtuous home from whence she had been betrayed; or if the witching power of music ever soothed her into a tender reverie, it was to dwell with fondness on the image of Antonio. But if Don Ambrosio, deceived by this transient calm, should attempt at such time to whisper his passion, she would start as from a dream, and recoil from him with involuntary shuddering.

She had passed one long day of more than ordinary sadness, and in the evening a band of these hired performers were exerting all the animating powers of song and dance to amuse her. But while the lofty saloon resounded with their warblings, and the light sound of feet upon its marble pavement kept time to the cadence of the song, poor Inez, with her face buried in the silken couch on which she reclined, was only rendered more wretched by the sound of gaiety.

At length her attention was caught by the voice of one of the singers, that brought with it some indefinite recollections. She raised her head, and cast an anxious look at the performers, who, as usual, were at the lower end of the saloon. One of them advanced a little before the others. It was a female, dressed in a fanciful, pastoral garb, suited to the character she was sustaining; but her countenance was not to be mistaken. It was the same ballad-singer that had twice crossed her path, and given her mysterious intimations of the lurking mischief that surrounded her. When the rest of the performances were concluded, she seized a tambourine, and tossing it aloft, danced alone to the melody of her own voice. In the course of her dancing she approached to where Inez reclined; and as she struck the tambourine, contrived, dexterously, to throw a folded paper on the couch. Inez seized it with avidity, and concealed it in her bosom. The singing and dancing were at an end; the motley crew retired; and Inez, left alone, hastened with anxiety to unfold the paper thus mysteriously conveyed. It was written in an agitated, and almost illegible, hand-writing; "Be on your guard! you are surrounded by treachery. Trust not to the forbearance of Don Ambrosio; you are marked out for his prey. An humble victim to his perfidy gives you this warning; she is encompassed by too many dangers to be more explicit. – Your father is in the dungeons of the inquisition!"

The brain of Inez reeled as she read this dreadful scroll. She was less filled with alarm at her own danger, than horror at her father's situation. The moment Don Ambrosio appeared, she rushed and threw herself at his feet, imploring him to save her father. Don Ambrosio started with astonishment; but immediately regaining his self-possession, endeavoured to soothe her by his blandishments, and by assurances that her father was in safety. She was not to be pacified; her fears were too much aroused to be trifled with. She declared her knowledge of her father's being a prisoner of the inquisition, and reiterated her frantic supplications that he would save him.

Don Ambrosio paused for a moment in perplexity, but was too adroit to be easily confounded. "That your father is a prisoner," replied he, "I have long known. I have concealed it from you, to save you from fruitless anxiety. You now know the real reason of the restraint I have put upon your liberty; I have been protecting instead of detaining you. Every exertion has been made in your father's favour; but I regret to say, the proofs of the offences of which he stands charged have been too strong to be controverted. Still," added he, "I have it in my power to save him; I have influence, I have means at my beck; it may involve me, it is true, in difficulties, perhaps in disgrace; but what would I not do in the hopes of being rewarded by your favour? Speak, beautiful Inez," said he, his eyes kindling with sudden eagerness, "it is with you to say the word that seals your father's fate. One kind word, say but you will be mine, and you will behold me at your feet, your father at liberty and in affluence, and we shall all be happy!"

Inez drew back from him with scorn and disbelief. "My father," exclaimed she, "is too innocent and blameless to be convicted of crime; this is some base, some cruel artifice!" Don Ambrosio repeated his asseverations, and with them also his dishonourable proposals; but his eagerness overshot its mark; her indignation and her incredulity were alike awakened by his base suggestions; and he retired from her presence checked and awed by the sudden pride and dignity of her demeanour.

The unfortunate Inez now became a prey to the most harrowing anxieties. Don Ambrosio saw that the mask had fallen from his face, and that the nature of his machinations was revealed. He had gone too far to retrace his steps, and assume the affectation of tenderness and respect; indeed he was mortified and incensed at her insensibility to his attractions, and now only sought to subdue her through her fears. He daily represented to her the dangers that threatened her father, and that it was in his power alone to avert them. Inez was still incredulous. She was too ignorant of the nature of the inquisition to know that even innocence was not always a protection from its cruelties; and she confided too surely in the virtue of her father to believe that any accusation could prevail against him.

At length, Don Ambrosio, to give an effectual blow to her confidence, brought her the proclamation of the approaching auto da fé, in which the prisoners were enumerated. She glanced her eye over it, and beheld her father's name, condemned to the stake for sorcery.

For a moment she stood transfixed with horror. Don Ambrosio seized upon the transient calm. "Think, now, beautiful Inez," said he, with a tone of affected tenderness, "his life is still in your hands; one word from you, one kind word, and I can yet save him."

"Monster! wretch!" cried she, coming to herself, and recoiling from him with insuperable abhorrence: "'tis you that are the cause of this – 'tis you that are his murderer!" Then, wringing her hands, she broke forth into exclamations of the most frantic agony.

The perfidious Ambrosio saw the torture of her soul, and anticipated from it a triumph. He saw that she was in no mood, during her present paroxysm, to listen to his words; but he trusted that the horrors of lonely rumination would break down her spirit, and subdue her to his will. In this, however, he was disappointed. Many were the vicissitudes of mind of the wretched Inez; one time she would embrace his knees with piercing supplications; at another she would shrink with nervous horror at his very approach; but any intimation of his passion only excited the same emotion of loathing and detestation.

At length the fatal day drew nigh. "To-morrow," said Don Ambrosio, as he left her one evening, "To-morrow is the auto da fé. To-morrow you will hear the sound of the bell that tolls your father to his death. You will almost see the smoke that rises from his funeral pile. I leave you to yourself. It is yet in my power to save him. Think whether you can stand to-morrow's horrors without shrinking. Think whether you can endure the after-reflection, that you were the cause of his death, and that merely through a perversity in refusing proffered happiness."

What a night was it to Inez! Her heart, already harassed and almost broken by repeated and protracted anxieties; her strength wasted and enfeebled. On every side horrors awaited her; her father's death, her own dishonour; there seemed no escape from misery or perdition. "Is there no relief from man – no pity in heaven?" exclaimed she. "What – what have we done that we should be thus wretched?"

As the dawn approached, the fever of her mind arose to agony; a thousand times did she try the doors and windows of her apartment, in the desperate hope of escaping. Alas! with all the splendour of her prison, it was too faithfully secured for her weak hands to work deliverance. Like a poor bird, that beats its wings against its gilded cage, until it sinks panting in despair, so she threw herself on the floor in hopeless anguish. Her blood grew hot in her veins, her tongue was parched, her temples throbbed with violence, she gasped rather than breathed; it seemed as if her brain was on fire. "Blessed Virgin!" exclaimed she, clasping her hands and turning up her strained eyes, "look down with pity, and support me in this dreadful hour!"

Just as the day began to dawn, she heard a key turn softly in the door of her apartment. She dreaded lest it should be Don Ambrosio; and the very thought of him gave her a sickening pang. It was a female, clad in a rustic dress, with her face concealed by her mantilla. She stepped silently into the room, looked cautiously round, and then, uncovering her face, revealed the well-known features of the ballad-singer. Inez uttered an exclamation of surprise, almost of joy. The unknown started back, pressed her finger on her lips enjoining silence, and beckoned her to follow. She hastily wrapped herself in her veil and obeyed. They passed with quick but noiseless steps through an antechamber, across a spacious hall, and along a corridor; all was silent; the household was yet locked in sleep. They came to a door, to which the unknown applied a key. Inez' heart misgave her; she knew not but some new treachery was menacing her; she laid her cold hand on the stranger's arm: "Whither are you leading me?" said she. "To liberty," replied the other, in a whisper.

"Do you know the passages about this mansion?"

"But too well!" replied the girl, with a melancholy shake of the head. There was an expression of sad veracity in her countenance that was not to be distrusted. The door opened on a small terrace, which was overlooked by several windows of the mansion.

"We must move across this quickly," said the girl, "or we may be observed."

They glided over it as if scarce touching the ground. A flight of steps led down into the garden; a wicket at the bottom was readily unbolted: they passed with breathless velocity along one of the alleys, still in sight of the mansion, in which, however, no person appeared to be stirring. At length they came to a low private door in the wall, partly hidden by a fig-tree. It was secured by rusty bolts, that refused to yield to their feeble efforts.

"Holy Virgin!" exclaimed the stranger, "what is to be done? one moment more, and we may be discovered."

She seized a stone that lay near by: a few blows, and the bolts flew back; the door grated harshly as they opened it, and the next moment they found themselves in a narrow road.

"Now," said the stranger, "for Grenada as quickly as possible! The nearer we approach it, the safer we shall be; for the road will be more frequented."

The imminent risk they ran of being pursued and taken gave super-natural strength to their limbs; they flew rather than ran. The day had dawned; the crimson streaks on the edge of the horizon gave tokens of the approaching sunrise; already the light clouds that floated in the western sky were tinged with gold and purple; though the broad plain of the Vega, which now began to open upon their view, was covered with the dark haze of morning. As yet they only passed a few straggling peasants on the road, who could have yielded them no assistance in case of their being overtaken. They continued to hurry forward, and had gained a considerable distance, when the strength of Inez, which had only been sustained by the fever of her mind, began to yield to fatigue. She slackened her pace, and faltered.

"Alas!" said she, "my limbs fail me! I can go no further!" "Bear up, bear up," replied her companion cheeringly; "a little further and we shall be safe: look! yonder is Grenada, just showing itself in the valley below us. A little further, and we shall come to the main road, and then we shall find plenty of passengers to protect us."

Inez, encouraged, made fresh efforts to get forward, but her weary limbs were unequal to the eagerness of her mind; her mouth and throat were parched by agony and terror; she gasped for breath, and leaned for support against a rock. "It is all in vain!" exclaimed she; "I feel as though I should faint."

"Lean on me," said the other; "let us get into the shelter of yon thicket, that will conceal us from the view; I hear the sound of water, which will refresh you."

With much difficulty they reached the thicket, which overhung a small mountain stream, just where its sparkling waters leaped over the rock and fell into a natural basin. Here Inez sank upon the ground exhausted. Her companion brought water in the palms of her hands, and bathed her pallid temples. The cooling drops revived her; she was enabled to get to the margin of the stream, and drink of its crystal current; then, reclining her head on the bosom of her deliverer, she was first enabled to murmur forth her heartfelt gratitude.

"Alas!" said the other, "I deserve no thanks; I deserve not the good opinion you express. In me you behold a victim of Don Ambrosio's arts. In early years he seduced me from the cottage of my parents; look! at the foot of yonder blue mountain in the distance lies my native village; but it is no longer a home for me. From thence he lured me when I was too young for reflection; he educated me, taught me various accomplish-ments, made me sensible to love, to splendour, to refinement; then, having grown weary of me, he neglected me, and cast me upon the world. Happily the accomplishments he taught me have kept me from utter want; and the love with which he inspired me has kept me from further degradation. Yes! I confess my weakness; all his perfidy and wrongs cannot efface him from my heart. I have been brought up to love him; I have no other idol; I know him to be base, yet I cannot help adoring him. I am content to mingle among the hireling throng that administer to his amusements, that I may still hover about him, and linger in those halls where I once reigned mistress. What merit, then, have I in assisting your escape? I scarce know whether I am acting from sympathy, and a desire to rescue another victim from his power; or jealousy, and an eagerness to remove too powerful a rival!"

While she was yet speaking, the sun rose in all its splendour; first lighting up the mountain summits, then stealing down height by height, until its rays gilded the domes and towers of Grenada, which they could partially see from between the trees, below them. Just then the heavy tones of a bell came sounding from a distance, echoing, in sullen clang, along the mountain. Inez turned pale at the sound. She knew it to be the great bell of the cathedral, rung at sunrise on the day of the auto da fé, to give note of funeral preparation. Every stroke beat upon her heart, and inflicted an absolute, corporeal pang. She started up wildly. "Let us be gone!" cried she; "there is not a moment for delay!"

"Stop!" exclaimed the other, "yonder are horsemen coming over the brow of that distant height; if I mistake not, Don Ambrosio is at their head. – Alas! 'tis he; we are lost. Hold!" continued she, "give me your scarf and veil; wrap yourself in this mantilla. I will fly up yon foot-path that leads to the heights. I will let the veil flutter as I ascend; perhaps they may mistake me for you, and they must dismount to follow me. Do you hasten forward – you will soon reach the main road. You have jewels on your fingers; bribe the first muleteer you meet to assist you on your way."

All this was said with hurried and breathless rapidity. The exchange of garments was made in an instant. The girl darted up the mountain-path, her white veil fluttering among the dark shrubbery; while Inez, inspired with new strength, or rather new terror, flew to the road, and trusted to Providence to guide her tottering steps to Grenada.

All Grenada was in agitation on the morning of this dismal day. The heavy bell of the cathedral continued to utter its clanging tones, that pervaded every part of the city, summoning all persons to the tremendous spectacle that was about to be exhibited. The streets through which the procession was to pass were crowded with the populace. The windows, the roofs, every place that could admit a face or a foothold, was alive with spectators. In the great square a spacious scaffolding, like an amphitheatre, was erected, where the sentences of the prisoners were to be read, and the sermon of faith to be preached; and close by were the stakes prepared, where the condemned were to be burnt to death. Seats were arranged for the great, the gay, the beautiful; for such is the horrible curiosity of human nature, that this cruel sacrifice was attended with more eagerness than a theatre, or even a bull feast.

As the day advanced, the scaffolds and balconies were filled with expecting multitudes; the sun shone brightly upon fair faces and gallant dresses; one would have thought it some scene of elegant festivity, instead of an exhibition of human agony and death. But what a different spectacle and ceremony was this from those which Grenada exhibited in the days of her Moorish splendour. "Her galas, her tournaments, her sports of the ring, her fêtes of St. John, her music, her Zambras, and admirable tilts of canes! Her serenades, her concerts, her songs in Generaliffe! The costly liveries of the Abencerrages, their exquisite inventions, the skill and valour of the Alabaces, the superb dresses of the Zegries, Mazas, and Gomeles!"* – All these were at an end. The days of chivalry were over. Instead of the prancing cavalcade, with neighing steed and lively trumpet; with burnished lance, and helm, and buckler; with rich confusion of plume, and scarf, and banner, where purple, and scarlet, and green, and orange, and every gay colour were mingled with cloth of gold and fair embroidery; instead of this crept on the gloomy pageant of superstition, in cowl and sackcloth; with cross and coffin, and frightful symbols of human suffering. In place of the frank, hardy knight, open and brave, with his lady's favour in his casque, and amorous motto on his shield, looking, by gallant deeds, to win the smile of beauty, came the shaven, unmanly monk, with downcast eyes, and head and heart bleached in the cold cloister, secretly exulting in this bigot triumph.

The sound of the bells gave notice that the dismal procession was advancing. It passed slowly through the principal streets of the city, bearing in advance the awful banner of the holy office. The prisoners walked singly, attended by confessors, and guarded by familiars of the inquisition. They were clad in different garments, according to the nature of their punishments; those who were to suffer death wore the hideous Samarra, painted with flames and demons. The procession was swelled by choirs of boys, by different religious orders and public dignitaries, and, above all, by the fathers of the faith, moving "with slow pace, and profound gravity, truly triumphing, as becomes the principal generals of that great victory."†

* Rodd's Civil Wars of Grenada.
† Gonsalvius, p. 135.

As the sacred banner of the inquisition advanced, the countless throng sunk on their knees before it; they bowed their faces to the very earth as it passed, and then slowly rose again, like a great undulating billow. A murmur of tongues prevailed as the prisoners approached, and eager eyes were strained, and fingers pointed, to distinguish the different orders of penitents, whose habits denoted the degree of punishment they were to undergo. But as those drew near whose frightful garb marked them as destined to the flames, the noise of the rabble subsided; they seemed almost to hold in their breaths; filled with that strange and dismal interest with which we contemplate a human being on the verge of suffering and death.

It is an awful thing – a voiceless, noiseless multitude! The hushed and gazing stillness of the surrounding thousands, heaped on walls, and gates, and roofs, and hanging, as it were, in clusters, heightened the effect of the pageant that moved drearily on. The low murmuring of the priests could now be heard in prayer and exhortation, with the faint responses of the prisoners, and now and then the voices of the choir at a distance, chanting the litanies of the saints.

The faces of the prisoners were ghastly and disconsolate. Even those who had been pardoned, and wore the Sanbenito, or penitential garment, bore traces of the horrors they had undergone. Some were feeble and tottering from long confinement; some crippled and distorted by various tortures; every countenance was a dismal page, on which might be read the secrets of their prison-house. But in the looks of those condemned to death there was something fierce and eager. They seemed men harrowed up by the past, and desperate as to the future. They were anticipating, with spirits fevered by despair, and fixed and clenched determination, the vehement struggle with agony and death which they were shortly to undergo. Some cast now and then a wild and anguished look about them upon the shining day; the "sun-bright palaces," the gay, the beautiful world, which they were soon to quit for ever; or a glance of sudden indignation at the thronging thousands, happy in liberty and life, who seemed, in contemplating their frightful situation, to exult in their own comparative security.

One among the condemned, however, was an exception to these remarks. It was an aged man, somewhat bowed down, with a serene, though dejected countenance, and a beaming, melancholy eye. It was the alchymist. The populace looked upon him with a degree of compassion, which they were not prone to feel towards criminals condemned by the inquisition; but when they were told that he was convicted of the crime of magic, they drew back with awe and abhorrence.

The procession had reached the grand square. The first part had already mounted the scaffolding, and the condemned were approaching. The press of the populace became excessive, and was repelled, as it were, in billows by the guards. Just as the condemned were entering the square, a shrieking was heard among the crowd. A female, pale, frantic, dishevelled, was seen struggling through the multitude. "My father! my father!" was all the cry she uttered, but it thrilled through every heart. The crowd instinctively drew back, and made way for her as she advanced.

The poor alchymist had made his peace with Heaven, and, by hard struggle, had closed his heart upon the world, when the voice of his child called him once more back to worldly thought and agony. He turned towards the well-known voice; his knees smote together; he endeavoured to stretch forth his pinioned arms, and felt himself clasped in the embraces of his child. The emotions of both were too agonizing for utterance. Convulsive sobs, and broken exclamations, and embraces more of anguish than tenderness, were all that passed between them. The procession was interrupted for a moment. The astonished monks and familiars were filled with involuntary respect at this agony of natural affection. Ejaculations of pity broke from the crowd, touched by the filial piety, the extraordinary and hopeless anguish of so young and beautiful a being.

Every attempt to soothe her, and prevail on her to retire, was unheeded; at length they endeavoured to separate her from her father by force. The movement roused her from her temporary abandonment. With a sudden paroxysm of fury, she snatched a sword from one of the familiars. Her late pale countenance was flushed with rage, and fire flashed from her once soft and languishing eyes. The guards shrunk back with awe. There was something in this filial frenzy, this feminine tenderness wrought up to desperation, that touched even their hardened hearts. They endeavoured to pacify her, but in vain. Her eye was eager and quick as the she-wolf's guarding her young. With one arm she pressed her father to her bosom, with the other she menaced every one that approached.

The patience of the guards was soon exhausted. They had held back in awe, but not in fear. With all her desperation the weapon was soon wrested from her feeble hand, and she was borne shrieking and struggling among the crowd. The rabble murmured compassion; but such was the dread inspired by the inquisition, that no one attempted to interfere.

The procession again resumed its march. Inez was ineffectually struggling to release herself from the hands of the familiars that detained her, when suddenly she saw Don Ambrosio before her. "Wretched girl!" exclaimed he with fury, "why have you fled from your friends? Deliver her," said he to the familiars, "to my domestics; she is under my protection."

His creatures advanced to seize her. "Oh no! oh no!" cried she, with new terrors, and clinging to the familiars, "I have fled from no friends. He is not my protector! He is the murderer of my father!"

The familiars were perplexed; the crowd pressed on with eager curiosity. "Stand off!" cried the fiery Ambrosio, dashing the throng from around him. Then turning to the familiars, with sudden moderation, "My friends," said he, "deliver this poor girl to me. Her distress has turned her brain; she has escaped from her friends and protectors this morning; but a little quiet and kind treatment will restore her to tranquillity."

"I am not mad! I am not mad!" cried she vehemently. "Oh, save me! – save me from these men! I have no protector on earth but my father, and him they are murdering!"

The familiars shook their heads; her wildness corroborated the assertions of Don Ambrosio, and his apparent rank commanded respect and belief. They relinquished their charge to him, and he was consigning the struggling Inez to his creatures. –

"Let go your hold, villain!" cried a voice from among the crowd, and Antonio was seen eagerly tearing his way through the press of people.

"Seize him! seize him!" cried Don Ambrosio to the familiars: "'tis an accomplice of the sorcerer's."

"Liar!" retorted Antonio, as he thrust the mob to the right and left, and forced himself to the spot.

The sword of Don Ambrosio flashed in an instant from the scabbard; the student was armed, and equally alert. There was a fierce clash of weapons; the crowd made way for them as they fought, and closed again, so as to hide them from the view of Inez. All was tumult and confusion for a moment; when there was a kind of shout from the spectators, and the mob again opening, she beheld, as she thought, Antonio weltering in his blood.

This new shock was too great for her already overstrained intellects. A giddiness seized upon her; every thing seemed to whirl before her eyes; she gasped some incoherent words, and sunk senseless upon the ground.

Days – weeks elapsed before Inez returned to consciousness. At length she opened her eyes, as if out of a troubled sleep. She was lying upon a magnificent bed, in a chamber richly furnished with pier glasses and massive tables inlaid with silver, of exquisite workmanship. The walls were covered with tapestry; the cornices richly gilded: through the door, which stood open, she perceived a superb saloon, with statues and crystal lustres, and a magnificent suite of apartments beyond. The casements of the room were open to admit the soft breath of summer, which stole in, laden with perfumes from a neighbouring garden; from whence, also, the refreshing sound of fountains and the sweet notes of birds came in mingled music to her ear.

Female attendants were moving, with noiseless step, about the chamber; but she feared to address them. She doubted whether this were not all delusion, or whether she was not still in the palace of Don Ambrosio, and that her escape, and all its circumstances, had not been but a feverish dream. She closed her eyes again, endeavouring to recall the past, and to separate the real from the imaginary. The last scenes of consciousness, however, rushed too forcibly, with all their horrors, to her mind to be doubted, and she turned shuddering from the recollection, to gaze once more on the quiet and serene magnificence around her. As she again opened her eyes, they rested on an object that at once dispelled every alarm. At the head of her bed sat a venerable form watching over her with a look of fond anxiety – it was her father!

I will not attempt to describe the scene that ensued; nor the moments of rapture which more than repaid all the sufferings that her affectionate heart had undergone. As soon as their feelings had become more calm, the alchymist stepped out of the room to introduce a stranger, to whom he was indebted for his life and liberty. He returned, leading in Antonio, no longer in his poor scholar's garb, but in the rich dress of a nobleman.

The feelings of Inez were almost overpowered by these sudden reverses, and it was some time before she was sufficiently composed to comprehend the explanation of this seeming romance.

It appeared that the lover, who had sought her affections in the lowly guise of a student, was only son and heir of a powerful grandee of Valentia. He had been placed at the university of Salamanca; but a lively curiosity and an eagerness for adventure had induced him to abandon the university, without his father's consent, and to visit various parts of Spain. His rambling inclination satisfied, he had remained incognito for a time at Grenada, until, by further study and self-regulation, he could prepare himself to return home with credit, and atone for his transgressions against paternal authority.

How hard he had studied does not remain on record. All that we know is his romantic adventure of the tower. It was at first a mere youthful caprice, excited by a glimpse of a beautiful face. In becoming a disciple of the alchymist, he probably thought of nothing more than pursuing a light love-affair. Further acquaintance, however, had completely fixed his affections; and he had determined to conduct Inez and her father to Valentia, and to trust to her merits to secure his father's consent to their union.

In the mean time he had been traced to his concealment. His father had received intelligence of his being entangled in the snares of a mysterious adventurer and his daughter, and likely to become the dupe of the fascinations of the latter. Trusty emissaries had been despatched to seize upon him by main force, and convey him without delay to the paternal home.

What eloquence he had used with his father to convince him of the innocence, the honour, and the high descent of the alchymist, and of the exalted worth of his daughter, does not appear. All that we know is, that the father, though a very passionate, was a very reasonable man, as appears by his consenting that his son should return to Grenada, and conduct Inez, as his affianced bride, to Valentia.

Away, then, Don Antonio hurried back, full of joyous anticipations. He still forbore to throw off his disguise, fondly picturing to himself what would be the surprise of Inez, when, having won her heart and hand as a poor wandering scholar, he should raise her and her father at once to opulence and splendour.

On his arrival he had been shocked at finding the tower deserted by its inhabitants. In vain he sought for intelligence concerning them; a mystery hung over their disappearance which he could not penetrate, until he was thunderstruck, on accidentally reading a list of the prisoners at the impending auto da fé, to find the name of his venerable master among the condemned.

It was the very morning of the execution. The procession was already on its way to the grand square. Not a moment was to be lost. The grand inquisitor was a relation of Don Antonio, though they had never met. His first impulse was to make himself known; to exert all his family influence, the weight of his name, and the power of his eloquence, in vindication of the alchymist. But the grand inquisitor was already proceeding, in all his pomp, to the place where the fatal ceremony was to be performed. How was he to be approached? Antonio threw himself into the crowd, in a fever of anxiety, and was forcing his way to the scene of horror, when he arrived just in time to rescue Inez, as has been mentioned.

It was Don Ambrosio that fell in their contest. Being desperately wounded, and thinking his end approaching, he had confessed, to an attending father of the inquisition, that he was the sole cause of the alchymist's condemnation, and that the evidence on which it was grounded was altogether false. The testimony of Don Antonio came in corroboration of this avowal; and his relationship to the grand inquisitor had, in all probability, its proper weight. Thus was the poor alchymist snatched, in a manner, from the very flames; and so great had been the sympathy awakened in his case, that for once a populace rejoiced at being disappointed of an execution.

The residue of the story may readily be imagined by every one versed in this valuable kind of history. Don Antonio espoused the lovely Inez, and took her and her father with him to Valentia. As she had been a loving and dutiful daughter, so she proved a true and tender wife. It was not long before Don Antonio succeeded to his father's titles and estates, and he and his fair spouse were renowned for being the handsomest and happiest couple in all Valentia.

As to Don Ambrosio, he partially recovered to the enjoyment of a broken constitution and a blasted name, and hid his remorse and disgraces in a convent; while the poor victim of his arts, who had assisted Inez in her escape, unable to conquer the early passion that he had awakened in her bosom, though convinced of the baseness of the object, retired from the world, and became a humble sister in a nunnery.

The worthy alchymist took up his abode with his children. A pavilion, in the garden of their palace, was assigned to him as a laboratory, where he resumed his researches, with renovated ardour, after the grand secret. He was now and then assisted by his son-in-law; but the latter slackened grievously in his zeal and diligence, after marriage. Still he would listen with profound gravity and attention to the old man's rhapsodies, and his quotations from Paracelsus, Sandivogius, and Pietro D'Abano, which daily grew longer and longer. In this way the good alchymist lived on quietly and comfortably, to what is called a good old age, that is to say, an age that is good for nothing, and, unfortunately for mankind, was hurried out of life in his ninetieth year, just as he was on the point of discovering the philosopher's stone.

Such was the story of the captain's friend, with which we whiled away the morning. The captain was, every now and then, interrupted by questions and remarks, which I have not mentioned, lest I should break the continuity of the tale. He was a little disturbed, also, once or twice, by the general, who fell asleep, and breathed rather hard, to the great horror and annoyance of Lady Lillycraft. In a long and tender love-scene, also, which was particularly to her ladyship's taste, the unlucky general, having his head a little sunk upon his breast,

kept making a sound at regular intervals, very much like the word *pish*,
long drawn out. At length he made an odd abrupt guttural sound, that
suddenly awoke him; he hemmed, looked about with a slight degree
of consternation, and then began to play with her ladyship's work-bag,
which, however, she rather pettishly withdrew. The steady sound of
the captain's voice was still too potent a soporific for the poor general;
he kept gleaming up and sinking in the socket, until the cessation of
the tale again roused him, when he started awake, put his foot down
upon Lady Lillycraft's cur, the sleeping Beauty, which yelped, and
seized him by the leg, and, in a moment, the whole library resounded
with yelpings and exclamations. Never did a man more completely
mar his fortunes while he was asleep. Silence being at length restored,
the company expressed their thanks to the captain, and gave various
opinions of the story. The parson's mind, I found, had been continually
running upon the leaden manuscripts, mentioned in the beginning, as
dug up at Grenada, and he put several eager questions to the captain
on the subject. The general could not well make out the drift of the
story, but thought it a little confused. "I am glad, however," said he,
"that they burnt the old chap of the tower; I have no doubt he was
a notorious imposter."

END OF VOL. I

BRACEBRIDGE HALL

Volume II

ENGLISH COUNTRY GENTLEMEN

His certain life, that never can deceive him,
  Is full of thousand sweets, and rich content;
The smooth-leav'd beeches in the field receive him
  With coolest shade, till noontide's heat be spent.
His life is neither tost in boist'rous seas,
Or the vexatious world; or lost in slothful ease.
Pleased and full blest he lives, when he his God can please.

PHINEAS FLETCHER

I take great pleasure in accompanying the squire in his perambulations about his estate, in which he is often attended by a kind of cabinet council. His prime minister, the steward, is a very worthy and honest old man, that assumes a right of way; that is to say, a right to have his own way, from having lived time out of mind on the place. He loves the estate even better than he does the squire; and thwarts the latter sadly in many of his projects of improvement, being a little prone to disapprove of every plan that does not originate with himself.

In the course of one of these perambulations, I have known the squire to point out some important alteration which he was contemplating, in the disposition or cultivation of the grounds; this of course would be opposed by the steward, and a long argument would ensue over a stile, or on a rising piece of ground, until the squire, who has a high opinion of the other's ability and integrity, would be fain to give up the point. This concession, I observed, would immediately mollify the old man, and, after walking over a field or two in silence, with his hands behind his back, chewing the cud of reflection, he would suddenly turn to the squire and observe, that "he had been turning the matter over in his mind, and, upon the whole, he believed he would take his honour's advice."

Christy, the huntsman, is another of the squire's occasional attendants, to whom he continually refers in all matters of local history, as to a chronicle of the estate, having, in a manner, been acquainted with many of the trees from the very time that they were acorns. Old Nimrod, as has been shown, is rather pragmatical in those points of knowledge on which he values himself; but the squire rarely contradicts him, and is, in fact, one of the most indulgent potentates that ever was hen-pecked by his ministry.

He often laughs about it himself, and evidently yields to these old men more from the bent of his own humour, than from any want of proper authority. He likes this honest independence of old age, and is well aware that these trusty followers love and honour him in their hearts. He is perfectly at ease about his own dignity and the respect of those around him; nothing disgusts him sooner than any appearance of fawning or sycophancy.

I really have seen no display of royal state that could compare with one of the squire's progresses about his paternal fields and through his hereditary woodlands, with several of these faithful adherents about him, and followed by a body-guard of dogs. He encourages a frankness and manliness of deportment among his dependents, and is the personal friend of his tenants; inquiring into their concerns, and assisting them in times of difficulty and hardship. This has rendered him one of the most popular, and of course one of the happiest of landlords.

Indeed, I do not know a more enviable condition of life, than that of an English gentleman, of sound judgment and good feelings, who passes the greater part of his time on an hereditary estate in the country. From the excellence of the roads and the rapidity and exactness of the public conveyances, he is enabled to command all the comforts and conveniences, all the intelligence and novelties of the capital, while he is removed from its hurry and distraction. He has ample means of occupation and amusement within his own domains; he may diversify his time by rural occupations, by rural sports, by study, and by the delights of friendly society collected within his own hospitable halls.

Or if his views and feelings are of a more extensive and liberal nature, he has it greatly in his power to do good, and to have that good immediately reflected back upon himself. He can render essential service to his country, by assisting in the disinterested administration of the laws; by watching over the opinions and principles of the lower orders around him; by diffusing among them those lights which may be important to their welfare; by mingling frankly among them, gaining their confidence, becoming the immediate auditor of their complaints, informing himself of their wants, making himself a channel through which their grievances may be quietly communicated to the proper sources of mitigation and relief; or by becoming, if need be, the intrepid and incorruptible guardian of their liberties – the enlightened champion of their rights.

All this, it appears to me, can be done without any sacrifice of personal dignity, without any degrading arts of popularity, without any truckling to vulgar prejudices, or concurrence in vulgar clamour; but by the steady influence of sincere and friendly counsel, of fair, upright, and generous deportment. Whatever may be said of English mobs and English demagogues, I have never met with a people more open to reason, more considerate in their tempers, more tractable by argument in the roughest times, than the English. They are remarkably quick at discerning and appreciating whatever is manly and honourable. They are by nature and habit methodical and orderly: and they feel the value of all that is regular and respectable. They may occasionally be deceived by sophistry, and excited into turbulence by public distresses and the misrepresentations of designing men; but open their eyes, and they will eventually rally round the land-marks of steady truth and deliberate good sense. They are fond of established customs, they are fond of long established names, and that love of order and quiet which characterizes the nation, gives a vast influence to the descendants of the old families, whose forefathers have been lords of the soil from time immemorial.

It is when the rich and well-educated and highly privileged classes neglect their duties, when they neglect to study the interests, and conciliate the affections, and instruct the opinions and champion the rights of the people, that the latter become discontented and turbulent, and fall into the hands of demagogues: the demagogue always steps in where the patriot is wanting. There is a common high-handed cant among the high-feeding, and, as they fancy themselves, high-minded men, about putting down the mob; but all true physicians know that it is better to sweeten the blood than attack the tumour, to apply the emollient rather than the cautery. It is absurd in a country like England, where there is so much freedom, and such a jealousy of right, for any man to assume an aristocratical tone, and to talk superciliously of the common people. There is no rank that makes him independent of the opinions and affections of his fellow-men, there is no rank nor distinction that severs him from his fellow-subject; and if, by any gradual neglect or assumption on the one side, and discontent and jealousy on the other, the orders of society should really separate, let those who stand on the eminence beware that the chasm is not mining at their feet. The orders of society in all well constituted governments are mutually bound together, and important to each other; there can be no such thing in a free government as a vacuum; and whenever one is likely to take place, by the drawing off of the rich and intelligent from the poor, the bad passions of society will rush in to fill up the space, and rend the whole asunder.

Though born and brought up in a republic, and more and more confirmed in republican principles by every year's observation and experience, yet I am not insensible to the excellence that may exist in other forms of government, nor to the fact that they may be more suitable to the situation and circumstances of the countries in which they exist: I have endeavoured rather to look at them as they are, and to observe how they are calculated to effect the end which they propose. Considering, therefore, the mixed nature of the government of this country, and its representative form, I have looked with admiration at the manner in which the wealth and influence and intelligence were spread over its whole surface; not as in some monarchies, drained from the country, and collected in towns and cities. I have considered the great rural establishments of the nobility, and the lesser establishments of the gentry, as so many reservoirs of wealth and intelligence distributed about the kingdom, apart from the towns, to irrigate, freshen, and fertilize the surrounding country. I have looked upon them too, as the august retreats of patriots and statesmen, where, in the enjoyment of honourable independence and elegant leisure, they might train up their minds to appear in those legislative assemblies, whose debates and decisions form the study and precedents of other nations, and involve the interests of the world.

I have been both surprised and disappointed, therefore, at finding, that on this subject I was often indulging in an Utopian dream, rather than a well-founded opinion. I have been concerned at finding that these fine estates were too often involved, and mortgaged, or placed in the hands of creditors, and the owners exiled from their paternal lands. There is an extravagance, I am told, that runs parallel with wealth; a lavish expenditure among the great; a senseless competition among the aspiring; a heedless, joyless dissipation, among all the upper ranks, that often beggars even these splendid establishments, breaks down the pride and principles of their possessors, and makes too many of them mere place-hunters, or shifting absentees. It is thus that so many are thrown into the hands of government; and a court, which ought to be the most pure and honourable in Europe, is so often degraded by noble, but importunate time-servers. It is thus, too, that so many become exiles from their native land, crowding the hotels of foreign countries, and expending upon thankless strangers the wealth so hardly drained from their laborious peasantry. I have looked upon these latter with a mixture of censure and concern. Knowing the almost bigoted fondness of an Englishman for his native home, I can conceive what must be their compunction and regret, when, amidst the sunburnt plains of France, they call to mind the green fields of England; the hereditary groves which they have abandoned, and the hospitable roof of their fathers, which they have left desolate, or to be inhabited by strangers. But retrenchment is no plea for an abandonment of country. They have risen with the prosperity of the land; let them abide its fluctuations, and conform to its fortunes. It is not for the rich to fly because the country is suffering: let them share, in their relative proportion, the common lot; they owe it to the land that has elevated them to honour and affluence. When the poor have to diminish their scanty morsel of bread; when they have to compound with the cravings of nature, and study with how little they can do, and not be starved; it is not then for the rich to fly, and diminish still further the resources of the poor, that they themselves may live in splendour in a cheaper country. Let them rather retire to their estates, and there practise retrenchment. Let them return to that noble simplicity, that practical good sense, that honest pride, which form the foundation of true English character, and from them they may again rear the edifice of fair and honourable prosperity.

On the rural habits of the English nobility and gentry; on the manner in which they discharge their duties on their patrimonial possessions, depend greatly the virtue and welfare of the nation. So long as they pass the greater part of their time in the quiet and purity of the country; surrounded by the monuments of their illustrious ancestors; surrounded by every thing that can inspire generous pride, noble emulation, and amiable magnanimous sentiment; so long they are safe, and in them the nation may repose its interests and its honour. But the moment that they become the servile throngers of court avenues, and give themselves up to the political intrigues and heartless dissipations of the metropolis, that moment they lose the real nobility of their natures, and become the mere leeches of the country.

That the great majority of nobility and gentry in England are endowed with high notions of honour and independence, I thoroughly believe. They have evidenced it lately on very important questions, and have given an example of adherence to principle, in preference to party and power, that must have astonished many of the venal and obsequious courts of Europe. Such are the glorious effects of freedom, when infused into a constitution. But it seems to me that they are apt to forget the positive nature of their duties, and to fancy that their eminent privileges are only so many means of self-indulgence. They should recollect, that in a constitution like that of England, the titled orders are intended to be as useful as they are ornamental, and it is their virtues alone that can render them both. Their duties are divided between the sovereign and the subject; surrounding and giving lustre and dignity to the throne, and at the same time tempering and mitigating its rays, until they are transmitted in mild and genial radiance to the people. Born to leisure and opulence, they owe the exercise of their talents, and the expenditure of their wealth, to their native country. They may be compared to the clouds; which, being drawn up by the sun, and ele-

A BACHELOR'S CONFESSIONS

"I'll live a private, pensive, single life."
THE COLLIER OF CROYDON

I was sitting in my room a morning or two since, reading, when some one tapped at the door, and Master Simon entered. He had an unusually fresh appearance; he had put on a bright green riding-coat, with a bunch of violets in the button-hole, and had the air of an old bachelor trying to rejuvenate himself. He had not, however, his usual briskness and vivacity; but loitered about the room with somewhat of absence of manner, humming the old song, – "Go, lovely rose, tell her that wastes her time and me;" and then, leaning against the window, and looking upon the landscape, he uttered a very audible sigh. As I had not been accustomed to see Master Simon in a pensive mood, I thought there might be some vexation preying on his mind, and I endeavoured to introduce a cheerful strain of conversation; but he was not in the vein to follow it up, and proposed that we should take a walk.

It was a beautiful morning of that soft vernal temperature, that seems to thaw all the frost out of one's blood, and to set all nature in a ferment. The very fishes felt its influence; the cautious trout ventured out of his dark hole to seek his mate, the roach and the dace rose up to the surface of the brook to bask in the sunshine, and the amorous frog piped from among the rushes. If ever an oyster can really fall in love, as has been said or sung, it must be on such a morning.

The weather certainly had its effect even upon Master Simon, for he seemed obstinately bent upon the pensive mood. Instead of stepping briskly along, smacking his dog-whip, whistling quaint ditties, or telling sporting anecdotes, he leaned on my arm, and talked about the approaching nuptials; from whence he made several digressions upon the character of womankind, touched a little upon the tender passion, and made sundry very excellent, though rather trite, observations upon disappointments in love. It was evident that he had something on his mind which he wished to impart, but felt awkward in approaching it. I was curious to see to what this strain would lead; but I was determined not to assist him. Indeed, I mischievously pretended to turn the conversation, and talked of his usual topics, dogs, horses, and hunting; but he was very brief in his replies, and invariably got back, by hook or by crook, into the sentimental vein.

At length we came to a clump of trees that overhung a whispering brook, with a rustic bench at their feet. The trees were grievously scored

163

with letters and devices, which had grown out of all shape and size by the growth of the bark; and it appeared that this grove had served as a kind of register of the family loves from time immemorial. Here Master Simon made a pause, pulled up a tuft of flowers, threw them one by one into the water, and at length, turning somewhat abruptly upon me, asked me if I had ever been in love. I confess the question startled me a little, as I am not over fond of making confessions of my amorous follies; and above all should never dream of choosing my friend Master Simon for a confidant. He did not wait, however, for a reply; the inquiry was merely a prelude to a confession on his own part, and after several circumlocutions and whimsical preambles, he fairly disburthened himself of a very tolerable story of his having been crossed in love.

The reader will, very probably, suppose that it related to the gay widow who jilted him not long since at Doncaster races; – no such thing. It was about a sentimental passion that he once had for a most beautiful young lady, who wrote poetry and played on the harp. He used to serenade her; and indeed he described several tender and gallant scenes, in which he was evidently picturing himself in his mind's eye as some elegant hero of romance, though, unfortunately for the tale, I only saw him as he stood before me, a dapper little old bachelor, with a face like an apple that has dried with the bloom on it.

What were the particulars of this tender tale I have already forgotten; indeed I listened to it with a heart like a very pebble stone, having hard work to repress a smile while Master Simon was putting on the amorous swain, uttering every now and then a sigh, and endeavouring to look sentimental and melancholy.

All that I recollect is, that the lady, according to his account, was certainly a little touched; for she used to accept all the music that he copied for her harp, and all the patterns that he drew for her dresses; and he began to flatter himself, after a long course of delicate attentions, that he was gradually fanning up a gentle flame in her heart, when she suddenly accepted the hand of a rich, boisterous, fox-hunting baronet, without either music or sentiment, who carried her by storm, after a fortnight's courtship.

Master Simon could not help concluding by some observation about "modest merit," and the power of gold over the sex. As a remembrance of his passion, he pointed out a heart carved on the bark of one of the trees; but which, in the process of time, had grown out into a large excrescence: and he showed me a lock of her hair, which he wore in a true lover's knot, in a large gold brooch.

I have seldom met with an old bachelor that had not, at some time or other, his nonsensical moment, when he would become tender and sentimental, talk about the concerns of the heart, and have some confession of a delicate nature to make. Almost every man has some little trait of romance in his life, which he looks back to with fondness, and about which he is apt to grow garrulous occasionally. He recollects himself as he was at the time, young and gamesome; and forgets that his hearers have no other idea of the hero of the tale, but such as he may appear at the time of telling it; peradventure, a withered, whimsical, spindle-shanked old gentleman. With married men, it is true, this is not so frequently the case; their amorous romance is apt to decline after marriage; why, I cannot for the life of me imagine; but with a bachelor, though it may slumber, it never dies. It is always liable to break out again in transient flashes, and never so much as on a spring morning in the country; or on a winter evening, when seated in his solitary chamber, stirring up the fire and talking of matrimony.

The moment that Master Simon had gone through his confession, and, to use the common phrase, "had made a clean breast of it," he became quite himself again. He had settled the point which had been worrying his mind, and doubtless considered himself established as a man of sentiment in my opinion. Before we had finished our morning's stroll, he was singing as blithe as a grasshopper, whistling to his dogs, and telling droll stories; and I recollect that he was particularly facetious that day at dinner, on the subject of matrimony, and uttered several excellent jokes, not to be found in Joe Miller, that made the bride elect blush and look down; but set all the old gentlemen at the table in a roar, and absolutely brought tears into the general's eyes.

ENGLISH GRAVITY

"Merrie England!"
ANCIENT PHRASE

There is nothing so rare as for a man to ride his hobby without molestation. I find the squire has not so undisturbed an indulgence in his humours as I had imagined; but has been repeatedly thwarted of late, and has suffered a kind of well-meaning persecution from a Mr. Faddy, an old gentleman of some weight, at least of purse, who has recently moved into the neighbourhood. He is a worthy and substantial manufacturer, who, having accumulated a large fortune by dint of steam-engines and spinning jennies, has retired from business, and set up for a country gentleman. He has taken an old country seat and refitted it, and painted and plastered it, until it looks not unlike his own manufactory. He has been particularly careful in mending the walls and hedges, and putting up notices of spring-guns and man-traps in every part of his premises. Indeed he shows great jealousy about his territorial rights, having stopped up a foot-path that led across his fields; and given warning, in staring letters, that whoever was found trespassing on those grounds would be prosecuted with the utmost rigour of the law. He has brought into the country with him all the practical maxims of town, and the bustling habits of business; and is one of those sensible, useful, prosing, troublesome, intolerable old gentlemen that go about wearying and worrying society with excellent plans for public utility.

He is very much disposed to be on intimate terms with the squire, and calls on him every now and then, with some project for the good of the neighbourhood, which happens to run diametrically opposite to some one or other of the squire's peculiar notions; but which is "too sensible a measure" to be openly opposed. He has annoyed him excessively by enforcing the vagrant laws; persecuting the gipsies, and endeavouring to suppress country wakes and holiday games; which he considers great nuisances, and reprobates as causes of the deadly sin of idleness.

There is evidently in all this a little of the ostentation of newly acquired consequence; the tradesman is gradually swelling into the aristocrat; and he begins to grow excessively intolerant of every thing that is not genteel. He has a great deal to say about "the common people;" talks much of his park, his preserves, and the necessity of enforcing the game laws more strictly; and makes frequent use of the phrase, "the gentry of the neighbourhood."

166

He came to the hall lately, with a face full of business, that he and the squire, to use his own words, "might lay their heads together," to hit upon some mode of putting a stop to the frolicking at the village on the approaching May-day. It drew, he said, idle people together from all parts of the neighbourhood, who spent the day fiddling, dancing, and carousing, instead of staying at home to work for their families.

Now, as the squire, unluckily, is at the bottom of these May-day revels, it may be supposed that the suggestions of the sagacious Mr. Faddy were not received with the best grace in the world. It is true, the old gentleman is too courteous to show any temper to a guest in his own house, but no sooner was he gone than the indignation of the squire found vent, at having his poetical cobwebs invaded by this buzzing, blue-bottle fly of traffic. In his warmth he inveighed against the whole race of manufacturers, who, I found, were sore disturbers of his comfort. "Sir," said he, with emotion, "it makes my heart bleed to see all our fine streams dammed up and bestrode by cotton mills; our valleys smoking with steam-engines, and the din of the hammer and the loom scaring away all our rural delights. What's to become of merry old England, when its manor houses are all turned into manu- factories, and its sturdy peasantry into pin-makers and stocking-weavers? I have looked in vain for merry Sherwood, and all the greenwood haunts of Robin Hood; the whole country is covered with manufacturing towns. I have stood on the ruins of Dudley Castle, and looked round, with an aching heart, on what were once its feudal domains of verdant and beautiful country. Sir, I beheld a mere campus phlegræ; a region of fire; reeking with coal-pits, and furnaces, and smelting-houses, vomiting forth flames and smoke. The pale and ghastly people, toiling among vile exhalations, looked more like demons than human beings; the clanking wheels and engines, seen through the murky atmosphere, looked like instruments of torture in this pandemonium. What is to become of the country with these evils rankling in its very core? Sir, these manufacturers will be the ruin of our rural manners; they will destroy the national character; they will not leave materials for a single line of poetry!"

The squire is apt to wax eloquent on such themes; and I could hardly help smiling at this whimsical lamentation over national industry and public improvement. I am told, however, that he really grieves at the growing spirit of trade, as destroying the charm of life. He con- siders every new short-hand mode of doing things, as an inroad of snug sordid method; and thinks that this will soon become a mere matter of fact world, where life will be reduced to a mathematical calculation of conveniences, and every thing will be done by steam.

He maintains also, that the nation has declined in its free and joyous spirit in proportion as it has turned its attention to commerce and manufactures; and that in old times, when England was an idler, it was also a merrier little island. In support of this opinion he adduces the frequency and splendour of ancient festivals and merry-makings, and the hearty spirit with which they were kept up by all classes of people. His memory is stored with the accounts given by Stow, in his Survey of London, of the holiday revels at the inns of court, the Christmas mummeries, and the masquings and bonfires about the streets. London, he says, in those days, resembled the continental cities in its picturesque manners and amusements. The court used to dance after dinner on public occasions. After the coronation dinner of Richard II, for example, the king, the prelates, the nobles, the knights, and the rest of the company danced in Westminster Hall to the music of the minstrels. The example of the court was followed by the middling classes, and so down to the lowest, and the whole nation was a dancing, jovial nation. He quotes a lively city picture of the times, given by Stow, which resembles the lively scenes one may often see in the gay city of Paris; for he tells us that on holidays, after evening prayers, the maidens in London used to assemble before the door, in sight of their masters and dames, and while one played on a timbrel, the others danced for garlands, hanged athwart the street.

"Where will we meet with such merry groups now-a-days?" the squire will exclaim, shaking his head mournfully; – "and then as to the gaiety that prevailed in dress throughout all ranks of society; and made the very streets so fine and picturesque. 'I have myself,' says Gervaise Markham, 'met an ordinary tapster in his silk stockings, garters deep fringed with gold lace, the rest of his apparel suitable, with cloak lined with velvet!' Nashe, too, who wrote in 1593, exclaims at the finery of the nation. 'England, the players stage of gorgeous attire, the ape of all nations superfluities, the continual masquer in outlandish habiliments.'"

Such are a few of the authorities quoted by the squire by way of contrasting what he supposes to have been the former vivacity of the nation with its present monotonous character. "John Bull," he will say, "was then a gay cavalier, with a sword by his side and a feather in his cap; but he is now a plodding citizen, in snuff-coloured coat and gaiters."

By the bye, there really appears to have been some change in the national character since the days of which the squire is so fond of talking; those days when this little island acquired its favourite old title of "merry England." This may be attributed in part to the growing hardships of the times, and the necessity of turning the whole attention to the means of subsistence; but England's gayest customs prevailed at times when her common people enjoyed comparatively few of the comforts and conveniences that they do at present. It may be still more attributed to the universal spirit of gain, and the calculating habits that commerce has introduced; but I am inclined to attribute it chiefly to the gradual increase of the liberty of the subject, and the growing freedom and activity of opinion.

A free people are apt to be grave and thoughtful. They have high and important matters to occupy their minds. They feel that it is their right, their interest, and their duty to mingle in public concerns, and to watch over the general welfare. The continual exercise of the mind on political topics gives intenser habits of thinking, and a more serious and earnest demeanour. A nation becomes less gay, but more intellectually active and vigorous. It evinces less play of the fancy, but more power of the imagination; less taste and elegance, but more grandeur of mind; less animated vivacity, but deeper enthusiasm.

It is when men are shut out of the regions of manly thought by a despotic government; when every grave and lofty theme is rendered perilous to discussion and almost to reflection; it is then that they turn to the safer occupations of taste and amusement; trifles rise to importance, and occupy the craving activity of intellect. No being is more void of care and reflection than the slave; none dances more gaily in his intervals of labour; but make him free, give him rights and interests to guard, and he becomes thoughtful and laborious.

The French are a gayer people than the English. Why? Partly from temperament, perhaps; but greatly because they have been accustomed to governments which surrounded the free exercise of thought with danger, and where he only was safe who shut his eyes and ears to public events, and enjoyed the passing pleasure of the day. Within late years they have had more opportunity of exercising their minds; and within late years the national character has essentially changed. Never did the French enjoy such a degree of freedom as they do at this moment: and at this moment the French are comparatively a grave people.

GIPSIES

What's that to absolute freedom; such as the very beggars
have; to feast and revel here today, and yonder tomorrow;
next day where they please, and so on still, the whole country or kingdom over? There's liberty! the birds of the air
can take no more.

JOVIAL CREW

Since the meeting with the gipsies, which I have related in a former
paper, I have observed several of them haunting the purlieus of the Hall,
in spite of a positive interdiction of the squire. They are part of a gang
that has long kept about this neighbourhood, to the great annoyance of
the farmers, whose poultry-yards often suffer from their nocturnal
invasions. They are, however, in some measure, patronised by the
squire, who considers the race as belonging to the good old times which,
to confess the private truth, seem to have abounded with good-for-
nothing characters.

This roving crew is called "Star-light Tom's Gang," from the name of
its chieftain, a notorious poacher. I have heard repeatedly of the misdeeds of this "minion of the moon;" for every midnight depredation that
takes place in park, or fold, or farm-yard, is laid to his charge. Star-light
Tom, in fact, answers to his name; he seems to walk in darkness, and,
like a fox, to be traced in the morning by the mischief he has done. He
reminds me of that fearful personage in the nursery rhyme:

> Who goes round the house at night?
> None but bloody Tom!
> Who steals all the sheep at night?
> None but one by one!

In short, Star-light Tom is the scape-goat of the neighbourhood; but so
cunning and adroit, that there is no detecting him. Old Christy and the
game-keeper have watched many a night in hopes of entrapping him;
and Christy often patrols the park with his dogs, for the purpose, but
all in vain. It is said that the squire winks hard at his misdeeds, having
an indulgent feeling towards the vagabond, because of his being very
expert at all kinds of games, a great shot with the cross-bow, and
the best morrice dancer in the country.

The squire also suffers the gang to lurk unmolested about the skirts
of his estate, on condition that they do not come about the house. The

approaching wedding, however, has made a kind of Saturnalia at the Hall, and has caused a suspension of all sober rule. It has produced a great sensation throughout the female part of the household; not a housemaid but dreams of wedding favours, and has a husband running in her head. Such a time is a harvest for the gipsies; there is a public foot-path leading across one part of the park, by which they have free ingress, and they are continually hovering about the grounds, telling the servant girls' fortunes, or getting smuggled in to the young ladies.

I believe the Oxonian amuses himself very much by furnishing them with hints in private, and bewildering all the weak brains in the house with their wonderful revelations. The general certainly was very much astonished by the communications made to him the other evening by the gipsy girl: he kept a wary silence towards us on the subject, and affected to treat it lightly; but I have noticed that he has since redoubled his attentions to Lady Lillycraft and her dogs.

I have seen also Phœbe Wilkins, the housekeeper's pretty and love-sick niece, holding a long conference with one of these old sibyls behind a large tree in the avenue, and often looking round to see that she was not observed. I make no doubt that she was endeavouring to get some favourable augury about the result of her love-quarrel with young Ready Money, as oracles have always been more consulted on love-affairs than upon any thing else. I fear, however, that in this instance the response was not so favourable as usual, for I perceived poor Phœbe returning pensively towards the house; her head hanging down, her hat in her hand, and the riband trailing along the ground.

At another time, as I turned a corner of a terrace, at the bottom of the garden, just by a clump of trees, and a large stone urn, I came upon a bevy of the young girls of the family, attended by this same Phœbe Wilkins. I was at a loss to comprehend the meaning of their blushing and giggling, and their apparent agitation, until I saw the red cloak of a gipsy vanishing among the shrubbery. A few moments after I caught sight of Master Simon and the Oxonian stealing along one of the walks of the garden, chuckling and laughing at their successful waggery; having evidently put the gipsy up to the thing, and instructed her what to say.

After all, there is something strangely pleasing in these tamperings with the future, even where we are convinced of the fallacy of the prediction. It is singular how willingly the mind will half deceive itself, and with what a degree of awe we will listen even to these babblers about futurity. For my part, I cannot feel angry with these poor vagabonds, that seek to deceive us into bright hopes and expectations. I have always been something of a castle-builder, and have found my liveliest pleasures to arise from the illusions which fancy has cast over common-place realities. As I get on in life, I find it more difficult to deceive myself in this delightful manner; and I should be thankful to any prophet, however false, that would conjure the clouds which hang over futurity into palaces, and all its doubtful regions into fairy-land.

The squire, who, as I have observed, has a private good will towards gipsies, has suffered considerable annoyance on their account. Not that they requite his indulgence with ingratitude, for they do not depredate very flagrantly on his estate; but because their pilferings and misdeeds occasion loud murmurs in the village. I can readily understand the old gentleman's humour on this point; I have a great toleration for all kinds of vagrant sunshiny existence, and must confess I take a pleasure in observing the ways of gipsies. The English, who are accustomed to them from childhood, and often suffer from their petty depredations, consider them as mere nuisances; but I have been very much struck with their peculiarities. I like to behold their clear olive complexions, their romantic black eyes, their raven locks, their lithe slender figures, and to hear them, in low silver tones, dealing forth magnificent promises of honours, and estates, of world's wealth, and ladies' love.

Their mode of life, too, has something in it very fanciful and picturesque. They are the free denizens of nature, and maintain a primitive independence, in spite of law and gospel; of county gaols and country magistrates. It is curious to see this obstinate adherence to the wild unsettled habits of savage life transmitted from generation to generation, and preserved in the midst of one of the most cultivated, populous, and systematic countries in the world. They are totally distinct from the busy, thrifty people about them. They seem to be, like the Indians of America, either above or below the ordinary cares and anxieties of mankind. Heedless of power, of honours, of wealth; and indifferent to the fluctuations of the times; the rise or fall of grain, or stock, or empires, they seem to laugh at the toiling, fretting world around them, and to live according to the philosophy of the old song:

> "Who would ambition shun,
>   And loves to lie i' the sun,
>   Seeking the food he eats,
>   And pleased with what he gets,
>   Come hither, come hither, come hither;
>   Here shall he see
>   No enemy,
>   But winter and rough weather."

In this way they wander from county to county; keeping about the purlieus of villages, or in plenteous neighbourhoods, where there are fat farms and rich country-seats. Their encampments are generally made in some beautiful spot; either a green shady nook of a road; or on the border of a common, under a sheltering hedge; or on the skirts of a fine spreading wood. They are always to be found lurking about fairs and races, and rustic gatherings, wherever there is pleasure, and throng, and idleness. They are the oracles of milk maids and simple serving girls; and sometimes have even the honour of perusing the white hands of gentlemen's daughters, when rambling about their fathers' grounds. They are the bane of good housewives and thrifty farmers, and odious in the eyes of country justices; but, like all other vagabond beings, they have something to commend them to the fancy. They are among the last traces, in these matter-of-fact days, of the motley population of former times; and are whimsically associated in my mind with fairies and witches, Robin Good Fellow, Robin Hood, and the other fantastical personages of poetry.

MAY-DAY CUSTOMS

Happy the age, and harmlesse were the dayes,
  (For then true love and amity was found)
When every village did a May-pole raise,
  And Whitson-ales and May-games did abound:
And all the lusty yonkers in a rout,
With merry lasses daunc'd the rod about,
Then friendship to their banquets bid the guests,
And poore men far'd the better for their feasts.

PASQUIL'S PALINODIA

The month of April has nearly passed away, and we are fast approaching that poetical day which was considered, in old times, as the boundary that parted the frontiers of winter and summer. With all its caprices, however, I like the month of April. I like these laughing and crying days, when sun and shade seem to run in billows over the landscape. I like to see the sudden shower coursing over the meadow, and giving all nature a greener smile; and the bright sunbeams chasing the flying cloud, and turning all its drops into diamonds.

I was enjoying a morning of the kind in company with the squire in one of the finest parts of the park. We were skirting a beautiful grove, and he was giving me a kind of biographical account of several of his favourite forest trees, when we heard the strokes of an axe from the midst of a thick copse. The squire paused and listened, with manifest signs of uneasiness. He turned his steps in the direction of the sound. The strokes grew louder and louder as we advanced; there was evidently a vigorous arm wielding the axe. The squire quickened his pace, but in vain; a loud crack and a succeeding crash told that the mischief had been done, and some child of the forest laid low. When we came to the place, we found Master Simon and several others standing about a tall and beautifully straight young tree, which had just been felled.

The squire, though a man of most harmonious dispositions, was completely put out of tune by this circumstance. He felt like a monarch witnessing the murder of one of his liege subjects, and demanded, with some asperity, the meaning of the outrage. It turned out to be an affair of Master Simon's, who had selected the tree, from its height and straightness, for a May-pole, the old one which stood on the village green being unfit for further service. If any thing could have soothed the ire of my worthy host, it would have been the reflection that his tree had fallen in so good a cause; and I saw that there was a great struggle between his fondness for his groves, and his devotion to

174

May-day. He could not contemplate the prostrate tree, however, without indulging in lamentation, and making a kind of funeral eulogy, like Mark Anthony over the body of Cæsar; and he forbade that any tree should thenceforward be cut down on his estate without a warrant from himself; being determined, he said, to hold the sovereign power of life and death in his own hands.

This mention of the May-pole struck my attention, and I inquired whether the old customs connected with it were really kept up in this part of the country. The squire shook his head mournfully; and I found I had touched on one of his tender points, for he grew quite melancholy in bewailing the total decline of old May-day. Though it is regularly celebrated in the neighbouring village, yet it has been merely resuscitated by the worthy squire, and is kept up in a forced state of existence at his expense. He meets with continual discouragements; and finds great difficulty in getting the country bumpkins to play their parts tolerably. He manages to have every year a "Queen of the May;" but as to Robin Hood, Friar Tuck, the Dragon, the Hobby Horse, and all the other motley crew that used to enliven the day with their mummery, he has not ventured to introduce them.

Still I look forward with some interest to the promised shadow of old May-day, even though it be but a shadow; and I feel more and more pleased with the whimsical, yet harmless hobby of my host, which is surrounding him with agreeable associations, and making a little world of poetry about him. Brought up, as I have been, in a new country, I may appreciate too highly the faint vestiges of ancient customs which I now and then meet with, and the interest I express in them may provoke a smile from those who are negligently suffering them to pass away. But with whatever indifference they may be regarded by those "to the manner born," yet in my mind the lingering flavour of them imparts a charm to rustic life, which nothing else could readily supply.

I shall never forget the delight I felt on first seeing a May-pole. It was on the banks of the Dee, close by the picturesque old bridge that stretches across the river from the quaint little city of Chester. I had already been carried back into former days by the antiquities of that venerable place; the examination of which is equal to turning over the pages of a black letter volume, or gazing on the pictures in Froissart. The May-pole on the margin of that poetic stream completed the illusion. My fancy adorned it with wreaths of flowers, and peopled the green bank with all the dancing revelry of May-day. The mere sight of this May-pole gave a glow to my feelings, and spread a charm over the country for the rest of the day; and as I traversed a part of the fair plain of Cheshire, and the beautiful borders of Wales, and looked from among swelling hills down a long green valley, through which "the Deva wound its wizard stream," my imagination turned all into a perfect Arcadia.

Whether it be owing to such poetical associations early instilled into my mind, or whether there is, as it were, a sympathetic revival and budding forth of the feelings at this season, certain it is, that I always experience, wherever I may be placed, a delightful expansion of the heart at the return of May. It is said that birds about this time will become restless in their cages, as if instinct with the season, conscious of the revelry that is going on in the groves, and impatient to break from their bondage, and join in the jubilee of the year. In like manner I have felt myself excited, even in the midst of the metropolis, when the windows, which had been churlishly closed all winter, were again thrown open to receive the balmy breath of May; when the sweets of the country were breathed into the town, and flowers were cried about the streets. I have considered the treasures of flowers thus poured in, as so many missives from nature inviting us forth to enjoy the virgin beauty of the year, before its freshness is exhaled by the heats of sunny summer.

One can readily imagine what a gay scene it must have been in jolly old London, when the doors were decorated with flowering branches, when every hat was decked with hawthorn, and Robin Hood, Friar Tuck, Maid Marian, the morrice dancers, and all the other fantastic masks and revellers, were performing their antics about the May-pole in every part of the city.

I am not a bigoted admirer of old times and old customs merely because of their antiquity. But while I rejoice in the decline of many of the rude usages and coarse amusements of former days, I cannot but regret that this innocent and fanciful festival has fallen into disuse. It seemed appropriate to this verdant and pastoral country, and calculated to light up the too pervading gravity of the nation. I value every custom that tends to infuse poetical feeling into the common people, and to sweeten and soften the rudeness of rustic manners, without destroying their simplicity. Indeed, it is to the decline of this happy simplicity that the decline of this custom may be traced; and the rural dance on the green and the homely May-day pageant have gradually disappeared, in proportion as the peasantry have become expensive and artificial in their pleasures, and too knowing for simple enjoyment.

Some attempts, the squire informs me, have been made of late years, by men of both taste and learning, to rally back the popular feeling to these standards of primitive simplicity; but the time has gone by, the feeling has become chilled by habits of gain and traffic, the country apes the manners and amusements of the town, and little is heard of

May-day at present, except from the lamentations of authors, who sigh after it from among the brick walls of the city:

"For O, for O, the Hobby Horse is forgot."

VILLAGE WORTHIES

Nay, I tell you, I am so well beloved in our town, that not
the worst dog in the street will hurt my little finger.

COLLIER OF CROYDON

As the neighbouring village is one of those out-of-the-way, but gossiping
little places, where a small matter makes a great stir, it is not to be supposed that the approach of a festival like that of May-day can be
regarded with indifference, especially since it is made a matter of
such moment by the great folks at the Hall. Master Simon, who is the
faithful factotum of the worthy squire, and jumps with his humour in
every thing, is frequent just now in his visits to the village, to give
directions for the impending fête; and as I have taken the liberty
occasionally of accompanying him, I have been enabled to get some
insight into the characters and internal politics of this very sagacious
little community.

Master Simon is in fact the Cæsar of the village. It is true the squire
is the protecting power, but his factotum is the active and busy agent.
He intermeddles in all its concerns, is acquainted with all the inhabitants
and their domestic history, gives counsel to the old folks in their business
matters, and the young folks in their love affairs, and enjoys the proud
satisfaction of being a great man in a little world.

He is the dispenser too of the squire's charity, which is bounteous;
and, to do Master Simon justice, he performs this part of his functions
with great alacrity. Indeed I have been entertained with the mixture of
bustle, importance, and kind-heartedness which he displays. He is of
too vivacious a temperament to comfort the afflicted by sitting down
moping and whining and blowing noses in concert; but goes whisking
about like a sparrow, chirping consolation into every hole and corner
of the village. I have seen an old woman, in a red cloak, hold him for
half an hour together with some long phthisical tale of distress, which
Master Simon listened to with many a bob of the head, smack of his
dog-whip, and other symptoms of impatience, though he afterwards
made a most faithful and circumstantial report of the case to the
squire. I have watched him too, during one of his pop visits into the
cottage of a superannuated villager, who is a pensioner of the squire,
where he fidgeted about the room without sitting down, made many
excellent off-hand reflections with the old invalid, who was propped
up in his chair, about the shortness of life, the certainty of death, and the
necessity of preparing for "that awful change;" quoted several texts of

178

scripture very incorrectly, but much to the edification of the cottager's
wife; and on coming out pinched the daughter's rosy cheek, and
wondered what was in the young men, that such a pretty face did not
get a husband.

He has also his cabinet councillors in the village, with whom he is
very busy just now, preparing for the May-day ceremonies. Among
these is the village tailor, a pale-faced fellow, that plays the clarionet
in the church choir; and, being a great musical genius, has frequent
meetings of the band at his house, where they "make night hideous"
by their concerts. He is, in consequence, high in favour with Master
Simon; and, through his influence, has the making, or rather marring, of
all the liveries of the Hall; which generally look as though they had
been cut out by one of those scientific tailors of the Flying Island of
Laputa, who took measure of their customers with a quadrant. The
tailor, in fact, might rise to be one of the monied men of the village,
was he not rather too prone to gossip, and keep holidays, and give
concerts, and blow all his substance, real and personal, through his
clarionet; which literally keeps him poor both in body and estate. He
has for the present thrown by all his regular work, and suffered the
breeches of the village to go unmade and unmended, while he is occupied in making garlands of party-coloured rags, in imitation of flowers,
for the decoration of the May-pole.

Another of Master Simon's councillors is the apothecary, a short
and rather fat man, with a pair of prominent eyes that diverge like
those of a lobster. He is the village wise man; very sententious, and
full of profound remarks on shallow subjects. Master Simon often
quotes his sayings, and mentions him as rather an extraordinary man;
and even consults him occasionally in desperate cases of the dogs and
horses. Indeed he seems to have been overwhelmed by the apothecary's
philosophy, which is exactly one observation deep, consisting of in-
disputable maxims, such as may be gathered from the mottos of tobacco-
boxes. I had a specimen of his philosophy in my very first conversation
with him; in the course of which he observed, with great solemnity and
emphasis, that "man is a compound of wisdom and folly;" upon which
Master Simon, who had hold of my arm, pressed very hard upon it,
and whispered in my ear, "that's a devilish shrewd remark!"

THE SCHOOLMASTER

There will no mosse stick to the stone of Sisiphus, no grasse
hang on the heeles of Mercury, no butter cleave on the bread
of a traveller. For as the eagle at every flight loseth a feather,
which maketh her bauld in her age, so the traveller in every
country loseth some fleece, which maketh him a beggar in
his youth, by buying that for a pound which he cannot sell
again for a penny — repentance.

LILLY'S EUPHUES

Among the worthies of the village that enjoy the peculiar confidence
of Master Simon is one who has struck my fancy so much, that I have
thought him worthy of a separate notice. It is Slingsby, the schoolmaster,
a thin elderly man, rather threadbare and slovenly, somewhat indolent in
manner, and with an easy, good-humoured look, not often met with in
his craft. I have been interested in his favour by a few anecdotes which
I have picked up concerning him.

He is a native of the village, and was a contemporary and playmate
of Ready Money Jack in the days of their boyhood. Indeed, they carried
on a kind of league of mutual good offices. Slingsby was rather puny,
and withal somewhat of a coward, but very apt at his learning: Jack,
on the contrary, was bully-boy out of doors, but a sad laggard at his
books. Slingsby helped Jack, therefore, to all his lessons; Jack fought
all Slingsby's battles; and they were inseparable friends. This mutual
kindness continued even after they left the school, notwithstanding the
dissimilarity of their characters. Jack took to ploughing and reaping, and
prepared himself to till his paternal acres; while the other loitered
negligently on in the path of learning, until he penetrated even into the
confines of Latin and mathematics.

In an unlucky hour, however, he took to reading voyages and travels,
and was smitten with a desire to see the world. This desire increased
upon him as he grew up; so, early one bright sunny morning he put all
his effects in a knapsack, slung it on his back, took staff in hand, and
called in his way to take leave of his early schoolmate. Jack was
just going out with the plough; the friends shook hands over the farm-
house gate; Jack drove his team afield, and Slingsby whistled "over the
hills and far away," and sallied forth gaily to "seek his fortune."

Years and years passed by, and young Tom Slingsby was forgotten;
when, one mellow Sunday afternoon in autumn, a thin man, somewhat advanced in life, with a coat out at elbows, a pair of old nankeen
gaiters, and a few things tied in a handkerchief, and slung on the end

of a stick, was seen loitering through the village. He appeared to regard several houses attentively, to peer into the windows that were open, to eye the villagers wistfully as they returned from church, and then to pass some time in the church-yard, reading the tomb-stones.

At length he found his way to the farm-house of Ready Money Jack, but paused ere he attempted the wicket; contemplating the picture of substantial independence before him. In the porch of the house sat Ready Money Jack, in his Sunday dress; with his hat upon his head, his pipe in his mouth, and his tankard before him, the monarch of all he surveyed. Beside him lay his fat house-dog. The varied sounds of poultry were heard from the well-stocked farm-yard; the bees hummed from their hives in the garden; the cattle lowed in the rich meadow; while the crammed barns and ample stacks bore proof of an abundant harvest.

The stranger opened the gate and advanced dubiously towards the house. The mastiff growled at the sight of the suspicious-looking intruder; but was immediately silenced by his master; who, taking his pipe from his mouth, awaited with inquiring aspect the address of this equivocal personage. The stranger eyed old Jack for a moment, so portly in his dimensions, and decked out in gorgeous apparel; then cast a glance upon his own threadbare and starveling condition, and the scanty bundle which he held in his hand; then giving his shrunk waistcoat a twitch to make it meet his receding waistband; and casting another look, half sad, half humorous, at the sturdy yeoman, "I suppose," said he, "Mr. Tibbets, you have forgot old times and old playmates."

The latter gazed at him with scrutinizing look, but acknowledged that he had no recollection of him.

"Like enough, like enough," said the stranger; "every body seems to have forgotten poor Slingsby!"

"Why, no sure! it can't be Tom Slingsby!"

"Yes, but it is, though!" replied the stranger, shaking his head.

Ready Money Jack was on his feet in a twinkling; thrust out his hand, gave his ancient crony the gripe of a giant, and slapping the other hand on a bench, "Sit down there," cried he, "Tom Slingsby!"

A long conversation ensued about old times, while Slingsby was regaled with the best cheer that the farm-house afforded; for he was hungry as well as wayworn, and had the keen appetite of a poor pedestrian. The early playmates then talked over their subsequent lives and adventures. Jack had but little to relate, and was never good at a long story. A prosperous life, passed at home, has little incident for narrative; it is only poor devils, that are tossed about the world, that are the true heroes of story. Jack had stuck by the paternal farm, followed the same plough that his forefathers had driven, and had waxed richer and richer as he grew older. As to Tom Slingsby, he was an exemplification of the old proverb, "a rolling stone gathers no moss." He had sought his fortune about the world, without ever finding it, being a thing oftener found at home than abroad. He had been in all kinds of situations, and had learnt a dozen different modes of making a living; but had found his way back to his native village rather poorer than when he left it, his knapsack having dwindled down to a scanty bundle.

As luck would have it, the squire was passing by the farm-house that very evening, and called there, as is often his custom. He found the two school-mates still gossiping in the porch, and, according to the good old Scottish song, "taking a cup of kindness yet, for auld lang syne." The squire was struck by the contrast in appearance and fortunes of these early playmates. Ready Money Jack, seated in lordly state, surrounded by the good things of this life, with golden guineas hanging to his very watch-chain, and the poor pilgrim Slingsby, thin as a weasel, with all his worldly effects, his bundle, hat, and walking-staff, lying on the ground beside him.

The good squire's heart warmed towards the luckless cosmopolite, for he is a little prone to like such half-vagrant characters. He cast about in his mind how he should contrive once more to anchor Slingsby in his native village. Honest Jack had already offered him a present shelter under his roof, in spite of the hints, and winks, and half remonstrances of the shrewd Dame Tibbets; but how to provide for his permanent maintenance was the question. Luckily the squire bethought himself that the village school was without a teacher. A little further conversation convinced him that Slingsby was as fit for that as for any thing else, and in a day or two he was seen swaying the rod of empire in the very school-house where he had often been horsed in the days of his boyhood.

Here he has remained for several years, and being honoured by the countenance of the squire and the fast friendship of Mr. Tibbets, he has grown into much importance and consideration in the village. I am told, however, that he still shows, now and then, a degree of restlessness, and a disposition to rove abroad again, and see a little more of the world; an inclination which seems particularly to haunt him about spring-time. There is nothing so difficult to conquer as the vagrant humour, when once it has been fully indulged.

Since I have heard these anecdotes of poor Slingsby, I have more than once mused upon the picture presented by him and his schoolmate Ready Money Jack, on their coming together again after so long a separation.

It is difficult to determine between lots in life, where each is attended with its peculiar discontents. He who never leaves his home repines at his monotonous existence, and envies the traveller, whose life is a constant tissue of wonder and adventure; while he, who is tossed about the world, looks back with many a sigh to the safe and quiet shore which he has abandoned. I cannot help thinking, however, that the man that stays at home, and cultivates the comforts and pleasures daily springing up around him, stands the best chance for happiness. There is nothing so fascinating to a young mind as the idea of travelling; and there is very witchcraft in the old phrase found in every nursery tale, of "going to seek one's fortune." A continual change of place and change of object promises a continual succession of adventure and gratification of curiosity. But there is a limit to all our enjoyments, and every desire bears its death in its very gratification. Curiosity languishes under repeated stimulants, novelties cease to excite surprise, until at length we cannot wonder even at a miracle. He who has sallied forth into the world like poor Slingsby, full of sunny anticipations, finds too soon how different the distant scene becomes when visited. The smooth place roughens as he approaches; the wild place becomes tame and barren; the fairy tints that beguiled him on still fly to the distant hill, or gather upon the land he has left behind, and every part of the landscape seems greener than the spot he stands on.

THE SCHOOL

> But to come down from great men and higher matters to my
> little children and poor school house again; I will, God willing,
> go forward orderly, as I purposed, to instruct children and
> young men both for learning and manners.
>
> ROGER ASCHAM

Having given the reader a slight sketch of the village schoolmaster,
he may be curious to learn something concerning his school. As the
squire takes much interest in the education of the neighbouring children, he put into the hands of the teacher, on first installing him in
office, a copy of Roger Ascham's Schoolmaster, and advised him, moreover, to con over that portion of old Peachem which treats of the duty
of masters, and which condemns the favourite method of making boys
wise by flagellation.

He exhorted Slingsby not to break down or depress the free spirit of
the boys, by harshness and slavish fear, but to lead them freely and
joyously on in the path of knowledge, making it pleasant and desirable
in their eyes. He wished to see the youth trained up in the manners
and habitudes of the peasantry of the good old times, and thus to lay
a foundation for the accomplishment of his favourite object, the revival
of old English customs and character. He recommended that all the
ancient holidays should be observed, and that the sports of the boys,
in their hours of play, should be regulated according to the standard
authorities laid down in Strutt, a copy of whose invaluable work,
decorated with plates, was deposited in the school-house. Above all,
he exhorted the pedagogue to abstain from the use of birch, an
instrument of instruction which the good squire regards with abhorrence,
as fit only for the coercion of brute natures, that cannot be reasoned with.

Mr. Slingsby has followed the squire's instructions to the best of
his disposition and abilities. He never flogs the boys, because he is
too easy, good-humoured a creature to inflict pain on a worm. He is
bountiful in holidays, because he loves holiday himself, and has a
sympathy with the urchins' impatience of confinement, from having
divers times experienced its irksomeness during the time that he was
seeing the world. As to sports and pastimes, the boys are faithfully
exercised in all that are on record, quoits, races, prison-bars, tipcat,
trap-ball, bandy-ball, wrestling, leaping, and what not. The only misfortune is, that having banished the birch, honest Slingsby has not
studied Roger Ascham sufficiently to find out a substitute, or rather

he has not the management in his nature to apply one; his school, therefore, though one of the happiest, is one of the most unruly in the country; and never was a pedagogue more liked or less heeded by his disciples than Slingsby.

He has lately taken a coadjutor worthy of himself, being another stray sheep that has returned to the village fold. This is no other than the son of the musical tailor, who had bestowed some cost upon his education, hoping to see him one day arrive at the dignity of an excise-man, or at least of a parish clerk. The lad grew up, however, as idle and musical as his father; and, being captivated by the drum and fife of a recruiting party, he followed them off to the army. He returned not long since, out of money, and out at the elbows, the prodigal son of the village. He remained for some time lounging about the place in half-tattered soldier's dress, with a foraging cap on one side of his head, jerking stones across the brook, or loitering about the tavern door, a burthen to his father, and regarded with great coldness by all warm householders.

Something, however, drew honest Slingsby towards the youth. It might be the kindness he bore to his father, who is one of the schoolmaster's great cronies; it might be that secret sympathy, which draws men of vagrant propensities towards each other, for there is something truly magnetic in the vagabond feeling; or it might be that he remembered the time, when he himself had come back like this youngster, a wreck to his native place. At any rate, whatever the motive, Slingsby drew towards the youth. They had many conversations in the village tap-room about foreign parts, and the various scenes and places they had witnessed during their wayfaring about the world. The more Slingsby talked with him the more he found him to his taste: and finding him almost as learned as himself, he forthwith engaged him as an assistant, or usher, in the school.

Under such admirable tuition the school, as may be supposed, flourishes apace; and if the scholars do not become versed in all the holiday accomplishments of the good old times, to the squire's heart's content, it will not be the fault of their teachers. The prodigal son has become almost as popular among the boys as the pedagogue himself. His instructions are not limited to school-hours; and having inherited the musical taste and talents of his father, he has bitten the whole school with the mania. He is a great hand at beating a drum, which is often heard rumbling from the rear of the school-house. He is teaching half the boys of the village, also, to play the fife, and the pandean pipes; and they weary the whole neighbourhood with their vague pipings, as they sit perched on stiles, or loitering about the barn-doors in the evenings. Among the other exercises of the school, also, he has introduced the ancient art of archery, one of the squire's favourite themes, with such success, that the whipsters roam in truant bands about the neighbourhood, practising with their bows and arrows upon the birds of the air, and the beasts of the field; and not unfrequently making a foray into the squire's domains, to the great indignation of the gamekeepers. In a word, so completely are the ancient English customs and habits cultivated at this school, that I should not be surprised if the squire should live to see one of his poetic visions realised, and a brood reared up, worthy successors to Robin Hood, and his merry gang of outlaws.

A VILLAGE POLITICIAN

I am a rogue if I do not think I was designed for the helm of
state; I am so full of nimble stratagems, that I should have
ordered affairs and carried it against the stream of a faction
with as much ease as a skipper would laver against the wind.

THE GOBLINS

In one of my visits to the village with Master Simon, he proposed that
we should stop at the inn, which he wished to show me, as a specimen
of a real country inn, the head-quarters of village gossip. I had remarked it before, in my perambulations about the place. It has a deep
old-fashioned porch, leading into a large hall, which serves for tap-
room and travellers'-room; having a wide fire-place, with high backed
settles on each side, where the wise men of the village gossip over their
ale, and hold their sessions during the long winter evenings. The landlord is an easy, indolent fellow, shaped a little like one of his own beer
barrels, and is apt to stand gossiping at his door, with his wig on one
side, and his hands in his pockets, whilst his wife and daughter attend
to customers. His wife, however, is fully competent to manage the
establishment; and, indeed, from long habitude, rules over all the
frequenters of the tap-room as completely as if they were her dependents instead of her patrons. Not a veteran ale-bibber but pays homage
to her, having, no doubt, been often in her arrears. I have already
hinted that she is on very good terms with Ready Money Jack. He
was a sweetheart of hers in early life, and has always countenanced
the tavern on her account. Indeed, he is quite the "cock of the walk"
at the tap-room.

As we approached the inn, we heard some one talking with great
volubility, and distinguished the ominous words "taxes," "poor's rates,"
and "agricultural distress." It proved to be a thin, loquacious fellow,
who had penned the landlord up in one corner of the porch, with his
hands in his pockets as usual, listening with an air of the most vacant
acquiescence.

The sight seemed to have a curious effect on Master Simon, as he
squeezed my arm, and altering his course, sheered wide of the porch,
as though he had not had any idea of entering. This evident evasion
induced me to notice the orator more particularly. He was meagre.
but active in his make, with a long, pale, bilious face; a black beard,
so ill-shaven as to bloody his shirt-collar, a feverish eye, and a hat
sharpened up at the sides into a most pragmatical shape. He had a

newspaper in his hand, and seemed to be commenting on its contents, to the thorough conviction of mine host.

At sight of Master Simon the landlord was evidently a little flurried, and began to rub his hands, edge away from his corner, and make several profound publican bows; while the orator took no other notice of my companion than to talk rather louder than before, and with, as I thought, something of an air of defiance. Master Simon, however, as I have before said, sheered off from the porch and passed on, pressing my arm within his, and whispering as we got by, in a tone of awe and horror, "That's a radical! he reads Cobbett!"

I endeavoured to get a more particular account of him from my companion, but he seemed unwilling even to talk about him, answering only in general terms, that he was "a cursed busy fellow, that had a confounded trick of talking, and was apt to bother one about the national debt, and such nonsense;" from which I suspected that Master Simon had been rendered wary of him by some accidental encounter on the field of argument; for these radicals are continually roving about in quest of wordy warfare, and never so happy as when they can tilt a gentleman logician out of his saddle.

On subsequent inquiry my suspicions have been confirmed. I find the radical has but recently found his way into the village, where he threatens to commit fearful devastations with his doctrines. He has already made two or three complete converts, or new lights; has shaken the faith of several others; and has grievously puzzled the brains of many of the oldest villagers, who had never thought about politics, or scarce any thing else, during their whole lives.

He is lean and meagre from the constant restlessness of mind and body; worrying about with newspapers and pamphlets in his pockets, which he is ready to pull out on all occasions. He has shocked several of the stanchest villagers by talking lightly of the squire and his family; and hinting that it would be better the park should be cut up into small farms and kitchen-gardens, or feed good mutton instead of worthless deer.

He is a great thorn in the side of the squire, who is sadly afraid that he will introduce politics into the village, and turn it into an unhappy, thinking community. He is a still greater grievance to Master Simon, who has hitherto been able to sway the political opinions of the place, without much cost of learning or logic; but has been very much puzzled of late to weed out the doubts and heresies already sown by this champion of reform. Indeed, the latter has taken complete command at the tap-room of the tavern, not so much because he has convinced, as because he has out-talked all the old established oracles. The apothecary, with all his philosophy, was as naught before him.

He has convinced and converted the landlord at least a dozen times; who, however, is liable to be convinced and converted the other way by the next person with whom he talks. It is true the radical has a violent antagonist in the landlady, who is vehemently loyal, and thoroughly devoted to the king, Master Simon, and the squire. She now and then comes out upon the reformer with all the fierceness of a cat-o'-mountain, and does not spare her own soft-headed husband, for listening to what she terms such "low-lived politics." What makes the good woman the more violent, is the perfect coolness with which the radical listens to her attacks, drawing his face up into a provoking, supercilious smile; and when she has talked herself out of breath, quietly asking her for a taste of her home-brewed.

The only person that is in any way a match for this redoubtable politician is Ready Money Jack Tibbets; who maintains his stand in the tap-room, in defiance of the radical and all his works. Jack is one of the most loyal men in the country, without being able to reason about the matter. He has that admirable quality for a tough arguer, also, that he never knows when he is beat. He has half a dozen old maxims, which he advances on all occasions, and though his antagonist may overturn them never so often, yet he always brings them anew to the field. He is like the robber in Ariosto, who, though his head might be cut off half a hundred times, yet whipped it on his shoulders again in a twinkling, and returned as sound a man as ever to the charge.

Whatever does not square with Jack's simple and obvious creed he sets down for "French politics;" for, notwithstanding the peace, he cannot be persuaded that the French are not still laying plots to ruin the nation, and to get hold of the Bank of England. The radical attempted to overwhelm him one day by a long passage from a newspaper; but Jack neither reads nor believes in newspapers. In reply he gave him one of the stanzas which he has by heart from his favourite, and indeed only author, old Tusser, and which he calls his Golden Rules:

> Leave princes' affairs undescanted on,
> And tend to such doings as stand thee upon;
> Fear God, and offend not the king nor his laws,
> And keep thyself out of the magistrate's claws.

When Tibbets had pronounced this with great emphasis, he pulled out a well-filled leathern purse, took out a handful of gold and silver, paid his score at the bar with great punctuality, returned his money, piece by piece, into his purse, his purse into his pocket, which he buttoned up; and then, giving his cudgel a stout thump upon the floor,

THE ROOKERY

But cawing rooks, and kites that swim sublime
In still repeated circles, screaming loud,
The jay, the pie, and e'en the boding owl,
That hails the rising moon, have charms for me.

COWPER

In a grove of tall oaks and beeches. that crowns a terrace-walk, just on the skirts of the garden, is an ancient rookery; which is one of the most important provinces in the squire's rural domains. The old gentleman sets great store by his rooks, and will not suffer one of them to be killed; in consequence of which they have increased amazingly; the tree-tops are loaded with their nests; they have encroached upon the great avenue, and have even established, in times long past, a colony among the elms and pines of the churchyard, which, like other distant colonies, has already thrown off allegiance to the mother-country.

The rooks are looked upon by the squire as a very ancient and honourable line of gentry, highly aristocratical in their notions, fond of place, and attached to church and state; as their building so loftily, keeping about churches and cathedrals, and in the venerable groves of old castles and manor-houses, sufficiently manifests. The good opinion thus expressed by the squire put me upon observing more narrowly these very respectable birds; for I confess, to my shame, I had been apt to confound them with their cousins-german the crows, to whom, at the first glance, they bear so great a family resemblance. Nothing, it seems, could be more unjust or injurious than such a mistake. The rooks and crows are, among the feathered tribes, what the Spaniards and Portuguese are among nations, the least loving, in consequence of their neighbourhood and similarity. The rooks are old-established housekeepers, high-minded gentlefolk, that have had their hereditary abodes time out of mind; but as to the poor crows, they are a kind of vagabond, predatory, gipsy race, roving about the country without any settled home; "their hands are against every body, and every body's against them," and they are gibbeted in every corn-field. Master Simon assures me that a female rook, that should so far forget herself as to consort with a crow, would inevitably be disinherited, and indeed would be totally discarded by all her genteel acquaintance.

The squire is very watchful over the interests and concerns of his sable neighbours. As to Master Simon, he even pretends to know many of them by sight, and to have given names to them; he points out several, which he says are old heads of families, and compares them to worthy old citizens, beforehand in the world, that wear cocked-hats, and silver buckles in their shoes. Notwithstanding the protecting benevolence of the squire, and their being residents in his empire, they seem to acknowledge no allegiance, and to hold no intercourse or intimacy. Their airy tenements are built almost out of the reach of gun-shot; and, notwithstanding their vicinity to the Hall, they maintain a most reserved and distrustful shyness of mankind.

There is one season of the year, however, which brings all birds in a manner to a level, and tames the pride of the loftiest highflyer; which is the season of building their nests. This takes place early in the spring, when the forest-trees first begin to show their buds; the long, withy ends of the branches to turn green; when the wild strawberry, and other herbage of the sheltered woodlands, put forth their tender and tinted leaves; and the daisy and the primrose peep from under the hedges. At this time there is a general bustle among the feathered tribes; an incessant fluttering about, and a cheerful chirping; indicative, like the germination of the vegetable world, of the reviving life and fecundity of the year.

It is then that the rooks forget their usual stateliness, and their shy and lofty habits. Instead of keeping up in the high regions of the air, swinging on the breezy tree-tops, and looking down with sovereign contempt upon the humble crawlers upon earth, they are fain to throw off for a time the dignity of the gentleman, to come down to the ground, and put on the pains-taking and industrious character of a labourer. They now lose their natural shyness, become fearless and familiar, and may be seen plying about in all directions, with an air of great assiduity, in search of building materials. Every now and then your path will be crossed by one of these busy old gentlemen, worrying about with awkward gait, as if troubled with the gout, or with corns on his toes, casting about many a prying look, turning down first one eye, then the other, in earnest consideration, upon every straw he meets with, until, espying some mighty twig, large enough to make a rafter for his air-castle, he will seize upon it with avidity, and hurry away with it to the tree-top; fearing, apparently, lest you should dispute with him the invaluable prize.

Like other castle-builders, these airy architects seem rather fanciful in the materials with which they build, and to like those most which come from a distance. Thus, though there are abundance of dry twigs on the surrounding trees, yet they never think of making use of them, but go foraging in distant lands, and come sailing home, one by one, from the ends of the earth, each bearing in his bill some precious piece of timber.

Nor must I avoid mentioning, what, I grieve to say, rather derogates from the grave and honourable character of these ancient gentlefolk, that, during the architectural season, they are subject to great dissensions among themselves; that they make no scruple to defraud and plunder each other; and that sometimes the rookery is a scene of hideous brawl and commotion, in consequence of some delinquency of the kind. One of the partners generally remains on the nest to guard it from depredation; and I have seen severe contests, when some sly neighbour has endeavoured to filch away a tempting rafter that had captivated his eye. As I am not willing to admit any suspicion hastily that should throw a stigma on the general character of so worshipful a people, I am inclined to think that these larcenies are very much discountenanced by the higher classes, and even rigorously punished by those in authority; for I have now and then seen a whole gang of rooks fall upon the nest of some individual, pull it all to pieces, carry off the spoils, and even buffet the luckless proprietor. I have concluded this to be some signal punishment inflicted upon him, by the officers of the police, for some pilfering misdemeanor; or, perhaps, that it was a crew of bailiffs carrying an execution into his house.

I have been amused with another of their movements during the building season. The steward has suffered a considerable number of sheep to graze on a lawn near the house, somewhat to the annoyance of the squire, who thinks this an innovation on the dignity of a park, which ought to be devoted to deer only. Be this as it may, there is a green knoll, not far from the drawing-room window, where the ewes and lambs are accustomed to assemble towards evening, for the benefit of the setting sun. No sooner were they gathered here, at the time when these politic birds were building, than a stately old rook, who Master Simon assured me was the chief magistrate of this community, would settle down upon the head of one of the ewes, who, seeming conscious of this condescension, would desist from grazing, and stand fixed in motionless reverence of her august burthen; the rest of the rookery would then come wheeling down, in imitation of their leader, until every ewe had two or three of them cawing, and fluttering, and battling upon her back. Whether they requited the submission of the sheep, by levying a contribution upon their fleece for the benefit of the rookery, I am not certain; though I presume they followed the usual custom of protecting powers.

The latter part of May is the time of great tribulation among the rookeries, when the young are just able to leave the nests, and balance themselves on the neighbouring branches. Now comes on the season of "rook shooting;" a terrible slaughter of the innocents. The squire, of course, prohibits all invasion of the kind on his territories; but I am told that a lamentable havoc takes place in the colony about the old church. Upon this devoted commonwealth the village charges "with all its chivalry." Every idle wight that is lucky enough to possess an old gun or blunderbuss, together with all the archery of Slingsby's school, takes the field on the occasion. In vain does the little parson interfere, or remonstrate, in angry tones, from his study window that looks into the churchyard; there is a continual popping from morning till night. Being no great marksmen, their shots are not often effective; but every now and then a great shout from the besieging army of bumpkins makes known the downfall of some unlucky, squab rook, which comes to the ground with the emphasis of a squashed apple-dumpling.

Nor is the rookery entirely free from other troubles and disasters. In so aristocratical and lofty-minded a community, which boasts so much ancient blood and hereditary pride, it is natural to suppose that questions of etiquette will sometimes arise, and affairs of honour ensue. In fact, this is very often the case; bitter quarrels break out between individuals, which produce sad scufflings on the tree-tops, and I have more than once seen a regular duel take place between two doughty heroes of the rookery. Their field of battle is generally the air; and their contest is managed in the most scientific and elegant manner; wheeling round and round each other, and towering higher and higher to get the 'vantage ground, until they sometimes disappear in the clouds before the combat is determined.

They have also fierce combats now and then with an invading hawk, and will drive him off from their territories by a *posse comitatis*. They are also extremely tenacious of their domains, and will suffer no other bird to inhabit the grove or its vicinity. There was a very ancient and respectable old bachelor owl that had long had his lodgings in a corner of the grove, but has been fairly ejected by the rooks; and has retired, disgusted with the world, to a neighbouring wood, where he leads the life of a hermit, and makes nightly complaints of his ill treatment.

The hootings of this unhappy gentleman may generally be heard in the still evenings, when the rooks are all at rest; and I have often listened to them of a moonlight night, with a kind of mysterious gratification. This gray-bearded misanthrope of course is highly respected by the squire; but the servants have superstitious notions about him; and it would be difficult to get the dairy-maid to venture after dark near to the wood which he inhabits.

Besides the private quarrels of the rooks, there are other misfortunes to which they are liable, and which often bring distress into the most respectable families of the rookery. Having the true baronial spirit of the good old feudal times, they are apt now and then to issue forth from their castles on a foray, and to lay the plebeian fields of the neighbouring country under contribution; in the course of which chivalrous expeditions they now and then get a shot from the rusty artillery of some refractory farmer. Occasionally, too, while they are quietly taking the air beyond the park boundaries, they have the incaution to come within the reach of the truant bowmen of Slingsby's school, and receive a flight shot from some unlucky urchin's arrow. In such case the wounded adventurer will sometimes have just strength enough to bring himself home, and, giving up the ghost at the rookery, will hang dangling "all abroad" on a bough, like a thief on a gibbet; an awful warning to his friends and an object of great commiseration to the squire.

But, maugre all these untoward incidents, the rooks have, upon the whole, a happy holiday life of it. When their young are reared, and fairly launched upon their native element the air, the cares of the old folks seem over, and they resume all their aristocratical dignity and idleness. I have envied them the enjoyment which they appear to have in their ethereal heights, sporting with clamorous exultation about their lofty bowers; sometimes hovering over them, sometimes partially alighting upon the topmost branches, and there balancing with outstretched wings, and swinging in the breeze. Sometimes they seem to take a fashionable drive to the church, and amuse themselves by circling in airy rings about its spire; at other times a mere garrison is left at home to mount guard in their strong hold at the grove, while the rest roam abroad to enjoy the fine weather. About sunset the garrison gives notice of their return; their faint cawing will be heard from a great distance, and they will be seen far off like a sable cloud, and then, nearer and nearer, until they all come soaring home. Then they perform several grand circuits in the air, over the Hall and garden, wheeling closer and closer, until they gradually settle down upon the grove when a prodigious cawing takes place, as though they were relating their day's adventures.

I like at such times to walk about these dusky groves, and hear the various sounds of these airy people roosted so high above me. As the gloom increases, their conversation subsides, and they seem to be gradually dropping asleep; but every now and then there is a querulous note, as if some one was quarrelling for a pillow, or a little more of the blanket. It is late in the evening before they completely sink to repose, and then their old anchorite neighbour, the owl, begins his lonely hootings from his bachelor's-hall, in the wood.

MAY-DAY

It is the choice time of the year,
For the violets now appear;
Now the rose receives its birth,
And pretty primrose decks the earth.
Then to the May-pole come away,
For it is now a holiday.

ACTÆON AND DIANA

As I was lying in bed this morning, enjoying one of those half-dreams, half reveries, which are so pleasant in the country, when the birds are singing about the window, and the sunbeams peeping through the curtains, I was roused by the sound of music. On going down stairs, I found a number of villagers dressed in their holiday clothes, bearing a pole, ornamented with garlands and ribands, and accompanied by the village band of music, under the direction of the tailor, the pale fellow who plays on the claironet. They had all sprigs of hawthorn, or, as it is called, "the May," in their hats, and had brought green branches and flowers to decorate the Hall door and windows. They had come to give notice that the May-pole was reared on the green, and to invite the household to witness the sports. The Hall, according to custom, became a scene of hurry and delighted confusion. The servants were all agog with May and music; and there was no keeping either the tongues or the feet of the maids quiet, who were anticipating the sports of the green, and the evening dance.

I repaired to the village at an early hour to enjoy the merry-making. The morning was pure and sunny, such as a May morning is always described. The fields were white with daisies, the hawthorn was covered with its fragrant blossoms, the bee hummed about every bank, and the swallow played high in the air about the village steeple. It was one of those genial days when we seem to draw in pleasure with the very air we breathe, and to feel happy we know not why. Whoever has felt the worth of worthy man, or has doted on lovely woman, will, on such a day, call them tenderly to mind, and feel his heart all alive with long-buried recollections. "For thenne," says the excellent romance of king Arthur, "lovers call ageyne to their mynde old gentilnes and old servyse, and many kind dedes that were forgotten by neglygence."

Before reaching the village, I saw the May-pole towering above the cottages, with its gay garlands and streamers, and heard the sound of music. I found that there had been booths set up near it, for the

196

reception of company; and a bower of green branches and flowers for the Queen of May, a fresh, rosy-cheeked girl of the village.

A band of morrice dancers were capering on the green in their fantastic dresses, jingling with hawks' bells, with a boy dressed up as Maid Marian, and the attendant fool rattling his box to collect contributions from the bystanders. The gipsy-women too were already plying their mystery in by-corners of the village, reading the hands of the simple country girls, and no doubt promising them all good husbands and tribes of children.

The squire made his appearance in the course of the morning, attended by the parson, and was received with loud acclamations. He mingled among the country people throughout the day, giving and receiving pleasure wherever he went. The amusements of the day were under the management of Slingsby, the schoolmaster, who is not merely lord of misrule in his school, but master of the revels to the village. He was bustling about with the perplexed and anxious air of a man who has the oppressive burthen of promoting other people's merriment upon his mind. He had involved himself in a dozen scrapes in consequence of a politic intrigue, which, by the bye, Master Simon and the Oxonian were at the bottom of, which had for object the election of the Queen of May. He had met with violent opposition from a faction of ale-drinkers, who were in favour of a bouncing bar-maid, the daughter of the innkeeper; but he had been too strongly backed not to carry his point, though it shows that these rural crowns, like all others, are objects of great ambition and heart-burning. I am told that Master Simon takes great interest, though in an underhand way, in the election of these May-day Queens, and that the chaplet is generally secured for some rustic beauty that has found favour in his eyes.

In the course of the day there were various games of strength and agility on the green, at which a knot of village veterans presided, as judges of the lists. Among these I perceived that Ready Money Jack took the lead, looking with a learned and critical eye on the merits of the different candidates; and though he was very laconic, and sometimes merely expressed himself by a nod, yet it was evident that his opinions far outweighed those of the most loquacious.

Young Jack Tibbets was the hero of the day, and carried off most of the prizes, though in some of the feats of agility, he was rivalled by the "prodigal son," who appeared much in his element on this occasion; but his most formidable competitor was the notorious gipsy, the redoubtable "Star-light Tom." I was rejoiced at having an opportunity of seeing this "minion of the moon" in broad daylight. I found him a tall, swarthy, good-looking fellow, with a lofty air, something like what I have seen in an Indian chieftain; and with a certain lounging, easy, and almost graceful carriage, which I have often remarked in beings of the lazaroni order, that lead an idle, loitering life, and have a gentlemanlike contempt of labour.

Master Simon and the old general reconnoitered the ground together, and indulged a vast deal of harmless raking among the buxom country girls. Master Simon would give some of them a kiss on meeting with them, and would ask after their sisters, for he is acquainted with most of the farmers' families. Sometimes he would whisper, and affect to talk mischievously with them, and, if bantered on the subject, would turn it off with a laugh, though it was evident he liked to be suspected of being a gay Lothario amongst them.

He had much to say to the farmers about their farms; and seemed to know all their horses by name. There was an old fellow, with a round ruddy face, and a night-cap under his hat, the village wit, who took several occasions to crack a joke with him in the hearing of his companions, to whom he would turn and wink hard when Master Simon had passed.

The harmony of the day, however, had nearly, at one time, been interrupted, by the appearance of the radical on the ground, with two or three of his disciples. He soon got engaged in argument in the very thick of the throng, above which I could hear his voice, and now and then see his meagre hand, half a mile out of the sleeve, elevated in the air in violent gesticulation, and flourishing a pamphlet by way of truncheon. He was decrying these idle nonsensical amusements in times of public distress, when it was every one's business to think of other matters, and to be miserable. The honest village logicians could make no stand against him, especially as he was seconded by his proselytes; when, to their great joy, Master Simon and the general came drifting down into the field of action. I saw that Master Simon was for making off, as soon as he found himself in the neighbourhood of this fireship; but the general was too loyal to suffer such talk in his hearing, and thought, no doubt, that a look and a word from a gentleman would be sufficient to shut up so shabby an orator. The latter, however, was no respecter of persons, but rather seemed to exult in having such important antagonists. He talked with greater volubility than ever, and soon drowned them in declamation on the subject of taxes, poor's rates, and the national debt. Master Simon endeavoured to brush along in his usual excursive manner, which had always answered amazingly well with the villagers; but the radical was one of those pestilent fellows that pin a man down to facts, and, indeed, he had two or three pamphlets in his pocket, to support every thing he advanced by printed documents. The general, too, found himself betrayed into a more serious action than his dignity could brook; and looked like a mighty Dutch Indiaman grievously peppered by a petty privateer. It was in vain that he swelled and looked big; and talked large, and endeavoured to make up by pomp of manner for poverty of matter; every home-thrust of the radical made him wheeze like a bellows, and seemed to let a volume of wind out of him. In a word, the two worthies from the Hall were completely dumb-founded, and this too in the presence of several of Master Simon's stanch admirers, who had always looked up to him as infallible. I do not know how he and the general would have managed to draw their forces decently from the field, had there not been a match at grinning through a horse-collar announced, whereupon the radical retired with great expression of contempt, and, as soon as his back was turned, the argument was carried against him all hollow.

"Did you ever hear such a pack of stuff, general?" said Master Simon; "there's no talking with one of these chaps when he once gets that confounded Cobbett in his head."

"S'blood, sir!" said the general, wiping his forehead, "such fellows ought all to be transported!"

In the latter part of the day the ladies from the Hall paid a visit to the green. The fair Julia made her appearance, leaning on her lover's arm, and looking extremely pale and interesting. As she is a great favourite in the village, where she has been known from childhood; and as her late accident had been much talked about, the sight of her caused very manifest delight, and some of the old women of the village blessed her sweet face as she passed.

While they were walking about, I noticed the schoolmaster in earnest conversation with the young girl that represented the Queen of May, evidently endeavouring to spirit her up to some formidable undertaking. At length, as the party from the Hall approached her bower, she came forth, faltering at every step, until she reached the spot where the fair Julia stood between her lover and Lady Lillycraft. The little Queen then took the chaplet of flowers from her head, and attempted to put it on that of the bride elect; but the confusion of both was so great, that the wreath would have fallen to the ground, had not the officer caught it, and, laughing, placed it upon the blushing brows of his mistress. There was something charming in the very embarrassment of these two young creatures, both so beautiful, yet so different in their kinds of beauty. Master Simon told me, afterwards, that the Queen of May was to have spoken a few verses which the schoolmaster had written for her; but that she had neither wit to understand, nor memory to recollect them. "Besides," added he, "between you and I, she murders the king's English abominably; so she has acted the part of a wise woman in holding her tongue, and trusting to her pretty face."

Among the other characters from the Hall was Mrs. Hannah, my Lady Lillycraft's gentlewoman: to my surprise she was escorted by old Christy the huntsman, and followed by his ghost of a greyhound; but I find they are very old acquaintances; being drawn together by some sympathy of disposition. Mrs. Hannah moved about with starched dignity among the rustics, who drew back from her with more awe than they did from her mistress. Her mouth seemed shut as with a clasp; excepting that I now and then heard the word "fellows!" escape from between her lips, as she got accidentally jostled in the crowd.

But there was one other heart present that did not enter into the merriment of the scene, which was that of the simple Phœbe Wilkins, the housekeeper's niece. The poor girl has continued to pine and whine for some time past, in consequence of the obstinate coldness of her lover; never was a little flirtation more severely punished. She appeared this day on the green, gallanted by a smart servant out of livery, and had evidently resolved to try the hazardous experiment of awakening the jealousy of her lover. She was dressed in her very best; affected an air of great gaiety; talked loud and girlishly, and laughed when there was nothing to laugh at. There was, however, an aching, heavy heart, in the poor baggage's bosom, in spite of all her levity. Her eye turned every now and then in quest of her reckless lover, and her cheek grew pale, and her fictitious gaiety vanished, on seeing him paying his rustic homage to the little May-day Queen.

My attention was now diverted by a fresh stir and bustle. Music was heard from a distance; a banner was seen advancing up the road, preceded by a rustic band playing something like a march, and followed by a sturdy throng of country lads, the chivalry of a neighbouring and rival village.

No sooner had they reached the green than they challenged the heroes of the day to new trials of strength and activity. Several gymnastic contests ensued for the honour of the respective villages. In the course of these exercises, young Tibbets and the champion of the adverse party had an obstinate match at wrestling. They tugged, and strained, and panted, without either getting the mastery, until both came to the ground, and rolled upon the green. Just then the disconsolate Phœbe came by. She saw her recreant lover in fierce contest, as she thought, and in danger. In a moment pride, pique, and coquetry were forgotten: she rushed into the ring, seized upon the rival champion by the hair, and was on the point of wreaking on him her puny vengeance, when a buxom, strapping country lass, the sweetheart of the prostrate swain, pounced upon her like a hawk, and would have stripped her of her fine plumage in a twinkling, had she also not been seized in her turn.

A complete tumult ensued. The chivalry of the two villages became embroiled. Blows began to be dealt, and sticks to be flourished. Phœbe was carried off from the field in hysterics. In vain did the sages of the village interfere. The sententious apothecary endeavoured to pour the soothing oil of his philosophy upon this tempestuous sea of passion, but was tumbled into the dust. Slingsby the pedagogue, who is a great lover of peace, went into the midst of the throng, as marshal of the day, to put an end to the commotion; but was rent in twain, and came out with his garment hanging in two strips from his shoulders: upon which the prodigal son dashed in with fury to revenge the insult which his patron had sustained. The tumult thickened; I caught glimpses of the jockey-cap of old Christy, like the helmet of a chieftain, bobbing about in the midst of the scuffle; while Mistress Hannah, separated from her doughty protector, was squalling and striking at right and left with a faded parasol; being tossed and tousled about by the crowd in such wise as never happened to maiden gentlewoman before.

At length I beheld old Ready Money Jack making his way into the very thickest of the throng; tearing it, as it were, apart, and enforcing peace *vi et armis*. It was surprising to see the sudden quiet that ensued. The storm settled down at once into tranquillity. The parties, having no real grounds of hostility, were readily pacified, and in fact were a little at a loss to know why and how they had got by the ears. Slingsby was speedily stitched together again by his friend the tailor, and resumed his usual good humour. Mrs. Hannah drew on one side to plume her rumpled feathers; and old Christy having repaired his damages, took her under his arm, and they swept back again to the Hall, ten times more bitter against mankind than ever.

The Tibbets family alone seemed slow in recovering from the agitation of the scene. Young Jack was evidently very much moved by the heroism of the unlucky Phœbe. His mother, who had been summoned to the field of action by news of the affray, was in a sad panic, and had need of all her management to keep him from following his mistress, and coming to a perfect reconciliation.

What heightened the alarm and perplexity of the good managing dame was, that the matter had aroused the slow apprehension of old Ready Money himself; who was very much struck by the intrepid interference of so pretty and delicate a girl, and was sadly puzzled to understand the meaning of the violent agitation in his family.

When all this came to the ears of the squire, he was grievously scandalized that his May-day fête should have been disgraced by such a brawl. He ordered Phœbe to appear before him, but the girl was so frightened and distressed, that she came sobbing and trembling, and, at the first question he asked, fell again into hysterics. Lady Lillycraft, who had understood that there was an affair of the heart at the bottom of this distress, immediately took the girl into great favour and protection, and made her peace with the squire. This was the only thing that disturbed the harmony of the day, if we except the discomfiture of Master Simon and the general by the radical. Upon the whole, therefore, the squire had very fair reason to be satisfied that he had rode his hobby throughout the day without any other molestation.

The reader, learned in these matters, will perceive that all this was but a faint shadow of the once gay and fanciful rites of May. The peasantry have lost the proper feeling for these rites, and have grown almost as strange to them as the boors of La Mancha were to the customs of chivalry in the days of the valorous Don Quixote. Indeed, I considered it a proof of the discretion with which the squire rides his hobby, that he had not pushed the thing any further, nor attempted to revive many obsolete usages of the day, which, in the present matter-of-fact times, would appear affected and absurd. I must say, though I do it under the rose, the general brawl in which this festival had nearly terminated, has made me doubt whether these rural customs of the good old times were always so very loving and innocent as we are apt to fancy them; and whether the peasantry in those times were really so Arcadian as they have been fondly represented. I begin to fear –

> —— "Those days were never; airy dreams
> Sat for the picture, and the poet's hand,
> Imparting substance to an empty shade,
> Impos'd a gay delirium for a truth.
> Grant it; I still must envy them an age
> That favoured such a dream."

THE MANUSCRIPT

Yesterday was a day of quiet and repose after the bustle of May-day. During the morning I joined the ladies in a small sitting-room, the windows of which came down to the floor, and opened upon a terrace of the garden, which was set out with delicate shrubs and flowers. The soft sunshine that fell into the room through the branches of trees that overhung the windows, the sweet smell of the flowers, and the singing of the birds, seemed to produce a pleasing, yet calming effect on the whole party, for some time elapsed without any one speaking. Lady Lillycraft and Miss Templeton were sitting by an elegant work-table, near one of the windows, occupied with some pretty lady-like work. The captain was on a stool at his mistress' feet, looking over some music, and poor Phœbe Wilkins, who has always been a kind of pet among the ladies, but who has risen vastly in favour with Lady Lillycraft, in consequence of some tender confessions, sat in one corner of the room, with swoln eyes, working pensively at some of the fair Julia's wedding ornaments.

The silence was interrupted by her ladyship, who suddenly proposed a task to the captain. "I am in your debt," said she, "for that tale you read to us the other day; I will now furnish one in return, if you'll read it: and it is just suited to this sweet May morning, for it is all about love!"

The proposition seemed to delight every one present. The captain smiled assent. Her ladyship rung for her page, and despatched him to her room for the manuscript. "As the captain," said she, "gave us an account of the author of his story, it is but right I should give one of mine. It was written by the parson of the parish where I reside. He is a thin, elderly man, of a delicate constitution, but positively one of the most charming men that ever lived. He lost his wife a few years since; one of the sweetest women you ever saw. He has two sons, whom he educates himself; both of whom already write delightful poetry. His parsonage is a lovely place, close by the church, all overrun with ivy and honeysuckles; with the sweetest flower-garden about it; for, you know, our country clergymen are almost always fond of flowers, and make their parsonages perfect pictures.

"His living is a very good one, and he is very much beloved, and does a great deal of good in the neighbourhood, and among the poor. And then such sermons as he preaches! Oh, if you could only hear one taken from a text in Solomon's Song, all about love and matrimony, one of the sweetest things you ever heard! He preaches it at least once a year, in spring time, for he knows I am fond of it. He always dines with me on Sundays, and often brings me some of the sweetest pieces of poetry, all about the pleasures of melancholy, and such subjects, that make me cry so, you can't think. I wish he would publish. I think he has some things as sweet as any thing in Moore or Lord Byron.

"He fell into very ill health some time ago, and was advised to go to the continent; and I gave him no peace until he went, and promised to take care of his two boys until he returned.

"He was gone for above a year, and was quite restored. When he came back, he sent me the tale I'm going to show you. – Oh, here it is!" said she, as the page put in her hands a beautiful box of satin-wood. She unlocked it, and from among several parcels of notes on embossed paper, cards of charades, and copies of verses, she drew out a crimson velvet case, that smelt very much of perfumes. From this she took a manuscript, daintily written on gilt-edged vellum paper, and stitched with a light blue riband. This she handed to the captain, who read the following tale, which I have procured for the entertainment of the reader.

ANNETTE DELARBRE

The soldier frae the war returns,
And the merchant from the main,
But I hae parted wi' my love,
And ne'er to meet again,
    My dear,
And ne'er to meet again.

When day is gone, and night is come,
And a' are boun to sleep,
I think on them that's far awa
The lee-lang night and weep,
    My dear,
The lee-lang night and weep.

           OLD SCOTCH BALLAD

In the course of a tour that I once made in Lower Normandy I remained for a day or two at the old town of Honfleur, which stands near the mouth of the Seine. It was the time of a fête, and all the world was thronging in the evening to dance at the fair, held before the chapel of Our Lady of Grace. As I like all kinds of innocent merry-making, I joined the throng.

The chapel is situated at the top of a high hill, or promontory, from whence its bell may be heard at a distance by the mariner at night. It is said to have given the name to the port of Havre de Grace, which lies directly opposite, on the other side of the Seine. The road up to the chapel went in a zig-zag course, along the brow of the steep coast; it was shaded by trees, from between which I had beautiful peeps at the ancient towers of Honfleur below, the varied scenery of the opposite shore, the white buildings of Havre in the distance, and the wide sea beyond. The road was enlivened by groups of peasant girls, in their bright crimson dresses, and tall caps; and I found all the flower of the neighbourhood assembled on the green that crowns the summit of the hill.

The chapel of Notre Dame de Grace is a favourite resort of the inhabitants of Honfleur and its vicinity, both for pleasure and devotion. At this little chapel prayers are put up by the mariners of the port previous to their voyages, and by their friends during their absence; and votive offerings are hung about its walls, in fulfilment of vows made during times of shipwreck and disaster. The chapel is surrounded by trees. Over the portal is an image of the Virgin and Child, with an inscription which struck me as being quite poetical:

205

"Etoile de la mer, priez pour nous!"
(Star of the sea, pray for us.)

On a level spot near the chapel, under a grove of noble trees, the populace dance on fine summer evenings; and here are held frequent fairs and fêtes, which assemble all the rustic beauty of the loveliest parts of Lower Normandy. The present was an occasion of the kind. Booths and tents were erected among the trees; there were the usual displays of finery to tempt the rural coquette, and of wonderful shows to entice the curious; mountebanks were exerting their eloquence; jugglers and fortune-tellers astonishing the credulous; while whole rows of grotesque saints, in wood and wax-work, were offered for the purchase of the pious.

The fête had assembled in one view all the picturesque costumes of the Pays d'Auge, and the Coté de Caux. I beheld tall, stately caps, and trim boddices, according to fashions which have been handed down from mother to daughter for centuries, the exact counterparts of those worn in the time of the Conqueror; and which surprised me by their faithful resemblance to those which I had seen in the old pictures of Froissart's Chronicles, and in the paintings of illuminated manuscripts. Any one, also, that has been in Lower Normandy, must have remarked the beauty of the peasantry, and that air of native elegance which prevails among them. It is to this country, undoubtedly, that the English owe their good looks. It was from hence that the bright carnation, the fine blue eye, the light auburn hair, passed over to England in the train of the Conqueror, and filled the land with beauty.

The scene before me was perfectly enchanting; the assemblage of so many fresh and blooming faces; the gay groups in fanciful dresses; some dancing on the green, others strolling about, or seated on the grass; the fine clumps of trees in the foreground, bordering the brow of this airy height, and the broad green sea, sleeping in summer tranquillity, in the distance.

Whilst I was regarding this animated picture, I was struck with the appearance of a beautiful girl, who passed through the crowd without seeming to take any interest in their amusements. She was slender and delicate in her form; she had not the bloom upon her cheek that is usual among the peasantry of Normandy, and her blue eyes had a singular and melancholy expression. She was accompanied by a venerable looking man, whom I presumed to be her father. There was a whisper among the bystanders, and a wistful look after her as she passed; the young men touched their hats, and some of the children followed her at a little distance, watching her movements. She approached the edge of the hill, where there is a little platform, from whence the people of Honfleur look out for the approach of vessels. Here she stood for some time waving her handkerchief, though there was nothing to be seen but two or three fishing-boats, like mere specks on the bosom of the distant ocean.

These circumstances excited my curiosity, and I made some inquiries about her, which were answered with readiness and intelligence by a priest of the neighbouring chapel. Our conversation drew together several of the bystanders, each of whom had something to communicate, and from them all I gathered the following particulars.

Annette Delarbre was the only daughter of one of the higher order of farmers, or small proprietors, as they are called, who lived at Pont l'Eveque, a pleasant village not far from Honfleur, in that rich pastoral part of Lower Normandy called the Pays d'Auge. Annette was the pride and delight of her parents, and was brought up with the fondest indulgence. She was gay, tender, petulant, and susceptible. All her feelings were quick and ardent; and having never experienced contradiction or restraint, she was little practised in self-control: nothing but the native goodness of her heart kept her from running continually into error.

Even while a child, her susceptibility was evinced in an attachment which she formed to a playmate, Eugene La Forgue, the only son of a widow who lived in the neighbourhood. Their childish love was an epitome of maturer passion; it had its caprices, and jealousies, and quarrels, and reconciliations. It was assuming something of a graver character as Annette entered her fifteenth, and Eugene his nineteenth year, when he was suddenly carried off to the army by the conscription.

It was a heavy blow to his widowed mother, for he was her only pride and comfort; but it was one of those sudden bereavements which mothers were perpetually doomed to feel in France, during the time that continual and bloody wars were incessantly draining her youth. It was a temporary affliction also to Annette, to lose her lover. With tender embraces, half childish, half womanish, she parted from him. The tears streamed from her blue eyes, as she bound a braid of her fair hair round his wrist; but the smiles still broke through; for she was yet too young to feel how serious a thing is separation, and how many chances there are, when parting in this wide world, against our ever meeting again.

Weeks, months, years flew by. Annette increased in beauty as she increased in years, and was the reigning belle of the neighbourhood. Her time passed innocently and happily. Her father was a man of some consequence in the rural community, and his house was the resort of the gayest of the village. Annette held a kind of rural court; she was always surrounded by companions of her own age, among whom she shone unrivalled. Much of their time was past in making lace, the prevalent manufacture of the neighbourhood. As they sat at this delicate and feminine labour, the merry tale and sprightly song went round: none laughed with a lighter heart than Annette; and if she sang, her voice was perfect melody. Their evenings were enlivend by the dance, or by those pleasant social games so prevalent among the French; and when she appeared at the village ball on Sunday evenings, she was the theme of universal admiration.

As she was a rural heiress, she did not want for suitors. Many advantageous offers were made her, but she refused them all. She laughed at the pretended pangs of her admirers, and triumphed over them with the caprice of buoyant youth and conscious beauty. With all her apparent levity, however, could any one have read the story of her heart, they might have traced in it some fond remembrance of her early playmate, not so deeply graven as to be painful, but too deep to be easily obliterated; and they might have noticed, amidst all her gaiety, the tenderness that marked her manner towards the mother of Eugene. She would often steal away from her youthful companions and their amusements, to pass whole days with the good widow; listening to her fond talk about her boy, and blushing with secret pleasure when his letters were read, at finding herself a constant theme of recollection and inquiry.

At length the sudden return of peace, which sent many a warrior to his native cottage, brought back Eugene, a young sun-burnt soldier, to the village. I need not say how rapturously his return was greeted by his mother, who saw in him the pride and staff of her old age. He had risen in the service by his merit; but brought away little from the wars, excepting a soldier-like air, a gallant name, and a scar across the forehead. He brought back, however, a nature unspoiled by the camp. He was frank, open, generous, and ardent. His heart was quick and kind in its impulses, and was perhaps a little softer from having suffered: it was full of tenderness for Annette. He had received frequent accounts of her from his mother; and the mention of her kindness to his lonely parent had rendered her doubly dear to him. He had been wounded; he had been a prisoner; he had been in various troubles, but he had always preserved the braid of her hair, which she had bound round his arm. It had been a kind of talisman to him; he had many a time looked upon it as he lay on the hard ground, and the thought that he might one day see Annette again, and the fair fields about his native village, had cheered his heart, and enabled him to bear up against every hardship.

He had left Annette almost a child; he found her a blooming woman. If he had loved her before, he now adored her. Annette was equally struck with the improvement which time had made in her lover. She noticed, with secret admiration, his superiority to the other young men of the village; the frank, lofty, military air, that distinguished him from all the rest at their rural gatherings. The more she saw him, the more her light, playful fondness of former years deepened into ardent and powerful affection. But Annette was a rural belle. She had tasted the sweets of dominion, and had been rendered wilful and capricious by constant indulgence at home, and admiration abroad. She was conscious of her power over Eugene, and delighted in exercising it. She sometimes treated him with petulant caprice, enjoying the pain which she inflicted by her frowns, from the idea how soon she would chase it away again by her smiles. She took a pleasure in alarming his fears, by affecting a temporary preference for some one or other of his rivals; and then would delight in allaying them by an ample measure of returning kindness. Perhaps there was some degree of vanity gratified by all this; it might be a matter of triumph to show her absolute power over the young soldier, who was the universal object of female admiration. Eugene, however, was of too serious and ardent a nature to be trifled with. He loved too fervently not to be filled with doubt. He saw Annette surrounded by admirers, and full of animation; the gayest among the gay at all their rural festivities, and apparently most gay when he was most dejected. Every one saw through this caprice but himself; every one saw that in reality she doted on him; but Eugene alone suspected the sincerity of her affection. For some time he bore this coquetry with secret impatience and distrust; but his feelings grew sore and irritable, and overcame his self-command. A slight misunderstanding took place; a quarrel ensued. Annette, unaccustomed to be thwarted and contradicted, and full of the insolence of youthful beauty, assumed an air of disdain. She refused all explanations to her lover, and they parted in anger. That very evening Eugene saw her, full of gaiety, dancing with one of his rivals; and as her eye caught his, fixed on her with unfeigned distress, it sparkled with more than usual vivacity. It was a finishing blow to his hopes, already so much impaired by secret distrust. Pride and resentment both struggled in his breast, and seemed to rouse his spirit to all its wonted energy. He retired from her presence with the hasty determination never to see her again.

A woman is more considerate in affairs of love than a man; because love is more the study and business of her life. Annette soon repented of her indiscretion; she felt that she had used her lover unkindly; she felt that she had trifled with his sincere and generous nature – and then he looked so handsome when he parted after their quarrel – his fine features lighted up by indignation. She had intended making up with him at the evening dance; but his sudden departure prevented her. She now promised herself that when next they met she would amply repay him by the sweets of a perfect reconciliation, and that, thenceforward, she would never – never tease him more! That promise was not to be fulfilled. Day after day passed; but Eugene did not make his appearance. Sunday evening came, the usual time when all the gaiety of the village assembled; but Eugene was not there. She inquired after him; he had left the village. She now became alarmed, and, forgetting all coyness and affected indifference, called on Eugene's mother for an explanation. She found her full of affliction, and learnt with surprise and consternation that Eugene had gone to sea.

While his feelings were yet smarting with her affected disdain, and his heart a prey to alternate indignation and despair, he had suddenly embraced an invitation which had repeatedly been made him by a relation, who was fitting out a ship from the port of Honfleur, and who wished him to be the companion of his voyage. Absence appeared to him the only cure for his unlucky passion; and in the temporary transports of his feelings, there was something gratifying in the idea of having half the world intervene between them. The hurry necessary for his departure left no time for cool reflection; it rendered him deaf to the remonstrances of his afflicted mother. He hastened to Honfleur just in time to make the needful preparations for the voyage; and the first news that Annette received of this sudden determination was a letter delivered by his mother, returning her pledges of affection, particularly the long-treasured braid of her hair, and bidding her a last farewell, in terms more full of sorrow and tenderness than upbraiding.

This was the first stroke of real anguish that Annette had ever received, and it overcame her. The vivacity of her spirits were apt to hurry her to extremes; she for a time gave way to ungovernable transports of affliction and remorse, and manifested, in the violence of her grief, the real ardour of her affection. The thought occurred to her that the ship might not yet have sailed; she seized on the hope with eagerness, and hastened with her father to Honfleur. The ship had sailed that very morning. From the heights above the town she saw it lessening to a speck on the broad bosom of the ocean, and before evening the white sail had faded from her sight. She turned full of anguish to the neighbouring chapel of Our Lady of Grace, and throwing herself on the pavement, poured out prayers and tears for the safe return of her lover.

When she returned home the cheerfulness of her spirits was at an end. She looked back with remorse and self-upbraiding at her past caprices; she turned with distaste from the adulation of her admirers, and had no longer any relish for the amusements of the village. With humiliation and diffidence she sought the widowed mother of Eugene; but was received by her with an overflowing heart; for she only beheld in Annette one who could sympathise in her doting fondness for her son. It seemed some alleviation of her remorse to sit by the mother all day, to study her wants, to beguile her heavy hours, to hang about her with the caressing endearments of a daughter, and to seek by every means, if possible, to supply the place of the son, whom she reproached herself with having driven away.

In the mean time the ship made a prosperous voyage to her destined port. Eugene's mother received a letter from him, in which he lamented the precipitancy of his departure. The voyage had given him time for sober reflection. If Annette had been unkind to him, he ought not to have forgotten what was due to his mother, who was now advanced in years. He accused himself of selfishness in only listening to the suggestions of his own inconsiderate passions. He promised to return with the ship, to make his mind up to his disappointment, and to think of nothing but making his mother happy——"And when he does return," said Annette, clasping her hands with transport, "it shall not be my fault if he ever leaves us again."

The time approached for the ship's return. She was daily expected, when the weather became dreadfully tempestuous. Day after day brought news of vessels foundered, or driven on shore, and the sea coast was strewed with wrecks. Intelligence was received of the looked-for ship having been seen dismasted in a violent storm, and the greatest fears were entertained for her safety.

Annette never left the side of Eugene's mother. She watched every change of her countenance with painful solicitude, and endeavoured to cheer her with hopes, while her own mind was racked by anxiety. She tasked her efforts to be gay; but it was a forced and unnatural gaiety: a sigh from the mother would completely check it; and when she could no longer restrain the rising tears, she would hurry away and pour out her agony in secret. Every anxious look, every anxious inquiry of the mother, whenever a door opened, or a strange face appeared, was an arrow to her soul. She considered every disappointment as a pang of her own infliction, and her heart sickened under the care-worn expression of the maternal eye. At length this suspense became insupportable. She left the village and hastened to Honfleur, hoping every hour, every moment, to receive some tidings of her lover. She paced the pier, and wearied the seamen of the port with her inquiries. She made a daily pilgrimage to the chapel of Our Lady of Grace; hung votive garlands on the wall, and passed hours either kneeling before the altar, or looking out from the brow of the hill upon the angry sea.

At length word was brought that the long-wished-for vessel was in sight. She was seen standing into the mouth of the Seine, shattered and crippled, bearing marks of having been sadly tempest-tossed. There was a general joy diffused by her return; and there was not a brighter eye, nor a lighter heart, than Annette's in the little port of Honfleur. The ship came to anchor in the river; and shortly after a boat put off for the shore. The populace crowded down to the pier-head to welcome it. Annette stood blushing, and smiling, and trembling, and weeping; for a thousand painfully pleasing emotions agitated her breast at the thoughts of the meeting and reconciliation about to take place. Her heart throbbed to pour itself out, and atone to her gallant lover for all its errors. At one moment she would place herself in a conspicuous situation, where she might catch his view at once, and surprise him by her welcome; but the next moment a doubt would come across her mind, and she would shrink among the throng, trembling and faint, and gasping with her emotions. Her agitation increased as the boat drew near, until it became distressing; and it was almost a relief to her when she perceived that her lover was not there. She presumed that some accident had detained him on board of the ship; and she felt that the delay would enable her to gather more self-possession for the meeting. As the boat neared the shore, many inquiries were made, and laconic answers returned. At length Annette heard some inquiries after her lover. Her heart palpitated; there was a moment's pause: the reply was brief, but awful. He had been washed from the deck, with two of the crew, in the midst of a stormy night, when it was impossible to render any assistance. A piercing shriek broke from among the crowd; and Annette had nearly fallen into the waves.

The sudden revulsion of feelings after such a transient gleam of happiness, was too much for her harassed frame. She was carried home senseless. Her life was for some time despaired of, and it was months before she recovered her health; but she never had perfectly recovered her mind: it still remained unsettled with respect to her lover's fate.

"The subject," continued my informer, "is never mentioned in her hearing; but she sometimes speaks of it herself, and it seems as though there were some vague train of impressions in her mind, in which hope and fear are strangely mingled; some imperfect idea of her lover's shipwreck, and yet some expectation of his return.

"Her parents have tried every means to cheer her, and to banish these gloomy images from her thoughts. They assemble round her the young companions in whose society she used to delight; and they will work, and chat, and sing, and laugh, as formerly; but she will sit silently among them, and will sometimes weep in the midst of their gaiety; and, if spoken to, will make no reply, but look up with streaming eyes, and sing a dismal little song, which she has learned somewhere, about a shipwreck. It makes every one's heart ache to see her in this way, for she used to be the happiest creature in the village.

"She passes the greater part of the time with Eugene's mother; whose only consolation is her society, and who dotes on her with a mother's tenderness. She is the only one that has perfect influence over Annette in every mood. The poor girl seems, as formerly, to make an effort to be cheerful in her company; but will sometimes gaze upon her with the most piteous look, and then kiss her gray hairs, and fall on her neck and weep.

"She is not always melancholy, however; she has occasional intervals when she will be bright and animated for days together; but there is a degree of wildness attending these fits of gaiety, that prevents their yielding any satisfaction to her friends. At such times she will arrange her room, which is all covered with pictures of ships and legends of saints; and will wreath a white chaplet, as if for a wedding, and prepare wedding ornaments. She will listen anxiously at the door, and look frequently out at the window, as if expecting some one's arrival. It is supposed that at such times she is looking for her lover's return; but, as no one touches upon the theme, or mentions his name in her presence, the current of her thoughts is mere matter of conjecture. Now and then she will make a pilgrimage to the chapel of Notre Dame de Grace; where she will pray for hours at the altar, and decorate the images with wreaths that she has woven; or will wave her handkerchief from the terrace, as you have seen, if there is any vessel in the distance."

Upwards of a year, he informed me, had now elapsed without effacing from her mind this singular taint of insanity; still her friends hoped it might gradually wear away. They had at one time removed her to a distant part of the country, in hopes that absence from the scenes connected with her story might have a salutary effect; but, when her periodical melancholy returned, she became more restless and wretched than usual, and, secretly escaping from her friends, set out on foot, without knowing the road, on one of her pilgrimages to the chapel.

This little story entirely drew my attention from the gay scene of the fête, and fixed it upon the beautiful Annette. While she was yet standing on the terrace the vesper-bell was rung from the neighbouring chapel. She listened for a moment, and then, drawing a small rosary from her bosom, walked in that direction. Several of the peasantry followed her in silence; and I felt too much interested not to do the same.

The chapel, as I said before, is in the midst of a grove, on the high promontory. The inside is hung round with little models of ships, and rude paintings of wrecks and perils at sea, and providential deliverances; the votive offerings of captains and crews that have been saved. On entering, Annette paused for a moment before a picture of the Virgin, which, I observed, had recently been decorated with a wreath of artificial flowers. When she reached the middle of the chapel she knelt down, and those who followed her involuntarily did the same at a little distance. The evening sun shone softly through the chequered grove into one window of the chapel. A perfect stillness reigned within; and this stillness was the more impressive, contrasted with the distant sound of music and merriment from the fair. I could not take my eyes off from the poor suppliant; her lips moved as she told her beads, but her prayers were breathed in silence. It might have been mere fancy excited by the scene, that, as she raised her eyes to heaven, I thought they had an expression truly seraphic. But I am easily affected by female beauty, and there was something in this mixture of love, devotion, and partial insanity, that was inexpressibly touching.

As the poor girl left the chapel, there was a sweet serenity in her looks; and I was told that she would return home, and in all probability be calm and cheerful for days, and even weeks; in which time it was supposed that hope predominated in her mental malady; and that when the dark side of her mind, as her friends call it, was about to turn up, it would be known by her neglecting her distaff or her lace, singing plaintive songs, and weeping in silence.

She passed on from the chapel without noticing the fête, but smiling and speaking to many as she passed. I followed her with my eye as she descended the winding road towards Honfleur, leaning on her father's arm. "Heaven," thought I, "has ever its store of balms for the hurt mind and wounded spirit, and may in time rear up this broken flower to be once more the pride and joy of the valley. The very delusion in which the poor girl walks may be one of those mists kindly diffused by Providence over the regions of thought, when they become too fruitful of misery. The veil may gradually be raised which obscures the horizon of her mind, as she is enabled steadily and calmly to contemplate the sorrows at present hidden in mercy from her view."

On my return from Paris, about a year afterwards, I turned off from the beaten route at Rouen, to revisit some of the most striking scenes of Lower Normandy. Having passed through the lovely country of the Pays d'Auge, I reached Honfleur on a fine afternoon, intending to cross to Havre the next morning, and embark for England. As I had no better way of passing the evening, I strolled up the hill to enjoy the fine prospect from the chapel of Notre Dame de Grace; and while there, I thought of inquiring after the fate of poor Annette Delarbre. The priest who had told me her story was officiating at vespers, after which I accosted him, and learnt from him the remaining circumstances. He told me that from the time I had seen her at the chapel, her disorder took a sudden turn for the worse, and her health rapidly declined. Her cheerful intervals became shorter and less frequent, and attended with more incoherency. She grew languid, silent, and moody in her melancholy; her form was wasted, her looks pale and disconsolate, and it was feared she would never recover. She became impatient of all sounds of gaiety, and was never so contented as when Eugene's mother was near her. The good woman watched over her with patient, yearning solicitude; and in seeking to beguile her sorrows, would half forget her own. Sometimes, as she sat looking upon her pallid face, the tears would fill her eyes, which, when Annette perceived, she would anxiously wipe them away, and tell her not to grieve, for that Eugene would soon return; and then she would affect a forced gaiety, as in former times, and sing a lively air; but a sudden recollection would come over her, and she would burst into tears, hang on the poor mother's neck, and entreat her not to curse her for having destroyed her son.

Just at this time, to the astonishment of every one, news was received of Eugene; who, it appeared, was still living. When almost drowned, he had fortunately seized upon a spar which had been washed from the ship's deck. Finding himself nearly exhausted, he had fastened himself to it, and floated for a day and night, until all sense had left him. On recovering, he had found himself on board a vessel bound to India, but so ill as not to move without assistance. His health had continued precarious throughout the voyage; on arriving in India he had experienced many vicissitudes, and had been transferred from ship to ship, and hospital to hospital. His constitution had enabled him to struggle through every hardship; and he was now in a distant port, waiting only for the sailing of a ship to return home.

Great caution was necessary in imparting these tidings to the mother, and even then she was nearly overcome by the transports of her joy. But how to impart them to Annette was a matter of still greater perplexity. Her state of mind had been so morbid; she had been subject to such violent changes, and the cause of her derangement had been of such an inconsolable and hopeless kind, that her friends had always forborne to tamper with her feelings. They had never even hinted at the subject of her griefs, nor encouraged the theme when she adverted to it, but had passed it over in silence, hoping that time would gradually wear the traces of it from her recollection, or, at least, would render them less painful. They now felt at a loss how to undeceive her even in her misery, lest the sudden recurrence of happiness might confirm the estrangement of her reason, or might overpower her enfeebled frame. They ventured, however, to probe those wounds which they formerly did not dare to touch, for they now had the balm to pour into them. They led the conversation to those topics which they had hitherto shunned, and endeavoured to ascertain the current of her thoughts in those varying moods that had formerly perplexed them. They found, however, that her mind was even more affected than they had imagined. All her ideas were confused and wandering. Her bright and cheerful moods, which now grew seldomer than ever, were all the effects of mental delusion. At such times she had no recollection of her lover's having been in danger, but was only anticipating his arrival. "When the winter has passed away," said she, "and the trees put on their blossoms, and the swallow comes back over the sea, he will return." When she was drooping and desponding, it was in vain to remind her of what she had said in her gayer moments, and to assure her that Eugene would indeed return shortly. She wept on in silence, and appeared insensible to their words. But at times her agitation became violent, when she would upbraid herself with having driven Eugene from his mother, and brought sorrow on her gray hairs. Her mind admitted but one leading idea at a time, which nothing could divert or efface; or if they ever succeeded in interrupting the current of her fancy, it only became the more incoherent, and increased the feverishness that preyed upon both mind and body. Her friends felt more alarm for her than ever, for they feared that her senses were irrecoverably gone, and her constitution completely undermined.

In the mean time Eugene returned to the village. He was violently affected when the story of Annette was told him. With bitterness of heart he upbraided his own rashness and infatuation that had hurried him away from her, and accused himself as the author of all her woes. His mother would describe to him all the anguish and remorse of poor Annette; the tenderness with which she clung to her, and endeavoured, even in the midst of her insanity, to console her for the loss of her son, and the touching expressions of affection that were mingled with her most incoherent wanderings of thought, until his feelings would be wound up to agony, and he would entreat her to desist from the recital. They did not dare as yet to bring him into Annette's sight; but he was permitted to see her when she was sleeping. The tears streamed down his sunburnt cheeks as he contemplated the ravages which grief and malady had made; and his heart swelled almost to breaking as he beheld round her neck the very braid of hair which she once gave him in token of girlish affection, and which he had returned to her in anger.

At length the physician that attended her determined to adventure upon an experiment; to take advantage of one of those cheerful moods when her mind was visited by hope, and to endeavour to ingraft, as it were, the reality upon the delusions of her fancy. These moods had now become very rare, for nature was sinking under the continual pressure of her mental malady, and the principle of reaction was daily growing weaker. Every effort was tried to bring on a cheerful interval of the kind. Several of her most favourite companions were kept continually about her; they chatted gaily, they laughed, and sang, and danced; but Annette reclined with languid frame and hollow eye, and took no part in their gaiety. At length the winter was gone; the trees put forth their leaves; the swallows began to build in the eaves of the house, and the robin and wren piped all day beneath the window. Annette's spirits gradually revived. She began to deck her person with unusual care; and bringing forth a basket of artificial flowers, she went to work to wreathe a bridal chaplet of white roses. Her companions asked her why she prepared the chaplet. "What!" said she with a smile, "have you not noticed the trees putting on their wedding dresses of blossoms? Has not the swallow flown back over the sea? Do you not know that the time is come for Eugene to return? that he will be home to-morrow, and that on Sunday we are to be married?"

Her words were repeated to the physician, and he seized on them at once. He directed that her idea should be encouraged and acted upon. Her words were echoed through the house. Every one talked of the return of Eugene as a matter of course; they congratulated her upon her approaching happiness, and assisted her in her preparations. The next morning the same theme was resumed. She was dressed out to receive her lover. Every bosom fluttered with anxiety. A cabriolet drove into the village. "Eugene is coming!" was the cry. She saw him alight at the door, and rushed with a shriek into his arms.

Her friends trembled for the result of this critical experiment; but she did not sink under it, for her fancy had prepared her for his return. She was as one in a dream, to whom a tide of unlooked-for prosperity, that would have overwhelmed his waking reason, seems but the natural current of circumstances. Her conversation, however, showed that her senses were wandering. There was an absolute forgetfulness of all past sorrow; a wild and feverish gaiety that at times was incoherent.

The next morning she awoke languid and exhausted. All the occurrences of the preceding day had passed away from her mind as though they had been the mere illusions of her fancy. She rose melancholy and abstracted, and as she dressed herself, was heard to sing one of her plaintive ballads. When she entered the parlour her eyes were swoln with weeping. She heard Eugene's voice without and started. She passed her hand across her forehead, and stood musing, like one endeavouring to recall a dream. Eugene entered the room, and advanced towards her; she looked at him with an eager, searching look, murmured some indistinct words, and, before he could reach her, sank upon the floor.

She relapsed into a wild and unsettled state of mind; but now that the first shock was over, the physician ordered that Eugene should keep continually in her sight. Sometimes she did not know him; at other times she would talk to him as if he were going to sea, and would implore him not to part from her in anger; and when he was not present, she would speak of him as if buried in the ocean, and would sit, with clasped hands, looking upon the ground, the picture of despair.

As the agitation of her feelings subsided, and her frame recovered from the shock which it had received, she became more placid and coherent. Eugene kept almost continually near her. He formed the real object round which her scattered ideas once more gathered, and which linked them once more with the realities of life. But her changeful disorder now appeared to take a new turn. She became languid and inert, and would sit for hours silent, and almost in a state of lethargy. If roused from this stupor, it seemed as if her mind would make some attempts to follow up a train of thought, but would soon become confused. She would regard every one that approached her with an anxious and inquiring eye, that seemed continually to disappoint itself. Sometimes, as her lover sat holding her hand, she would look pensively in his face without saying a word, until his heart was overcome; and after these transients fits of intellectual exertion, she would sink again into lethargy.

By degrees this stupor increased; her mind appeared to have subsided into a stagnant and almost deathlike calm. For the greater part of the time her eyes were closed; her face almost as fixed and passionless as that of a corpse. She no longer took any notice of surrounding objects. There was an awfulness in this tranquillity that filled her friends with apprehension. The physician ordered that she should be kept perfectly quiet; or that, if she evinced any agitation, she should be gently lulled, like a child, by some favourite tune.

She remained in this state for hours, hardly seeming to breathe, and apparently sinking into the sleep of death. Her chamber was profoundly still. The attendants moved about it with noiseless tread; every thing was communicated by signs and whispers. Her lover sat by her side watching her with painful anxiety, and fearing that every breath which stole from her pale lips would be the last.

At length she heaved a deep sigh; and from some convulsive motions, appeared to be troubled in her sleep. Her agitation increased, accompanied by an indistinct moaning. One of her companions, remembering the physician's instructions, endeavoured to lull her by singing, in a low voice, a tender little air, which was a particular favourite of Annette's. Probably it had some connexion in her mind with her own story; for every fond girl has some ditty of the kind, linked in her thoughts with sweet and sad remembrances.

As she sang, the agitation of Annette subsided. A streak of faint colour came into her cheeks; her eyelids became swoln with rising tears, which trembled there for a moment, and then, stealing forth, coursed down her pallid cheek. When the song was ended, she opened her eyes and looked about her, as one awaking in a strange place.

"Oh, Eugene! Eugene!" said she, "it seems as if I have had a long and dismal dream: what has happened, and what has been the matter with me?"

The questions were embarrassing; and before they could be answered, the physician, who was in the next room, entered. She took him by the hand, looked up in his face, and made the same inquiry. He endeavoured to put her off with some evasive answer; – "No, no!" cried she, "I know I've been ill, and I have been dreaming strangely. I thought Eugene had left us – and that he had gone to sea – and that he was drowned! – But he *has* been to sea!" added she earnestly, as recollection kept flashing upon her, "and he has been wrecked – and we were all so wretched – and he came home again one bright morning – and – Oh!" said she, pressing her hand against her forehead with a sickly smile, "I see how it is; all has not been right here, I begin to recollect – but it is all past now – Eugene is here! and his mother is happy – and we shall never – never part again – shall we, Eugene?"

She sunk back in her chair exhausted; the tears streamed down her cheeks. Her companions hovered round her, not knowing what to make of this sudden dawn of reason. Her lover sobbed aloud. She opened her eyes again, and looked upon them with an air of the sweetest acknowledgment. "You are all so good to me!" said she, faintly.

The physician drew the father aside. "Your daughter's mind is restored," said he; "she is sensible that she has been deranged; she is growing conscious of the past, and conscious of the present. All that now remains is to keep her calm and quiet until her health is re-established, and then let her be married, in God's name!"

"The wedding took place," continued the good priest, "but a short time since; they were here at the last fête during their honey-moon, and a handsomer and happier couple was not to be seen as they danced under yonder trees. The young man, his wife, and mother, now live on a fine farm at Pont L'Eveque; and that model of a ship which you see yonder, with white flowers wreathed round it, is Annette's offering of thanks to our Lady of Grace, for having listened to her prayers and protected her lover in the hour of peril."*

The captain having finished, there was a momentary silence. The tender-hearted Lady Lillycraft, who knew the story by heart, had led the way in weeping, and indeed had often begun to shed tears before they had come to the right place.

The fair Julia was a little flurried at the passage where wedding preparations were mentioned; but the auditor most affected was the simple Phœbe Wilkins. She had gradually dropt her work in her lap, and sat sobbing through the latter part of the story, until towards the end, when the happy reverse had nearly produced another scene of hystericks. "Go, take this case to my room again, child," said Lady Lillycraft kindly, "and don't cry so much."

"I won't, an't please your ladyship, if I can help it; – but I'm glad they made all up again, and were married!"

By the way, the case of this love-lorn damsel begins to make some talk in the household, especially among certain little ladies, not far in their teens, of whom she has made confidants. She is a great favourite with them all, but particularly so since she has confided to them her love secrets. They enter into her concerns with all the violent zeal and overwhelming sympathy with which little boarding-school ladies engage in the politics of a love affair.

---

* Whoever has seen the pathetic ballet of Nina, may be reminded of it by some of the passages in the latter part of the above tale. The story, it is true, was sketched before seeing that ballet; but in re-writing it, the author's memory was haunted by the inimitable performance of Bigottini, in Nina, and the vivid recollection of it may have produced an occasional similarity. He is in some measure prompted to make this acknowledgment, for the purpose of expressing his admiration of the wonderful powers of that actress; who has given a dignity and pathos to the ballet, of which he had not supposed it capable.

I have noticed them frequently clustering about her in private conferences, or walking up and down the garden terrace under my window,
listening to some long and dolorous story of her afflictions; of which I
could now and then distinguish the ever-recurring phrases "says he,"
and "says she."

I accidentally interrupted one of these little councils of war, when
they were all huddled together under a tree, and seemed to be earnestly
considering some interesting document. The flutter at my approach
showed that there were some secrets under discussion; and I observed
the disconsolate Phœbe crumbling into her bosom either a love-letter
or an old valentine, and brushing away the tears from her cheeks.

The girl is a good girl, of a soft melting nature, and shows her concern at the cruelty of her lover only in tears and drooping looks; but with
the little ladies who have espoused her cause, it sparkles up into fiery
indignation: and I have noticed on Sunday many a glance darted at the
pew of the Tibbetses, enough even to melt down the silver buttons on
old Ready Money's jacket.

TRAVELLING

A citizen, for recreation sake,
To see the country would a journey take
Some dozen mile, or very little more;
Taking his leave with friends two months before,
With drinking healths, and shaking by the hand,
As he had travail'd to some new-found land.
DOCTOR MERRIE-MAN, 1609

The squire has lately received another shock in the saddle, and been almost unseated by his marplot neighbour the indefatigable Mr. Faddy, who rides his jog-trot hobby with equal zeal; and is so bent upon improving and reforming the neighbourhood, that the squire thinks, in a little while, it will be scarce worth living in. The enormity that has just discomposed my worthy host, is an attempt of the manufacturer to have a line of coaches established, that shall diverge from the old route, and pass through the neighbouring village.

I believe I have mentioned that the Hall is situated in a retired part of the country, at a distance from any great coach road; insomuch that the arrival of a traveller is apt to make every one look out of the window, and to cause some talk among the ale-drinkers at the little inn. I was at a loss, therefore, to account for the squire's indignation at a measure apparently fraught with convenience and advantage, until I found that the conveniences of travelling were among his greatest grievances.

In fact, he rails against stage-coaches, post-chaises, and turnpike-roads, as serious causes of the corruption of English rural manners. They have given facilities, he says, to every hum-drum citizen to trundle his family about the kingdom, and have sent the follies and fashions of town whirling, in coach-loads, to the remotest parts of the island. The whole country, he says, is traversed by these flying cargoes; every by-road is explored by enterprising tourists from Cheapside and the Poultry, and every gentleman's park and lawns invaded by cockney sketchers of both sexes, with portable chairs and portfolios for drawing.

He laments over this as destroying the charm of privacy, and interrupting the quiet of country life; but more especially as affecting the simplicity of the peasantry, and filling their heads with half-city notions. A great coach inn, he says, is enough to ruin the manners of a whole village. It creates a horde of sots and idlers; makes gapers and gazers and newsmongers of the common people, and knowing jockeys of the country bumpkins.

The squire has something of the old feudal feeling. He looks back with regret to the "good old times," when journeys were only made on horseback, and the extraordinary difficulties of travelling, owing to bad roads, bad accommodations, and highway robbers, seemed to separate each village and hamlet from the rest of the world. The lord of the manor was then a kind of monarch in the little realm around him. He held his court in his paternal hall, and was looked up to with almost as much loyalty and deference as the king himself. Every neighbourhood was a little world within itself, having its local manners and customs, its local history, and local opinions. The inhabitants were fonder of their homes, and thought less of wandering. It was looked upon as an expedition to travel out of sight of the parish steeple; and a man that had been to London was a village oracle for the rest of his life.

What a difference between the mode of travelling in those days and at present! At that time, when a gentleman went on a distant visit, he sallied forth like a knight-errant on an enterprise, and every family excursion was a pageant. How splendid and fanciful must one of those domestic cavalcades have been, when the beautiful dames were mounted on palfries magnificently caparisoned, with embroidered harness, all tinkling with silver bells; attended by cavaliers richly attired on prancing steeds, and followed by pages and serving-men, as we see them represented in old tapestry. The gentry, as they travelled about in those days, were like moving pictures. They delighted the eyes and awakened the admiration of the common people, and passed before them like superior beings; and indeed they were so; there was a hardy and healthful exercise connected with this equestrian style, that made them generous and noble.

In his fondness for the old style of travelling, the squire makes most of his journeys on horseback, though he laments the modern deficiency of incident on the road, from the want of fellow-wayfarers, and the rapidity with which every one else is whirled along in coaches and post-chaises. In the "good old times," on the contrary, a cavalier jogged on through bog and mire, from town to town, and hamlet to hamlet, conversing with friars and franklens, and all other chance companions of the road; beguiling the way with travellers' tales, which then were truly wonderful, for every thing beyond one's neighbourhood was full of marvel and romance; stopping at night at some "hostel," where the bush over the door proclaimed good wine, or a pretty hostess made bad wine palatable; meeting at supper with travellers like himself; discussing their day's adventures, or listening to the song or merry story of the host, who was generally a boon companion, and presided at his own board; for, according to old Tusser's "Innholder's Posie,"

"At meales my friend who vitleth here
    And sitteth with his host,
Shall both be sure of better cheere,
    And 'scape with lesser cost."

The squire is fond, too, of stopping at those inns which may be met with, here and there, in ancient houses of wood and plaster, or calimanco houses, as they are called by antiquaries, with deep porches, diamond-paned bow-windows, panneled rooms, and great fire-places. He will prefer them to more spacious and modern inns, and will cheerfully put up with bad cheer and bad accommodations in the gratification of his humour. They give him, he says, the feeling of old times, insomuch that he almost expects, in the dusk of the evening, to see some party of weary travellers ride up to the door, with plumes and mantles, trunk-hose, wide boots, and long rapiers.

The good squire's remarks brought to mind a visit that I once paid to the Tabard Inn, famous for being the place of assemblage from whence Chaucer's pilgrims set forth for Canterbury. It is in the borough of Southwark, not far from London Bridge, and bears, at present, the name of "the Talbot." It has sadly declined in dignity since the days of Chaucer, being a mere rendezvous and packing place of the great waggons that travel into Kent. The court-yard, which was anciently the mustering-place of the pilgrims previous to their departure, was now lumbered with huge waggons. Crates, boxes, hampers, and baskets, containing the good things of town and country, were piled about them; while, among the straw and litter, the motherly hens scratched and clucked, with their hungry broods at their heels. Instead of Chaucer's motley and splendid throng, I only saw a group of waggoners, and stable-boys enjoying a circulating pot of ale; while a longbodied dog sat by, with head on one side, ear cocked up, and wistful gaze, as if waiting for his turn at the tankard.

Notwithstanding this grievous declension, however, I was gratified at perceiving that the present occupants were not unconscious of the poetical renown of their mansion. An inscription over the gateway proclaimed it to be the inn where Chaucer's pilgrims slept on the night previous to their departure, and at the bottom of the yard was a magnificent sign, representing them in the act of sallying forth. I was pleased, too, at noticing, that though the present inn was comparatively modern, yet the form of the old inn was preserved. There were galleries round the yard, as in old times, on which opened the chambers of the guests. To these ancient inns have antiquaries ascribed the present forms of our theatres. Plays were originally acted in inn-yards. The guests lolled over the galleries which answered to our modern dress-circle; the critical mob clustered in the yard instead of the pit; and the groups gazing from the garret windows, were no bad representatives of the gods of the shilling gallery. When, therefore, the drama grew important enough to have a house of its own, the architects took a hint for its construction from the yard of the ancient "hostel."

I was so well pleased at finding these remembrances of Chaucer and his poem, that I ordered my dinner in the little parlour of the Talbot. Whilst it was preparing, I sat at the window, musing and gazing into the court-yard, and conjuring up recollections of the scenes depicted in such lively colours by the poet, until, by degrees, bales, boxes and hampers, boys, waggoners, and dogs, faded from sight, and my fancy peopled the place with the motley throng of Canterbury pilgrims. The galleries once more swarmed with idle gazers in the rich dresses of Chaucer's time, and the whole cavalcade seemed to pass before me. There was the stately knight on sober steed, who had ridden in Christendom and heathenesse, and had "foughten for our faith at Tramissene;" – and his son, the young squire, a lover, and a lusty bachelor, with curled locks and gay embroidery; a bold rider, a dancer, and a writer of verses, singing and fluting all day long, and "fresh as the month of May;" – and his "knot-headed" yeoman; a bold forester, in green, with horn, and baudrick, and dagger, a mighty bow in hand, and a sheaf of peacock arrows shining beneath his belt; – and the coy, smiling, simple nun, with her gray eyes, her small red mouth and fair forehead, her dainty person clad in featly cloak and " 'ypinched wimple," her coral beads about her arm, her golden brooch with a love motto, and her pretty oath "by Saint Eloy;" – and the merchant, solemn in speech and high on horse, with forked beard and "Flaundrish bever hat;" — and the lusty monk, "full fat and in good point," with berry brown palfrey, his hood fastened with gold pin, wrought with a love-knot, his bald head shining like glass, and his face glistening as though it had been anointed; – and the lean, logical, sententious clerke of Oxenforde, upon his half-starved, scholar-like horse; – and the bowsing sompnour, with fiery-cherub face, all knobbed with pimples, an eater of garlick and onions, and drinker of "strong wine, red as blood," that carried a cake for a buckler, and babbled Latin in his cups; of whose brimstone visage "children were sore aferd;" – and the buxom wife of Bath, the widow of five husbands, upon her ambling nag, with her hat broad as a buckler, her red stockings and sharp spurs; – and the slender, choleric reeve of Norfolk, bestriding his good gray stot; with close-shaven beard, his hair cropped round his ears, long, lean, calfless legs, and a rusty blade by his side, – and the jolly Limitour, with lisping tongue and twinkling eye, well beloved of franklens and housewives, a great promoter of marriages among young women, known at the taverns in every town, and by every "hosteler and gay tapstere." In short, before I was roused from my reverie by the less poetical, but more substantial apparition of a smoking beef-steak, I had seen the whole cavalcade issue forth from the hostel-gate, with the brawny, double-jointed, red-haired miller, playing the bagpipes before them, and the ancient host of the Tabard giving them his fare-well God-send to Canterbury.

When I told the squire of the existence of this legitimate descendant of the ancient Tabard Inn, his eyes absolutely glistened with delight. He determined to hunt it up the very first time he visited London, and to eat a dinner there, and drink a cup of mine host's best wine, in memory of old Chaucer. The general, who happened to be present, immediately begged to be of the party, for he liked to encourage these long-established houses, as they are apt to have choice old wines.

POPULAR SUPERSTITIONS

Farewell rewards and fairies
    Good housewives now may say;
For now fowle sluts in dairies
    Do fare as well as they:
And though they sweepe their hearths no lesse
    Than maids were wont to doe,
Yet who of late for cleanlinesse
    Finds sixpence in her shooe?

BISHOP CORBET

I have mentioned the squire's fondness for the marvellous, and his predeliction for legends and romances. His library contains a curious collection of old works of this kind, which bear evident marks of having been much read. In his great love for all that is antiquated, he cherishes popular superstitions, and listens, with very grave attention, to every tale, however strange; so that, through his countenance, the household, and, indeed, the whole neighbourhood, is well stocked with wonderful stories; and if ever a doubt is expressed of any one of them, the narrator will generally observe, that "the squire thinks there's something in it."

The Hall of course comes in for its share, the common people having always a propensity to furnish a great superannuated building of the kind with supernatural inhabitants. The gloomy galleries of such old family mansions; the stately chambers, adorned with grotesque carvings and faded paintings; the sounds that vaguely echo about them; the moaning of the wind; the cries of rooks and ravens from the trees and chimney-tops; all produce a state of mind favourable to superstitious fancies.

In one chamber of the Hall, just opposite a door which opens upon a dusky passage, there is a full length portrait of a warrior in armour; when, on suddenly turning into the passage, I have caught a sight of the portrait, thrown into strong relief by the dark pannelling against which it hangs, I have more than once been startled, as though it were a figure advancing towards me.

To superstitious minds, therefore, predisposed by the strange and melancholy stories that are connected with family paintings, it needs but little stretch of fancy, on a moonlight night, or by the flickering light of a candle, to set the old pictures on the walls in motion, sweeping in their robes and trains about the galleries.

To tell the truth, the squire confesses that he used to take a pleasure in his younger days in setting marvellous stories afloat, and connecting

them with the lonely and peculiar places of the neighbourhood. Whenever he read any legend of a striking nature, he endeavoured to trans-
plant it, and give it a local habitation among the scenes of his boyhood.
Many of these stories took root, and he says he is often amused with
the odd shapes in which they will come back to him in some old
woman's narrative, after they have been circulating for years among the
peasantry, and undergoing rustic additions and amendments. Among
these may doubtless be numbered that of the crusader's ghost, which
I have mentioned in the account of my Christmas visit; and another
about the hard-riding squire of yore, the family Nimrod, who is sometimes heard on stormy winter nights, galloping, with hound and horn,
over a wild moor a few miles distant from the Hall. This I apprehend
to have had its origin in the famous story of the wild huntsman, the
favourite goblin in German tales; though, by-the-bye, as I was talking on
the subject with Master Simon the other evening in the dark avenue, he
hinted, that he had himself once or twice heard odd sounds at night, very
like a pack of hounds in cry; and that once, as he was returning rather
late from a hunting-dinner, he had seen a strange figure galloping
along this same moor; but as he was riding rather fast at the time, and
in a hurry to get home, he did not stop to ascertain what it was.

Popular superstitions are fast fading away in England, owing to the
general diffusion of knowledge, and the bustling intercourse kept up
throughout the country: still they have their strong holds and lingering
places, and a retired neighbourhood like this is apt to be one of them.
The parson tells me that he meets with many traditional beliefs and
notions among the common people, which he has been able to draw
from them in the course of familiar conversation, though they are rather
shy of avowing them to strangers, and particularly to "the gentry," who
are apt to laugh at them. He says there are several of his old parishioners
who remember when the village had its bar-guest, or bar-ghost; a spirit
supposed to belong to a town or village, and to predict any impending
misfortune by midnight shrieks and wailings. The last time it was heard
was just before the death of Mr. Bracebridge's father, who was much
beloved throughout the neighbourhood; though there are not wanting
some obstinate unbelievers, who insisted that it was nothing but the
howling of a watch-dog. I have been greatly delighted, however, at
meeting with some traces of my old favourite, Robin Good-fellow,
though under a different appellation from any of those by which I have
heretofore heard him called. The parson assures me that many of the
peasantry believe in household goblins, called Dobbies, which live
about particular farms and houses, in the same way that Robin Good-
fellow did of old. Sometimes they haunt the barns and outhouses, and

now and then will assist the farmer wonderfully, by getting in all his hay or corn in a single night. In general, however, they prefer to live within doors, and are fond of keeping about the great hearths, and basking at night, after the family have gone to bed, by the glowing embers. When put in particular good humour by the warmth of their lodgings, and the tidiness of the housemaids, they will overcome their natural laziness, and do a vast deal of household work before morning; churning the cream, brewing the beer, or spinning all the good dame's flax. All this is precisely the conduct of Robin Good-fellow, described so charmingly by Milton:

> "Tells how the drudging goblin sweat
> To earn his cream-bowl duly set,
> When in one night, ere glimpse of morn,
> His shadowy flail had thresh'd the corn
> That ten day labourers could not end;
> Then lays him down the lubber-fiend,
> And stretch'd out all the chimney's length
> Basks at the fire his hairy strength,
> And crop-full, out of door he flings
> Ere the first cock his matin rings."

But beside these household Dobbies, there are others of a more gloomy and unsocial nature, that keep about lonely barns at a distance from any dwelling-house, or about ruins and old bridges. These are full of mischievous, and often malignant tricks, and are fond of playing pranks upon benighted travellers. There is a story, among the old people, of one that haunted a ruined mill, just by a bridge that crosses a small stream; how that late one night, as a traveller was passing on horseback, the Dobbie jumped up behind him, and grasped him so close round the body that he had no power to help himself, but expected to be squeezed to death: luckily his heels were loose, with which he plied the sides of his steed, and was carried, with the wonderful instinct of a traveller's horse, straight to the village inn. Had the inn been at any greater distance, there is no doubt but he would have been strangled to death; as it was, the good people were a long time in bringing him to his senses, and it was remarked that the first sign he showed of returning consciousness was to call for a bottom of brandy.

These mischievous Dobbies bear much resemblance in their natures and habits to those sprites which Heywood in his Hierarchie calls pugs or hobgoblins:

"——Their dwellings be
In corners of old houses least frequented,
Or beneath stacks of wood, and these convented,
Make fearfull noise in butteries and in dairies;
Robin Goodfellow some, some call them faries.
In solitarie rooms these uprores keep,
And beate at doores, to wake men from their slepe,
Seeming to force lockes, be they nere so strong,
And keeping Christmasse gambols all night long.
Pots, glasses, trenchers, dishes, pannes and kettles
They will make dance about the shelves and settles,
As if about the kitchen tost and cast,
Yet in the morning, nothing found misplac't.
Others such houses to their use have fitted
In which base murthers have been once committed.
Some have their fearful habitations taken
In desolat houses, ruin'd and forsaken."

In the account of our unfortunate hawking expedition, I mentioned an instance of one of these sprites supposed to haunt the ruined grange that stands in a lonely meadow, and has a remarkable echo. The parson informs me also, that the belief was once very prevalent, that a household Dobbie kept about the old farm-house of the Tibbetses. It has long been traditional, he says, that one of these good-natured goblins is attached to the Tibbets' family, and came with them when they moved into this part of the country; for it is one of the peculiarities of these household sprites, that they attach themselves to the fortunes of certain families, and follow them in ali their removals.

There is a large old-fashioned fire-place in the farm-house, which affords fine quarters for a chimney-corner sprite that likes to lie warm; especially as Ready Money Jack keeps up rousing fires in the winter time. The old people of the village recollect many stories about this goblin that were current in their young days. It was thought to have brought good luck to the house, and to be the reason why the Tibbetses were always beforehand in the world, and why their farm was always in better order, their hay got in sooner, and their corn better stacked than that of their neighbours. The present Mrs. Tibbets, at the time of her courtship, had a number of these stories told her by the country gossips; and when married, was a little fearful about living in a house where such a hobgoblin was said to haunt: Jack, however, who has always treated this story with great contempt, assured her that there

Traveler and Goblin

An engraving reproduced in the Geoffrey Crayon edition of *Bracebridge Hall*
(New York: G. P. Putnam's Sons, 1868).

was no spirit kept about his house that he could not at any time lay in the Red sea with one flourish of his cudgel. Still his wife has never got completely over her notions on the subject, but has a horse-shoe nailed on the threshold, and keeps a branch of rauntry, or mountain-ash, with its red berries suspended from one of the great beams in the parlour, – a sure protection from all evil spirits.

These stories, however, as I before observed, are fast fading away, and in another generation or two will probably be completely forgotten. There is something, however, about these rural superstitions that is extremely pleasing to the imagination; particularly those which relate to the good-humoured race of household demons, and indeed to the whole fairy mythology. The English have given an inexpressible charm to these supersitions, by the manner in which they have associated them with whatever is most home-felt and delightful in rustic life, or refreshing and beautiful in nature. I do not know a more fascinating race of beings than these little fabled people that haunted the southern sides of hills and mountains, lurked in flowers and about fountain heads, glided through key-holes into ancient halls, watched over farm-houses and dairies, danced on the green by summer moonlight, and on the kitchen hearth in winter. They seem to me to accord with the nature of English housekeeping and English scenery. I always have them in mind when I see a fine old English mansion, with its wide hall and spacious kitchen; or a venerable farm-house, in which there is so much fire-side comfort and good housewifery. There was something of national character in their love of order and cleanliness; in the vigilance with which they watched over the economy of the kitchen, and the functions of the servants; munificently rewarding, with silver sixpence in shoe, the tidy housemaid, but venting their direful wrath, in midnight bobs and pinches, upon the sluttish dairymaid. I think I can trace the good effects of this ancient fairy sway over household concerns, in the care that prevails to the present day among English housemaids, to put their kitchens in order before they go to bed.

I have said, too, that these fairy superstitions seemed to me to accord with the nature of English scenery. They suit these small landscapes, which are divided by honeysuckled hedges into sheltered fields and meadows, where the grass is mingled with daisies, buttercups, and hare-bells. When I first found myself among English scenery, I was continually reminded of the sweet pastoral images which distinguish their fairy mythology; and when for the first time a circle in the grass was pointed out to me as one of the rings where they were formerly supposed to have held their moonlight revels, it seemed for a moment as if fairy land were no longer a fable. Brown, in his Britannia's Pastorals, gives a picture of the kind of scenery to which I allude:

> "———A pleasant mead
> Where fairies often did their measures tread;
> Which in the meadows makes such circles green
> As if with garlands it had crowned been.
> Within one of these rounds was to be seen
> A hillock rise, where oft the fairy queen
> At twilight sat."

And there is another picture of the same, in a poem ascribed to Ben Jonson.

> "By wells and rills in the meadowes green,
>   We nightly dance our hey-day guise,
> And to our fairy king and queen
>   We chant our moonlight minstrelsies."

Indeed it seems to me, that the older British poets, with that true feeling for nature which distinguishes them, have closely adhered to the simple and familiar imagery which they found in these popular superstitions, and have thus given to their fairy mythology those continual allusions to the farm-house and the dairy, the green meadow and the fountain-head, that fill our minds with the delightful associations of rural life. It is curious to observe how the most beautiful fictions have their origin among the rude and ignorant. There is an indescribable charm about the illusions with which chimerical ignorance once clothed every subject. These twilight views of nature are often more captivating than any which are revealed by the rays of enlightened philosophy. The most accomplished and poetical minds, therefore, have been fain to search back into these accidental conceptions of what are termed barbarous ages, and to draw from them their finest imagery and machinery. If we look through our most admired poets, we shall find that their minds have been impregnated by these popular fancies, and that those have succeeded best who have adhered closest to the simplicity of their rustic originals. Such is the case with Shakspeare in his Mid-summer-Night's Dream, which so minutely describes the employments and amusements of fairies, and embodies all the notions concerning them which were current among the vulgar. It is thus that poetry in England has echoed back every rustic note, softened into perfect melody; it is thus that it has spread its charms over every-day life, displacing nothing, taking things as it found them, but tinting them up with its own magical hues, until every green hill and fountain head, every fresh meadow, nay, every humble flower, is full of song and story.

I am dwelling too long, perhaps, upon a threadbare subject; yet it brings up with it a thousand delicious recollections of those happy days of childhood, when the imperfect knowledge I have since obtained had not yet dawned upon my mind, and when a fairy tale was true history to me. I have often been so transported by the pleasure of these recollections, as almost to wish that I had been born in the days when the fictions of poetry were believed. Even now I cannot look upon those fanciful creations of ignorance and credulity, without a lurking regret that they have all passed away. The experience of my early days tells me, that they were sources of exquisite delight; and I sometimes question whether the naturalist who can dissect the flowers of the field, receives half the pleasure from contemplating them, that he did who considered them the abode of elves and fairies. I feel convinced that the true interests and solid happiness of man are promoted by the advancement of truth; yet I cannot but mourn over the pleasant errors which it has trampled down in its progress. The fauns and sylphs, the household sprite, the moonlight revel, Oberon, Queen Mab, and the delicious realms of fairy land, all vanish before the light of true philosophy; but who does not sometimes turn with distaste from the cold realities of morning, and seek to recall the sweet visions of the night?

THE CULPRIT

From fire, from water, and all things amiss,
Deliver the house of an honest justice.

THE WIDOW

The serenity of the Hall has been suddenly interrupted by a very important occurrence. In the course of this morning a posse of villagers was seen trooping up the avenue, with boys shouting in advance. As it drew near, we perceived Ready Money Jack Tibbets striding along, wielding his cudgel in one hand, and with the other grasping the collar of a tall fellow, whom, on still nearer approach, we recognised for the redoubtable gipsy hero, Starlight Tom. He was now, however, completely cowed and crest-fallen, and his courage seemed to have quailed in the iron gripe of the lion-hearted Jack.

The whole gang of gipsy-women and children came draggling in the rear; some in tears, others making a violent clamour about the ears of old Ready Money, who, however, trudged on in silence with his prey, heeding their abuse as little as a hawk that has pounced upon a barn-door hero regards the outcries and cacklings of his whole feathered seraglio.

He had passed through the village on his way to the Hall, and of course had made a great sensation in that most excitable place, where every event is a matter of gaze and gossip. The report flew like wildfire, that Starlight Tom was in custody. The ale-drinkers forthwith abandoned the tap-room; Slingsby's school broke loose, and master and boys swelled the tide that came rolling at the heels of old Ready Money and his captive.

The uproar increased as they approached the Hall; it aroused the whole garrison of dogs, and the crew of hangers-on. The great mastiff barked from the dog-house; the stag-hound and the greyhound, and the spaniel issued barking from the hall-door, and my Lady Lillycraft's little dogs ramped and barked from the parlour window. I remarked, however, that the gipsy dogs made no reply to all these menaces and insults, but crept close to the gang, looking round with a guilty, poaching air, and now and then glancing up a dubious eye to their owners; which shows that the moral dignity, even of dogs, may be ruined by bad company!

When the throng reached the front of the house, they were brought to a halt by a kind of advanced guard, composed of old Christy, the gamekeeper, and two or three servants of the house, who had been brought out by the noise. The common herd of the village fell back with respect; the boys were driven back by Christy and his compeers; while Ready Money Jack maintained his ground and his hold of the prisoner, and was surrounded by the tailor, the schoolmaster, and several other dignitaries of the village, and by the clamorous brood of gipsies, who were neither to be silenced nor intimidated.

By this time the whole household were brought to the doors and windows, and the squire to the portal. An audience was demanded by Ready Money Jack, who had detected the prisoner in the very act of sheep-stealing on his domains, and had borne him off to be examined before the squire, who is in the commission of the peace.

A kind of tribunal was immediately held in the servants' hall, a large chamber, with a stone floor and a long table in the centre, at one end of which, just under an enormous clock, was placed the squire's chair of justice, while Master Simon took his place at the table as clerk of the court. An attempt had been made by old Christy to keep out the gipsy gang, but in vain; and they, with the village worthies, and the household, half filled the hall. The old housekeeper and the butler were in a panic at this dangerous irruption. They hurried away all the valuable things and portable articles that were at hand, and even kept a dragon watch on the gipsies, lest they should carry off the house clock, or the deal table.

Old Christy, and his faithful coadjutor the gamekeeper, acted as constables to guard the prisoner, triumphing in having at last got this terrible offender in their clutches. Indeed I am inclined to think the old man bore some peevish recollection of having been handled rather roughly by the gipsy in the chance-medley affair of May-day.

Silence was now commanded by Master Simon; but it was difficult to be enforced in such a motley assemblage. There was a continual snarling and yelping of dogs, and, as fast as it was quelled in one corner, it broke out in another. The poor gipsy curs, who, like errant thieves, could not hold up their heads in an honest house, were worried and insulted by the gentlemen dogs of the establishment, without offering to make resistance; the very curs of my Lady Lillycraft bullied them with impunity.

The examination was conducted with great mildness and indulgence by the squire, partly from the kindness of his nature, and partly, I suspect, because his heart yearned towards the culprit, who had found great favour in his eyes, as I have already observed, from the skill he had at various times displayed in archery, morrice dancing, and other obsolete accomplishments. Proofs, however, were too strong. Ready Money Jack told his story in a straight-forward independent way, nothing daunted by the presence in which he found himself. He had suffered from various depredations on his sheepfold and poultry-yard, and had at length kept watch, and caught the delinquent in the very act of making off with a sheep on his shoulders.

Tibbets was repeatedly interrupted, in the course of his testimony, by the culprit's mother, a furious old beldame, with an insufferable tongue, and who, in fact, was several times kept, with some difficulty, from flying at him tooth and nail. The wife, too, of the prisoner, whom I am told he does not beat above half a dozen times a week, completely interested Lady Lillycraft in her husband's behalf, by her tears and supplications; and several of the other gipsy women were awakening strong sympathy among the young girls and maid-servants in the back-ground. The pretty black-eyed gipsy-girl, whom I have mentioned on a former occasion as the sibyl that read the fortunes of the general, endeavoured to wheedle that doughty warrior into their interests, and even made some approaches to her old acquaintance, Master Simon; but was repelled by the latter with all the dignity of office, having assumed a look of gravity and importance suitable to the occasion.

I was a little surprised at first, to find honest Slingsby, the schoolmaster, rather opposed to his old crony Tibbets, and coming forward as a kind of advocate for the accused. It seems that he had taken compassion on the forlorn fortunes of Starlight Tom, and had been trying his eloquence in his favour the whole way from the village, but without effect. During the examination of Ready Money Jack, Slingsby had stood like "dejected pity at his side," seeking every now and then, by a soft word, to soothe any exacerbation of his ire or to qualify any harsh expression. He now ventured to make a few observations to the squire in palliation of the delinquent's offence; but poor Slingsby spoke more from the heart than the head, and was evidently actuated merely by a general sympathy for every poor devil in trouble, and a liberal toleration for all kinds of vagabond existence.

The ladies, too, large and small, with the kind-heartedness of the sex, were zealous on the side of mercy, and interceded strenuously with the squire; insomuch that the prisoner, finding himself unexpectedly surrounded by active friends, once more reared his crest, and seemed disposed for a time to put on the air of injured innocence. The squire, however, with all his benevolence of heart, and his lurking weakness towards the prisoner, was too conscientious to swerve from the strict path of justice. There was abundant concurring testimony that made the proof of guilt incontrovertible, and Starlight Tom's mittimus was made out accordingly.

The sympathy of the ladies was now greater than ever; they even made some attempts to mollify the ire of Ready Money Jack; but that sturdy potentate had been too much incensed by the repeated incursions that had been made into his territories by the predatory band of Starlight Tom, and he was resolved, he said, to drive the "varment reptiles" out of the neighbourhood. To avoid all further importunities, as soon as the mittimus was made out, he girded up his loins, and strode back to his seat of empire, accompanied by his interceding friend, Slingsby, and followed by a detachment of the gipsy gang, who hung on his rear, assailing him with mingled prayers and execrations.

The question now was, how to dispose of the prisoner; a matter of great moment in this peaceful establishment, where so formidable a character as Starlight Tom was like a hawk entrapped in a dove-cote. As the hubbub and examination had occupied a considerable time, it was too late in the day to send him to the county prison, and that of the village was sadly out of repair from long want of occupation. Old Christy, who took great interest in the affair, proposed that the culprit should be committed for the night to an upper loft of a kind of tower in one of the out-houses, where he and the gamekeeper would mount guard. After much deliberation this measure was adopted; the premises in question were examined and made secure, and Christy and his trusty ally, the one armed with a fowling-piece, the other with an ancient blunderbuss, turned out as sentries to keep watch over this donjon-keep.

Such is the momentous affair that has just taken place, and it is an event of too great moment in this quiet little world, not to turn it completely topsy-turvy. Labour is at a stand. The house has been a scene of confusion the whole evening. It has been beleagured by gipsy women, with their children on their backs, wailing and lamenting; while the old virago of a mother has cruised up and down the lawn in front, shaking her head and muttering to herself, or now and then breaking into a paroxysm of rage, brandishing her fist at the Hall, and denouncing ill luck upon Ready Money Jack, and even upon the squire himself.

Lady Lillycraft has given repeated audiences to the culprit's weeping wife, at the Hall door; and the servant maids have stolen out to confer with the gipsy women under the trees. As to the little ladies of the family, they are all outrageous at Ready Money Jack, whom they look upon in the light of a tyrannical giant of fairy tale. Phœbe Wilkins, contrary to her usual nature, is the only one that is pitiless in the affair. She thinks Mr. Tibbets quite in the right; and thinks the gipsies deserve to be punished severely for meddling with the sheep of the Tibbetses.

In the mean time the females of the family have evinced all the provident kindness of the sex, ever ready to soothe and succour the distressed, right or wrong. Lady Lillycraft has had a mattress taken to the outhouse, and comforts and delicacies of all kinds have been taken to the prisoner; even the little girls have sent their cakes and sweetmeats; so that, I'll warrant, the vagabond has never fared so well in his life before. Old Christy, it is true, looks upon every thing with a wary eye; struts about with his blunderbuss with the air of a veteran campaigner, and will hardly allow himself to be spoken to. The gipsy women dare not come within gunshot, and every tatterdemallion of a boy has been frightened from the park. The old fellow is determined to lodge Starlight Tom in prison with his own hands; and hopes, he says, to see one of the poaching crew made an example of.

I doubt, after all, whether the worthy squire is not the greatest sufferer in the whole affair. His honourable sense of duty obliges him to be rigid, but the overflowing kindness of his nature makes this a grievous trial to him.

He is not accustomed to have such demands upon his justice in his truly patriarchal domain; and it wounds his benevolent spirit, that while prosperity and happiness are flowing in thus bounteously upon him, he should have to inflict misery upon a fellow-being.

He has been troubled and cast down the whole evening; took leave of the family, on going to bed, with a sigh, instead of his usual hearty and affectionate tone; and will, in all probability, have a far more sleepless night than his prisoner. Indeed this unlucky affair has cast a damp upon the whole household, as there appears to be an universal opinion that the unlucky culprit will come to the gallows.

Morning. – The clouds of last evening are all blown over. A load has been taken from the squire's heart, and every face is once more in smiles. The gamekeeper made his appearance at an early hour, completely shame-faced and crest-fallen. Starlight Tom had made his escape in the night; how he had got out of the loft no one could tell: the Devil they think must have assisted him. Old Christy was so mortified that he would not show his face, but had shut himself up in his strong-hold at the dog-kennel, and would not be spoken with. What has particularly relieved the squire is, that there is very little likelihood of the culprit's being retaken, having gone off on one of the old gentleman's best hunters.

FAMILY MISFORTUNES

"The night has been unruly; where we lay,
The chimneys were blown down."

MACBETH

We have for a day or two past had a flaw of unruly weather, which has intruded itself into this fair and flowery month, and for a time has quite marred the beauty of the landscape. Last night the storm attained its crisis; the rain beat in torrents against the casements, and the wind piped and blustered about the old Hall with quite a wintry vehemence. The morning, however, dawned clear and serene; the face of the heavens seemed as if newly washed, and the sun shone with a brightness that was undimmed by a single vapour. Nothing over-head gave traces of the recent storm; but on looking from my window I beheld sad ravage among the shrubs and flowers; the garden walks had formed the channels for little torrents; trees were lopped of their branches, and a small silver stream that wound through the park, and ran at the bottom of the lawn, had swelled into a turbid, yellow sheet of water.

In an establishment like this, where the mansion is vast, ancient, and somewhat afflicted with the infirmities of age, and where there are numerous and extensive dependencies, a storm is an event of a very grave nature, and brings in its train a multiplicity of cares and disasters.

While the squire was taking his breakfast in the great hall, he was continually interrupted by some bearer of ill tidings from some part or other of his domains; he appeared to me like the commander of a besieged city, after some grand assault, receiving at his head-quarters reports of damages sustained in the various quarters of the place. At one time the housekeeper brought him intelligence of a chimney blown down, and a desperate leak sprung in the roof over the picture-gallery, which threatened to obliterate a whole generation of his ancestors. Then the steward came in with a doleful story of the mischief done in the woodlands; while the gamekeeper bemoaned the loss of one of his finest bucks, whose bloated carcass was seen floating along the swoln current of the river.

When the squire issued forth, he was accosted, before the door, by the old, paralytic gardener, with a face full of trouble, reporting, as I supposed, the devastation of his flower-beds, and the destruction of his wall-fruit. I remarked, however, that his intelligence caused a peculiar expression of concern not only with the squire and Master Simon, but with the fair Julia and Lady Lillycraft, who happened to be present.

239

From a few words which reached my ear, I found there was some tale of domestic calamity in the case, and that some unfortunate family had been rendered houseless by the storm. Many ejaculations of pity broke from the ladies; I heard the expressions of "poor helpless beings," and "unfortunate little creatures," several times repeated; to which the old gardener replied by very melancholy shakes of the head.

I felt so interested, that I could not help calling to the gardener, as he was retiring, and asking what unfortunate family it was that had suffered so severely? The old man touched his hat, and gazed at me for an instant, as if hardly comprehending my question. "Family!" replied he: "there be no family in the case, your honour; but here have been sad mischief done in the rookery!"

I had noticed the day before that the high and gusty winds which prevailed had occasioned great disquiet among these airy householders; their nests being all filled with young, who were in danger of being tilted out of their tree-rocked cradles. Indeed, the old birds themselves seemed to have hard work to maintain a foothold; some kept hovering and cawing in the air; or if they ventured to alight, they had to hold fast, flap their wings, and spread their tails, and thus remain see-sawing on the topmost twigs.

In the course of the night, however, an awful calamity had taken place in this most sage and politic community. There was a great tree, the tallest in the grove, which seemed to have been the kind of court-end of the metropolis, and crowded with the residences of those whom Master Simon considers the nobility and gentry. A decayed limb of this tree had given way with the violence of the storm, and had come down with all its air-castles.

One should be well aware of the humours of the good squire and his household, to understand the general concern expressed at this disaster. It was quite a public calamity in this rural empire, and all seemed to feel for the poor rooks as for fellow-citizens in distress.

The ground had been strewed with the callow young, which were now cherished in the aprons and bosoms of the maid servants, and the little ladies of the family. I was pleased with this touch of nature: this feminine sympathy in the sufferings of the offspring, and the maternal anxiety of the parent birds.

It was interesting, too, to witness the general agitation and distress that seemed to prevail throughout the feathered community. The common cause that was made of it; and the incessant hovering, and fluttering, and lamenting, that took place in the whole rookery. There is a chord of sympathy that runs through the whole feathered race as to any misfortunes of the young; and the cries of a wounded bird in the breeding season will throw a whole grove in a flutter and an alarm. Indeed, why should I confine it to the feathered tribe? Nature seems to me to have implanted an exquisite sympathy on this subject, which extends through all her works. It is an invariable attribute of the female heart, to melt at the cry of early helplessness, and to take an instinctive interest in the distresses of the parent and its young. On the present occasion the ladies of the family were full of pity and commiseration; and I shall never forget the look that Lady Lillycraft gave the general, on his observing that the young birds would make an excellent curry, or an especial good rook-pie.

LOVERS' TROUBLES

"The poor soul sat singing by a sycamore tree,
    Sing all a green willow;
Her hand on her bosom, her head on her knee,
    Sing willow, willow, willow;
Sing all a green willow must be my garland."
                                        OLD SONG

The fair Julia having nearly recovered from the effects of her hawking disaster, it begins to be thought high time to appoint a day for the wedding. As every domestic event in a venerable and aristocratic family connexion like this is a matter of moment, the fixing upon this important day has, of course, given rise to much conference and debate.

Some slight difficulties and demurs have lately sprung up, originating in the peculiar humours that are prevalent at the Hall. Thus, I have overheard a very solemn consultation between Lady Lillycraft, the parson, and Master Simon, as to whether the marriage ought not to be postponed until the coming month.

With all the charms of the flowery month of May, there is, I find, an ancient prejudice against it as a marrying month. An old proverb says, "To wed in May is to wed poverty." Now, as Lady Lillycraft is very much given to believe in lucky and unlucky times and seasons, and indeed is very superstitious on all points relating to the tender passion, this old proverb seems to have taken great hold upon her mind. She recollects two or three instances in her own knowledge of matches that took place in this month, and proved very unfortunate. Indeed, an own cousin of hers, who married on a May-day, lost her husband by a fall from his horse, after they had lived happily together for twenty years.

The parson appeared to give great weight to her ladyship's objections, and acknowledged the existence of a prejudice of the kind, not merely confined to modern times, but prevalent likewise among the ancients. In confirmation of this, he quoted a passage from Ovid, which had a great effect on Lady Lillycraft, being given in a language which she did not understand. Even Master Simon was staggered by it; for he listened with a puzzled air; and then, shaking his head, sagaciously observed that Ovid was certainly a very wise man.

From this sage conference I likewise gathered several other important pieces of information relative to weddings; such as that, if two were celebrated in the same church, on the same day, the first would be happy, the second unfortunate. If, on going to church, the bridal party should meet the funeral of a female, it was an omen that the bride would die first; if of a male, the bridegroom. If the newly married couple were to dance together on their wedding-day, the wife would thenceforth rule the roast; with many other curious and unquestionable facts of the same nature, all which made me ponder more than ever upon the perils which surround this happy state, and the thoughtless ignorance of mortals as to the awful risks they run in venturing upon it. I abstain, however, from enlarging upon this topic, having no inclination to promote the increase of bachelors.

Notwithstanding the due weight which the squire gives to traditional saws and ancient opinions, yet I am happy to find that he makes a firm stand for the credit of this loving month, and brings to his aid a whole legion of poetical authorities; all which, I presume, have been conclusive with the young couple, as I understand they are perfectly willing to marry in May, and abide the consequences. In a few days, therefore, the wedding is to take place, and the Hall is in a buzz of anticipation. The housekeeper is bustling about from morning till night, with a look full of business and importance, having a thousand arrangements to make, the squire intending to keep open house on the occasion; and as to the house-maids, you cannot look one of them in the face, but the rogue begins to colour up and simper.

While, however, this leading love affair is going on with a tranquillity quite inconsistent with the rules of romance, I cannot say that the under-plots are equally propitious. The "opening bud of love" between the general and Lady Lillycraft seems to have experienced some blight in the course of this genial season. I do not think the general has ever been able to retrieve the ground he lost, when he fell asleep during the captain's story. Indeed, Master Simon thinks his case is completely desperate, her ladyship having determined that he is quite destitute of sentiment.

The season has been equally unpropitious to the love-lorn Phœbe Wilkins. I fear the reader will be impatient at having this humble amour so often alluded to; but I confess I am apt to take a great interest in the love troubles of simple girls of this class. Few people have an idea of the world of care and perplexity that these poor damsels have in managing the affairs of the heart.

We talk and write about the tender passion; we give it all the colourings of sentiment and romance, and lay the scene of its influence in high life; but, after all, I doubt whether its sway is not more absolute among females of a humbler sphere. How often, could we but look into the heart, should we find the sentiment throbbing in all its violence, in the bosom of the poor lady's-maid, rather than in that of the brilliant beauty she is decking out for conquest; whose brain is probably bewildered with beaux, ball-rooms, and wax-light chandeliers.

With these humble beings love is an honest, engrossing concern. They have no ideas of settlements, establishments, equipages, and pin-money. The heart – the heart is all-in-all with them, poor things! There is seldom one of them but has her love cares, and love secrets; her doubts, and hopes, and fears, equal to those of any heroine of romance, and ten times as sincere. And then, too, there is her secret hoard of love documents; – the broken sixpence, the gilded brooch, the lock of hair, the unintelligible love-scrawl, all treasured up in her box of Sunday finery, for private contemplation.

How many crosses and trials is she exposed to from some lynx-eyed dame, or staid old vestal of a mistress, who keeps a dragon watch over her virtue, and scouts the lover from the door. But then, how sweet are the little love scenes, snatched at distant intervals of holiday, and fondly dwelt on through many a long day of household labour and confinement. If in the country – it is the dance at the fair or wake, the interview in the churchyard after service, or the evening stroll in the green lane. If in town, it is perhaps merely a stolen moment of delicious talk between the bars of the area, fearful every instant of being seen; – and then, how lightly will the simple creature carol all day afterwards at her labour!

Poor baggage! after all her crosses and difficulties, when she marries, what is it but to exchange a life of comparative ease and comfort, for one of toil and uncertainty? Perhaps, too, the lover for whom in the fondness of her nature she has committed herself to fortune's freaks, turns out a worthless churl, the dissolute, hard-hearted husband of low life; who, taking to the ale-house, leaves her to a cheerless home, to labour, penury, and child-bearing.

When I see poor Phœbe going about with drooping eye, and her head hanging "all o' one side," I cannot help calling to mind the pathetic little picture drawn by Desdemona: –

> "My mother had a maid, called Barbara;
> She was in love; and he she loved proved mad,
> And did forsake her: she had a song of willow,
> An old thing 'twas; but it express'd her fortune,
> And she died singing it."

I hope, however, that a better lot is in reserve for Phœbe Wilkins, and that she may yet "rule the roast," in the ancient empire of the Tibbetses! She is not fit to battle with hard hearts or hard times. She was, I am told, the pet of her poor mother, who was proud of the beauty of her child, and brought her up more tenderly than a village girl ought to be; and, ever since she has been left an orphan, the good ladies at the Hall have completed the softening and spoiling of her.

I have recently observed her holding long conferences in the church-yard, and up and down one of the lanes near the village, with Slingsby the schoolmaster. I at first thought the pedagogue might be touched with the tender malady so prevalent in these parts of late; but I did him injustice. Honest Slingsby, it seems, was a friend and crony of her late father, the parish clerk; and is on intimate terms with the Tibbets family: prompted, therefore, by his good-will towards all parties, and secretly instigated, perhaps, by the managing dame Tibbets, he has undertaken to talk with Phœbe upon the subject. He gives her, however, but little encouragement. Slingsby has a formidable opinion of the aristocratical feeling of old Ready Money, and thinks, if Phœbe were even to make the matter up with the son, she would find the father totally hostile to the match. The poor damsel, therefore, is reduced almost to despair; and Slingsby, who is too good-natured not to sym-pathise in her distress, has advised her to give up all thoughts of young Jack, and has proposed as a substitute his learned coadjutor, the prodigal son. He has even, in the fulness of his heart, offered to give up the school-house to them; though it would leave him once more adrift in the wide world.

THE HISTORIAN

Hermione.	Pray you sit by us,

Hermione.   Pray you sit by us,
And tell's a tale.
    Mamilius.   Merry, or sad shall't be?
  Hermione. As merry as you will.
    Mamilius.   A sad tale's best for winter.
I have one of sprites and goblins.
    Hermione.   Let's have that, sir.

WINTER'S TALE

As this is a story-telling age, I have been tempted occasionally to give the reader one of the many tales that are served up with supper at the Hall. I might, indeed, have furnished a series almost equal in number to the Arabian Nights; but some were rather hackneyed and tedious; others I did not feel warranted in betraying into print; and many more were of the old general's relating, and turned principally upon tiger-hunting, elephant-riding, and Seringapatam, enlivened by the wonderful deeds of Tippoo Saib, and the excellent jokes of Major Pendergast.

I had all along maintained a quiet post at a corner of the table, where I had been able to indulge my humour undisturbed; listening attentively when the story was very good, and dozing a little when it was rather dull, which I consider the perfection of auditorship.

I was roused the other evening from a slight trance into which I had fallen during one of the general's histories, by a sudden call from the squire to furnish some entertainment of the kind in my turn. Having been so profound a listener to others, I could not in conscience refuse; but neither my memory nor invention being ready to answer so unexpected a demand, I begged leave to read a manuscript tale from the pen of my fellow-countryman, the late Mr. Diedrich Knickerbocker, the historian of New York. As this ancient chronicler may not be better known to my readers than he was to the company at the Hall, a word or two concerning him may not be amiss, before proceeding to his manuscript.

Diedrich Knickerbocker was a native of New York, a descendant from one of the ancient Dutch families which originally settled that province, and remained there after it was taken possession of by the English in 1664. The descendants of these Dutch families still remain in villages and neighbourhoods in various parts of the country, retaining, with singular obstinacy, the dresses, manners, and even language of their ancestors, and forming a very distinct and curious feature in the motley population of the state. In a hamlet whose spire may be seen from New York, rising from above the brow of a hill on the opposite side of the Hudson, many of the old folks, even at the present day, speak English with an accent, and the Dominie preaches in Dutch; and so completely is the hereditary love of quiet and silence maintained, that in one of these drowsy little villages, in the middle of a warm summer's day, the buzzing of a stout blue-bottle fly will resound from one end of the place to the other.

With the laudable hereditary feeling thus kept up among these worthy people, did Mr. Knickerbocker undertake to write a history of his native city, comprising the reign of its three Dutch governors during the time that it was yet under the domination of the Hogenmogens of Holland. In the execution of this design the little Dutchman has displayed great historical research, and a wonderful consciousness of the dignity of his subject. His work, however, has been so little understood, as to be pronounced a mere work of humour, satirising the follies of the times, both in politics and morals, and giving whimsical views of human nature.

Be this as it may: – among the papers left behind him were several tales of a lighter nature, apparently thrown together from materials which he had gathered during his profound researches for his history, and which he seems to have cast by with neglect, as unworthy of publication. Some of these have fallen into my hands by an accident which it is needless at present to mention; and one of these very stories, with its prelude in the words of Mr. Knickerbocker, I undertook to read, by way of acquitting myself of the debt which I owed to the other story-tellers at the Hall. I subjoin it for such of my readers as are fond of stories.*

* I find that the tale of Rip Van Winkle, given in the Sketch Book, has been discovered by divers writers in magazines, to have been founded on a little German tradition, and the matter has been revealed to the world as if it were a foul instance of plagiarism marvellously brought to light. In a note which follows that tale I had alluded to the superstition on which it was founded, and I thought a mere allusion was sufficient, as the tradition was so notorious as to be inserted in almost every collection of German legends. I had seen it myself in three. I could hardly have hoped, therefore, in the present age, when every source of ghost and goblin story is ransacked, that the origin of the tale would escape discovery. In fact, I had considered popular traditions of the kind as fair foundations for authors of fiction to build upon, and had made use of the one in question accordingly. I am not disposed to contest the matter, however, and indeed consider myself so completely overpaid by the public for my trivial performances, that I am content to submit to any deduction which, in their afterthoughts, they may think proper to make.

THE HAUNTED HOUSE

FROM THE MSS. OF THE LATE

DIEDRICH KNICKERBOCKER

Formerly almost every place had a house of this kind. If a
house was seated on some melancholy place, or built in some
old romantic manner, or if any particular accident had happened in it, such as murder, sudden death, or the like, to be
sure that house had a mark set on it, and was afterwards
esteemed the habitation of a ghost.

BOURNE'S ANTIQUITIES

In the neighbourhood of the ancient city of the Manhattoes there stood,
not very many years since, an old mansion, which, when I was a boy,
went by the name of the Haunted House. It was one of the very few
remains of the architecture of the early Dutch settlers, and must have
been a house of some consequence at the time when it was built. It
consisted of a centre and two wings, the gable ends of which were
shaped like stairs. It was built partly of wood, and partly of small
Dutch bricks, such as the worthy colonists brought with them from
Holland, before they discovered that bricks could be manufactured
elsewhere. The house stood remote from the road, in the centre of
a large field, with an avenue of old locust* trees leading up to it,
several of which had been shivered by lightning, and two or three
blown down. A few apple trees grew straggling about the field; there
were traces also of what had been a kitchen-garden; but the fences
were broken down, the vegetables had disappeared, or had grown
wild and turned to little better than weeds, with here and there a
ragged rose-bush, or a tall sunflower shooting up from among brambles,
and hanging its head sorrowfully, as if contemplating the surrounding
desolation. Part of the roof of the old house had fallen in, the windows
were shattered, the pannels of the doors broken, and mended with rough
boards, and there were two rusty weathercocks at the ends of the house
which made a great jingling and whistling as they whirled about, but
always pointed wrong. The appearance of the whole place was forlorn
and desolate at the best of times; but, in unruly weather, the howling
of the wind about the crazy old mansion, the screeching of the weathercocks, the slamming and banging of a few loose window-shutters, had

* Acacias.

altogether so wild and dreary an effect, that the neighbourhood stood perfectly in awe of the place, and pronounced it the rendezvous of hobgoblins. I recollect the old building well; for I remember how many times, when an idle, unlucky urchin, I have prowled round its precincts, with some of my graceless companions, on holiday afternoons, when out on a freebooting cruise among the orchards. There was a tree standing near the house that bore the most beautiful and tempting fruit; but then it was on enchanted ground, for the place was so charmed by frightful stories that we dreaded to approach it. Sometimes we would venture in a body, and get near the Hesperian tree, keeping an eye upon the old mansion, and darting fearful glances into its shattered windows; when, just as we were about to seize upon our prize, an exclamation from one of the gang, or an accidental noise, would throw us all into a panic, and we would scamper headlong from the place, nor stop until we had got quite into the road. Then there were sure to be a host of fearful anecdotes told of strange cries and groans, or of some hideous face suddenly seen staring out of one of the windows. By degrees we ceased to venture into these lonely grounds, but would stand at a distance and throw stones at the building; and there was something fearfully pleasing in the sound as they rattled along the roof, or sometimes struck some jingling fragments of glass out of the windows.

The origin of this house was lost in the obscurity that covers the early period of the province, while under the government of their high mightinesses the states-general. Some reported it to have been a country residence of Wilhelmus Kieft, commonly called the Testy, one of the Dutch governors of New Amsterdam; others said that it had been built by a naval commander who served under Van Tromp, and who, on being disappointed of preferment, retired from the service in disgust, became a philosopher through sheer spite, and brought over all his wealth to the province, that he might live according to his humour, and despise the world. The reason of its having fallen to decay was likewise a matter of dispute; some said that it was in chancery, and had already cost more than its worth in legal expenses; but the most current, and, of course, the most probable account, was that it was haunted, and that nobody could live quietly in it. There can, in fact, be very little doubt that this last was the case, there were so many corroborating stories to prove it, – not an old woman in the neighbourhood but could furnish at least a score. There was a gray-headed curmudgeon of a negro that lived hard by, who had a whole budget of them to tell, many of which had happened to himself. I recollect many a time stopping with my schoolmates, and getting him to relate some. The old crone lived in a hovel, in the midst of a small patch of potatoes, and Indian corn, which his master had given him on setting him free. He would come to us, with his hoe in his hand, and as we sat perched, like a row of swallows, on the rail of the fence, in the mellow twilight of a summer evening, he would tell us such fearful stories, accompanied by such awful rollings of his white eyes, that we were almost afraid of our own footsteps as we returned home afterwards in the dark.

Poor old Pompey! many years are past since he died, and went to keep company with the ghosts he was so fond of talking about. He was buried in a corner of his own little potatoe patch; the plough soon passed over his grave, and levelled it with the rest of the field, and nobody thought any more of the gray-headed negro. By singular chance I was strolling in that neighbourhood several years afterwards, when I had grown up to be a young man, and I found a knot of gossips speculating on a skull which had just been turned up by a ploughshare. They of course determined it to be the remains of some one that had been murdered, and they had raked up with it some of the traditionary tales of the haunted house. I knew it at once to be the relic of poor Pompey, but I held my tongue; for I am too considerate of other people's enjoyment ever to mar a story of a ghost or a murder. I took care, however, to see the bones of my old friend once more buried in a place where they were not likely to be disturbed. As I sat on the turf and watched the interment, I fell into a long conversation with an old gentleman of the neighbourhood, John Josse Vandermoere, a pleasant gossiping man, whose whole life was spent in hearing and telling the news of the province. He recollected old Pompey, and his stories about the Haunted House; but he assured me he could give me one still more strange than any that Pompey had related; and on my expressing a great curiosity to hear it, he sat down beside me on the turf, and told the following tale. I have endeavoured to give it as nearly as possible in his words; but it is now many years since, and I am grown old, and my memory is not over good. I cannot therefore vouch for the language, but I am always scrupulous as to facts.

D. K.

DOLPH HEYLIGER

"I take the town to concord, where I dwell,
All Kilborn be my witness, if I were not
Begot in bashfulness, brought up in shamefacedness:
Let 'un bring a dog but to my vace that can
Zay I have beat 'un, and without a vault;
Or but a cat will swear upon a book,
I have as much as zet a vire her tail,
And I'll give him or her a crown for 'mends."

TALE OF A TUB

In the early time of the province of New York, while it groaned under the tyranny of the English governor, Lord Cornbury, who carried his cruelties towards the Dutch inhabitants so far as to allow no Dominie, or schoolmaster, to officiate in their language, without his special licence; about this time, there lived in the jolly, little old city of the Manhattoes a kind motherly dame, known by the name of Dame Heyliger. She was the widow of a Dutch sea captain, who died suddenly of a fever, in consequence of working too hard, and eating too heartily, at the time when all the inhabitants turned out in a panic, to fortify the place against the invasion of a small French privateer.* He left her with very little money, and one infant son, the only survivor of several children. The good woman had need of much management to make both ends meet, and keep up a decent appearance. However, as her husband had fallen a victim to his zeal for the public safety, it was universally agreed that "something ought to be done for the widow;" and on the hopes of this "something" she lived tolerably for some years; in the meantime every body pitied and spoke well of her, and that helped along.

She lived in a small house, in a small street, called Garden-street, very probably from a garden which may have flourished there some time or other. As her necessities every year grew greater, and the talk of the public about doing "something for her" grew less, she had to cast about for some mode of doing something for herself, by way of helping out her slender means, and maintaining her independence, of which she was somewhat tenacious.

Living in a mercantile town, she had caught something of the spirit, and determined to venture a little in the great lottery of commerce. On a sudden, therefore, to the great surprise of the street, there

* 1705.

appeared at her window a grand array of gingerbread kings and queens, with their arms stuck a-kimbo, after the invariable royal manner. There were also several broken tumblers, some filled with sugar-plums, some with marbles; there were, moreover, cakes of various kinds, and barley-sugar, and Holland dolls, and wooden horses, with here and there gilt-covered picture-books, and now and then a skein of thread, or a dangling pound of candles. At the door of the house sat the good old dame's cat, a decent demure-looking personage, that seemed to scan every body that passed, to criticise their dress, and now and then to stretch her neck, and look out with sudden curiosity, to see what was going on at the other end of the street; but if by chance any idle vaga-bond dog came by, and offered to be uncivil – hoity-toity! – how she would bristle up, and growl, and spit, and strike out her paws! she was as indignant as ever was an ancient and ugly spinster on the approach of some graceless profligate.

But though the good woman had to come down to those humble means of subsistence, yet she still kept up a feeling of family pride, having descended from the Vanderspiegels, of Amsterdam; and she had the family arms painted and framed, and hung over her mantel-piece. She was, in truth, much respected by all the poorer people of the place; her house was quite a resort of the old wives of the neighbourhood; they would drop in there of a winter's afternoon, as she sat knitting on one side of her fire-place, her cat purring on the other, and the tea-kettle singing before it; and they would gossip with her until late in the evening. There was always an arm chair for Peter de Groodt, some-times called Long Peter, and sometimes Peter Longlegs, the clerk and sexton of the little Lutheran church, who was her great crony, and indeed the oracle of her fire-side. Nay, the Dominie himself did not disdain, now and then, to step in, converse about the state of her mind, and take a glass of her special good cherry-brandy. Indeed, he never failed to call on new year's day, and wish her a happy new year; and the good dame, who was a little vain on some points, always piqued herself on giving him as large a cake as any one in town.

I have said that she had one son. He was the child of her old age; but could hardly be called the comfort, for, of all unlucky urchins, Dolph Heyliger was the most mischievous. Not that the whipster was really vicious; he was only full of fun and frolic, and had that daring, gamesome spirit, which is extolled in a rich man's child, but execrated in a poor man's. He was continually getting into scrapes; his mother was incessantly harassed with complaints of some waggish pranks which he had played off; bills were sent in for windows that he had broken; in a word, he had not reached his fourteenth year before he was pronounced, by all the neighbourhood, to be a "wicked dog, the wickedest dog in the street!" Nay, one old gentleman, in a claret-coloured coat, with a thin red face, and ferret eyes, went so far as to assure dame Heyliger, that her son would, one day or other, come to the gallows!

Yet, notwithstanding all this, the poor old soul loved her boy. It seemed as though she loved him the better the worse he behaved; and that he grew more in her favour, the more he grew out of favour with the world. Mothers are foolish, fond-hearted beings; there's no reasoning them out of their dotage; and, indeed, this poor woman's child was all that was left to love her in this world; – so we must not think it hard that she turned a deaf ear to her good friends, who sought to prove to her that Dolph would come to a halter.

To do the varlet justice, too, he was strongly attached to his parent. He would not willingly have given her pain on any account; and when he had been doing wrong, it was but for him to catch his poor mother's eye fixed wistfully and sorrowfully upon him, to fill his heart with bitterness and contrition. But he was a heedless youngster, and could not, for the life of him, resist any new temptation to fun and mischief. Though quick at his learning, whenever he could be brought to apply himself, yet he was always prone to be led away by idle company, and would play truant to hunt after birds' nests, to rob orchards, or to swim in the Hudson.

In this way he grew up, a tall, lubberly boy; and his mother began to be greatly perplexed what to do with him, or how to put him in a way to do for himself; for he had acquired such an unlucky reputation, that no one seemed willing to employ him.

Many were the consultations that she held with Peter de Groodt, the clerk and sexton, who was her prime councillor. Peter was as much perplexed as herself, for he had no great opinion of the boy, and thought he would never come to good. He at one time advised her to send him to sea; a piece of advice only given in the most desperate cases; but Dame Heyliger would not listen to such an idea; she could not think of letting Dolph go out of her sight. She was sitting one day knitting by her fire-side, in great perplexity, when the sexton entered with an air of unusual vivacity and briskness. He had just come from a funeral. It had been that of a boy of Dolph's years, who had been apprentice to a famous German doctor, and had died of a consumption. It is true, there had been a whisper that the deceased had been brought to his end by being made the subject of the doctor's experiments, on which he was apt to try the effects of a new compound, or a quieting draught. This, however, it is likely was a mere scandal; at any rate, Peter de Groodt did not think it worth mentioning; though,

had we time to philosophise, it would be a curious matter for speculation, why a doctor's family is apt to be so lean and cadaverous, and a
butcher's so jolly and rubicund.

Peter de Groodt, as I said before, entered the house of Dame
Heyliger with unusual alacrity. He was full of a bright idea that had
popped into his head at the funeral, and over which he had chuckled
as he shovelled the earth into the grave of the doctor's disciple. It
had occurred to him, that, as the situation of the deceased was vacant
at the doctor's, it would be the very place for Dolph. The boy had
parts, and could pound a pestle, and run an errand with any boy in the
town, and what more was wanted in a student?

The suggestion of the sage Peter was a vision of glory to the mother.
She already saw Dolph, in her mind's eye, with a cane at his nose, a
knocker at his door, and an M.D. at the end of his name – one of the
established dignitaries of the town.

The matter, once undertaken, was soon effected: the sexton had some
influence with the doctor, they having had much dealing together in
the way of their separate professions; and the very next morning he
called and conducted the urchin, clad in his Sunday clothes, to undergo
the inspection of Dr. Karl Lodovick Knipperhausen.

They found the doctor seated in an elbow chair, in one corner of his
study, or laboratory, with a large volume, in German print, before him.
He was a short fat man, with a dark square face, rendered more dark
by a black velvet cap. He had a little nobbed nose, not unlike the
ace of spades, with a pair of spectacles gleaming on each side of his
dusky countenance, like a couple of bow windows.

Dolph felt struck with awe on entering into the presence of this
learned man; and gazed about him with boyish wonder at the furniture of this chamber of knowledge; which appeared to him almost as the
den of a magician. In the centre stood a claw-footed table, with pestle
and mortar, phials and gallipots, and a pair of small burnished scales. At
one end was a heavy clothes-press, turned into a receptacle for drugs
and compounds; against which hung the doctor's hat and cloak, and
gold-headed cane, and on the top grinned a human skull. Along the
mantel-piece were glass vessels, in which were snakes and lizards,
and a human fœtus preserved in spirits. A closet, the doors of which
were taken off, contained three whole shelves of books, and some too of
mighty folio dimensions; a collection, the like of which Dolph had never
before beheld. As, however, the library did not take up the whole of
the closet, the doctor's thrifty housekeeper had occupied the rest with
pots of pickles and preserves; and had hung about the room, among

awful implements of the healing art, strings of red pepper and corpulent cucumbers, carefully preserved for seed.

Peter de Groodt, and his protegé, were received with great gravity and stateliness by the doctor, who was a very wise, dignified little man, and never smiled. He surveyed Dolph from head to foot, above, and under, and through his spectacles, and the poor lad's heart quailed as these great glasses glared on him like two full moons. The doctor heard all that Peter de Groodt had to say in favour of the youthful candidate; and then, wetting his thumb with the end of his tongue, he began deliberately to turn over page after page of the great black volume before him. At length, after many hums and haws, and strokings of the chin, and all that hesitation and deliberation with which a wise man proceeds to do what he intended to do from the very first, the doctor agreed to take the lad as a disciple; to give him bed, board, and clothing, and to instruct him in the healing art; in return for which he was to have his services until his twenty-first year.

Behold, then, our hero, all at once transformed from an unlucky urchin, running wild about the streets, to a student of medicine, diligently pounding a pestle, under the auspices of the learned Doctor Karl Lodovick Knipperhausen. It was a happy transition for his fond old mother. She was delighted with the idea of her boy's being brought up worthy of his ancestors; and anticipated the day when he would be able to hold up his head with the lawyer, that lived in the large house opposite; or, peradventure, with the Dominie himself.

Doctor Knipperhausen was a native of the Palatinate in Germany; from whence, in company with many of his countrymen, he had taken refuge in England, on account of religious persecution. He was one of nearly three thousand Palatines, who came over from England in 1710, under the protection of Governor Hunter. Where the doctor had studied, how he had acquired his medical knowledge, and where he had received his diploma, it is hard at present to say, for nobody knew at the time; yet it is certain that his profound skill and abstruse knowledge were the talk and wonder of the common people, far and near.

His practice was totally different from that of any other physician; consisting in mysterious compounds, known only to himself, in the preparing and administering of which, it was said, he always consulted the stars. So high an opinion was entertained of his skill, particularly by the German and Dutch inhabitants, that they always resorted to him in desperate cases. He was one of those infallible doctors, that are always effecting sudden and surprising cures, when the patient has been given up by all the regular physicians; unless, as is shrewdly observed, the case has been left too long before it was put into their hands. The doctor's library was the talk and marvel of the neighbourhood, I might almost say of the entire burgh. The good people looked with reverence at a man that had read three whole shelves full of books, and some of them too as large as a family Bible. There were many disputes among the members of the little Lutheran church, as to which was the wisest man, the doctor or the Dominie. Some of his admirers even went so far as to say, that he knew more than the governor himself – in a word, it was thought that there was no end to his knowledge!

No sooner was Dolph received into the doctor's family, than he was put in possession of the lodging of his predecessor. It was a garret-room of a steep-roofed Dutch house, where the rain pattered on the shingles, and the lightning gleamed, and the wind piped through the crannies in stormy weather; and where whole troops of hungry rats, like Don Cossacks, galloped about, in defiance of traps and ratsbane.

He was soon up to his ears in medical studies, being employed, morning, noon, and night, in rolling pills, filtering tinctures, or pounding the pestle and mortar in one corner of the laboratory; while the doctor would take his seat in another corner, when he had nothing else to do, or expected visitors, and, arrayed in his morning gown and velvet cap, would pore over the contents of some folio volume. It is true, that the regular thumping of Dolph's pestle, or, perhaps, the drowsy buzzing of the summer flies, would now and then lull the little man into a slumber; but then his spectacles were always wide awake, and studiously regarding the book.

There was another personage in the house, however, to whom Dolph was obliged to pay allegiance. Though a bachelor, and a man of such great dignity and importance, yet the doctor was, like many other wise men, subject to petticoat government. He was completely under the sway of his houskeeper; a spare, busy, fretting housewife, in a little, round, quilted German cap, with a huge bunch of keys jingling at the girdle of an exceedingly long waist. Frau Ilsé (or Frow Ilsy as it was pronounced) had accompanied him in his various migrations from Germany to England, and from England to the province; managing his establishment and himself too: ruling him, it is true, with a gentle hand, but carrying a high hand with all the world beside. How she had acquired such ascendancy I do not pretend to say. People, it is true, did talk – but have not people been prone to talk ever since the world began? Who can tell how women generally contrive to get the upper hand? A husband, it is true, may now and then be master in his own house; but who ever knew a bachelor that was not managed by his housekeeper?

Dolph Heyliger and The Doctor

An engraving reproduced in the Geoffrey Crayon edition of *Bracebridge Hall* (New York: G. P. Putnam's Sons, 1868).

Indeed, Frau Ilsy's power was not confined to the doctor's household. She was one of those prying gossips that knew every one's business better than they do themselves; and whose all-seeing eyes, and all-telling tongues, are terrors throughout a neighbourhood.

Nothing of any moment transpired in the world of scandal of this little burgh, but it was known to Frau Ilsy. She had her crew of cronies, that were perpetually hurrying to her little parlour with some precious bit of news; nay, she would sometimes discuss a whole volume of secret history, as she held the street-door ajar, and gossiped with one of these garrulous crones in the very teeth of a December blast.

Between the doctor and the housekeeper it may easily be supposed that Dolph had a busy life of it. As Frau Ilsy kept the keys, and literally ruled the roast, it was starvation to offend her, though he found the study of her temper more perplexing even than that of medicine. When not busy in the laboratory, she kept him running hither and thither on her errands; and on Sundays he was obliged to accompany her to and from church, and carry her Bible. Many a time has the poor varlet stood shivering and blowing his fingers, or holding his frost-bitten nose, in the church-yard, while Ilsy and her cronies were huddled together, wagging their heads, and tearing some unlucky character to pieces.

With all his advantages, however, Dolph made very slow progress in his art. This was no fault of the doctor's, certainly, for he took unwearied pains with the lad, keeping him close to the pestle and mortar, or on the trot about town with phials and pill-boxes; and if he ever flagged in his industry, which he was rather apt to do, the doctor would fly into a passion, and ask him if he ever expected to learn his profession, unless he applied himself closer to the study. The fact is, he still retained the fondness for sport and mischief that had marked his childhood; the habit, indeed, had strengthened with his years, and gained force from being thwarted and constrained. He daily grew more and more untractable, and lost favour in the eyes both of the doctor and the housekeeper.

In the mean time the doctor went on, waxing wealthy and renowned. He was famous for his skill in managing cases not laid down in the books. He had cured several old women and young girls of witchcraft; a terrible complaint, nearly as prevalent in the province in those days as hydrophobia is at present. He had even restored one strapping country girl to perfect health, who had gone so far as to vomit crooked pins and needles; which is considered a desperate stage of the malady. It was whispered, also, that he was possessed of the art of preparing love-powders; and many applications had he in consequence from love-sick patients of both sexes. But all these cases formed the mysterious part of his practice, in which, according to the cant phrase, "secrecy and honour might be depended on." Dolph, therefore, was obliged to turn out of the study whenever such consultations occurred, though it is said he learnt more of the secrets of the art at the key-hole, than by all the rest of his studies put together.

As the doctor increased in wealth, he began to extend his possessions, and to look forward, like other great men, to the time when he should retire to the repose of a country seat. For this purpose he had purchased a farm, or as the Dutch settlers called it, a *bowerie,* a few miles from town. It had been the residence of a wealthy family, that had returned some time since to Holland. A large mansion-house stood in the centre of it, very much out of repair, and which, in consequence of certain reports, had received the appellation of the Haunted House. Either from these reports, or from its actual dreariness, the doctor had found it impossible to get a tenant; and, that the place might not fall to ruin before he could reside in it himself, he had placed a country boor, with his family, in one wing, with the privilege of cultivating the farm on shares.

The doctor now felt all the dignity of a landholder rising within him. He had a little of the German pride of territory in his composition, and almost looked upon himself as owner of a principality. He began to complain of the fatigue of business; and was fond of riding out "to look at his estate." His little expeditions to his lands were attended with a bustle and parade that created a sensation throughout the neighbourhood. His wall-eyed horse stood stamping, and whisking off the flies, for a full hour before the house. Then the doctor's saddle-bags would be brought out and adjusted; then, after a little while, his cloak would be rolled up and strapped to the saddle; then his umbrella would be buckled to the cloak; while, in the mean time, a group of ragged boys, that observant class of beings, would gather before the door. At length the doctor would issue forth, in a pair of jack-boots that reached above his knees, and a cocked hat flapped down in front. As he was a short, fat man, he took some time to mount into the saddle; and when there, he took some time to have the saddle and stirrups properly adjusted, enjoying the wonder and admiration of the urchin crowd. Even after he had set off, he would pause in the middle of the street, or trot back two or three times to give some parting orders; which were answered by the housekeeper from the door, or Dolph from the study, or the black cook from the cellar, or the chambermaid from the garret window; and there were generally some last words bawled after him, just as he was turning the corner.

The whole neighbourhood would be aroused by this pomp and circumstance. The cobbler would leave his last; the barber would thrust out his frizzed head, with a comb sticking in it; a knot would collect at the grocer's door, and the word would be buzzed from one end of the street to the other, "The doctor's riding out to his country seat!"

These were golden moments for Dolph. No sooner was the doctor out of sight, than pestle and mortar were abandoned; the laboratory was left to take care of itself, and the student was off on some madcap frolic.

Indeed, it must be confessed, the youngster, as he grew up, seemed in a fair way to fulfil the prediction of the old, claret-coloured gentleman. He was the ringleader of all holiday sports, and midnight gambols; ready for all kinds of mischievous pranks, and hare-brained adventures.

There is nothing so troublesome as a hero on a small scale, or rather, a hero in a small town. Dolph soon became the abhorrence of all drowsy, housekeeping, old citizens, who hated noise, and had no relish for waggery. The good dames, too, considered him as little better than a reprobate, gathered their daughters under their wings whenever he approached, and pointed him out as a warning to their sons. No one seemed to hold him in much regard, excepting the wild striplings of the place, who were captivated by his open-hearted, daring manners, and the negroes, who always look upon every idle, do-nothing youngster, as a kind of gentleman. Even the good Peter de Groodt, who had considered himself a kind of patron of the lad, began to despair of him; and would shake his head dubiously, as he listened to a long complaint from the housekeeper, and sipped a glass of her raspberry brandy.

Still his mother was not to be wearied out of her affection by all the waywardness of her boy; nor disheartened by the stories of his misdeeds, with which her good friends were continually regaling her. She had, it is true, very little of the pleasure which rich people enjoy, in always hearing their children praised; but she considered all this ill-will as a kind of persecution which he suffered, and she liked him the better on that account. She saw him growing up a fine, tall, good-looking youngster, and she looked at him with the secret pride of a mother's heart. It was her great desire that Dolph should appear like a gentleman, and all the money she could save went towards helping out his pocket and his wardrobe. She would look out of the window after him, as he sallied forth in his best array, and her heart would yearn with delight; and once, when Peter de Groodt, struck with the youngster's gallant appearance on a bright Sunday morning, observed, "Well, after all, Dolph does grow a comely fellow!" the tear of pride started into the mother's eye: "Ah, neighbour! neighbour!" exclaimed she, "they may say what they please; poor Dolph will yet hold up his head with the best of them!"

Dolph Heyliger had now nearly attained his one-and-twentieth year, and the term of his medical studies was just expiring; yet it must be confessed that he knew little more of the profession than when he first entered the doctor's doors. This, however, could not be from any want of quickness of parts, for he showed amazing aptness in mastering other branches of knowledge, which he could only have studied at intervals. He was, for instance, a sure marksman, and won all the geese and turkeys at Christmas-holidays. He was a bold rider; he was famous for leaping and wrestling; he played tolerably on the fiddle; could swim like a fish; and was the best hand in the whole place at fives or ninepins.

All these accomplishments, however, procured him no favour in the eyes of the doctor, who grew more and more crabbed and intolerant the nearer the term of apprenticeship approached. Frau Ilsy, too, was for ever finding some occasion to raise a windy tempest about his ears; and seldom encountered him about the house, without a clatter of the tongue; so that at length the jingling of her keys, as she approached, was to Dolph like the ringing of the prompter's bell, that gives notice of a theatrical thunder-storm. Nothing but the infinite good humour of the heedless youngster enabled him to bear all this domestic tyranny without open rebellion. It was evident that the doctor and his housekeeper were preparing to beat the poor youth out of the nest, the moment his term should have expired; a short hand mode which the doctor had of providing for useless disciples.

Indeed the little man had been rendered more than usually irritable lately, in consequence of various cares and vexations which his country estate had brought upon him. The doctor had been repeatedly annoyed by the rumours and tales which prevailed concerning the old mansion; and found it difficult to prevail even upon the countryman and his family to remain there rent free. Every time he rode out to the farm he was teased by some fresh complaint of strange noises and fearful sights, with which the tenants were disturbed at night; and the doctor would come home fretting and fuming, and vent his spleen upon the whole household. It was indeed a sore grievance, that affected him both in pride and purse. He was threatened with an absolute loss of the profits of his property; and then, what a blow to his territorial consequence, to be the landlord of a haunted house!

It was observed, however, that with all his vexation, the doctor never proposed to sleep in the house himself; nay, he could never be prevailed upon to remain on the premises after dark, but made the best of his way for town as soon as the bats began to flit about in the twilight. The fact was, the doctor had a secret belief in ghosts, having passed the early part of his life in a country where they particularly abound; and indeed the story went, that, when a boy, he had once seen the devil upon the Hartz mountains in Germany.

At length the doctor's vexations on this head were brought to a crisis. One morning, as he sat dozing over a volume in his study, he was suddenly startled from his slumbers by the bustling in of the housekeeper.

"Here's a fine to do!" cried she, as she entered the room. "Here's Claus Hopper come in, bag and baggage, from the farm, and swears he'll have nothing more to do with it. The whole family have been frightened out of their wits; for there's such racketing and rummaging about the old house, that they can't sleep quiet in their beds!"

"Donner und Blitzen!" cried the doctor, impatiently; "will they never have done chattering about that house? What a pack of fools, to let a few rats and mice frighten them out of good quarters!"

"Nay, nay," said the housekeeper, wagging her head knowingly, and piqued at having a good ghost-story doubted, "there's more in it than rats and mice. All the neighbourhood talks about the house; and then such sights have been seen in it! Peter de Groodt tells me, that the family that sold you the house, and went to Holland, dropped several strange hints about it, and said, 'they wished you joy of your bargain;' and you know yourself there's no getting any family to live in it."

"Peter de Groodt's a ninny – an old woman," said the doctor, peevishly; "I'll warrant he's been filling these people's heads full of stories. It's just like his nonsense about the ghost that haunted the church belfry, as an excuse for not ringing the bell that cold night when Hermanus Brinkherhoff's house was on fire. Send Claus to me."

Claus Hopper now made his appearance: a simple country lout, full of awe at finding himself in the very study of Dr. Knipperhausen, and too much embarrassed to enter in much detail of the matters that had caused his alarm. He stood twirling his hat in one hand, resting sometimes on one leg, sometimes on the other, looking occasionally at the doctor, and now and then stealing a fearful glance at the death's head that seemed ogling him from the top of the clothes-press.

The doctor tried every means to persuade him to return to the farm, but all in vain; he maintained a dogged determination on the subject; and at the close of every argument or solicitation would make the same brief, inflexible reply, "Ich kan nicht, mynheer." The doctor was a "little pot, and soon hot;" his patience was exhausted by these continual vexations about his estate. The stubborn refusal of Claus Hopper seemed to him like flat rebellion; his temper suddenly boiled over, and Claus was glad to make a rapid retreat to escape scalding.

When the bumpkin got to the housekeeper's room, he found Peter de Groodt, and several other true believers, ready to receive him. Here he indemnified himself for the restraint he had suffered in the study, and opened a budget of stories about the haunted house that astonished all his hearers. The housekeeper believed them all, if it was only to spite the doctor for having received her intelligence so uncourteously. Peter de Groodt matched them with many a wonderful legend of the times of the Dutch dynasty, and of the Devil's Stepping-stones; and of the pirate that was hanged at Gibbet Island, and continued to swing there at night long after the gallows was taken down; and of the ghost of the unfortunate Governor Leisler, who was hanged for treason, which haunted the old fort and the government-house. The gossiping knot dispersed, each charged with direful intelligence. The sexton disburdened himself at a vestry meeting that was held that very day, and the black cook forsook her kitchen, and spent half of the day at the street-pump, that gossiping place of servants, dealing forth the news to all that came for water. In a little time the whole town was in a buzz with tales about the haunted house. Some said that Claus Hopper had seen the devil, while others hinted that the house was haunted by the ghosts of some of the patients whom the doctor had physicked out of the world, and that was the reason why he did not venture to live in it himself.

All this put the little doctor in a terrible fume. He threatened vengeance on any one who should affect the value of his property by exciting popular prejudices. He complained loudly of thus being in a manner dispossessed of his territories by mere bugbears; but he secretly determined to have the house exorcised by the Dominie. Great was his relief, therefore, when, in the midst of his perplexities, Dolph stepped forward and undertook to garrison the haunted house. The youngster had been listening to all the stories of Claus Hopper and Peter de Groodt; he was fond of adventure, he loved the marvellous, and his imagination had become quite excited by these tales of wonder. Besides, he had led such an uncomfortable life at the doctor's, being subjected to the intolerable thraldom of early hours, that he was delighted at the prospect of having a house to himself, even though it should be a haunted one. His offer was eagerly accepted, and it was determined that he should mount guard that very night. His only stipulation was, that the enterprise should be kept secret from his mother; for he knew the poor soul would not sleep a wink if she knew that her son was waging war with the powers of darkness.

When night came on he set out on this perilous expedition. The old black cook, his only friend in the household, had provided him with a little mess for supper, and a rush-light; and she tied round his neck an amulet, given her by an African conjurer, as a charm against evil spirits. Dolph was escorted on his way by the doctor and Peter de Groodt, who had agreed to accompany him to the house, and to see him safe lodged. The night was overcast, and it was very dark when they arrived at the grounds which surrounded the mansion. The sexton led the way with a lantern. As they walked along the avenue of acacias, the fitful light, catching from bush to bush, and tree to tree, often startled the doughty Peter, and made him fall back upon his followers; and the doctor grappled still closer hold of Dolph's arm, observing that the ground was very slippery and uneven. At one time they were nearly put to total rout by a bat, which came flitting about the lantern; and the notes of the insects from the trees, and the frogs from a neighbouring pond, formed a most drowsy and doleful concert.

The front door of the mansion opened with a grating sound, that made the doctor turn pale. They entered a tolerably large hall, such as is common in American country-houses, and which serves for a sitting room in warm weather. From hence they went up a wide staircase, that groaned and creaked as they trod, every step making its particular note, like the key of a harpsichord. This led to another hall on the second story, from whence they entered the room where Dolph was to sleep. It was large, and scantily furnished; the shutters were closed; but as they were much broken, there was no want of a circulation of air. It appeared to have been that sacred chamber, known among Dutch housewives by the name of "the best bed-room;" which is the best furnished room in the house, but in which scarce any body is ever permitted to sleep. Its splendour, however, was all at an end. There were a few broken articles of furniture about the room, and in the centre stood a heavy deal table and a large arm-chair, both of which had the look of being coeval with the mansion. The fire-place was wide, and had been faced with Dutch tiles, representing scripture stories; but some of them had fallen out of their places, and lay shattered about the hearth. The sexton had lit the rushlight; and the doctor, looking fearfully about the room, was just exhorting Dolph to be of good cheer, and to pluck up a stout heart, when a noise in the chimney, like voices and struggling, struck a sudden panic into the sexton. He took to his heels with the lantern; the doctor followed hard after him; the stairs groaned and creaked as they hurried down, increasing their agitation and speed by its noises. The front door slammed after them; and Dolph heard them scrambling down the avenue, till the sound of their feet was lost in the distance. That he did not join in this precipitate retreat might have been owing to his possessing a little more courage than his companions, or perhaps that he had caught a glimpse of the cause of their dismay, in a nest of chimney swallows, that came tumbling down into the fire-place.

Being now left to himself, he secured the front door by a strong bolt and bar; and having seen that the other entrances were fastened, he returned to his desolate chamber. Having made his supper from the basket which the good old cook had provided, he locked the chamber door, and retired to rest on a mattress in one corner. The night was calm and still; and nothing broke upon the profound quiet, but the lonely chirping of a cricket from the chimney of a distant chamber. The rushlight, which stood in the centre of the deal table, shed a feeble yellow ray, dimly illumining the chamber, and making uncouth shapes and shadows on the walls, from the clothes which Dolph had thrown over a chair.

With all his boldness of heart there was something subduing in this desolate scene; and he felt his spirits flag within him, as he lay on his hard bed and gazed about the room. He was turning over in his mind his idle habits, his doubtful prospects, and now and then heaving a heavy sigh, as he thought on his poor old mother; for there is nothing like the silence and loneliness of night to bring dark shadows over the brightest mind. By-and-by he thought he heard a sound as if some one was walking below stairs. He listened, and distinctly heard a step on the great staircase. It approached solemnly and slowly, tramp – tramp – tramp! It was evidently the tread of some heavy personage; and yet how could he have got into the house without making a noise? He had examined all the fastenings, and was certain that every entrance was secure. Still the steps advanced, tramp – tramp – tramp! It was evident that the person approaching could not be a robber, the step was too loud and deliberate; a robber would either be stealthy or precipitate. And now the footsteps had ascended the staircase; they were slowly advancing along the passage, resounding through the silent and empty apartments. The very cricket had ceased its melancholy note, and nothing interrupted their awful distinctness. The door, which had been locked on the inside, slowly swung open, as if self-moved. The footsteps entered the room; but no one was to be seen. They passed slowly and audibly across it, tramp – tramp – tramp! but whatever made the sound was invisible. Dolph rubbed his eyes, and stared about him; he could see to every part of the dimly-lighted chamber; all was vacant; yet still he heard those mysterious footsteps, solemnly walking about the chamber. They ceased, and all was dead silence. There was something more appalling in this invisible visitation, than there would have been in any thing that addressed itself to the eyesight. It was awfully vague and indefinite. He felt his heart beat against his ribs; a cold sweat broke out upon his forehead; he lay for some time in a state of violent agitation; nothing, however, occurred to increase his alarm. His light gradually burnt down into the socket, and he fell asleep. When he awoke it was broad daylight; the sun was peering through the cracks of the window-shutters, and the birds were merrily singing about the house. The bright cheery day soon put to flight all the terrors of the preceding night. Dolph laughed, or rather tried to laugh, at all that had passed, and endeavoured to persuade himself that it was a mere freak of the imagination, conjured up by the stories he had heard; but he was a little puzzled to find the door of his room locked on the inside, not-withstanding that he had positively seen it swing open as the footsteps had entered. He returned to town in a state of considerable perplexity; but he determined to say nothing on the subject, until his doubts were either confirmed or removed by another night's watching. His silence was a grievous disappointment to the gossips who had gathered at the doctor's mansion. They had prepared their minds to hear direful tales; and they were almost in a rage at being assured that he had nothing to relate.

The next night, then, Dolph repeated his vigil. He now entered the house with some trepidation. He was particular in examining the fastenings of all the doors, and securing them well. He locked the door of his chamber, and placed a chair against it; then having despatched his supper, he threw himself on his mattress and endeavoured to sleep. It was all in vain; a thousand crowding fancies kept him waking. The time slowly dragged on, as if minutes were spinning themselves out into hours. As the night advanced, he grew more and more nervous; and he almost started from his couch when he heard the mysterious footstep again on the staircase. Up it came, as before, solemnly and slowly, tramp – tramp – tramp! It approached along the passage; the door again swung open, as if there had been neither lock nor impedi-ment, and a strange looking figure stalked into the room. It was an elderly man, large and robust, clothed in the old Flemish fashion. He had on a kind of short cloak, with a garment under it, belted round the waist; trunk hose, with great bunches or bows at the knees; and a pair of russet boots, very large at top, and standing widely from his legs. His hat was broad and slouched, with a feather trailing over one side. His iron-gray hair hung in thick masses on his neck; and he had a short grizzled beard. He walked slowly round the room, as if examin-ing that all was safe; then, hanging his hat on a peg beside the door, he sat down in the elbow-chair, and, leaning his elbow on the table, he fixed his eyes on Dolph with an unmoving and deadening stare.

Dolph was not naturally a coward; but he had been brought up in an implicit belief in ghosts and goblins. A thousand stories came swarming to his mind that he had heard about this building; and as he looked at this strange personage, with his uncouth garb, his pale visage, his grizzly beard, and his fixed, staring, fish-like eye, his teeth began to chatter, his hair to rise on his head, and a cold sweat to break out all over his body. How long he remained in this situation he could not tell, for he was like one fascinated. He could not take his gaze off from the spectre; but lay staring at him, with his whole intellect absorbed in the contemplation. The old man remained seated behind the table, without stirring, or turning an eye, always keeping a dead steady glare upon Dolph. At length the household cock, from a neighbouring farm, clapped his wings, and gave a loud cheerful crow that rung over the fields. At the sound the old man slowly rose, and took down his hat from the peg; the door opened, and closed after him; he was heard to go slowly down the staircase, tramp – tramp – tramp! – and when he had got to the bottom, all was again silent. Dolph lay and listened earnestly; counted every footfall; listened, and listened if the steps should return, until, exhausted with watching and agitation, he fell into a troubled sleep.

Daylight again brought fresh courage and assurance. He would fain have considered all that had passed as a mere dream; yet there stood the chair in which the unknown had seated himself; there was the table on which he had leaned; there was the peg on which he had hung his hat; and there was the door, locked precisely as he himself had locked it, with the chair placed against it. He hastened down stairs, and examined the doors and windows; all were exactly in the same state in which he had left them, and there was no apparent way by which any being could have entered and left the house, without leaving some trace behind. "Pooh!" said Dolph to himself, "it was all a dream:" – but it would not do; the more he endeavoured to shake the scene off from his mind, the more it haunted him.

Though he persisted in a strict silence as to all that he had seen and heard, yet his looks betrayed the uncomfortable night that he had passed. It was evident that there was something wonderful hidden under this mysterious reserve. The doctor took him into the study, locked the door, and sought to have a full and confidential communication; but he could get nothing out of him. Frau Ilsy took him aside into the pantry, but to as little purpose; and Peter de Groodt held him by the button for a full hour, in the churchyard, the very place to get at the bottom of a ghost story, but came off not a whit wiser than the rest. It is always the case, however, that one truth concealed makes a dozen current lies. It is like a guinea locked up in a bank, that has a dozen paper representatives. Before the day was over, the neighbourhood was full of reports. Some said that Dolph Heyliger watched in the haunted house, with pistols loaded with silver bullets; others, that he had a long talk with a spectre without a head; others, that Doctor Knipperhausen and the sexton had been hunted down the Bowery-lane, and quite into town, by a legion of ghosts of their customers. Some shook their heads; and thought it a shame that the doctor should put Dolph to pass the night alone in that dismal house, where he might be spirited away, no one knew whither; while others observed, with a shrug, that if the devil did carry off the youngster, it would but be taking his own.

These rumours at length reached the ears of the good Dame Heyliger, and, as may be supposed, threw her into a terrible alarm. For her son to have exposed himself to danger from living foes, would have been nothing so dreadful in her eyes, as to dare alone the terrors of the Haunted House. She hastened to the doctor's, and passed a great part of the day in attempting to dissuade Dolph from repeating his vigil; she told him a score of tales, which her gossiping friends had just related to her, of persons who had been carried off, when watching alone, in old ruinous houses. It was all to no effect. Dolph's pride, as well as curiosity, was piqued. He endeavoured to calm the apprehensions of his mother, and to assure her that there was no truth in all the rumours she had heard. She looked at him dubiously, and shook her head; but finding his determination was not to be shaken, she brought him a little thick Dutch Bible, with brass clasps, to take with him, as a sword wherewith to fight the powers of darkness; and, lest that might not be sufficient, the housekeeper gave him the Heidelburgh catechism by way of dagger.

The next night, therefore, Dolph took up his quarters for the third time in the old mansion. Whether dream or not, the same thing was repeated. Towards midnight, when every thing was still, the same sound echoed through the empty halls – tramp – tramp – tramp! The stairs were again ascended; the door again swung open; the old man entered; walked round the room; hung up his hat, and seated himself by the table. The same fear and trembling came over poor Dolph, though not in so violent a degree. He lay in the same way, motionless and fascinated, staring at the figure, which regarded him as before with a dead, fixed, chilling gaze. In this way they remained for a long time, till, by degrees, Dolph's courage began gradually to revive. Whether alive or dead, this being had certainly some object in his visitation; and he recollected to have heard it said, that spirits have no power to speak until they are spoken to. Summoning up resolution, therefore, and making two or three attempts, before he could get his parched tongue in motion, he addressed the unknown in the most solemn form of adjuration that he could recollect, and demanded to know what was the motive of his visit.

No sooner had he finished, than the old man rose, took down his hat, the door opened, and he went out, looking back upon Dolph just as he crossed the threshold, as if expecting him to follow. The youngster did not hesitate an instant. He took the candle in his hand, and the Bible under his arm, and obeyed the tacit invitation. The candle emitted a feeble, uncertain ray; but still he could see the figure before him, slowly descending the stairs. He followed, trembling. When it had reached the bottom of the stairs, it turned through the hall towards the back-door of the mansion. Dolph held the light over the balustrades; but, in his eagerness to catch a sight of the unknown, he flared his feeble taper so suddenly, that it went out. Still there was sufficient light from the pale moonbeams, that fell through a narrow window, to give him an indistinct view of the figure, near the door. He followed, therefore, down stairs, and turned towards the place; but when he had got there, the unknown had disappeared. The door remained fast barred and bolted; there was no other mode of exit; yet the being, whatever he might be, was gone. He unfastened the door, and looked out into the fields. It was a hazy, moonlight night, so that the eye could distinguish objects at some distance. He thought he saw the unknown in a footpath that led from the door. He was not mistaken; but how had he got out of the house? He did not pause to think, but followed on. The old man proceeded at a measured pace, without looking about him, his footsteps sounding on the hard ground. He passed through the orchard of apple-trees that stood near the house, always keeping the footpath. It led to a well, situated in a little hollow, which had supplied the farm with water. Just at this well Dolph lost sight of him. He rubbed his eyes and looked again; but nothing was to be seen of the unknown. He reached the well, but nobody was there. All the surrounding ground was open and clear; there was no bush nor hiding-place. He looked down the well and saw, at a great depth, the reflection of the sky in the still water. After remaining here for some time, without seeing or hearing any thing more of his mysterious conductor, he returned to the house, full of awe and wonder. He bolted the door, groped his way back to bed, and it was long before he could compose himself to sleep.

His dreams were strange and troubled. He thought he was following the old man along the side of a great river, until they came to a vessel that was on the point of sailing; and that his conductor led him on board and vanished. He remembered the commander of the vessel, a short swarthy man, with crisped black hair, blind of one eye, and lame of one leg; but the rest of his dream was very confused. Sometimes he was sailing; sometimes on shore; now amidst storms and tempests, and now wandering quietly in unknown streets. The figure of the old man was strangely mingled up with the incidents of the dream; and the whole distinctly wound up by his finding himself on board of the vessel again, returning home, with a great bag of money!

When he woke, the gray, cool light of dawn was streaking the horizon, and the cocks passing the *réveil* from farm to farm throughout the country. He rose more harassed and perplexed than ever. He was singularly confounded by all that he had seen and dreamt, and began to doubt whether his mind was not affected, and whether all that was passing in his thoughts might not be mere feverish fantasy. In his present state of mind, he did not feel disposed to return immediately to the doctor's, and undergo the cross-questioning of the household. He made a scanty breakfast, therefore, on the remains of last night's provisions, and then wandered out into the fields to meditate on all that had befallen him. Lost in thought, he rambled about, gradually approaching the town, until the morning was far advanced, when he was roused by a hurry and bustle around him. He found himself near the water's edge, in a throng of people, hurrying to a pier, where there was a vessel ready to make sail. He was unconsciously carried along by the impulse of the crowd, and found that it was a sloop, on the point of sailing up the Hudson to Albany. There was much leave-taking, and kissing of old women and children, and great activity in carrying on board baskets of bread and cakes, and provisions of all kinds, notwithstanding the mighty joints of meat that dangled over the stern; for a voyage to Albany was an expedition of great moment in those days. The commander of the sloop was hurrying about, and giving a world of orders, which were not very strictly attended to; one man being busy in lighting his pipe, and another in sharpening his snicker-snee.

The appearance of the commander suddenly caught Dolph's attention. He was short and swarthy, with crisped black hair; blind of one eye, and lame of one leg – the very commander he had seen in his dream! Surprised and aroused, he considered the scene more attentively, and recalled still further traces of his dream: the appearance of the vessel, of the river, and of a variety of other objects, accorded with the imperfect images vaguely rising to recollection.

As he stood musing on these circumstances, the captain suddenly called to him in Dutch, "Step on board, young man, or you'll be left behind!" He was startled by the summons; he saw that the sloop was cast loose, and was actually moving from the pier; it seemed as if he was actuated by some irresistible impulse; he sprang upon the deck, and the next moment the sloop was hurried off by the wind and tide. Dolph's thoughts and feelings were all in tumult and confusion. He had been strongly worked upon by the events that had recently befallen him, and could not but think that there was some connexion between his present situation and his last night's dream. He felt as if he was under supernatural influence; and he tried to assure himself with an old and favourite maxim of his, that "one way or other, all would turn out for the best." For a moment, the indignation of the doctor at his departure, without leave, passed across his mind, but that was matter of little moment; then he thought of the distress of his mother at his strange disappearance, and the idea gave him a sudden pang. He would have entreated to be put on shore; but he knew with such wind and tide the entreaty would have been in vain. Then the inspiring love of novelty and adventure came rushing in full tide through his bosom; he felt himself launched strangely and suddenly on the world, and under full way to explore the regions of wonder that lay up this mighty river, and beyond those blue mountains that had bounded his horizon since childhood. While he was lost in this whirl of thought, the sails strained to the breeze; the shores seemed to hurry away behind him; and, before he perfectly recovered his self-possession, the sloop was ploughing her way past Spiking-devil and Yonkers, and the tallest chimney of the Manhattoes had faded from his sight.

I have said that a voyage up the Hudson in those days was an undertaking of some moment; indeed, it was as much thought of as a voyage to Europe is at present. The sloops were often many days on the way; the cautious navigators taking in sail when it blew fresh, and coming to anchor at night; and stopping to send the boat ashore for milk for tea; without which it was impossible for the worthy old lady passengers to subsist. And then there were the much-talked-of perils of the Tappaan-zee, and the highlands. In short, a prudent Dutch burgher would talk of such a voyage for months, and even years, beforehand; and never undertook it without putting his affairs in order, making his will, and having prayers said for him in the Low Dutch churches.

In the course of such a voyage, therefore, Dolph was satisfied he would have time enough to reflect, and to make up his mind as to what he should do when he arrived at Albany. The captain, with his blind eye, and lame leg, would, it is true, bring his strange dream to mind, and perplex him sadly for a few moments; but of late his life had been made up so much of dreams and realities, his nights and days had been so jumbled together, that he seemed to be moving continually in a delusion. There is always, however, a kind of vagabond consolation in a man's having nothing in this world to lose; with this Dolph comforted his heart, and determined to make the most of the present enjoyment.

In the second day of the voyage they came to the highlands. It was the latter part of a calm, sultry day that they floated gently with the tide between these stern mountains. There was that perfect quiet which prevails over nature in the languor of summer heat; the turning of a plank, or the accidental falling of an oar on deck, was echoed from the mountain-side, and reverberated along the shores; and if by chance the captain gave a shout of command, there were airy tongues that mocked it from every cliff.

Dolph gazed about him in mute delight and wonder at these scenes of nature's magnificence. To the left the Dunderberg reared its woody precipices, height over height, forest over forest, away into the deep summer sky. To the right strutted forth the bold promontory of Anthony's Nose, with a solitary eagle wheeling about it; while beyond, mountain succeeded mountain, until they seemed to lock their arms together, and confine this mighty river in their embraces. There was a feeling of quiet luxury in gazing at the broad, green bosoms here and there scooped out among the precipices; or at woodlands high in air, nodding over the edge of some beetling bluff, and their foliage all transparent in the yellow sunshine.

In the midst of his admiration, Dolph remarked a pile of bright, snowy clouds peering above the western heights. It was succeeded by another and another, each seemingly pushing onwards its predecessor, and towering, with dazzling brilliancy, in the deep blue atmosphere: and now muttering peals of thunder were faintly heard rolling behind the mountains. The river, hitherto still and glassy, reflecting pictures of the sky and land, now showed a dark ripple at a distance, as the breeze came creeping up it. The fish-hawks wheeled and screamed, and sought their nests on the high dry trees; the crows flew clamorously to the crevices of the rocks, and all nature seemed conscious of the approaching thunder-gust.

The clouds now rolled in volumes over the mountain tops; their summits still bright and snowy, but the lower parts of an inky blackness. The rain began to patter down in broad and scattered drops; the wind freshened, and curled up the waves; at length it seemed as if the bellying clouds were torn open by the mountain tops, and complete torrents of rain came rattling down. The lightning leaped from cloud to cloud, and streamed quivering against the rocks, splitting and rending the stoutest forest trees. The thunder burst in tremendous explosions; the peals were echoed from mountain to mountain; they crashed upon Dunderberg, and rolled up the long defile of the high-lands, each headland making a new echo, until old Bull-hill seemed to bellow back the storm.

For a time the scudding rack and mist, and the sheeted rain, almost hid the landscape from the sight. There was a fearful gloom, illumined still more fearfully by the streams of lightning which glittered among the rain-drops. Never had Dolph beheld such an absolute warring of the elements; it seemed as if the storm was tearing and rending its way through this mountain defile, and had brought all the artillery of heaven into action.

The vessel was hurried on by the increasing wind, until she came to where the river makes a sudden bend, the only one in the whole course of its majestic career.* Just as they turned the point, a violent flaw of wind came sweeping down a mountain-gully, bending the forest before it, and, in a moment, lashing up the river into white froth and foam. The captain saw the danger, and cried out to lower the sail. Before the order could be obeyed, the flaw struck the sloop, and threw her on her beam-ends. Every thing now was fright and confusion: the flapping of the sails, the whistling and rushing of the wind, the bawling of the captain and crew, the shrieking of the passengers, all mingled with the rolling and bellowing of the thunder. In the midst of the uproar the sloop righted; at the same time the mainsail shifted, the boom came sweeping the quarter-deck, and Dolph, who was gazing unguardedly at the clouds, found himself, in a moment, floundering in the river.

For once in his life one of his idle accomplishments was of use to him. The many truant hours which he had devoted to sporting in the Hudson had made him an expert swimmer; yet with all his strength and skill, he found great difficulty in reaching the shore. His disappearance from the deck had not been noticed by the crew, who were all occupied by their own danger. The sloop was driven along with inconceivable rapidity. She had hard work to weather a long promontory on the east-ern shore, round which the river turned, and which completely shut her from Dolph's view.

It was on a point of the western shore that he landed, and, scrambling up the rocks, he threw himself, faint and exhausted, at the foot of a tree. By degrees the thunder-gust passed over. The clouds rolled away

* This must have been the bend at West point.

to the east, where they lay piled in feathery masses, tinted with the
last rosy rays of the sun. The distant play of the lightning might be still
seen about their dark bases, and now and then might be heard the faint
muttering of the thunder. Dolph rose, and sought about to see if any
path led from the shore, but all was savage and trackless. The rocks
were piled upon each other; great trunks of trees lay shattered about,
as they had been blown down by the strong winds which draw through
these mountains, or had fallen through age. The rocks too, were overhung with wild vines and briars, which completely matted themselves
together, and opposed a barrier to all ingress; every movement that he
made shook down a shower from the dripping foliage. He attempted to
scale one of these almost perpendicular heights; but, though strong
and agile, he found it an Herculean undertaking. Often he was supported
merely by crumbling projections of the rock, and sometimes he clung
to roots and branches of trees, and hung almost suspended in the air.
The wood-pigeon came cleaving his whistling flight by him, and the
eagle screamed from the brow of the impending cliff. As he was thus
clambering, he was on the point of seizing hold of a shrub to aid his
ascent, when something rustled among the leaves, and he saw a snake
quivering along like lightning, almost from under his hand. It coiled
itself up immediately, in an attitude of defiance, with flattened head,
distended jaws, and quickly vibrating tongue, that played like a little
flame about its mouth. Dolph's heart turned faint within him, and he
had well nigh let go his hold, and tumbled down the precipice. The
serpent stood on the defensive but for an instant; it was an instinctive
movement of defence; and, finding there was no attack, it glided away
into a cleft of the rock. Dolph's eye followed it with fearful intensity;
and he saw at a glance that he was in the vicinity of a nest of adders,
that lay knotted, and writhing, and hissing in the chasm. He hastened
with all speed to escape from so frightful a neighbourhood. His imagination was full of this new horror; he saw an adder in every curling vine,
and heard the tail of a rattle-snake in every dry leaf that rustled.

At length he succeeded in scrambling to the summit of a precipice; but
it was covered by a dense forest. Wherever he could gain a look out
between the trees, he saw that the coast rose in heights and cliffs, one
rising beyond another, until huge mountains overtopped the whole.
There were no signs of cultivation; nor any smoke curling amongst the
trees to indicate a human residence. Every thing was wild and solitary.
As he was standing on the edge of a precipice that overlooked a deep
ravine fringed with trees, his feet detached a great fragment of rock;
it fell, crashing its way through the tree tops, down into the chasm.
A loud whoop, or rather yell, issued from the bottom of the glen; the

endeavoured to retreat quietly, not caring to entrust himself to these half-human beings in so savage and lonely a place. It was too late; the Indian, with that eagle quickness of eye so remarkable in his race, perceived something stirring among the bushes on the rock; he seized one of the guns that leaned against the tree; one moment more, and Dolph might have had his passion for adventure cured by a bullet. He hallooed loudly, with the Indian salutation of friendship. The whole party sprang upon their feet; the salutation was returned, and the straggler was invited to join them at the fire.

On approaching he found to his consolation, that the party was composed of white men, as well as Indians. One, who was evidently the principal personage, or commander, was seated on a trunk of a tree before the fire. He was a large stout man, somewhat advanced in life, but hale and hearty. His face was bronzed almost to the colour of an Indian's; he had strong but rather jovial features, an aquiline nose, and a mouth shaped like a mastiff's. His face was half thrown in shade by a broad hat, with a buck's tail in it. His gray hair hung short in his neck. He wore a hunting frock, with Indian leggings, and mockasins, and a tomahawk in the broad wampum belt round his waist. As Dolph caught a distinct view of his person and features, he was struck with something that reminded him of the old man of the Haunted House. The man before him, however, was different in his dress and age; he was more cheery too in his aspect, and it was hard to define where the vague resemblance lay; but a resemblance there certainly was. Dolph felt some degree of awe in approaching him; but was assured by the frank, hearty welcome with which he was received. As he cast his eyes about, too, he was still further encouraged, by perceiving that the dead body, which had caused him some alarm, was that of a deer; and his satisfaction was complete in discerning, by the savoury steams which issued from a kettle, suspended by a hooked stick over the fire, that there was a part cooking for the evening's repast.

He now found that he had fallen in with a rambling hunting party; such as often took place in those days among the settlers along the river. The hunter is always hospitable; and nothing makes men more social and unceremonious than meeting in the wilderness. The commander of the party poured him out a dram of cheering liquor, which he gave him with a merry leer, to warm his heart; and ordered one of his followers to fetch some garments from a pinnace, which was moored in a cove close by; while those in which our hero was dripping might be dried before the fire.

Dolph found, as he had suspected, that the shot from the glen, which had come so near giving him his quietus when on the precipice, was from the party before him. He had nearly crushed one of them by the fragment of rock which he had detached; and the jovial old hunter, in the broad hat and buck tail, had fired at the place where he saw the bushes move, supposing it to be some wild animal. He laughed heartily at the blunder; it being what is considered an exceeding good joke among hunters; "but, faith, my lad," said he, "if I had but caught a glimpse of you to take sight at, you would have followed the rock. Antony Vander Heyden is seldom known to miss his aim." These last words were at once a clue to Dolph's curiosity; and a few questions let him completely into the character of the man before him, and of his band of woodland rangers. The commander in the broad hat and hunting frock was no less a personage than the Heer Antony Vander Heyden, of Albany, of whom Dolph had many a time heard. He was, in fact, the hero of many a story; being a man of singular humours and whimsical habits, that were matters of wonder to his quiet Dutch neighbours. As he was a man of property, having had a father before him, from whom he inherited large tracts of wild land, and whole barrels full of wampum, he could indulge his humours without control. Instead of staying quietly at home; eating and drinking at regular meal-times; amusing himself by smoking his pipe on the bench before the door; and then turning into a comfortable bed at night; he delighted in all kinds of rough, wild expeditions. He was never so happy as when on a hunting party in the wilderness, sleeping under trees or bark sheds, or cruising down the river, or on some woodland lake, fishing and fowling, and living the Lord knows how.

He was a great friend to Indians, and to an Indian mode of life, which he considered true natural liberty and manly enjoyment. When at home he had always several Indian hangers-on, who loitered about his house, sleeping like hounds in the sunshine, or preparing hunting and fishing-tackle for some new expedition, or shooting at marks with bows and arrows.

Over these vagrant beings Heer Antony had as perfect command as a huntsman over his pack; though they were great nuisances to the regular people of his neighbourhood. As he was a rich man, no one ventured to thwart his humours; indeed, he had a hearty, joyous manner about him, that made him universally popular. He would troll a Dutch song as he tramped along the street; hail every one a mile off; and when he entered a house, he would slap the good man familiarly on the back, shake him by the hand till he roared, and kiss is wife and daughters before his face — in short, there was no pride nor ill humour about Heer Antony.

Besides his Indian hangers on, he had three or four humble friends among the white men, who looked up to him as a patron, and had the run of his kitchen, and the favour of being taken with him occasionally on his expeditions. It was with a medley of such retainers that he was at present on a cruise along the shores of the Hudson, in a pinnace which he kept for his own recreation. There were two white men with him, dressed partly in the Indian style, with mocassins and hunting shirts; the rest of his crew consisted of four favourite Indians. They had been prowling about the river, without any definite object, until they found themselves in the highlands; where they had passed two or three days, hunting the deer which still lingered among these mountains.

"It is a lucky circumstance, young man," said Antony Vander Heyden, "that you happened to be knocked overboard to-day; as tomorrow morning we start early on our return homewards; and you might then have looked in vain for a meal among these mountains – but come, lads, stir about! stir about! Let's see what prog we have for supper; the kettle has boiled long enough; my stomach cries cupboard; and I'll warrant our guest is in no mood to dally with his trencher."

There was a bustle now in the little encampment; one took off the kettle and turned a part of the contents into a huge wooden bowl. Another prepared a flat rock for a table; while a third brought various utensils from the pinnace; and Heer Antony himself brought a flask or two of precious liquor from his own private locker; knowing his boon companions too well to trust any of them with the key.

A rude but hearty repast was soon spread; consisting of venison smoking from the kettle, with cold bacon, boiled Indian corn, and mighty loaves of good brown household bread. Never had Dolph made a more delicious repast; and when he had washed it down by two or three draughts from the Heer Antony's flask, and felt the jolly liquor sending its warmth through his veins, and glowing round his very heart, he would not have changed his situation, no, not with the governor of the province.

The Heer Antony, too, grew chirping and joyous; told half a dozen fat stories, at which his white followers laughed immoderately, though the Indians, as usual, maintained an invincible gravity.

"This is your true life, my boy!" said he, slapping Dolph on the shoulder; "a man is never a man till he can defy wind and weather, range woods and wilds, sleep under a tree, and live on bass-wood leaves!"

And then would he sing a stave or two of a Dutch drinking song, swaying a short, squab Dutch bottle in his hand, while his myrmidons would join in chorus, until the woods echoed again; – as the good old song has it:

"They all with a shout made the elements ring,
    So soon as the office was o'er;
To feasting they went, with true merriment,
    And tippled strong liquor gillore."

In the midst of his joviality, however, Heer Antony did not lose
sight of discretion. Though he pushed the bottle without reserve to
Dolph, yet he always took care to help his followers himself, knowing
the beings he had to deal with; and he was particular in granting but
a moderate allowance to the Indians. The repast being ended, the
Indians having drunk their liquor, and smoked their pipes, now wrapped
themselves in their blankets, stretched themselves on the ground, with
their feet to the fire, and soon fell asleep, like so many tired hounds.
The rest of the party remained chatting before the fire, which the gloom
of the forest, and the dampness of the air from the late storm, rendered
extremely grateful and comforting. The conversation gradually moder-
ated from the hilarity of supper-time, and turned upon hunting adventures, and exploits and perils in the wilderness; many of which were so
strange and improbable, that I will not venture to repeat them, lest the
veracity of Antony Vander Heyden and his comrades should be brought
into question. There were many legendary tales told, also, about the
river, and the settlements on its borders; in which valuable kind of lore
the Heer Antony seemed deeply versed. As the sturdy bush-beater sat
in a twisted root of a tree, that served him for a kind of arm-chair,
dealing forth these wild stories, with the fire gleaming on his strongly
marked visage, Dolph was again repeatedly perplexed by something
that reminded him of the phantom of the Haunted House; some vague
resemblance that could not be fixed upon any precise feature or linea-
ment, but which pervaded the general air of his countenance and figure.

The circumstance of Dolph's falling overboard being again discussed,
led to the relation of divers disasters and singular mishaps that had
befallen voyagers on this great river, particularly in the earlier periods
of colonial history; most of which the Heer deliberately attributed to
supernatural causes. Dolph stared at this suggestion; but the old gentleman assured him that it was very currently believed by the settlers
along the river, that these highlands were under the dominion of supernatural and mischievous beings, which seemed to have taken some
pique against the Dutch colonists in the early time of the settlement.
In consequence of this, they have ever since taken particular delight
in venting their spleen, and indulging their humours, upon the Dutch
skippers; bothering them with flaws, head-winds, counter-currents, and
all kinds of impediments; insomuch, that a Dutch navigator was always

obliged to be exceedingly wary and deliberate in his proceedings; to come to anchor at dusk; to drop his peak, or take in sail, whenever he saw a swag-bellied cloud rolling over the mountains; in short, to take so many precautions, that he was often apt to be an incredible time in toiling up the river.

Some, he said, believed these mischievous powers of the air to be evil spirits conjured up by the Indian wizards, in the early times of the province, to revenge themselves on the strangers who had dispossessed them of their country. They even attributed to their incantations the misadventure which befell the renowned Hendrick Hudson, when he sailed so gallantly up this river in quest of a northwest passage, and, as he thought, run his ship aground; which they affirm was nothing more nor less than a spell of these same wizards, to prevent his getting to China in this direction.

The greater part, however, Heer Antony observed, accounted for all the extraordinary circumstances attending this river, and the perplexities of the skippers which navigated it, by the old legend of the Storm-ship which haunted Point-no-point. On finding Dolph to be utterly ignorant of this tradition, the Heer stared at him for a moment with surprise, and wondered where he had passed his life, to be uninformed on so important a point of history. To pass away the remainder of the evening, therefore, he undertook the tale, as far as his memory would serve, in the very words in which it had been written out by Mynheer Selyne, an early poet of the New Nederlandts. Giving then, a stir to the fire, that sent up its sparks among the trees like a little volcano, he adjusted himself comfortably in his root of a tree; and throwing back his head, and closing his eyes for a few moments, to summon up his recollection, he related the following legend.

THE STORM-SHIP

In the golden age of the province of the New Netherlands, when it was under the sway of Wouter Van Twiller, otherwise called the Doubter, the people of the Manhattoes were alarmed one sultry afternoon, just about the time of the summer solstice, by a tremendous storm of thunder and lightning. The rain descended in such torrents as absolutely to spatter up and smoke along the ground. It seemed as if the thunder rattled and rolled over the very roofs of the houses; the lightning was seen to play about the church of St. Nicholas, and to strive three times, in vain, to strike its weathercock. Garret Van Horne's new chimney was split almost from top to bottom; and Doffue Mildeberger was struck speechless from his bald-faced mare, just as he was riding into town. In a word, it was one of those unparalleled storms, that only happen once within the memory of that venerable personage, known in all towns by the appellation of "the oldest inhabitant."

Great was the terror of the good old women of the Manhattoes. They gathered their children together, and took refuge in the cellars; after having hung a shoe on the iron point of every bed-post, lest it should attract the lightning. At length the storm abated; the thunder sunk into a growl, and the setting sun, breaking from under the fringed borders of the clouds, made the broad bosom of the bay to gleam like a sea of molten gold.

The word was given from the fort that a ship was standing up the bay. It passed from mouth to mouth, and street to street, and soon put the little capital in a bustle. The arrival of a ship, in those early times of the settlement, was an event of vast importance to the inhabitants. It brought them news from the old world, from the land of their birth, from which they were so completely severed. To the yearly ship, too, they looked for their supply of luxuries, of finery, of comforts, and almost of necessaries. The good vrouw could not have her new cap nor new gown until the arrival of the ship; the artist waited for it for his tools, the burgomaster for his pipe and his supply of Hollands, the schoolboy for his top and marbles, and the lordly landholder for the bricks with which he was to build his new mansion. Thus every one, rich and poor, great and small, looked out for the arrival of the ship. It was the great yearly event of the town of New Amsterdam; and from one end of the year to the other, the ship – the ship – the ship – was the continual topic of conversation.

The news from the fort, therefore, brought all the populace down to the battery, to behold the wished-for sight. It was not exactly the time when she had been expected to arrive, and the circumstance was a matter of some speculation. Many were the groups collected about the battery. Here and there might be seen a burgomaster, of slow and pompous gravity, giving his opinion with great confidence to a crowd of old women and idle boys. At another place was a knot of old weather-beaten fellows, who had been seamen or fishermen in their times, and were great authorities on such occasions; these gave different opinions, and caused great disputes among their several adherents: but the man most looked up to, and followed and watched by the crowd, was Hans Van Pelt, an old Dutch sea captain retired from service, the nautical oracle of the place. He reconnoitred the ship through an ancient telescope, covered with tarry canvas, hummed a Dutch tune to himself, and said nothing. A hum, however, from Hans Van Pelt had always more weight with the public than a speech from another man.

In the mean time the ship became more distinct to the naked eye: she was a stout, round, Dutch-built vessel, with high bow and poop, and bearing Dutch colours. The evening sun gilded her bellying canvas, as she came riding over the long waving billows. The centinel who had given notice of her approach, declared, that he first got sight of her when she was in the centre of the bay; and that she broke suddenly on his sight, just as if she had come out of the bosom of the black thunder-cloud. The bystanders looked at Hans Van Pelt, to see what he would say to this report: Hans Van Pelt screwed his mouth closer together, and said nothing; upon which some shook their heads, and others shrugged their shoulders.

The ship was now repeatedly hailed, but made no reply, and passing by the fort, stood on up the Hudson. A gun was brought to bear on her, and, with some difficulty, loaded and fired by Hans Van Pelt, the garrison not being expert in artillery. The shot seemed absolutely to pass through the ship, and to skip along the water on the other side, but no notice was taken of it! What was strange, she had all her sails set, and sailed right against wind and tide, which were both down the river. Upon this Hans Van Pelt, who was likewise harbour-master, ordered his boat, and set off to board her; but after rowing two or three hours, he returned without success. Sometimes he would get within one or two hundred yards of her, and then, in a twinkling, she would be half a mile off. Some said it was because his oars-men, who were rather pursy and short-winded, stopped every now and then to take breath, and spit on their hands; but this it is probable was a mere scandal. He got near enough, however, to see the crew; who were all dressed in the Dutch style, the officers in doublets and high hats and feathers. Not a word was spoken by any one on board; they stood as motionless as so many statues, and the ship seemed as if left to her own government. Thus she kept on, away up the river, lessening and lessening in the evening sunshine, until she faded from sight, like a little white cloud melting away in the summer sky.

The appearance of this ship threw the governor into one of the deepest doubts that ever beset him in the whole course of his administration. Fears were entertained for the security of the infant settlements on the river, lest this might be an enemy's ship in disguise, sent to take possession. The governor called together his council repeatedly, to assist him with their conjectures. He sat in his chair of state, built of timber from the sacred forest of the Hague, and smoked his long jasmin pipe, and listened to all that his counsellors had to say on a subject about which they knew nothing; but in spite of all the conjecturing of the sagest and oldest heads, the governor still continued to doubt.

Messengers were despatched to different places on the river; but they returned without any tidings – the ship had made no port. Day after day, and week after week, elapsed, but she never returned down the Hudson. As, however, the council seemed solicitous for intelligence, they had it in abundance. The captains of the sloops seldom arrived without bringing some report of having seen the strange ship at different parts of the river; sometimes near the Pallisadoes, sometimes off Croton Point, and sometimes in the highlands; but she never was reported as having been seen above the highlands. The crews of the sloops, it is true, generally differed among themselves in their accounts of these apparitions; but that may have arisen from the uncertain situations in which they saw her. Sometimes it was by the flashes of the thunder-storm lighting up a pitchy night, and giving glimpses of her careering across Tappaan Zee, or the wide waste of Haverstraw Bay. At one moment she would appear close upon them, as if likely to run them down, and would throw them into great bustle and alarm; but the next flash would show her far off, always sailing against the wind. Sometimes, in quiet moonlight nights, she would be seen under some high bluff of the highlands, all in deep shadow, excepting her top-sails glittering in the moonbeams; by the time, however, that the voyagers would reach the place, there would be no ship to be seen; and when they had past on for some distance, and looked back, behold! there she was again, with her top-sails in the moonshine! Her appearance was always just after, or just before, or just in the midst of unruly weather; and she was known by all the skippers and voyagers of the Hudson by the name of "the storm-ship."

These reports perplexed the governor and his council more than ever; and it would be endless to repeat the conjectures and opinions that

were uttered on the subject. Some quoted cases in point, of ships seen
off the coast of New England, navigated by witches and goblins. Old
Hans Van Pelt, who had been more than once to the Dutch colony at
the Cape of Good Hope, insisted that this must be the flying Dutchman
which had so long haunted Table Bay; but being unable to make port,
had now sought another harbour. Others suggested, that, if it really
was a supernatural apparition, as there was every natural reason to
believe, it might be Hendrick Hudson, and his crew of the Half-moon;
who, it was well known, had once run aground in the upper part of the
river, in seeking a north-west passage to China. This opinion had very
little weight with the governor, but it passed current out of doors; for
indeed it had already been reported, that Hendrick Hudson and his
crew haunted the Kaatskill Mountain; and it appeared very reasonable
to suppose, that his ship might infest the river where the enterprise was
baffled, or that it might bear the shadowy crew to their periodical revels
in the mountain.

Other events occurred to occupy the thoughts and doubts of the
sage Wouter and his council, and the storm-ship ceased to be a subject
of deliberation at the board. It continued, however, to be a matter
of popular belief and marvellous anecdote through the whole time of
the Dutch government, and particularly just before the capture of
New Amsterdam, and the subjugation of the province by the English
squadron. About that time the storm-ship was repeatedly seen in the
Tappaan-Zee, and about Weehawk, and even down as far as Hoboken;
and her appearance was supposed to be ominous of the approaching
squall in public affairs, and the downfall of Dutch domination.

Since that time we have no authentic accounts of her; though it is
said she still haunts the highlands, and cruises about Point-no-point
People who live along the river, insist that they sometimes see her in
summer moonlight; and that in a deep still midnight they have heard
the chant of her crew, as if heaving the lead; but sights and sounds
are so deceptive along the mountainous shores, and about the wide
bays and long reaches of this great river, that I confess I have very
strong doubts upon the subject.

It is certain, nevertheless, that strange things have been seen in
these highlands in storms, which are considered as connected with the
old story of the ship. The captains of the river craft talk of a little
bulbous-bottomed Dutch goblin, in trunk hose and sugar-loafed hat,
with a speaking-trumpet in his hand, which they say keeps about the
Dunderberg.* They declare that they have heard him, in stormy

---

* *i.e.* the "Thunder-Mountain," so called from its echoes.

weather, in the midst of the turmoil, giving orders in low Dutch for the piping up of a fresh gust of wind, or the rattling off of another thunder-clap. That sometimes he has been seen surrounded by a crew of little imps in broad breeches and short doublets; tumbling head over heels in the rack and mist, and playing a thousand gambols in the air; or buzzing like a swarm of flies about Anthony's Nose; and that, at such times, the hurry-scurry of the storm was always greatest. One time a sloop, in passing by the Dunderberg, was overtaken by a thunder-gust, that came scouring round the mountain, and seemed to burst just over the vessel. Though tight and well ballasted, yet she laboured dreadfully, until the water came over the gunwale. All the crew were amazed, when it was discovered that there was a little white sugarloaf-hat on the mast head, which was known at once to be the hat of the Heer of the Dunderberg. Nobody, however, dared to climb to the mast-head, and get rid of this terrible hat. The sloop continued labouring and rocking, as if she would have rolled her mast overboard. She seemed in continual danger either of upsetting or of running on shore. In this way she drove quite through the highlands, until she had passed Pollopol's Island, where, it is said, the jurisdiction of the Dunderberg potentate ceases. No sooner had she passed this bourne, than the little hat, all at once, spun up into the air like a top; whirled up all the clouds into a vortex, and hurried them back to the summit of the Dunderberg; while the sloop righted herself, and sailed on as quietly as if in a mill-pond. Nothing saved her from utter wreck but the fortunate circumstance of having a horse-shoe nailed against the mast; a wise precaution against evil spirits, which has since been adopted by all the Dutch captains that navigate this haunted river.

There is another story told of this foul-weather urchin, by Skipper Daniel Ouslesticker, of Fishkill, who was never known to tell a lie. He declared, that, in a severe squall, he saw him seated astride of his bowsprit, riding the sloop ashore, full butt against Anthony's Nose, and that he was exorcised by Dominie Van Gieson, of Esopus, who happened to be on board, and who sung the hymn of St. Nicholas; whereupon the goblin threw himself up in the air like a ball, and went off in a whirlwind, carrying away with him the night-cap of the Dominie's wife; which was discovered the next Sunday morning hanging on the weather-cock of Esopus' church steeple, at least forty miles off! After several events of this kind had taken place, the regular skippers of the river, for a long time, did not venture to pass the Dunderberg, without lowering their peaks, out of homage to the Heer of the mountain; and it was observed that all such as paid this tribute of respect were suffered to pass unmolested.*

"Such," said Antony Vander Heyden, "are a few of the stories written down by Selyne the poet, concerning this storm-ship; which he affirms to have brought this colony of mischievous imps into the province, from some old ghost-ridden country of Europe. I could give you a host more, if necessary; for all the accidents that so often befall the river craft in the highlands are said to be tricks played off by these imps of the Dunderberg; but I see that you are nodding, so let us turn in for the night." –

The moon had just raised her silver horns above the round back of Old Bull Hill, and lit up the gray rocks and shagged forests, and glittered on the waving bosom of the river. The night dew was falling, and the late gloomy mountains began to soften and put on a gray aerial tint in the dewy light. The hunters stirred the fire, and threw on fresh fuel to qualify the damp of the night air. They then prepared a bed of branches and dry leaves under a ledge of rocks for Dolph; while Antony Vander Heyden, wrapping himself up in a huge coat made of skins, stretched himself before the fire. It was some time, however, before Dolph could close his eyes. He lay contemplating the strange scene before him: the wild woods and rocks around; the fire throwing fitful gleams on the faces of the sleeping savages; and the Heer Antony, too, who so singularly, yet vaguely, reminded him of the nightly visitant

* Among the superstitions which prevailed in the colonies, during the early times of the settlements, there seems to have been a singular one about phantom ships. The superstitious fancies of men are always apt to turn upon those objects which concern their daily occupations. The solitary ship, which, from year to year, came like a raven in the wilderness, bringing to the inhabitants of a settlement the comforts of life from the world from which they were cut off, was apt to be present to their dreams, whether sleeping or waking. The accidental sight from shore of a sail gliding along the horizon in those, as yet, lonely seas, was apt to be a matter of much talk and speculation. There is mention made in one of the early New England writers, of a ship navigated by witches, with a great horse that stood by the mainmast. I have met with another story, somewhere, of a ship that drove on shore, in fair, sunny, tranquil weather, with sails all set and a table spread in the cabin, as if to regale a number of guests, yet not a living being on board. These phantom ships always sailed in the eye of the wind; or ploughed their way with great velocity, making the smooth sea foam before their bows, when not a breath of air was stirring.

Moore has finely wrought up one of these legends of the sea into a little tale, which, within a small compass, contains the very essence of this species of supernatural fiction. I allude to his Spectre-Ship bound to Deadman's Isle.

to the Haunted House. Now and then he heard the cry of some animal from the forest; or the hooting of the owl; or the notes of the whip-poor-will, which seemed to abound among these solitudes; or the splash of a sturgeon, leaping out of the river, and falling back full length on its placid surface. He contrasted all this with his accustomed nest in the garret room of the doctor's mansion; where the only sounds he heard at night were the church clock telling the hour; the drowsy voice of the watchman, drawling out all was well; the deep snoring of the doctor's clubbed nose from below stairs; or the cautious labours of some carpenter rat gnawing in the wainscot. His thoughts then wandered to his poor old mother: what would she think of his mysterious disappearance – what anxiety and distress would she not suffer? This was the thought that would continually intrude itself to mar his present enjoyment. It brought with it a feeling of pain and compunction, and he fell asleep with the tears yet standing in his eyes.

Were this a mere tale of fancy, here would be a fine opportunity for weaving in strange adventures among these wild mountains, and roving hunters; and, after involving my hero in a variety of perils and difficulties, rescuing him from them all by some miraculous contrivance; but as this is absolutely a true story, I must content myself with simple facts, and keep to probabilities.

At an early hour of the next day, therefore, after a hearty morning's meal, the encampment broke up, and our adventurers embarked in the pinnace of Antony Vander Heyden. There being no wind for the sails, the Indians rowed her gently along, keeping time to a kind of chant of one of the white men. The day was serene and beautiful; the river without a wave; and as the vessel cleft the glassy water, it left a long, undulating track behind. The crows, who had scented the hunters' banquet, were already gathering and hovering in the air, just where a column of thin, blue smoke, rising from among the trees, showed the place of their last night's quarters. As they coasted along the bases of the mountains, the Heer Antony pointed out to Dolph a bald eagle, the sovereign of these regions, who sat perched on a dry tree that projected over the river; and, with eye turned upwards, seemed to be drinking in the splendour of the morning sun. Their approach disturbed the monarch's meditations. He first spread one wing, and then the other; balanced himself for a moment; and then, quitting his perch with dignified composure, wheeled slowly over their heads. Dolph snatched up a gun, and sent a whistling ball after him that cut some of the feathers from his wing; the report of the gun leaped sharply from rock to rock, and awakened a thousand echoes; but the monarch of the air sailed calmly on, ascending higher and higher, and wheeling widely as he ascended, soaring up the green bosom of the woody mountain, until he disappeared over the brow of a beetling precipice. Dolph felt in a manner rebuked by this proud tranquillity, and almost reproached himself for having so wantonly insulted this majestic bird. Heer Antony told him, laughing, to remember that he was not yet out of the territories of the lord of the Dunderberg; and an old Indian shook his head, and observed, that there was bad luck in killing an eagle; the hunter, on the contrary, should always leave him a portion of his spoils.

Nothing, however, occurred to molest them on their voyage. They passed pleasantly through magnificent and lonely scenes, until they came to where Pollopol's Island lay, like a floating bower, at the extremity of the highlands. Here they landed, until the heat of the day should abate, or a breeze spring up, that might supersede the labour of the oar. Some prepared the mid-day meal, while others reposed under the shade of the trees in luxurious summer indolence, looking drowsily forth upon the beauty of the scene. On the one side were the highlands, vast and cragged, feathered to the top with forests, and throwing their shadows on the glassy water that dimpled at their feet. On the other side was a wide expanse of the river, like a broad lake, with long sunny reaches, and green headlands; and the distant line of Shawungunk mountains waving along a clear horizon, or chequered by a fleecy cloud.

But I forbear to dwell on the particulars of their cruise along the river. This vagrant amphibious life, careering across silver sheets of water; coasting wild woodland shores; banqueting on shady promontories, with the spreading tree over head, the river curling its light foam to one's feet, and distant mountain, and rock, and tree, and snowy cloud, and deep blue sky, all mingling in summer beauty before one; all this, though never cloying in the enjoyment, would be but tedious in narration.

When encamped by the water-side, some of the party would go into the woods and hunt; others would fish; sometimes they would amuse themselves by shooting at a mark, by leaping, by running, by wrestling; and Dolph gained great favour in the eyes of Antony Vander Heyden, by his skill and adroitness in all these exercises, which the Heer considered as the highest of manly accomplishments.

Thus did they coast jollily on, choosing only the pleasant hours for voyaging; sometimes in the cool morning dawn, sometimes in the sober evening twilight, and sometimes when the moonshine spangled the crisp curling waves that whispered along the sides of their little bark. Never had Dolph felt so completely in his element; never had he met with any thing so completely to his taste as this wild, hap-hazard life.

He was the very man to second Antony Vander Heyden in his rambling humours, and gained continually on his affections. The heart of the old bush-whacker yearned towards the young man, who seemed thus growing up in his own likeness; and as they approached the end of their voyage, he could not help inquiring a little into his history. Dolph frankly told him his course of life, his severe medical studies, his little proficiency, and his very dubious prospects. The Heer was shocked to find that such amazing talents and accomplishments were to be cramped and buried under a doctor's wig. He had a sovereign contempt for the healing art, having never had any other physician than the butcher. He bore a mortal grudge to all kinds of study also, ever since he had been flogged about an unintelligible book when he was a boy. But to think that a young fellow like Dolph, of such wonderful abilities, who could shoot, fish, run, jump, ride, and wrestle, should be obliged to roll pills, and administer juleps for a living – 'twas monstrous! He told Dolph never to despair, but to "throw physic to the dogs;" for a young fellow of his prodigious talents could never fail to make his way. "As you seem to have no acquaintance in Albany," said Heer Antony, "you shall go home with me, and remain under my roof until you can look about you; and in the meantime we can take an occasional bout at shooting and fishing, for it is a pity such talents should lie idle."

Dolph, who was at the mercy of chance, was not hard to be persuaded. Indeed, on turning over matters in his mind, which he did very sagely and deliberately, he could not but think that Antony Vander Heyden was, "some how or other," connected with the story of the Haunted House; that the misadventure in the highlands, which had thrown them so strangely together, was, "some how or other," to work out something good: in short, there is nothing so convenient as this "some how or other" way of accommodating one's self to circumstances; it is the main stay of a heedless actor, and tardy reasoner, like Dolph Heyliger; and he who can, in this loose, easy way, link foregone evil to anticipated good, possesses a secret of happiness almost equal to the philosopher's stone.

On their arrival at Albany, the sight of Dolph's companion seemed to cause universal satisfaction. Many were the greetings at the river-side, and the salutations in the streets; the dogs bounded before him; the boys whooped as he passed; every body seemed to know Antony Vander Heyden. Dolph followed on in silence, admiring the neatness of this worthy burgh; for in those days Albany was in all its glory, and inhabited almost exclusively by the descendants of the original Dutch settlers, for it has not as yet been discovered and colonized by the restless people of New England. Every thing was quiet and orderly; every thing was conducted calmly and leisurely; no hurry, no bustle, no struggling and scrambling for existence. The grass grew about the unpaved streets, and relieved the eye by its refreshing verdure. Tall sycamores or pendent willows shaded the houses, with caterpillars swinging, in long silken strings, from their branches, or moths, fluttering about like coxcombs, in joy at their gay transformation. The houses were built in the old Dutch style, with the gable ends towards the street. The thrifty housewife was seated on a bench before her door, in close crimped cap, bright flowered gown, and white apron, busily employed in knitting. The husband smoked his pipe on the opposite bench, and the little pet negro girl, seated on the step at her mistress' feet, was industriously plying her needle. The swallows sported about the eaves, or skimmed along the streets, and brought back some rich booty for their clamorous young; and the little housekeeping wren flew in and out of a Lilliputian house, or an old hat nailed against the wall. The cows were coming home, lowing through the streets, to be milked at their owner's door; and if, perchance, there were any loiterers, some negro urchin, with a long goad, was gently urging them homewards.

As Dolph's companion passed on, he received a tranquil nod from the burghers, and a friendly word from their wives; all calling him familiarly by the name of Antony; for it was the custom in this strong hold of the patriarchs, where they had all grown up together from childhood, to call every one by the christian name. The Heer did not pause to have his usual jokes with them, for he was impatient to reach his home. At length they arrived at his mansion. It was of some magnitude, in the Dutch style, with large iron figures on the gables, that gave the date of its erection, and showed that it had been built in the earliest times of the settlement.

The news of Heer Antony's arrival had preceded him, and the whole household was on the look out. A crew of negroes, large and small, had collected in front of the house to receive him. The old, white-headed ones, who had grown gray in his service, grinned for joy, and made many awkward bows and grimaces, and the little ones capered about his knees. But the most happy being in the household was a little, plump, blooming lass, his only child, and the darling of his heart. She came bounding out of the house; but the sight of a strange young man with her father called up, for a moment, all the bashfulness of a home-bred damsel. Dolph gazed at her with wonder and delight; never had he seen, as he thought, any thing so comely in the shape of woman. She was dressed in the good old Dutch taste, with long stays, and full, short petticoats, so admirably adapted to show and set off the female form. Her hair, turned up under a small round cap, displayed the fairness of her forehead; she had fine blue, laughing eyes; a trim, slender waist, and soft swel——but, in a word, she was a little Dutch divinity; and Dolph, who never stopt half-way in a new impulse, fell desperately in love with her.

Dolph was now ushered into the house with a hearty welcome. In the interior was a mingled display of Heer Antony's taste and habits, and of the opulence of his predecessors. The chambers were furnished with good old mahogany; the beaufets and cupboards glittered with embossed silver, and painted china. Over the parlour fire-place was, as usual, the family coat of arms, painted and framed; above which was a long, duck fowling-piece, flanked by an Indian pouch, and a powder-horn. The room was decorated with many Indian articles, such as pipes of peace, tomahawks, scalping knives, hunting pouches, and belts of wampum; and there were various kinds of fishing tackle, and two or three fowling-pieces in the corners. The household affairs seemed to be conducted, in some measure, after the master's humours; corrected, perhaps, by a little quiet management of the daughter's. There was a great degree of patriarchal simplicity, and good-humored indulgence. The negroes came into the room without being called, merely to look at their master, and hear of his adventures; they would stand listening at the door until he had finished a story, and then go off on a broad grin, to repeat it in the kitchen. A couple of pet negro children were playing about the floor with the dogs, and sharing with them their bread and butter. All the domestics looked hearty and happy; and when the table was set for the evening repast, the variety and abundance of good household luxuries bore testimony to the open-handed liberality of the Heer, and the notable housewifery of his daughter.

In the evening there dropped in several of the worthies of the place, the Van Rennsellaers, and the Gansevoorts, and the Rosebooms, and others of Antony Vander Heyden's intimates, to hear an account of his expedition; for he was the Sindbad of Albany, and his exploits and adventures were favourite topics of conversation among the inhabitants. While these sat gossiping together about the door of the hall, and telling long twilight stories, Dolph was cozily seated, entertaining the daughter on a window-bench. He had already got on intimate terms; for those were not times of false reserve and idle ceremony: and, besides, there is something wonderfully propitious to a lover's suit, in the delightful dusk of a long summer evening; it gives courage to the most timid tongue, and hides the blushes of the bashful. The stars alone twinkled brightly; and now and then a fire-fly streamed his transient light before the window, or, wandering into the room, flew gleaming about the ceiling.

What Dolph whispered in her ear that long summer evening it is impossible to say. His words were so low and indistinct, that they never reached the ear of the historian. It is probable, however, that they were to the purpose; for he had a natural talent at pleasing the sex, and was never long in the company with a petticoat without paying proper court to it. In the mean time the visitors, one by one, departed; Antony Vander Heyden, who had fairly talked himself silent, sat nodding alone in his chair by the door, when he was suddenly aroused by a hearty salute with which Dolph Heyliger had unguardedly rounded off one of his periods, and which echoed through the still chamber like the report of a pistol. The Heer started up, rubbed his eyes, called for lights, and observed, that it was high time to go to bed; though, on parting for the night, he squeezed Dolph heartily by the hand, looked kindly in his face, and shook his head knowingly; for the Heer well remembered what he himself had been at the youngster's age.

The chamber in which our hero was lodged was spacious, and pannelled with oak. It was furnished with clothes presses, and mighty chests of drawers, well waxed, and glittering with brass ornaments. These contained ample stock of family linen; for the Dutch housewives had always a laudable pride in showing off their household treasures to strangers.

Dolph's mind, however, was too full to take particular note of the objects around him; yet he could not help continually comparing the free, open-hearted cheeriness of this establishment, with the starveling, sordid, joyless housekeeping, at Doctor Knipperhausen's. Still there was something that marred the enjoyment; the idea that he must take leave of his hearty host, and pretty hostess and cast himself once more adrift upon the world. To linger here would be folly; he should only get deeper in love: and for a poor varlet, like himself, to aspire to the daughter of the great Heer Vander Heyden – it was madness to think of such a thing! The very kindness that the girl had shown towards him prompted him, on reflection, to hasten his departure; it would be a poor return for the frank hospitality of his host, to entangle his daughter's heart in an injudicious attachment. In a word, Dolph was, like many other young reasoners, of exceeding good hearts, and giddy heads; who think after they act, and act differently from what they think; who make excellent determinations over night, and forget to keep them the next morning.

"This is a fine conclusion, truly, of my voyage," said he, as he almost buried himself in a sumptuous feather-bed, and drew the fresh white sheets up to his chin. "Here am I, instead of finding a bag of money to carry home, launched in a strange place, with scarcely a stiver in my pocket; and, what is worse, have jumped ashore up to my very ears in love into the bargain. However," added he, after some pause, stretching himself, and turning himself in bed, "I'm in good quarters for the present, at least; so I'll e'en enjoy the present moment, and let the next take care of itself. I dare say all will work out, 'some how or other,' for the best."

As he said these words, he reached out his hand to extinguish the candle, when he was suddenly struck with astonishment and dismay, for he thought he beheld the phantom of the Haunted House, staring on him from a dusky part of the chamber. A second look reassured him, as he perceived that what he had taken for the spectre was, in fact, nothing but a Flemish portrait, that hung in a shadowy corner, just behind a clothes press. It was, however, the precise representation of his nightly visitor. The same cloak and belted jerkin, the same grizzled beard and fixed eye, the same broad slouched hat, with a feather hanging over one side. Dolph now called to mind the resemblance he had frequently remarked between his host and the old man of the Haunted House; and was fully convinced that they were in some way connected, and that some especial destiny had governed his voyage. He lay gazing on the portrait with almost as much awe as he had gazed on the ghostly original, until the shrill house clock warned him of the lateness of the hour. He put out the light; but remained for a long time turning over these curious circumstances and coincidences in his mind, until he fell asleep. His dreams partook of the nature of his waking thoughts. He fancied that he still lay gazing on the picture, until, by degrees, it became animated; that the figure descended from the wall, and walked out of the room; that he followed it, and found himself by the well, to which the old man pointed, smiled on him, and disappeared.

In the morning, when Dolph waked, he found his host standing by his bed-side, who gave him a hearty morning's salutation, and asked him how he had slept. Dolph answered cheerily; but took occasion to inquire about the portrait that hung against the wall. "Ah," said Heer Antony, "that's a portrait of old Killian Vander Spiegel, once a burgomaster of Amsterdam, who, on some popular troubles, abandoned Holland, and came over to the province during the government of Peter Stuyvesant. He was my ancestor by the mother's side, and an old miserly curmudgeon he was. When the English took possession of New Amsterdam, in 1664, he retired into the country. He fell into a melancholy, apprehending that his wealth would be taken from him, and that he would come to beggary. He turned all his property into cash, and used to hide it away. He was for a year or two concealed in various places, fancying himself sought after by the English, to strip him of his wealth; and finally was found dead in his bed one morning, without any one being able to discover where he had concealed the greater part of his money."

When his host had left the room, Dolph remained for some time lost in thought. His whole mind was occupied by what he had heard. Vander Spiegel was his mother's family name; and he recollected to have heard her speak of this very Killian Vander Spiegel as one of her ancestors. He had heard her say, too, that her father was Killian's rightful heir, only that the old man died without leaving any thing to be inherited. It now appeared that Heer Antony was likewise a descendant, and perhaps an heir also, of this poor rich man; and that thus the Heyligers and the Vander Heydens were remotely connected. "What," thought he, "if, after all, this is the interpretation of my dream, that this is the way I am to make my fortune by this voyage to Albany, and that I am to find the old man's hidden wealth in the bottom of that well? But what an odd round-about mode of communicating the matter! Why the plague could not the old goblin have told me about the well at once, without sending me all the way to Albany, to hear a story that was to send me all the way back again?"

These thoughts passed through his mind while he was dressing. He descended the stairs, full of perplexity, when the bright face of Marie Vander Heyden suddenly beamed in smiles upon him, and seemed to give him a clue to the whole mystery. "After all," thought he, "the old goblin is in the right. If I am to get his wealth, he means that I shall marry his pretty descendant; thus both branches of the family will be again united, and the property go on in the proper channel."

No sooner did this idea enter his head, than it carried conviction with it. He was now all impatience to hurry back and secure the treasure, which, he did not doubt, lay at the bottom of the well, and which he feared every moment might be discovered by some other person. "Who knows," thought he, "but this night-walking old fellow of the Haunted House may be in the habit of haunting every visitor, and may give a hint to some shrewder fellow than myself, who will take a shorter cut to the well than by the way of Albany?" He wished a thousand times that the babbling old ghost was laid in the Red Sea, and his rambling portrait with him. He was in a perfect fever to depart. Two or three days elapsed before any opportunity presented for returning down the river. They were ages to Dolph, notwithstanding that he was basking in the smiles of the pretty Marie, and daily getting more and more enamoured.

At length the very sloop from which he had been knocked overboard prepared to make sail. Dolph made an awkward apology to his host for his sudden departure. Antony Vander Heyden was sorely astonished. He had concerted half a dozen excursions into the wilderness; and his Indians were actually preparing for a grand expedition to one of the lakes. He took Dolph aside, and exerted his eloquence to get him to abandon all thoughts of business and to remain with him, but in vain; and he at length gave up the attempt, observing, "that it was a thousand pities so fine a young man should throw himself away." Heer Antony, however, gave him a hearty shake by the hand at parting, with a favourite fowling-piece, and an invitation to come to his house whenever he revisited Albany. The pretty little Marie said nothing; but as he gave her a farewell kiss, her dimpled cheek turned pale, and a tear stood in her eye.

Dolph sprang lightly on board of the vessel. They hoisted sail; the wind was fair; they soon lost sight of Albany, and its green hills, and embowered islands. They were wafted gaily past the Kaatskill mountains, whose fairy heights were bright and cloudless. They passed prosperously through the highlands, without any molestation from the Dunderberg goblin and his crew; they swept on across Haverstraw Bay, and by Croton Point, and through the Tappaan Zee, and under the Pallisadoes, until, in the afternoon of the third day, they saw the promontory of Hoboken, hanging like a cloud in the air; and, shortly after, the roofs of the Manhattoes rising out of the water.

Dolph's first care was to repair to his mother's house; for he was continually goaded by the idea of the uneasiness she must experience on his account. He was puzzling his brains, as he went along, to think how he should account for his absence, without betraying the secrets of the Haunted House. In the midst of these cogitations, he entered the street in which his mother's house was situated, when he was thunderstruck at beholding it a heap of ruins.

There had evidently been a great fire, which had destroyed several large houses, and the humble dwelling of poor dame Heyliger had been involved in the conflagration. The walls were not so completely destroyed, but that Dolph could distinguish some traces of the scene of his childhood. The fire-place, about which he had often played, still remained, ornamented with Dutch tiles, illustrating passages in Bible history, on which he had many a time gazed with admiration. Among the rubbish lay the wreck of the good dame's elbow-chair, from which she had given him so many a wholesome precept; and hard by it was the family Bible, with brass clasps; now, alas! reduced almost to a cinder.

For a moment Dolph was overcome by this dismal sight, for he was seized with the fear that his mother had perished in the flames. He was relieved, however, from this horrible apprehension, by one of the neighbours who happened to come by, and who informed him that his mother was yet alive.

The good woman had, indeed, lost every thing by this unlooked-for calamity; for the populace had been so intent upon saving the fine furniture of her rich neighbours, that the little tenement and the little all of poor dame Heyliger had been suffered to consume without interruption; nay, had it not been for the gallant assistance of her old crony, Peter de Groodt, the worthy dame and her cat might have shared the fate of their habitation.

As it was, she had been overcome with fright and affliction, and lay ill in body, and sick at heart. The public, however, had showed her its wonted kindness. The furniture of her rich neighbours being, as far as possible, rescued from the flames; themselves duly and ceremoniously visited and condoled with on the injury of their property, and their ladies commiserated on the agitation of their nerves; the public, at length, began to recollect something about poor dame Heyliger. She forthwith became again a subject of universal sympathy; every body pitied her more than ever; and if pity could but have been coined into cash – good Lord! how rich she would have been!

It was now determined, in good earnest, that something ought to be done for her without delay. The Dominie, therefore, put up prayers for her on Sunday, in which all the congregation joined most heartily. Even Cobus Groesbeek, the alderman, and Mynheer Milledollar, the great Dutch merchant, stood up in their pews, and did not spare their voices on the occasion; and it was thought the prayers of such great men could not but have their due weight. Doctor Knipperhausen, too, visited her professionally, and gave her abundance of advice gratis, and was universally lauded for his charity. As to her old friend, Peter de Groodt, he was a poor man, whose pity, and prayers, and advice, could be of but little avail, so he gave her all that was in his power – he gave her shelter.

To the humble dwelling of Peter de Groodt, then, did Dolph turn his steps. On his way thither, he recalled all the tenderness and kindness of his simple-hearted parent, her indulgence of his errors, her blindness to his faults; and then he bethought himself of his own idle, harum-scarum life. "I've been a sad scapegrace," said Dolph, shaking his head sorrowfully. "I've been a complete sink-pocket, that's the truth of it! – But," added he briskly, and clasping his hands, "only let her live – only let her live – and I'll show myself indeed a son!"

As Dolph approached the house he met Peter de Groodt coming out of it. The old man started back aghast, doubting whether it was not a ghost that stood before him. It being bright daylight, however, Peter soon plucked up heart, satisfied that no ghost dare show his face in such clear sunshine. Dolph now learned from the worthy sexton the consternation and rumour to which his mysterious disappearance had given rise. It had been universally believed that he had been spirited away by those hobgoblin gentry that infested the Haunted House; and old Abraham Vandozer, who lived by the great Button-wood trees, at the three mile stone, affirmed, that he had heard a terrible noise in the air, as he was going home late at night, which seemed just as if a flight of wild-geese were over-head, passing towards the northward. The Haunted House was, in consequence, looked upon with ten times more awe than ever; nobody would venture to pass a night in it for the world, and even the doctor had ceased to make his expeditions to it in the daytime.

It required some preparation before Dolph's return could be made known to his mother, the poor soul having bewailed him as lost; and her spirits having been sorely broken down by a number of comforters, who daily cheered her with stories of ghosts, and of people carried away by the devil. He found her confined to her bed, with the other member of the Heyliger family, the good dame's cat, purring beside her, but sadly singed, and utterly despoiled of those whiskers which were the glory of her physiognomy. The poor woman threw her arms about Dolph's neck: "My boy! my boy! art thou still alive?" For a time she seemed to have forgotten all her losses and troubles in her joy at his return. Even the sage grimalkin showed indubitable signs of joy at the return of the youngster. She saw, perhaps, that they were a forlorn and undone family, and felt a touch of that kindliness which fellow-sufferers only know. But, in truth, cats are a slandered people; they have more affection in them than the world commonly gives them credit for.

The good dame's eyes glistened as she saw one being, at least, beside herself, rejoiced at her son's return. "Tib knows thee! poor dumb beast!" said she, smoothing down the mottled coat of her favourite; then recollecting herself, with a melancholy shake of the head, "Ah, my poor Dolph!" exclaimed she, "thy mother can help thee no longer! She can no longer help herself! What will become of thee, my poor boy!"

"Mother," said Dolph, "don't talk in that strain; I've been too long a charge upon you; it's now my part to take care of you in your old days. Come! be of good heart! You, and I, and Tib, will all see better days. I'm here, you see, young, and sound, and hearty; then don't let us despair; I dare say things will all, some how or other, turn out for the best."

While this scene was going on with the Heyliger family, the news was carried to Doctor Knipperhausen, of the safe return of his disciple. The little doctor scarcely knew whether to rejoice or be sorry at the tidings. He was happy at having the foul reports which had prevailed concerning his country mansion thus disproved; but he grieved at having his disciple, of whom he had supposed himself fairly disencumbered, thus drifting back, a heavy charge upon his hands. While he was balancing between these two feelings, he was determined by the counsels of Frau Ilsy, who advised him to take advantage of the truant absence of the youngster, and shut the door upon him for ever.

At the hour of bed-time, therefore, when it was supposed the recreant disciple would seek his old quarters, every thing was prepared for his reception. Dolph, having talked his mother into a state of tranquillity, sought the mansion of his quondam master, and raised the knocker with a faltering hand. Scarcely, however, had it given a dubious rap, when the doctor's head, in a red night-cap, popped out of one window, and the housekeeper's, in a white night-cap, out of another. He was now greeted with a tremendous volley of hard names and hard language, mingled with invaluable pieces of advice, such as are seldom ventured to be given excepting to a friend in distress, or a culprit at the bar. In a few moments, not a window in the street but had its particular night-cap, listening to the shrill treble of Frau Ilsy, and the guttural croaking of Dr. Knipperhausen; and the word went from window to window, "Ah! here's Dolph Heyliger come back, and at his old pranks again." In short, poor Dolph found he was likely to get nothing from the doctor but good advice; a commodity so abundant as even to be thrown out of the window; so he was fain to beat a retreat, and take up his quarters for the night under the lowly roof of honest Peter de Groodt.

The next morning, bright and early, Dolph was out at the Haunted House. Every thing looked just as he had left it. The fields were grass-grown and matted, and it appeared as if nobody had traversed them since his departure. With palpitating heart he hastened to the well. He looked down into it, and saw that it was of great depth, with water at the bottom. He had provided himself with a strong line, such as the fishermen use on the banks of Newfoundland. At the end was a heavy plummet and a large fish-hook. With this he began to sound the bottom of the well, and to angle about in the water. He found that the water was of some depth; there appeared also to be much rubbish, stones from the top having fallen in. Several times his hook got entangled, and he came near breaking his line. Now and then, too, he hauled up mere trash, such as the skull of a horse, an iron hoop, and a shattered iron-bound bucket. He had now been several hours employed without finding any thing to repay his trouble, or to encourage him to proceed.

He began to think himself a great fool, to be thus decoyed into a wild-goose-chase by mere dreams, and was on the point of throwing line and all into the well, and giving up all further angling.

"One more cast of the line," said he, "and that shall be the last." As he sounded, he felt the plummet slip, as it were, through the interstices of loose stones; and as he drew back the line, he felt that the hook had taken hold of something heavy. He had to manage his line with great caution, lest it should be broken by the strain upon it. By degrees the rubbish that lay upon the article which he had hooked gave way; he drew it to the surface of the water, and what was his rapture at seeing something like silver glittering at the end of his line! Almost breathless with anxiety, he drew it up to the mouth of the well, surprised at its great weight, and fearing every instant that his hook would slip from its hold, and his prize tumble again to the bottom. At length he landed it safe beside the well. It was a great silver porringer, of an ancient form, richly embossed, and with armorial bearings, similar to those over his mother's mantel-piece, engraved on its side. The lid was fastened down by several twists of wire; Dolph loosened them with a trembling hand, and, on lifting the lid, behold! the vessel was filled with broad golden pieces, of a coinage which he had never seen before! It was evident he had lit on the place where old Killian Vander Spiegel had concealed his treasure.

Fearful of being seen by some straggler, he cautiously retired, and buried his pot of money in a secret place. He now spread terrible stories about the Haunted House, and deterred every one from approaching it, while he made frequent visits to it in stormy days, when no one was stirring in the neighbouring fields; though, to tell the truth, he did not care to venture there in the dark. For once in his life he was diligent and industrious, and followed up his new trade of angling with such perseverance and success, that in a little while he had hooked up wealth enough to make him, in those moderate days, a rich burgher for life.

It would be tedious to detail minutely the rest of his story. To tell how he gradually managed to bring his property into use without exciting surprise and inquiry – how he satisfied all scruples with regard to retaining the property, and at the same time gratified his own feelings by marrying the pretty Marie Vander Heyden – and how he and Heer Antony had many a merry and roving expedition together.

I must not omit to say, however, that Dolph took his mother home to live with him, and cherished her in her old days. The good dame, too, had the satisfaction of no longer hearing her son made the theme of censure; on the contrary, he grew daily in public esteem; every body spoke well of him and his wines; and the lordliest burgomaster was never known to decline his invitation to dinner. Dolph often related, at his own table, the wicked pranks which had once been the abhorrence of the town; but they were now considered excellent jokes, and the gravest dignitary was fain to hold his sides when listening to them. No one was more struck with Dolph's increasing merit than his old master the doctor; and so forgiving was Dolph, that he absolutely employed the doctor as his family physician, only taking care that his prescriptions should be always thrown out of the window. His mother had often her junto of old cronies to take a snug cup of tea with her in her comfortable little parlour; and Peter de Groodt, as he sat by the fireside, with one of her grandchildren on his knee, would many a time congratulate her upon her son turning out so great a man; upon which the good old soul would wag her head with exultation, and exclaim, "Ah, neighbour, neighbour! did I not say that Dolph would one day or other hold up his head with the best of them?"

Thus did Dolph Heyliger go on, cheerily and prosperously, growing merrier as he grew older and wiser, and completely falsifying the old proverb about money got over the devil's back; for he made good use of his wealth, and became a distinguished citizen, and a valuable member of the community. He was a great promoter of public institutions, such as beef-steak societies and catch-clubs. He presided at all public dinners, and was the first that introduced turtle from the West Indies. He improved the breed of race-horses and game-cocks, and was so great a patron of modest merit, that anyone, who could sing a good song, or tell a good story, was sure to find a place at his table.

He was a member, too, of the corporation, made several laws for the protection of game and oysters, and bequeathed to the board a large silver punch-bowl, made out of the identical porringer before-mentioned, and which is in the possession of the corporation to this very day.

Finally, he died, in a florid old age, of an apoplexy at a corporation feast, and was buried with great honours in the yard of the little Dutch church in Garden-street, where his tombstone may still be seen, with a modest epitaph in Dutch, by his friend Mynheer Justus Benson, an ancient and excellent poet of the province.

The foregoing tale rests on better authority than most tales of the kind, as I have it at second hand from the lips of Dolph Heyliger himself. He never related it till towards the latter part of his life, and then in great confidence, (for he was very discreet) to a few of his particular cronies at his own table, over a supernumerary bowl of punch; and, strange as the hobgoblin parts of the story may seem, there never was a single doubt expressed on the subject by any of his guests. It may

THE WEDDING

No more, no more, much honor aye betide
The lofty bridegroom, and the lovely bride;
That all of their succeeding days may say,
Each day appears like to a wedding-day.

BRAITHWAITE

Notwithstanding the doubts and demurs of Lady Lillycraft, and all the grave objections that were conjured up against the month of May, yet the wedding has at length happily taken place. It was celebrated at the village church, in presence of a numerous company of relatives and friends, and many of the tenantry. The squire must needs have something of the old ceremonies observed on the occasion; so at the gate of the church-yard, several little girls of the village, dressed in white, were in readiness with baskets of flowers, which they strewed before the bride; and the butler bore before her the bride cup, a great silver embossed bowl, one of the family reliques from the days of the hard drinkers. This was filled with rich wine, and decorated with a branch of rosemary, tied with gay ribands, according to ancient custom.

"Happy is the bride that the sun shines on," says the old proverb; and it was as sunny and auspicious a morning as heart could wish. The bride looked uncommonly beautiful; but, in fact, what woman does not look interesting on her wedding-day? I know no sight more charming and touching than that of a young and timid bride, in her robes of virgin white, led up trembling to the altar. When I thus behold a lovely girl, in the tenderness of her years, forsaking the house of her fathers, and the home of her childhood; and, with the implicit confiding, and the sweet self-abandonment, which belong to woman, giving up all the world for the man of her choice; when I hear her, in the good old language of the ritual, yielding herself to him, "for better for worse, for richer for poorer, in sickness and in health, to love, honour, and obey, till death us do part," it brings to my mind the beautiful and affecting self-devotion of Ruth: "Whither thou goest I will go, and where thou lodgest I will lodge; thy people shall be my people, and thy God my God."

The fair Julia was supported on the trying occasion by Lady Lilly-craft, whose heart was overflowing with its wonted sympathy in all matters of love and matrimony. As the bride approached the altar, her face would be one moment covered with blushes, and the next deadly pale; and she seemed almost ready to shrink from sight among her female companions.

I do not know what it is that makes every one serious, and, as it were, awe-struck at a marriage ceremony; which is generally considered as an occasion of festivity and rejoicing. As the ceremony was performing, I observed many a rosy face among the country girls turn pale, and I did not see a smile throughout the church. The young ladies from the Hall were almost as much frightened as if it had been their own case, and stole many a look of sympathy at their trembling companion. A tear stood in the eye of the sensitive Lady Lillycraft; and as to Phœbe Wilkins, who was present, she absolutely wept and sobbed aloud; but it is hard to tell, half the time, what these fond foolish creatures are crying about.

The captain, too, though naturally gay and unconcerned, was much agitated on the occasion; and, in attempting to put the ring upon the bride's finger, dropped it on the floor; which Lady Lillycraft has since assured me is a very lucky omen. Even Master Simon had lost his usual vivacity, and had assumed a most whimsically solemn face, which he is apt to do on all occasions of ceremony. He had much whispering with the parson and parish-clerk, for he is always a busy personage in the scene; and he echoed the clerk's amen with a solemnity and devotion that edified the whole assemblage.

The moment, however, that the ceremony was over, the transition was magical. The bride cup was passed round, according to ancient usage, for the company to drink to a happy union; every one's feelings seemed to break forth from restraint; Master Simon had a world of bachelor pleasantries to utter, and as to the gallant general, he bowed and cooed about the dulcet Lady Lillycraft, like a mighty cock pigeon about his dame.

The villagers gathered in the church-yard, to cheer the happy couple as they left the church; and the musical tailor had marshalled his band, and set up a hideous discord, as the blushing and smiling bride passed through a lane of honest peasantry to her carriage. The children shouted and threw up their hats; the bells rung a merry peal that set all the crows and rooks flying and cawing about the air, and threatened to bring down the battlements of the old tower; and there was a continual popping off of rusty firelocks from every part of the neighbourhood.

The prodigal son distinguished himself on the occasion, having hoisted a flag on the top of the school-house, and kept the village in a hubbub from sun-rise, with the sound of drum and fife and pandean pipe; in which species of music several of his scholars are making wonderful proficiency. In his great zeal, however, he had nearly done mischief; for on returning from church, the horses of the bride's carriage took fright from the discharge of a row of old gun-barrels, which he had mounted as a park of artillery in front of the school-house, to give the captain a military salute as he passed.

The day passed off with great rustic rejoicings. Tables were spread under the trees in the park, where all the peasantry of the neighbourhood were regaled with roast beef and plum-pudding, and oceans of ale. Ready Money Jack presided at one of the tables, and became so full of good cheer, as to unbend from his usual gravity, to sing a song out of all tune, and give two or three shouts of laughter, that almost electrified his neighbours, like so many peals of thunder. The schoolmaster and the apothecary vied with each other in making speeches over their liquor; and there were occasional glees and musical performances by the village band, that must have frightened every faun and dryad from the park. Even old Christy, who had got on a new dress, from top to toe, and shone in all the splendor of bright leather breeches, and an enormous wedding favour in his cap, forgot his usual crustiness, became inspired by wine and wassel, and absolutely danced a hornpipe on one of the tables, with all the grace and agility of a mannikin hung upon wires.

Equal gaiety reigned within doors, where a large party of friends were entertained. Every one laughed at his own pleasantry, without attending to that of his neighbours. Loads of bride-cake were distributed. The young ladies were all busy in passing morsels of it through the wedding ring to dream on, and I myself assisted a fine little boarding-school girl in putting up a quantity for her companions, which I have no doubt will set all the little heads in the school gadding, for a week at least.

After dinner all the company, great and small, gentle and simple, abandoned themselves to the dance: not the modern quadrille, with its graceful gravity, but the merry, social, old country dance; the true dance, as the squire says, for a wedding occasion; as it sets all the world jigging in couples, hand in hand, and makes every eye and every heart dance merrily to the music. According to frank old usage, the gentlefolks of the Hall mingled for a time in the dance of the peasantry, who had a great tent erected for a ball-room; and I think I never saw Master Simon more in his element than when figuring about among his rustic admirers, as master of the ceremonies; and, with a mingled air of protection and gallantry, leading out the quondam Queen of May; all blushing at the signal honour conferred upon her.

In the evening the whole village was illuminated, excepting the house of the radical, who has not shown his face during the rejoicings. There was a display of fireworks at the school-house, got up by the prodigal son, which had well nigh set fire to the building. The squire is so much pleased with the extraordinary services of this last-mentioned worthy, that he talks of enrolling him in his list of valuable retainers, and promoting him to some important post on the estate; peradventure to be falconer, if the hawks can ever be brought into proper training.

There is a well-known old proverb, that says, "one wedding makes many," – or something to the same purpose; and I should not be surprised if it holds good in the present instance. I have seen several flirtations among the young people, that have been brought together on this occasion; and a great deal of strolling about in pairs, among the retired walks and blossoming shrubberies of the old garden; and if groves were really given to whispering, as poets would fain make us believe, Heaven knows what love-tales the grave-looking old trees about this venerable country seat might blab to the world.

The general, too, has waxed very zealous in his devotions within the last few days, as the time of her ladyship's departure approaches. I observed him casting many a tender look at her during the wedding-dinner, while the courses were changing; though he was always liable to be interrupted in his adoration by the appearance of any new delicacy. The general, in fact, has arrived at that time of life, when the heart and the stomach maintain a kind of balance of power; and when a man is apt to be perplexed in his affections between a fine woman and a truffled turkey. Her ladyship was certainly rivalled through the whole of the first course by a dish of stewed carp; and there was one glance, which was evidently intended to be a point-blank shot at her heart, and could scarcely have failed to effect a practicable breach, had it not unluckily been diverted away to a tempting breast of lamb, in which it immediately produced a formidable incision.

Thus did this faithless general go on, coquetting during the whole dinner, and committing an infidelity with every new dish; until, in the end, he was so overpowered by the attentions he had paid to fish, flesh, and fowl; to pastry, jelly, cream, and blanc-mange, that he seemed to sink within himself; his eyes swam beneath their lids, and their fire was so much slackened, that he could no longer discharge a single glance that would reach across the table. Upon the whole, I fear the general ate himself into as much disgrace, at this memorable dinner, as I have seen him sleep himself into on a former occasion.

I am told, moreover, that young Jack Tibbets was so touched by the wedding ceremony, at which he was present, and so captivated by the sensibility of poor Phœbe Wilkins, who certainly looked all the better for her tears, that he had a reconciliation with her that very day, after dinner, in one of the groves of the park, and danced with her in the evening; to the complete confusion of all Dame Tibbets' domestic politics. I met them walking together in the park, shortly after the reconciliation must have taken place. Young Jack carried himself gaily and manfully; but Phœbe hung her head, blushing, as I approached. However, just as she passed me, and dropped a curtesy, I caught a shy gleam of her eye from under her bonnet; but it was immediately cast down again. I saw enough in that single gleam, and in the involuntary smile that dimpled about her rosy lips, to feel satisfied that the little gipsy's heart was happy again.

What is more, Lady Lillycraft, with her usual benevolence and zeal in all matters of this tender nature, on hearing of the reconciliation of the lovers, undertook the critical task of breaking the matter to Ready Money Jack. She thought there was no time like the present, and attacked the sturdy old yeoman that very evening in the park, while his heart was yet lifted up with the squire's good cheer. Jack was a little surprised at being drawn aside by her ladyship, but was not to be flurried by such an honour: he was still more surprised by the nature of her communication, and by this first intelligence of an affair that had been passing under his eye. He listened, however, with his usual gravity, as her ladyship represented the advantages of the match, the good qualities of the girl, and the distress which she had lately suffered; at length his eye began to kindle, and his hand to play with the head of his cudgel. Lady Lillycraft saw that something in the narrative had gone wrong, and hastened to mollify his rising ire by reiterating the soft-hearted Phœbe's merit and fidelity, and her great unhappiness; when old Ready Money suddenly interrupted her by exclaiming, that if Jack did not marry the wench, he'd break every bone in his body! The match, therefore, is considered a settled thing; Dame Tibbets and the housekeeper have made friends, and drunk tea together; and Phœbe has again recovered her good looks and good spirits, and is carolling from morning till night like a lark.

But the most whimsical caprice of Cupid is one that I should be almost afraid to mention, did I not know that I was writing for readers well experienced in the waywardness of this most mischievous deity. The morning after the wedding, therefore, while Lady Lillycraft was making preparations for her departure, an audience was requested by her immaculate handmaid, Mrs. Hannah, who, with much primming of the mouth, and many maidenly hesitations, requested leave to stay behind, and that Lady Lillycraft would supply her place with some other servant. Her ladyship was astonished: "What! Hannah going to quit her, that had lived with her so long!"

"Why, one could not help it; one must settle in life some time or other."

The good lady was still lost in amazement; at length the secret was gasped from the dry lips of the maiden gentlewoman: "she had been some time thinking of changing her condition, and at length had given her word, last evening, to Mr. Christy, the huntsman."

How, or when, or where this singular courtship had been carried on, I have not been able to learn; nor how she has been able, with the vinegar of her disposition, to soften the stony heart of old Nimrod. So, however, it is, and it has astonished every one. With all her ladyship's love of match-making, this last fume of Hymen's torch has been too much for her. She has endeavoured to reason with Mrs. Hannah, but all in vain; her mind was made up, and she grew tart on the least contradiction. Lady Lillycraft applied to the squire for his interference. "She did not know what she should do without Mrs. Hannah, she had been used to have her about her so long a time."

The squire, on the contrary, rejoiced in the match, as relieving the good lady from a kind of toilet-tyrant, under whose sway she had suffered for years. Instead of thwarting the affair, therefore, he has given it his full countenance; and declares that he will set up the young couple in one of the best cottages on his estate. The approbation of the squire has been followed by that of the whole household; they all declare, that if ever matches are really made in heaven, this must have been; for that old Christy and Mrs. Hannah were as evidently formed to be linked together as ever were pepper-box and vinegar-cruet.

As soon as this matter was arranged, Lady Lillycraft took her leave of the family at the Hall; taking with her the captain and his blushing bride, who are to pass the honeymoon with her. Master Simon accompanied them on horseback, and indeed means to ride on ahead to make preparations. The general, who was fishing in vain for an invitation to her seat, handed her ladyship into her carriage with a heavy sigh; upon which his bosom friend, Master Simon, who was just mounting his horse, gave me a knowing wink, made an abominably wry face, and leaning from his saddle, whispered loudly in my ear, "it won't do!" Then putting spurs to his horse, away he cantered off. The general stood for some time waving his hat after the carriage as it rolled down the avenue, until he was seized with a fit of sneezing, from exposing his head to the cool breeze. I observed that he returned rather thoughtfully to the house; whistling softly to himself, with his hands behind his back, and an exceedingly dubious air.

The company have now almost all taken their departure. I have determined to do the same to-morrow morning; and I hope my reader may not think that I have already lingered too long at the Hall. I have been tempted to do so, however, because I thought I had lit upon one of the retired places where there are yet some traces to be met with of old

English character. A little while hence, and all these will probably have passed away. Ready Money Jack will sleep with his fathers. The good squire, and all his peculiarities, will be buried in the neighbouring church. The old Hall will be modernised into a fashionable country-seat, or peradventure a manufactory. The park will be cut up into petty farms and kitchen-gardens. A daily coach will run through the village; it will become, like all other common-place villages, thronged with coachmen, post-boys, tipplers, and politicians; and Christmas, May-day, and all the other hearty merry-makings of the "good old times" will be forgotten.

THE AUTHOR'S FAREWELL

And so, without more circumstance at all,
I hold it fit that we shake hands, and part.
HAMLET

Having taken leave of the Hall and its inmates, and brought the history of my visit to something like a close, there seems to remain nothing further than to make my bow and exit. It is my foible, however, to get on such companionable terms with my reader in the course of a work, that it really costs me some pain to part with him, and I am apt to keep him by the hand, and have a few farewell words at the end of my last volume.

When I cast an eye back upon the work I am just concluding, I cannot but be sensible how full it must be of errors and imperfections; indeed, how should it be otherwise, writing as I do, about subjects and scenes with which, as a stranger, I am but partially acquainted? Many will, doubtless, find cause to smile at very obvious blunders which I may have made; and many may, perhaps, be offended at what they may conceive prejudiced representations. Some will think I might have said much more on such subjects as may suit their peculiar tastes; whilst others will think I had done wiser to have left those subjects entirely alone.

It will, probably, be said, too, by some, that I view England with a partial eye. Perhaps I do; for I can never forget that it is my "father land." And yet the circumstances under which I have viewed it have by no means been such as were calculated to produce favourable impressions. For the greater part of the time that I have resided in it, I have lived almost unknowing and unknown; seeking no favours, and receiving none; "a stranger and a sojourner in the land," and subject to all the chills and neglects that are the common lot of the stranger.

When I consider these circumstances, and recollect how often I have taken up my pen, with a mind ill at ease, and spirits much dejected and cast down; I cannot but think I was not likely to err on the favourable side of the picture. The opinions I have given of English character have been the result of much quiet, dispassionate, and varied observation. It is a character not to be hastily studied, for it always puts on a repulsive and ungracious aspect to a stranger. Let those, then, who condemn my representations as too favourable, observe this people as closely and deliberately as I have done, and they will, probably, change their opinion. Of one thing, at any rate, I am certain, that I have spoken honestly and sincerely, from the convictions of my mind, and the dictates of my heart. When I first published my former writings, it was with no hope of gaining favour in English eyes, for I little thought they were to become current out of my own country; and had I merely sought popularity among my own countrymen, I should have taken a more direct and obvious way, by gratifying rather than rebuking the angry feelings that were then prevalent against England.

And here let me acknowledge my warm, my thankful feelings, at the effect produced by one of my trivial lucubrations. I allude to the essay in the Sketch-Book, on the subject of the literary feuds between England and America. I cannot express the heartfelt delight I have experienced, at the unexpected sympathy and approbation with which those remarks have been received on both sides of the Atlantic. I speak this not from any paltry feelings of gratified vanity; for I attribute the effect to no merit of my pen. The paper in question was brief and casual, and the ideas it conveyed were simple and obvious. "It was the cause; it was the cause" alone. There was a predisposition on the part of my readers to be favourably affected. My countrymen responded in heart to the filial feelings I had avowed in their name towards the parent country; and there was a generous sympathy in every English bosom towards a solitary individual, lifting up his voice in a strange land, to vindicate the injured character of his nation. There are some causes so sacred as to carry with them an irresistible appeal to every virtuous bosom; and he needs but little power of eloquence, who defends the honour of his wife, his mother, or his country.

I hail, therefore, the success of that brief paper, as showing how much good may be done by a kind word, however feeble, when spoken in season – as showing how much dormant good feeling actually exists in each country, towards the other, which only wants the slightest spark to kindle it into a genial flame – as showing, in fact, what I have all along believed and asserted, that the two nations would grow together in esteem and amity, if meddling and malignant spirits would but throw by their mischievous pens, and leave kindred hearts to the kindly impulses of nature.

I once more assert, and I assert it with increased conviction of its truth, that there exists, among the great majority of my countrymen, a favourable feeling towards England. I repeat this assertion, because I think it a truth that cannot too often be reiterated, and because it has met with some contradiction. Among all the liberal and enlightened minds of my countrymen, among all those which eventually give a tone to national opinion, there exists a cordial desire to be on terms of courtesy and friendship. But, at the same time, there exists in those very minds a distrust of reciprocal good will on the part of England. They have been rendered morbidly sensitive by the attacks made upon their country by the English press; and their occasional irritability on this subject has been misinterpreted into a settled and unnatural hostility.

For my part, I consider this jealous sensibility as belonging to generous natures. I should look upon my countrymen as fallen indeed from that independence of spirit which is their birth-gift; as fallen indeed from that pride of character which they inherit from the proud nation from which they sprung, could they tamely sit down under the infliction of contumely and insult. Indeed the very impatience which they show as to the misrepresentations of the press, proves their respect for English opinion, and their desire for English amity; for there is never jealousy where there is not strong regard.

It is easy to say that these attacks are all the effusions of worthless scribblers, and treated with silent contempt by the nation; but alas! the slanders of the scribbler travel abroad, and the silent contempt of the nation is only known at home. With England, then, it remains, as I have formerly asserted, to promote a mutual spirit of conciliation; she has but to hold the language of friendship and respect, and she is secure of the good will of every American bosom.

In expressing these sentiments I would utter nothing that should commit the proper spirit of my countrymen. We seek no boon at England's hands. We ask nothing as a favour. Her friendship is not necessary, nor would her hostility be dangerous to our well-being. We ask nothing from abroad that we cannot reciprocate. But with respect to England, we have a warm feeling of the heart, the glow of consanguinity that still lingers in our blood. Interest apart – past differences forgotten – we extend the hand of old relationship. We merely ask, do not estrange us from you; do not destroy the ancient tie of blood; do not let scoffers and slanderers drive a kindred nation from your side: we would fain be friends; do not compel us to be enemies.

There needs no better rallying ground for international amity, than that furnished by an eminent English writer: "There is," says he, "a sacred bond between us of blood and of language, which no circumstances can break. Our literature must always be theirs; and though their laws are no longer the same as ours, we have the same Bible, and we address our common Father in the same prayer. Nations are too ready to admit that they have natural enemies; why should they be less willing to believe that they have natural friends?"*

---

* From an article (said to be by Robert Southey, Esq.), published in the Quarterly Review. It is to be lamented that that publication should so often forget the generous text here given!

To the magnanimous spirits of both countries must we trust to carry such a natural alliance of affection into full effect. To pens more powerful than mine I leave the noble task of promoting the cause of national amity. To the intelligent and enlightened of my own country, I address my parting voice, entreating them to show themselves superior to the petty attacks of the ignorant and the worthless, and still to look with dispassionate and philosophic eye to the moral character of England, as the intellectual source of our rising greatness; while I appeal to every generous-minded Englishman from the slanders which disgrace the press, insult the understanding, and belie the magnanimity of his country: and I invite him to look to America, as to a kindred nation, worthy of its origin; giving, in the healthy vigour of its growth, the best of comments on its parent stock; and reflecting, in the dawning brightness of its fame, the moral effulgence of British glory.

I am sure that such appeal will not be made in vain. Indeed I have noticed, for some time past, an essential change in English sentiment with regard to America. In parliament, that fountain-head of public opinion, there seems to be an emulation, on both sides of the house, in holding the language of courtesy and friendship. The same spirit is daily becoming more and more prevalent in good society. There is a growing curiosity concerning my country; a craving desire for correct information, that cannot fail to lead to a favourable understanding. The scoffer, I trust, has had his day; the time of the slanderer is gone by. The ribald jokes, the stale commonplaces, which have so long passed current when America was the theme, are now banished to the ignorant and the vulgar, or only perpetuated by the hireling scribblers and traditional jesters of the press. The intelligent and high-minded now pride themselves upon making America a study.

But however my feelings may be understood or reciprocated on either side of the Atlantic, I utter them without reserve, for I have ever found that to speak frankly is to speak safely. I am not so sanguine as to believe that the two nations are ever to be bound together by any romantic ties of feeling; but I believe that much may be done towards keeping alive cordial sentiments, were every well disposed mind occasionally to throw in a simple word of kindness. If I have, indeed, produced any such effect by my writings, it will be a soothing reflection to me, that for once, in the course of a rather negligent life, I have been useful; that for once, by the casual exercise of a pen which has been in general but too unprofitably employed, I have awakened a chord of sympathy between the land of my fathers and the dear land that gave me birth.

In the spirit of these sentiments I now take my farewell of the paternal

EDITORIAL APPENDIX

Textual Commentary,
Discussions, and Lists by
Herbert F. Smith

LIST OF ABBREVIATIONS

The following symbols have been used in the editorial apparatus to designate the manuscripts and previously published texts of *Bracebridge Hall.*

MSA	Manuscript used to set the 1822 Van Winkle first American edition; the portion extant, Volume II complete, is in the Alderman Library, University of Virginia
MSE	Manuscript used to set, or more closely related to, the 1822 John Murray first English edition; portions of both volumes are extant in the New York Public Library, the Columbia University Library, and the Alderman Library, University of Virginia
1A	First American edition (Van Winkle, 1822)
1E	First English edition (John Murray, 1822)
1Ea, 1Eb, 1Ec	Succeeding states of 1E
2E	Second English edition (John Murray, 1822)
2A	Second American edition (Van Winkle, 1822)
2A22	First impression
2A26	Reimpression, 1826
3E	Third English edition (John Murray, 1823)
3E23	First impression
3E24	Reimpression, 1824
3E25	Reimpression, 1825
3E29	Reimpression, 1829
4E	Fourth English edition (Murray's Home and Colonial Library, 1845)
1F	First French edition
1F23	First impression (Baudry and Didot, 1823)
1F27	Reimpression (Galignani, 1827)
1F34	Reimpression (Baudry, 1834)

3A	Third American edition
3A30	First impression (Carey and Lea, 1830)
3A31	Reimpression (Carey and Lea, 1831)
3A33	Reimpression (Carey and Lea, 1833)
3A35a	Reimpression (Carey and Lea, 1835)
3A35b	Reimpression ("A New Edition," Carey, Lea, and Blanchard, 1835; copyright dated 1836)
3A36	Reimpression (Carey, Lea, and Blanchard, 1836)
3A38	Reimpression (Carey, Lea, and Blanchard, 1838)
3A39	Reimpression (Carey, Lea, and Blanchard, 1839)
3A41	Reimpression (Lea and Blanchard, 1841)
ARE	Author's Revised Edition (Putnam, 1849)
ARE49	First impression
ARE53	Reimpression (Putnam, 1853)
ARE59	Reimpression (Putnam, 1859)
T	Twayne edition

GENEALOGICAL TABLE

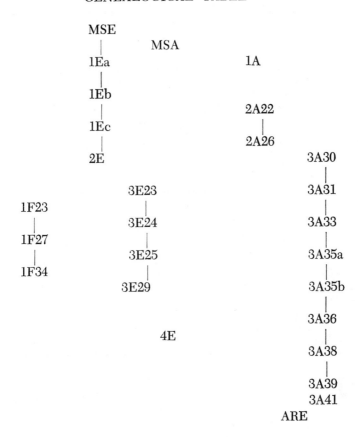

EXPLANATORY NOTES

The numbers indicate page and line respectively. Chapter numbers, chapter or section titles, epigraphs, texts, quotations and footnotes are included in the line count. The quotation from the text to the left of the bracket is the matter under discussion.

t.p. Under this . . . CHRISTMAS ORDINARY] The quotation is from *The Christmas Ordinary, A Private Show*, by W. R., Master of Arts (London, 1682), scene vii, p. 11.

4.28 Tintern Abbey] The ruins of this abbey in Monmouthshire provided the subject of Wordsworth's well-known poem. Irving visited the abbey on his trip to Wales in 1815.

4.30 Conway Castle] This fortress castle was built by the conquering Edward I in Wales, ca. 1284.

5.31–32 St. John's Gate . . . Gentleman's Magazine] *The Gentleman's Magazine* was founded in 1731 by Edward Cave under the pseudonym of Sylvanus Urban. It ran continuously until 1914. The original press was set up near St. John's Gate, an engraving of which served as the frontispiece. The gate is the chief entrance to St. John's Priory.

6.2 Gog and Magog] Gogmagog was the chief of the giants of Albion whom Brute destroyed. The statues called Gog and Magog in the Guildhall in London are actually of Gogmagog and Corineus, one of Brute's lieutenants, who wrestled with Gogmagog and threw him into the sea.

6.5–6 Mr. Newberry's shop] This shop was originally operated by John Newberry (1713–1767), a publisher of children's books.

8.2–5 The ancientest . . . MERRY BEGGARS.] The quotation is from Richard Brome, *The Jovial Crew or the Merry Beggars* (London, 1652), IV, i, the Cook speaking.

10.5–9 For freshest . . . Magistrates] Unidentified.

11.2–7 A decayed . . . JOVIAL CREW] From Brome, *The Jovial Crew or the Merry Beggars*, IV, i. See note 8.2–5 above.

11.33–35 Novelist's Magazine, the Sporting Magazine, the Racing Calendar . . . the Newgate Calendar] These are all popular magazines: *The Sporting Magazine or Monthly Calendar of the Transactions of the Turf, the Chace, etc.* (London, 1793–1870); *The Racing Calendar; containing an account of the Plates, Matches, and Sweepstakes, run for in Great Britain and Ireland* (London, 1773–); *Novelist's Magazine*

318

(London, 1780–1788); *The Newgate Calendar, or Malefactor's Bloody Register* (London, ca. 1774–).

13.1–2 *casting*, and *imping*, and *gleaming*, and *enseaming* ... the *rangle*] These are all terms used in falconry. "Casting" is the vomit or the purge given a hawk to clean its gorge; "imping" is the repairing of the hawk's wing with adscititious feathers to improve its flying capacity; "enseaming" is to cleanse the hawk of superfluous fat; "gleaming" is the purging of the hawk's vomit or "casting"; "rangle" is the gravel given to the hawk to improve its digestion.

15.2–4 Verily old ... their abode.] Unidentified.

19.11–12 "Master, go ... and loyalty!"] From Shakespeare's *As You Like It*, II, iii, 69–70. See also the Discussions of Adopted Readings and List of Emendations.

20.2–9 She was ... CHAUCER.] The quotation is from the General Prologue of Chaucer's *Canterbury Tales*, lines 143–49, describing the Prioress.

23.2–6 Rise up ... SOLOMON] The quotation is from the Song of Solomon, 2:10–12.

24.31 Sir Peter Lely's portraits] Lely (1618–1680) painted portraits of Charles I, Cromwell, Charles II, and many lords and ladies of the time. The hairstyle of his portraits of ladies is extremely meticulous and decorative.

26.2–13 My Infelice's ... DEKKER] The quotation is from Thomas Dekker, *The Honest Whore* (in collaboration with Thomas Middleton), part I (London, 1604), V, i, 34–37, 41–47.

27.6–7 Rippon spurs] Rippon is the name of a town in Yorkshire (now spelled Ripon) famous formerly for the manufacture of spurs.

28.16–17 the fair Mrs. Philips, the once celebrated Orinda] Mrs. Katherine Philips (1631–1664) was called "the matchless Orinda." She was the earliest English writer of sentimental verse.

30.2–6 I've worn ... THE ORDINARY] The quotation is from William Cartwright's *The Ordinary* (London: Moseley, 1651), I, iv, 372–76.

30.34 Seringapatam] The town of Seringapatam, located on an island in the Cauvery River, was the capital of Mysore in southern India. The British besieged the town in 1799 successfully, capturing the forces of Sultan Ryder Ali and killing his son Tipu (Tipoo) Sahib during the third Mysore War. This was, of course, a minor engagement in terms of the battles of the Napoleonic wars.

31.32–35 Why, soldiers ... to die!] The quotation is from the first lines of a song now commonly entitled "How Stands the Glass Around." In *Abbotsford and Newstead Abbey* (1835), "Singing and Souvenirs," Irving wrote that Scott quoted the song to him from "a manuscript picked up on the field of Waterloo, containing copies of several songs popular at the time in France. . . . He adverted . . . to the . . . song, said to have been composed by General Wolfe, and sung by him at the mess-table on the eve of the storming of Quebec, in which he fell so gloriously" (*Works*, III, 541).

31.39–40 Tippoo Saib] See the note at 30.34.

33.2–3 Little dogs and all! LEAR] The quotation is from Shakespeare's *King Lear*, III, vi, 60.

36.2–10 My purse . . . OF HUNTING] The quotation is from Dame Juliana Berners or Barnes (b. 1388?), supposed author of *The Booke of Haulking, Hunting (with measure of blowing) and Fysshing* (London, 1563), sig. 33ʳ. In the original line 3 reads, "It parteth men of muche stryfe." All but the fishing text was first published in the *Book of St. Albans* (1486), which was reprinted in 1595 as *The Gentleman's Academie* by Gervase Markham. See the note at 68.38. It is impossible to discover exactly what text Irving was quoting from in this and other references of the type.

37.11 Pinner of Wakefield] George-a-Green is the merry pinner, or pinder (pound-keeper) of Wakefield, subject of a play, probably by Robert Greene, first published in 1599.

39.28–29 Tusser's "Hundred Points of good Husbandrie,"] Thomas Tusser, *Hundreth Good Pointes of Husbandrie*, first published in 1557; enlarged editions in 1570 and 1573.

40.2–6 The Bachelor . . . OLD BALLADS] The quotation is from Thomas Evans, *Old Ballads, Historical and Narrative, with Some of Modern Date*, 4 vols. (London, 1784), III, 222, ballad no. XXVIII, "The batchellor's plea against matrimony," stanza one.

43.2–8 Believe me . . . SIDNEY] The quotation is from Sir Philip Sidney, *Poems from the Countess of Pembroke's Arcadia*, the third eclogue. The text may be found in *The Poems of Sir Philip Sidney*, ed. William A. Ringler, Jr. (Oxford, 1962), p. 103.

43.29–30 old play . . . "The City Night-cap;"] Robert Davenport, *The City-Night-Cap; or Crede quod habes, et habes* (London, 1661).

43.33 Griselda] See also "patient Grizzle" at 46.17. The type of the long-suffering woman, most notably treated in English by Chaucer in the "Clerk's Tale" and by Dekker (in collaboration with Chettle and Haughten) in *Patient Grissil*, first printed in 1603.

44.15–28 She's modest . . . sweet character.] Davenport, *The City-Night-Cap*, act I, pp. 1–2.

44.36–40 ——Hast thou . . . was made?] *Ibid.*, act I, p. 4.

45.7–25 ——Farewell, Lorenzo . . . a throne.] *Ibid.*, act III, p. 21. Irving omitted three and a half lines from the original after the eleventh line of his text, "Strewing your path with flowers.—"

45.30–46.2 ——Oh, Abstemia . . . no more.] *Ibid.*, act V, p. 49. Irving miscopied "dead" for "dread" in the eleventh line of this quotation. See the Discussions of Adopted Readings and the List of Emendations.

46.8–14 Thou wealth ... in thee.] *Ibid.*, act V, p. 58.

46.17 patient Grizzle] See above, note 43.33.

47.10–15 "She that ... she dies."] The quotation is from Jeremy Taylor, *XXV Sermons* (London, 1653), Sermon XVIII, "The Marriage Ring; or the Mysteriousness and Duties of Marriage, Part II." The text may be found in Jeremy Taylor, *Discourses on Various Subjects* (Boston: Wells and Lilly, 1816), p. 365. In this text the sentence "She must have no focus but blushings" is found in place of Irving's "She must have no painting but blushings."

47.23–30 "There is ... displease her."] *Ibid.*, Sermon XVII, "The Marriage Ring; or, the Mysteriousness and Duties of Marriage. Part I" (p. 344).

48.17 the Wandering Jew, the Man with the Iron Mask ... the Invisible Girl ... the Pigfaced Lady] The wandering Jew is common to the literature and folktales of many Western countries, doomed to wander the earth until Christ's second coming, often, according to the legends, because he chided Christ while he was bearing the cross, urging him to go faster. He appears in many German works (including Goethe's), and notably in Eugène Sue's *Le Juif Errant*, and in one of the ballads of Percy's *Reliques*. The Man in the Iron Mask was a state prisoner in the reign of Louis XIV, confined at Pignerol, on the island of St. Marguerite, and finally in the Bastille, whose name was concealed and who wore a mask covered with black velvet. He has been variously identified as Count Mattioli, an Italian agent, and as the younger twin brother of Louis XIV, among many others. The Pigfaced Lady is the subject of a legend common to several European languages. In the usual form, a lady of rank insults a commoner by calling her child a pig, and receives her reward when her own daughter is born with a pig's face. The story then proceeds to detail the troubles in finding a nursemaid and husband. Another legend has the pig-faced girl born to a man who converts to Judaism during the Commonwealth as a result of his confusion over the variety of Christian sects. When the father and daughter are reconverted by a priest she is miraculously restored. See *The Book of Days: a Miscellany of Popular Antiquities*, ed. R. Chambers (London, 1888), II, 255–57. The Invisible girl remains unidentified and unseen.

49.3–4 "I'll cross it, though it blast me!" HAMLET] The line quoted is from *Hamlet*, I, i, 127.

50.8 upper Benjamin] A close-fitting man's overcoat popular in the early nineteenth century.

52.21–22 slammerkin] A slovenly female, a slattern. This use of the word by Irving is cited in the *OED*, which describes the word as chiefly dialect.

52.35 Hunt]   Henry Hunt (1773–1835) was an English radical politician. In 1819 he presided at the reform meeting in Manchester which was broken up by soldiers and came to be called the Peterloo Massacre.

54.9 Belcher handkerchiefs]   A neckerchief with blue ground and large white spots, named after a celebrated pugilist, Jim Belcher. Sometimes applied to any multicolored handkerchief worn around the neck.

54.10–11 sworn at Highgate]   A popular custom at Highgate, a suburb of North London, was to have travelers to London swear any of a variety of mock oaths on a ram's or stag's horn attached to a five-foot pole. These were all oaths of self-indulgence: "I shall not drink small beer while I can get strong," etc.

57.2 "A living gallery of aged trees."]   The quotation is from John Evelyn, *Silva: or, A Discourse of Forest-Trees*, first published in 1664, from Book IV, "Dendrologia, An Historical Account of the Sacredness and Use of Standing Groves." The text may be found in the "fifth edition . . . with notes by A. Hunter . . . with the editor's last corrections" (London, 1825), II, 356. It refers to "the royal walk of Elms in St. James park."

58.1–6 "As the fall . . . and pity."]   *Ibid.*, II, 349–50.

58.7–14 "Methinks I . . . blown down."]   *Ibid.*, II, 350. In the text consulted the parenthetical remark "(happening on the 26th of November, 1703)" follows the word "hurricane."

59.26–30 Penshurst . . . Hagley . . . Windsor Forest]   Three of the most famous and beautiful parks in England. Penshurst, Sidney's home in southwest Kent, is sung in the *Arcadia*, and in poems by Ben Jonson, Edmund Waller, and Robert Southey. Hagley in Worcestershire is no less beautiful. Windsor Forest in Berkshire, and once spreading over into Surrey, was the largest and most imposing of the three.

61.2–6 Printed bookes . . . MICRO-COSMOGRAPHIE, 1628]   The quotation is from John Earle, *Micro-cosmography, or a Piece of the World Discovered in Essays and Characters* (London, 1628), Sig. C_2^v–C_3; in this edition the word "all" is missing from the phrase "be all moth eaten." See also the List of Emendations.

61.36–37 Perigord pie, or a *Paté de Strasbourg*.]   A Perigord pie is a truffled partridge pie; *paté de Strasbourg* is *paté de foie gras*.

61.39–62.4 "silk linings . . . jealousies."*]   The quotation is from Isaac Disraeli, *The Curiosities of Literature* (five series, 1791–1834) in the chapter entitled "The Bibliomania." The text may be found in the edition published by A. C. Armstrong and Son (New York, 1881), I, 57–58.

62.15 Strutt, Brand, and Douce]   Joseph Strutt (1749–1802), John

Brand (1744–1806), and Francis Douce (1757–1834) were all well-known antiquarians.

63.7 Dibdin's Bibliographical Tour] Thomas Frognall Dibdin, *A Bibliographical, Antiquarian and Picturesque Tour* (London, 1821).

63.36–37 Captain Morris's, or George Stevens', or Anacreon Moore's bacchanalian songs] Captain Thomas Morris (fl. 1806) and George Alexander Stevens (1710–1784) were both known for their published songs of a popular nature, many of them drinking songs. Thomas Moore (1779–1852) also wrote many such songs; his nickname "Anacreon" derived from his translation of Anacreon's *Odes*. He was a good friend of Irving's and perhaps the "onlie begetter" of *Bracebridge Hall*.

65.4 —"Love and . . . Beaumont and Fletcher] The quotation is from John Fletcher, *Monsieur Thomas* (first published 1639), V, ii, 54–55. The text may be found in *The Works of Francis Beaumont and John Fletcher*, ed. A. H. Bullen et al. (London, 1912). There is general agreement among scholars that the play was written by Fletcher alone.

68.2–7 A coach . . . TAYLOR, THE WATER POET] The quotation is from John Taylor, English poet and pamphleteer and Thames waterman, "The World runnes on Wheels," in *All the Works of John Taylor the Water Poet Being 63 in Number Collected into One Volume by the Author with Sundry New Additions, Corrected, Revised and Newly Imprinted* (London, 1630), p. 240.

68.38 Peachem, Markam] Henry Peacham (1576?–1643?) is best known as the author of *The Compleat Gentleman*, first published in 1622. Gervase (or Jervis) Markham (1568?-1637) has been described as "the earliest English hackney writer." A minor poet and collaborator in the theater, he is better known for his popular treatises in prose, among which are *Discourse on Horsemanship* (1593), *The Complete Farrier* (1639), and *Country Contentments* (1611). These and others of his prose works are often shameless plagiarisms of his own and other men's works. In 1595 he reprinted Juliana Berners' *Book of St. Albans* under the title *The Gentleman's Academie*. See notes to 36.2–10 and 74.6.

69.13–21 "It was . . . impotent people."] Thomas Nashe, *Quaternio, or a Fourfold Way to a Happy Life* (London, 1633), p. 31. In this text the last line reads "and decrepit, aged, and impotent people."

69.35–70.2 "It is . . . the curvetty."] *Ibid.* Significant variants from this text include ". . . Gentleman at age of fifteene" (69.35); "anone" [anon] for "and one"; and "advance to yorke" for "advance, to yorke."

71.2–4 I will . . . MARSTON] The quotation is from John Marston, *Parasitaster; or The Fawne* (1606), act IV. The text may be found in *The Plays of John Marston*, ed. H. H. Wood (Edinburgh, 1934–1938).

71.31–34 "Men and . . . Arthurs dayes."] The quotation is from Sir

Thomas Malory, *Le Morte d'Arthur,* first printed by Caxton in 1485. The text may be found in *The Works of Sir Thomas Malory,* ed. Eugene Vinaver (Oxford, 1948), III, 120. Irving's text has the word "betwene" for "betwyxte" and "lo" for "so."

73.2–6 Ne is . . . SPENSER] The quotation is from Edmund Spenser, *The Fairie Queene,* VI, ii, 32, 1–4. The text may be found in *The Poetical Works of Edmund Spenser,* ed. J. C. Smith and E. de Selincourt (Oxford, 1912), p. 345.

73.27 Braithwate] Richard Brathwaite (1588?–1673), English poet and satirist, best known for his *Barnabæ Itinerarium, or Barnabee's Journal* (1638). Irving perhaps had in mind here his two works on manners, *The English Gentleman* (1630) and *The English Gentlewoman* (1631).

73.33 tassel-gentel held by jesses] A tassel gentel or tercel-gentle was a trained male hawk; jesses were the short straps, usually of leather, which held the bird's legs.

74.6 Juliana Barnes; the Gentleman's Academie, by Markham] See notes at 36.2–10 and 68.38.

75.9 Sir Watkyn Williams Wynne] Sir Watkins Williams Wynn, third baronet (1692–1749), was the first to add the name Wynn to Williams, the original family surname, upon inheriting Wynnstay from his kinsman Sir John Wynn. The third baronet was succeeded by his son, Sir Watkins Williams Wynn, fourth baronet (1749–1789), who in turn was succeeded by his son of the same name, fifth baronet (1772–1840).

75.12 Snowden . . . Penmanmawr] Snowden is the highest mountain in northern Britain; Penmanmawr is a precipitous headland on Conway Bay, like Wynnstay, in North Wales.

76.2–10 The soaring . . . PLEASANT DELITES] The quotation is from the poem, "The Lover compareth him self to the painful Falcon," in Clement Robinson et al., *A Handful of Pleasant Delights, containing sundry new Sonnets and delectable Histories in divers kinds of metre* (1584), ed. Edward Arber (London, 1878), pp. 62–63. Irving's text has the word "about" for "unknown" in the Arber edition.

76.16–19 "In peascod . . . a-field," &c.] Probably from "A matter of fond Cupid, and vain Venus," by Thomas Chuchyard, first printed in *A Pleasante Laberinthe called Churchyardes Chance* (London, 1580), p. 13. This text reads as follows: "In peascod time when hound to horne giv's eare til Buck be kilde / And little laddes with pipes of corne, sat keepyng beastes a filde."

78.10-16 Webster's Duchess . . . That answers."] The quotation is from John Webster, *The Duchess of Malfi* (ca. 1614), V, iii, 3–5, 7–9. The missing line reads, "So hollow, and so dismal, and withal."

78.39 *Bekker's Monde enchanté.] Balthasar Bekker, *Le Monde En-

chanté (Amsterdam, 1694), I, 171. This is the French translation of Bekker's Dutch text of 1691. See also the note to 86.29–87.13.

81.2–9 O 'tis . . . DRYDEN] The quotation is from John Dryden (with Nathaniel Lee), *Oedipus*, III, i. The text may be found in *Dryden: The Dramatic Works*, ed. Montague Summers (London, 1932), IV, 282–83. The second line of Irving's quotation, "Or if to be, to wander after death!" is not included in this text.

82.37 Demonolatria of Nicholas Remigius] Nicholas Rémy or Remi (1530–1612) published the *Demonolatria* first in Leyden, 1595.

82.38–39 Joachimus Camerarius] Joachim Camerarius (1500–1574), a scholar and classicist and devotee of astrology.

82.41 °Aubrey's Miscel.] The incident is reported in "Corps-Candles in Wales," in John Aubrey, *Miscellanies*, 2d ed. (London, 1721), pp. 176–78.

83.2 Blefkénius, Scheffer] Blefkénius is probably Dithmar Blefken, traveler and author of *Islandia* (Leyden, 1607), which is included in *Purchas his Pilgrims*, part III (1625), as *Dithmar Blefkens his Voyages, and Historie of Island and Groenland*. Scheffer is probably the author of *Lapponia* (1674), a compendium of Lapland superstition and magical practices.

83.19 Philo the Rabbi] Philo Judaeus, who flourished in the first century A.D., was a Hellenistic Jewish philosopher nurtured in Greek culture but faithful to the Jewish religion. Most of his works have been lost, but three studies of the Pentateuch remain extant.

83.26 St. Jerome] Eusebius Sophronius Hieronymus, St. Jerome (ca. 340–420), best known for his translation and revision of the Vulgate Bible, the most learned of the Latin Fathers of the church.

83.28 Lactantius] Lucius Caelius (or Caecilius) Firmianus (ca. 240–ca. 320), the most classical of the Latin Fathers of the church; Renaissance writers thought of him as the Christian Cicero.

83.30–31 Clemens Alexandrinus] Clement of Alexandria, Titus Flavius Clemens (150?–215?), after Origen the principal representative of the early theological school of Alexandria. Not a heretical Gnostic, he believed that knowledge and contemplation are in the foreground of the spiritual life, which seems to be Irving's point in this passage.

84.11–12 "——walk the . . . we sleep."] The quotation is from John Milton, *Paradise Lost*, IV, 677–78.

84.20–22 "Nothing . . . care of it."] It has not been determined which of St. Jerome's many writings contains the quoted sentence.

86.25 Rabbi Eleazer] Putative author of the *Pirkê De Rabbi Eliezer* (*The Chapters of Rabbi Eliezer the Great*) lived in the last half of the first century A.D. and into the second century.

86.29–87.13 According to Eleazer . . . beasts and animals."] Irving's text bears some resemblance to *Pirkê De Rabbi Eliezer* (*The Chapters of Rabbi Eliezer the Great*), ed. Gerald Friedlander (New York: Hermon Press, 1965), chap. IV, "The Sin of Adam and Eve," p. 99. However, it is much more likely that Irving drew his text from Bekker's *Le Monde Enchanté* (cited in 78.39), I, 159–60. Apparently he translated directly from the French translation of Bekker, including a parenthetical remark by Bekker which he treats as if it were part of Eliezer's text. Bekker quotes Eliezer thus, the quotation in italics, his own interpolation in roman: "*Il les fit venir tous trois devant lui; il chargea par son Arrêt Eve et Adam de neuf malédictions, et les condamna à la mort; mais il précipita Sammaël et toute sa bande du Ciel sejour de sa Santété en bas; il coupa les piés au Serpent* (car il avoit auparavant la figure d'un Chameau, et Sammaël état monté sur lui) *et il le maudit entre toutes les bêtes et les animaux.*"

88.2–5 ——True Gentrie . . . MIRROR FOR MAGISTRATES]   Unidentified.

88.10 Peachem]   See note for 68.38.

88.12 Chesterfield]   Philip Dormer Stanhope, 4th Earl of Chesterfield (1694–1773), famous wit, statesman, intimate of Pope and Swift, is best known for the worldly wisdom imparted in his *Letters to His Son* (1774), to which the squire objects.

89.9–12 "Surrey," says Camden . . . of his time.]   Unidentified.

89.13–16 his person was . . . fund of wit.]   This seems to be a paraphrase of Surrey's poem "Of the Death of the Same Sir T. W.," which includes the phrase "A visage, sterne, and milde," and all of the other comments, though phrased differently. The text may be found in Alexander Chalmers, *The Works of the English Poets* (London, 1810), II, 336.

89.19–22 "They were . . . and style."]   The quotation is from George Puttenham, *The Arte of English Poesie* (1589). The text may be found in *Elizabethan Critical Essays*, ed. G. Gregory Smith (Oxford, 1904), II, 62–63. Irving omits "as novices newly crept out of the schools of *Dante, Arioste,* and *Petrarch,* they" after "Italian poetry."

90.6 Edward the Black Prince]   Eldest son of Edward III of England, Edward the Black Prince (1330–1376) fought at Crécy while still a boy, perhaps winning his *soubriquet* there for the color of his armor— though the first mention of it does not occur until the sixteenth century. He won a great victory at Poitiers in 1356 and was created Prince of Aquitaine in 1362. He was the father of Richard II.

90.16–17 the Life of the Chevalier Bayard, by Godefroy]   Pierre du Terrail, Chevalier de Bayard, was the chevalier "sans peur et sans reproche" (1476–1524). The "Life" was written by J. Joffrey, probably Bayard's secretary, "Le Loyal Serviteur." It was first published in 1527 and not translated into English until 1825.

90.20–29 "Ah, Sir Lancelot . . . in the rest."] Malory, *Morte d'Arthur*,
ed. Vinaver, III, 1259.

91.2–8 Each city . . . MERRY BEGGARS] The quotation is from Richard
Brome, *The Jovial Crew*, from a song in act I. The only significant
variant from the 1652 text is "nay-cock" for "way-cock" in line 5.

94.11–15 "Cupid's Solicitor . . . will deceive."] The title and the verse
quoted have not been identified.

95.2–5 ——Come, do not . . . SUCKLING] The quotation is from act IV
of *The Goblins*, in *A Collection of All the Incomparable Pieces written
by Sir John Suckling* (London, 1653), p. 117.

97.24–26 "All hail . . . shall be."] The quotation may be found in John
Aubrey, *Miscellanies*, 2d ed., p. 202.

98.11–12 "Author of Waverley"] Sir Walter Scott.

100.2–8 What a life . . . Lilly's Gallathea] The quotation is from John
Lyly, *Gallathea* (1592), II, iii. The text may be found in *The Complete
Works of John Lyly*, ed. R. Warwick Bond (Oxford, 1902), p. 442.
The words "encorporation, circination, sementation" follow "rubifica-
tion" in Bond's edition. They were included in the first American edition
of *Bracebridge Hall* but were omitted from the copy-text.

105.31–32 Abencerrages] A Moorish family prominent in fifteenth-
century Grenada, whose feuds with the rival family of the Zegris and
whose cruel treatment at the hands of the latter are celebrated in the
work that was a major source for "The Student of Salamanca," namely,
Gines Perez de Hita, *Guerra civiles de Grenada* (1595), translated by
Thomas Rodd as *The Civil Wars of Grenada* (London, 1803). Rodd
quotes dozens of ballads like the one described here.

110.8–9 Theophrastus, and Geber, and Albertus Magnus] Theophrastus
(ca. 372–286 B.C.), Greek philosopher, student of Plato and Aristotle,
whom he succeeded as leader of the peripatetic school; Geber (ca.
720–813 A.D.), Arabian alchemist sometimes identified with Jabir ibn
Haijan, reputed author of hundreds of alchemical writings; Albertus
Magnus (1193?–1280), the greatest of the scholastics and author of
the *Summa Theologiae*, was, like the other two mentioned here, a
writer on alchemical matters.

112.10 Pietro d'Abano] Pietro d'Abano or Petrus de Abano was a scholar
and astrologer, author of many treatises on medicine, philosophy, and
astronomy. He owes most of his modern fame to the harsh treatment
he received at the hands of the Inquisition who first burned him, then
dried his bones and incinerated them as well. His best-known work,
Conciliator differentiarum philosophorem, was first published in Venice
in 1476.

112.17 Geber, and Alfarabius, and Avicenna] For Geber, see 110.8–9;
Alfarabius was an alchemical scholar and adept who was born in Asia

Minor and died in 954 A.D. He is alleged to have learned seventy languages and written many books, none of which survive. Avicenna (980–1026), on the other hand, was a deeply learned man in philosophy, theology, and the occult. Appointed Grand Vizier by the Sultan Magdal Boulet because of his great learning, he was later dismissed for debauchery. He wrote nearly one hundred works on philosophy, mathematics, and medicine, including no less than seven treatises on the philosopher's stone.

113.3–4 Sierra Morena] A mountain range in southern Spain, flanking the great central plateau along the northern boundary of Andalusia.

114.29–30 Sandivogius, and Philalethes, and Dominus de Nuysment] Michael Sandivogius was an alchemist whose best-known work was translated into English as *A New Light of Alchymie* (1650). Eirenaeus Philalethes was the pseudonym of an alchemist who flourished in the second half of the seventeenth century. Virtually nothing is known of him, although some have tried to identify him with Thomas Vaughan, twin brother of the English poet, Henry Vaughan. Dominus de Nuysment or Nuysement or Nuisement was the author, among other alchemical treatises, of *Poeme philosophic de la Verité de la Phisique Minerale*... etc. (Paris, 1620).

117.6–11 Pontanus...Flamel...Cartilaceus Bernard de Treves] "The alchemist Pontanus says in his *Épître* that he went astray more than two hundred times, although he was working on the true material, because he did not know the Fire of the Philosophers" (Emile Grillat de Givry, *Picture Museum of Sorcery, Magic and Alchemy*, trans. J. Courtenay Locke [New York, 1963], p. 370).

Nicholas Flamel (1330?–1419?) is alleged to have purchased a book written by one "Abraham the Jew, Priest, Prince, Levite, Astrologer, and Philosopher," which was addressed "to the nations of the Jews dispersed by the wrath of God in France." The book contained the alchemical secrets, but Flamel could not understand it until he had studied for about the length of time Irving suggests with the help of learned Spanish Jews. Fortunately the story has a happy ending; he came to understand the work, succeeded in transmuting mercury to silver, and became one of the richest men in France, doubtless by leasing his patents. Cartilaceus is probably Johannes Hiskia Cardilucius, author of the *Magnalia Medico-Chymica* (Nurenberg, 1676).

Bernard of Treviso or Bernard Trevison (1406–1490) was an Italian nobleman who devoted his life to alchemy. He spent huge sums of money in travel, study, and experiments, all without success. The three-year period Irving refers to is probably a true believer's version of the three-year stint near the end of Bernard's life when he worked continuously in his laboratory without undressing, rarely resting, in an apoplexy of belief that the secret was at his fingertips.

117.40 Rosycrucian doctrines] "The Rosicrucians first appeared in Germany in the fourteenth century. They were thought to have been founded by a Crusader who had learned great secrets from the Arabians, including those of the philosopher's stone and the elixir of life. . . . The doctrine of the Rosicrucians was a system of theosophy directed to the discovery of the ultimate secrets of Nature; indeed, not only of things natural and visible, but of the supernatural and invisible. . . . The Rosicrucians regarded light and darkness, controlled by divine influence, as the original principles of creation, itself a miraculous process in which innumerable angels—favorable (of light) and adverse (of darkness)—participated in producing Nature in all her forms. Creation was the alchemy of Nature" (Richard B. Pilcher, *Lecture on Alchemists in Art and Literature* [London, 1933], pp. 32–33).

119.1 Behmen] Jakob Boehme or Behmen (1575–1624), German theosophist, may have been a Rosicrucian. His major work, *Aurora* (1612), is a series of meditations on God, man, and nature. It was condemned by religious authorities and brought much persecution to its author.

123.32 Flamel] See 117.6–11.

123.34–35 King Kalid . . . Morienus] Morien was born in Rome in the twelfth century but settled in Egypt at an early age where he became a student of Adfar, a famous Alexandrian philosopher. Upon Adfar's death he traveled to Jerusalem where he became a recluse. When Adfar's papers came into the hands of Kalid, the Sultan of Egypt, he called for Morien to help him decipher the secret of transmutation revealed within them. Morien did manage to decipher the papers and perform a transmutation, but he refused a reward and returned to his hermitage. Later they met again. Morien tried to convert Kalid to Christianity, but failing that, the two of them took up the study of alchemy together.

123.36 Elardus] Unidentified.

124.3–13 "Thou shalt see . . . as a salamander!"] Heinrich Khunrath, Khünrath, Kunrath, or Kunrade (1560–1605) was a follower of Paracelsus and author of several theosophic or mystical books. The most famous was the *Amphitheatrum Sapientiae Æternae Solius Verae* (Hanover, 1609, but dated 1602 on the title page), to which Irving refers as the "Amphitheatre of the Eternal Wisdom." However, no edition of the work was available in English at the time of Irving's writing; he doubtless gathered the quotation from some compendium of alchemical writings.

125.40–42 *and* 126.37–42 Here are the . . . HOWELL's LETTERS] The quotation is from James Howell, *Epistolae Ho-Elianae; Familiar Letters,*

Domestic and Foreign, 4 vols. (London, 1645–1655). The text may be found in *The Familiar Letters of James Howell* (Temple Classics Edition, London, 1903), I, 52–53. Interestingly, Irving's transcription omits the clause, "for the prime Courtesans in *Madrid* and elsewhere are had hence" after "the beautifull'st females of all Spain."

133.19 Apollonius Thyaneus] Apollonius of Tyana (fl. first century A.D.), a wandering Pythagorean philosopher and mystic whose writings have not survived, but whose place in the history of alchemy rivals that of the mythical Hermes Trismegistes.

135.10–11 Paracelsus, Sandivogius, Raymond Lully] Theophrastus Bombastus von Hohenheim (1493–1541) coined the name Paracelsus for himself. He is a watershed figure between alchemy and chemistry, often writing in the mystic lunacy of the former, but also compounding some new chemical combinations and encouraging research in pharmacology and medicine. For Sandivogius, see note at 114.29–30.

Raymond Lully (or Lull) (ca. 1232–1315) was a Spanish theologian who combined religious mysticism with Aristotelian logic to produce the "Lullian method" of mechanically acquiring knowledge and resolving all problems. Not an alchemist himself, his name was used by his followers to justify alchemy.

135.36 Hermes Trismegistes] The mythical father of alchemy and supposed author of the original "hermetic" wisdom, combining magic, astrology, alchemy, and metaphysics. During part at least of the seventeenth century, Hermes was believed to have been a Christian philosopher, although modern scholarship now identifies the writings found under his name with North African (particularly Egyptian) mystiques of metal and ceramic coloring and mnemonic systems.

135.41 De Nuysement] See 114.29–30.

140.18 Adonis] Beloved of Aphrodite, the beautiful youth Adonis, when killed in a boar hunt, had the rose of the anemone spring up from his blood or from the tears Aphrodite shed over him. After death he was shared as a lover between Aphrodite and Persephone.

140.20 Acis wooed his Galatea] Galatea was a nereid who was beloved by the cyclops Polyphemus, but who spurned him for the youth Acis. Alas, poor Acis was crushed under a rock by his enormous rival.

140.25–26 Diana . . . Endymion] Endymion was another beautiful youth, this time thrown into perpetual sleep and embraced every night by Diana. The legend forms the basis for Drayton's "Endimion and Phoebe" (1593) and Keats's "Endymion" (1818).

140.26 Cupid and Psyche] Psyche was so beautiful that Venus became jealous of her. She sent Cupid to make her fall in love with some ugly creature, but Cupid fell in love with her himself. He placed her in a palace and visited her only in the dark.

142.12–17 "Her galas . . . and Gomeles!"]   See above at 105.31–32. The text may be found in Rodd, *The Civil Wars of Grenada*, p. 270.

147.39–40 "With slow pace . . . that great victory."]   Reginald Gonsalvius Montanus, *Sanctae inquisitionis hispanicae* (Heidelberg, 1567), appeared in English the next year as *A Discovery and playne Declaration of Sundry Subtill practices of the Holy Inquisition of Spayne* (London, 1568). The text may be found with several changes of wording on p. 47 of this edition; Irving doubtless used another translation.

157.2–9 His   certain . . . PHINEAS FLETCHER]   The   quotation   is   from Phineas Fletcher, *The Purple Island* (1633), canto XII, stanza 5. In the 1633 text line 4 reads "noon-tides rage is spent"; line 6 reads "Of troublous world, nor lost," but Irving probably used a different edition. See also the List of Emendations.

163.2–3 "I'll live . . . COLLIER OF CROYDON]   The quotation is from William Haughton, *Grim the Collier of Croydon* (London, 1622), "by I.T.," act IV, scene 1. The text may be found in *Anonymous Plays*, ed. John S. Farmer (London, 1908), p. 162.

163.10–11 "Go, lovely rose . . . and me"]   The first line of Edmund Waller's best-known poem, "Go, lovely rose" (1645).

167.25 campus phlegræ]   The Phlegraen Fields or Plain, in Italian, Campi Flegrei, a volcanic region west of Naples, named for the ancient Phlegra in Macedonia. See also the Discussions of Adopted Readings under this entry.

168.18 Stow]   Probably the comment refers to John Stow, *Survey of London and Westminster* (1598).

168.26–29 'I have myself . . . lined with velvet!']   Unidentified. For Gervase Markham, see 68.38.

168.29–32 Nashe, too . . . outlandish habiliments.' "]   The quotation is from Thomas Nashe, *Christs Teares over Ierusalem* (1593). The text may be found in *The Works of Thomas Nashe*, ed. R. B. McKerrow (Oxford, 1958), II, 142, lines 18–20.

170.2–7 What's that . . . JOVIAL CREW]   Richard Brome, *The Jovial Crew or the Merry Beggars*, act II. Cited above at 8.2–5 and 91.2–8.

170.24–27 Who goes round . . . one by one!]   Variants of this anonymous verse may be found in Andrew Lang, *The Nursery Rhyme Book* (London, 1947), p. 186, and Barbara Ireson, *The Faber Book of Nursery Rhymes* (London, 1958), p. 211.

172.34–41 "Who would . . . rough weather."]   *As You Like It*, II, v. 40–47. Irving's text differs from the first folio and from the modern Kittredge text in "would" for "doth" in the first line and "Lie" for "live" in the second.

174.2–10 Happy the age . . . PASQUIL'S PALINODIA]   The quotation is from

[W. Fennor?], *Pasquils Palinodia; and his progresse to the taverne* (London, 1619), Sig. B₃.

177.3 "For O, for O, the Hobby Horse is forgot."] *Hamlet*, III, ii, 145; see also *Love's Labours Lost*, III, i, 29–30. *OED* suggests the line is probably from an old ballad now lost.

178.2–4 Nay, I tell you . . . COLLIER OF CROYDON] From Haughton, *Grim the Collier of Croydon*, V, i (Farmer edition, p. 167).

180.2–9 There will . . . LILLY'S EUPHUES] The quotation is from John Lyly, *Euphues and His England*; the text may be found in *The Complete works of John Lyly*, ed. Bond, p. 26.

184.2–6 But to come . . . ROGER ASCHAM] The quotation is from Roger Ascham, *The Scholemaster* (1570). The text may be found in the edition edited by J. E. B. Mayor (London, 1863), pp. 67–68.

184.12 Peachem] Henry Peacham; see note for 68.38.

184.24 Strutt] Joseph Strutt, *The Sports and Pastimes of the People of England* (1801).

187.2–6 I am a rogue . . . THE GOBLINS] The quotation is from Sir John Suckling, *The Goblins*; the text may be found in *A Collection of . . . Suckling*, p. 109.

188.10 Cobbett] William Cobbett (1763–1835), English radical political writer.

189.21 the robber in Ariosto] The reference is to Ludovico Ariosto, *Orlando Furioso*, canto XV, especially stanzas LXXXII–LXXXIV, in which Astolpho hews the felon Orrilo with "a thousand blows," and Orrilo persistently puts himself back together again.

189.32–35 Leave princes' affairs . . . magistrate's claws.] The quotation is from Thomas Tusser, *Hundred Points of Good Husbandrie*, first published in 1557 and augmented in several later editions; the lines quoted first appeared in the edition of 1573, chapter X. The text may be found in a modern edition with an introduction by Sir Walter Scott and a benediction by Rudyard Kipling (London, 1931), p. 20.

191.2–6 But cawing rooks . . . COWPER] The text is from William Cowper, "The Sofa," in *The Task* (1785), book I, lines 203–6.

196.2–8 It is the choice . . . ACTÆON AND DIANA] The quotation is from R. Cox, *Actaeon and Diana* (London, 1656), p. 3.

202.26–31 "Those days . . . such a dream."] Unidentified.

205.2–14 The soldier . . . OLD SCOTCH BALLAD] Unidentified.

206.18–19 Froissart's Chronicles] Jean Froissart's *Chronicle* deals with the period 1326–1400, chiefly concerning France, England, Scotland, and Flanders and touching also on Germany, Italy, and Spain and even so far afield as Hungary and the Balkans. Much of the charm of the *Chronicle* comes from the first-hand nature of the material Froissart gathered in courts and on byways, among noblemen, heralds, and the many kings he knew, including England's Edward III and Richard II.

222.2–8 A citizen . . . DOCTOR MERRIE-MAN, 1609] The quotation is from S[amuel] R[owlands], *Doctor Merrie-Man his Medicines against Melancholy Humours* (1607); reprinted as *Doctor Merry-Man: or nothing but mirth* in 1609. The text may be found in *The Complete Works of Samuel Rowlands* (Hunterian Club Facsimile Edition, 1880), II, 3, lines 1–6.

224.1–4 "At meales . . . lesser cost."] Tusser, *Hundred Points of Good Husbandrie*; the text may be found in the edition cited above at 189.32–35, p. 184.

227.2–10 Farewell rewards . . . BISHOP CORBET] Richard Corbet (1582–1635), bishop of Oxford and Norwich, was a noted wit and poet. *The Fairies' Farewell*, from which Irving quotes here, was his most serious and best-known work. The text may be found in *The Poems of Richard Corbet*, ed. J. A. W. Bennet and H. R. Trevor-Roper (Oxford, 1955), p. 49.

229.11–20 "Tells how . . . matin rings."] John Milton, *L'Allegro*, lines 105–14. Irving has "lays" for the original "lies" in the sixth line of the quotation.

230.1–17 "——Their dwellings . . . ruin'd and forsaken."] The quotation is from Thomas Heywood, *The hierarchie of the blessed angells. Their names, orders, and offices. The fall of Lucifer with his angells* (London, 1635), book IX, "The Angell," pp. 574–75.

232.1–9 Brown, in his . . . At twilight sat."] The quotation is from William Browne, *Brittania's Pastorals*, book I (1613). The text may be found in William Browne, *The Whole Works*, ed. W. Carew Hazlitt (Darmstadt, 1970), song 2, p. 66. Irving omitted two lines after line four of his quotation: "Or like the Circle where the Signes we tracke, / And learned Shepherds call't the *Zodiacke*"

232.12–15 "By wells . . . moonlight minstrelsies."] The lines quoted are from a poem entitled "Robin Good-fellow." It is found in many collections and often ascribed to Ben Jonson, notably by Thomas Percy in his *Reliques of Ancient English Poetry* (1765). Irving's source was probably John Brand's augmented reprint of Henry Bourne's *Antiquitates vulgares* (Newcastle, 1725), published as *Observations on the Popular Antiquities of Great Britain* (1777). The text of Irving's quotation may be found in the edition of Brand edited by Sir Henry Ellis (New York, 1970), II, 516. It is very likely that Brand's book was used extensively by Irving in the composition of *Bracebridge Hall*. The poem Irving quotes at 232.3–9, citing Browne's *Brittania's Pastorals*, appears in Brand with the same two lines missing (*ibid.*, II,

480). Other references to Tusser, Camden, Nashe, and Jonson in Brand are echoed by Irving.

234.2–4 From fire . . . THE WIDOW] The quotation is from Thomas Middleton, *The Widow* (1652), I, i, 29–30.

236.24 "dejected pity at his side"] The quotation is from William Collins, "The Passions: an Ode for Music," line 49.

239.2–4 "The night . . . MACBETH] The quotation is from *Macbeth*, II, iii, 60–61. Irving has "the chimneys" for "our chimneys."

242.2–7 "The poor soul . . . OLD SONG] See *Othello*, IV, iii, 40–43, 50, and the note at IV, iii, 40–43 in the Furness variorum edition of *Othello*. See also the next note. Thomas Heywood, in the song from *The Green Willow*, Shakespeare in *Othello*, and Percy in the *Reliques* ("Willow, willow, willow") all probably draw from a popular tradition of willow songs.

244.34–38 "My mother . . . died singing it."] The quotation is from *Othello*, IV, ii, 26–30. See the note above.

246.2–9 *Hermione* . . . WINTER'S TALE] The quotation is from *The Winter's Tale*, II, i, 22–25. Irving omits "good" before "sir" in the last half line.

248.4–10 Formerly almost every . . . BOURNE'S ANTIQUITIES] The quotation has not been found in Henry Bourne's *Antiquitates vulgares* (1725), or in John Brand's augmented reprint, *Observations on Popular Antiquities* (1777). See notes 232.1–9 and 232.12–15 above.

251.2–10 "I take . . . TALE OF A TUB] The quotation is from Ben Jonson, *The Tale of a Tub* (1633), III, i, 67–74. The copy-text reads "of" for "to" in the first line of the quotation. See the List of Emendations and the Discussions of Adopted Readings.

278.3–6 "They all . . . liquor gillore."] Unidentified.

279.26–27 Mynheer Selyne] Probably Henricus Selyns (1636–1701), pastor of the Dutch Church of New York, and somewhat celebrated as a local historian. Perhaps in calling him a "poet," Irving implies his historiography is of the Diedrich Knickerbocker type.

285.40–42 Moore . . . Spectre-Ship bound to Deadman's Isle] Irving is probably referring to Thomas Moore's poem, "Written on Passing Deadman's Island in the Gulf of St. Lawrence Late in the evening, September, 1804." The poem may be found in *The Poetical Works of Thomas Moore* (London, 1852), p. 130.

301.2–6 No more . . . BRAITHWAITE] The quotation is of the last lines of the epithalamium in Richard Braithwaite's *A Strappado for the Devell* (1615). Irving has "wedding-day" for "marriage-day" in the fourth line.

308.2–4 And so . . . HAMLET] The quotation is from *Hamlet*, I, v, 127–28.

TEXTUAL COMMENTARY

In the editing of this text, an unmodernized critical edition based upon the first state of the first English edition (Murray, 1822), the procedures established by W. W. Greg and modified by Fredson Bowers have been followed, with particular attention to the CEAA *Statement of Editorial Principles*.[1] These procedures are useful not only for the important distinction between accidental variants (variants that affect the form of the text, i.e., punctuation, spelling, capitalization) and substantive variants (variants that affect the meaning), but as a general theory pertinent to many circumstances in the creation of a critical edition. Nevertheless, in the application of the general theory to the specific case of *Bracebridge Hall*, situations arise in which the theory must be modified to accommodate the unusual circumstances of this particular text. When necessary, this commentary includes discussion of relevant portions of these theories as they apply to this text.

As with any edition, this one presents problems in three general areas, which determine the three divisions of the commentary: the identification and comparison of different forms of the text, the choice of copy-text, and the principles of emendation. However, before entering into detailed commentary upon these matters, one larger question pertinent to all of them should be raised: Should one see *Bracebridge Hall* as primarily an English work by a man living and writing in England, who only happened to be an American by birth, or as an American work, by an American writer, who only happened to be living in England at the time and writing on English themes? This question, of course, breaks down easily into several subsidiary but practical questions. Should one favor English spellings over American? Should later additions be included in the text? What should be the treatment of substantive variants made by Irving in the Author's Revised Edition? But such specifics are better deferred for the moment, in favor of a more philosophical overview to start with.

1. W. W. Greg, "The Rationale of Copy-Text," *Studies in Bibliography* 3 (1950–1951), 19–36; Fredson Bowers, "Some Principles for Scholarly Editions of Nineteenth-Century American Authors," *Studies in Bibliography* 17 (1964), 223–28; Center for Editions of American Authors, Modern Language Association of America, *Statement of Editorial Principles* (1967). The terminology used in this commentary is that set forth by Fredson Bowers in *Principles of Bibliographical Description* (Princeton: Princeton University Press, 1949).

Irving's American birth to the contrary notwithstanding, virtually all of the evidence suggests that *Bracebridge Hall* should, must, be seen as primarily English, at least at the time of its composition. As the evidence cited in the Introduction to this volume suggests, Irving was chiefly concerned with his English reception. He was willing to submit a corrupt text to his American readers to preserve his copyright in America while he laboriously corrected the manuscript submitted to his English publisher, John Murray, and later painstakingly corrected proofs for the first English edition. His eye was on the English reading public, and particularly on John Murray, Sir Walter Scott, and the English literati. In spite of his brother Ebenezer's fears for the American reception of the Christmas sketches in *The Sketch Book*, they provided the very topic suggested by Thomas Moore for expansion into *Bracebridge Hall*, a suggestion eagerly adopted by Irving. A good argument could be made for preferring the American form of *The Sketch Book* over the English; Irving was still, in 1819, truly a transatlantic writer. Conditions had changed by 1822 though, and the primacy of the English form of *Bracebridge Hall* over the American at that date is beyond dispute.

But Irving took the blue pencil to *Bracebridge Hall* in 1848–1849, and this time for an edition (the Author's Revised Edition) aimed directly at the American reading public. If the 1822 text is English in its orientation, this one, so far as possible, is American. The question follows, then: Which text, when they differ, has primacy—the one expressing Irving's first (English) intention, or the one expressing his latest and last (American) intention? Should this edition give full weight to revisions which are undoubtedly authorial but are intended to produce a subtly different book from Irving's first intent?[2] This is not a simple question, and not one to be resolved solely by recourse to the Greg-Bowers-CEAA principles of emendation of authorial variants in later editions by distinction between accidental and substantive variants. These would be substantive variants, but variants created by a "new" author, twenty-six years older and home to stay at Sunnyside, writing a "new" book, as part of his collected works, intended for a "new" audience, the American reading public. The answer to this question, as will be seen, requires analysis of several specific instances and examples. These will be given in due time, but for the moment it should be stated that the decision was to favor the English nature of *Bracebridge Hall* even where the variants of the Author's Revised Edition are almost surely authorial and substantive.

2. This is to ignore for the moment the fact that Irving took a corrupt text to mark for the ARE; such corruptions could, in general, be corrected.

THE TEXTS

In the discussion that follows the symbols used to designate texts are those given in the key which appears on pages 315–316.[3] Over a period of some five years, all of the texts except the 1834 Baudry (1F34), the 1824 and 1829 Murray (3E24 and 3E29), and the 1841 Lea and Blanchard (3A41) have been examined and collated. The following collations were made (all sight collations unless otherwise described): (1) MSA against 1A; (2) MSE against 1Ea; (3) 1Ea against 1A; (4) 1Ea against 2E (combined sight and machine); (5) 1Ea against 1Eb; (6) 2E against 1Ec; (7) 1Ea against 3E (twice, substantives only, 3E23, 3E25); (8) 1Ea against 1F27 (substantives only); (9) 1Ea against 2A26 (substantives only); (10) 2A against 2A26 (substantives only); (11) 1Ea against ARE (three times: ARE 1849, 1853, 1859); (12) ARE49 against ARE53 (machine); (13) ARE53 against ARE59 (machine); (14) 1Ea against 4E (substantives only); (15) 1Ea against 3A30 (substantives only); (16) 1Ea against 1Ea (machine); (17) 2E against 2E (machine, three copies); (18) 3A30 against 3A33 (machine); (19) 3A33 against 3A35 (machine); (20) 3A35 against 3A36 (machine); (21) 3A35 against 3A39 (Vol. II only, machine); (22) 1F23 against T proofs.[4]

3. For aid in interpreting the relationships between the texts and the significance of the earliest forms of the text, the reader may wish to consult the schematic diagram of the genealogy of the texts, p. 317 and the Index to Earliest Extant Texts, pp. 420–422, along with the three appendices concerning precopy-texts and early copy-text variants.

4. The specific texts used for these collations were the following, listed by collation numbers in the text: (1) MSE (NYPL, Columbia Univ., Univ. of Virginia) vs 1Ea, Texas Ir 8br; (2) MSA (Alderman Library, University of Virginia) vs. 1A Texas 60–1517; (3) 1Ea, Texas Ir 8br vs. 1A, Texas 60–1517; (4) 1Ea, Texas Ir 8br vs. 2E, Univ. of Victoria PS2057/A1/1822; (5) 1Ea, Texas Ir 8br vs. 1Eb, Columbia B812/Ir8/05/1822g; (6) 2E Univ. of Victoria PS2057/A1/1822 vs. 1Ec, UCLA PS2057/.A1/1822; (7) 1Ea, Texas Ir 8br, vs. 2E23, Wisconsin (accession number) C29504, and 2E25, Texas (uncataloged) "John Anstice, 1834," on title page, Vol. I; (8) 1Ea, Texas Ir 8br vs. 1F27, Yale Za/Ir8/822g (microfilm); (9) 1Ea, Texas Ir 8br vs. 2A26, Wisconsin (accession number) C17300; (10) 2A22, Boston Public Library A.4470.15 vs. 2A26, Wisconsin (accession number) C17300; (11) 1Ea, Texas Ir 8br vs. ARE49, personal copy belonging to Ralph Aderman, Dept. of English, Univ. of Wisconsin, Milwaukee (imprint date on title page is 1850), ARE53, Wisconsin PS2057/A1./1853, ARE59, Oberlin College 817.1/Ir8.1859; (12) ARE49, personal copy belonging to Ralph Aderman, Dept. of English, Univ. of Wisconsin, Milwaukee (imprint date on title page is 1850) vs. ARE53, Wisconsin PS2057/A1./1853; (13) ARE53, Wisconsin PS2057/A1./1853 vs. ARE59, Oberlin College 817.1 Ir8./1859; (14) 1Ea, Texas Ir 8br vs. 4E, Texas (uncataloged, unmarked); (15) 1Ea, Texas Ir 8br vs. 3A30, NYPL 687321 and 687322; (16) 1Ea (first), Texas Ir 8br vs. 1Ea (second), Texas (accession number) 3122; (17) 2E (first), Univ. of Victoria PS2057/A1/1822

These collations revealed a clear genealogy for the various texts, which is interesting in itself and informative for the bibliographer. Collation 1 revealed an extraordinary number of variants, accidental and substantive, relevant to the choice of copy-text and discussed below. Collations 2 and 3 revealed what one would expect—that Irving exercised no control over the correction of proof for 1A. This matter is also significant for choice of copy-text. The collations of what was thought to be the four identified states of the first English edition (and a survey made of twenty-nine copies of this edition)[5] documented the progress

vs. 2E (second), Univ. of Indiana PS2057/.A1/1822 (Xerox), and 2E (third), Univ. of Pennsylvania AC8. Ir844/.822bb; (18) 3A30, NYPL 687321 and 687322 *vs.* 3A33, Univ. of Mississippi PS2057/.A1/1833; (19) 3A33, Univ. of Mississippi PS2057/.A1/1833 *vs.* 3A35, Univ. of Wisconsin, Milwaukee PS2050/.E35/V.4 (2 vols in 1); (20) 3A35, Univ. of Wisconsin, Milwaukee PS2050/.E35/V.4 (2 vols in 1) *vs.* 3A36, personal copy of Ralph Aderman, Dept of English, Univ. of Wisconsin, Milwaukee; (21) 3A35, personal copy of Ralph Aderman, Dept of English, Univ. of Wisconsin, Milwaukee *vs.* Harvard A1.1968.321, Gift of Samuel R. Green, November 22, 1858; (22) IF23, personal copy of H. F. Smith, Dept. of English, University of Victoria *vs.* T (proofs).

No further bibliographical description of these texts is given here, since full collations are given of the major texts in BAL (10109–10111) and because a detailed physical description of all these editions will appear in the full-scale Irving bibliography to be published as the last volume of the Twayne edition.

5. For the survey, twenty-one copies of 1E were checked at nine points for the following choices: 1E I, 122.5 (T, 52.33) whig or Whig; 1E I, 158.3 (T 65.30) Tibbets or Tibbetses; 1E I 204.2 (T 82.37) Remigius or Remegius; 1E I, 383.11 (T, 150.34) intellects, or intellects.; 1E I, 384.22 (T, 151.22) As she or [As omitted] she; 1E II, 42.13 (T, 172.23) goals or gaols; 1E II, 165.6 (T, 221.17) money's jacket. or Ready-money's jacket. or Money's jacket.; 1E II, 354.6 (T, 292.33) Spiegle/pro- or Spiegel/the or Speigle/pro-; 1E II text ends on p. 404 or p. 403.

As a result of this survey of twenty-one copies and full collation of eight other copies of 1E, the three states of 1E and the hitherto unsuspected 2E were determined to be consistent within the sample of a total of twenty-nine copies. The copies surveyed or collated are divided within these three states and two editions as follows:

1Ea: Newberry Y255.I72; Library of Congress PS2057/A1/1822a; Princeton 3797/.32; NYPL, "Irving Case" copy and Berg Collection copy number 1; Texas Ir 8br and accession number 3122.

1Eb: Univ. of Minnesota Y8/Ir8/ObrM; Columbia B812Ir8/05/1822g; New York Univ.; Duke Univ. A13/TR.R/817.24/172B; Boston Athenaeum; Harvard A1.1868.302; Chicago PS2058/1822a/Rare Book; Univ. of Michigan RBR/828/I72.

1Ec: Univ. of Pennsylvania Ac8/Ir844/822bb/c.2; Univ. of Illinois 817/Ir8b.1822; Rice Univ; Library of Congress PS2057/.A1/1822a/copy 2; NYPL, Berg Collection copy number 2; UCLA; Univ. of California, Berkeley.

2E: Univ. of Pennsylvania AC8/Ir844/822bb/c.1; Univ. of North Carolina V817/I72b/1822; NYPL stacks copy NBO; NYPL rare book room copy; Univ. of of the text during its first printing and gave some suggestion concerning the numbers and timing of the various revisions made. Jacob Blanck left open the question of priority among the states that he identified; this problem has now been resolved.[6] The first state (1Ea) may now clearly be identified as the one with its text ending at page 403 in Volume II and without the paragraph added by Irving to the last essay (see above p. 000). Two exemplars machine collated with this pagination were identical; seven copies surveyed for nine checkpoints were identical. Since the paragraph missing in 1Ea was undoubtedly added by Irving when he sent sheets of 1E to America for the publication of 2A (in which the paragraph appears), this priority may be confidently asserted. It follows as well that the second state (1Eb) includes those copies which are identical to 1Ea except for the added paragraph; this conclusion was confirmed by collation and by the survey. The identification of a third state (1Ec) is more tentative, since intermediates may exist, but collation and the survey suggest that copies that have "gaols" at 1E II, 42.13 (172.23), "Spiegel" at 1E II, 354.6 (292.33), and "Remigius" at 1E I, 204.2 (82.37) are of this state. This must be a later state than 1Ea because all copies have the added paragraph; it must be later than 1Eb because all its variants differ from both earlier states.

What was thought to be the fourth state of 1E differed strikingly from the other three states. Machine collation showed that it was in fact a new edition in masquerade (2E), since it was completely reset. Certainly Murray did not consider it a new edition, never identifying it as such. Almost certainly it was the "run-on of 1000" copies mentioned in the letter from Murray's heirs to Blanck cited in note 38 of the Introduction to this text (see above, p. xxvii). Thus, even though it is technically the second English edition, it is comparable at all

---

Victoria PS2057/A1/1822; Princeton Ex/3797/.32; Indiana Univ. PS2057/.A1/1822.

It should be noted that this survey was undertaken with every expectation that intermediates would appear among these states. When none did so, additional collations were made of copies of 1Ea and 2E (collations 15 and 16 above). Exemplars of each of these two editions were found to be consistent within the state except for type shifting and wear. The editor is still not convinced that intermediates do not exist, especially in 1Ec, but further investigation of the matter seemed to have reached an extreme point of diminishing returns. Thus the hypothesis of three discernible states and a concealed second edition is allowed to stand until further evidence modifies it. It should also be noted that a sample of twenty-nine copies from a printing of four thousand is not particularly relevant statistically. Without going into the details of the standard deviation in such a case, and the appropriate formulae, one can say that the numbers of copies printed in each state were probably fairly sizeable, but that the almost even division of copies in the sample is only illusory in any statistical sense.

6. BAL, V, 19–20.

points with the three earlier states of 1E. Although some of the reset-tings include no changes except in spacing, and others seem designed only to repair damaged type, justify lines, or reset passages that had an awkward number of hyphenated compounds at the ends of lines, about one hundred of the reset pages of 2E include textual variants, accidental or substantive. The variants prove beyond question that 2E is later than all three states of 1E, since it includes all the variants of 1Ec and many more as well. One of the corrections in 1Ec, "Spiegel," at II. 354.6 (292.33), is "corrected" in 2E erroneously to "Speigle." Machine collation of three copies of 2E showed them to be identical except for type wear and movement, suggesting that this "edition" is likely to have a constant form, although intermediates are of course possible.

Identifying the chronology of the three states of 1E and 2E is useful chiefly in establishing the earliest state over which Irving had control of accidentals. As was remarked in the Introduction, no clear evidence indicates that Irving had anything to do with any revisions to 1E later than the added paragraph at the end of 1Eb. This supposition is sup-ported by the form of 2A, which is clearly drawn from 1Ea and 1Eb. 2A is different from all three states of 1E and 2E—it was reset, after all, and in an American print shop, and very possibly by compositors who had set 1A only a few months before. But for all the evidences of an American house style and the dozens of errors in the text which crept in, since the author had no opportunity to oversee the proofs, the text of 2A follows the text of 1Ea at a number of cruxes. Perhaps the most important of these is at 172.23, where 2A reads "goals," for "gaols," like 1Ea and 1Eb, and unlike 1Ec. A dozen other points sug-gest strongly that 2A was not drawn from 2E, but "goals" for "gaols" is the only sure indicator that 1Ea and 1Eb and not 1Ec supplied the text. The point should be evidence enough, since we have Irving's word that he would send sheets to Ebenezer as soon as possible to set a new American edition. All of the evidence indicates that he was much more interested in quickly getting a better text of *Bracebridge Hall* into print in America than in getting a perfect text. Therefore it seems reason-able to assume that he sent off an early set of sheets with a minimum of correction on them.

Collation of the second American (2A) with the first English (1E) edition revealed several other interesting substantive variants, which fall into two categories. First and most important, 2A includes a single change, apparently made for this edition, which was not added to later English texts and was possibly made by Irving. That is the inser-tion at 3.9 of "to my European readers," set off by commas and not included in the T text. A similar phrase appears in 1A, and it is possible that the compositors of 2A added it without Irving's authority. But since it is not identical to the 1A reading, and since Irving was sensitive to the fact that he was preparing an American edition for the press, it seems likely that it is from his hand. If so, the text of 2A presents us with the interesting picture of the author looking over the first and last pages in his text and making two additions as a sop to his American readers, but not bothering with any further correction of the English material in between.

Comparison of the two texts also revealed many examples of accidental and substantive variants in 2A which were clearly compositors' errors or corrections. There is no reason whatsoever to believe that Irving had any hand in the correction of this edition. Nor is it likely that he corrected the sheets of 1E used to set it, since none of the "corrections" made for 1Ec appear, and none of the 2A "corrections" found their way into 2E. But the American compositors of 2A, perhaps more familiar than the English with American family and place names, corrected "Gansevorts" to "Gansevoorts" at 290.29 and "Polopol's" to "Pollopol's" at 287.11, for example. More significant variants are those which had no justification but were repeated, as we shall see, in the ARE. These include a range of variants, from simple changes like "further" to "farther," for example, at 8.17 and 145.13, and "when" to "where" at 152.37, to some rather long and complicated omissions, like those at 195.31 and 223.40 These, perhaps unimportant in themselves, became significant with the collation of ARE with 1E.

Those three collations of ARE against 1E, the later ones checking on the accuracy of the first, revealed a pattern of variants which was at first puzzling, but became immensely informative when compared to the list of variants recorded between 1E and 2A. The two lists corresponded at sixty-six points, suggesting strongly that Irving had used a copy of one of the texts generated by 2A to mark up for the ARE. Moreover, only sixteen of those corresponding variants were found in the first volume, fifty in the second, and the Volume I variants were all relatively minor compared to the substantial omissions and changes of Volume II. The pattern strongly suggests an interesting hypothesis: that Irving did use an American text for ARE, that he corrected the first half of it rather carefully, perhaps even comparing it with MSE (see Discussions of Adopted Readings, 82.25–26), but that he became careless with time and corrected the second volume without referring to any other text, allowing a number of errors to creep into ARE.

Although the evidence is strong that the procedure described here is correct, it does not explain why Irving should have chosen a text that even his first examination would indicate to him was more corrupt than any of the English forms of the work to use as the foundation for printer's copy for his Author's Revised Edition. After all, several aspects of some form of 1E would inevitably recommend that text to him to mark up for a printer—not the least of them the fact that 1E is the only text of *Bracebridge Hall* besides 1A that exists in a generous format, with wide margins and ample space between the lines. Why then should he choose a cramped copy, the duodecimo 2A or the even more corrupt and less readable 3A? While the choice might have been made on purely irrelevant issues— an American text the only one at hand, or the one most battered and therefore easiest to spare—the American texts had one strong advantage that might have been foremost in his mind at the time: they had been de-Anglicized to some extent, particularly in their punctuation and spelling. Although no complete collation was made of accidental variants in 2A and 3A and either ARE or 1E, spot-checking of these texts indicated that a far higher degree of correspondence exists between the texts in the American line than between 1E and either 2A or 3A. Thus the American text may have recommended itself to Irving for marking because it corresponded more closely to Putnam's house style.

A number of changes were made for style which are less clearly matters of Putnam's requirements, but may represent Irving's sensitivity to the simplification of standard English and American prose between 1822 and 1849. Emendations in ARE for style and grammar are scattered in roughly equal proportions through the text, but are far from being consistently applied, suggesting that they were made by Irving himself rather than the publisher's editor. The most condensed group of changes appears at 104.4–13, a revision from indirect quotation to direct address in "The Student of Salamanca." Further striking groups of revisions are, first, in "Annette Delarbre" at 215.28–36, changing tenses primarily, and second, the consistent cutting of the forest wanderings of Dolph Heyliger at 273.26–35. None of these variants significantly affects the meaning of the text by reflecting second thoughts about the characters or changes of that sort, although the Dolph Heyliger variants do suggest that Irving intended to play down the Gothic element in Dolph's adventures.[7]

Once these collations had brought to light the imperfect transmission of the ARE text, an attempt to identify the specific text Irving used as copy for ARE became important. To that end four machine collations were made of texts in the Carey, Lea, Blanchard American line. They revealed nothing positive, and the question remains open. One bit of evidence suggests that he used the 1826 Van Winkle edition. This is

---

7. The point adds a minor corroboration of the argument advanced by William L. Hedges, *Washington Irving: An American Study, 1802–1832* (Baltimore: Johns Hopkins Press, 1965), p. 195.

the reading "with a" at 171.39, which is peculiar to 2A22, 2A26, and ARE. All other texts, including 1E and all the American texts after 2A26, have "with what a."[8] But this is surely too slender a reed to build a supposition on. Nor did the machine collations of later editions of ARE prove very interesting. Beyond countless points that might be valuable for the book collector—broken letters, type wear, and the like—only sixteen textual variants were discovered, and only two of those were substantive: "of" for "or" at ARE 83.29 (52.10) and "here's" for "there's" at ARE 411.6 (261.23). Two of the fourteen accidental variants were in titles or running heads, and all of them resulted from broken or dropped punctuation.

Collation of the later English and French texts revealed a few interesting points. Two sight collations were made for substantive variants in the 1823 and 1825 Murray reprints (3E23 and 3E25), since no machine was available at the time. Sight collations were also made between 1E and the Galignani edition of 1827 and the Murray edition of 1845 (1F27 and 4E). No copy of the 1823 Baudry edition (1F23) could be found until late in the research for this work, so it has been collated with the T proofs. These collations proved that the text of the third English edition (3E) was drawn from the third impression of the Murray first edition (1Ec), and that the French line of texts was derived from 3E23, while 4E follows the text of 3E25. Each new printing generated some new variants, and the genealogy was simple to establish. None of the variants seemed authorial, but a few of them deserve some discussion. Two variants found in all texts after 3E23 in the English and French lines and nowhere else, at 309.9 and 311.36, seem to have been made for the same purpose. Both qualify the amount of credit Irving deserved for his contribution to Anglo-American good feeling as a result of *The Sketch Book*. One cannot but wonder if the rather biting expression of amusement at Irving's "good-natured vanity" remarked in the *Blackwood's* review of *Bracebridge Hall* (quoted above in the Introduction, pp. xxix–xxx) contributed to this sudden expression of modesty. One also wonders if the revisions are Irving's; they are the kind of qualification that a cautious editor might make as easily as a cautious author, and are not repeated in later editions not taking their text from this line.

Another interesting emendation in the English descent of the text occurs at 187.38. In 3E23 and the editions following it the word "bloody" and the phrase in which it appears is deleted. In the Author's Revised

8. It is highly unlikely that Irving used 2A22 for his ARE revision; some twenty corrections were made between 2A22 and 2A26, in none of which is 2A22 preferable, and all correspond to the ARE text.

Edition the word "bloody" is changed to "leave marks of blood on." Both variants reflect the increasing sensitivity to the word "bloody," which, according to the *Oxford English Dictionary*, was first used as a profane epithet in literature in 1840. Although Irving's use of the word here clearly does not have any such sense, yet the editor (probably) of 3E23 and Irving himself in 1848 or 1849 had become sensitized to the word to the point that neither was willing to let it stand as it was, though each chose a different way to revise it. Clearly this was a case of revision under genteel social duress; the T text retains the 1E reading.

CHOICE OF COPY-TEXT

The choice of copy-text for *Bracebridge Hall* was particularly difficult. Two forms of a manuscript exist, one (designated MSA) for the text of Volume II as it appears in 1A, the other (designated MSE) corresponding to some two-thirds of the text of 1E. In addition, no less than three printed texts (1A, 1E, 2A) might be considered as copy-text for all or part of the text, and one of those (1E) exists in at least three states and in a concealed second edition, 2E. To sort out these texts, one must examine them in detail.[9]

Although both manuscripts are incomplete, MSA has an archival purity denied MSE. It is known that Irving mailed MSA for Volume II to his brother Ebenezer from London on February 25, 1822; that it had a more fortunate crossing than the now-missing MSA for Volume I, arriving only eight days after it, near the beginning of April, though Volume I had been mailed almost a month before, on January 29, 1822; that Irving wrote a table of contents for it and had it paged by Ebenezer, 1 to 355, consecutively without omissions, from the title page to the last page of text; that it was set in type by three compositors, named Flanagan, John McReady, and John Connor; and that it was kept intact until it was deposited in the Barrett Collection of the Alderman Library of the University of Virginia.

MSE, on the other hand, has had a checkered career. Unlike MSA, which is a fair-copy manuscript written at one time, MSE shows evidence of being revised over a period of many months, both before and after the drafting of MSA. Irving undoubtedly presented MSE to Murray's printers, probably in installments, and most of it bears the marks of having been used to set type for 1E. Two segments, including fourteen pages of "St. Mark's Eve" and seventy-six pages of "The Student of

---

9. An Index to Earliest Extant Texts is printed below, pp. 420–422. It lists the extant manuscripts (with their locations) and the earliest printed forms for the entire work.

Salamanca," are apparently an earlier draft and were not used to set type for 1E. Two versions of MSE exist for parts of "Falconry" and "Hawking," one of which was used to set 1E, the other, wildly variant, was not. None of these segments are part of the missing first volume of MSA, since their texts are closer to the text of 1E at many cruxes. Only one page of manuscript of Volume I, from "The Author," has been tentatively identified as from MSA, since it corresponds to the printed text of 1A at several cruxes, but it bears no distinguishing marks, and therefore the identification must remain tentative.

MSE was partially paged, through "Family Reliques," but at that point Irving apparently decided to shift the position of "The Widow" from fifth to sixth place in 1E, and gave up his pagination as a result. He probably did number the sketches, and perhaps paged them individually, but the handwriting is not conclusive. He worked hard on MSE after MSA was drafted, producing a substantial number of variants from MSA, but gave it to Murray long before he was satisfied with it. Most of it was used by compositors who will ever be nameless, and who were probably frustrated by an author who insisted on making so many corrections in proof that many of their page-end and gathering notations are inexact. Just one piece of ambiguous internal evidence suggests that Irving possibly referred to MSE while correcting copy for ARE (see Discussions of Adopted Readings, 82.25–26). About one-third of MSE descended to the collection of Bishop Hurst, to be deposited with the Seligman Collection in the New York Public Library; close to two-thirds stayed with the Irving family until 1885, when that portion was deposited in the Columbia University Library. A smaller segment was preserved by Clifton Waller Barrett, to rest finally with MSA in the University of Virginia Library.

The physical similarity of MSA and MSE suggests that they were produced at approximately the same time. The basic sheet size is 4½" by 7", although many sheets have been cut and pasted together to make extralength sheets, or torn or cut at either end. The remains of what appear to be thread holes on the left-hand side of many sheets in both MSA and MSE suggest that some of the paper, perhaps all of it, came from bound notebooks. With only a very few exceptions, the sheets are written on one side only, which would have been the right-hand page of a notebook. Three kinds of paper are found. The most common is a high-rag-content wove paper with a Bath crest on the left-hand top corner; some one-half or more of both MSA and MSE pages are of this type, with almost all of MSA consisting of this paper. Another wove paper without a crest but with a high rag content was used less frequently, and a third kind of wove paper with a higher pulp content, thus deteriorating markedly more than the other varieties, appears even more rarely. No pattern of use among these papers is discernible; the fragmentary nature of the manuscripts and their long history in the hands of collectors and the Irving family have probably destroyed all hope of reconstructing any such pattern.

The relationship of MSA and MSE to each other presents no problem, although the evidence of it is entirely circumstantial. MSE was a working manuscript, most of it probably a first draft. It is possible, of course, that there was an ur-manuscript from which it was drafted, but most of it appears to be written from no model, and there seems no reason to hypothesize such a manuscript. Excisions and interlineations are common, and they are of the kind that would very likely arise in the heat of composition, rather than while copying. MSA, on the other hand, was a fair copy drafted from an intermediate stage of MSE. One could cite hundreds of instances which suggest this relationship, but perhaps this one example, from the opening of "Travelling" (222.9–13) will suffice:

[MSE]

The Squire has lately received another shock
in the Saddle, and been almost unseated
⟨from his hobby⟩ by his marplot neighbour
the indefatigable Mr Faddy, who rides his
jog trot hobby with equal zeal; and is so
bent upon improving and reforming the
neighbourhood, that the Squire thinks in a
little while it will be scarce worth living in.

[MSA]

The Squire has lately received
another shock in the Saddle, and
been almost unseated by his marplot
neighbour the indefatigable Mr Faddy
who rides his jog trot hobby with
equal zeal; and is ↑so↓ bent upon improving
and reforming the neighbourhood, that the
Squire thinks in a little while it will
be scarce worth living in.

These are two fairly clean passages, only one cancellation in MSE, one careted interpolation in MSA.[10] But, if one can reconstruct Irving's

10. Editorial symbols used above and in subsequent transcriptions from manuscript pages are the following: ⟨ ⟩ restored cancellations; ↑ ↓ interlinear insertions.

writing, he must conclude that the cancellation of "from his hobby" seems much more likely to arise from the heat of composition than from faulty copying. Irving began the passage with the riding of hobby-horses in mind, no doubt, but as he continued, he saw that Mr. Faddy, not the squire, was to be the more proper Uncle Toby for this occasion, and the emphasis should fall on his hobbyhorse, not the squire's. The passage in MSA, on the other hand, copies MSE perfectly, with the exception of the "so," which slipped past the hurrying copyist, Irving, only to be inserted later when the sense of the sentence required it.

Obviously, then, MSE was the working draft, MSA the fair copy of the work as it was in the period around December, 1821, and January and February, 1822. MSA represents a fixed state of the composition completed some three months before the publication of the work both in England and America. After Irving mailed it, nothing more could be done for it, nothing for the American publication it became, until he mailed the corrected sheets of 1E to be used in setting 2A. MSE, on the other hand, continued as a working draft and as a final draft for the English publication of the book. Irving deleted many passages from MSE which appear in MSA and 1A, changed the word order from the MSA form, transposed whole sections and chapters, and added material not found in MSA and 1A, including no less than four new chapters, two of them extant in MSE. Thus, what has survived of MSE is both earlier and later than MSA, and represents both his earliest intentions for the work and his latest extant in manuscript form. An example will illustrate this mixed character of MSE. Here is a segment from the "May Day" chapter (197.31–35) as it appears in MSE and MSA:

[MSE]

Among these
I perceived that Ready Money Jack took
the lead, looking with a learned 〈eye upon
the efforts of the〉 and critical eye on the merits
⟨candidates↓
of the different 〈antagonists〉 : 〈He had His hat
↑was↓
drawn a little on one side over his brow,
which gave additional effect to his decisions:〉
and though he was very laconic and
〈sententious and〉 sometimes merely expressed
↑himself↓
〈his opinion〉 by a nod, yet it was evident
↑that↓ his opinions 〈out〉 far outweighed those of the
most loquacious.

[MSA]

Among these I perceived that Ready Money
Jack took the lead, looking with a
learned and critical eye on the merits
of the different candidates. His hat was
drawn a little on one side over his brow,
which gave additional effect to his decisions;
and though he was very laconic and   ⟨sententious⟩
sometimes merely expressed   ⟨his⟩
himself by a nod; yet it was evident
that his opinions far outweighed those of
the most loquacious.

Comparison of the two versions shows the mixed nature of MSE. The
cancellation, in lines 2 and 3 of the above transcription, of "eye upon
the efforts of the" is almost surely a result of original composition, not
repeated when the passage was copied for MSA. Similarly, the cancellation of "his opinion," in line 9 above, rids the passage of a
repetition in a stylistically satisfactory manner. Furthermore, it is a
repetition which Irving almost duplicated in MSA, there having to
cancel only the "his" (line 8 above). Perhaps he made both revisions
while copying MSA; perhaps not. The point remains that such revisions
must have been made before or during the writing of MSA. They are
quite different from the cancellation in MSE of the detail of the arrangement of Jack's hat, lines 4–6 above; that change must have taken place
after MSA had been sent off to America. Again and again the evidence
suggests this mixed nature for MSE: it is earlier than MSA, which was
drafted from it in an early stage; it is later than MSA, showing later
major revisions of that draft.

   If the relationship of the two manuscripts to each other is complex,
the relationship of each manuscript to the earliest printed editions is
what one might expect. Since MSA was a fair copy, drafted as printer's
copy for a compositor thousands of miles away who could not possibly consult with the author, it would be reasonable to expect that it
should be eminently readable. Such is indeed the case. It would be no
less reasonable to expect that the text printed from it would conform
to it except for compositors' errors. Such is emphatically not the case.
Transcribed here are two pages of MSA, one, leaf 10 (corresponding
approximately to 159.30–160.3), as rough as any leaf in MSA, the other,
leaf 143 (corresponding approximately to 203.9–24) perfectly clean,
without interlineations or cancellations of any sort. Following these two
leaves is a table of variants for the two leaves in the corresponding text

of 1A. (The interested reader may himself check the correspondence in
the T text, based on 1Ea.) It is striking how carelessly written and
punctuated Irving's draft of MSA is, strongly suggesting that he intended
that the compositor make the appropriate corrections. Should an editor
attempt to use MSA as partial copy-text for an edition of *Bracebridge
Hall* (heaven forbid!), he would be hard put to defend his choice.
As we shall see, the problem is exponentially greater with a manuscript
which was definitely not a fair copy.

[MSA leaf 10]

should really separate, let them that stand
on the eminence beware that the chasm is
not mining at their feet. The orders of Society
in all well constituted governments, are
mutually bound together and important to
each other; there can be no such thing in a free
government as a vacuum; and where-ever
one is ⟨made by this⟩ likely to take place by the
drawing off of the rich and intelligent from
the poor, the bad passions of society will rush
in, to fill up the space, and rend the whole
asunder.

⟨Without pretending to disrupt the nature of this
government on general principles of⟩

↑born and↓

Though brought up in a republic
more confirmed in republican principles by
any years observation and experience; yet I
am not insensible to the excellence that may
exist in other forms of government; nor to the
fact that they may be more suitable to the
situation and circumstances of the countries in
which they exist. ⟨Considering the⟩

I have endeavoured rather to look at them
as they are, and to observe how they are calculated to effect the end which they propose.

[MSA leaf 143]

Lady Lillycraft and Miss Templeton were
sitting by an elegant work table near
one of the windows, occupied with some
pretty lady like work. The Captain was
on a stool at his mistress' feet, looking

over some music, and poor phoebe Wilkins, who has always been a kind of
pet among the ladies, but who had
risen vastly in favour with Lady
Lillycraft, in consequence of some
tender confessions, sat in one corner,
with swoln eyes; working pensively
at some of the fair Julia's wedding
ornaments. The silence was interrupted by her ladyship, who suddenly
proposed a task to the Captain. "I am
in your debt said she," for that tale
you read to us the other day; I will
now furnish one, in return, if
you'll read it; and it is just suited
to this swett may morning, for it is
all about love!"

The proposition seemed to delight
every one present. The Captain smiled assent. Her Ladyship rang for
her page in green, and dispatched

Variants in the texts of MSA, leaves 10 and 143 (Alderman Library)
and the corresponding texts of 1A, II, 15.18–16.16, and II, 139.14–140.16.
A caret ∧ indicates lack of a punctuation mark.

		MSA leaf 10	1A, II, 15.18–16.16
line	3	Society [?]	society
	4	governments,	governments∧
	5	together∧	together,
	7	where-ever	wherever
	15	years	year's
	15	experience;	experience,
		MSA leaf 143	1A II, 139.14–140.16
line	4	lady like	ladylike
	8	ladies;	ladies,
	16	Captain	captain
	17	debt∧	debt,"
	19	one,	one∧
	21	swett	sweet
	21	may	May
	24	Captain	captain
	26	dispatched	despatched

The physical difficulties Irving experienced in the publication of the Murray 1822 edition (1E) have been discussed in the Introduction. Irving, just getting over an illness, was troubled by what amounted to a deadline for the text, both to preserve his copyright and to cash in on the popularity of *The Sketch Book;* he was juggling revision of various states of the manuscript and the printed text simultaneously and probably worrying about getting a revised text to Ebenezer for the publication of 2A. As a result, there is no clear point at which an editor can say, "Here is the finished text of *Bracebridge Hall.*" The text seems to have been in a constant flux from March through May of 1822, with heavy revision being made by Irving in manuscript, and in proof (which is no longer extant), and continued into 1Eb and 2A, and possibly even through 1Ec and 2E. Furthermore, his revisions and corrections were extremely uneven, ranging from what seems to have been casual proof-reading of some sketches or passages to almost total rewriting of others. Therefore it is extremely difficult to generalize about the relationship of MSE to 1E.

Suggestive of this range of treatment of the various segments of MSE and 1E are the three transcriptions of pages of manuscript reproduced here. A list of variants has been appended. These pages were chosen as typical of good manuscript—manuscript with few or no substantive variants. A total of 206 pages of 1E text was set from such good manuscript—interestingly enough, 180 pages in Volume I, only 26 in Volume II. The criterion for this division was solely the number of substantive variants between MSE and 1E—an average of slightly more than one per page of 1E text was perhaps arbitrarily given this classification. The curious disparity in the number of pages of good manuscript in the two volumes is only partly explained by the amount of manuscript surviving for the two volumes. Volume I has extant manuscript corresponding to 297 pages of 1E text out of a total of 393 pages, while Volume II has extant manuscript for only 139 pages of 1E text out of a total of 404 pages. Even allowing for the fact that more of MSE for Volume II than for Volume I is missing, it seems that Irving corrected the second volume in proof much more heavily than he did the first.

The number of accidental variants recorded on these sample pages of MSE is roughly typical of both good manuscript and bad, although leaf 53 has more than usual. Six to eight accidentals per page of 1E text seems typical of MSE generally, as it is of MSA. The number is important to the question of choice of copy-text for this edition. To quote the CEAA *Statement of Editorial Principles,* "if it is shown that an author exerted closest control over and paid closest attention to both his accidentals and substantives in heavily-revised galleys (now missing) which intervene between first print and a 'fat' manuscript filled with

cancellations—and regarded these galleys as his 'fair-copy manuscript'—
then first print will be chosen as copy-text, with regard to the potential
authority of accidentals in the manuscript." The case in favor of first
print as copy-text could hardly be clearer, it seems. MSE is a "fat"
manuscript indeed in comparison to MSA, yet both received substantial
correction of accidentals at the hands of their compositors. Irving paid
little attention to punctuation and capitalization, assuming that his
eccentricities would be regularized by compositor or editor, while he
devoted his full attention to revision of substantives.

[MSE leaf 52]

The Widows retinue.
"Little dogs and all!"
Lear

In giving an account of the arrival of
Lady Lillycraft at the Hall I ought to have
mentioned the entertainment which I derived
from witnessing the unpacking of her
carriage, and the disposing of her ⟨motley⟩
retinue. There is something extremely
amusing to me in the number of factitious
⟨comforts and conveniences⟩ wants; the loads
of imaginary ⟨comforts and⟩ conveniences, but
real incumbrances, with which the luxu-
                    ↑burthen↓
rious are apt to ⟨encumber⟩ themselves. I like
to watch the whimsical stir and display
⟨in⟩ about one of ⟨the⟩ ↑these↓ petty progresses. The
number of robustious footmen and retainers
of all kinds bustling about, with looks of
infinite gravity and importance, to do
almost nothing. The number of heavy

[MSE leaf 53]

trunks and ⟨packs and⟩ parcel and ban-
boxes belonging to my lady; and the solicitude exhibited about some ⟨odd⟩ humble
odd looking box, by my ladies maid. The
cushions piled in the carriage to make a
soft seat still softer, and to prevent the
dreaded possibility of a jolt. The smelling
bottles, the cordials; the baskets of biscuit

and fruit, the ⟨*illegible* novels *illegible*⟩ new
publications; all ⟨providently⟩ provided to
guard against hunger ⟨leisure [?]⟩ fatigue or
ennui; the led horses to vary the mode
of travelling, and all this preparation and
parade to move perhaps some very
good for nothing personage about a little
↑space↓
⟨scrap⟩ of earth! ⟨It reminds me of
the vast bustle and painstaking of the
⟨*illegible* usually⟩ redoubtable Balzoni
and his myrmidons of the nile; to
transport some egyptian mummy; or
perhaps to trundle off some mutilated
statue at the rate of a few inches in
an hour.⟩
   I do not mean to apply the latter part
of these observations to Lady Lillycraft for whose

[MSE leaf 54]

simple kind heartedness I have a very
great respect, and who is really a most
amiable and worthy being. I cannot
refrain, however, from mentioning some of
the motley retinue she has brought with
                                   ↑the↓
her; and which indeed bespeak ⟨*that*⟩   ever-
flowing kindness of her nature, which requires her to be surrounded with objects on
which to lavish it.
   In the first place her ladyship has a
pamperd coachman, with a red face and
cheeks that hang down like dew-laps. He
evidently domineers over her a little with
respect to the fat horses; and only drives
out when he thinks proper, and when he
thinks it will be good for the cattle.
   She has a favourite page to attend
upon her person. A handsome boy of about
twelve years of age but a mischievous ⟨varlet⟩
varlet; very much spoiled and in a fair
way to be good for nothing. He is dressed in

Variants in the texts of MSE, leaves 52–54 (Columbia University Library) and the corresponding texts of 1Ea, I, 73–75.9. A caret ∧ indicates the lack of a punctuation mark. See T 33.1–36.

MSE leaf 52		1Ea I, 73
line	1	Widows	Widow's
	5	Hall∧	Hall,
	10	wants;	wants,

MSE leaf 53		
line	1	parcel	parcels
	1	ban-/boxes	bandboxes
	4	odd looking	odd-looking
	4	ladies	lady's
	4	maid. The	maid; the
	7	jolt. The	jolt; the
	7	smelling / bottles∧	smelling-bottles,
	7	cordials;	cordials,
	10	fatigue∧	fatigue,
	13	move∧ perhaps∧	move, perhaps,
	14	good for nothing	good-for-nothing
	16–23	It . . . hour. [Sentence lightly canceled with one vertical line.]	*omitted*

MSE leaf 54		
line	6	which∧ indeed∧	which, indeed,
	10	place∧	place,
	11	pamperd	pampered
	16	∧good for the cattle.∧	"good for the cattle."
	18	person. A	person: a
	20	varlet:	varlet,

These sample leaves average a few more accidental variants per page than the sample pages transcribed from MSA, though they are not as legible as the MSA pages. Once again we might expect that the variants between manuscript and printed text represent compositors' errors; but as was the case with MSA, such a conclusion is doubtful at best. The MSE variants in these pages have as little to recommend them as did the MSA variants reproduced above. Indeed, they have less authority, since Irving did have the opportunity with 1E to review compositors' changes and did not choose to correct them to his MSE form. In fact, none of these

of an "airy nothing" I called to mind
the fine description of an echo in Webster's
Dutchess of Malfy:

— "Yond side o' th' river lies a wall
Piece of a cloister, which in my opinion
Gives the best echo that you ever heard;
So plain in the distinction of our words,
That many have supposed it a Spirit
That answers."

I was startled from this musing by a
prodigious bawling, shouting and yelping.
A flight of crows, alarmed by the
approach of our forces, had suddenly rose from
a meadow; a cry was put up by the
rabble rout on foot, "now chrissty!"
now is your time chrissty!" The old man
partly in a pet and partly in a flurry had
slipt of the hood from the falcon; and
away flew the crows. and away soared
the hawk. Vol. I. P 193

My attention however, was attracted
for a time to the party in the meadow

possible emendations of the 1E text has been made for the T text, although all, including the less justifiable ones, were considered. But decisions to emend or not to emend are quite separate from the larger question of choice of copy-text. The editor has the right, indeed the obligation, to emend copy-text from precopy-text variants where the evidence suggests that the earlier text has been misconstrued or corrupted by the compositor. To choose such an early, obviously uncorrected text as these pages of manuscript represent as copy-text, however, would be to ignore the evidence of the manuscript itself that Irving intended his manuscript to be corrected extensively for apostrophes, hyphens, commas, spelling, and even such grammatical niceties as parallelism, subject-verb agreement, and the like. That his compositors did not always succeed, and in fact sometimes even compounded his grammatical felonies, complicates the editor's problem of emendation not a little, but is essentially irrelevant to the question of choice of copy-text. This sampling of manuscript pages shows that even Irving's good manuscript is a poor choice for copy-text; it follows that bad manuscript is a worse choice.

The last piece of evidence in this series, the facsimile of the leaf from MSE bearing the compositor's mark for the beginning of gathering O, page 193 of Volume I of 1E, illustrates how widely divergent MSE can be from the text of 1E and how many of these changes were made in page proof. Virtually all of the paragraph following the quotation from *The Duchess of Malfi* was rewritten: some details were added, others removed, some to disappear, others to be worked into other parts of the chapter. A comparison with 78.7–33 will show how much was changed. The revisions were so extensive that the compositor's mark noting the beginning of the new gathering is out of place by more than half a page in 1E. Such extensive revision, amounting virtually to a rewriting of the text in proof, was going on at the same time as revision of other parts of the manuscript. All of this shows how busy Irving was during this period and helps to explain why he was more careless than usual about his accidentals.

It is also interesting to observe the kinds of changes that Irving made between the rewriting of MSE and the correcting of proof. Once again, they suggest an author harried to the limits of his endurance and busy not with periods and semicolons but with the correction of what would have appeared as monumental blunders of style and narration. The page above is a good case in point; the text of the MSE segment is perhaps comprehensible, but certainly graceless in comparison to the finished text of 1E. An even more striking example occurs in the chapter "May-Day." Part of the text of MSE describing the encounter between Master Simon and General Harbottle and the village radical reads this way in MSE (see 198.27–30):

The honest
⟨country folks⟩ ↗village logicians↗ ⟨*illegible*⟩ could make no stand
against him↗ especially as he was seconded by his proselytes↗
when to their great joy
Master Simon and the General got embroiled in the discussion. I saw that ⟨Master⟩
the former rather entered into it with an
ill grace, from which I ⟨concluded⟩ ↑was persuaded↑ that he
must before this have had a brush with
the radical;

The cancellations and interlineations in MSE are all stylistic, evidence
of Irving's care for detail—the telling irony of "village logicians" is
preferable to the more innocuous "country folks"; the added clause about
the radical's proselytes and the revised verb at the end are certainly
unexceptionable as stylistic revisions. Unfortunately, they are to this
passage but cosmetic brushes in a narrative that needed major surgery.
Only two chapters before this one, in "A Village Politician," Geoffrey
Crayon had already made essentially the same comment about Master
Simon's unwillingness to tangle with the radical in argument, and had
himself observed this earlier "brush with the radical." Irving noticed
the repetition in proof and corrected it:

The
honest village logicians could make no stand
against him, especially as he was seconded by
his proselytes; when to their great joy, Master
Simon and the general came drifting
down into the field of action. I saw that
Master Simon was for making off, as soon as
he found himself in the neighbourhood of this
fireship; [1E, II, 104–105]

The correction is a particularly good one, continuing the metaphor
of a naval engagement that Irving had introduced in the first encounter with the radical two chapters before, where Master Simon was
described as "sheering off" from the encounter.
    One could easily multiply the examples. The text of *Bracebridge Hall*
is long and complex, with a plethora of characters; the writing and
revising of the text, on the other hand, was feverish and disjointed.
It is to be expected that confusion and inconsistency should be the
result, and it is understandable why Irving's attention was directed to
matters far more crucial to his reputation as a writer than consistency

in spelling, punctuation, and capitalization. Especially during that critical final examination of proofs must his eye have been on the gross blunder rather than the delicate nuance. In such a state he was willing to pass with his tacit approval any number of accidental variants from his own admittedly eccentric pointing and spelling.

Thus, in spite of the fragmentary state of MSE, the hurried and doubtless disjointed correction it received in proof, and the wide disparity of correction of various parts of it, certain conclusions may be drawn about its relationship with 1E. To begin with, it is unquestionably a "fat" manuscript, including cancellations and additions dating back to its origin and preceding the fair-copy draft of MSA. It is both a first draft and printer's copy, and as printer's copy it served to produce page proofs which were often very different from the finished pages of 1E. Therefore, in terms of substantive variants it must be viewed as only a preliminary document of Irving's intention for *Bracebridge Hall*, in virtually all instances superseded by the corrections made in proof as evidenced by the published text of 1E. As to its authority for accidentals, although no indications exist that Irving paid any attention to correction of accidentals in proof, the sheer number of accidental variants between MSE and 1E argues strongly that he gave tacit approval to whatever changes in pointing, spelling, and capitalization were made by John Murray's compositors. Thus, even the good manuscript segments would seem a poor choice for copy-text. If Irving did not attempt to revise his proofs to correspond to the punctuation, spelling, and capitalization of his manuscript, neither did he revise such matters with any consistency between the creation of his first draft and the delivery of copy to the printer.

To recapitulate, all versions of the text before the appearance of 1E on May 23, 1822, are best regarded as precopy-text. MSA, widely variant from the text of MSE, even more so from the text of 1E, represents an artificial fixing of the text perpetrated upon it by the needs of international copyright and the commercial necessities generated by the success of *The Sketch Book*. The same is true for 1A, except that it has even less authority, since Irving had no control over its appearance. MSE, composed before MSA was drafted from it and revised extensively afterward, has unquestionably more authority than either, but is itself little more than a draft of the text as Irving later corrected it in proofs and less close, therefore, to Irving's intention than is the text of 1E. Unless the corrected proofs of 1E should come to light, no form earlier than the first printing of 1E can possibly claim priority as copy-text.

Modern principles of bibliography presume that under these circumstances the earliest printed text ought to serve as copy-text. But, once again, the circumstances surrounding *Bracebridge Hall* appear to be exceptional. It is obvious that Irving made the one change that distinguishes 1Eb from 1Ea, the paragraph added at 311.15–28. It is known that he then sent the sheets of this text to America where they were published as 2A, thus making 1Eb and 2A the earliest texts of the paragraph. One must also consider that ambiguous statement in the letter to Brevoort of June 11, 1822, quoted in the Introduction; that he "was enabled to improve the work while printing," especially in the light of the many variants appearing in 1Ec and 2E.[11] Did Irving indeed continue to correct the text of *Bracebridge Hall* after he had gone over the proofs, while the book was in press? Or, did he make extensive corrections to the sheets he transmitted to America, thus making that text a first printing of sorts? Should a text produced obviously later than 1Ea be considered as copy-text under these circumstances? Once again the questions are crucial, and may be answered only after a thorough examination of the texts in question.

Since 1Ea and 1Eb are identical except for the added paragraph in 1Eb, and 1Ea clearly precedes 1Eb, 1Ea should be preferred as copy-text for all the text except the single addition. The text of 1Eb should be preferred as copy-text for the added paragraph over the text of 2A, since Irving had the opportunity to oversee the printing of 1Eb when he added the paragraph, but could exercise no control over the printing of 2A. 2A was set in an American house style, and dozens of errors crept into it. Some corrections were made to its text as well, but these were almost certainly not authorial. Already mentioned are the "American" corrections "Gansevoort" for "Gansevort" (290.29), and "Pollopol's" for "Polopol's" (287.11), neither of which found their way into any succeeding English texts, and were therefore almost certainly changed by the American compositors of 2A. Even more striking is the variant "Cobbett" for "Cobbet," corrected in 2A (199.17). But both MSA and MSE read "Cobbet." The most crucial point, however, is at 172.23 where 2A, like 1Ea–b, reads "goals" and 1Ec–2E read "gaols." It must be concluded that 2A was indeed set from a copy of 1Ea, marked by Irving with the added paragraph (and possibly the one added phrase at 3.9; see Discussions of Adopted Readings), but that all other variants in this text were produced by its American compositors and/or editors.

11. PMI (I, 78) noted enigmatically that "Mr. Irving sent the last proof of *Bracebridge Hall* to press in London, May 11, 1822. He had made great alterations and additions as the work was printing." May 11 is one month earlier than the date of the letter to Brevoort, which mentions three weeks as the launching date for the book, but PMI seems no more precise in his distinction between printing and composition than Irving was. The exact details remain unresolvable by this kind of evidence.

The only other contribution by Irving was not to the text. That is the apologetic "Advertisement to the Second Edition," printed only in the second American edition and its 1826 reprint.

Therefore, on the one occasion on which it is known that Irving looked again at the text of *Bracebridge Hall* after it appeared in sheets, he did not extensively correct it. If he did not make the corrections on the sheets which he sent to Ebenezer and they were not adopted for 2A, it seems reasonable to suppose that he did not make the corrections that appeared in 1Ec, at least not at this time. Thus, the corrections for 1Ec must have been made after the copy for 2A had been mailed, and the evidence that suggests that Irving did at least examine the sheets for the 2A changes does not apply to the 1Ec corrections. There is then no external evidence that the corrections for 1Ec are authorial. Is there any internal evidence? At least twenty variants may be ascribed to 1Ec, seven in Volume I, thirteen in Volume II. It seems unlikely the author would be involved in changes so minor.

T	1Ea–b	1Ec
9.29	pannel	panel
28.9	ladies	ladies'
40.5	alwaies	alwaies.
42.19	Tippo	Tippoo
112.41	believe	believed
119.33	son;"	son,"
150.34	intellects,	intellects.
172.23	goals	gaols
199.17	Cobbet	Cobbett
221.16	Tibbets's	Tibbetses
229.38	Heirarchie	Hierarchie
237.41	Tibbets's	Tibbetses
258.6	be	he
267.8	Knypper-	Knipper-
275.21	haunted house	Haunted House
288.18	Anthony	Antony
291.25	Knypperhausen's	Knipperhausen's
292.33	Spiegle	Spiegel
297.40	scull	skull
310.39	*."	*?"

If Irving was not involved in the few minor corrections in 1Ec, might he not have been called in for the heavier correction they seemed to provoke, the changes which led to 2E. Here the evidence of Irving's manuscripts suggests, although certainly not conclusively, that he took little or no part in the revision. If all cases be excluded where the manuscript form is either ambiguous or different from both 1Ec and 2E, we find that of all variants in 1Ea–1Ec and 2E which have manuscript equivalents, slightly more than half of the 1Ea readings follow the manuscripts. The evidence is, then, inconclusive. But, of the 2E readings with manuscript support, all but seven are the same type: the name "Ready Money Jack," almost always capitalized and without a hyphen before "Money" in the manuscripts. Thus, only seven 2E readings are supported by the manuscripts if this one case is excluded, while five times as frequently the manuscripts support 1Ea readings. The evidence remains inconclusive, but seems to suggest that Irving probably did not have a hand in the revision, beyond perhaps suggesting that his punctuation and capitalization of Ready Money Jack's name be followed.

Much more significant is the ratio of accidentals to substantives. Although 2E includes hundreds of variants and resettings of type, only five of these could be considered substantive, and they are all changes of only a letter or two: indeed, it is questionable whether they affect the meaning enough to be considered substantive.

T	1Ea–c	2E
65.12	pailing	paling
65.30	Tibbets	Tibbetses
84.27	yielded	yields
128.20	woods	wood
174.35	Simon's	Simon

Even keeping in mind that revisions this late in publication are not likely to be major whether made by the author or not, since resetting is difficult if the spacing is changed much, this is very little evidence upon which to build a hypothesis of authorial intervention. Irving may have suggested some of them, but that is not to say that he authorized the changes *in toto*. That is, this disguised second edition could only be considered as a possible copy-text if it were demonstrable that Irving continued correction from his manuscripts consistently through the earlier states (as we presume he did in the case of the added paragraph in 1Eb) with the intention of perfecting or completing his own intentions for the text. More than a reasonable doubt intrudes upon such a supposition in this case; therefore, 2E may not be considered as copy-text, although it may be quite possible and desirable to emend from it, since *in part* it may serve to bear out Irving's final intentions.

The one text that Irving did correct and did see through printing after 1822 was the Author's Revised Edition (ARE). Although bibliography since Greg's seminal "The Rationale of Copy-Text" has turned away from the old-fashioned practice of preferring the later edition to the text closest to the author's hand, it would seem to be true that for some authors at least one ought not to dismiss out of hand a late edition revised by the author. If a case can be made for choice of copy-text from the author's latest text rather than his earliest, surely *Bracebridge Hall* must be a prime instance. We have seen how correction of the manuscripts and early editions was ongoing and undefinitive; with the ARE we clearly have a conscious effort on the part of the author to fix his text for posterity. If 1Ea is to be the preferred copy-text, it must justify itself no less against this late challenger than the earlier ones.

The argument against the choice of the ARE as copy-text rests on three grounds: biographical, philosophical, and theoretical. As was mentioned in the Introduction, Irving's work on the ARE was feverish—no less so, we might assume, than his hectic three months of labor under John Murray's eye for 1Ea. We have his own word for the "fagging of the pen" involved. It is also well known that his major interest during this period was not the works like *Bracebridge Hall* which had been in print for years and which had already achieved a measure of success, but the new works like *Mahomet* which probably could only be published under the protective coloration and support of the other volumes in a uniform edition. Under these circumstances it might be expected that Irving's care with works like *Bracebridge Hall* would be less than perfect. Major revision, including extensive rewriting, would be unlikely. Indeed, comparison of the texts indicates that this was precisely the case. As was mentioned above, he seems to have taken a copy of one of the American texts of *Bracebridge Hall* and marked it up for the printers without even noticing that it was corrupt at a number of points; he apparently skimmed it more and more superficially as he went along, noticing few of the corruptions of Volume II; and he made no effort at all toward any major changes. In all, his work on the text of *Bracebridge Hall* seems superficial and perfunctory. Here was no Henry James, raising the technique of revision to the level of the art of creation; here was a professional engaged in a kind of hackwork, doing enough to justify the rubric "Author's Revised Edition," but little more.

The philosophical argument against the choice of ARE as copy-text was broached at the beginning of this introduction. The writing of *Bracebridge Hall* was done by a man who had been a guest of Sir Walter Scott, an intimate of Tom Moore, a frequenter of Samuel Rogers' soirees. He had denigrated the first American appearance of the work with a corrupt text, made fun of the fulsome praises of American critics, but danced attendance on men like William Gifford, the savage reviewer of the *Quarterly*. The text of *Bracebridge Hall* is unrelieved with anything American until "Dolph Heyliger," and that suffers by comparison with "Rip Van Winkle" and "The Legend of Sleepy Hollow." But when Irving set out to revise the work for the ARE he was once again in residence in America, had written three books about the West, was about to begin what he considered as his crowning work, the *Life of Washington,* and needed to satisfy an American editor, American critics, and an American reading public. It is a wonder under the circumstances that the work managed to retain as much of its English flavor as it did. What changes of form were made were almost always unfortunate, sometimes ludicrous. Perhaps a single example will illustrate this point. The spelling change from "reliques" to "relics" is more than a change of form, English to American; "Family Reliques" has a certain dignity in the context of this volume, "Family Relics" is absurd. One could perhaps justify adopting the American forms of ARE if the English forms of 1E had been forced upon Irving by his English printers, but such is definitely not the case. Both MSE and MSA, though somewhat inconsistent, overwhelmingly favor English forms.

The theoretical argument against adoption of ARE as copy-text is the familiar one of Greg's "The Rationale of Copy-Text." This is the argument that a distinction should be made between accidental and substantive variants, variants of form and variants of meaning, and that the editor should follow the earliest available text for accidental variants. The theory is peculiarly appropriate to the case of *Bracebridge Hall;* since, as we have seen, Irving paid little attention to his accidentals in his manuscripts and his earliest printings, how much less attention must he have paid when revising for the ARE? The selection of ARE as copy-text would affect only the treatment of accidentals; however striking or valuable the substantive variants of ARE may be, the matter is not relevant to this question, since late variants may be emended. As a matter of fact, the indication from collation of the texts is that Irving paid almost no attention whatsoever to his accidentals for ARE. The one passage in the text where it is likely that he did change some punctuation was at 104.4–12, where a paragraph in indirect address is changed to direct address, necessitating some changes in punctuation. Such changes in accidentals may, also, of course, be emended.[12] In sum, then, nothing in the text of the ARE form of *Bracebridge Hall* favors any kind of treatment thoretically different from that urged by Greg, while the events surrounding the creation of the ARE text and the different philosophy it represents argue against its adoption as copy-text.

12. See Greg, "Rationale of Copy-Text," pp. 26, 29–30.

PRINCIPLES OF EMENDATION

Since 1Ea is to be copy-text, along with the paragraph added at 311:15–28 from 1Eb, the next problem is that of emendation. Emendations may be considered from four sources: first, MSE; second, MSA and 1A; third, 1Ec and 2E; and fourth, ARE. Emendations made for the T text without sources, i.e., solely on the authority of the T editor, are chiefly regularizations and will be discussed below. The other texts of *Bracebridge Hall* have no authority. Their relationship to the 1Ea text is indicated for specific emendations and rejected substantive variants in the Discussions of Adopted Readings, but no emendations have been made on their authority alone.

The same reasons that were cited in opposition to the choice of MSE as copy-text make it a fertile field for possible emendations of 1Ea. A "fat" text, including readings from the beginning of the composition of *Bracebridge Hall*, hundreds of cancellations and interlineations, careless handwriting and devil-may-care punctuation and spelling, it was a compositor's nightmare. Small wonder that from time to time the compositor misread Irving's hand, or that Irving failed to restore readings from his manuscript, when so much original composition was being done in proof. Still, one does not emend casually from a manuscript so much at variance from a text which was supervised by the author. Each variant must be weighed on its own merits; yet certain principles of emendation or rejection of emendations inevitably arise. Reasons for the rejection or acceptance of individual variants are given in the Discussions of Adopted Readings. At this point the general principles only will be discussed.

The first principle of emendation from MSE concerns the variation in the closeness of the manuscript to the text. The relative quantities of good manuscript and bad have already been mentioned. It follows that variants in good manuscript are much more likely to be adopted than variants in manuscript which is totally different from the text of 1Ea. Though the number of accidental variants is so great that MSE remains a poor choice for copy-text even where it is fairly close to the text of 1Ea, the editor would be unwise not to consider the possibility that substantive variants which are scribal errors might slip by Irving in the correction of proof. Very few such emendations have been made,[13] but the manuscript has been scoured for such variants; it may be confidently asserted that these are all that exist.

A second principle of emendation from MSE has been the assertion of consistent forms by Irving in manuscript over either inconsistent or

---

13. Examples may be found at 26.22; 31.13; 61.35; 98.7; and 223.18.

otherwise variant forms in 1Ea. That is, if Irving spelled, punctuated, or capitalized a form one way frequently enough so that it might be assumed that the form was preferred by him, variants in the form of 1Ea text have been emended to correspond to the manuscript form. The clearest example is his treatment of "by the bye," which is always spelled with the final "e" in MSE and MSA, and always found with the final "e" omitted in 1Ea. "Morrice" in "morrice dancer" is another constant form in MSE which is inconsistently rendered in 1Ea, and has been restored to the MSE form. On the other hand, Irving was inconsistent with "holiday," obviously preferring some form of "holyday," but not consistently enough so that one could confidently assert that one form represented a clear preference. In this case the usual 1Ea reading, "holiday," has been adopted. Perhaps the most striking example of this kind of emendation has been the treatment of the many uses of "Ready Money Jack." The evidence of MSE is slightly equivocal; "Ready Money Jack" is by far the preferred form there, but there are traces of a hyphen from time to time between "Ready" and "Money," and Irving's capital M's are not always distinguishable from his small m's. Still, more than half the appearances of the name in MSE are as "Ready Money Jack," while there seems no consistency in the manuscript appearance of other forms of the name, "Ready-money Jack," "Ready-Money Jack," and "ready-money Jack," to suggest that Irving settled on another form consistently at any point in the composition. Virtually all instances in MSA are "Ready Money," and 1A was set fairly consistently in that form. Further corroboration of that form comes from the attempt at correction in 2E, if indeed Irving had any hand in that. On balance, it seemed that "Ready Money Jack" was the form Irving preferred, and the T text has been emended accordingly.

A third principle has been followed in one recurring situation in which a compositor of 1E has rather arbitrarily imposed a regular system of punctuation where Irving used more varied punctuation. This was the case with thirty-eight colons in the copy-text which have been emended to commas, periods, or semicolons, following the text of MSE, often with support from MSA and 1A. This old-fashioned use of the colon in the 1E text begins on page 43 of the first volume and appears sporadically through page 61 of Volume II, then disappears until page 243 and appears, again sporadically, through the remainder of the second volume. Where possible, Irving's punctuation of MSE or MSA has been restored. Where that was equally impossible, or where, in two instances, no manuscript was extant, the punctuation has been regularized and noted. The majority of these colons appear where Irving's own punctuation was a semicolon, and perhaps the compositor misread these for colons, although they seem clear in the manuscript. This kind of emendation has only been made where the colon was inconsistent with Irving's habitual usage.

Other emendations have been made from MSE, but these are the only ones which might represent a principle of emendation—in other words, which fit into a class or type of change. All others, as well as these mentioned above, were weighed on their own merits and found desirable. As for the alternative case, variants in MSE which were rejected, no separate list has been published with this text. As may be seen from the list of variants given above, p. 354, the number of accidental variants in even the best manuscript would yield a staggering list, while often the substantive text of MSE is almost totally different from the form printed in 1E. It is hoped that the examples shown will indicate adequately the nature of MSE in comparison to the 1E text.

It has been noted that MSA and the text set from it, 1A, represent an intermediate stage in the development of the text of *Bracebridge Hall*, and therefore have almost no value in terms of establishing what was Irving's final intention for his text. In general, then, variants peculiar to MSA and 1A and not found in 1E and later texts carry very little authority. The exception to this rule might occur where the text changes very slightly in all forms of the manuscripts and the early editions. In those instances we might expect that a finished draft, intended for publication, might possibly carry more authority than the earlier draft of a manuscript, not nearly so clearly written, which was subsequently marked up further and then handed over to a compositor to be set in type. One might carry this line of reasoning even a bit further. In the case of the chapter epigraphs and quotations in the text, might not Irving have given even more care to his American manuscript than he did subsequently to MSE? After all, in this case he would be giving a final form to these texts, and he knew, of course, that he would not be able to supervise the setting of his manuscript or to correct proofs. Surely under these circumstances the fair copy MSA might have more authority than the less clear MSE. Then, as has been shown, with the great number of corrections made for 1E, it is possible that Irving neglected to correct his proofs of such passages in 1E as carefully as he had drafted his fair copy of MSA of the same texts. This is all extremely hypothetical, but it is justified by a number of readings in MSA and 1A which seem preferable to the corresponding texts in MSE and 1E. Most of these are accidentals, but one interesting substantive occurs which tends to support this hypothesis. At 19.12, Irving quotes Adam's speech from *As You Like It* (II, iii, 70) incorrectly in MSE and 1E, substituting "love" for "truth." The passage appears correctly in 1A. Although MSA is not extant for this part of the text, it seems likely that Irving did transmit the passage correctly in manuscript, but neglected to correct his error in MSE.

Only one other substantive emendation was made solely on the basis of MSA and 1A, at 267.17, and one reading from these texts supports a variant reading from MSE at 223.18. But many accidentals have been adopted from MSA, particularly when there has been a considerable agreement in the texts of MSA, MSE, and 1A, and when the MSE text is heavily canceled. And, since the entire MSA for Volume I is not extant, on some occasions the 1A reading has been adopted over 1E, usually when MSE supports 1A, but on occasion also where MSE is not extant. The largest number of the latter case were emendations of the arbitrary colons mentions above. The most striking example of an emendation based on 1A and supported by MSE is at 20.12, "naïveté" for "nature." MSE is equivocal—the word there surely looks more like "nature" than "naïveté," but could be read "naivete" without accents. Since "naïveté" is the 1A reading, and seems preferable in the context, we might assume that Irving wrote the word more clearly in the missing MSA. A parallel emendation occurs at 57.19, where the 1A reading casts suspicion on the 1E text, which was set from a nearly illegible MSE text.

Since there are more than a thousand substantive variants and many thousands of accidental variants, between the MSA and 1A texts and the 1E texts, in almost all of which the MSA and 1A form is inferior, no effort has been made to indicate all of these variants. To do so would require nearly one hundred pages of text listing variants ranging from a single word to passages extending over many pages. To allow the reader the opportunity to gauge the kinds of changes Irving made between the composition of MSA and its printed form in 1A and his finished text in 1E, two appendices have been added to this work. The first is a reprinting of the 1A text of the opening essay of this volume, "The Author." This chapter was chosen as a typical example; some parts of the book have many fewer variants; most have many more. It is intended only as a representative selection illustrating the various kinds of emendations made between the composition of MSA and the printing of 1E. A second appendix lists an extremely selective group of variants between 1A and 1E on the basis of their literary interest, and insights they present about Irving's methods of composition. It should be noted that these few examples are culled from well over a thousand substantive variants and are in no way particularly representative.

Emendations based on the text of 1Ec and 2E have been made, in general, when the forms of the later states are supported by the manuscripts, are obvious corrections of typographical errors even when no manuscript is extant, or recommend themselves on the grounds of consistency with forms generally preferred by Irving in texts over which he unquestionably had some control. In other words, they have not been treated as authorial, although they have been used to support editorial decisions based on either secure texts or common sense. In practice, this means that Irving's obsolete spelling "camelion," although not common since the seventeenth century, has not been emended to the 2E form, "chameleon," since the obsolete spelling is supported by MSE. The same is true for "pannel" at 9.29 and "pannelling" at 222.31, since the double "n" spelling is supported by MSA. On the other hand, "Tippoo" is adopted from the 1Ec and 2E texts, although no manuscript exists, since that use conforms to Irving's practice. "Goals" at 172.23 has been emended to "gaols," the 1Ec and 2E form, although no manuscript exists, simply because it was undoubtedly what Irving meant to write. For the same reason "believed" at 117.41 has been adopted instead of "believe," obviously a slip on Irving's part or the printer's.

Other emendations of accidentals from 1Ec and 2E are even harder to categorize. In general, again, these two later states of 1E are not considered authorial and emendation has been made only where the form of the later states is supported by some kind of external evidence. The case of "Ready Money Jack" has already been discussed; other examples of preferences of one form over another based on the support of manuscript include "hostler" at 51.16 in the copy-text and in MSE, preferred to "ostler" in 2E; "paling" at 65.12, the spelling in 2E and MSE, preferred to "pailing," the copy-text form; and "old-fashioned," in 2E, preferred over the copy-text "old fashioned" at 24.33 because MSE has just the hint of a hyphen. This part of the editing has been very conservative, on the grounds that the evidence seems to suggest that Irving played little or no part in the revisions of 1Ec and 2E. However, an appendix supplies a list of all accidental variants discovered in 1Ec and 2E which were not adopted and therefore are not present in the List of Emendations. Substantive variants of 1Ec and 2E are supplied in the List of Rejected Substantives. The form of the later state of 1E and the concealed second edition can thus be reconstructed should the reader wish to do so.

Although no emendations have been made from the texts published between 1E and the ARE, these texts have been consulted and their variants are listed among the rejected substantives or are cited in the notes to variants where their texts support an emendation. Additional important examples of rejected substantives are those variants in the American texts which correspond with readings in the ARE. While such a correspondence certainly does not prove that the ARE variants are not authorial, it casts a strong suspicion on them. Two such variants, both with support from MSE, have been adopted (82.26); others, when they are clearly corrections which Irving would approve, have recommended themselves even where there is no manuscript evidence (for example, 287.11, 288.18, 290.29). Variants in the later English and French editions are more clearly a textual dead end; they, too, are listed among the rejected substantives.

The most difficult problem, both theoretical and practical, raised by this edition of *Bracebridge Hall* is the question of emendations from ARE. While the possibility and practicality of choosing ARE as copy-text may be convincingly dismissed on historical, philosophical, and theoretical grounds, the same factors would seem to argue for accepting vast numbers of emendations from ARE. As the events surrounding the revisions for ARE suggest that Irving's revision of his text for ARE was hurried, they also leave no doubt that he did indeed revise, and that his principal interest was in substantive revision. The philosophical argument—that Irving was converting an English text into an American form—is perhaps relevant only to accidentals; the hundreds of substantive revisions made for this edition, once one makes allowance for those generated by the corrupt transmission through the American line of texts, remain convincingly authorial. And the theoretical argument is perhaps the most telling. Greg argued forcefully that where revision by the author is certain, and where the original reading and the later reading are both authorial, "then the later reading should be presumed to be due to revision and admitted into the text, whether the editor himself considers it an improvement or not." His statement is unusually categorical in an essay otherwise moderate when dealing with the details of editing. He modified it only slightly with a statement about "indifferent" variants, which might be "treated as fortuitous and refused admission to the text."[14]

Most variants in ARE are instances of authorial change of original readings. Among these readings, one may make a further division for convenience: revisions which are essentially corrections, and revisions which change the style or form. The first classification presents no problem. Corrections which are indisputably authorial have something like a presumptive right to be adopted. Perhaps the clearest example of this kind of revision is the variant at 227.22, in which Irving excised a duplicate reference to the location of Antony Vander Heyden's pinnace.

Stylistic revisions are not so easily dealt with. One might dismiss them as fortuitous, or indifferent, except that there are so many of them they are clearly not fortuitous, and they are so much of a type they are clearly not indifferent. There are several hundred such variants,

14. Greg, "Rationale of Copy-Text," p. 32.

most of them deletions of words which are stylistically unnecessary or positively redundant. Time and again Irving blue-penciled the extraneous "yet," "that," and "there is," and "there are." He made numerous substitutions of "who" and "whom" for "that," and dropped redundant "froms" before "thence" and "whence." Evidently he was making a coherent effort to tighten his style and to make his text more modern and graceful. To the modern ear they are distinct improvements.

Perhaps paradoxically, it is just that aura of modernity such emendations have that makes the editor uneasy when he contemplates adopting them for a modern text. Since they are closer to his own usage, he suspects that he prefers them for the wrong reason. As Bowers writes, "One may flatly assert that any text that is modernized can never pretend to be scholarly, no matter at what audience it is aimed."[15] May not this injunction to the modern editor be applied to the author's own modernizing of his text if he had no other purpose in mind? Might not Irving's own emendations for ARE be no less guilty than a modernized text in the matter of destroying the characteristics of the original composition? Then too there is the transatlantic nature of these revisions. If they are aimed at creating an American text out of the English original, might not the result be such a bastardization that they must be rejected to retain the English flavor? Certainly there is no question here of a right form and a wrong. Deletion of "from" before "whence" and "thence," for example, is correct in modern English, but the *OED* gives examples of the redundant "from" through the nineteenth century, including one from Dickens' *Bleak House*, 1853. Other revisions that are matters of usage seem similarly arbitrary. The ARE text is undoubtedly less wordy and more lucid than the text of 1E, but it is no less true of the substantive variants in this text than it is of the accidentals that "nothing [in the earlier text] . . . is likely to cause a present-day reader any difficulty, whereas an attempt at modernization is certain to destroy a number of values of the original."[16]

In some sense, the otherwise useful distinction between substantive and accidental variants seems to break down when it is the author himself who sets out, not to corrupt his own text perhaps, but to deprive it of the distinctive flavor of the original. Under these circumstances, might not the modern editor presume to reject substantive variants which are hardly less formal in nature than spelling, punctuation, and capitalization? If we are to grant the value of retaining the spellings "camelion" and "relique," how justify choosing a prose style which is antithetical to such antiquarianisms? There is, of course, much to be said for eclecti-

15. Bowers, "Principles for Scholarly Editors," p. 223.
16. *Ibid.*

cism in textual editing, and the arguments of Greg and others are most convincing on this point; but it would seem reasonable that with *some* authors and in *some* instances the principles might be altered to allow for retention of a more homogeneous style.

The T text has excluded all such stylistic ARE variants when their only purpose was clearly to make the narration conform more closely to the standards of American English for 1849 than the standards for the period of original composition. This has been done with a full awareness that such a decision is arbitrary, and that another text might reasonably be created adopting all the variants that have here been rejected. Naturally, these variants are listed in the table of Rejected Variants. Thus, a re-creation of the ARE text in all but its accidentals is possible from this volume.

It is fortunate for the editor of *Bracebridge Hall* that modern bibliographical theory imposes a conservative treatment of the text. All of the texts of *Bracebridge Hall* are a mass of inconsistencies of one sort or another; neither in 1822 nor in 1849 did Irving manage a coherent overview of his text to rid it of its inconsistencies of grammar, style, and punctuation. The impulse toward regularization of his forms is almost overwhelming, but once begun, such a task would become endless and, eventually, self-defeating. Who, for instance, would not want to correct the dangling participle that begins the sketch "The School": "Having given the reader a slight sketch of the village schoolmaster, he may be curious to learn something of his school." But of course, if the work is to remain Irving's, such locutions must go uncorrected.

Regularization in this edition has generally been of the most obvious and limited sort, and even then has only been attempted when the evidence is conclusive that Irving himself intended to regularize and failed simply because the work was too long and his efforts were distracted by the press of events. In practice, this amounts to the regularization of a few common forms like "Ready Money Jack," "morrice dancers," "holiday," and the restoration of Irving's manuscript punctuation where other punctuation was inserted by the compositor for no apparent reason. Asterisks after quotations have been regularized to appear after the period. In the copy-text they appear in an unusual location, before the period ending the sentence and often after the quotation mark. This awkward practice seems to have resulted from Irving's inconsistent placing of them in the manuscript, sometimes above the period, sometimes before it, sometimes after it. Reasonable practice has also been followed for the plural and possessive of the Tibbets family name where necessary, since both Irving and Murray's compositor were apparently unable to resolve the question. No restoration was done in the many quotations in the text and epigraphs except where there was clear evidence that the error was typographical or that Irving at one time or another had used the proper form. For the correct forms of quotations the reader is directed to the explanatory notes to this volume.

One constant temptation to regularize was Irving's inconsistent hyphenation of compound words. In the list of end-of-line compound words given in this text, it should be noted that "church-yard," for example, appears in the text both as one word and as a hyphenated compound. Every effort has been made to gather evidence of Irving's preferred practice from manuscript use and use in 1Ea where the word is not at the end of a line, but where his usage was inconsistent, the form of the nearest repetition of the word (or an analogous word) has been adopted. In the case of compound words broken by the end of a line in the T text, the list gives the form used in 1Ea.

In preparing the Twayne text, proof was read six times, and following the last revises a set of the unbound pages of the book was again scanned under the Hinman collating machine against a set of final revised page proof, in an effort to detect and correct any possible new errors resulting from last-minute resettings.

Although the text of the first impression of the Murray 1822 edition is faithfully and critically rendered, and all emendations are recorded, no effort has been made to reproduce the appearance of the copy-text— that is, typographical details like the precise arrangement of the title and half-title pages and other preliminary matter, pagination and lineation, the footnote symbols as they appear in the copy-text, the display capitals and the capitalized text letters following them, and the running heads. Also, in keeping with modern typographical design, periods found in the copy-text at the ends of lines in the title page, after chapter titles and after ascriptions in epigraphs, have been deleted throughout. Except for these details, the Introduction, Textual Commentary, Discussions of Adopted Readings, Lists of Emendations, of Rejected Substantives and of End-of-Line Hyphenation, are designed to provide the reader with all the data needed to reconstruct the copy-text and to follow the steps by which the Twayne text of *Bracebridge Hall* was established.

DISCUSSIONS OF ADOPTED READINGS

In these discussions of decisions to emend or not to emend, the symbols used to designate texts are those given in the key which appears on pages 315–316.

The page and line figures are keyed in each case to a word or words in the text to which the discussion or comment refers. A bracket separates the key word or words from the comment that follows. Most of these discussions concern emendations made for this edition; sources of these emendations may be found in the List of Emendations, pp. 383–392. A smaller number of discussions are of decisions not to emend on the basis of substantive variants in texts after the copy-text; the history of these variants may be found in the List of Rejected Substantives, pp. 393–414. A still smaller group of discussions concern decisions not to emend from postcopy-text accidentals or from portions of the text which are unchanged in all editions. These are listed here:

9.28	treat, has
9.29	sliding-pannel
29.14	lot: a
30.17	rouge.
43.30	intitled
63.13	Bibliographical

t.p.5 Humourists]   All of the English-generated texts except for 1F have the "-*or*" spelling, while the American texts with the exception of ARE have the "-*our*" spelling. However, the word is an exception to the usual distinction between "American" and "English" spellings of "-*or*" or "-*our*" words. It is often spelled on the analogy of its Latin root, "humorosus" by English writers who otherwise use the "-*our*" spelling generally. The T text prints "Humourists" principally because it was Irving's more frequent form in manuscript, and because the only extant manuscript title page (for Volume II of MSA) spells it that way.

t.p.6 A Medley]   This final subtitle for the work appears in all the American texts and in none of the English. Probably its disappearance from the English line of texts is an oversight, perhaps on Irving's part, perhaps on Murray's. But "Medley," however well it describes the contents of *Bracebridge Hall*, and continues the tradition of the earlier *Salmagundi*, has deprecatory overtones. Pope (*Dunciad*, 42) lumps

"Journals, Medleys, Merc'ries, Magazines" among the "monsters" escaped from the "Cave of Poverty and Poetry." Perhaps Murray excised it on the grounds that it slighted the work.

verso of p. following the t.p. ADVERTISEMENT TO THE SECOND EDITION] Printed only in 2A, this advertisement is not properly part of the text, but is reprinted among the rejected substantives, p. 393. The circumstances which made it necessary are discussed above in the Introduction, pp. xxi–xxxi and in the Textual Commentary, pp. 345–359.

3.4 at] This is the first of many slight substantive variants made for 3E25 and continued into 4E. They are often clustered several on a single page (see 40.34, 40.37, and 41.2, for example, all of which were on a single page which was reset for 3E25), and most of them have little effect on the text. Some others are less fortunate (48.14, "mystical" for "mysterious" is a good example), strongly suggesting that they are not authorial. There are enough of them to demonstrate that 4E was set from a late reprinting of 3E, in spite of a few variants between these two editions, and, because most of them are indifferent, to suggest that Irving had no hand in the 1845 Murray text.

3.9 marvel] The American line of texts adds the qualifying phrase, "to my European readers," which is appropriate only to an American audience. Perhaps the addition is authorial, but even so, its parochial nature makes it inappropriate to the English form of the text. For these reasons it is not included in the T text.

3.17 criticism] This is the first of many indifferent or inferior variants found only in the American line of texts. Relatively few are present in the first volume, but their number increases remarkably in Volume II, as Irving became more careless in his correction for ARE. Evidence of his flagging enthusiasm for the job of correcting the errors and changes that crept into 2A may be seen at 8.2 and 13.23, for example, where Irving changed the 2A and 3A "ancient" and "rather as" back to his original "ancientest" and "as rather." That kind of correction is not found in Volume II.

5.21–22 countries," that] This is an obvious improvement, undoubtedly authorial, found only in the ARE text. The parallelism of this clause and the one before it requires the concluding clause found only in ARE. It is likely that the 1E compositor misread Irving's comma for a period.

6.27 poetical] 3E, 4E, and 1F have "political," an inferior reading in the light of the parallel structure of "poetically" and "politically" at 6.35.

8.17 further] Irving seems to have used "further" and "farther" indiscriminately, as far as one can tell from his careless manuscript. The word, here and elsewhere in the text, was set variously by compositors in England and America, with the Americans generally favoring "further" and the English "farther." The T text makes no attempt to regularize, following the copy-text in each use.

9.28 treat, has]   The treatment in the three states of 1E and 2E of the comma here, the variant "aught" for "ought" in the same line, and the spelling of "sliding-pannel" in line 29, illustrate the inconsistency of compositorial changes in the later impressions of the 1822 John Murray edition. In the third impression "pannel" was changed to "panel." This correction was continued into the concealed "second edition" when the comma after "treat" was removed. Meanwhile, the misprint or antiquated spelling of "ought" for "aught" went undetected through all impressions of this edition. The T text preserves the comma splice and the spelling "pannel"—both justified by Irving's known practice— and corrects "ought" to "aught."

9.28 aught]   See discussion above at 9.28.

9.29 sliding-pannel]   See 9.28.

10.1 loiterings]   ARE "wanderings" seems inferior to "loiterings," found in all other texts, yet it might well be authorial. The *OED* reveals no significant change in usage between 1822 and 1849 that might explain the substitution. The T text follows the copy-text on the grounds that the variant is at best indifferent, at worst inferior.

13.11 great-great]   MSE reads "great ⟨great⟩ great," which perhaps accounts for the missing hyphen in the copy-text.

14.15 countries]   MSE reads "countries," as do both the earliest texts, 1A and 1E. That all subsequent texts read "counties" may be coincidental, or may be accounted for by the familiarity of the phrase "sporting counties." The T text follows the copy-text because Irving's intention was unequivocal, based on the manuscript and early textual evidence.

18.12 halls]   There are many interesting facets to the transmission of the text from 1E and 2E to 3E and the texts it generated (1F and 4E). 3E includes many more variants than any other new setting of the text except ARE, where most of the variants are unquestionably authorial. But the evidence for authorial changes in 3E is not convincing. Most of them are indifferent and are exactly the type one might expect from a compositor with a short memory but a good capacity to carry the sense, if not the exact wording, from his original. They tend to come in clusters, as in this case in which the List of Rejected Substantives includes three quite insignificant variants plus this one, "walls" for "halls," in the space of two paragraphs of text. And, when they do affect the sense of the text, as this variant does, they detract rather than add. The 3E sense of servants thronging the walls rather than the halls of fashionable town residences makes little sense.

19.12 truth]   Since "truth" is the correct word in the quotation, from *As You Like It*, II, iii, 69–70, it seems proper to emend the copy-text here, even though "truth" appears in only one text over which Irving had some control, 1A, and the manuscript for that setting is missing.

20.12 naïveté]   "Naïveté" is clearly a superior reading. The word in MSE could be read equally well as "nature" or "naivete," without the accent, but the context indicates that "naïveté" was surely Irving's intention. That he never corrected it is more an indication of the carelessness of his proofreading than a support for the copy-text reading.

21.37 past]   This is the first of several peculiar past tenses (another is at 61.21). The usage is slightly antiquarian, but not unknown in the early nineteenth century, and Irving's preference, as expressed in the manuscripts, is unexceptionable.

24.7 has]   The logic of the sentence and the paragraph requires a past tense rather than the pluperfect of the copy-text and all other texts except 4E and ARE. MSE is indistinct; it could read "has" or "had."

24.33 old-fashioned]   A trace of a hyphen appears in MSE. Irving is somewhat inconsistent in his use of the hyphen in this word. It appears without the hyphen one other time in the copy-text, at 9.16, and five times with it.

26.22 character]   This is a problematic emendation. The copy-text and all later texts read "characters," while MSE and 1A read "character." This segment of MSE is relatively clean and includes few unmarked variants from the 1E text, which is relatively close to the 1A text. The sense of the sentence, "character and habits that have prevailed" seems to be making a distinction between the singular "character" and plural "habits." When all the evidence is weighed, it seems likely that Irving's intention was the singular, "character," but that he missed the correction while reading proof for the Murray edition (rapidly, it will be recalled, *per fretum febris*), and that thereafter the slight change in meaning escaped his notice during the ARE revisions.

28.9 ladies']   The fact that this correction of an obvious error is found only in 1Ec of the three states of the 1822 Murray edition and not in 2E prompts several explanations, none entirely satisfactory. This variant and a few others are inconsistent with the pattern that suggests that 2E was a complete resetting of 1E. But the mass of evidence supports the chronology hypothesized in the Textual Commentary. Furthermore, this variant alone cannot be explained away in terms of multiple resettings; apparently this gathering was reset only once, for this one correction. One can only hypothesize that perhaps several uncorrected sheets remained, which were bound in with the otherwise corrected 2E gatherings, perhaps for the entire impression, perhaps only for a relatively few copies, which just happened to be the ones examined for this edition. No completely satisfactory explanation is available with the evidence currently at hand.

28.12 evidence]   For ARE Irving substituted "evidence" for "the marks," found in all other texts, doubtless because of the ungracefulness of the repetition which follows: "and are scored, and marked with notes of admiration." The T text follows his final intention here, since it appears to be the kind of stylistic change he might well have made in 1822 had he corrected proof more carefully.

29.14 lot: a]   Irving's intention for the punctuation here is doubtful. MSE has "lot—a," but Irving often overused the dash as a full or part stop, trusting to his compositors to supply more appropriate punctuation. The 1A compositor corrected to "lot. A," which is not quite as satisfactory as the 1E "lot: a," since what follows is syntactically dependent upon "her lot." The T text here accepts the colon not authorized by the manuscript, since it fits the sense better than any other punctuation would.

30.10 general]   Here and at 30.13 the copy-text has been emended for consistency; all later occurrences of this form are in lowercase. Irving's capital G is almost indistinguishable from his small g, but MSE would seem to support the T text.

30.17 rouge.]   The precopy-text MSE "rouge on her face" is a tempting emendation, since the sense of this sentence is slightly ambiguous—is the rouge for her hair? But there can be little doubt that Irving canceled the prepositional phrase in proofs.

31.13 to]   The copy-text "the" persists in all following texts, in spite of the fact that MSE clearly reads "to," and is preferable in terms of the sense of the sentence. The misreading by the 1E compositor probably came as a result of the "the" in "half the seats" which is directly below the "to" in MSE.

31.18 Lillycraft]   Apparently Lady Lillycraft was first named Lady Jocelyne; then, for some reason, Irving changed the name. This appearance of the old name in the copy-text is unique, and was not corrected until the ARE; but there is another reference to Lady Jocelyne in 1A (at 1A, I, 70.10), in a passage which is not found in any later text. Both references are undoubtedly slips by Irving and not references to a character otherwise unmentioned.

31.29 Windsor Terrace . . . Kensington Garden]   MSE supports the T emendations; the words are not hyphenated, and, although Irving's capitals are hard to distinguish from initial small g's and t's, here they seem to justify the emendations.

32.14 loyalty]   The ARE "royalty" must be a misprint, since the sentence would require "royalism" or something of that sort to make sense.

34.34 fill]   The grammatical intention of the sentence is debatable, particularly in view of Irving's well-known habit of setting comma splices between verb and subject. In this case the sense seems to call for the plural verb, since it is both the yelping of the dogs and Lady Lillycraft's lamentation that fill the room.

37.15 Ready Money]   All texts except ARE capitalize both words and omit the hyphen at the first appearance of Jack's nickname (at 36.19), but consistency ends there. For this and the next emendation, 39.19, all forms for later texts are listed; these two entries in the List of Emendations represent what we might call the normal distribution of hyphens and capitals. Later entries in the List of Emendations cite only the early texts, except where there is interesting variation in later texts.

38.13 holiday]   Irving was not as consistent in the spelling of this word as he was with "morrice," although it usually appears in MSE as some form of "holyday," sometimes hyphenated, sometimes as two words. Since the 1E compositor regularized all uses except this one to "holiday," the text emends to that form here.

39.34 acquaintances, and]   MSE has no punctuation here. It was probably the compositor, not Irving, who had second thoughts about overpunctuation with the semicolon in 1Ea–c, and who replaced it with a comma, but since Irving is on record as opposing too "highly pointed" texts, the 2E emendation recommends itself to the T text.

43.30 intitled]   What seems to be an inconsistency between this spelling and "entitled" at 48.28 and "intitled" at 52.26 is possibly intended as a distinction in the meaning of the words in different contexts. The T text follows the copy-text in each case.

46.1 dread]   This undoubtedly unintentional error by Irving went uncorrected in all editions. "Dead sea" is so familiar a phrase that it could easily escape attention, though the correct "dread sea" of the T text is a superior reading.

48.5 chiefly]   This is an example of a punctuation variant which seriously affects the meaning of the text. If "chiefly" modifies "promotes," as it must if the comma is present, the sentence, however awkwardly, emphasizes the squire's fondness for storytelling to the point of making it almost an obsession. If it modifies "because," as it must with the comma omitted, the squire's balance of character is restored.

49.32 hard-drinking]   The alteration of this colorful expression to "hardened" in ARE seems particularly unfortunate. One wonders if Irving were under some social pressure from temperance advocates. See 187.38 for another example of an emendation in ARE which was possibly socially induced.

55.35 toper] ARE "topers" must be a misprint, as only the one man is mentioned.

57.19 bearing] MSE could read "bearing," "having," or "leaving," all three of which fit the context more or less well. The T text choice is based on the likelihood that Irving made the word clearer in his (missing) MSA draft than in MSE.

60.15 as] ARE has "as those"; MSE has "as" followed by "those" with a line through it. It is probably coincidental that the ARE form is a return to an earlier rejected form. This case sheds no light on the question raised at 82.25–26, since the passage is not very similar in 1A, and "those" is not present in that text.

61.35 seems] MSE "seems" provides a consistency in tense missing in all later texts.

63.13 Bibliographical] MSE, the copy-text, and all texts in the English line have the capital B, all the American texts including ARE have a small b. The temptation to emend is almost overwhelming, but Irving seems to have intended a specific reference to Dibdin's work, rather than a general bibliographical expedition. The single capital letter hardly serves his case well, but the T text respects his intention, as given unequivocally in MSE.

65.11 Well-scoured] The antiquated spelling of the copy-text is suspect, since MSE may be even more of a misspelling. Furthermore, though MSE looks very much like "scowerd," it might well be "scoured."

65.30 Tibbetses] This is the first of a number of instances of confusion exhibited by Irving and the 1E compositors over the formation of the plural and possessive for the Tibbets family. They have been regularized according to modern usage in the T text, since that seems to be what Irving was groping toward.

74.20 scholars;] There are two forms of MSE for this passage. The earlier one corresponds to the 1A reading, "scholars." with a sentence differing considerably from the 1E text following. The later manuscript is the basis for the T text reading.

74.21 trouble] ARE "labor" was surely inserted by a cliché-bound compositor.

82.25–26 , in fact,] This variant and the one following it on the List of Emendations, while they are insignificant textually, are extremely hard to explain in terms of the genesis of the various later editions of *Bracebridge Hall*. They are the only variants in which MSE, 1A, and all the texts in the American line correspond but are at variance with the text of 1E and the English imprints generated by that edition. Furthermore, MSE shows that the 1E text ("indeed" here, "and to act" below) has been excised and the new text corresponding to the American line interlined. This combination of evidence, assuming it is not a coincidence, would seem to damage the otherwise attractive and necessary hypothesis that 2A was set from sheets of 1E. For, if that were so, why should the texts here vary in the first place, and why should the manuscript have been revised after the setting of 1E to correspond with the American text? No explanation is completely satisfactory, but the fact that this anomaly stands alone suggests that it does not destroy the hypothesis of the setting of 2A. Possible explanations include: (1) Complete coincidence; MSE was marked up by Irving after the setting of 1E and the mailing of the sheets for 2A. Such an explanation seems highly unlikely, since Irving must have had *some* reason for making the corrections. (2) Irving sent MSE to America along with the sheets of 1Ea for the setting of 2A, having made this one revision. Again unlikely, since this correspondence in variants is unique. (3) These changes in MSE were made during the revisions for ARE. Irving had MSE before him for reference while he marked a copy of one of the American imprints. On this one occasion he marked the manuscript to make it correspond with the printed text of his American copy for no very good reason—perhaps forgetting for the moment which text he was marking. The variants in 2A were a result of some flaw in the printing of the sheets upon which the text of 2A was based, so that the compositors had to consult a copy of 1A, in which the text appears in this form. On the whole, this explanation seems the most likely.

82.26 acting]   See discussion at 82.25–26.

84.27 yielded]   The 2E variant "yields" seems at first glance an attractive emendation. Deeper analysis of the passage, however, contradicts the impulse and offers further evidence of the nonauthorial nature of 2E variants. If one can set aside the doubtful punctuation of the sentence (in particular the semicolon after "discussion"), it becomes clear that "yielded" is not intended as the verb accompanying "attention." Rather, it is adjectival, and "attention" and "prevalence" are the twin subjects of the verb "prove." Thus the 2E reading is a snare, confusing the passage even more than the copy-text does.

104.4 said that all]   This and the following variants (to 104.13) included in the List of Rejected Substantives are all the result of a single intention on Irving's part—to change this conversation from indirect to direct address—for the ARE. Interestingly, the page in MSE that would contain this paragraph is missing from the otherwise complete portion of the manuscript in the Alderman Library for pages 225 to 271 of the first volume of 1E. Its absence suggests that Irving marked it up for ARE.

120.14 philosopher's]   This passage is not present in MSE, but other examples of this word in MSE and MSA indicate that when Irving bothered to put in the apostrophe at all, it was usually in this form. The T text has regularized to reflect his intention.

121.25 him$_\wedge$]   The comma alters the meaning of the sentence in a way that Irving must not have intended. Therefore the T text follows the 2E reading even though it is not authorial. The passage is not extant in MSE.

128.20 woods]   Although "wood" seems superior in this context, avoiding what appears to be a subject-verb disagreement and a non-euphonious gaggle of sibillants, "woods" is collective and therefore grammatically satisfactory. Although "wood" has the authority of ARE to support it, that authority is damaged by its coincident appearance in the American line of texts after 1822. On balance, the evidence supports "woods," the T reading.

140.22 fauns]   While "faun" and "fawn" are each allowable spellings for the other, both context and the manuscript evidence support the T reading, "faun." MSE is not extant for this use, but both MSE and MSA support an identical emendation made at 303.12.

145.40 splendour]   Since the MSE spelling "splendour" is clear for this variant and for the same word at 146.11 and 147.12, the sudden reversion to an "-or" spelling in the copy-text for this one word and one area in the text seems inexplicable. If one adds to the mystery the case at 143.38 where another use of "splendour" was reset in 2E to the "-or" spelling, the mystery deepens.

157.28 advice."]   The footnote here, added only to ARE, was a belated admission on Irving's part of the influence that Scott and Abbotsford had on *Bracebridge Hall.* This influence is discussed above in the Introduction, pp. xv–xvii.

159.20 high-feeding]   MSA omits the hyphen in this word and in the parallel "high-handed" and "high-minded." 1A omits the hyphen in all three words, but the 1E compositor added hyphens to two of the three, omitting only this one. Since Irving was quite casual in his hyphenation, the   text has been regularized to the English standard usage.

167.25 phlegræ]   Apparently the 3E25 compositor remembered his Ovid (*Metamorphoses* X, 151) better than Irving had. See the discussion of this phrase in the Explanatory Notes.

170.3 today]   Irving's spelling of "today" and "tomorrow" is inconsistent, sometimes hyphenated, sometimes not. The 1E form has been emended in the T text to correspond with manuscript usage, but there has been no effort to regularize.

170.35 morrice]   Manuscript spelling is invariably "morrice." Since Irving was keenly aware of the word's origin in "moorish," his intention has been restored in the T text.

171.21 Ready Money]   It is interesting to note what confusion occurs at the first recurrence of this name in the second volume. Irving may have had trouble himself; the word here is smeared with an inky thumbprint in MSA (though it seems to read "Ready-money"), and is most ambiguous in MSE—the hyphen is faint, if present, the *m* may be capitalized, perhaps not.

171.39 what]   The omission of this word in both impressions of 2A and in ARE may be coincidental, or it may indicate that it was a copy of 2A26 that Irving used to mark up for ARE.

209.17 for]   This slight variant changes the meaning of the sentence in which it appears. Annette "affecting a temporary preference" *to* another man makes her appear far more of a coquette than the ARE "affecting a temporary preference" *for* someone else—presumably the affectation is communicated to Eugene.

215.28 appeared]   This variant and the eight following on the List of Rejected Substantives are all a part of Irving's revision of tense describing Eugene's adventures. The ARE form is unquestionably more immediate, direct, exciting. The T text, in following the 1E text, retains the distance and calm of the original version.

223.18 when]   MSE could easily be misread as "where," although a closer look indicates the "when" was Irving's intention. MSA has "when" written much more clearly following a comma which was aparently misread as a period by the 1A compositor, who has "When" beginning a sentence fragment.

232.5 makes]   The ARE variant listed among the rejected substantives, if authorial, was perhaps an attempt to correct an apparent lack of agreement between verb and subject. If so, it was done without reference to the original poem, which reads "made" here. See the entry under this citation in the Explanatory Notes.

251.2 to]   Irving seems to have miscopied this word as "of" from the first, and the error was passed from edition to edition without a change. Some of the editors perhaps thought the intention was the obsolete verb, "to concord," meaning to agree; more likely most of them never considered the meaning of the passage. It is interesting to note that the editor or compositor of 1A capitalized the word "Concord," perhaps in an effort to make some sense of the passage, if only to New Englanders.

267.17 exposed]   The precopy-text reading is undoubtedly superior. MSE for this passage is not extant, but probably had a word variously decipherable as "exposed" or "opposed," and, as was the case with "nature"—"naïveté" (20.12), the compositor made the wrong choice. No later text made the correction because "opposed" does make some sense.

267.19 Haunted House] The phrase is capitalized regularly elsewhere except at 275.21, in all instances in which it is clear the specific haunted house mentioned in the story is intended.

273.25–26 it was an instinctive movement of defence;] One is sorely tempted to allow emendations like this one and such others, also rejected, at 273.28 and 274.41–42. In all such cases Irving is undoubtedly improving his narrative, reducing a wordy analysis to a simple but exciting statement of the action. To do so, however, is to tamper with the flavor of the 1822 text, which is more that of the casual storyteller, however amateur, than the accomplished artist in fiction.

276.2 fragment] The ARE "fragments" is in error; a passage earlier in the text (273.40) states that it was a "great fragment" that Dolph dropped accidentally on the party.

276.39–40 daughters] The ARE text slightly modifies the character of Antony Vander Heyden. To kiss a casual friend's wife and daughter before his face is slightly more arch than to kiss his wife and daughters. If this variant is indeed authorial it may indicate some second thoughts on Irving's part about Vander Heyden's character. The T text follows the copy-text because of some doubt about the authority of the variant and the wisdom of Irving's hypothetical second thoughts.

277.22 pinnace;] The location of the pinnace is given in almost identical language at 275.38. Irving seems here to have been correcting an oversight for ARE, and the T text follows his ARE revision.

292.33 Spiegel] MSA and 1A consistently spell the whole name Vanderspiegel.

303.12 faun] See the discussion in this list under 140.22.

309.8–9 , at the effect produced by one of my trivial lucubrations] It is possible that this slight modification to the 1E text, along with the similar variant at 311.36, was a result of the ironic comment in *Blackwood's* quoted above in the Introduction (pp. xxix-xxx). Either author or editor might have made the revision, so the T text follows the copy-text.

311.15–28 I am sure . . . a study.] Perhaps this variant like the two discussed in the entry above on this list was provoked by the *Blackwood's* review.

LIST OF EMENDATIONS

In this list of changes in the copy-text, the symbols used to designate the sources of the readings are those given in the key which appears on pages 315–316.

These notes identify all emendations of the copy-text. The numbers before each note indicate the page and line. Chapter numbers, chapter titles, epigraphs, text, quotations, and footnotes are included in the line count. Only running heads and rules added by the printer to separate running heads from the text are omitted from the count.

The reading to the left of the bracket is the portion of the text under consideration and represents an accepted reading that differs from the copy-text. The source of the reading is identified by symbol after the bracket. Other texts with the same reading are also given by symbol when the emendation has been made from a text later than the copy-text. Emendations of accidentals based on precopy-texts (MSA, MSE, and 1A) do not list later texts with the same readings, since these are always coincidental.

The reading after the semicolon is the rejected copy-text reading; the symbols following it include the copy-text itself and all other forms of the text with the same reading in the case of all substantive variants and for most accidentals. Emendations of accidentals based on pre-copy-texts (MSA, MSE, and 1A) list only the copy-text reading and symbol: later forms of these variants differ widely and pointlessly— many house styles and many changes in usage intervene. When other alternative readings are available (except in the case of precopy-text accidental variants), they are recorded after the copy-text reading along with the symbols for the text in which they are found. When a reading is consistent through all reprintings of an edition, only the major symbol is given. Thus 2A means that the text under discussion is identical in the Van Winkle 1822 printing of the second American edition and the 1826 reprint; 1E means that all states of the Murry 1822 edition have the same reading.

The swung (wavy) dash ∼ represents the same word that appears before the bracket, and is used in recording punctuation variants; the caret ∧ indicates that a mark of punctuation is omitted. An asterisk * is placed before an entry when the reading is discussed in the Discussion of Adopted Readings, pp. 372–382.

*t.p.5   Humourists] 1A, 2A, 1F, 3A; Humorists 1E, 2E, 3E, 4E, ARE

*t.p.6   A Medley] 1A, 2A, 3A, ARE; *omitted* 1E, 2E, 3E, 4E, 1F

4.28   Abbey] 1A, 2A, 4E, 3A, ARE; abbey 1E, 2E, 3E, 1F

4.30   Castle] 1A, 2A, 4E, 3A, ARE; castle 1E, 2E, 3E, 1F

*5.21–22   countries," that] ARE; countries." 1E, 2A, 2E, 3E, 4E, 1F, 3A

8.8   Hall] MSE, 1A, 2A, 3A, ARE; hall 1E, 2E, 3E, 4E, 1F

8.26   humourist] MSE, 1A, 2A, 3E, 4E, 1F, 3A; humorist 1E, 2E, ARE

9.5   Hall] MSE, 1A, 2A, 3A, ARE; hall 1E, 2E, 3E, 4E, 1F

*9.28   aught] 2A, 2E, 3E, 4E, 1F, 3A, ARE; ought 1E

11.33   Novelist's] 2A, 3A, ARE; Novelists' 1E, 2E, 3E, 4E, 1F; Novellist's 1A; Novellists MSE

12.9   Hall] MSE, 1A; hall 1E, 2A, 2E, 3E, 4E, 1F, 3A, ARE

*13.11   great-great] ARE; ∼ ∧ ∼ 1E, 2A, 2E, 3E, 4E, 1F, 3A

15.14   By the bye] MSE, 1A; By the by 1E, 2A, 2E, 3E, 4E, 1F, 3A, ARE

17.36   mistress∧] MSE, ARE; ∼, 1E

*19.12   truth] 1A, 3E, 4E, 1F; love MSE, 1E, 2E, 2A, 3A, ARE

19.15–16   George III∧] ARE; ∼. 1E, 2A, 2E, 3E, 4E, 1F, 3A

20.4   bled;] MSE, 1A; ∼: 1E

*20.12   naïveté] 1A; nature 1E, 2A, 2E, 3E, 4E, 1F, 3A, ARE

21.20   Grandison. Every] MSE, 1A; ∼: ∼ 1E

21.24   arm-chairs∧] MSE, 1A; ∼, 1E

21.24   sofas∧] MSE, 1A; ∼, 1E

*24.7   has] 4E, ARE; had 1A, 1E, 2A, 2E, 3E, 1F, 3A

*24.33   old-fashioned] 2E; ∼ ∧ ∼ 1Ea–c

*26.22   character] MSE, 1A; characters 1E, 2A, 2E, 3E, 4E, 1F, 3A, ARE

*28.9   ladies'] 1Ec, 2A, 3E, 4E, 1F, 3A, ARE; ∼ ∧ 1Ea–b, 2E; ladies MSE

*28.12   evidence] ARE; the marks MSE, 1A, 1E, 2A, 2E, 3E, 4E, 1F, 3A

*30.10   general] 1A, 2A, 3A, ARE; General 1E, 2E, 3E, 4E, 1F

30.13   general's] 2A, 3A, ARE; General's 1A, 1E, 2E, 3E, 4E, 1F

31.1   promoted,] 2E; ∼∧ 1Ea–c

*31.13   to] MSE, 1A; the 1E, 2A, 2E, 3E, 4E, 1F, 3A, ARE

*31.18   Lillycraft] ARE; Jocelyne MSE, 1A, 1E, 2A, 2E, 3E, 4E, 1F, 3A

*31.29   Windsor Terrace] MSE; Windsor-terrace 1E, 2E, 3E, 4E, 1F, ARE; Windsor terrace 1A, 2A, 3A

*31.29   Kensington Garden] MSE, 1A; Kensington-/garden 1E,
                2E, 3E, 4E, 1F; Kensington garden 2A, 3A, ARE
34.32   household;] MSE, 1A; ~: 1E
*34.34   fill] ARE; fills MSE, 1A, 1E, 2A, 2E, 3E, 4E, 1F, 3A
37.12   champion,] MSE, 1A; ~; 1E
*37.15   Ready Money] 1A, 2E, 3E, 4E, 1F; ready money 1E;
                Ready-money 2A, 3A, ARE
37.21   character;] MSE, 1A; ~: 1E
37.30   by the bye] MSE, 1A; by the by 1E, 2A, 2E, 3E, 4E,
                1F, 3A, ARE
38.1   night,"*] 1A, 2A, 2E, 3E, 4E, 1F, 3A, ARE; ~*," 1E
*38.13   holiday] 2A, 3A, ARE; holyday MSE, 1A, 1E, 2E, 3E,
                4E, 1F
39.13   up,] 2E; ~ ∧ 1Ea–c
39.19   Ready Money] MSE, 1A, 2E, 3E, 4E, 1F; Ready-money
                1E; Ready-Money 2A, 3A, ARE
*39.34   acquaintances, and] 2E; ~; ~, 1Ea–c; ~ ∧ ~ ∧ MSE
40.5   alwaies.] 1Ec, 2E; ~∧ MSE, 1Ea–b
40.15   other's] 1A; others' 1E, 2A, 2E, 3E, 4E, 1F, ARE; others
                MSE
40.31   companion. He] MSE, 1A; ~: he 1E
42.19   Tippoo] 1Ec, 2E; Tippo 1Ea–b
*46.1   dread] T; dead 1A, 1E, 2A, 2E, 3E, 4E, 1F, 3A, ARE
47.25   accidents;] 1A; ~: 1E
*48.5   ∧ chiefly∧] 1A, ARE; ∧ ~, 1E, 2E, 3E, 4E, 1F; , ~,
                2A, 3A
52.39   information. Nobody] MSE, 1A; ~: nobody 1E
53.36–37   storm. The] MSE, 1A; ~: the 1E
*57.19   bearing] 1A; leaving 1E, 2A, 2E, 3E, 4E, 1F, 3A, ARE
59.3   taste; it] MSE; ~: ~ 1E; ~. It 1A
61.6   MICRO] T; Mico MSE, 1A, 1E, 2A, 2E, 3E, 4E, 1F,
                3A, ARE
*61.35   seems] MSE, 1A; seemed 1E, 2A, 2E, 3E, 4E, 1F, 3A,
                ARE
62.4   jealousies."*] MSE, 1A, 2A, 2E, 3E, 4E, 1F, 3A, ARE;
                ~*." 1E
65.5–6   Ready Money] MSE, 1A, 2E, 4E; Ready money 1Ea–c;
                Ready-money 3E, 1F; Ready-Money 2A, 3A, ARE
*65.11   Well-scoured] 1A, 2A, 3E25, 4E, 3A, ARE; Well-scowered
                1E, 2E, 3E23, 1F; Well-scowerd MSE.
65.12   paling] MSE, 2E, 2A, 3E, 4E, 1F, 3A, ARE; pailing
                1Ea–c
65.28   Ready Money] MSE, 2E; Ready money 1Ea–c

°65.30   Tibbetses] 2E; Tibbets 1Ea–c, 2A, 3E, 4E, 1F, 3A, ARE;
                Tibbets' MSE, 1A
66.4   Ready Money] MSE, 2E; Ready money 1Ea–c
66.39   Tibbetses] 2E; Tibbets 1Ea–c; Tibbets' MSE, 1A
67.15   Tibbetses] 2E; Tibbets 1Ea–c; Tibbets' 1A
67.21   Ready Money] 2E; Ready-money 1Ea–c
67.26   Ready Money's] 2E; Ready-money's 1Ea–c
67.32   Ready Money] 2E; Ready-money 1Ea–c
71.34   dayes."°] MSE, 2A, 3E, 4E, 1F, 3A, ARE; ∼°." 1E, 2E
73.20   favourite] MSE, 2E; favorite 1Ea–c
°74.20   scholars;] MSE; ∼: 1E
78.13   heard;] MSE, 1A; ∼: 1E
78.21   honoured.°] 2A, 3E, 4E, 1F, 3A; ∼°. 1E, 2E; ∼.° ARE
82.8   attempt.°] MSE, 1A, 2A, 3E, 4E, 1F, 3A, ARE; ∼°.
                1E, 2E
°82.25–26   , in fact,] MSE, 1A, 2A, 3A, ARE; indeed 1E, 2E, 3E,
                4E, 1F
°82.26   acting] MSE, 1A, 2A, 3A, ARE; and to act 1E, 2E, 3E,
                4E, 1F
90.3–4   son," said he, "] 1A, 2A, 4E, 3A, ARE; ∼ ∧∧ ∼ ∼,∧
                1E, 2E, 3E, 1F
96.42   Ready Money] MSE, 1A; Ready-money 1E, 2A, 2E, 3E,
                4E, 1F, 3A; Ready-Money ARE
97.11   are∧] MSE, 1A; ∼, 1E
98.7   quiet∧] MSE, 1A; ∼, 1E
102.3   Wherever] MSE, 1A, 2A, 3E, 4E, 1F, 3A, ARE; Where-/
                ever 1E, 2E
103.22   out. It] MSE, 1A; ∼: ∼ 1E
112.12   elixir.°] 1A, 2A, 3E, 4E, 1F, 3A, ARE; ∼°. 1E, 2E
113.39   laboratory;] 1A, 2E, 2A, 3A, ARE; ∼, 1Ea–c, 3E, 4E, 1F
116.11   snow∧] 1A; ∼, 1E
117.30   murmur;] 1A; ∼: 1E
117.41   believed] 1A, 1Ec, 2E, 2A, 3E, 4E, 1F, 3A, ARE; believe
                1Ea–b
119.33   son,] 1Ec, 2E; ∼; 1Ea–b
119.33   enthusiasm;] 1Ec, 2E; ∼, 1Ea–b
°120.14   philosopher's] 1A, 2A, 3E, 4E, 1F, 3A, ARE; philos-
                ophers' 1E, 2E
120.34   recognised,] 1A; ∼ ∧ 1E
120.34–35   rival. He] 1A; ∼: he 1E
121.10   ladder. He] 1A; ∼: he 1E
121.22   fierce∧] 1A; ∼, 1E
121.22   combat∧] 1A; ∼, 1E

121.24   shadow. His] 1A; ∼: his 1E

*121.25   him] 2E; ∼, 1Ea–c

121.26   weapon;] 1A; ∼: 1E

123.32–33   philosopher's] 1A, 2E, 2A, 3E, 4E, 1F, 3A, ARE; philos-
                      ophers' 1Ea–c

124.4   Kuhnrade,*] 1A, 2A, 3E, 4E, 1F, 3A, ARE; ∼*, 1E, 2E

124.34   tenderness;] 1A; ∼: 1E

125.17   philosopher's] 1A, 2A, 3E, 4E, 1F, 3A, ARE; philos-
                      ophers' 1E, 2E

125.39   Valentia.*] 1A, 2A, 3E, 4E, 1F, 3A, ARE; ∼*. 1E, 2E

127.25   were] ARE; was MSE, 1A, 1E, 2A, 2E, 3E, 4E, 1F, 3A

133.24   simplicity,] MSE, 1A; ∼; 1E

135.16   philosopher's] 1A, 2A, 3A; philosophers' 1E, 2E, 3E,
                      4E, 1F, ARE; philosophers MSE

135.42   God∧] 2E; ∼, 1Ea–c

139.28   thing;] MSE; ∼: 1E

*140.22   fauns] 4E, ARE; fawns 1E, 2A, 2E, 3E, 1F, 3A

142.13   liberty;] MSE; ∼: 1E

143.27   shrinking.] MSE, 1A; ∼? 1E

145.4   sunrise;] MSE; ∼: 1E

145.11–12   fatigue. She] MSE; ∼: she 1E

145.20   terror;] MSE; ∼: 1E

145.36   parents;] MSE; ∼: 1E

145.37   village;] MSE; ∼: 1E

*145.40   splendour] MSE; splendor 1E

146.4   idol;] MSE; ∼: 1E

146.11   splendour] MSE; splendor 1E

146.27   forward –] MSE; ∼: 1E

146.28   fingers;] MSE; ∼: 1E

147.12   splendour] MSE; splendor 1E

147.17   Gomeles!"*] 1A, 2A, 3E, 4E, 1F, 3A, ARE; ∼*!" 1E,
                      2E; ∼!*" MSE

147.40   victory."†] T; ∼."* 1A, 2A, 3E, 4E, 1F, 3A, ARE;
                      ∼*." 1E, 2E; ∼.*" MSE

150.34   intellects.] 1Ec, 2E; ∼, 1Ea–b

153.32   philosopher's stone] 1A, ARE; Philosophers' Stone 1E,
                      2E; Philosopher's Stone 2A, 3E, 4E, 1F, 3A

157.4   leav'd] MSA, 1A; leaved 1E

157.6   boist'rous seas,] MSA, 1A; boisterous seas∧ 1E

157.8   lives,] MSA, 1A; ∼∧ 1E

157.29   honour's] 1A; honor's 1E; honours MSA

157.33   trees∧] MSA, 2E; ∼, 1Ea–c

*159.20   high-feeding] T; ∼ ∧ ∼ MSA, 1A, 1E

163.10	Go,] 3E, 4E, 1F, ARE; Go$_\wedge$ MSA, MSE, 1E, 2A, 2E, 3A; go$_\wedge$ 1A
166.12	it,] MSE; it; 1E; it$_\wedge$ MSA, 1A *with a changed text following.*
168.13	II] T; II. 1E; II MSE
168.39	By the bye] MSE; By the by 1E
°170.3	today] MSA; to-day 1E; to day 1A; to-/day MSE
170.3	tomorrow] MSA, MSE; to-morrow 1A, 1E
170.4	please,] MSA, MSE, 1A; ~; 1E
°170.35	morrice] MSA, MSE, 1A; morris- 1E
°171.21	Ready Money] T; Ready-money 1E; Ready-Money 1A, ARE
171.32	Master] 2E; master 1Ea–c
172.23	gaols] 1Ec, 2E, 2A26, 3E, 4E, 1F, 3A; goals 1Ea–b, 2A22; jails ARE
173.8	milk maids] MSA, MSE; milk-/maids 1E; milkmaids 1A, ARE
174.12	day$_\wedge$] MSA, MSE, 1A; ~, 1E
176.22	morrice] MSA, MSE, 1A; morris- 1E
176.35	green$_\wedge$] MSA, MSE, 1A; ~, 1E
176.35	pageant] MSE; ~, MSA, 1A, 1E
179.23	short$_\wedge$] MSA, MSE; ~, 1A, 1E
179.24	eyes$_\wedge$] MSA, MSE, 1A; ~, 1E
180.10	village$_\wedge$] MSA, MSE, 1A; ~, 1E
180.11	Simon$_\wedge$] MSE; ~, MSA, 1A, 1E
180.18	Ready Money] MSE, 1A, 2E; Ready-money MSA, 1Ea–c
180.34	plough;] MSA, MSE, 1A; ~: 1E
181.5	Ready Money] MSA, MSE, 1A, 2E; Ready-money 1Ea–c
181.8	Ready Money] MSA, MSE, 1A, 2E; Ready-money 1Ea–c
181.32	Ready Money] MSA, MSE, 1A, 2E; Ready-money 1Ea–c
182.15	Ready Money] MSA, MSE, 1A, 2E; Ready-money 1Ea–c
182.33	squire$_\wedge$] MSE, MSA; ~, 1A, 1E
182.41–42	Ready Money] MSA, MSE, 1A, 2E; Ready-money 1Ea–c
183.11	place$_\wedge$] MSA, MSE, 1A; ~, 1E
183.12	object$_\wedge$] MSA, MSE, 1A; ~, 1E
183.17	world$_\wedge$] MSA, MSE, 1A; ~, 1E
184.3	school house] MSA, MSE, 1A; school-house 1E
185.3	liked$_\wedge$] MSA, MSE, 1A; ~, 1E
185.3	heeded$_\wedge$] MSA, MSE; ~, 1A, 1E
185.21	other,] MSA, MSE, 1A; ~; 1E
185.22	be$_\wedge$] MSA, MSE, 1A; ~, 1E
185.31	tuition$_\wedge$] MSA, MSE, 1A; ~, 1E
187.4	affairs$_\wedge$] MSA, MSE, 1A; ~, 1E

187.4   faction_∧] MSA, MSE, 1A; ~, 1E

187.23   Ready Money Jack] 1A, 2E; Ready-money Jack 1Ea–c; Ready-money-Jack MSA; Ready-Money Jack MSE

187.39   sides_∧] MSA, MSE, 1A; ~, 1E

188.8   porch_∧] MSA, MSE, 1A; ~, 1E

189.14   Ready Money] 2E; Ready-money MSE, 1Ea–c; Ready money MSA

189.24   creed_∧] MSA, MSE, 1A; ~, 1E

191.7   beeches_∧] MSE; ~, 1E

193.9   that] 1Ec, 2E; tha 1Ea–b

194.6   takes] ARE; take MSE, 1E, 2A, 2E, 3E, 4E, 1F, 3A

194.11   downfall] MSE, 2A, 3A, ARE; downfal 1E, 2E, 3E, 4E, 1F

195.13   friends_∧] MSE; ~, 1E

197.3   morrice] MSA, MSE, 1A; morris- 1E

197.13   wherever] MSA, MSE, 1A; where-/ever 1E

197.19   by the bye] MSA, MSE, 1A; by the by 1E

197.31   Ready Money] 2E; Ready-money 1Ea–c; Ready money MSA, MSE

198.37   poor's] MSA, 1A, 2A, 3E25, 4E, 3A; poors' 1E, 2E, 3E23, 1F; poors MSE

199.17   Cobbett] 1Ec, 2E, 1A, 2A, 4E, 1F, 3A, ARE; Cobbet 1Ea–b, 3E

201.20   Ready Money] 2E; Ready-money 1Ea–c; Ready money MSA, MSE

201.39   Ready Money] 2E; Ready-money MSA, MSE, 1Ea–c

202.29   Impos'd] MSA, MSE, 1A; Imposed 1E

202.31   favoured] MSA, MSE, 1A; favour'd 1E

*209.17   for] ARE; to MSA, MSE, 1A, 1E, 2A, 2E, 3E, 4E, IF, 3A

220.13   peril."*] 2A, 3E, 4E, 1F; ~*." 1E, 2E

221.16   Tibbetses] 1Ec, 2E; Tibbets's 1Ea–b, 2A, 3E, 4E, 1F, 3A, ARE

221.17   Ready Money's] 2E; Ready-money's MSA, MSE, 1Ea–b; Ready-Money's 1Ec

*223.18   when] MSA, MSE; where 1E; When 1A

228.10   yore,] MSA, 1A; ~; 1E

228.10   Nimrod,] MSA, 1A; ~; 1E

228.14   by-the-bye] MSA, 1A; by-the-by 1E

229.38   Hierarchie] 2E; Heirarchie 1Ea–c

230.22   Tibbetses] T; Tibbets MSA, 1A, 1E

230.30   Ready Money] 2E; Ready-money 1Ea–c

230.33   Tibbetses] T; Tibbets MSA, 1A, 1E

233.23	recall] MSA, 1A, 4E, 3A, ARE; recal 1E, 2A, 2E, 3E, 1F
234.8	Ready Money] 1A, 2E; Ready-money MSA, 1Ea–c
234.16	Ready Money] MSA, 1A, 2E; Ready-money 1Ea–c
234.24–25	Ready Money] MSA, 1A, 2E; Ready-money 1Ea–c
235.2	Ready Money] MSA, 1A, 2E; Ready-money 1Ea–c
235.8	Ready Money] MSA, 1A, 2E; Ready-money 1Ea–c
235.39	morrice] MSA, 1A; morris 1E
235.40–41	Ready Money] MSA, 1A, 2E; Ready-money 1Ea–c
236.23	Ready Money] MSA, 1A, 2E; Ready-money 1Ea–c
236.42	Ready Money] MSA, 1A, 2E; Ready-money 1Ea–c
237.31	Ready Money] 1A, 2E; Ready-money MSA, 1Ea–c
237.36	Ready Money] 1A, 2E; Ready-money MSA, 1Ea–c
237.41	Tibbetses] 1Ec, 2E; Tibbets's MSA, 1A, 1Ea–b
242.36	observed$_\wedge$] MSE; ~, 1E
244.40–245.1	Tibbetses] T; Tibbets MSE, 1E
245.16	Ready Money] MSE, 2E; Ready-money 1Ea–c
246.17	Tippoo] MSE, 2A, 4E, 3A, ARE; Tibboo 1E, 2E, 3E, 1F
247.27	stories.*] 2A, 3E, 4E, 1F, 3A; ~*. 1E, 2E
*251.2	to] T; of MSA, 1A, 1E, 2A, 2E, 3E, 4E, 1F, 3A, ARE
251.20	privateer.*] 1A, 2A, 3E, 4E, 1F, 3A, ARE; ~*. 1E, 2E
252.39	scrapes;] MSA, 1A; ~: 1E
252.41	off;] MSA, 1A; ~: 1E
258.6	he] MSA, 1A, 1Ec, 2E; be 1Ea–b
261.14	Blitzen] MSA, 1A; blitzen 1E
262.33	Groodt;] MSA, 1A; ~: 1E
267.8	Knipperhausen] MSA, 1A, 1Ec, 2E, 2A, 4E, 3A, ARE; Knypperhausen 1Ea–b, 3E, 1F
*267.17	exposed] MSA, 1A; opposed 1E, 2A, 2E, 3E, 4E, 1F, 3A, ARE
*267.19	Haunted House] 1A, 2E; haunted house MSA, 1Ea–c
270.16–17	pang. He] MSA, 1A; ~; he 1E
272.17	career.*] 1A, 2A, 3E, 4E, 1F, 3A, ARE; ~*. 1E, 2E; ~* MSA
275.2–3	late; the] T; ~: ~ 1E; ~. The MSA, 1A
275.4	rock; he] T; ~: ~ 1E; ~. He MSA, 1A
275.7	friendship. The] MSA, 1A; ~: the 1E
275.21	Haunted House] MSA, 1A, 1Ec, 2E; haunted house 1Ea–b
276.26	life,] MSA, 1A; ~; 1E
276.28	hangers-on,] MSA, 1A; ~; 1E
277.8	without] MSA, 1A, 2E; with / out 1Ea–c
*277.22	pinnace;] ARE; pinnace, which was moored close by; and MSA, 1A, 1E, 2A, 2E, 3E, 4E, 1F, 3A

280.28	severed. To] MSA, 1A; ~: to 1E
281.41	feathers. Not] MSA, 1A; ~: not 1E
283.40	Dunderberg.°] 2A, 3E, 4E, 1F, 3A, ARE; ~°. 1E, 2E; ~° MSA
284.6	Nose] 1A, 2A, 3E, 4E, 1F, 3A, ARE; nose 1E, 2E
284.29	Fishkill] MSA, 1A, ARE; Fish-Hill 1E, 2A, 2E, 3E, 4E, 1F, 3A
284.31	Nose] 1A, 2A, 3E, 4E, 1F, 3A, ARE; nose 1E, 2E
285.2	unmolested.°] 2A, 3E, 4E, 1F, 3A, ARE; ~°. 1E, 2E; ~° MSA
287.11	Pollopol's] MSA, 2A, 3A, ARE; Polopol's 1E, 2E, 3E, 4E, IF; Pollopel's 1A
287.24	river. This] MSA, 1A; ~: this 1E
287.32	fish;] MSA, 1A; ~: 1E
287.35	exercises,] MSA, 1A; ~; 1E
288.4	approached] MSA, 1A; approached to 1E, 2A, 2E, 3E, 4E, 1F, 3A, ARE
288.18	Antony] MSA, 1A, 1Ec, 2E, 2A, 2E, 4E, 1F, 3A, ARE; Anthony 1Ea–b
288.32	philosopher's] MSA, 1A, 2A, 3E, 4E, 1F, 3A, ARE; philosophers' 1E, 2E
290.29	Gansevoorts] MSA, 1A, 2A, 3A, ARE; Gansevorts 1E, 2E, 3E, 4E, 1F
291.2	say. His] MSA, 1A; ~: his 1E
291.25	Knipperhausen's] 1Ec, 2E, 2A, 4E, 3A, ARE; Knypperhausen's MSA, 1A, 1Ea–b, 3E, 1F
292.5	itself.] MSA, 1A; ~: 1E
°292.33	Spiegel] 1Ec, 2A, 3E, 4E, 1F, 3A, ARE; Spiegle 1Ea–b; Speigle 2E
293.16	round-about] 1A, 2E; round about MSA, 1Ea–c
295.26	Knipperhausen] 2A, 4E, 3A, ARE; Knypperhausen 1E, 2E, 3E
297.1	Knipperhausen] 2A, 4E, 3A, ARE; Knypperhausen 1E, 2E, 3E
297.22	Knipperhausen] 2A, 4E, 3A, ARE; Knypperhausen 1E, 2E, 3E
297.28	at] MSA, 1A, 2A, 3E, 4E, 1F, 3A, ARE; of 1E, 2E
297.40	skull] MSA, 1A, 1Ec, 2E, 2A, 3E, 4E, 1F, 3A, ARE; scull 1Ea–b
298.21	Spiegel] 2A, 3E, 4E, 1F, 3A, ARE; Spiegle 1E, 2E
303.6	Ready Money] MSA, 1A, 2E; Ready-money 1Ea–c; Ready money MSE

°303.12   faun] MSA, MSE, 3E, 4E, ARE; fawn 1A, 1E, 2E, 2A,
               3A
305.10–11   Ready Money] MSA, 1A, 2E; Ready-money 1Ea–c, MSE
305.24   Ready Money] MSA, 1A, 2E; Ready-money 1Ea-c; ready-
               money MSE
305.27   drunk] MSE, ARE; drank 1A, 1E, 2A, 2E, 3E, 4E,
               1F, 3A
306.6   Nimrod. So] MSA, MSE, 1A; ~: so 1E
306.19   household;] MSA, MSE, 1A, 2E; ~: 1Ea–c
307.2   Ready Money] MSA; Ready-money MSE, 1E; Ready
               money 1A
307.2   fathers. The] MSA, MSE, 1A; ~: the 1E
310.23   hands. We] T; ~: we 1E
310.39   friends?"°] 1Ec–d, 2A, 2E, 3E, 1F, 3A; ~°." 1Ea–b;
               ~."° ARE
°311.15–28   I am sure . . . a study.] 1Eb–c, 2E, 2A, 3E, 4E, 1F, 3A,
               ARE; omitted 1Ea

LIST OF REJECTED SUBSTANTIVES

This list provides a historical record of all substantive variants in texts following the copy-text through the Author's Revised Edition and its reprintings through 1859. A key to the symbols used to designate texts appears on pages 315–316.

The reading to the left of the bracket is the portion of the text under consideration and represents the copy-text reading. The source of the reading in the copy-text and all other texts which follow the copy-text is identified by symbol after the bracket. The reading after the semicolon is the rejected variant. The symbols following it identify all the texts after the copy-text in which it is found. If yet another reading exists, it is given along with the symbols for the texts in which it is found after the second semicolon. When a reading is consistent through all printings of an edition, only the major symbol is given.

This list includes precopy-text variants (MSA, MSE, and 1A) only when they are or may be pertinent to later variants. For examples of precopy-text variants, see Appendices 1 and 2, pp. 423–434. An asterisk *
is placed before an entry when the reading is discussed in the Discussions of Adopted Readings, pp. 372–382.

*verso of   *blank*] 1E, 2E, 3E, 4E, 1F, 3A, ARE; ADVERTISE-
p. following   MENT / TO / THE SECOND EDITION. / The
the title p.   manuscript for the first edition of this work was transmitted to America at a time when the author was suffering under a long and obstinate indisposition, and much depression of spirits. He was conscious of the imperfections of the work, but was advised by his physician to commit it to the press, and relieve his mind from it, as a necessary step to the recovery of his health. In the course of publication in England, however, an improved state of health and spirits enabled him to make considerable alterations and additions; which will account for the material difference that will be perceived between the first and second editions of the work, as published in America. ; 2A

*3.4   at] 1E, 2E, 2A, 2E23, 2E24, 1F, 3A, ARE; on 2E25, 3E
*3.9   marvel] 1E, 2E, 3E, 4E, 1F, marvel, at least to the European part of my readers, 1A; marvel, to my European readers, 2A, 3A, ARE

*3.17   criticism] 1E, 2E, 3E, 1F; criticisms 2A, 3A, ARE
3.17   with] 1E, 2A, 2E, 3E, 4E, 1F, 3A; of ARE
3.18   which has been] 1E, 2A, 2E, 3E, 4E, 1F, 3A; *omitted*
                 ARE
3.29   and] 1E, 2E, 2A, 3E23, 3E24, 1F, 3A, ARE; *omitted*
                 3E25, 4E
3.36   that are] 1E, 2A, 2E, 3E, 4E, 1F, 3A; *omitted* ARE
4.21   in anticipation] 1E, 2A, 2E, 3E, 4E, 1F, 3A; anticipation
                 ARE
5.20   that had been] 1E, 2A, 2E, 3E, 4E, 1F, 3A; *omitted*
                 ARE
*6.27   poetical] 1E, 2E, 2A, 3A, ARE; political 3E, 4E, 1F
6.35   than] 1E, 2A, 2E, 3E, 4E, 1F, 3A; that ARE
8.2   ancientest] 1E, 2E, 3E, 4E, 1F, ARE; ancient 2A, 3A
*8.17   further] 1E, 2E; farther 1A, 2A, 3E, 4E, 1F, 3A, ARE
8.20   partly] 1E, 2E, 2A, 3E23, 4E, 1F, 3A; party 3E24, 3E25
9.33   an old gentleman] 1E, 2A, 2E, 3E, 4E, 1F, 3A; *omitted*
                 ARE
9.39   further] 1E, 2E, ARE; farther 2A, 3E, 4E, 1F, 3A
*10.1   loiterings] 1E, 2E, 2A, 3E, 4E, 1F, 3A; wanderings ARE
13.4   this] 1E, 2A, 2E, 3E, 1F, 3A, ARE; his 4E
13.11   bestrode] 1E, 2A, 2E, 3E, 1F, 3A, ARE; bestrid 4E
13.13   for] 1E, 2A, 2E, 3E, 4E, 3A, ARE; of 1F
13.23   as rather] 1E, 2E, 3E, 4E, 1F, ARE; rather as 2A, 3A
13.27   it] 1E, 2A, 2E, 3E, 1F, 3A, ARE; *omitted* 4E
*14.15   countries] 1E, 2E; counties 2A, 3E, 4E, 1F, 3A, ARE
15.19   that] 1E, 2A, 2E, 3E, 4E, 1F, 3A; *omitted* ARE
16.21   on] 1E, 2A, 2E, 3E, 4E, 1F, 3A; upon ARE
17.27   that amounts] 1E, 2A, 2E, 3E, 4E, 1F, 3A; which
                 amounts ARE
17.35   a] 1E, 2E, 2A, 3A, ARE; *omitted* 3E, 4E, 1F
17.37   often] 1E, 2E, 2A, 3A, ARE; *omitted* 3E, 4E, 1F
18.7   both] 1E, 2E, 2A, 3A, ARE; *omitted* 3E, 4E, 1F
*18.12   halls] 1E, 2E, 2A, 3A, ARE; walls 3E, 4E, 1F
18.14   epitomes] 1E, 2A, 2E, 3E, 4E, 1F, 3A; epitome ARE
18.20   home] 1E, 2E, 3E, 4E, 1F, 3A, ARE; *omitted* 2A
18.34   churchyard] 1E, 2E, 3E, 4E, 1F, 3A; church ARE;
                 church yard 2A
20.12   she has] 1E, 2A, 2E, 3E, 4E, 1F, 3A; *omitted* ARE
20.15   frizzed] 1E, 2E, 2A, 3A, ARE; frizzled 3E, 4E, 1F
21.23   that] 1E, 2A, 2E, 3E, 4E, 1F, 3A; who ARE
*21.37   past] 1E, 2A, 2E, 3E, 4E, 1F, 3A; passed 1A, ARE
21.38   has] 1E, 2A, 2E, 3E, 4E, 1F, 3A; *omitted* ARE

22.8	to] 1E, 2A, 2E, 3E, 4E, 1F, 3A; *omitted* 1A, ARE
22.8	an especial] 1E, 2E, 2A, 3A, ARE; a special 3E, 4E, 1F
24.19	at] 1E, 2A, 2E, 3E, 1F, 3A, ARE; of 4E
24.21	that she] 1E, 2A, 2E, 3E, 4E, 1F, 3A; she ARE
24.40	I have had] 1E, 2A, 2E, 3E, 4E, 1F, 3A; *omitted* ARE
26.21	the kind] 1E, 2E, 2A, 3A, ARE; this kind 3E, 4E, 1F
26.26	that] 1E, 2A, 2E, 3E, 4E, 1F, 3A; which ARE
30.4	infidels] 1E, 2E, 2A, 3A, ARE; individuals 3E, 4E, 1F
30.9	had been] 1E, 2A, 2E, 3E, 4E, 1F, 3A; *omitted* ARE
30.16	frizzed] 1E, 2E, 2A, 3A, ARE; frizzled 3E, 4E, 1F
30.18	lithe] 1E, 2E, 2A, 3A, ARE; little 3E, 4E, 1F
30.21	curtsy] 1E, 2A, 2E, 3E, 4E, 1F, 3A; courtesy ARE
31.11	of first-rate] 1E, 2E, 2A, 3A, ARE; of the first-rate, 3E, 4E, 1F
31.21	in] 1E, 2A, 2E, 3E, 4E, 3A, ARE; at 1F
32.10	of] 1E, 2A, 2E, 3E, 4E, 1F, 3A; at ARE
*32.14	loyalty] 1E, 2A, 2E, 3E, 4E, 1F, 3A; royalty ARE
34.22	most] 1E, 2A, 2E, 3E, 4E, 1F, 3A; *omitted* ARE
36.21	the] 1E, 2A, 2E, 3E, 1F, 3A, ARE; *omitted* 4E
37.6	owned] 1E, 2E, 3E, 4E, 1F, ARE; own 2A, 3A
38.11	yet] 1E, 2A, 2E, 3E, 4E, 1F, 3A; *omitted* ARE
38.33	once] 1E, 2A, 2E, 3E, 4E, 1F, 3A; *omitted* ARE
39.5	found that they had] 1E, 2A, 2E, 3E, 4E, 1F, 3A; *omitted* ARE
40.7	that is] 1E, 2A, 2E, 3E, 4E, 1F, 3A; *omitted* ARE
40.22	blade] 1E, 2E, 2A, 3A, ARE; gallant 3E, 4E, 1F
40.34	on] 1E, 2E, 2A, 3E23, 3E24, 1F, 3A, ARE; in 3E25, 4E
40.37	a] 1E, 2E, 2A, 3E23, 3E24, 1F, 3A, ARE; *omitted* 3E25, 4E
40.39	wag] 1E, 2A, 2E, 3E, 1F, 3A, ARE; wig 4E
41.2	that] 1E, 2E, 2A, 3E23, 3E24, 1F, 3A, ARE; who 3E25, 4E
41.35	the] 1E, 2E, 2A, 3E23, 3E24, 1F, 3A, ARE; what 3E25, 4E
42.6	but a] 1E, 2E, 2A, 3A, ARE; but, as Major Pendergast says, a 3E, 4E, 1F
43.9	round] 1E, 2E, 3E, 4E, 1F; around 2A, 3A, ARE
44.23	but] 1E, 2A, 2E, 3E, 4E, 1F, 3A; *omitted* ARE
44.29	has] 1E, 2A, 2E, 3E, 4E, 1F, 3A; had ARE
44.38	thorough] 1E, 2E, 2A, 3E23, 3E24, 1F, 3A, ARE; through 3E25, 4E
45.1	by false] 1E, 2E, 3E, 4E, 1F, ARE; by no false 2A, 3A
46.17	stand] 1E, 2A, 2E, 3E, 4E, 1F, 3A; stands ARE

46.23   round] 1E, 2E, 3E, 4E, 1F; around 2A, 3A, ARE
46.32   that] 1E, 2A, 2E, 3E, 4E, 1F, 3A; which ARE
48.14   mysterious] 1E, 2E, 2A, 3E23, 3E24, 1F, 3A, ARE; mys-
             tical 3E25, 4E
48.18   that] 1E, 2A, 2E, 3E, 4E, 1F, 3A; who ARE
48.19   that] 1E, 2A, 2E, 3E, 4E, 1F, 3A; who ARE
48.27   that] 1E, 2A, 2E, 3E, 4E, 1F, 3A; whom ARE
49.7   but I] 1E, 2A, 2E, 3E, 4E, 1F, 3A; but ARE
49.29   now] 1E, 2E, 3E, 4E, 1F, 3A, ARE; new 2A
°49.32   hard-drinking] 1E, 2A, 2E, 3E, 4E, 1F, 3A; hardened
             ARE
50.20   finishing his] 1E, 2E, 2A, 3A, ARE; finishing 3E, 4E, 1F
51.19   dog, and] 1E, 2E, 2A, 3A, ARE; dog, 3E, 4E, 1F
52.10   or] 1E, 2A, 2E, 3E, 4E, 1F, 3A, ARE49, ARE53; of
             ARE59
53.24   confounded] 1E, 2A, 2E, 3E, 1F, 3A, ARE; confound-
             edly 4E
53.26   terrible] 1E, 2A, 2E, 3E, 1F, 3A, ARE; terrible high 4E
54.12   on] 1E, 2E, 3E, 4E, 1F, 3A, ARE; o 2A
54.16   of] 1E, 2A, 2E, 3E, 4E, 1F, 3A; omitted ARE
54.35   that] 1E, 2A, 2E, 3E, 4E, 1F, 3A; who ARE
55.7   up to] 1E, 2E, 2A, 3A, ARE; versed in 3E, 4E, 1F
55.17   credits] 1E, 2A, 2E, 3E, 4E, 1F, 3A; credit ARE
55.25   was] 1E, 2A, 2E, 3E, 4E, 1F, 3A; was now ARE
°55.35   toper] 1E, 2A, 2E, 3E, 4E, 1F, 3A; topers ARE
57.4   that] 1E, 2A, 2E, 3E, 4E, 1F, 3A; omitted ARE
57.11   that] 1E, 2A, 2E, 3E, 4E, 1F, 3A; which ARE
57.25   that the squire] 1E, 2A, 2E, 3E, 4E, 1F, 3A; he ARE
58.20   among] 1E, 2A, 2E, 3E, 1F, 3A, ARE; amongst 4E
58.28   from] 1E, 2A, 2E, 3E, 4E, 1F, 3A; omitted ARE
59.12   earth shall] 1E, 2A, 2E, 3E, 4E, 1F, 3A; earth will ARE
59.13   and shall] 1E, 2A, 2E, 3E, 4E, 1F, 3A; and ARE
59.22   that] 1E, 2A, 2E, 3E, 4E, 1F, 3A; which ARE
59.27   the gallant, the amiable, the elegant Sir Philip] 1E, 2E,
             2A, 3A, ARE; omitted 3E, 4E, 1F
59.39   that] 1E, 2A, 2E, 3E, 4E, 1F, 3A; which ARE
°60.15   as] 1E, 2A, 2E, 3E, 4E, 1F, 3A; as those ARE
60.19   which rise] 1E, 2A, 2E, 3E, 4E, 1F, 3A; rising ARE
60.21   all nature] 1E, 2E, 2A, 3A, ARE; all great natures 3E,
             4E, 1F; all natures 1A
60.34   would] 1E, 2A, 2E, 3E, 1F, 3A, ARE; should 4E
61.13   that] 1E, 2A, 2E, 3E, 4E, 1F, 3A; which ARE
61.21   past] 1E, 2A, 2E, 3E, 4E, 1F, 3A; passed ARE

62.2	expressions] 1E, 2A, 2E, 3E23, 3E24, 1F, 3A, ARE; expression 3E25, 4E
62.20	that] 1E, 2A, 2E, 3E, 4E, 1F, 3A; who ARE
62.21	several] 1E, 2A, 2E, 3E, 4E, 1F, 3A; some ARE
63.40	you] 1E, 2E, 3E, 4E, 1F, 3A, ARE; yon 2A
65.7	built of] 1E, 2E, 3E, 4E, 1F, ARE; built with 2A, 3A
66.1	that] 1E, 2A, 2E, 3E, 4E, 1F, 3A; who ARE
66.42	faithfully been] 1E, 2A, 2E, 3E, 4E, 3A, ARE; been faithfully 1F
67.12	another] 1E, 2A, 2E, 3E24, 3E25, 4E, 3A, ARE; other 3E23, 1F
67.20	her] 1E, 2E, 3E, 4E, 1F, ARE; the 2A, 3A
67.28	those] 1E, 2E, 3E, 4E, 1F, ARE; these 2A; the 3A
67.33	perplexed] 1E, 2A, 2E, 3E23, 3E24, 1F, 3A, ARE; perplexing 3E25, 4E
68.2–3	of one] 1E, 2E, 3E, 4E, 1F, ARE; *omitted* 2A, 3A
69.10	riding in] 1E, 2E, 2A, 3A, ARE; using 3E, 4E, 1F
70.16	that blows] 1E, 2A, 2E, 3E, 4E, 1F, 3A; *omitted* ARE
72.6	his] 1E, 2E, 2A, 3A, ARE; the 3E, 4E, 1F
73.9	there is] 1E, 2A, 2E, 3E, 4E, 1F, 3A; *omitted* ARE
73.9	that] 1E, 2A, 2E, 3E, 4E, 1F, 3A; *omitted* ARE
73.32	her] 1E, 2E, 3E, 4E, 1F, ARE; a 2A, 3A
*74.21	trouble] 1E, 2A, 2E, 3E, 4E, 1F, 3A; labor ARE
77.7	council] 1E, 2E; counsel 3E, 2A, 4E, 1F, 3A, ARE
77.42	that lay] 1E, 2A, 2E, 3E, 4E, 1F, 3A; *omitted* ARE
78.1	this] 1E, 2A, 2E, 3E, 1F, 3A, ARE; the 4E
78.13	you] 1E, 2A, 2E, 3A, ARE; you have, 3E, 4E, 1F
78.24	rose] 1E, 2A, 2E, 3A, ARE; risen 3E, 4E, 1F
78.32	from] 1E, 2A, 2E, 3E, 4E, 1F, 3A; *omitted* ARE
82.30	exaltation] 1E, 2A, 2E, 3E, 4E, 1F, 3A; exaltations ARE
83.7	that] 1E, 2A, 2E, 3E, 4E, 1F, 3A; which ARE
*84.27	yielded] 1Ea–c, 2A, 3E, 4E, 1F, 3A, ARE; yields 2E
85.7	fleshly] 1E, 2A, 2E, 3E, 1F, 3A; fleshy 1A, 4E, ARE
85.12	there is] 1E, 2A, 2E, 3E, 4E, 1F, 3A; *omitted* ARE
85.13	that] 1E, 2A, 2E, 3E, 4E, 1F, 3A; *omitted* ARE
85.25	idea] 1E, 2A, 2E, 3E24, 3E25, 4E, 1F, 3A, ARE; ideas 3E23
85.35	that] 1E, 2A, 2E, 3E, 4E, 1F, 3A; whom ARE
85.36	that] 1E, 2A, 2E, 3E, 4E, 1F, 3A; who ARE
86.4	bounds] 1E, 2A, 2E, 3E23, 3E24, 1F, 3A, ARE; bonds 3E25, 4E
86.8	fleshly] 1E, 2A, 2E, 3E23, 3E24, 1F, 3A, ARE; fleshy 3E25, 4E

86.36	name] 1E, 2A, 2E, 3A, ARE; names 3E, 4E, 1F
88.15	youth] 1E, 2A, 2E, 3E, 4E, 1F, 3A; youth; and ARE
88.25–26	that ... that ... that] 1E, 2A, 2E, 3E, 4E, 1F, 3A; who ... who ... who ARE
89.40	cool-blooded] 1E, 2A, 2E, 3E, 4E, 1F, 3A; cold-blooded ARE
90.8	towards] 1E, 2E, 3E, 4E, 1F; toward 2A, 3A, ARE
90.9	into] 1E, 2E, 3E, 4E, 1F; in 2A, 3A, ARE
90.29	in the] 1E, 2A, 2E, 3E, 4E, 1F, 3A; in ARE
91.11	from] 1E, 2A, 2E, 3E, 4E, 1F, 3A; omitted 1A, ARE
91.20	that were] 1E, 2A, 2E, 3E, 4E, 1F, 3A; omitted ARE
91.22	tinkled] 1E, 2A, 2E, 3E, 4E, 3A, ARE; tingled 1F
93.34	driven] 1E, 2A, 2E, 3E24, 3E25, 4E, 1F, 3A, ARE; omitted 3E23
93.37	after] 1E, 2A, 2E, 3E, 4E, 1F, 3A; afterwards ARE
95.15	that] 1E, 2A, 2E, 3E, 4E, 1F, 3A; which ARE
96.33	him] 1E, 2A, 2E, 3E23, 3E24, 1F, 3A, ARE; him of 3E25, 4E
96.42	very] 1E, 2A, 2E, 3E, 1F, 3A, ARE; omitted 4E
100.7	compassed] 1E, 2E, 3E, 4E, 1F, 3A, ARE; compose 2A
100.25	in general,] 1E, 2A, 2E, 3E, 4E, 1F, 3A; omitted ARE
101.23	but] 1E, 2A, 2E, 3E, 4E, 1F, 3A; but a ARE
101.29	yet] 1E, 2A, 2E, 3E, 4E, 1F, 3A; omitted ARE
101.30	he] 1E, 2A, 2E, 3E, 4E, 1F, 3A; omitted ARE
102.39	from] 1E, 2A, 2E, 3E, 4E, 1F, 3A; omitted ARE
103.3	that] 1E, 2A, 2E, 3E, 4E, 1F, 3A; which ARE
103.9	that led] 1E, 2A, 2E, 3E, 4E, 1F, 3A; leading ARE
103.16	it was] 1E, 2A, 2E, 3E, 4E, 1F, 3A; omitted ARE
°104.4	said that all] 1E, 2A, 2E, 3E, 4E, 1F, 3A; said, "All ARE
104.6	He] 1E, 2A, 2E, 3E, 4E, 1F, 3A; I ARE
104.6	his] 1E, 2A, 2E, 3E, 4E, 1F, 3A; my ARE
104.7	lived] 1E, 2A, 2E, 3E, 4E, 1F, 3A; live ARE
104.7	they had] 1E, 2A, 2E, 3E, 4E, 1F, 3A; we have ARE
104.8	they had] 1E, 2A, 2E, 3E, 4E, 1F, 3A; we have ARE
104.9	worked] 1E, 2A, 2E, 3E, 4E, 1F, 3A; work ARE
104.10	believed] 1E, 2A, 2E, 3E, 4E, 1F, 3A; believe ARE
104.10	to be one that] 1E, 2A, 2E, 3E, 4E, 1F, 3A; omitted ARE
104.10	dealt] 1E, 2A, 2E, 3E, 4E, 1F, 3A; deals ARE
104.11	were] 1E, 2A, 2E, 3E, 4E, 1F, 3A; they are ARE
104.12	" said the Gitano, "] 1E, 2A, 2E, 3E, 4E, 1F, 3A; omitted ARE
104.12	we] 1E, 2A, 2E, 3E, 4E, 1F, 3A; we Gitanas ARE

104.12	that] 1E, 2A, 2E, 3E, 4E, 1F, 3A; to ARE
104.13	much] 1E, 2A, 2E, 3E, 4E, 1F, 3A; *omitted* ARE
104.19	sat] 1E, 2E, 3E, 4E, 1F, 3A, ARE; set 2A
105.7	that there was] 1E, 2A, 2E, 3E, 4E, 1F, 3A; *omitted* ARE
105.25	that] 1E, 2A, 2E, 3E, 4E, 1F, 3A; *omitted* ARE
106.12	He found, however, that she] 1E, 2A, 2E, 3E, 4E, 1F, 3A; She ARE
106.12	out] 1E, 2A, 2E, 3E, 4E, 1F, 3A; out, however, ARE
106.16	, however,] 1E, 2A, 2E, 3E, 4E, 1F, 3A; *omitted* ARE
106.40–41	It was evident that he was] 1E, 2A, 2E, 3E, 4E, 1F, 3A; He was evidently ARE
107.11	his] 1E, 2A, 2E, 3E23, 3E24, 1F, 3A, ARE; the 3E25, 4E
107.21	at] 1E, 2A, 2E, 3E, 4E, 3A, ARE; of 1F
107.28	enough] 1E, 2A, 2E, 3E, 4E, 1F, 3A; *omitted* ARE
108.1	vehemence] 1E, 2A, 2E, 3E, 4E, 3A, ARE; violence 1F
109.1	Ay] 1E, 2E, 3E, 4E, 1F; Ah 2A, 3A, ARE; Aye MSE
109.18	that] 1E, 2A, 2E, 3E, 4E, 1F, 3A; which ARE
109.24	most] 1E, 2A, 2E, 3E23, 3E24, 1F, 3A, ARE; more 3E25, 4E
109.33	against a] 1E, 2A, 2E, 3A, ARE; against the 3E, 4E, 1F
110.37	those] 1E, 2E, 3E, 4E, 1F; these 2A, 3A, ARE
112.13	had] 1E, 2A, 2E, 3E, 4E, 1F, 3A; *omitted* ARE
112.18	was] 1E, 2A, 2E, 3A, ARE; is 3E, 4E, 1F
113.32	that were] 1E, 2A, 2E, 3E, 4E, 1F, 3A; *omitted* ARE
115.8	further] 1E, 2A, 2E, 3A, ARE; farther 3E, 4E, 1F
116.31	that] 1E, 2A, 2E, 3E, 4E, 1F, 3A; which ARE
116.33	dream of] 1E, 2E, 3E, 4E, 1F, 3A, ARE; dream 2A
117.42	exaltation] 1E, 2A, 2E, 3E23, 3E24, 1F, 3A, ARE; exultation 3E25, 4E
118.5	lest] 1E, 2E, 3E, 4E, 1F, 3A, ARE; less 2A
118.32	alleys] 1E, 2A, 2E, 3A, ARE; valleys 3E, 4E, 1F
119.13	alleys] 1E, 2A, 2E, 3A, ARE; valleys 3E, 4E, 1F
120.3	woman] 1E, 2A, 2E, 3E23, 3E24, 1F, 3A, ARE; women 3E25, 4E
120.7	sprung] 1E, 2A, 2E, 3E, 4E, 1F, 3A; sprang 1A, ARE
121.6	covert] 1E, 2A, 2E, 3A, ARE; cover 3E, 4E, 1F
121.25	would] 1E, 2A, 2E, 3E, 1F, 3A, ARE; could 4E
121.28	a] 1E, 2E, 3E, 4E, 1F, 3A, ARE; *omitted* 2A
123.4	with] 1E, 2A, 2E, 3A, ARE; with the 3E, 4E, 1F
123.10	traces] 1E, 2E, 3E, 4E, 1F, ARE; graces 2A, 3A
123.20	towards] 1E, 2E, 3A, ARE; toward 2A, 3E, 4E, 1F
124.5	into] 1E, 2A, 2E, 3E23, 3E24, 1F, 3A, ARE; in 3E25, 4E

124.7   temperate] 1E, 2A, 2E, 3E, 4E, 3A, ARE; temperated 1F
124.29   besides] 1E, 2E, 3E, 4E, 1F; beside 1A, 2A, 3A, ARE
124.38   entwining of] 1E, 2A, 2E, 3A, ARE; entwining the
             3E, 4E, 1F

126.31   by] 1E, 2A, 2E, 3E23, 3E24, 1F, 3A, ARE; with 3E25, 4E
128.15   Spanish] 1E, 2A, 2E, 3E23, 3E24, 1F, 3A, ARE; Spaniards
             3E25, 4E
°128.20   woods] 1Ea–c, 2A22, 3E, 4E, 1F; wood 2E, 2A26, 3A,
             ARE

128.25   or to] 1E, 2A, 2E, 3E23, 3E24, 1F, 3A, ARE; or 3E25, 4E
129.27   open] 1E, 2A, 2E, 3E, 4E, 1F, 3A; opened ARE
130.9   further] 1E, 2A, 2E, 3E23, 3E24, 1F, 3A, ARE; farther
             1A, 3E25, 4E

130.36   from] 1E, 2A, 2E, 3E, 4E, 1F, 3A; *omitted* ARE
131.27   suite] 1E, 2A, 2E, 3E, 4E, 1F, 3A; suit ARE
131.29   at] 1E, 2A, 2E, 3E, 4E, 1F, 3A; on ARE
132.21–22   that had been] 1E, 2A, 2E, 3E, 4E, 1F, 3A; *omitted*
             ARE

132.32   from] 1E, 2A, 2E, 3E, 4E, 1F, 3A; *omitted* ARE
133.16   avowed] 1E, 2A, 2E, 3E, 4E, 1F, 3A; allowed ARE
134.13   slight] 1E, 2A, 2E, 3E, 4E, 1F, 3A; little ARE
136.4   times been expressly] 1E, 2A, 2E, 3E, 1F, 3A, ARE;
             times expressly been 4E

136.7   and] 1E, 2A, 2E, 3E, 4E, 1F, 3A; *omitted* ARE
136.7   bush, and] 1E, 2A, 2E, 3E, 4E, 1F, 3A; bush, ARE
136.7   dream, and] 1E, 2A, 2E, 3E, 4E, 1F, 3A; dream, ARE
138.10   into] 1E, 2A, 2E, 3E, 4E, 1F, 3A; in ARE
139.24   It was in vain that] 1E, 2A, 2E, 3E, 4E, 1F, 3A; In
             vain ARE

139.33   by] 1E, 2A, 2E, 3E, 4E, 1F, 3A; *omitted* ARE
139.37   the] 1E, 2A, 2E, 3E, 4E, 1F, 3A; *omitted* ARE
141.6   from] 1E, 2A, 2E, 3E, 4E, 1F, 3A; *omitted* ARE
142.18   me] 1E, 2A, 2E, 3E, 1F, 3A, ARE; *omitted* 4E
143.25   from his] 1E, 2E, 3E, 4E, 1F, ARE; from the 2A, 3A
145.7   of] 1E, 2A, 2E, 3E, 4E, 1F, 3A; of the ARE
145.13   further] 1E, 2E; farther 2A, 3E, 4E, 1F, 3A, ARE
145.14   further] 1E, 2E; farther 2A, 3E, 4E, 1F, 3A, ARE
145.16   further] 1E, 2E; farther 2A, 3E, 4E, 1F, 3A, ARE
145.24   from the] 1E, 2A, 2E, 3E, 4E, 1F, 3A; from ARE
145.38   From thence he lured me] 1E, 2A, 2E, 3E, 4E, 1F, 3A;
             He lured me thence ARE
146.2   further] 1E, 2E, 3E, 4E, 1F; farther 2A, 3A, ARE
146.38   that was] 1E, 2A, 2E, 3E, 4E, 1F, 3A; *omitted* ARE

146.39   procession] 1E, 2A, 2E, 3E24, 3E25, 4E, 1F, 3A, ARE;
          possession 3E23
147.37   boys, by] 1E, 2E, 3E, 4E, 1F; boys, 2A, 3A, ARE
148.29   which] 1E, 2A, 2E, 3E, 4E, 1F, 3A; *omitted* ARE
148.38   upon] 1E, 2A, 2E, 3E, 4E, 3A, ARE; on 1F
149.4   among] 1E, 2A, 2E, 3A, ARE; from 3E, 4E, 1F
149.30   eye] 1E, 2A, 2E, 3E, 4E, 3A, ARE; ear 1F
150.34   intellects] 1E, 2A, 2E, 3A, ARE; intellect 3E, 4E, 1F
151.5   from] 1E, 2A, 2E, 3E, 4E, 1F, 3A; *omitted* ARE
151.16   As] 1Ea–c, 2A, 3E, 4E, 1F, 3A, ARE; *omitted* 2E
151.20   moments] 1E, 2A, 2E, 3E23, 3E24, 1F, 3A, ARE; moment
          3E25, 4E
151.21   that] 1E, 2A, 2E, 3E, 4E, 1F, 3A; *omitted* 1A, ARE
152.1   Further] 1E; Farther 2A, 2E, 3E, 4E, 1F, 3A, ARE
152.22   by] 1E, 2A, 2E, 3E, 4E, 1F, 3A; of ARE
152.37   when] 1E, 2E, 3E, 4E, 1F; where 2A, 3A, ARE
152.39   their] 1E, 2A, 2E, 3E23, 3E24, 1F, 3A; the 3E25, 4E,
          ARE
154.9   yelped, and] 1E, 2A, 2E, 3E, 4E, 1F, 3A; yelped, ARE
154.19   of] 1E, 2A, 2E, 3E, 4E, 1F, 3A; in ARE
157.13   that] 1E, 2A, 2E, 3E, 4E, 1F, 3A; who ARE
157.29   advice."] 1E, 2A, 2E, 3E, 4E, 1F, 3A; advice." *The
          reader who has perused a little work published by
          the author several years subsequently to Bracebridge
          Hall, narrating a visit to Abbotsford, will detect the
          origin of the above anecdote in the conference between
          Sir Walter Scott and his right-hand man, Tommy
          Purdie. Indeed, the author is indebted for several of
          his traits of the Squire to observations made on Sir
          Walter Scott during that visit: though he had to be
          cautious and sparing in drawing from that source.
          ARE
157.36–37 ever was] 1E, 2A, 2E, 3E, 4E, 1F, 3A; was ever 1A,
          ARE
158.29   which may be] 1E, 2A, 2E, 3E, 4E, 1F, 3A; *omitted*
          ARE
159.9–10 customs, they are fond of] 1E, 2A, 2E, 3E, 4E, 1F, 3A;
          customs and ARE
159.20   high-feeding] T; high fed 3E, 4E, 1F; high feeding 1E,
          2A, 2E, 3A, ARE
159.25   to] 1E, 2A, 2E, 3E, 4E, 1F, 3A; *omitted* ARE
159.28   fellow-subject] 1E, 2E, 3E, 4E, 1F; fellow-subjects 2A,
          3A, ARE

159.40	yet] 1E, 2A, 2E, 3E, 4E, 1F, 3A; *omitted* ARE
161.6	further] 1E, 2E, 3E, 4E, 1F; farther 1A, 2A, 3A, ARE
161.32	fancy] 1E, 2A, 2E, 3E, 4E, 1F, 3A; consider ARE
161.37	subject] 1E, 2E, 3E, 4E, 1F; subjects 2A, 3A, ARE
162.2	from which] 1E, 2A, 2E, 3E, 4E, 1F, 3A; whence ARE
163.6	had put on] 1E, 2A, 2E, 3E, 4E, 1F, 3A; were ARE
163.16	that we should take] 1E, 2A, 2E, 3E, 4E, 1F, 3A; *omitted* ARE
163.17	that] 1E, 2A, 2E, 3E, 4E, 1F, 3A; which ARE
163.18	and to] 1E, 2A, 2E, 3E, 4E, 1F, 3A; and ARE
163.24	even] 1E, 2A, 2E, 3E, 4E, 1F, 3A; *omitted* ARE
163.28	from] 1E, 2A, 2E, 3E, 4E, 1F, 3A; *omitted* ARE
163.31	that] 1E, 2A, 2E, 3E, 4E, 1F, 3A; *omitted* ARE
163.33	see to] 1E, 2A, 2E, 3E, 4E, 1F, 3A; see ARE
163.33	lead] 1E, 2A, 2E, 3E, 4E, 1F, 3A; lead to ARE
163.33	I was] 1E, 2E, 3E, 4E, 1F; *omitted* ARE; was 2A, 3A
163.38	that overhung] 1E, 2A, 2E, 3E, 4E, 1F, 3A; overhanging ARE
164.1	which had] 1E, 2A, 2E, 3E, 4E, 1F, 3A; *omitted* ARE
164.36	about] 1E, 2A, 2E, 3E23, 3E24, 1F, 3A, ARE; upon 3E25, 4E
164.42	that] 1E, 2A, 2E, 3E, 4E, 1F, 3A; who ARE
165.4	life,] 1E, 2E, 3E, 4E, 1F; life, to 1A, 2A, 3A, ARE
165.4	to] 1E, 2E, 3E, 4E, 1F; *omitted* 1A, 2A, 3A, ARE
165.16	that] 1E, 2A, 2E, 3E, 4E, 1F, 3A; *omitted* ARE
166.17	that] 1E, 2A, 2E, 3E, 4E, 1F, 3A; which ARE
166.18	was] 1E, 2A, 2E, 3A, ARE; should be 3E, 4E, 1F
166.22	that] 1E, 2A, 2E, 3E, 4E, 1F, 3A; who ARE
166.34	consequence] 1E, 2A, 2E, 3E23, 3E24, 1F, 3A, ARE; confidence 3E25, 4E
166.34	tradesman] 1E, 2A, 2E, 3E, 1F, 3A, ARE; tradesmen 4E
167.5	spent] 1E, 2E, 3E, 4E, 1F, 3A, ARE; spend 2A
167.16	bestrode] 1E, 2A, 2E, 3E23, 3E24, 1F, 3A, ARE; bestrid 3E25, 4E
°167.25	phlegrae] 1E, 2A, 2E, 3E23, 3E24, 1F, 3A, ARE; phlegraeus 3E25, 4E
167.38	spirit] 1E, 2A, 2E, 3E, 4E, 1F, 3A; *omitted* ARE
168.29	1593] 1E, 2E, 3E, 4E, 1F, 3A, ARE; 1793 2A
169.4	that] 1E, 2A, 2E, 3E, 4E, 1F, 3A; which ARE
169.10	that it is] 1E, 2A, 2E, 3E, 4E, 1F, 3A; it ARE; it is 1A
169.24	but] 1E, 2E, 3E, 4E, 1F, 3A, ARE; but to 2A
170.10	in spite of] 1E, 2A, 2E, 3E, 4E, 1F, 3A; notwithstanding ARE

170.19–20   that takes place] 1E, 2A, 2E, 3E, 4E, 1F, 3A; *omitted* ARE

170.37   that] 1E, 2A, 2E, 3E, 4E, 1F, 3A; *omitted* ARE

171.32   caught] 1E, 2A, 2E, 3E, 4E, 1F, 3A; caught a ARE

*171.39   what] 1E, 2E, 3E, 4E, 1F, 3A; *omitted* 2A, ARE

171.39   even] 1E, 2E, 3E, 4E, 1F, 3A, ARE; *omitted* 2A

172.20   wealth] 1E, 2A, 2E, 3E23, 3E24, 1F, 3A, ARE; worth 3E25, 4E

172.24   this] 1E, 2A, 2E, 3E23, 3E24, 1F, 3A, ARE; the 3E25, 4E

172.31   of the] 1E, 2E, 3E, 4E, 1F; of 2A, 3A, ARE

174.22   we] 1E, 2E, 3E, 4E, 1F; he 2A, 3A, ARE

174.35   Simon's] 1Ea–c, 2A, 3E, 4E, 1F, 3A, ARE; Simon 2E

174.40   his fondness] 1E, 2A, 2E, 3E23, 3E24, 1F, 3A, ARE; this fondness 3E25, 4E

176.5   , as it were,] 1E, 2A, 2E, 3E, 4E, 1F, 3A; *omitted* ARE

176.10   that is] 1E, 2A, 2E, 3E, 4E, 1F, 3A; *omitted* ARE

176.27   cannot but] 1E, 2A, 2E, 3E, 4E, 1F, 3A; *omitted* ARE

176.31   that] 1E, 2A, 2E, 3E, 4E, 1F, 3A; which ARE

179.7   that] 1E, 2A, 2E, 3E, 4E, 1F, 3A, who ARE

181.23   his] 1E, 2E, 3E, 4E, 1F; its 2A, 3A, ARE

182.27   further] 1E, 2A, 2E, 3E, 1F, 3A, ARE; farther 4E

183.6   man that] 1E, 2A, 2E, 3E, 4E, 1F, 3A; man who ARE

183.20   that] 1E, 2A, 2E, 3E, 4E, 1F, 3A; which ARE

184.22   and that] 1E, 2A, 2E, 3E, 4E, 1F, 3A; and ARE

184.23   should be] 1E, 2A, 2E, 3E, 4E, 1F, 3A; *omitted* ARE

184.27   with abhorrence,] 1E, 2A, 2E, 3E, 4E, 1F, 3A; *omitted* ARE

184.32   holiday] 1E, 2A, 2E, 3E23, 3E24, 1F, 3A, ARE; holidays 3E25, 4E

185.6   that has] 1E, 2A, 2E, 3E, 4E, 1F, 3A; *omitted* ARE

185.8   to see him one day] 1E, 2E, 3E, 4E, 1F; one day to see him 2A, 3A, ARE

185.11   he] 1E, 2A, 2E, 3E, 4E, 1F, 3A; *omitted* ARE

185.12   at the] 1E, 2A, 2E, 3E, 4E, 1F, 3A; at ARE

187.3   state; I] 1E, 2A, 2E, 3E, 4E, 1F, 3A; state; ARE

187.16   at his] 1E, 2A, 2E, 3E, 4E, 1F, 3A; at his own ARE

187.21   instead of] 1E, 2A, 2E, 3E, 4E, 1F, 3A; and not ARE

187.38   bloody] 1E, 2A, 2E, 3A; to leave marks of blood on ARE; black, ill-shaven beard 3E, 4E, 1F

188.8   before said] 1E, 2A, 2E, 3E, 1F, 3A, ARE; said before 4E

188.26   or] 1E, 2A, 2E, 3E, 4E, 1F, 3A; nor ARE

188.42   naught] 1E, 2A, 2E, 3E, 4E, 3A, ARE; nought 1F

189.13   that is] 1E, 2A, 2E, 3E23, 3E24, 1F, 3A; *omitted* ARE;
                who is 3E25, 4E
189.20   never] 1E, 2A, 2E, 3E, 4E, 1F, 3A; ever ARE
189.20   to] 1E, 2A, 2E, 3E23, 3E24, 1F, 3A, ARE; into 3E25, 4E
191.29   that] 1E, 2A, 2E, 3E, 4E, 1F, 3A; who ARE
191.34   that] 1E, 2A, 2E, 3E, 4E, 1F, 3A; who ARE
192.11   buds;] 1E, 2A, 2E, 3E, 4E, 1F, 3A; buds, and ARE
193.9   that had] 1E, 2A, 2E, 3E, 1F, 3A, ARE; that has 4E
193.10   willing] 1E, 2A, 2E, 3E, 4E, 1F, 3A; willing hastily ARE
193.10–11   hastily that should throw a stigma on] 1E, 2A, 2E, 3E,
                4E, 1F, 3A; derogatory to ARE
193.12   that] 1E, 2A, 2E, 3E, 4E, 1F, 3A; *omitted* ARE
193.12   are very much] 1E, 2A, 2E, 3E, 4E, 1F, 3A; *omitted*
                ARE
193.17   some] 1E, 2A, 2E, 3E, 4E, 1F, 3A; a ARE
193.30   conscious] 1E, 2A, 2E, 3E, 4E, 1F, 3A; unconscious ARE
193.40   leave the] 1E, 2E, 3E, 4E, 1F, ARE; leave their 2A, 3A
194.4   that is] 1E, 2A, 2E, 3E, 4E, 1F, 3A; *omitted* ARE
194.19   take place] 1E, 2A, 2E, 3E, 4E, 1F, 3A; *omitted* ARE
194.28   There was a] 1E, 2A, 2E, 3E, 4E, 1F, 3A; A ARE
194.29   that had long had] 1E, 2A, 2E, 3E, 4E, 1F, 3A; had for
                a long time ARE
195.3   to] 1E, 2A, 2E, 3E, 4E, 1F, 3A; *omitted* ARE
195.8   within the] 1E, 2A, 2E, 3E, 4E, 1F, 3A; within ARE
195.31   upon the grove] 1E, 2E, 3E, 4E, 1F; *omitted* 2A, 3A,
                ARE
195.36–37   seem to be gradually dropping] 1E, 2A, 2E, 3E, 4E, 1F,
                3A; gradually drop ARE
196.21   delighted] 1E, 2A, 2E, 3A, ARE; delightful 3E, 4E, 1F
196.39   I found that there had been booths] 1E, 2A, 2E, 3E,
                4E, 1F, 3A; Booths had been ARE
197.20   for] 1E, 2A, 2E, 3E, 4E, 1F, 3A; for its ARE
197.28   that] 1E, 2A, 2E, 3E, 4E, 1F, 3A; who ARE
197.31   I perceived that] 1E, 2A, 2E, 3E, 4E, 1F, 3A; *omitted*
                ARE
197.34   yet] 1E, 2A, 2E, 3E, 4E, 1F, 3A; *omitted* ARE
197.34   that] 1E, 2A, 2E, 3E, 4E, 1F, 3A; *omitted* ARE
198.30   I saw that] 1E, 2A, 2E, 3E, 4E, 1F, 3A; *omitted* ARE
198.35   seemed to exult] 1E, 2A, 2E, 3E, 4E, 1F, 3A; exulted
                ARE
198.39   had] 1E, 2A, 2E, 3E, 4E, 1F, 3A; *omitted* ARE
199.3–4   It was in vain that] 1E, 2A, 2E, 3E, 4E, 1F, 3A; In
                vain ARE

199.11	there not been] 1E, 2A, 2E, 3E, 4E, 1F, 3A; not ARE
199.12	horse-collar] 1E, 2A, 2E, 3E, 4E, 1F, 3A; horse-collar been ARE
199.28	the young girl that represented] 1E, 2A, 2E, 3E, 4E, 1F, 3A; *omitted* ARE
199.41	that] 1E, 2A, 2E, 3E, 4E, 1F, 3A; *omitted* ARE
200.7	by] 1E, 2A, 2E, 3E23, 3E24, 1F, 3A, ARE; from 3E25, 4E
200.28	seen] 1E, 2A, 2E, 3E, 4E, 1F, 3A; *omitted* ARE
201.13–14	which his patron had sustained] 1E, 2A, 2E, 3E, 4E, 1F, 3A; sustained by his patron ARE
201.16	Mistress] 1E, 2A, 2E, 3E, 1F, 3A, ARE; Mrs. 4E
202.3	that] 1E, 2A, 2E, 3E, 4E, 1F, 3A; *omitted* 1A, ARE
202.18	further] 1E, 2A, 2E, 3E23, 3E24, 1F, 3A; farther 3E25, 4E, ARE
203.6	that fell] 1E, 2A, 2E, 3E, 4E, 1F, 3A; falling ARE
203.7	smell of the] 1E, 2A, 2E, 3E, 4E, 1F, 3A; smell of ARE
203.7–8	singing of the] 1E, 2A, 2E, 3E, 4E, 1F, 3A; singing of ARE
203.8	seemed to produce] 1E, 2A, 2E, 3E, 4E, 1F, 3A; produced ARE
203.9	party, for some] 1E, 2A, 2E, 3E, 4E, 1F, 3A; party. Some ARE
203.14	with] 1E, 2A, 2E, 3E, 1F, 3A, ARE; of 4E
203.24	rung] 1E, 2A, 2E, 3E23, 3E24, 1F, 3A; rang 1A, 3E25, 4E, ARE
203.27	parson] 1E, 2A, 2E, 3A, ARE; clergyman 3E, 4E, 1F
204.6	in] 1E, 2E, 3E, 4E, 1F; of 2A, 3A, ARE
204.13	from] 1E, 2A, 2E, 3E, 4E, 1F, 3A; *omitted* ARE
205.15	that I once made] 1E, 2A, 2E, 3E, 4E, 1F, 3A; *omitted* ARE
205.21	from] 1E, 2A, 2E, 3E, 4E, 1F, 3A; *omitted* ARE
205.29	their] 1E, 2A, 2E, 3E, 4E, 1F, 3A; *omitted* ARE
206.18	which I had seen] 1E, 2A, 2E, 3E, 4E, 1F, 3A; *omitted* ARE
206.23	from] 1E, 2A, 2E, 3E, 4E, 1F, 3A; *omitted* ARE
206.35	in her form; she had not] 1E, 2A, 2E, 3E, 4E, 1F, 3A; , without ARE
206.35	that is] 1E, 2A, 2E, 3E, 4E, 1F, 3A; *omitted* ARE
207.1	from] 1E, 2A, 2E, 3E, 4E, 1F, 3A; *omitted* ARE
207.15	and was brought] 1E, 2A, 2E, 3E, 4E, 1F, 3A; who brought her ARE
207.18	or] 1E, 2A, 2E, 3E, 4E, 1F, 3A; nor ARE
209.5	which] 1E, 2A, 2E, 3E, 4E, 1F, 3A; *omitted* ARE

210.19	relation] 1E, 2A, 2E, 3E, 4E, 1F, 3A; relative 1A, ARE
211.4	at] 1E, 2A, 2E, 3E, 4E, 1F, 3A; on ARE
211.28	sea] 1E, 2E, 3E, 4E, 1F; *omitted* 2A, 3A, ARE
211.30	seen] 1E, 2A, 2E, 3A, ARE; *omitted* 3E, 4E, 1F
212.11	There was a general joy] 1E, 2A, 2E, 3E, 4E, 1F, 3A; A general joy was ARE
212.13	Honfleur. The] 1E, 2A, 2E, 3E23, 3E24, 1F, 3A, ARE; Honfleur, as the 3E25, 4E
212.26	she] 1E, 2A, 2E, 3E, 4E, 1F, 3A; *omitted* ARE
213.19	she has] 1E, 2A, 2E, 3E, 4E, 1F, 3A; there are ARE
213.20	there is] 1E, 2A, 2E, 3E, 4E, 1F, 3A; *omitted* ARE
213.21	attending] 1E, 2A, 2E, 3E, 4E, 1F, 3A; attends ARE
214.2	was rung] 1E, 2A, 2E, 3E, 4E, 1F, 3A; rang ARE
214.26	that] 1E, 2A, 2E, 3E, 4E, 1F, 3A; *omitted* ARE
214.28	that] 1E, 2A, 2E, 3E, 4E, 1F, 3A; *omitted* ARE
214.33	eye] 1E, 2A, 2E, 3E, 4E, 1F, 3A; eyes ARE
°215.28	appeared] 1E, 2A, 2E, 3E, 4E, 1F, 3A; appears ARE
215.29	which had been] 1E, 2A, 2E, 3E, 4E, 1F, 3A; *omitted* ARE
215.30	he had] 1E, 2A, 2E, 3E, 4E, 1F, 3A; he ARE
215.31	sense had] 1E, 2A, 2E, 3E, 4E, 1F, 3A; sense ARE
215.32	he had] 1E, 2A, 2E, 3E, 4E, 1F, 3A; he ARE
215.33	health had] 1E, 2A, 2E, 3E, 4E, 1F, 3A; health ARE
215.34	he had] 1E, 2A, 2E, 3E, 4E, 1F, 3A; he ARE
215.35	had been] 1E, 2A, 2E, 3E, 4E, 1F, 3A; was ARE
215.36	had] 1E, 2A, 2E, 3E, 4E, 1F, 3A; *omitted* ARE
216.14	that] 1E, 2A, 2E, 3E, 4E, 1F, 3A; which ARE
216.14–15	, however, that] 1E, 2A, 2E, 3E, 4E, 1F, 3A; *omitted* ARE
216.15	was] 1E, 2A, 2E, 3E, 4E, 1F, 3A; *omitted* ARE
216.32	that] 1E, 2A, 2E, 3E, 4E, 1F, 3A; *omitted* ARE
217.23	she] 1E, 2A, 2E, 3E, 4E, 1F, 3A; *omitted* ARE
218.9–10	started. She] 1E, 2A, 2E, 3E, 4E, 1F, 3A; started; passed ARE
218.23	which] 1E, 2A, 2E, 3E, 4E, 1F, 3A; *omitted* ARE
218.38	face] 1E, 2A, 2E, 3E, 4E, 1F, 3A; face was ARE
218.41	apprehension] 1E, 2E, 3E, 4E, 1F; apprehensions, 2A, 3A, ARE
219.7	that] 1E, 2A, 2E, 3E, 4E, 1F, 3A; *omitted* ARE
220.16	had often begun] 1E, 2A, 2E, 3E, 4E, 1F, 3A; often began ARE
220.34–41	°Whoever ... capable.] 1E, 2A22, 2E, 3E, 4E, 1F; *omitted* 2A26, 3A, ARE

222.2	recreation] 1E, 2A, 2E, 3E, 1F, 3A, ARE; recreation's 4E
222.14	just] 1E, 2E, 3E, 4E, 1F; thus 2A, 3A, ARE
223.31	else] 1E, 2A, 2E, 3A, ARE; *omitted* 3E, 4E, 1F
223.39–40	like himself; discussing their day's adventures] 1E, 2E, 3E, 4E, 1F; *omitted* 2A, 3A, ARE
224.9	will] 1E, 2E, 3E, 4E, 1F; would 2A, 3A, ARE
224.15	that] 1E, 2A, 2E, 3E, 4E, 1F, 3A; *omitted* ARE; which 1A
224.38	yet] 1E, 2A, 2E, 3E, 4E, 1F, 3A; *omitted* ARE
225.11	bales, boxes] 1E, 2E, 3E, 4E, 1F; boxes, bales 2A, 3A, ARE
226.12	mine] 1E, 2A, 2E, 3E23, 3E24, 1F, 3A, ARE; my 3E25, 4E
227.35	that are] 1E, 2A, 2E, 3E, 4E, 1F, 3A; *omitted* ARE
227.39	To tell the truth, the] 1E, 2A, 2E, 3E, 4E, 1F, 3A; The ARE
228.11	on] 1E, 2E, 3E, 4E, 1F, ARE; in 2A, 3A
229.22	that] 1E, 2A, 2E, 3E, 4E, 1F, 3A; which ARE
229.26	that] 1E, 2A, 2E, 3E, 4E, 1F, 3A; which ARE
229.28	Dobbie] 1E, 2A, 2E, 3E, 4E, 1F, 3A; goblin ARE
230.4	and in] 1E, 2A, 2E, 3E23, 3E24, 1F, 3A, ARE; and 3E25, 4E
230.21	that the belief was] 1E, 2A, 2E, 3E, 4E, 1F, 3A; of a belief ARE
230.32	goblin that were] 1E, 2A, 2E, 3E, 4E, 1F, 3A; goblin, ARE
231.7	however,] 1E, 2A, 2E, 3E, 4E, 1F, 3A; *omitted* ARE
231.9	that is] 1E, 2A, 2E, 3E, 4E, 1F, 3A; *omitted* ARE
231.14–15	in rustic life, or refreshing and beautiful in] 1E, 2E, 3E, 4E, 1F; *omitted* 2A, 3A, ARE
231.20	hearth] 1E, 2E, 3E, 4E, 1F, 3A, ARE; heart 2A
231.20	seem to me to] 1E, 2E, 3E, 4E, 1F; *omitted* ARE; seem to 2A, 3A
231.27	servants] 1E, 2A, 2E, 3A, ARE; servant 3E, 4E, 1F
231.33	, too,] 1E, 2A, 2E, 3E, 4E, 1F, 3A; *omitted* ARE
231.33	seemed to me to] 1E, 2A, 2E, 3E, 4E, 1F, 3A; *omitted* ARE
231.35	honeysuckled] 1E, 2A, 2E, 3E, 4E, 1F, 3A; honeysuckle ARE
°232.5	makes] 1E, 2A, 2E, 3E, 4E, 1F, 3A; make ARE
232.21	that] 1E, 2A, 2E, 3E, 4E, 1F, 3A; which ARE
233.13	that] 1E, 2A, 2E, 3E, 4E, 1F, 3A; *omitted* ARE

235.32	gentlemen] 1E, 2A, 2E, 3E23, 3E24, 1F, 3A, ARE; gentle-man 3E25, 4E
236.38	There was abundant] 1E, 2A, 2E, 3E, 4E, 1F, 3A; Abundant ARE
236.38	concurring] 1E, 2A, 2E, 3E23, 3E24, 1F, 3A, ARE; concurrent 3E25, 4E
236.38	that] 1E, 2A, 2E, 3E, 4E, 1F, 3A; *omitted* ARE
237.1–2	that had been made] 1E, 2A, 2E, 3E, 4E, 1F, 3A; *omitted* ARE
237.38	that is] 1E, 2A, 2E, 3E, 4E, 1F, 3A; *omitted* ARE
237.42	have] 1E, 2E, 3E, 4E, 1F; *omitted* 2A, 3A, ARE
239.6	has] 1E, 2A, 2E, 3E, 4E, 1F, 3A; *omitted* ARE
239.12	that was] 1E, 2A, 2E, 3E, 4E, 1F, 3A; *omitted* ARE
239.16	that] 1E, 2A, 2E, 3E, 4E, 1F, 3A; which ARE
239.23	some bearer] 1E, 2A, 2E, 3E, 4E, 1F, 3A; bearers ARE
240.13–14	which prevailed] 1E, 2A, 2E, 3E, 4E, 1F, 3A; *omitted* ARE
240.18	alight, they] 1E, 2A, 2E, 3E, 4E, 1F, 3A; alight, ARE
240.26	the storm] 1E, 2E, 3E, 4E, 1F, ARE; this storm, 2A, 3A
240.26	had come] 1E, 2A, 2E, 3E, 4E, 1F, 3A; came ARE
240.38	that seemed to prevail] 1E, 2A, 2E, 3E, 4E, 1F, 3A; prevalent ARE
240.40	that took place] 1E, 2A, 2E, 3E, 4E, 1F, 3A; *omitted* ARE
241.3	seems to me to have] 1E, 2A, 2E, 3E, 4E, 1F, 3A; has ARE
242.14	that are] 1E, 2A, 2E, 3E, 4E, 1F, 3A; *omitted* ARE
242.23	seems to have] 1E, 2A, 2E, 3E, 4E, 1F, 3A; has ARE
243.8	risks] 1E, 2A, 2E, 3E, 4E, 1F, 3A; risk ARE
243.12	yet] 1E, 2A, 2E, 3E, 4E, 1F, 3A; *omitted* ARE
243.36	that] 1E, 2A, 2E, 3E, 4E, 1F, 3A; *omitted* ARE
243.41	a] 1E, 2A, 2E, 3E, 4E, 1F; an 3A, ARE
244.2	out] 1E, 2A, 2E, 3E, 4E, 3A, ARE; our 1F
246.11	that are] 1E, 2A, 2E, 3E, 4E, 1F, 3A; *omitted* ARE
247.5	little] 1E, 2E, 3E, 4E, 1F; *omitted* 2A, 3A, ARE
247.20	which he had] 1E, 2A, 2E, 3E, 4E, 1F, 3A; *omitted* ARE
247.25	owed] 1E, 2A, 2E, 3E23, 3E24, 1F, 3A, ARE; owe 3E25, 4E
247.28–42	°I . . . make.] 1E, 2A, 2E, 3E, 4E, 1F, 3A; *omitted* 1A, ARE
247.38	had] 1E, 2E, 3E, 4E, 1F; *omitted* 2A, 3A
248.8	on] 1E, 2E, 3E, 4E, 1F, ARE; upon 2A, 3A

248.27	among] 1E, 2A, 2E, 3E, 4E, 1F, 3A; among the 1A, ARE
248.31	there were] 1E, 2A, 2E, 3E, 4E, 1F, 3A; *omitted* ARE
248.31–32	, which] 1E, 2A, 2E, 3E, 4E, 1F, 3A; *omitted* ARE
248.35–36	weathercocks,] 1E, 2A, 2E, 3E, 4E, 1F, 3A; weathercocks, and ARE
249.3	I remember how] 1E, 2A, 2E, 3E, 4E, 1F, 3A; *omitted* ARE
249.4	precincts] 1E, 2A, 2E, 3E, 4E, 1F, 3A; precinct ARE
249.27	that] 1E, 2A, 2E, 3E, 4E, 1F, 3A; *omitted* ARE
249.39	There was a] 1E, 2A, 2E, 3E, 4E, 1F, 3A; A ARE
249.40	that] 1E, 2A, 2E, 3E, 4E, 1F, 3A; who ARE
249.40	, who] 1E, 2A, 2E, 3E, 4E, 1F, 3A; *omitted* ARE
250.5	he] 1E, 2A, 2E, 3E, 4E, 1F, 3A; *omitted* ARE
252.8	that] 1E, 2A, 2E, 3E, 4E, 1F, 3A; who ARE
252.17	having] 1E, 2A, 2E, 3E, 4E, 1F, 3A; being ARE
253.20	yet] 1E, 2A, 2E, 3E, 4E, 1F, 3A; *omitted* ARE
253.37	apprentice] 1E, 2A, 2E, 3E23, 3E24, 1F, 3A, ARE; apprenticed 3E25, 4E
254.5	He was full of a] 1E, 2A, 2E, 3E, 4E, 1F, 3A; A ARE
254.5	that] 1E, 2A, 2E, 3E, 4E, 1F, 3A; *omitted* ARE
254.6	and] 1E, 2A, 2E, 3E, 4E, 1F, 3A; *omitted* ARE
255.26	from] 1E, 2A, 2E, 3E, 4E, 1F, 3A; *omitted* ARE
256.3	that] 1E, 2A, 2E, 3E, 4E, 1F, 3A; who ARE
256.28	yet] 1E, 2A, 2E, 3E, 4E, 1F, 3A; *omitted* ARE
257.2	that] 1E, 2A, 2E, 3E, 4E, 1F, 3A; who ARE
257.10	crones] 1E, 2A, 2E, 3A, ARE; cronies 3E, 4E, 1F
257.27	the] 1E, 2A, 2E, 3A, ARE; his 3E, 4E, 1F
258.14	had] 1E, 2A, 2E, 3E, 4E, 1F, 3A; *omitted* ARE
258.16	had] 1E, 2A, 2E, 3E, 4E, 1F, 3A; *omitted* ARE
259.34	pride] 1E, 2A, 2E, 3E, 1F, 3A, ARE; joy 4E
260.6	any] 1E, 2E, 3E, 4E, 1F, ARE; *omitted* 2A, 3A
261.23	there's] 1E, 2A, 2E, 3E, 4E, 1F, 3A, ARE49; here's ARE53, ARE59
262.11	that was] 1E, 2A, 2E, 3E, 4E, 1F, 3A; *omitted* ARE
262.11	and] 1E, 2A, 2E, 3E, 4E, 1F, 3A; that ARE
262.17	of] 1E, 2E, 3E, 4E, 1F; *omitted* 2A, 3A, ARE
263.14	to total rout by a] 1E, 2E, 3E, 4E, 1F, ARE; to a total rout by 2A; to a total rout by a 3A
263.20	hence] 1E, 2A, 2E, 3E, 4E, 1F, 3A; this ARE
263.23	from] 1E, 2A, 2E, 3E, 4E, 1F, 3A; *omitted* ARE
263.31	heavy] 1E, 2A, 2E, 3E, 1F, 3A, ARE; *omitted* 4E
263.35	had] 1E, 2A, 2E, 3E, 4E, 1F, 3A; *omitted* ARE

264.7	he] 1E, 2A, 2E, 3E, 4E, 1F, 3A; *omitted* ARE
265.20	they] 1E, 2A, 2E, 3E, 4E, 1F, 3A; *omitted* ARE
266.1	he] 1E, 2A, 2E, 3E, 4E, 1F, 3A; *omitted* ARE
266.21	with] 1E, 2E, 3E, 4E, 1F; by 2A, 3A, ARE
267.13	but be] 1E, 2E, 3E, 4E, 1F; be but 2A, 3A, ARE
268.14	descending] 1E, 2E, 3E, 4E, 1F; descend 2A, 3A, ARE
268.22	had got] 1E, 2A, 2E, 3E, 4E, 1F, 3A; arrived ARE; got 1A
268.27	that] 1E, 2A, 2E, 3E, 4E, 1F, 3A; *omitted* ARE
268.31	that stood near the house] 1E, 2A, 2E, 3E, 4E, 1F, 3A; *omitted* ARE
269.3	that was] 1E, 2A, 2E, 3E, 4E, 1F, 3A; *omitted* ARE
269.25	there] 1E, 2A, 2E, 3E, 4E, 1F, 3A; *omitted* ARE
270.2	called] 1E, 2E, 3E, 4E, 1F; called out 2A, 3A, ARE
270.8	that] 1E, 2A, 2E, 3E, 4E, 1F, 3A; which ARE
270.9	think that] 1E, 2A, 2E, 3E, 4E, 1F, 3A; think ARE
270.10	he was] 1E, 2A, 2E, 3E, 4E, 1F, 3A; *omitted* ARE
270.11	and he] 1E, 2A, 2E, 3E, 4E, 1F, 3A; and ARE
272.30	which] 1E, 2A, 2E, 3E, 4E, 1F, 3A; *omitted* ARE
272.38	point on] 1E, 2A, 2E, 3E, 4E, 3A, ARE; point of 1F
272.39	rocks, he] 1E, 2A, 2E, 3E, 4E, 1F, 3A; rocks, ARE
273.2	still] 1E, 2E, 3E, 4E, 1F; *omitted* 2A, 3A, ARE
273.3	their] 1E, 2E, 3E, 4E, 1F; the 2A, 3A, ARE
*273.25–26	it was an instinctive movement of defence;] 1E, 2A, 2E, 3E, 4E, 1F, 3A; *omitted* ARE
273.26	attack, it] 1E, 2A, 2E, 3E, 4E, 1F, 3A; attack, ARE
273.28	he saw at a glance that he was in the vicinity of] 1E, 2A, 2E, 3E, 4E, 1F, 3A; saw ARE
273.29	that lay] 1E, 2A, 2E, 3E, 4E, 1F, 3A; *omitted* ARE
273.30	to escape] 1E, 2A, 2E, 3E, 4E, 1F, 3A; *omitted* ARE
273.31	was] 1E, 2A, 2E, 3E, 4E, 1F, 3A; *omitted* ARE
273.31	horror; he] 1E, 2A, 2E, 3E, 4E, 1F, 3A; horror, ARE
273.35	saw that the coast rose in] 1E, 2A, 2E, 3E, 4E, 1F, 3A; beheld ARE
273.37	nor any] 1E, 2A, 2E, 3E, 4E, 1F, 3A; no ARE
273.37	amongst] 1E, 2A, 2E, 3E, 4E, 1F, 3A; among ARE; from among 1A
273.39	that overlooked] 1E, 2A, 2E, 3E, 4E, 1F, 3A; overlooking ARE
274.7	further] 1E; farther 1A, 2A, 2E, 3E, 4E, 1F, 3A, ARE
274.14	yet] 1E, 2A, 2E, 3E, 4E, 1F, 3A; *omitted* ARE
274.19–20	hopes that here might be some] 1E, 2A, 2E, 3E, 4E, 1F, 3A; hope of a ARE

274.23	It was with] 1E, 2A, 2E, 3E, 4E, 1F, 3A; With ARE
274.23	that] 1E, 2A, 2E, 3E, 4E, 1F, 3A; *omitted* ARE
274.24	towards] 1E, 2A, 2E, 3E, 4E, 1F, 3A; toward ARE
274.28	that overhung] 1E, 2A, 2E, 3E, 4E, 1F, 3A; overhanging ARE
274.28	from] 1E, 2A, 2E, 3E, 4E, 1F, 3A; *omitted* ARE
274.29–30	that stood] 1E, 2A, 2E, 3E, 4E, 1F, 3A; *omitted* ARE
274.37	full] 1E, 2A, 2E, 3E, 4E, 1F, 3A; *omitted* ARE
274.41–42	Dolph began to doubt whether he was not in a worse condition than before; here] 1E, 2A, 2E, 3E, 4E, 1F, 3A; Here ARE
275.8	sprang] 1E, 2A, 2E, 3E, 1F, 3A, ARE; sprung 4E
275.10	that] 1E, 2A, 2E, 3E, 4E, 1F, 3A; *omitted* ARE
275.11	who was] 1E, 2A, 2E, 3E, 4E, 1F, 3A; *omitted* ARE
275.16	shade] 1E, 2A, 2E, 3E, 4E, 1F, 3A; shadow ARE
275.20–21	he was struck with something that] 1E, 2A, 2E, 3E, 4E, 1F, 3A; something ARE
275.22	his] 1E, 2A, 2E, 3E, 4E, 1F, 3A; *omitted* ARE
275.26	the] 1E, 2A, 2E, 3E, 4E, 1F, 3A; a ARE
275.26–27	with which he was received. As he cast his eyes about, too, he] 1E, 2A, 2E, 3E, 4E, 1F, 3A; received. He ARE
275.29	the] 1E, 2A, 2E, 3E, 4E, 1F, 3A; *omitted* ARE
275.30	which issued] 1E, 2A, 2E, 3E, 4E, 1F, 3A; *omitted* ARE
275.32	he now found that he had] 1E, 2A, 2E, 3E, 4E, 1F, 3A; He had, in fact, ARE
275.36	him] 1E, 2A, 2E, 3E, 4E, 1F, 3A; *omitted* ARE
275.38	which was] 1E, 2A, 2E, 3E, 4E, 1F, 3A; *omitted* ARE
*276.2	fragment] 1E, 2A, 2E, 3E, 4E, 1F, 3A; fragments ARE
276.14	being a man of] 1E, 2A, 2E, 3E, 4E, 1F, 3A; his ARE
276.15	, that were] 1E, 2A, 2E, 3E, 4E, 1F, 3A; being ARE
276.22	He was never] 1E, 2A, 2E, 3E, 4E, 1F, 3A; Never ARE
276.35	he had a] 1E, 2A, 2E, 3E, 4E, 1F, 3A; his ARE
276.36	about him, that] 1E, 2A, 2E, 3E, 4E, 1F, 3A; *omitted* ARE
276.38	house, he] 1E, 2A, 2E, 3E, 4E, 1F, 3A; house ARE
*276.39–40	daughters] 1E, 2A, 2E, 3E, 4E, 1F, 3A; daughter ARE
277.3	It was with] 1E, 2A, 2E, 3E, 4E, 1F, 3A; With ARE
277.3	that] 1E, 2A, 2E, 3E, 4E, 1F, 3A; *omitted* ARE
277.5	which he] 1E, 2A, 2E, 3E, 4E, 1F, 3A; *omitted* ARE
277.12	a lucky circumstance] 1E, 2A, 2E, 3E, 4E, 1F, 3A; lucky for you ARE
277.15	these] 1E, 2E, 3E, 4E, 1F; the 2A, 3A, ARE

278.1   in chorus] 1E, 2A, 2E, 3E, 4E, 1F, 3A; in the chorus
                 ARE
278.9   yet] 1E, 2A, 2E, 3E, 4E, 1F, 3A; *omitted* ARE
278.10   he] 1E, 2A, 2E, 3E, 4E, 1F, 3A; *omitted* ARE, 1A (*sen-
                 tence in 1A changed elsewhere*)
278.25   a kind of] 1E, 2A, 2E, 3E, 4E, 1F, 3A; an ARE
278.31   being again discussed,] 1E, 2A, 2E, 3E, 4E, 1F, 3A;
                 omitted ARE
278.35   this] 1E, 2A, 2E, 3E23, 3E24, 1F, 3A, ARE; the 3E25, 4E
278.36   that] 1E, 2A, 2E, 3E, 4E, 1F, 3A; *omitted* ARE
278.40   since] 1E, 2A, 2E, 3E, 4E, 1F, 3A; *omitted* ARE
279.15   run] 1E, 2A, 2E, 3E23, 3E24, 1F, 3A, ARE; ran 3E25, 4E
279.16   these] 1E, 2A, 2E, 3E, 1F, 3A, ARE; those 4E
279.20   which] 1E, 2A, 2E, 3E, 4E, 1F, 3A; who ARE
280.2–3   it was] 1E, 2A, 2E, 3E, 4E, 1F, 3A; *omitted* ARE
280.6   descended] 1E, 2A, 2E, 3E, 4E, 1F, 3A; fell ARE
280.14   that] 1E, 2A, 2E, 3E, 4E, 1F, 3A; which ARE
280.19   sunk] 1E, 2A, 2E, 3E, 4E, 1F, 3A; sank ARE
282.11   and smoked] 1E, 2E, 3E, 4E, 1F; smoking 2A, 3A, ARE
282.12   listened] 1E, 2A, 2E, 3E, 4E, 1F, 3A; listening ARE
282.34   would reach] 1E, 2A, 2E, 3E, 4E, 1F, 3A; reached ARE
282.35   there would be no ship] 1E, 2A, 2E, 3E, 4E, 1F, 3A;
                 no ship was ARE
282.35   past] 1E, 2A, 2E, 3E, 1F, 3A; passed 1A, 4E, ARE
282.39   by all] 1E, 2A, 2E, 3E, 4E, 1F, 3A; among ARE
282.42–283.1   that were] 1E, 2A, 2E, 3E, 4E, 1F, 3A; *omitted* ARE
283.19   to be] 1E, 2A, 2E, 3E, 4E, 1F, 3A; *omitted* ARE
284.6   Anthony's] 1E, 2E, 3E, 4E, 1F; Antony's 2A, 3A, ARE
284.10   yet] 1E, 2A, 2E, 3E, 4E, 1F, 3A; *omitted* ARE
284.13   which was] 1E, 2A, 2E, 3E, 4E, 1F, 3A; *omitted* ARE
284.16–17   overboard. She] 1E, 2A, 2E, 3E, 4E, 1F, 3A; overboard,
                 and ARE
284.21   , all at once] 1E, 2A, 2E, 3E, 4E, 1F, 3A; *omitted* ARE
284.26   which has since been] 1E, 2A, 2E, 3E, 4E, 1F, 3A;
                 since ARE
284.31   Anthony's] 1E, 2E, 3E, 4E, 1F; Antony's 2A, 3A, ARE
284.33   sung] 1E, 2A, 2E, 3E, 4E, 1F, 3A; sang ARE
284.38   After several] 1E, 2A, 2E, 3E, 4E, 1F, 3A; Several ARE
284.38   had] 1E, 2A, 2E, 3E, 4E, 1F, 3A; having ARE
285.5   this colony] 1E, 2A, 2E, 3E, 4E, 1F, 3A; a crew ARE
285.18   up] 1E, 2A, 2E, 3E, 4E, 1F, 3A; *omitted* ARE
285.18   made] 1E, 2A, 2E, 3E, 4E, 1F, 3A; *omitted* ARE
286.7   he heard] 1E, 2A, 2E, 3E, 4E, 1F, 3A; *omitted* ARE

286.13	was the thought that] 1E, 2A, 2E, 3E, 4E, 1F, 3A; thought ARE
288.3	towards] 1E, 2E, 3E, 4E, 1F; toward 2A, 3A, ARE
288.21	pity] 1E, 2A, 2E, 3E, 4E, 1F, 3A; pity that ARE
288.41	for it had not] 1E, 2A, 2E, 3E, 4E, 1F, 3A; not having ARE; had not 1A
289.23	every one] 1E, 2A, 2E, 3E, 4E, 1F, 3A; each other ARE
291.25–26	there was something that] 1E, 2A, 2E, 3E, 4E, 1F, 3A; something ARE
292.12	that hung] 1E, 2A, 2E, 3E, 4E, 1F, 3A; hanging ARE
292.18	that] 1E, 2A, 2E, 3E, 4E, 1F, 3A; *omitted* ARE
292.29	Dolph] 1E, 2A, 2E, 3E, 4E, 1F, 3A; he ARE
292.40	that he would] 1E, 2A, 2E, 3E, 4E, 1F, 3A; he ARE
294.14	Albany, and] 1E, 2A, 2E, 3E, 4E, 1F, 3A; Albany, ARE
295.1	and who] 1E, 2A, 2E, 3E, 4E, 1F, 3A; and ARE
295.30	of but] 1E, 2A, 2E, 3E, 4E, 1F, 3A; but of ARE
296.6	at] 1E, 2A, 2E, 3E, 4E, 1F, 3A; near ARE
296.9	flight] 1E, 2A, 2E, 3E, 4E, 1F, 3A; flock ARE
296.40	things will] 1E, 2A, 2E, 3E24, 3E25, 4E, 1F, 3A, ARE; things with 3E23
297.2	scarcely] 1E, 2A, 2E, 3E, 4E, 1F, 3A; scarce ARE
297.6	he was] 1E, 2A, 2E, 3E, 4E, 1F, 3A; *omitted* ARE
297.30	and it] 1E, 2A, 2E, 3E, 4E, 1F, 3A; and ARE
297.36	He found that the] 1E, 2A, 2E, 3E, 4E, 1F, 3A; The ARE
297.37	appeared also to be] 1E, 2A, 2E, 3E, 4E, 1F, 3A; was also ARE
298.16–17	, similar to those over his mother's mantel-piece, engraved on its side] 1E, 2A, 2E, 3E, 4E, 1F, 3A; engraved on its side, similar to those over his mother's mantel-piece ARE
298.21	old] 1E, 2E, 3E, 4E, 1F; *omitted* 2A, 3A, ARE
301.8	that were] 1E, 2A, 2E, 3E, 4E, 1F, 3A; *omitted* ARE
301.8	yet] 1E, 2A, 2E, 3E, 4E, 1F, 3A; *omitted* ARE
302.32	rung] 1E, 2A, 2E, 3E, 4E, 1F, 3A; rang ARE
303.3	rejoicings] 1E, 2E, 3E, 4E, 1F; rejoicing 2A, 3A, ARE
303.22	a fine] 1E, 2E, 3E, 4E, 1F; a few fine 2A, 3A, ARE
303.23	girl] 1E, 2E, 3E, 4E, 1F; girls 2A, 3A, ARE
303.29	jigging] 1E, 2A, 2E, 3E24, 3E25, 4E, 3A, ARE; gigging 3E23, 1F
304.4	that] 1E, 2A, 2E, 3E, 4E, 1F, 3A; which ARE
304.7	that have been] 1E, 2A, 2E, 3E, 4E, 1F, 3A; *omitted* ARE

304.25   diverted] 1E, 2E, 3E, 4E, 1F; directed 2A, 3A, ARE
305.6   that dimpled] 1E, 2A, 2E, 3E, 4E, 1F, 3A; dimpling
                    ARE
305.32   experienced] 1E, 2A, 2E, 3E, 1F, 3A, ARE; acquainted
                    4E
309.7   that were] 1E, 2A, 2E, 3E, 4E, 1F, 3A; *omitted* ARE
*309.8–9   , at the effect produced by one of my trivial lucubrations]
                    1E, 2A, 2E, 3A, ARE; for the manner in which one of
                    my trivial lucubrations has been received 3E, 4E, 1F
309.14   this not] 1E, 2A, 2E, 3E, 1F, 3A, ARE; not this 4E
309.37   towards] 1E, 2E, 3E, 4E, 1F; toward 2A, 3A, ARE
311.23   is] 1E, 2A, 2E, 3E, 1F, 3A, ARE; has 4E
311.24   have] 1E, 2A, 2E, 3E23, 3E24, 1F, 3A, ARE; had 3E25
                    4E
311.36   produced any] 1E, 2A, 2E, 3A, ARE; contributed in any
                    degree to produce 3E, 4E, 1F
312.2   are lowering] 1E, 2A, 2E, 3E, 4E, 1F, 3A; lower ARE
312.2   hope that] 1E, 2A, 2E, 3E, 4E, 1F, 3A; hope ARE
312.6   oh] 1E, 2A, 2E, 3E23, 3E24, 1F, 3A, ARE; O 3E25, 4E

LIST OF COMPOUND WORDS
HYPHENATED
AT END OF LINE

List I includes all compound and possible compound words that are hyphenated at the end of the line in the copy-text. Each word is listed in its editorially accepted form after the page and line number of its appearance in the T text. The decision whether to retain the hyphen or print the word as a single-word compound was based on three different criteria, applied serially. First, usage elsewhere in the copy-text; sometimes this proved an inconsistent test, as with the word "churchyard," unhyphenated at 18.34 and 36.20–21, for example, and hyphenated elsewhere; where the usage was inconsistent the form of the word nearest in the text was chosen. Second, usage in the manuscripts; unfortunately Irving was almost totally inconsistent about this matter in his manuscripts, varying between spelling compounds as one word, two words, or hyphenated, with no discernible principles at all. Nevertheless, where the manuscript could be followed, it was. Finally, for some fifteen cases where no other use of the word could be found in the copy-text and where the manuscript was not helpful, recourse was made to the *Oxford English Dictionary*. Decisions based on that search were deliberately conservative on the grounds that Irving intended an antiquarian flavor to this text; where an eighteenth-century usage conflicted with a post-1822 usage, the earlier was chosen.

List II presents all compounds, or possible compounds, that are hyphenated or separated as two words at the end of the line in the T text. They are listed in the form in which they would have appeared in the T text had they come in midline.

LIST I

5.6–7	supernatural	15.15	housekeeper
5.13	grown-up	16.26	soft-hearted
5.28	three-cornered	16.30	second-hand
5.29	bedroom	17.31	clock-work
6.6	Church-yard	18.26	fellow-domestics
9.29	sliding-pannel	19.4	churchyard
13.32	footman	21.5	gold-laced

21.22–23	tender-hearted	74.30–31	wrong-headed
21.31	ladylike	74.34	book-knowledge
22.3	now-/a-days	76.32	riding-hat
22.11	love-quarrels	77.10	horseback
24.25	housekeeper	77.22	footman
24.32	picture-gallery	81.10	supper-table
26.25	jack-boots	95.29	barley-meal
33.14	odd-looking	95.35	hemp-seed
33.20	good-/for-nothing	99.15	well-cushioned
34.36	waiting-gentlewoman	100.19	eyebrows
37.3	watch-chain	109.40	bed-chamber
37.41–42	farm-house	123.13	broken-down
39.27	home-brewed	125.42	rosemary
39.36	gentleman	134.12	well-known
40.40	bachelor-like	136.14	birthright
43.14	romance-read	140.24	wood-nymph
49.20	half-drowned	143.28	after-reflection
50.7	driving-whip	151.27	overpowered
50.30	tradesman	159.19	high-handed
50.36	long-lived	159.27	fellow-men
51.15	lurking-places	164.33–34	fox-hunting
52.33	newspaper	164.35	fortnight
53.13	mantel-piece	166.10–11	steam-engines
54.11	Highgate	167.17	steam-engines
55.20	night-caps	171.6	foot-path
56.5	elbow-chair	171.16	housekeeper's
56.17	wax-topped	178.35	superannuated
56.28–29	coach-door	181.5	farm-house
59.32–33	long-enduring	181.11	well-stocked
60.15	noble-spirited	181.38	playmates
62.6	black-letter	182.15	playmates
62.9–10	quaintly-carved	182.41	schoolmate
62.10	reading-desk	183.10	witchcraft
62.39	church-yard	185.14	half-tattered
65.24	old-fashioned	185.19	schoolmaster's
65.35	good-looking	186.1	barn-doors
66.36	housekeeper	187.12	travellers'-room
68.15	cross-grained	193.2	gentlefolk
70.8–9	horsewomen	195.21	outstretched
73.16	clothyard	196.11	sunbeams
73.22	gunpowder	196.37	May-pole
74.7	well-known	197.6	bystanders
74.25	fox-hunt	199.5	home-thrust

200.26	May-day		252.4–5	barley-sugar
202.1	May-day		252.8	demure-looking
203.3	sitting-room		257.19	church-yard
203.7	overhung		257.42	love-sick
203.33	flower-garden		258.11	mansion-house
205.38	shipwreck		258.32	jack-boots
207.4	fishing-boats		260.13	ninepins
211.29	looked-for		260.31	countryman
212.8	long-/wished-for		262.10–11	Stepping-stones
217.4	sunburnt		262.14	government-house
217.28	to-morrow		263.32	fire-place
222.24	post-chaises		265.8	window-shutters
224.22	mustering-place		265.31	footstep
224.28	stable-boys		266.1	elbow-chair
225.10	court-yard		269.28	leave-taking
225.21	knot-headed		274.15	half-drowned
227.36	moonlight		278.31	overboard
228.37	Robin Good-fellow		279.2	counter-currents
229.6	housemaids		281.22	thunder-cloud
231.36	buttercups		283.28	Point-no-point
232.21	fountain-head		283.30	moonlight
232.33–34	Midsummer-Night's		284.18	highlands
233.19	household		284.28	foul-weather
234.11	Starlight		284.37	night-cap
234.13	lion-hearted		287.12	highlands
234.22	ale-drinkers		287.42	hap-hazard
234.28	stag-hound		289.8	housewife
235.9	sheep-stealing		291.25	housekeeping
235.26	chance-medley		293.31	night-walking
237.20	fowling-piece		294.37	elbow-chair
238.9	tatterdemallion		295.37	sink-pocket
239.25	head-quarters		299.11	grandchildren
239.36	flower-beds		299.21	beef-steak
240.14	householders		299.23	game-cocks
240.19	see-sawing		302.37	hubbub
244.30	child-bearing		302.42	gun-barrels
247.11–12	Hogen-mogens		307.4–5	country-seat
247.41	after-thoughts		307.6	kitchen-gardens
248.36	window-shutters		307.7	common-place
249.39	gray-headed		307.8	post-boys
251.14	schoolmaster		307.9	merry-makings

LIST II

5.6–7	supernatural	74.30–31	wrong-headed
9.2–3	manor-house	78.4–5	Robin-/good-fellow
11.13–14	bachelor-looking	80.5–6	housekeeper
11.34–35	Newgate	84.8–9	moonshine
12.12–13	landscapes	85.7–8	prison-house
16.35–36	housekeepers'	91.14–15	footpath
18.33–34	tombstone	93.35–36	self-complacency
19.16–17	gentleman	97.18–19	sweetheart's
21.22–23	tender-hearted	99.15–16	elbow-chair
21.34–35	easy-tempered	120.11–12	spell-bound
21.40–41	love-tales	144.24–25	overlooked
22.8–9	love-affairs	145.1–2	supernatural
29.14–15	sunshine	146.24–25	footpath
33.16–17	smelling-bottles	146.31–32	mountain-path
34.28–29	ladyship	151.36–37	self-regulation
36.20–21	churchyard	164.33–34	fox-hunting
37.41–42	farm-house	166.10–11	steam-engines
38.12–13	village-green	170.15–16	good-for-nothing
39.1–2	Bartholomew-fair	171.16–17	lovesick
40.32–33	namby-pamby	179.31–32	tobacco-boxes
40.34–35	handkerchiefs	180.34–35	farm-house
40.39–40	Bracebridge	185.8–9	exciseman
41.29–30	churchyard	187.11–12	tap-room
43.26–27	handwriting	187.14–15	landlord
50.11–12	now-a-/days	189.6–7	cat-o'-mountain
50.24–25	window-glass	189.28–29	newspaper
51.22–23	tortoise-shell	191.28–29	housekeepers
52.21–22	slammerkin	192.1–2	cocked-hats
53.16–17	bed-room	202.19–20	matter-of-fact
59.1–2	tree-fanciers	223.2–3	horseback
59.32–33	long-enduring	224.7–8	diamond-paned
62.9–10	quaintly-carved	224.13–14	trunk-hose
65.11–12	milking-tubs	226.7–8	farewell
67.8–9	somebody	228.41–42	Good-fellow
67.28–29	cobwebs	230.21–22	household
70.8–9	horsewomen	232.33–34	Mid-summer-Night's
70.28–29	gentleman	234.21–22	wildfire
71.14–15	ladyship	236.18–19	schoolmaster
72.17–18	gentlewoman	238.36–37	gentleman's
73.24–25	sunshiny	239.28–29	picture-gallery
74.7–8	sportsmen	244.5–6	pin-money
74.25–26	gamekeeper	244.13–14	lynx-eyed

245.6–7	churchyard		272.5–6	highlands
247.11–12	Hogen-mogens		273.8–9	overhung
248.35–36	weather-cocks		278.37–38	supernatural
252.4–5	barley-sugar		279.20–21	Storm-ship
258.39–40	chambermaid		285.41–42	supernatural
259.7–8	mad-cap		292.33–34	burgomaster
259.35–36	gentleman		279.40–41	iron-bound
262.10–11	Stepping-stones		303.22–23	boarding-school
264.36–37	footsteps		304.15–16	wedding-dinner
265.13–14	notwithstanding		307.4–5	country-seat

INDEX TO EARLIEST EXTANT TEXTS

This index lists the earliest forms extant for all known forms of the text of *Bracebridge Hall*. It does not attempt to describe variant forms except where the variant is an omission of considerable length. The following abbreviations have been used for this list:

MSEc	Manuscript used to set 1E, Columbia University Library
MSEn	Manuscript used to set 1E, New York Public Library
MSEv	Manuscript used to set 1E, Alderman Library, University of Virginia
MSA	Manuscript used to set 1A, Alderman Library, University of Virginia
1A	First American edition, Van Winkle, 1822
1E	First English edition, John Murray, 1822
1Eb	Second state of 1E
2A	Second American edition, Van Winkle, 1822
ARE	Author's Revised Edition, Putnam, 1849.

3.1–6.22	*THE AUTHOR*. . . . ruin.	1A, 1E
6.23–6.38	Having been. . . . will permit	MSA?[1] 1A, 1E
6.39–7.6	I have. . . . GEOFFREY CRAYON.	1A, 1E
8.1–9.6	*THE HALL*. . . . feudal homage.	MSEc, 1A, 1E
9.6–9.10	An old. . . . old style.	1E
9.11–9.25	I am. . . . before me.	MSEc, 1A, 1E
9.26–10.9	I would. . . . glee.* Mirror for Magistrates	1E
11.1–18.8	*THE BUSY*. . . . national character.	MSEc, 1A, 1E
18.9–18.30	These observations. . . . affection?	1E
18.31–19.12	I love. . . . and loyalty!"	MSEc, 1A, 1E
19.13–19.19	NOTE–I. . . . a menial.	1E
20.1–42.8	*THE WIDOW*. . . . to it.	MSEc, 1A, 1E
42.8–48.33	I should. . . . present day.	1A, 1E
49.1–64.7	*THE STOUT*. . . . the ears.	MSEc, 1A, 1E
64.8–64.32	I have. . . . modern guinea.	1E
65.1–67.4	*THE FARM HOUSE*. . . . the villagers;	MSEc, 1A, 1E
67.4–67.22	and her. . . . as to	MSEn, 1A, 1E
67.22–67.38	what might. . . . opposite.	1A, 1E

308.1–311.14   *THE AUTHOR'S*. . . . British
                                                    glory.   1E
311.15–311.28   I am sure. . . . a study.   1Eb, 2A
311.29–312.8   But however. . . . within thee!"   1E

[1] Identical to 1A text, but bears no 1A compositors' marks.

[2] Widely variant from 1E text; no 1E compositors' marks.

[3] A single manuscript leaf, bearing part of this text only; widely variant from all texts.

APPENDIX I

Printed here is the first essay of the first volume from the first American edition of *Bracebridge Hall* (Van Winkle, 1822), "The Author." The reprinting of this one part of the precopy-text is intended to serve as a sample illustrating the extensive rewriting that was done for the first English edition. The chapter was chosen as a typical example; some chapters have fewer variants, most have many more.

THE AUTHOR

WORTHY READER!

IN again taking pen in hand I would fain make a few observations at the outset, by way of bespeaking a right understanding. The volumes which I have already published have met with a reception far beyond my most sanguine expectations. I would willingly attribute this to their intrinsic merits; but, in spite of the vanity of authorship, I cannot but be sensible that their success has, in a great measure, been owing to a less flattering cause. It has been a matter of marvel, at least to the European part of my readers, that a man from the wilds of America should express himself in tolerable English. I was looked upon as something new and strange in literature; a kind of demi-savage, with a feather in his hand instead of on his head, and there was a curiosity to hear what such a being had to say about civilized society.

This novelty is now at an end, and with it, in all probability, the feeling of indulgence which it produced. I must now expect to bear the scrutiny of sterner criticism, and to be measured by the same standard with contemporary writers; and the very indulgence that has been shown to my previous writings, will cause these to be treated with the greater rigour.

I am aware that I often travel over a beaten ground, and treat of subjects that have been already discussed by abler pens. Indeed, various authors have been mentioned as my models, to whom I should feel flattered if I thought I bore the slightest resemblance. I write after no model that I am conscious of; and I write with no idea of imitation or competition. In venturing occasionally on subjects that have already been almost exhausted by English authors, I do it, not with the presumption of challenging a comparison, but because I trust there will be some new interest given to them, when discussed by the pen of a stranger. If, therefore, I should occasionally be found dwelling with fondness on topics that are trite and commonplaced with the reader, I beg the circumstances under which I write may be kept in recollection. I have been born and brought up in a new country; yet educated from infancy in the literature of an old one. My mind has gradually been filled with historical and poetical associations, which were connected with places, and manners, and customs of Europe, but could rarely be applied to those of my own country. With a mind thus peculiarly prepared, the most trivial and commonplaced objects and scenes, on first landing in Europe, were full of interest and novelty.

Indeed, it is difficult to describe the whimsical medley of ideas that rush at once upon a stranger in such peculiar predicament. He for the first time sees a world about which he has been thinking in every stage of his existence. The recollections of infancy, youth, and manhood; of the nursery, the school, and the study, some swarming upon him; distracting his attention between great and little objects, and each perhaps producing equal delight.

Such, for instance, was the odd confusion of associations that kept breaking upon me as I first approached London. One of my earliest wishes had been to see it; I had heard so much of it in childhood; I had read so much about it in the earliest books that had been put in my infant hands; I was familiar with the names of its streets, and squares, and public places, before I knew those of my native city. It was, to me, the great centre of the world, round which every thing seemed to revolve. I recollect contemplating so wistfully, when a boy, a paltry little print of the Thames, and London Bridge, and St. Paul's, that was in front of a magazine; even the venerable wood-cut of St. John's gate, that has stood time out of mind on the title page of the Gentleman's Magazine, was not without its charms for me.

How my bosom thrilled when the towers of Westminster Abbey were pointed out to me, rising above the rich groves of St. James' Park, with a thin blue haze about their gray pinnacles.

I could not behold this great mausoleum of what is most illustrious in our paternal history without feeling all my enthusiasm in a glow; nor can I forbear to mention, on the other hand, the delightful, yet childish interest with which I first peeped into Mr. Newberry's shop in St. Paul's church yard; that fountain head of literature. Mr. Newberry was the first that ever filled my infant mind with the idea of a great and good man. He published all the picture books of the day, Tom Thumb's Folio, Giles Gingerbread, and Jack the Giant Killer; and out of his abundant love for children, he demanded nothing for the paper and print, and only a penny halfpenny for the binding!

But what have most especially attracted my attention, and have afforded a continually recurring source of pleasure, have been those peculiarities which distinguish an old country and an old state of society from a new one. I have never yet grown so familiar with the crumbling monuments of foregone ages, as to blunt the intense interest with which I at first beheld them. Accustomed always to scenes where history was in a manner in anticipation; where every thing in art was new and progressive, and where the works of man gave no ideas but those of young existence and prospective improvement, there was something inexpressibly touching in these enormous piles, gray with antiquity, and sinking to decay. I cannot describe the mute but deepfelt enjoyment with which I have contemplated a vast monastic ruin, like Fentern Abbey, buried in the bosom of a quiet valley, as though it had existed merely for itself. Or a warrior pile, like Conway Castle, standing in stern loneliness on its rocky promontory, a mere hollow, yet threatening phantom of departed power. They spread a grand and melancholy, and, to me, an unusual charm over the landscape, giving proofs of the transient and perishing glories of art, among the ever springing and reviving fertility of nature.

In like manner have I been affected by every thing antique and obsolete in manners and customs; and I mention these circumstances as an apology for often recurring to such themes; and betraying, occasionally, a provincial ignorance and delight respecting them, which must provoke a smile from my wiser and more experienced reader. Having been brought up, also, in the comparative simplicity of a republic, I am apt to be struck with even the ordinary circumstances attendant on an aristocratical state of society. I have amused myself occasionally, therefore, by pointing out some of the eccentricities, and some of the poetical characteristics of the latter, without pretending to decide on its merits, compared with any other form of government. My only aim is to paint manners and characters, such as I see them. I am no politician. The more I have considered politics, the more I have found it full of perplexity; and as in religion, I have contented myself with the faith in which I have been brought up; regulating my own conduct by its precepts; but leaving to abler heads the task of making converts.

I shall continue on, therefore, in the course I have hitherto pursued; looking at things poetically rather than politically, describing them as they are, rather than pretending to point out how they should be, and endeavouring to see the world in as pleasant a light, as circumstances will permit.

I have always had an opinion that much good might be done by keeping mankind in good humour with one another. I may be wrong in my philosophy, but I shall continue to practise it until convinced of its fallacy. When I discover the world to be all that it has been represented by sneering cynics and whining poets, I will turn to and abuse it also; in the mean while, worthy reader, I hope you will not think lightly of me, because I cannot believe this to be so very bad a world as it is represented.

Thine truly,

GEOFFREY CRAYON.

APPENDIX II

Selected Precopy-Text variants

To supplement Appendix I in giving the reader a sense of the kinds of changes made between the writing of the first American edition of *Bracebridge Hall* and the copy-text, this list includes a sampling of variants which the editor hopes is illustrative of the kinds of changes Irving made in the text. It is a small sample—twenty-one substantive variants selected from well over a thousand—but combined with the 1A text of "The Author" in Appendix I it should document Irving's motivation for the rewriting of his text as well as his thoroughness.

A quite different system of notation has been used for this one list. The page and line numbers refer to the place in the T text where the 1A variant would occur. The text enclosed in square brackets is the 1A text. Where the text has been deleted entirely from the 1E text, the words immediately before and after it indicate where it would appear had it been retained. Where it has been rewritten for 1E, the appropriate text is enclosed in ⟨ ⟩ and printed after it. If the 1E revision is lengthy, only the first and last two words are given, along with inclusive page and line numbers from the T text. Explanatory notes are provided for all of these selected variants. They are printed immediately after the list with the same page and line numbers.

20.9–10 CHAUCER [I am much better pleased with Lady Lillycraft than I fancied I should have been.] Notwithstanding

31.40 Seringapatam. [He insists that Bonaparte was no general; and that he was a great coward for running away from the army after the battle of Leipsick, and for not putting himself in the way of being shot on the field of Waterloo.] I am

32.16–18 [and with everything about him. He goes about from dinner to dinner and country seat to country seat, and wonders how people can be dissatisfied in a country where a man has nothing to do but to dine out at other people's expense and to loll on sofas.] ⟨and apt . . . agricultural distress.⟩

33.21–22 earth! [It reminds me of the vast bustle and pains-taking of the redoubtable Belzoni, and his myrmidons of the Nile, to transport some Egyptian mummy; or, perhaps, to trundle off some mutilated statue at the rate of a few inches in an hour.] I

49.2 [A TALE OF MYSTERY] ⟨A STAGECOACH ROMANCE⟩

59.30 Hagley [, treading in the footsteps of a Pope and a Lyttleton]; or

61.7–19 [In the account of my Christmas visit to the Hall I made some
mention of the parson, who is a kind of family chaplain to the
Squire; and was his chum at Oxford. A farther acquaintance with
the little man has increased my esteem for him. He is a scholar without arrogance or pedantry; very ignorant of the world, having lived
almost entirely among books; and those too, old books, so that his
mind is as antiquated as the Squire's garden, where one finds formal
flower beds and peacocks cut in yew.] ⟨The squire . . . and peacocks.⟩

71.28–72.9 [It may, however, be nothing but a little venerable flirtation,
the general being a veteran dangler, and the good lady habituated
to these kind of attentions. Master Simon, however, thinks the general,
now that he is growing old, is desirous of getting into warm winter
quarters, and I doubt whether the former, with all his admiration of
the veteran, would be pleased at his winning the lady; as he looks
upon Lady Lillycraft's house as one of his strong holds.

   Among other symptoms that look suspicious,] ⟨It would . . . Thus for
instance⟩

73.7–29 [Among the many recreations of the good old times which the
Squire has endeavoured to revive on his estate, is that of hawking.
He decries shooting as a skulking solitary treacherous sport in comparison; but hawking, he says, was the noble art of hunting carried
into the skies. It was the stately amusement of gentlemen, for in
old times, he says, according to the Welsh saying,] ⟨There are. . . in
those times⟩

78.17–21 [Upon hearing this quotation, the parson mentioned a beautiful appellation which the Jews had of old for the echo; which they
called Bathkool, that is to say "the daughter of the voice."*

   *Note, They said it was an oracle, supplying in the second temple
the want of the Urim and Thummim with which the first temple
was honoured.

                                           Bekker, Le Monde Enchanté]
⟨The parson . . . was honoured*.⟩

138.3–6 [Now that he had her in his power he was determined to
protract the pleasure of pursuit.] ⟨He had . . . her virtue.⟩

167.9–12 [After he was gone the Squire could not contain his indigna-
tion] ⟨It is . . . found vent⟩

172.28–29 [Indians] ⟨Indians of America⟩

174.9–10 [Then lords of castles, mannors, townes, and towers,
            Rejoic'd when they beheld the farmers flourish,
         And would come downe unto the summer-bowers
         To see the country-gallants dance the Morrice.]
                                           PASQUIL'S PALINODIA

198.29–32   [got embroiled in the discussion. I saw that the former
rather entered into it with an ill grace, from which I was persuaded
that he must before this have had a brush with the radical;] ⟨came
drifting . . . this fireship⟩

212.19–26   [placed herself in a conspicuous place, where she might at
once catch his view, and surprize him by her welcome; the next
moment she shrunk among the throng, trembling, and faint, and
gasping with her emotions.

It was almost a relief to her when she perceived that her lover
was not in the boat; she presumed that he had remained on board
to prepare for his return home, and she felt as if] ⟨would place . . .
felt that⟩

233.23   of the night? [*** In an old play entitled the Mayds Metamorphosis, there is a scene resembling in many respects Nick Bottom's
dialogue with the fairies in Midsummer's Night's Dream. The edition
that I saw was printed in 1600, and was bound up in the same
volume with an edition of Midsummer's Night's Dream published in
the same year. Which of these plays was written first I do not know;
though it is very possible Shakespeare may have taken his idea from
the other play, and improved upon it; as he took the . . . of his witch
scenes in Macbeth from a play of Marlow's. I subjoin the scene
alluded to from the Mayds Metamorphosis.

Mopso.	But soft, who comes here?
	[*Enter the Fairies, singing and dancing*]
	By the moone we sport and play
	With the night begins our day;
	As we dance the deaw doth fall,
	Trip it little urchins all:
	Lightly as the little Bee,
	Two by two and three by three:
	And about go we, and about go we.
Joculo.	What Mawmets are these?
Frisco.	O they be the Fayries that haunt these woods.
Mopso.	O we shall be pincht most cruelly.
1st. Fay.	Will you have any musicke sir?
2d. Fay.	Will you have any fine musicke sir?
3d. Fay.	Most daintie musicke?
Mopso.	We must set a face on it now, there's no flying
	No sir; we are very merry I thank you.
1st. Fay.	O but you shall sir.
Fris.	No. I pray you save your labour.
2d. Fay.	O sir, it shall not cost you a penny.
Joculo.	Where be your fiddles?

3d. Fay.   You shall have most daintie instruments sir.

Mopso.   I pray you what might I call you?

1st. Fay.   My name is Penny.

Mopso.   I am sorry I cannot purse you.

Frisco.   I pray you what might I call you?

2d. Fay.   My name is Cricket.

Frisco   I would I were a chimney for your sake.

       ❂   ❂   ❂   ❂   ❂   ❂

1st. Fay.   I do come about the coppes
             Leaping upon flowers toppes:
             Then I get upon a flie
             She carries me above the skie:
             And trip and goe.

2d. Fay.   When a deaw drop falleth downe,
             And doth light upon my crowne,
             Then I shake my head and skip:
             And about I trip.

3d. Fay.   When I feele a gyrle a sleepe,
             Underneath her frocke I peepe,
             There to sport, and there I play,
             Then I byte her like a flea,
             And about I skip.

Joculo.   I, I thought I should have you.

1st. Fay.   Wilt please you daunce, sir?

Joculo.   Indeed, sir, I cannot handle my legges.

2d. Fay.   O you must needs daunce and sing,
             Which if you refuse to doo,
             We will pinch you blacke and blew,
             And about we goe.

    [*They all daunce in a ring, and sing as follows*]
             Round about, round about in a fine ring a
             Thus we daunce, thus we daunce, and thus we sing a,
             Trip and go, too and fro, over this greene a:
             All about, in and out, for our brave queen a &c.]

246.2–247.42   [I have foreborne to recount various tales which have been told during the evenings at the Hall, because some of them were rather hackneyed and tedious, and others I did not feel warranted in betraying into print. I was suddenly startled lately by a call from the Squire to furnish a story in my turn, and having been a profound listener to those of others, I could not in conscience refuse; so I begged leave to read a manuscript tale from the pen of the late Mr. Deidrich Knickerbocker, the historian of New-York.

As some curiosity was expressed about the author, I had to explain, "that he was a native of New-York, a descendant of one of the ancient Dutch families that originally settled that province, and remained there after it was taken possession of by the English, in 1664. The... descendants of these Dutch families still remained in villages and neighbourhoods in various parts of the country; retaining with singular fidelity, the dresses, manners, and even language of their ancestors, and forming a very distinct and curious feature in the population of the state.

That Mr. Knickerbocker had written a history of his native city, comprising the reign of the three first governors who held a delegated sway under the Hogen Mogens of Holland. That in this the worthy little Dutchman had displayed great historical research, and a wonderful sense of the dignity of his subject; but that his work had been so little understood as to be pronounced a mere work of humour; satirizing the follies of the times in politics and morals, and giving whimsical views of human nature.

That among the papers left behind him were several tales of a lighter nature, apparently thrown together from materials which he had gathered during his profound researches for the history; and which he seemed to have thrown by with neglect, as unworthy of publicity. That these had fallen into my hands by an accident which it was needless to mention, and one of those stories, with its prelude, in the words of Mr. Knickerbocker, I now undertook to read, by way of acquitting myself of the debt which I owed to the other story-tellers in company.] ⟨*Hermione.* Pray ... to make.⟩

277.40–278.6 [And then he would sit, with his hat on one side, swaying a short squab Dutch bottle in his hand, and sing a stave or two of a Dutch drinking song, to which his myrmidons would join in chorus.

With all his joviality, however, he mingled discretion.] ⟨And then ... of discretion.⟩

301.6–10 BRAITHWAITE

[The fair Julia having recovered from the effects of her fall, the day for the wedding was at length appointed. As it drew near, there rose several doubts and conversations between Lady Lillycraft, Master Simon, and the parson, on the subject of marrying in the month of May; against which I find there is an ancient prejudice, as being an unfortunate month for matrimony. From the discussions that took place on these occasions, I picked up much valuable information relative to weddings. Such as, that if there were two celebrated in the same church, on the same day, the first would be happy, the second otherwise. If, in going to church, they should meet the funeral of a female, the bride would die first; if of a male, the bridegroom. If the

new married couple were to dance together on their wedding day,
the wife would thenceforth rule the roast; with many more curious
facts of the same kind; which made me ponder, more than ever,
upon the perils which surround this happy state; and how little men
know the awful risks they run in venturing upon it. I abstain, however, from enlarging on this topic, as I have no wish to promote the
increase of bachelors.

The Squire, however, though he gave due weight to all these
ancient saws, yet had a host of poetical authorities in favour of this
loving month, which I suppose were conclusive with the young
couple, as I found they were perfectly willing to marry in May, and
abide the consequences.

The wedding has accordingly taken place at the village church,]
⟨Notwithstanding the . . . village church,⟩

Notes to Appendix II

20.9–10   This variant is representative of two common kinds of changes
made between 1A and 1E: the exclusion for 1E of indifferent intro-
ductory statements to new chapters, and the reduction of the personal
element—the character of Geoffrey Crayon—from prominence.

31.40 *and* 32.16–18   One of the regretable losses in the transition from
1A to 1E is the further development of the character of General
Harbottle, as typified in these two variants. Enough is left in the 1E
text to suggest his blimpish character adequately, but he is toned
down a good deal in his final form. One wonders if Murray perhaps
suggested to Irving that the caricature might raise British hackles.

33.21–22   The text of 1E does not include a number of somewhat far-
fetched comparisons of which this example is typical. The comparison
certainly has a certain baroque character, is somewhat pedantic, and
might even have been sensitive to the British character, the rape of
the Elgin marbles being an event of the fairly recent past. For any
of these reasons and probably others, Irving decided to excise it.

49.2   In this subtitle to "The Stout Gentleman" we can observe a clear
improvement by Irving. "A Tale of Mystery" gives the wrong tone to
the clever and subtle story; "A Stagecoach Romance" identifies the
theme of travelers' psychology and is as reticent about the central
issue of the story as the other subtitle is outspoken and melodramatic.

59.30   Irving's reasons for excising this passage in 1E can only be
guessed at. Perhaps the allusion seemed a bit too recondite, although
it would be even more so for the American audience of 1A. Pope's
association with Hagley is not obvious; Irving would have been
much closer to a recognizable allusion if he had recalled the name

of James Thomson, whose poem "Summer" (1727) in *The Seasons* (1730) is placed in Hagley. Hagley was in the possession of the Lyttelton family from 1564, but the Lyttelton Irving probably had in mind here was George, first Baron Lyttelton (1709–1773).

61.7–19   A comparison of the two texts will illustrate how much more sympathetic is Irving's second thought about, in this case, the squire's chaplain. The phenomenon is repeated in the 1E text for most of the minor characters. Where the 1A portraits are often sharply critical, the 1E text has been toned down to a gentle and mellow, almost loving, caricature. It is likely that this sea-change does not represent pressure upon Irving by Murray or the exigencies of publication for an English audience. In general the softening is an improvement, although one might wish an exception were made for cases like General Harbottle.

71.28–72.9   The major addition to the 1E text here is the quotation from Malory. It is interesting to note how often Irving added to his text with material from his commonplace book, often, as is apparently the case here, of only peripheral or doubtful relevance.

73.7–29   The traditionalism of the squire, bordering on pedantry, is one of his characteristics found much more strongly in the 1E text than in 1A. Here the squire is allowed in the 1E text a disquisition on archery and the degeneration of the English character as a result of the introduction of gunpowder, all as a preamble to the main topic of the chapter, falconry.

78.17–21   This passage in the text gave Irving more trouble in the rewriting for 1E than any other. The 1A text is awkward and digressive in the reflective passages, like this one, downright confusing in the action which follows. This passage and its context is described with more detail about Irving's continued corrections in the Textual Commentary, pp. 000–000.

138.3–6   "The Student of Salamanca" was almost entirely rewritten between the drafting of MSA and the publication of 1E. Its 1A form is almost unreadable, with gaping holes in the narration, little attention paid to motivation, and a plethora of melodramatic clichés. It is impossible to characterize the rewriting adequately here, since it is the extent of the changes that marks the differences most strongly. This one very brief example indicates Irving's effort to qualify one character's motivation from the bald statement of melodrama to a consideration of more complex problems of motivation.

167.9–12   Revisions for the 1E text often were concerned with the squire's character. Here Irving is careful to insert a brief reference to the squire's hospitality even in the face of the despicable Mr. Faddy.

172.28–29   The qualifying phrase "of America" was added in proof to

1E. MSA, MSE, and 1A do not have it. The fact that it was kept in all later editions, including ARE, suggests that Irving was shedding his American provincialism.

174.9–10   The dropping of the last four lines of the poem is typical of several epigraphs which are shorter in 1E than in 1A.

198.29–32   The 1A text forgets that only a few chapters earlier Geoffrey Crayon was present at a "brush with the radical." The passage is discussed at greater length in the Textual Commentary, pp. 000–000.

212.19–26   Typical of the variants in "Annette Delarbre," this one adds several gratuitous heartthrobs to the general distress of the story.

233.23   The longest single deletion from the 1A text is this scene from the close of the second act of *The Maydes Metamorphosis* (1600), supposedly by Lyly, but more likely by John Day. The text may be found in *A Collection of Old English Plays*, ed. A. H. Bullen (New York, 1964), I, 127–29. Irving bowdlerized the text with the omission signified by the line of asterisks of the following:

> *Io.*   I pray you, prettie little fellow, whats your name?
>
> *3 Fay.*   My name is little, little *Pricke*.
>
> *Io.*   Little, little *Pricke?* ô you are a daungerous Fayrie,
>   And fright all the little wenches in the Country
>   Out of their beds.
>   I care not whose hand I were in, so I were out of
>   yours.

Murray may have objected to such an egregious example of padding, but it is more likely that Irving himself excised the material.

246.2–247.42   This short and undistinguished chapter in 1A was enlarged considerably and turned into a pleasant essay, interesting and valuable in its own right, where the 1A text is nothing more than an introduction to "Dolph Heyliger."

277.40–278.8   The addition of the sample chorus to the 1E passage is typical of Irving's revisions for "Dolph Heyliger." The original story was improved in the rewriting in many ways, but often the technique was one of expansion, documentation, and specification, as was the case here.

301.6–10   Most of the matter from these two paragraphs was simply moved to the chapter "Lovers' Troubles," pp. 242–245, which was not printed in 1A. In "The Wedding" this material detracts from the thrust of the narrative, which is about the festivities associated with the wedding. In "Lovers' Troubles" it adds character and interest to an essay more appropriately chosen.

APPENDIX III

Variants in the later states of the 1822 John Murray edition, not otherwise recorded in the List of Rejected Substantives or List of Emendations to the copy-text.

This list includes all variants found in the later states of 1E and 2E which are not listed elsewhere in this text. The numbers given first indicate page and line in the T text; chapter titles, epigraphs, text. quotations and footnotes are included in the line count. The reading to the left of the bracket is the portion of the text under consideration; the reading after the bracket is the variant in the later state or states of 1E and 2E, followed by the symbol for the state in which it is found. An asterisk indicates that the variant is considered in the Discussions of Adopted Readings.

*9.28	treat, has] ~∧ ~ 2E
*9.29	-pannel] panel 1Ec, 2E
35.3	confidence, to] ~∧ ~ 2E
39.39–40	quarter-staff∧ when] ~, ~ 2E
40.30	camelion] chameleon 2E
47.6–7	imperfection∧ incident] ~, ~ 2E
51.16	hostler] ostler 2E
52.33	whig] Whig 2E
57.2	trees."] ~!" 2E
64.18	kissed] kiss'd 2E
70.20	carriage."] ~!" 2E
72.20	Simon∧ or] ~, ~ 2E
82.37	Remigius] Remegius 2E
89.13	Wyat, his] ~∧ ~ 2E
104.27	beauty.] ~, 2E
108.37	he, wildly] ~∧ ~ 2E
123.40	man∧ delighted] ~, ~ 2E
124.9	chrystal] crystal 2E
140.39	performed,] ~∧ 2E
140.39	saloons,] ~∧ 2E
143.38	splendour] splendor 2E
146.6	him,] ~∧ 2E
151.22	she] As she 2E
152.21	splendour] splendor 2E

174.35	Simon's] Simon 2E
187.8	me, as] ~$_\wedge$ ~ 2E
192.6	Hall, they] ~$_\wedge$ ~ 2E
206.21	elegance$_\wedge$ which] ~, ~ 2E
225.19	locks$_\wedge$] ~, 2E
225.24	mouth$_\wedge$] ~, 2E
227.31	pannelling] paneling 2E
244.34	called] call'd 2E
259.42	neighbour! neighbour] ~, ~ 2E
266.15	farm, clapped] ~$_\wedge$ ~ 2E
297.15	head,] ~$_\wedge$ 2E